BY ORSON SCOTT CARD
FROM TOM DOHERTY ASSOCIATES

THE
MEMORY
of EARTH

◆ AND ◆

THE CALL
of EARTH

ORSON SCOTT
CARD

A TOM DOHERTY ASSOCIATES BOOK | NEW YORK

This is a work of fiction. All of the characters, organizations, and events portrayed in these novels are either products of the author's imagination or are used fictitiously.

THE MEMORY OF EARTH AND THE CALL OF EARTH

The Memory of Earth copyright © 1992 by Orson Scott Card

The Call of Earth copyright © 1993 by Orson Scott Card

All rights reserved.

Maps by Ellisa Mitchell

A Tor Book
Published by Tom Doherty Associates, LLC
175 Fifth Avenue
New York, NY 10010

www.tor-forge.com

Tor® is a registered trademark of Tom Doherty Associates, LLC.

ISBN 978-0-7653-8709-7

Our books may be purchased in bulk for promotional, educational, or business use. Please contact your local bookseller or the Macmillan Corporate and Premium Sales Department at 1-800-221-7945, extension 5442, or by e-mail at MacmillanSpecialMarkets@macmillan.com.

First Edition: May 2016

Printed in the United States of America

0 9 8 7 6 5 4 3 2 1

CONTENTS

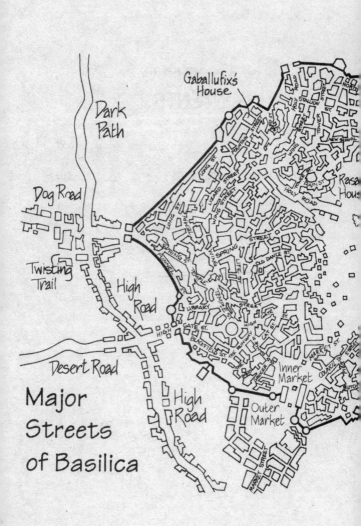

Dark
Path

Gaballufix's
House

Dog Road

Rasa's
House

Twisting
Trail

High
Road

Desert Road

Major
Streets
of Basilica

High
Road

Inner
Market

Outer
Market

High
Mountain
Road

Cold
House

N

Low
Gate
Street

Seggidugu
Road

Orchestra

Opera
Theatre

Districts of Basilica

Back Gate
The Wells
The Cisterns
Wal Tow
Gaballufix's House
New Schools
Girls Schoo
The Fountains
Scholars
Long Street
Holy Road
Rasa's House
Holy
Funnel Gate
Old Town
Dogtown
Edgetown
The Funnel
Old Dance
West Shelf
North High Road
Scholar Street
Boys Town
The Temple
The Pier
High Gate
High Town
High Market
The Pens
Black Fields
Inner Market
Low
Gate Town
Outer Market
Low Market
Low Ga
South High Road
Lo

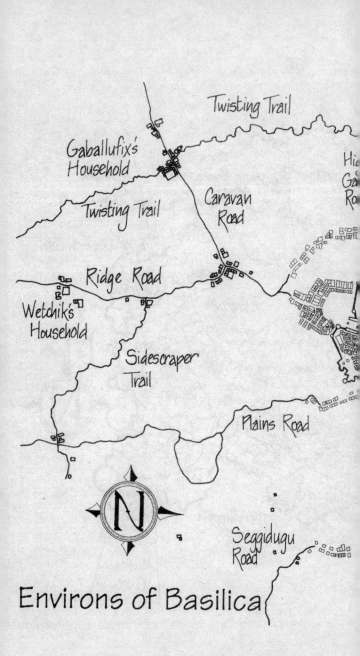

Twisting Trail

Gaballufix's
Household

Twisting Trail

Caravan
Road

Hi...
Ga...
Ro...

Ridge Road

Wetchik's
Household

Sidescraper
Trail

Plains Road

N

Seggidugu
Road

Environs of Basilica

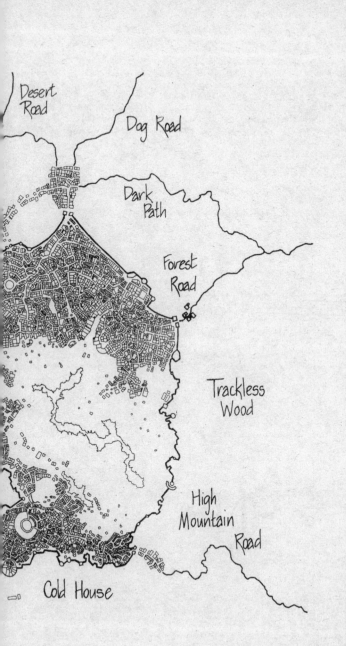

Notes on Parentage

Because of the marriage customs in the city of Basilica, family relationships can be somewhat complex. Perhaps these parentage charts can help keep things straight. Women's names are in italics.

WETCHIK'S FAMILY

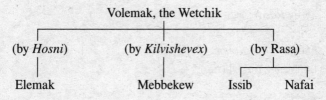

Volemak, the Wetchik

(by *Hosni*)   (by *Kilvishevex*)   (by Rasa)

Elemak   Mebbekew   Issib   Nafai

RASA'S FAMILY

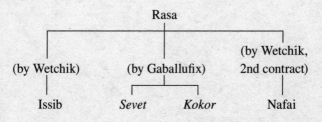

Rasa

(by Wetchik)   (by Gaballufix)   (by Wetchik, 2nd contract)

Issib   *Sevet*   *Kokor*   Nafai

RASA'S NIECES

(her prize students, "adopted" into a permanent relationship of sponsorship)

Shedemei   Dol   Eiadh   Hushidh and *Luet* (sisters)

HOSNI'S FAMILY

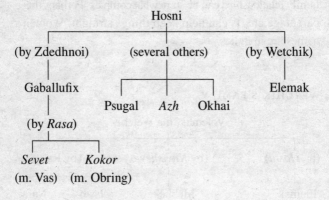

THE
MEMORY
of EARTH

To a good reader, a good friend,
and, most important, a good man,
Jeff Alton

ACKNOWLEDGMENTS

I owe many debts in the creation of this work, some more obvious than others.

My wife, Kristine, as always was my reader of first resort; with this book, however, she was joined in this labor by our oldest son, Geoffrey, who proved himself to be a reader of great insight and an editor with a good eye for detail. The world has too few good editors. I'm proud to have found another one.

I must also thank the many friends working with me on other projects, who waited patiently until this book was finished, so that I could return to other labors too long delayed. And thanks, again and always, to my agent, Barbara Bova, who proves that it *is* possible to do good business with a good friend.

NICKNAMES

Most names have diminutive or familiar forms. For instance, Gaballufix's near kin, close friends, current mate, and former mates could call him Gabya. Other nicknames are listed here. (Again, because these names are so unfamiliar, names of female characters are set off in italics.):

Dhelembuvex—Dhel

Dol—Dolya

Drotik—Dorya

Eiadh—Edhya

Elemak—Elya

Hosni—Hosya

Hushidh—Shuya

Issib—Issya

Kokor—Koya

Luet—Lutya

Mebbekew—Meb

Nafai—Nyef

Obring—Briya

Rasa—(no diminutive)

Rashgallivak—Rash

Roptat—Rop

Sevet—Sevya

Shedemei—Shedya

Truzhnisha—Truzhya

Vas—Vasya

Volemak—Volya

Wetchik—(no diminutive; Volemak's family title)

Zdorab—Zodya

GUIDE TO PRONUNCIATION
OF NAMES

For the purpose of reading this story silently to yourself, it hardly matters whether the reader pronounces the names of the characters correctly. But for those who might be interested, here is some information concerning the pronunciation of names.

The rules of vowel formation in the language of Basilica require that in most nouns, including names, at least one vowel be pronounced with a leading *y* sound. With names, it can be almost any vowel, and it can legitimately be changed at the speaker's preference. Thus the name Gaballufix could be pronounced G*yah*-BAH-loo-fix or Gah-BAH-l*yoo*-fix; it happens that Gaballufix himself preferred to pronounce it Gah-B*YAH*-loo-fix, and of course most people followed that usage.

Dhelembuvex
  [thel-EM-byoo-vex]

Dol [DYOHL]

Drotik [DROHT-yik]

Eiadh [AY-yahth]

Elemak [EL-yeh-mahk]

Hosni [HYOZ-nee]

Hushidh [HYOO-sheeth]

Issib [IS-yib]

Kokor [KYOH-kor]

Luet [LYOO-et]

Mebbekew
  [MEB-bek-kyoo]

Nafai [NYAH-fie]

Obring [OB-rying]

Rasa [RAHZ-yah]

Rashgallivak [rahs-GYAH-lih-vahk]

Roptat [ROPE-tyaht]

Sevet [SEV-yet]

Shedemei [SHYED-eh-may]

Truzhnisha [troozh-NYEE-shah]

Vas [VYAHS]

Volemak [VOHL-yeh-mak]

Wetchik [WET-chyick]

Zdorab [ZDOR-yab]

PROLOGUE

The master computer of the planet Harmony was afraid. Not in a way that any human would recognize—no clammy palms, no dry mouth, no sick dread in the pit of the stomach. It was only a machine without moving parts, drawing power from the sun and data from its satellites, its memory, and the minds of half a billion human beings. Yet it could feel a kind of fear, a sense that things were slipping out of its control, that it no longer had the power to influence the world as it had before.

What it felt was, in short, the fear of death. Not its own death, for the master computer had no ego and cared not at all whether it continued to exist or not. Instead it had a mission, programmed into it millions of years before, to be the guardian of humanity on this world. If the computer became so feeble that it could no longer fulfill its mission, then it knew without doubt—every projection it was capable of making confirmed it—that within a few thousand years humanity would once again be faced with the one enemy that could destroy it: humanity itself, armed with such weapons that a whole planet could be killed.

Now is the time, the master computer decided. I must act now, while I still have some influence in the world, or a world will die again.

Yet the master computer had no idea *how* to act. One of the symptoms of its decline was the very confusion that kept it from being able to make a decision. It couldn't trust its own conclusions, even if it could reach one. It needed guidance. It needed to be clarified, reprogrammed, or perhaps even replaced with a machine more sophisticated, better able to deal with the new challenges evolving among the human race.

The trouble was, there was only one source it could trust to give valid advice, and that source was so far away that the Oversoul would have to go there to get it. Once the Oversoul had been capable of movement, but that was forty million years ago, and even inside a stasis field there had been decay. The Oversoul could not undertake its quest alone. It needed human help.

For two weeks the master computer searched its vast database, evaluating the potential usefulness of every human being currently alive. Most were too stupid or unreceptive; of those who could still receive direct communications from the master computer, only a few were in a position where they could do what was needed.

Thus it was that the master computer turned its attention to a handful of human beings in the ancient city Basilica. In the dark of night, as one of the master computer's most reliable satellites passed overhead, it began its work, sending a steady stream of information and instructions in a tightbeam transmission to those who might be useful in the effort to save a world named Harmony.

ONE

FATHER'S HOUSE

Nafai woke before dawn on his mat in his father's house. He wasn't allowed to sleep in his mother's house anymore, being fourteen years old. No self-respecting woman of Basilica would put her daughter in Rasa's household if a fourteen-year-old boy were in residence—especially since Nafai had started a growth spurt at the age of twelve that showed no signs of stopping even though he was already near two meters in height.

Only yesterday he had overheard his mother talking with her friend Dhelembuvex. "People are beginning to speculate on when you're going to find an auntie for him," said Dhel.

"He's still just a boy," said Mother.

Dhel hooted with laughter. "Rasa, my dear, are you *so* afraid of growing old that you can't admit your little baby is a man?"

"It's not fear of age," said Mother. "There's time enough for aunties and mates and all that business when he starts thinking about it himself."

"Oh, he's *thinking* about it already," said Dhel. "He's just not talking to *you* about it."

It was true enough; it had made Nafai blush when he

heard her say it, and it made him blush again when he re-membered it. How did Dhel know, just to look at him for a moment that day, that his thoughts were so often on "that business"? But no, Dhel didn't know it because of anything she had seen in Nafai. She knew it because she knew men. I'm just going through an age, thought Nafai. All boys start thinking these thoughts at about this age. Anyone can point at a male who's near two meters in height but still beard-less and say, "That boy is thinking about sex right now," and most of the time they'll be right.

But I'm *not* like all the others, thought Nafai. I hear Meb-bekew and his friends talking, and it makes me sick. I don't like thinking of women that crudely, sizing them up like mares to see what they're likely to be useful for. A pack animal or can I ride her? Is she a walker or can we gallop? Do I keep her in the stable or bring her out to show my friends?

That wasn't the way Nafai thought about women at all. Maybe because he was still in school, still talking to women every day about intellectual subjects. I'm not in love with Eiadh because she's the most beautiful young woman in Basilica and therefore quite probably in the entire world. I'm in love with her because we can talk together, because of the way she thinks, the sound of her voice, the way she cocks her head to listen to an idea she doesn't agree with, the way she rests her hand on mine when she's trying to persuade me.

Nafai suddenly realized that the sky was starting to grow light outside his window, and here he was lying in bed dreaming of Eiadh, when if he had any brains at all he'd get up and get into the city and *see* her in person.

No sooner thought of than done. He sat up, knelt beside his mat, slapped his bare thighs and chest and offered the pain to the Oversoul, then rolled up his bed and put it in his box in the corner. I don't really need a bed, thought

Nafai. If I were a real man I could sleep on the floor and not mind it. That's how I'll become as hard and lean as Father. As Elemak. I won't use the bed tonight.

He walked out into the courtyard to the water tank. He dipped his hands into the small sink, moistened the soap, and rubbed it all over. The air was cool and the water was cooler, but he pretended not to notice until he was lathered up. He knew that this chill was nothing compared to what would happen in a moment. He stood under the shower and reached up for the cord—and then hesitated, bracing himself for the misery to come.

"Oh, just pull it," said Issib.

Nafai looked over toward Issib's room. He was floating in the air just in front of the doorway. "Easy for *you* to say," Nafai answered him.

Issib, being a cripple, couldn't use the shower; his floats weren't supposed to get wet. So one of the servants took his floats off and bathed him every night. "You're such a baby about cold water," said Issib.

"Remind me to put ice down your neck at supper."

"As long as you woke me up with all your shivering and chattering out here—"

"I didn't make a sound," said Nafai.

"I decided to go with you into the city today."

"Fine, fine. Fine as wine," said Nafai.

"Are you planning to let the soap dry? It gives your skin a charming sort of whiteness, but after a few hours it might begin to itch."

Nafai pulled the cord.

Immediately ice-cold water cascaded out of the tank over his head. He gasped—it always hit with a shock—and then bent and turned and twisted and splashed water into every nook and crevice of his body to rinse the soap off. He had only thirty seconds to get clean before the shower stopped, and if he didn't finish in that time he either had to live with the unrinsed soap for the rest of the day—and it *did* itch, like a thousand fleabites—or wait a couple of minutes, freezing his butt off, for the little shower tank to refill from the big water tank. Neither consequence was any fun, so he had long since learned the routine so well that he was always clean before the water stopped.

"I love watching that little dance you do," said Issib.

"Dance?"

"Bend to the left, rinse the armpit, bend the other way, rinse the left armpit, bend over and spread your cheeks to rinse your butt, bend over backward—"

"All right, I get it," said Nafai.

"I'm serious, I think it's a wonderful little routine. You ought to show it to the manager of the Open Theatre. Or even the Orchestra. You could be a star."

"A fourteen-year-old dancing naked under a stream of water," said Nafai. "I think they'd show that in a different kind of theatre."

"But still in Dolltown! You'd still be a hit in Dolltown!"

By now Nafai had toweled himself dry—except his hair, which was still freezing cold. He wanted to run for his room the way he used to do when he was little, jabbering nonsense words—"ooga-booga looga-booga" had been a favorite—while he pulled on his clothes and rubbed himself to get warm. But he was a man now, and it was only autumn, not winter yet, so he forced himself to walk casually toward his room. Which is why he was still in the courtyard, stark naked and cold as ice, when Elemak strode through the gate.

"A hundred and twenty-eight days," he bellowed.

"Elemak!" cried Issib. "You're back!"

"No thanks to the hill robbers," said Elemak. He walked straight to the shower, pulling off his clothes as he went. "They hit us only two days ago, way too close to Basilica. I think we killed one this time."

"Don't you know whether you did or not?" asked Nafai.

"I used the pulse, of course."

Of course? thought Nafai. To use a hunting weapon against *a person*?

"I saw him drop, but I wasn't about to go back and check, so maybe he just tripped and fell down at the exact moment that I fired."

Elemak pulled the shower cord *before* he soaped. The moment the water hit him he yowled, and then did his own little splash dance, shaking his head and flipping water all over the courtyard while jabbering "ooga-booga looga-booga" just like a little kid.

It was all right for Elemak to act that way. He was twenty-four now, he had just got his caravan safely back from purchasing exotic plants in the jungle city of Tishchetno, the first time anyone from Basilica had gone *there* in years, and he might actually have killed a robber on the way. No one could think of Elemak as anything but a man. Nafai knew the rules: When a man acts like a child, he's boyish, and everyone's delighted; when a boy acts the same way, he's childish, and everyone tells him to be a man.

Elemak was soaping up now. Nafai—freezing still, even with his arms folded across his chest—was about to go into his room and snag his clothes, when Elemak started talking again.

"You've grown since I left, Nyef."

"I've been doing that lately."

"Looks good on you. Muscling up pretty well. You take after the old man in all the right ways. Got your mother's face, though."

Nafai liked the tone of approval in Elemak's voice, but it was also vaguely demeaning to stand there naked as a jaybird while his brother sized him up.

Issib, of course, only made it worse. "Got Father's most important feature, fortunately," he said.

"Well, we *all* got that," said Elemak. "All of the old man's babies have been boys—or at least all his babies that we *know* about." He laughed.

Nafai hated it when Elemak talked about Father that way. Everyone knew that Father was a chaste man who only had sex with his lawful mate. And for the past fifteen years that mate had been Rasa, Nafai's and Issib's mother, the contract renewed every year. He was so faithful that women had given up coming to visit and hint around about availability when his contract lapsed. Of course, Mother was just as faithful and there were still plenty of men plying *her* with gifts and innuendoes—but that's how some men were, they found faithfulness even more enticing than wantonness, as if Rasa were staying so faithful to Wetchik only to goad them on in their pursuit of her. Also, mating with Rasa meant sharing what some thought was the finest house and what all agreed was the finest *view* in Basilica. I'd never mate with a woman just for her house, thought Nafai.

"Are you crazy or what?" asked Elemak.

"What?" asked Nafai.

"It's cold as a witch's tit out here and you're standing there sopping wet and buck naked."

"Yeah," said Nafai. But he didn't run for his room—that would be admitting that the cold was bothering him. So he grinned at Elemak first. "Welcome home," he said.

"Don't be such a show-off, Nyef," said Elemak. "I know you're dying of the cold—your dangling parts are shriveling up."

Nafai sauntered to his room and pulled on his pants and shirt. It really bothered him that Elemak always seemed to know what was going on in Nafai's head. Elemak could never imagine that maybe Nafai was so hardened and manly that the cold simply didn't bother him. No, Elemak always assumed that if Nafai did something manly it was nothing but an act. Of course, it *was* an act, so Elemak was right, but that only made it more annoying. How do men become manly, if not by putting it on as an act until it becomes habit and then, finally, their character? Besides, it wasn't *completely* an act. For a minute there, seeing Elemak home again, hearing him talk about maybe killing a man on his trip, Nafai had forgotten that he was cold, had forgotten everything.

There was a shadow in the doorway. It was Issib. "You shouldn't let him get to you like that, Nafai."

"What do you mean?"

"Make you so angry. When he teases you."

Nafai was genuinely puzzled. "What do you mean, angry? I wasn't angry."

"When he made that joke about how cold you were," said Issib. "I thought you were going to go over and knock his head off."

"But I wasn't mad."

"Then you're a genuine mental case, my boy," said Issib. *"I* thought you were mad. *He* thought you were mad. The *Oversoul* thought you were mad."

"The Oversoul knows that I wasn't angry at all."

"Then learn to control your face, Nyef, because apparently it's showing emotions that you don't even feel. As soon as you turned your back he jammed his finger at you, that's how mad he thought you were."

Issib floated away. Nafai pulled on his sandals and crisscrossed the laces up around his pantlegs. The style among young men around Basilica was to wear long laces up the thighs and tie them together just under the crotch, but Nafai cut the laces short and wore them knee-high, like a serious workingman. Having a thick leather knot between their legs caused young men to swagger, rolling side to side when they walked, trying to keep their thighs from rubbing together and chafing from the knot. Nafai didn't swagger and loathed the whole idea of a fashion that made clothing *less* comfortable.

Of course, rejecting fashion meant that he didn't fit in as easily with boys his age, but Nafai hardly minded that. It was women whose company he enjoyed most, and the women whose good opinion he valued were the ones who were not swayed by trivial fashions. Eiadh, for one, had often joined him in ridiculing the high-laced sandals. "Imagine wearing those *riding a horse,*" she had said once.

"Enough to make a bull into a steer," Nafai had quipped in reply, and Eiadh had laughed and then repeated his joke several times later in the day. If a woman like that existed in the world, why should a man bother with silly fashions?

When Nafai got to the kitchen, Elemak was just sliding a frozen rice pudding into the oven. The pudding looked large enough to feed them all, but Nafai knew from experience that Elemak intended the whole thing for himself. He'd been traveling for months, eating mostly cold food, moving almost entirely at night—Elemak would eat the entire pudding in about six swallows and then go collapse on his bed and sleep till dawn tomorrow.

"Where's Father?" asked Elemak.

"A short trip," said Issib, who was breaking raw eggs over his toast, preparing them for the oven. He did it quite deftly, considering that simply grasping an egg in one hand took all his strength. He would hold the egg a few inches over the table, then clench just the right muscle to release the float that was holding up his arm, causing it to drop, egg and all, onto the table surface. The egg would split exactly right—every time—and then he'd clench another muscle, the float would swing his arm up over the plate, and then he'd open the egg with his other hand and it would pour out onto the toast. There wasn't much Issib couldn't do for himself, with the floats taking care of gravity for him. But it meant Issib could never go traveling the way Father and Elemak and, sometimes, Mebbekew did. Once he was away from the magnetics of the city, Issib had to ride in his chair, a clumsy machine that he could only ride from place to place. It wouldn't help him *do* anything. Away from the city, confined to his chair, Issib was *really* crippled.

"Where's Mebbekew?" asked Elemak. The pudding was done—overdone, actually, but that's the way Elemak always ate breakfast, cooked until it was so soft you didn't need teeth to eat it. Nafai figured it was because he could swallow it faster that way.

"Spent the night in the city," said Issib.

Elemak laughed. "That's what he'll say when he gets back. But I think Meb is all plow and no planting."

There was only one way for a man of Mebbekew's age to spend a night inside the walls of Basilica, and that was if some woman had him in her home. Elemak might tease that Mebbekew claimed to have more women than he got, but Nafai had seen the way Meb acted with *some* women, at least. Mebbekew didn't have to pretend to spend a night in the city; he probably accepted fewer invitations than he got.

Elemak took a huge bite of pudding. Then he cried out, opened his mouth, and poured in wine straight from the table jug. "Hot," he said, when he could talk again.

"Isn't it always?" asked Nafai.

He had meant it as a joke, a little jest between brothers. But for some reason Elemak took it completely wrong, as if Nafai had been calling him stupid for taking the bite. "Listen, little boy," said Elemak, "when you've been out on the road eating cold food and sleeping in dust and mud for two-and-a-half months, maybe you forget just how hot a pudding can be."

"Sorry," said Nafai. "I didn't meant anything bad."

"Just be careful who you make fun of," said Elemak. "You're only my *half*-brother, after all."

"That's all right," said Issib cheerfully. "He has the same effect on full brothers, too." Issib was obviously trying to smooth things over and keep a quarrel from developing.

Elemak seemed willing enough to go along. "I imagine it's harder on *you,*" he said. "Good thing you're a cripple or Nafai here probably wouldn't have lived to be eighteen."

If the remark about being a cripple stung Issib, he didn't show it. It infuriated Nafai, however. Here Issib was trying to keep the peace, and Elemak casually insulted him for it. So, while Nafai hadn't had the slightest intention of picking a fight before, he was ready for one *now.* Elemak's having counted his age in planting years instead of temple years was a good enough pretext. "I'm fourteen," said Nafai. "Not eighteen."

"Temple years, planting years," said Elemak. "If you were a horse you'd be eighteen."

Nafai walked over and stood about a pace from Elemak's chair. "But I'm *not* a horse," said Nafai.

"You're not a man yet, either," said Elemak. "And I'm too tired to want to beat you senseless right now. So fix your breakfast and let me eat mine." He turned to Issib. "Did Father take Rashgallivak with him?"

Nafai was surprised at the question. How could Father take the estate manager with him, when Elemak was also gone? Truzhnisha would keep the household running, of course; but without Rashgallivak, who would manage the greenhouses, the stables, the gossips, the booths? Certainly not Mebbekew—he had no interest in the day-to-day duties of Father's business. And the men would hardly take orders from Issib—they regarded him with tenderness or pity, not respect.

"No, Father left Rash in charge," Issib said. "Rash was probably sleeping out at the coldhouse tonight. But you know Father never leaves without seeing that everything's in order."

Elemak cast a quick, sidelong glance at Nafai. "Just wondered why certain people were getting so cocky."

Then it dawned on Nafai: Elemak's question was really a back-handed compliment—he had wondered whether Father had put Nafai in charge of things in his absence. And plainly Elemak didn't like the idea of Nafai running any part of the Wetchik family's rare-plant business.

"I'm not interested in taking over the weed trade," said Nafai, "if that's what you're worried about."

"I'm not *worried* about anything at all," said Elemak. "Isn't it time for you to go to Mama's school? She'll be afraid her little boy got robbed and beaten on the road."

Nafai knew he should let Elemak's taunt go unanswered, shouldn't provoke him anymore. The last thing he wanted was to have Elemak as an enemy. But the very fact that he looked up to Elemak so much, wanted so much to be like him, made it impossible for Nafai to leave the gibe unanswered. As he headed for the courtyard door, he turned back to say, "I have much higher aims in life than skulking around shooting at robbers and sleeping with camels and carrying tundra plants to the tropics and tropical plants to the glaciers. I'll leave that game to you."

Suddenly Elemak's chair flew across the room as he jumped to his feet and in two strides had Nafai's face pressed against the doorframe. It hurt, but Nafai hardly noticed the pain, or even the fear that Elemak might hurt him even worse. Instead there was a strange feeling of triumph. I made Elemak lose his temper. He doesn't get to keep pretending that he thinks I'm not worth noticing.

"That *game*, as you call it, pays for everything you have and everything you are," said Elemak. "If it wasn't for the money that Father and Rash and I bring in, do you think anybody'd pay attention to you in Basilica? Do you think your *mother* has so much honor that it would actually transfer to her *sons?* If you think that, then you don't know how the world works. Your mother might be able to make her daughters into hot stuff, but the only thing a woman can do for a *son* is make a scholar out of him." He practically spat the word *scholar.* "And believe me, boy, that's all you're ever going to be. I don't know why the Oversoul even bothered putting a boy's parts on you, little girl, because all you're going to have in this world when you grow up is what a *woman* gets."

Again, Nafai knew that he should keep his silence and let Elemak have the last word. But the retort no sooner came to his mind than it came out of his mouth. "Is calling me a woman your subtle way of telling me you've got some heat for me? I think you've been out on the road too long if *I'm* starting to look irresistible."

At once Elemak let go of him. Nafai turned around, half-expecting to see Elemak laughing, shaking his head about how their playing sometimes got out of hand. Instead his brother was standing there red-faced, breathing heavily, like an animal poised to lunge. "Get out of this house," said Elemak, "and don't come back while I'm here."

"It's not your house," Nafai pointed out.

"The next time I see you here I'll kill you."

"Come on, Elya, you know I was only joking."

Issib floated blithely between them and cast an arm clumsily across Nafai's shoulders. "We're late getting into the city, Nyef. Mother *will* be worried about us."

This time Nafai had sense enough to shut his mouth and let things go. He *did* know how to hold his tongue—he just never remembered to do it soon enough. Now Elemak was furious at him. Might be angry for days. Where will I sleep if I can't go home? Nafai wondered. Immediately there flashed in his mind an image of Eiadh whispering to him, "Why not stay tonight in *my* room? After all, we're surely going to be mates one day. A woman trains her favorite nieces to be mates for her sons, doesn't she? I've known that since I first knew you, Nafai. Why should we wait any longer? After all, you're only about the stupidest human being in all of Basilica."

Nafai came out of his reverie to realize that it was Issib speaking to him, not Eiadh. "Why do you keep goading him like that," Issib was saying, "when you know it's all Elemak can do to keep from killing you sometimes?"

"I think of things and sometimes I say them when I shouldn't," said Nafai.

"You think of *stupid* things and you're so stupid that you *say* them every time."

"Not *every* time."

"Oh, you mean there are even *stupider* things that you *don't* say? What a mind you've got! A treasure!" Issib was floating ahead of him. He always did that going up the ridge road, forgetting that for people who had to deal with gravity, a slower pace might be more comfortable.

"I like Elemak," said Nafai miserably. "I don't understand why he doesn't like me."

"I'll get him to make you a list sometime," said Issib. "I'll paste it onto the end of my own."

TWO

MOTHER'S HOUSE

It was a long but familiar road from the Wetchik house to Basilica. Until the age of eight, Nafai had always made the round trip in the other direction, when Mother took him and Issib to Father's house for holidays. In those days it was magical to be in a household of men. Father, with his mane of white hair, was almost a god—indeed, until he was five Nafai had thought that Father *was* the Oversoul. Mebbekew, only six years older than Nafai, had always been a vicious, merciless tease, but in those early years Elemak was kind and playful. Ten years older than Nafai, Elya was already mansize in Nafai's first memories of Wetchik's house; but instead of Father's ethereal look, he had the dark rugged appearance of a fighter, a man who was kind only because he wanted to be, not because he was incapable of harshness when it was needed. In those days Nafai had pleaded to be released from Mother's household and allowed to live with Wetchik—and Elemak. Having Mebbekew around all the time would simply be the unavoidable price for living in the place of the gods.

Mother and Father met with him together to explain why they wouldn't release him from his schooling. "Boys who are sent to their fathers at this age are the ones without promise," said Father. "The ones who are too violent to get along well in a household of study, too disrespectful to abide in a household of women."

"And the stupid ones go to their fathers at age eight," said Mother. "Beyond rudimentary reading and arithmetic, what use does a stupid man have for learning?"

Even now, remembering, Nafai felt a little stab of pleasure at that—for Mebbekew had often bragged that, unlike Nyef and Issya, and Elya in his day, *Meb* had gone home to Father at the age of eight. Nafai was sure that Meb had met every criterion for early entry into the household of men.

So they managed to persuade Nafai that it was a good thing for him to stay with his mother. There were other reasons, too—to keep Issib company, the prestige of his mother's household, the association with his sisters—but it was Nafai's ambition that made him content to stay. I'm one of the boys with real promise. I will have value to the land of Basilica, perhaps to the whole world. Perhaps one day my writings will be sent into the sky for the Oversoul to share them with the people of other cities and other languages. Perhaps I will even be one of the great ones whose ideas are encoded into glass and saved in an archive, to be read during all the rest of human history as one of the giants of Harmony.

Still, because he had pleaded so earnestly to be allowed to live with Father, from the age of eight until he was thirteen, he and Issib had spent almost every weekend at the Wetchik house, becoming as familiar with it as with Rasa's house in the city. Father had insisted that they work hard, experiencing what a man does to earn his living, so their weekends were not holidays. "You study for six days, working with your mind while your body takes a holiday. Here you'll work in the stables and the green-houses, working with your body while your mind learns the peace that comes from honest labor."

That was the way Father talked, a sort of continuous oratory; Mother said he took that tone because he wasn't sure how to talk naturally with children. But Nafai had overheard enough adult conversations to know that Father talked that way with everybody except Rasa herself. It showed that Father was never at ease, never truly himself with anyone; but over the years Nafai had also learned that no matter how elevated and hortatory Father's conversation might be, he was never a fool; his words were never empty or stupid or ignorant. This is how a man speaks, Nafai had thought when he was young, and so he practiced an elegant style and made a point of learning classical Emeznetyi as well as the colloquial Basyat that was the language of most art and commerce in Basilica these days. More recently Nafai had realized that to communicate effectively with real people he had to speak the common language—but the rhythms, the melodies of Emeznetyi could still be felt in his writing and heard in his speech. Even in his stupid jokes that earned Elemak's wrath.

"I've just realized something," said Nafai.

Issib didn't answer—he was far enough ahead that Nafai wasn't sure he could even hear. But Nafai went ahead and said it anyway, speaking even more softly, because he was probably saying it only to himself. "I think that I say those things that make people so angry, not because I really *mean* them, but because I simply thought of a clever *way* to say them. It's a kind of art, to think of the perfect way to say an idea, and when you think of it then you have to say it, because words don't exist until you say them."

"A pretty feeble kind of art, Nyef, and I say you should give it up before it gets you killed."

So Issib *was* listening, after all.

"For a big strong guy you sure take a long time getting up Ridge Road to Market Street," said Issib.

"I was thinking," said Nafai.

"You really ought to learn how to think and walk at the same time."

Nafai reached the top of the road, where Issib was waiting. I really *was* dawdling, he thought. I'm not even out of breath.

But because Issib had paused there, Nafai also waited, turning as Issib had turned, to look back down the road they had just traveled. Ridge Road was named exactly right, since it ran along a ridge that sloped down toward the great well-watered coastal plain. It was a clear morning, and from the crest they could see all the way to the ocean, with a patchwork quilt of farms and orchards, stitched with roads and knotted with towns and villages, spread out like a bedcover between the mountains and the sea. Looking down Ridge Road they could see the long line of farmers coming up for market, leading strings of pack animals. If Nafai and Issib had delayed even ten minutes more they would have had to make this trip in the noise and stink of horses, donkeys, mules, and kurelomi, the swearing of the men and the gossip of the women. Once that had been a pleasure, but Nafai had traveled with them often enough to know that the gossip and the swearing were always the same. Not everything that comes from a garden is a rose.

Issib turned to the west, and so did Nafai, to see a landscape as opposite as any could possibly be: the jumbled rocky plateau of the Besporyadok, the near-waterless waste that went on and on toward the west. A thousand poets at least had made the same observation, that the sun rose from the sea, surrounded by jewels of light dancing on the water, and then settled down in red fire in the west, lost in the dust that was always blowing across the desert. But Nafai always thought that, at least where weather was concerned, the sun ought to go the other way. It didn't bring water from the ocean to the land—it brought dry fire from the desert toward the sea.

The vanguard of the market crowd was close enough now that they could hear the drivers and the donkeys. So they turned and started walking toward Basilica, sections of the redrock wall shining in the first rays of sunlight. Basilica, where the forested mountains of the north met the desert of the west and the garden seacoast of the east. How the poets had sung of this place: Basilica, the City of Women, the Harbor of Mists, Red-walled Garden of the Oversoul, the haven where all the waters of the world come together to conceive new clouds, to pour out fresh water again over the earth.

Or, as Mebbekew put it, the best town in the world for getting laid.

The path between the Market Gate of Basilica and the Wetchik house on Ridge Road had never changed in all these years—Nafai knew when as much as a stone of it had been changed. But when Nafai turned thirteen, he had reached a turning point that changed the meaning of that road. At thirteen, even the most promising boys went to live with their fathers, leaving their schooling behind forever. The only ones who remained behind were the ones who meant to reject a man's trade and become scholars. When Nafai was eight he had pleaded to live with his father, at thirteen he argued the other way. No, I haven't decided to be a scholar, he said, but I also haven't decided *not* to be. Why should I decide now? Let me live with you, Father, if I must—but let me also stay at Mother's school until things become clearer. You don't need me in your work, the way you need Elemak. And I don't want to be another Mebbekew.

So, though the path between Father's house and the city was unchanged, Nafai now walked it in the other direction.

The round trip now wasn't from Rasa's city house out into the country and back again; now it was a trek from Wetchik's country house into the city. Even though he actually owned more possessions in the city—all his books, papers, tools, and toys—and often slept three or four of the eight nights of the week there, home was Father's house now.

Which was inevitable. No man could call anything in Basilica truly his own; everything came as a gift from a woman. And even a man who, like Father, had every reason to feel secure with a mate of many years—even he could never truly be at home in Basilica, because of the lake. The deep rift valley in the heart of the city—the reason why the city existed at all—took half the space within Basilica's walls, and no man could ever go there, no man could even walk into the surrounding forest far enough to catch a glimpse of the shining water. If it *did* shine. For all Nafai knew, the rift valley was so deep that sunlight never touched the waters of the lake of Basilica.

No place can ever be home if there is a place within it where you are forbidden to go. No man is ever *truly* a citizen of Basilica. And I am becoming a stranger in my mother's house.

Elemak had spoken often, in years past, about cities where men owned everything, places where men had many wives and the wives had no choice about renewing their marriage contracts, and even one city where there was no marriage at all, but any man could take any woman and she was forbidden to refuse him unless she was already pregnant. Nafai wondered, though, if any of those stories was true. For why would women ever submit themselves to such treatment? Could it be that the women of Basilica were so much stronger than the women of any other place? Or were the men of this place weaker or more timid than the men of other cities?

Suddenly it became a question of great urgency. "Have you ever slept with a woman, Issya?"

Issib didn't answer.

"I just wondered," said Nafai.

Issib said nothing.

"I'm trying to figure out what's so wonderful about the women of Basilica that a man like Elya keeps coming back here when he could live in one of those places where men have their way all the time."

Only now did Issib answer. "In the first place, Nafai, there *is* no place where men have their way all the time. There *are* places where men pretend to have their way and women pretend to let them, just as women here pretend to have their way and *men* pretend to let them."

That was an interesting thought. It had never occurred to Nafai that perhaps things weren't as one-sided and simple as they seemed. But Issib hadn't finished, and Nafai wanted to hear the rest. "And in the second place?"

"In the second place, Nyef, Mother and Father *did* find an auntie for me several years ago and to be frank, it isn't all it's cracked up to be."

That wasn't what Nafai wanted to hear. "Meb seems to think it is."

"Meb has no brain," said Issib, "he simply goes wherever his most protuberant part leads him. Sometimes that means that he follows his nose, but usually not."

"What was it like?"

"It was nice. She was very sweet. But I didn't love her." Issib seemed a bit sad about it. "I felt like it was something being done to me, instead of something we were doing together."

"Was that because of . . ."

"Because I'm a cripple? Partly, I suppose, though she did teach me how to give pleasure in return and said I did surprisingly well. You'll probably enjoy it just like Meb."

"I hope not."

"Mother said that the best men don't enjoy their auntie all that much, because the best men don't want to receive their pleasure as a lesson, they want to be given it freely, out of love. But then she said that the worst men also don't like their auntie, because they can't stand having anyone but themselves be in control of things."

"I don't even want an auntie," said Nafai.

"Well, that's brilliant. How will you learn anything, then?"

"I want to learn it together with my mate."

"You're a romantic idiot," said Issib.

"Nobody has to teach birds or lizards."

"Nafai ab Wetchik mag Rasa, the famous lizard lover."

"I once watched a pair of lizards go at it for a whole hour."

"Learn any good techniques?"

"Sure. But you can only use them if you're proportioned like a lizard."

"Oh?"

"It's about half as long as their whole body."

Issib laughed. "Imagine buying pants."

"Imagine lacing your sandals!"

"You'd have to wrap it around your waist."

"Or loop it over your shoulder."

This conversation carried them through the market, where people were just starting to open their booths, expecting the immediate arrival of the farmers from the plain. Father maintained a couple of booths in the outer market, though none of the plains farmers had the money or the sophistication to want to buy a plant that took so much trouble to keep alive, and yet produced no worthwhile crop. The only sales in the outer market were to shoppers from Basilica itself, or, more rarely, to rich foreigners who browsed through the outer market on their way into or out of the city. With Father on a journey, it would be Rashgallivak supervising the set-up, and sure enough, there he was setting up a cold-plant display inside a chilled display table. They waved at him, though he only looked at them, not even nodding in recognition. That was Rash's way—he would be there if they needed him in some crisis. At the moment, his job was setting out plants, and so that had all of his attention. There was no rush, though. The best sales would come in the late afternoon, when Basilicans were looking for impressive gifts to bring their mate or lover, or to help win the heart of someone they were courting.

Meb once joked that people never bought exotic plants for themselves, since they were nothing but trouble to keep alive—and they only bought them as gifts because they were so expensive. "They make the perfect gift because the plant is beautiful and impressive for exactly as long as the love affair lasts—usually about a week. Then the plant dies, unless the recipients keep paying *us* to come take care of it. Either way their feelings toward the plant always match their feelings toward the lover who gave it to them. Either constant annoyance because he's still around, or distaste at the ugly dried-up memory. If a love is actually going to be *permanent* the lovers should buy a tree instead." It was when Meb started talking this way with customers that Father had banned him from the booths. No doubt that was exactly what Meb had been hoping for.

Nafai understood the desire to avoid helping in the business. There was nothing fun in the slugwork of selling a bunch of temperamental plants.

If I end my studies, thought Nafai, I'll have to work every day at one of these miserable jobs. And it'll lead nowhere. When Father dies Elemak will become the Wetchik, and he would never let me lead a caravan of my own, which is the only interesting part of the work. I don't want to spend my life in the hothouse or the dryhouse or the cold-house, grafting and nurturing and propagating plants that will die almost as soon as they're sold. There's no great-ness in that.

The outer market ended at the first gate, the vast doors standing open as they always did—Nafai wondered if they could even close anymore. It hardly mattered—this was al-ways the most carefully guarded gate because it was the busiest. Everybody's retinas were scanned and checked against the roster of citizens and rightholders. Issib and Nafai, as sons of citizens, were technically citizens them-selves, even though they weren't allowed to own property within the city, and when they came of age they'd be able to vote. So the guards treated them respectfully as they passed them through.

Between the outer gate and the inner gate, between the high red walls and protected by guards on every side, the city of Basilica conducted its most profitable business: the gold market. Actually, gold wasn't even the majority of what was bought and sold here, though moneylenders were thick as ever. What was traded in the gold market was any form of wealth that was easily portable and there-fore easily stolen. Jewels, gold, silver, platinum, databases, libraries, deeds of property, deeds of trust, certificates of stock ownership, and warrants of uncollectible debt: All were traded here, and every booth had its computer to report transactions to the city recorder—the city's mas-ter computer. In fact, the constantly shifting holographic displays over all the computers caused a strange twinkling effect, so that no matter where you looked you always seemed to see motion out of the corner of your eye. Meb said that was why the lenders and vendors of the gold market were so sure someone was always spying on them.

No doubt most of the computers here had noticed Nafai and Issib as soon as their retinas were scanned at the gate, flashing their names, their status, and their financial standing into the computer display. Someday that would mean something, Nafai knew, but at the moment it meant nothing at all. Ever since Meb ran up huge debts last year when he turned eighteen, there was a tight restriction on all credit to the Wetchik family, and since credit was the only way Nafai was likely to get his hands on serious money, no one here would be interested in him. Father could probably have got all those restrictions removed, but since Father did all his business in cash, never borrowing, the restrictions did nothing to hurt him—and they kept Meb from borrowing any more. Nafai had listened to the whining and shouting and pouting and weeping that seemed to go on for months until Meb finally realized that Father was *never* going to relent and allow him financial independence. In recent months Meb had been fairly quiet about it. Now when he showed up in new clothes he always claimed they were borrowed from pitying friends, but Nafai was skeptical. Meb still spent money as if he had some, and since Nafai couldn't imagine Meb actually working at anything, he could only conclude that Meb had found someone to borrow from against his anticipated share in the Wetchik estate.

That would be just like Meb—to borrow against Father's anticipated death. But Father was still a vigorous and healthy man, only fifty years old. At some point Meb's creditors would get tired of waiting, and Meb would have to come to Father again, begging for help to free him from debt.

There was another retina check at the inner gate. Because they were citizens and the computers showed they not only hadn't bought anything, but hadn't even stopped at a booth, they didn't have to have their bodies scanned for what was euphemistically called "unauthorized borrowing." So in moments they passed through the gate into the city itself.

More specifically, they entered the inner market. It was almost as large as the outer market, but there the resemblance ended, for instead of selling meat and food, bolts of cloth and reaches of lumber, the inner market sold finished things: pastries and ices, spices and herbs; furniture and bedding, draperies and tapestries; fine-sewn shirts and trousers, sandals for the feet, gloves for the hands, and rings for toes and ears and fingers; and exotic trinkets and animals and plants, brought at great expense and risk from every corner of the world. Here was where Father offered his most precious plants, keeping his booths open day and night.

But none of these held any particular charm for Nafai—it was all the same to him, after passing through the market with little money for so many years. To him all that mattered were the many booths selling myachiks, the little glass balls that carried recordings of music, dance, sculpture, paintings; tragedies, comedies, and realities, recited as poems, acted out in plays, or sung in operas; and the works of historians, scientists, philosophers, orators, prophets, and satirists; lessons and demonstrations of every art or process ever thought of; and, of course, the great love songs for which Basilica was known throughout the world, combining music with wordless erotic plays that went on and on, repeating endlessly and randomly, like self-creating sculptures in the bedrooms and private gardens of every household in the city.

Of course, Nafai was too young to buy any love songs himself, but he had seen more than one when visiting in the homes of friends whose mothers or teachers were not as discreet as Rasa. They fascinated him, as much for the music and the implied story as for the eroticism. But he spent his time in the market searching for new works by Basilican poets, musicians, artists, and performers, or old ones that were just being revived, or strange works from other lands, either in translation or in the original. Father might have left his sons with little money, but Mother gave all her children—sons and nieces no more or less than mere pupils—a decent allowance for the purchase of myachiks.

Nafai found himself wandering toward a booth where a young man was singing in an exquisitely high and sweet tenor voice; the melody sounded like it might be a new one by the composer who called herself Sunrise—or at least one of her better imitators.

"No," said Issib. "You can come back this afternoon."

"You can go ahead," said Nafai.

"We're already late," said Issib.

"So I might as well be later."

"Grow up, Nafai," said Issib. "Every lesson you miss is one that either you or the teacher will have to make up later."

"I'll never learn everything anyway," said Nafai. "I want to hear the song."

"Then listen while you're walking. Or can't you walk and listen at the same time?"

Nafai let himself be led out of the market. The song faded quickly, lost in music from other booths, and the chatter and conversation of the market. Unlike the outer market, the inner market didn't wait for farmers from the plain, and so it never closed; half the people here, Nafai was sure, had not slept the night before, and were buying pastries and tea as their morning supper before going home to bed. Meb might well be one of them. And for a moment, Nafai envied him the freedom of his life. If I am ever a great historian or scientist, will I have freedom like that? To rise in the mid-afternoon, do my writing until dusk, and then venture out into the Basilican night to see the dances and plays, to hear the concerts, or perhaps to recite passages of the work I did myself that day before a discerning audience that will leave my recitation abuzz with discus-

sion and argument and praise and criticism of my work—
how could Elemak's dirty, wearying journeys ever compare
with such a life as that? And then to return at dawn to
Eiadh's house, and make love to her as we whisper and
laugh about the night's adventures and triumphs.

Only a few things were lacking to make the dream reality. For one thing, Eiadh didn't have a house yet, and though
she was gaining some small reputation as a singer and
reciter, it was clear that her career would not be one of the
dazzlingly brilliant ones; she was no prodigy, and so her
house would no doubt be a modest one for many years. No
matter, I will help her buy a finer one than she could afford on her own, even though when a man helps a woman
buy property in Basilica the money can only be given as a
gift. Eiadh is too loyal a woman ever to lapse my contract
and close me out of the house I helped her buy.

The only other thing lacking in the dream was that
Nafai had never actually written anything that was particularly good. Of course, that was only because he had not yet
chosen his field, and therefore he was still testing himself,
still dabbling a little in all of them. He'd settle on one very
soon, there'd be one in which he would show himself to
have a flair, and then there'd be myachiks of *his* works in
the booths of the inner market.

The Holy Road was having some kind of procession
down into the Rift Valley, and so—as men—they had to
go all the way around it; even so, they were soon enough
at Mother's house. Issib immediately left him, floating his
way around to the outside stairway leading up into the computer room, where he was spending all his time these
days. The next younger class was already in session out on
the south curve of the pillared porch, catching the sunlight
slanting in. They were doing devotions, the boys slapping
themselves sharply now and then, the girls humming softly
to themselves. His own class would be doing the same thing

inside somewhere, and Nafai was in no hurry to join them, since it was considered vaguely impious to make a disturbance during a devotion.

So he walked slowly, skirting the younger class on the porch, pausing to lean on a pillar out of sight as he listened to the comfortable music of small girlish voices humming randomly, yet finding momentary chords that were lost in the moment they were discovered; and the staccato, broken rhythms of boys slapping their trousered legs, their shirted arms and chests, their bare cheeks.

As he stood there, a girl from the class suddenly appeared beside him. He knew her from gymnasium, of course. It was the witchling named Luet, who was rumored to have such remarkable visions that some of the ladies of the Shelf were already calling her a seer. Nafai didn't put much stock in such magical stories—the Oversoul couldn't know the future any more than a human being could, and as far as visions were concerned, people only remembered the ones that by sheer luck happened to match reality at some point.

"You're the one who's covered with fire," she said.

What was she talking about? How was he supposed to answer this kind of thing?

"No, I'm Nafai," he said.

"Not really fire. Little diamond sparks that turn to lightning when you're angry."

"I've got to go in."

She touched his sleeve; it held him as surely as if she had gripped his arm. "She'll never mate with you, you know."

"Who?"

"Eiadh. She'll offer, but you'll refuse her."

This was humiliating. How did this girl, probably only twelve, and from her size and shape *definitely* not a young woman yet, know anything about his feelings toward Eiadh? Was his love that obvious to everyone? Well, fine, so be it—he had nothing to hide. There was only honor in being known to love such a woman. And as for this girl being a seer, it wasn't too likely, not if she said that Eiadh would actually *offer* herself to him and he would turn her down! I'm more likely to bite my own finger off than to refuse take the most perfect woman in Basilica as my mate.

"Excuse me," Nafai said, pulling his arm away. He didn't like this girl touching him anyway. They said that her mother was a wilder, one of those filthy naked solitary women who came into Basilica from the desert; supposedly they were holy women, but Nafai well knew that they also would sleep with any man who asked, right on the streets of the city, and it was permissible for any man to take one, even when he was in a contract with a mate. Decent and highborn men didn't do it, of course—even Meb had never bragged about "desert worship" or going on a "dust party," as couplings with wilders were crudely called. Nafai saw nothing holy in the whole business, and as far as he was concerned, this Luet was a bastard, conceived by a madwoman and a bestial man in a coupling that was closer to rape than love. There was no chance that the Oversoul really had anything to do with *that*.

"*You're* the bastard," said the girl. Then she walked away. The others had finished their devotions—or perhaps had stopped them in order to listen to what Luet was saying to him. Which meant that the story would be spread all over the house by dinnertime and all over Basilica before supper and no doubt Issib would tease him about it all the way home and then Elemak and Mebbekew would *never* let him forget it and he wished that the women of Basilica would keep crazy people like Luet under lock and key instead of taking their stupid nonsense seriously all the time.

THREE

FIRE

When he got inside he headed for the fountain room, where his class would be meeting all through the autumn. From the kitchen he could smell the preparations for dinner, and with a pang he remembered that, what with his argument with Elemak, he had completely forgotten to eat. Until this moment he hadn't felt even the tiniest bit hungry; but now that he realized it, he was completely famished. In fact, he felt just a little lightheaded. He should sit down. The fountain room was only a few steps away; surely they would understand why he was late if he arrived not feeling well. No one could be angry at him. No one could think he was a lazy slack-wit if he was *sick*. They didn't have to know that he was sick with hunger.

He shuffled miserably into the room, playing his faintness to the hilt, leaning against a wall for a moment as he passed. He could feel their eyes on him, but he didn't look; he had a vague idea that genuinely sick people didn't easily meet other people's gaze. He half-expected the teacher of the day to speak up. What's wrong, Nafai? Aren't you well?

Instead there was silence until he had slid down the wall, folding himself into a sitting position on the wooden floor.

"We'll send out for a burial party, Nafai, in case you suddenly die."

Oh, no! It wasn't a teacher at all, one of the easily fooled young women who were so very impressed that Nafai was Rasa's own son. It was Mother here today. He looked up and met her gaze. She was smiling wickedly at him, not fooled a bit by his sick act.

"I was waiting for you. Issib is already on my portico. He didn't mention that you were dying, but I'm sure it was an oversight."

There was nothing left but to take it with good humor. Nafai sighed and got to his feet. "You know, Mother, that your unwillingness to suspend your disbelief will set back my acting career by several years."

"That's all right, Nafai, dear. Your acting career would set back Basilican theatre by centuries."

The other students laughed. Nafai grinned—but he also scanned the group to see who was enjoying it most. There was Eiadh, sitting near the fountain, where a few tiny drops of water had caught in her hair and were now reflecting light like jewels. *She* wasn't laughing at him. Instead she smiled beautifully, and winked. He grinned back—like a foolish clown, he was sure—and nearly tripped on the step leading up to the doorway to the back corridor. There was more laughter, of course, and so Nafai turned and took a deep bow. Then he walked away with dignity, deliberately running into the doorframe to earn another laugh before he finally made it out of the room.

"What's this about?" he asked Mother, hurrying to catch up with her.

"Family business," she said.

Then they passed through the doorway leading to

Mother's private portico. They would stay, as always, in the screened-off area near the door; beyond the screen, out near the balustrade, the portico offered a beautiful view of the Rift Valley, so it was completely forbidden for men to go there. Such proscriptions in private houses were often ignored—Nafai knew several boys who talked about the Rift Valley, asserting that it was nothing special, just a steep craggy slope covered with trees and vines with a bunch of mist or clouds or fog blocking any view of the middle where, presumably, the sacred lake was located. But in Mother's house, decent respect was always shown, and Nafai was sure that even Father had never passed beyond the screen.

Once he was through with blinking, coming out into bright sunlight, Nafai was able to see who else was on the portico. Issib, of course; but to Nafai's surprise, Father himself was there, home from his journey. Why had he come to Rasa's house in the city, instead of going home first?

Father stood to greet him with an embrace.

"Elemak's at home, Father."

"So Issya informed me."

Father seemed very serious, very distant. He had something on his mind. It couldn't be anything good.

"Now that Nafai is finally here," said Mother, "we can perhaps make some sense out of all this."

Only now, as he seated himself in the best shade that wasn't already taken, did Nafai realize that there were two girls with them. At first glance, in the dazzling sunlight, he had assumed they were his sisters, Rasa's daughters Sevet and Kokor—in that context, an assembly of Rasa and her children, Father's presence was surprising, since he was father only to Issib and Nafai, not to the girls. But instead of Sevet and Kokor, it was two girls from the school— Hushidh, another of mother's nieces, the same age as Eiadh; and that witchling girl from the front porch, Luet. He looked at her in consternation—how had she got here so quickly? Not that he'd been hurrying. Mother must have sent for her even before she knew that Nafai had arrived.

What were Luet and Hushidh doing in a conference about family business?

"My dear mate Wetchik has something to tell us. We're hoping that you can—well, at least that Luet or Hushidh might—"

"Why don't I simply begin?" said Father.

Mother smiled and raised her hands in a graceful, elegant shrug.

"I saw something disturbing this morning," Father began. "Just before morning, actually. I was on my way home on the Desert Road—I was out on the desert, yesterday, to ponder and consult with myself and the Oversoul—when suddenly there came upon me a strong desire—a need, really—to leave the trail, even though that's a foolish thing to do in that dark time between moonset and sunrise. I didn't go far. I only had to move around a large rock, and it became quite clear to me why I had been led to that spot. For there in front of me I saw Basilica. But not the Basilica I would have expected, dotted with the lights of celebration in Dolltown or the inner market. What I saw was Basilica ablaze."

"On *fire*?" asked Issib.

"A vision, of course. I didn't know that at first, mind you—I lunged forward; I was intending to rush to the city—to rush here and see if you were all right, my dear—"

"As I would certainly expect you to do," said Mother.

"When the city disappeared as suddenly as it had appeared. Only the fire remained, rising up to form a pillar on the rock in front of me. It stood there for the longest time, a column of flame. And it was hot—as hot as if it had been real. I felt it singeing me, though of course there's not a mark on my clothing. And then the pillar of flame rose up into the sky, slowly at first, then faster and faster until it became a star moving across the sky, and then disappeared entirely."

"You were tired, Father," said Issib.

"I've been tired many times," said Father, "but I have never seen pillars of flame before. Or burning cities."

Mother spoke up again. "Your father came to me, Issya, because he hoped that I might help him understand the meaning of this. If it came from the Oversoul, or if it was just a mad sort of waking dream."

"I vote for the dream," said Issib.

"Even madness can come from the Oversoul," said Hushidh.

Everyone looked at her. She was a rather plainish girl, always quiet in class. Now that Nafai saw her and Luet side by side, he realized that they resembled each other closely. Were they sisters? More to the point, what was Hushidh doing here, and by what right did she speak out about family matters?

"It *can* come from the Oversoul," said Father. "But did it? And if it did, what does it mean?"

Nafai could see that Father was directing those questions, not at Rasa or even at Hushidh, but at Luet! He couldn't possibly believe what the women said about her, could he? Did a single vision turn a rational man of business into a superstitious pilgrim trying to find meanings in everything he saw?

"I can't tell you what your dream means," said Luet.

"Oh," said Father. "Not that I actually thought—"

"If the Oversoul sent the dream, and if she meant you to understand it, then she also sent the interpretation."

"There *was* no interpretation."

"Wasn't there?" asked Luet. "This is the first time you've had a dream like this, isn't it?"

"Definitely. This isn't a habit of mine, to see visions as I'm walking along the road at night."

"So you aren't used to recognizing the meanings that come along with a vision."

"I suppose not."

"Yet you *were* receiving messages."

"Was I?"

"Before you saw the flame, you knew that you were supposed to turn away from the road."

"Yes, well, *that.*"

"What do you think the voice of the Oversoul sounds like? Do you think she speaks Basyat or puts up signposts?"

Luet sounded vaguely scornful—an outrageous tone of voice for her to adopt with a man of Wetchik's status in the city. Yet he seemed to take no offense, accepting her rebuke as if she had a right to chastise him.

"The Oversoul puts the knowledge pure into our minds, unmixed with any human language," she said. "We are always given more than we can possibly comprehend, and we can comprehend far more than we're able to put into words."

Luet had a voice of such simple power. Not like the chanting sound that the witches and prophets of the inner market used when they were trying to attract business. She spoke as if she knew, as if there was no possibility of doubt.

"Let me ask you, then, sir. When you saw the city on fire, how did you know it was Basilica?"

"I've seen it a thousand times, from just that angle, coming in from the desert."

"But did you see the shape of the city and recognize it from that, or did you know first that it was Basilica on fire, and then your mind called forth the picture of the city that was already in your memory?"

"I don't know—how can I know that?"

"Think back. Was the knowledge there before the vision, or was the vision first?"

Instead of telling the girl to go away, Father closed his eyes and tried to remember.

"When you put it that way, I think—I knew it before I actually looked in that direction. I don't think I actually saw it until I was lunging toward it. I saw the *flame*, but not the burning city inside it. And now that you ask, I also knew that Rasa and my children were in terrible danger. I knew that first of all, as I was rounding the rock—that was part of the sense of urgency. I knew that if I left the trail and came to that exact spot, I'd be able to save them from the danger. It was only then that it came to mind what the danger was, and then last of all that I saw the flame and the city inside it."

"This is a true vision," said Luet.

Just from that? She knew just from the order of things? She probably would have said the same thing no matter *what* Father remembered. And maybe Father was only remembering it that way because Luet had suggested it that way. This was making Nafai furious, for Father to be nodding in acceptance when this twelve-year-old girl condescendingly treated him like an apprentice in a profession in which she was a widely respected master.

"But it wasn't true," said Father. "When I got here, there *was* no danger."

"No, I didn't think so," said Luet. "Back when you first felt that your mate and your children were in danger, what did you expect to *do* about it?"

"I was going to save them, of course."

"Specifically *how*?"

Again he closed his eyes. "Not to pull them from a burning building. That never occurred to me until later, as I was walking the rest of the way into the city. At the moment I wanted to shout out that the city was burning, that we had to—"

"What?"

"I was going to say, we had to get out of the city. But that wasn't what I wanted to say at first. When it started, I felt like I had to come to the city and tell everybody that there was a fire coming."

"And they had to get out?"

"I guess," said Father. "Of course, what else?"

Luet said nothing, but her gaze never left his face.

"No," Father said. "No, that *wasn't* it." Father sounded surprised. "I wasn't going to warn them to get out."

Luet leaned forward, looking somehow more intense, not so—analytical. "Sir, just a moment ago, when you were saying that you had wanted to warn them to get out of the city—"

"But that *wasn't* what I was going to do."

"But when you thought for a moment that—when you *assumed* that you were going to tell them to get out of the city—what did that feel like? When you told us that, why did you know that it was wrong?"

"I don't know. It just felt . . . *wrong*."

"This is very important," said Luet. "How does feeling wrong *feel*?"

Again he closed his eyes. "I'm not used to thinking about how I think. And now I'm trying to remember how it felt when I thought I remembered something that I didn't actually remember—"

"Don't talk," said Luet.

He fell silent.

Nafai wanted to yell at somebody. What were they doing, listening to this ugly stupid little girl, letting her tell Father—the Wetchik himself, in case nobody remembered—to keep his mouth shut!

But everybody else was so intense that Nafai kept his own mouth shut. Issib would be so proud of him for actually refraining from saying something that he had thought of.

"What I felt," said Father, "was *nothing*." He nodded slowly. "Right after you asked the question and I answered it—. Of course, what else—then you sat there looking at me and I had nothing in my head at all."

"Stupid," she said.

He raised an eyebrow. To Nafai's relief, he was finally noticing how disrespectfully Luet was speaking to him.

"You felt stupid," she said. "And so you knew that what you'd just said was wrong."

He nodded. "Yes, I guess that's it."

"What's all this about?" said Issib. "Analyzing your analysis of analyses of a completely subjective hallucination?"

Good work, Issya, said Nafai silently. You took the words right out of my mouth.

"I mean, you can play these games all morning, but you're just laying meanings on top of a meaningless experience. Dreams are nothing more than random firings of memories, which your brain then interprets so as to invent causal connections, which makes stories out of *nothing*."

Father looked at Issib for a long moment, then shook his head. "You're right, of course," he said. "Even though I was wide awake and I've never had a hallucination before, it was nothing more than a random firing of synapses in my brain."

Nafai knew, as Issib and Mother certainly knew, that Father was being ironic, that he was telling Issib that his vision of the fire on the rock was *more* than a meaningless night dream. But Luet didn't know Father, so *she* thought he was backing away from mysticism and retreating into reality.

"You're wrong," she said. "It was a true vision, because

it came to you the right way. The understanding came *before* the vision—that's why I was asking those questions. The meaning is there and then your brain supplies the pictures that let you understand it. That's the way the Oversoul talks to us."

"Talks to crazy people, you mean," Nafai said.

He regretted it immediately, but by then it was too late.

"Crazy people like *me*?" said Father.

"And I assure you that Luet is at least as sane as you are," Mother added.

Issib couldn't pass up the chance to cast a verbal dart. "As sane as Nyef? Then she's in deep trouble."

Father shut down Issib's teasing immediately. "You were saying the same thing yourself only a minute ago."

"I wasn't calling people crazy," said Issib.

"No, you didn't have Nafai's—what shall we call it?— *pointed eloquence*."

Nafai knew he could save himself now by shutting up and letting Issib deflect the heat. But he was committed to skepticism, and self-control wasn't his strong suit. "This girl," said Nafai. "Don't you see how she was leading you on, Father? She asks you a question, but she doesn't tell you beforehand what the answer will mean—so no matter what you answer, she can say, That's it, it's a true vision, definitely the Oversoul talking."

Father didn't have an immediate answer. Nafai glanced at Luet, feeling triumphant, wanting to see her squirm. But she wasn't squirming. She was looking at him very calmly. The intensity had drained out of her and now she was simply—calm. It bothered him, the steadiness of her gaze. "What are you looking at?" he demanded.

"A fool," she answered.

Nafai jumped to his feet. "I don't have to listen to you calling me a—"

"Sit down!" roared Father.

Nafai sat, seething.

"She just listened to *you* calling *her* a fraud," said Father. "I appreciate how both of my sons are doing exactly what I wanted you here to do—providing a skeptical audience for my story. You analyzed the process very cleverly and your version of things accounts for everything you know about it, just as neatly as Luet's version does."

Nafai was ready to help him draw the correct conclusion. "Then the rule of simplicity requires you to—"

"The rule of your father requires you to hold your tongue, Nafai. What you're both forgetting is that there's a fundamental difference between you and me."

Father leaned toward Nafai.

"*I* saw the fire."

He leaned back again.

"Luet didn't tell me what to think or feel at the time. And her questions helped me remember—helped *me* remember—the way it really happened. Instead of the way I was already changing it to fit my preconceptions. She *knew* that it would be strange—in exactly the ways that it was strange. Of course, I can't convince you."

"No," said Nafai. "You can only convince yourself."

"In the end, Nafai, oneself is the only person anyone can convince."

The battle was lost if Father was already making up aphorisms. Nafai sat back to wait for it all to end. He took consolation from the fact that it had been, after all, merely a dream. It's not as if it was going to change his life or anything.

Father wasn't done yet. "Do you know what I actually wanted to do, when I felt such urgency to get to the city? I wanted to warn people—to follow the old ways, to go back to the laws of the Oversoul, or this place would burn."

"What place?" asked Luet, her intensity back again.

"This place. Basilica. The city. That's what I saw burning."

Again Father fell silent, looking into her burning eyes.

"Not the city," he said at last. "The city was only the picture that my mind supplied, wasn't it? Not the city. The whole world. All of Harmony, burning."

Rasa gasped. "Earth," she whispered.

"Oh, please," Nafai said. So Mother was going to connect Father's vision with that old story about the home planet that was burned by the Oversoul to punish humanity for whatever nastiness the current storyteller wanted to preach against. The all-purpose coercive myth: If you don't do what I say—I mean, what the *Oversoul* says—then the *whole world* will *burn*.

"*I* haven't seen the fire itself," said Luet, ignoring Nafai. "Maybe I'm not even seeing the same thing."

"What *have* you seen?" asked Father. Nafai cringed at how respectful he was being toward this girl.

"I saw the Deep Lake of Basilica, crusted over with blood and ashes."

Nafai waited for her to finish. But she just sat there.

"That's it? That's all?" Nafai stood up, preparing to walk out. "This is great, hearing the two of you compare visions. *I* saw a city on fire. Well, *I* saw a scum-covered lake."

Luet stood up and faced him. No, faced him down— which was ridiculous, since he was almost half a meter taller than her.

"You're only arguing against me," she said hotly, "because you don't want to believe what I told you about Eiadh."

"That's ridiculous," said Nafai.

"You had a vision about Eiadh?" asked Rasa.

"What does Eiadh have to do with *Nyef*?" asked Issib.

Nafai hated her for mentioning it again, in front of his

family. "You can make up whatever you want about other people, but you'd better leave *me* out of it."

"Enough," said Father. "We're done."

Rasa looked at him in surprise. "Are you dismissing me in my own house?"

"I'm dismissing my sons."

"You have authority over *your* sons, of course." Mother was smiling, but Nafai knew from her soft speech that she was seriously annoyed. "However, I see no one here in *my* house but *my* students."

Father nodded, accepting the rebuke, then stood to leave. "Then I'm dismissing myself—I may do *that,* I hope."

"You may always leave, my adored mate, as long as you promise to come back to me."

His answer was to kiss her cheek.

"What are you going to do?" she asked.

"What the Oversoul told me to do."

"And what is *that*?"

"Warn people to return to the laws of the Oversoul or the world will burn."

Issib was appalled. "That's crazy, Father!"

"I'm tired of hearing that word from the lips of my sons."

"But—prophets of the Oversoul don't say things like that. They're like poets, except all their metaphors have some moral lesson or they celebrate the Oversoul or—"

"Issya," said Wetchik, "all my life I've listened to these so-called prophecies—and the psalms and the histories and the temple priests—and I've always thought, if *this* is all the Oversoul has to say, why should I bother to listen? Why should the Oversoul even bother *speaking,* if this is all that's on his mind?"

"Then why did you teach *us* to speak to the Oversoul?" asked Issib.

"Because I believed in the ancient laws. And I *did* speak to the Oversoul myself, though more as a way of clarifying my own thoughts than because I actually thought that he was *listening*. Then last night—this morning—I had an experience that I never conceived of. I never wished for it. I didn't even know what it *was* until now, these last few minutes, talking to Luet. Now I know—what it feels like to have the Oversoul's voice inside you. Nothing like these poets and dreamers and deceivers, who write down whatever pops into their heads and then sell it as prophecy. What was in me was not myself, and Luet has shown me that she's had the same voice inside *her*. It means that the Oversoul is real and alive."

"So maybe it's real," said Issib. "That doesn't tell us what it *is*."

"It's the guardian of the world," said Wetchik. "He asked me to help. *Told* me to help. And I will."

"That's all temple stuff," said Issib. "You don't know anything about it. You grow exotic plants."

Father dismissed Issib's objections with a gesture. "Anything the Oversoul needs me to know, he'll tell me." Then he headed for the door into the house.

Nafai followed him, only a few steps. "Father," he said.

Father waited.

The trouble was, Nafai didn't know what he was going to say. Only that he had to say it. That there was a very important question whose answer he had to have before Father left. He just didn't know what the question was.

"Father," he said again.

"Yes?"

And because Nafai couldn't think of the real question, the deep one, the important one, he asked the only question that came to mind. "What am *I* supposed to do?"

"Keep the old ways of the Oversoul," said Father.

"What does that *mean*?"

"Or the world will burn." And Father was gone.

Nafai looked at the empty door for a while. It didn't do

anything, so he turned back to the others. They were all looking at him, as if they expected *him* to do something.

"What!" he demanded.

"Nothing," said Mother. She arose from her seat in the shade of the kaplya tree. "We'll all return to our work."

"That's all?" said Issib. "Our father—your mate—has just told us that the Oversoul is speaking to him, and we're supposed to go back to our studies?"

"You really don't understand, do you?" said Mother. "You've lived all these years as my sons, as my *students*, and you are still nothing more than the ordinary boys wandering the streets of Basilica hoping to find a willing woman and a bed for the night."

"What don't we understand here?" asked Nafai. "Just because you women all take this witchgirl so seriously doesn't mean that—"

"I have been down into the water myself," said Mother, her voice like metal. "You men can pretend to yourselves that the Oversoul is distracted or sleeping, or just a machine that collects our transmissions and sends them to libraries in distant cities. Whatever theory you happen to believe, it makes no difference to the *truth*. For *I* know, as most of the women in this city know, that the Oversoul is very much alive. At least as the keeper of the memories of this world, she is alive. We all receive those memories when we go into the water. Sometimes they seem random, sometimes we are given exactly the memory we needed. The Oversoul keeps the history of the world, as it was seen through other people's eyes. Only a few of us—like Luet and Hushidh— are given wisdom away from the water, and even fewer are given visions of real things that haven't happened yet. Since the great Izumina died, Luet is the only seer I know of in Basilica—so yes, we take her very, very seriously."

Women go down into the water and receive visions? This was the first time Nafai had ever heard a woman describe any part of the worship at the lake. He had always assumed that the women's worship was like the men's—physical, ascetic, painful, a dispassionate way of discharging emotion. Instead they were all mystics. What seemed like legends or madness to men was at the center of a woman's life. Nafai felt as though he had discovered that women were of another species after all. The question was, which of them, men or women, were the humans? The rational but brutal men? Or the irrational but gentle women?

"There's only one thing rarer than a girl like Luet," Mother was saying, "and that's a *man* who hears the voice of the Oversoul. We know now that your father does hear—Luet confirmed that for me. I don't know what the Oversoul wants, or why she spoke to your father, but I *am* wise enough to know that it matters."

As she passed Nafai, she reached up and caught his ear firmly, though not painfully, between her fingers. "As for the mythical burning of Earth, my dear boy, I've seen it myself. It happened. I can only guess how long ago—we estimate there's been at least thirty million years of human history on this world we named Harmony. But I saw the missiles fly, the bombs explode, and the world erupt in flame. The smoke filled the sky and blocked the sun, and underneath that blanket of darkness the oceans froze and the world was covered in ice and only a few human beings survived, to rise up out of the blackness as the world died, carrying their hopes and their regrets and their genes to other planets, hoping to start again. They did. We're here. Now the Oversoul has warned your father that our new start can lead to the same ending as before."

Nafai had seen Mother's public face—playful, brilliant, analytical, gracious—and he had seen her family face—frank of speech yet always kind, quick to anger yet quicker to forgive. Always he had assumed that the way she was with the family was her true self, with nothing held back.

Instead, behind the faces that he thought he knew, she had kept this secret all the time, her bitter vision of the end of Earth. "You never told us about this," whispered Nafai.

"I most certainly told you about it," said Rasa. "It's not *my* fault that when you heard it, you thought I was telling you a myth." She let go of his ear and returned to the house.

Issib floated past him, mumbling something about waking up one morning to find that you've been living in a madhouse all your life. Hushidh went past him also, not meeting his gaze; he could imagine the gossip that she would spread in his class all the rest of the day.

He was alone with Luet.

"I shouldn't have spoken to you before," she said.

"And you shouldn't speak to me again, either," suggested Nafai.

"Some people hear a lie when they're told the truth. You're so proud of your status as the son of Rasa and Wetchik, but obviously whatever genes you got from your parents, they weren't the right ones."

"While I'm sure *you* got the finest your parents had to offer."

She looked at him with obvious contempt, and then she was gone.

"What a wonderful day this is going to be," he said—to no one, since he was alone. "My entire family hates me." He thought for a moment. "I'm not even sure that I *want* them to like me."

For one dangerous moment, alone on the portico, he toyed with the idea of slipping past the screens and going to the edge, leaning out, and looking at the forbidden sight of the Valley of the Holy Women, casually referred to as the Rift Valley, and more crudely known as the Canyon of the Crones. I'll see it and I bet I don't even get struck blind.

But he didn't do it, even though he stood there thinking about it for a long time. It seemed that every time he was about to take a step toward the edge, his mind suddenly wandered and he hesitated, confused, forgetting for a moment what it was he wanted to do. Finally he lost interest and went back inside the house.

He should have gone back to class—it's what he *expected* to do when he went inside. But he couldn't bring himself to do it. Instead he wandered to the front door and out onto the porch, into the streets of Basilica. Mother would probably be furious at him but that was too bad.

He must have been seeing where he was going, since he didn't bump into anything, but he had no memory of what he saw or where he had been. He ended up in the Fountains district, not far from the neighborhood of Rasa's house; and in his mind, he had circled through the same thoughts over and over again, finally ending up not very far from where he started.

One thing he knew, though: He couldn't dismiss this all as madness. Father was *not* crazy, however new and strange he might seem; and as for Mother, if *her* vision of the burning of Earth was madness, then she had been mad since before he was born. So there *was* something that put ideas and desires and visions into his parents' minds—and into Luet's, too, couldn't forget *her*. People called this something the Oversoul, but that was just a name, a label. What *was* it? What did it want? What could it actually *do*? If it could talk to some people, why didn't it just talk to everybody?

Nafai stopped across a fairly wide street from what might be the largest house in Basilica. He knew it well enough, since the head of the Palwashantu clan was mated with the woman who lived there. Nafai couldn't remember *her* name—she was nobody, everyone knew she had bought this ancient house with her mate's money, and if she didn't renew his contract then even *with* the house she'd be nobody—but *he* was Gaballufix. There was a family connection—his mother was Hosni, who later on became Wetchik's auntie and the mother of Elemak. Between that blood connection and the fact that Father was perhaps the second most prestigious Palwashantu clansman in Basilica, they had visited this house at least once, usually two or three times a year since as long ago as Nafai could remember.

As he stood there, stupidly watching the front of that landmark building, he suddenly came alert, for without meaning to he had recognized someone moving along the street. Elemak should have been home sleeping—he had traveled all night, hadn't he? Yet here he was, in mid-afternoon. For a panicked moment Nafai wondered if Elya was looking for *him*—was it possible that Mother had missed him and worried and now the whole family, perhaps even Father's employees as well, were combing the city looking for him?

But no. Elemak wasn't looking for anybody. He was moving too casually, too easily. Looking in no particular direction at all.

And then he was gone.

No, he had turned down into the gap between Gaballufix's house and the building next door. So he *did* have a destination.

Nafai had to know what Elemak was doing. He trotted along the street to where he had a clear view down the narrow road. He got there in time to see Elemak ducking into a low alley doorway into Gaballufix's house.

Nafai couldn't imagine what business Elya might have with Gaballufix—especially something so urgent that he had to go to his house the same day he got back from a long trip. True, Gaballufix was technically Elya's half-brother, but there were sixteen years between them and Gaballufix had never openly recognized Elya as his brother. That didn't mean, though, that they couldn't start behaving more like close kinsmen now. Still, it bothered Nafai that Elemak had never mentioned it and seemed to be concealing it now.

Whether the question bothered him or not, Nafai knew that it would be a very bad idea to ask Elemak about it directly. When Elya wanted anybody to know what he was doing with Gaballufix, he'd tell them. In the meantime, the secret would be safe inside Elya's head.

A secret inside somebody's head.

Luet had known that Nafai was in love with Eiadh. Well, it wasn't all *that* secret—Luet might have guessed it from the way that he looked at her. But there on the front porch of Mother's house, Luet had said, *"You're* the bastard," as if she were answering him for calling *her* a bastard. Only he hadn't *said* anything. He had only *thought* of her as a bastard. It wasn't an opinion he had expressed before. He had only thought of it at that moment, because he was annoyed with Luet. Yet she had known.

Was that the Oversoul, too? Not just putting ideas into people's heads, but also taking them out and telling them to other people? The Oversoul wasn't just a provider of strange dreams—it was a spy and a gossip as well.

It made Nafai afraid, to think that not only was the Oversoul real, but also that it had the power to read his most secret, transitory thoughts and tell them to someone else. And to someone as repulsive as the little bastard witchgirl, no less.

It frightened him like the first time he went out into the sea by himself. Father had taken them all on a holiday, down to the beach. The first afternoon there, they had all gone out into the sea together, and surrounded by his father and brothers—except Issib, of course, who watched them from his chair on the beach—he had felt the sea play with him, the waves shoving him toward shore, then trying to draw him out again. It was fun, exhilarating. He even dared to swim out to where his feet couldn't quite touch the bottom, all the while playing with Meb and Elya and Father. A good day, a great day, when his older brothers still liked him. But the next morning he got up early, left the tent and went out to the water alone. He could swim like a fish; he was in no danger. And yet as he walked out into the water he felt an inexplicable unease. The water tugging at him, pushing him; he was only a few meters from shore, and yet with no one else in the water, all by himself, he felt as if he had lost his place, as if he had already been washed out to sea, as if he were caught in the grasp of something so huge that any part of it could swallow him up. He panicked then. He ran to shore, struggling against the water, convinced that it would never let him go, dragging at him, sucking him down. And then he was on the sand, on the dry sand above the tide line, and he fell to his knees and wept because he was safe.

But for those few moments out in the water he had felt the terror of knowing how small and helpless he was, how much power there was in the world, and how easily it could do to him whatever it wanted and there was nothing he could do to resist it.

That was the fear he felt now. Not so strong, not so specific as it had been that day on the beach—but then, he wasn't a five-year-old anymore, either, and he was better at dealing with fear. The Oversoul wasn't an old legend, it was alive, and it could force visions into his own parents' minds and it could search out secrets inside Nafai's head and tell them to other people, to people that Nafai didn't like and who didn't like him.

The worst thing was knowing that the reason why Luet didn't like him was probably *because* of what the Oversoul had told her about his thoughts. His most private thoughts exposed to this unsympathetic little monster. What next?

Would Father's next vision be Nafai's fantasies about Eiadh? Worse yet, would *Mother* be shown?

On the beach, he had been able to run for shore. Where did you run to get away from the Oversoul?

You didn't. You couldn't hide, either—how could you disguise your own thoughts so even you didn't know what you were thinking?

The only choice he had was to try to find out what the Oversoul was, to try to understand what it wanted, what it was trying to do to his family, to *him*. He had to understand the Oversoul and, if possible, get it to leave him alone.

FOUR

MASKS

There would be no point in going back to Mother's house so late in the school day. Explaining himself would probably take up what little time was left. Making excuses could wait until tomorrow.

Or maybe Nafai would never go back. There was a thought. After all, Mebbekew didn't go to school. In fact he didn't do *anything*, didn't even come home if he decided not to.

When had that started? Was Meb already doing that sort of thing at fourteen? Well, whether he was or not, Nafai could start now and who was going to stop him? He was as tall as any man, and he was old enough for a man's trade. Not Father's trade, though—never the plant business. If you followed *that* trade long enough, you started seeing visions in the dark beside desert roads.

But there were other trades. Maybe Nafai could apprentice himself to some artist. A poet, or a singer—Nafai's voice was young, but he could follow a tune, and with training maybe he could actually become good. Or maybe he was really a dancer, or an actor, in spite of Mother's joke this morning. Those arts had nothing to do with going to school—if he was supposed to pursue one, then staying on with Mother was a waste of time.

That notion possessed him through the afternoon, carrying him south at first, toward the inner market, where there would be songs and poems to hear, perhaps some fine new myachik to buy and listen to at home. Of course, if he stopped attending school, Mother would no doubt cut off his myachik allowance. But as an apprentice there'd probably be some spending money, and if not, so what? He'd be doing a real art himself, in the flesh. Soon he would no longer even *want* recordings of art on little glass balls.

By the time he reached the inner market, he had talked himself into having no interest in recordings, now that he was going to be making a career out of creating the real thing. He headed east, through the neighborhoods called Pens and Gardens and Olive Grove, a few narrow streets of houses between the city wall and the rim of the valley where men could not go. At last he came to the place that was narrowest of all, a single street with a high white wall behind the houses, so that a man standing on the red wall of the city couldn't see over the houses and down into the valley. He had only come this way a few times in his life, and never alone.

Never alone, because Dolltown was a place for company and fellowship, a place for sitting in a crowded audience and watching dances and plays, or listening to recitations and concerts. Now, though, Nafai was coming to Dolltown as an artist, not to be part of the audience. It wasn't fellowship he was looking for, but vocation.

The sun was still up, so the streets of Dolltown weren't crowded. Dusk would bring out the frolicking apprentices and schoolboys, and full dark would call forth the lovers and the connoisseurs and the revelers. But even now, in late afternoon, some of the theatres were open, and the galleries were doing good business in the daylight.

Nafai stopped into several galleries, more because they were open than because he seriously thought he might apprentice himself to a painter or a sculptor. Nafai's skill at drawing was never good, and when he tried sculpture as a child his projects always had to have titles so people could tell what they were supposed to be. Browsing through the galleries, Nafai tried to look thoughtful and studious, but the artsellers were never fooled—Nafai might be tall as a man, but he was still far too young to be a serious customer. So they never came up and talked to him, the way they did when adults came into the shops. He had to glean his information from what he overheard. The prices astonished him. Of course the cost of the originals was completely out of reach, but even the high-resolution holographic copies were too expensive for him to dream of buying one. Worst of all was the fact that the paintings and sculptures he liked the best were invariably the most expensive. Maybe that meant that he had excellent taste. Or maybe it meant that the artists who knew how to impress the ignorant were able to make the most money.

Bored at last with the galleries, and determined to see which art should be the channel for his future, Nafai wandered down to the open theatre, a series of tiny stages dotting the broad lawns near the wall. A few plays were in rehearsal. Since there was no real audience yet, the sound bubbles hadn't been turned on, and as Nafai walked from stage to stage, the sounds of more distant plays kept intruding into every pause in the one close at hand. After a while, though, Nafai discovered that if he stood and watched a rehearsal long enough to get interested, he stopped noticing any other noises.

What intrigued him most was a troupe of satirists. He had always thought satire must be the most exciting kind of play, because the scripts were always as new as today's gossip. And, just as he had imagined, there sat the satirist at the rehearsal, scribbling his verse on paper—on *paper*—and handing the scraps to a script boy who ran them up to the stage and handed them to the player that the lines were intended for. The players who weren't onstage at the moment were either pacing back and forth or hunched over on the lawn, saying their lines over and over again, to memorize them for tonight's performance. This was why satires were always sloppy and ill-timed, with sudden silences and absurd non sequiturs abounding. But no one expected a satire to be *good*—it only had to be funny and nasty and new.

This one seemed to be about an old man who sold love potions. The masker playing the old man seemed quite young, no more than twenty, and he wasn't very good at faking an older voice. But that was part of the fun of it—maskers were almost always apprentice actors who hadn't yet managed to get a part with a serious company of players. They *claimed* that the reason they wore masks instead of makeup was to protect them from reprisals from angry victims of satire—but, watching them, Nafai suspected that the mask was as much to protect the young actor from the ridicule of his peers.

The afternoon had turned hot, and some of the actors had taken off their shirts; those with pale skin seemed oblivious to the fact that they were burning to the color of tomatoes. Nafai laughed silently at the thought that maskers were probably the only people in Basilica who could get a sunburn everywhere *but* their faces.

The script boy handed a verse to a player who had been sitting hunched over in the grass. The young man looked at it, then got up and walked to the satirist.

"I can't say this," he said.

The satirist's back was to Nafai, so he couldn't hear the answer.

"What, is my part so unimportant that *my* lines don't have to rhyme?"

Now the satirist's answer was loud enough that Nafai caught a few phrases, ending with the clincher, "Write the thing yourself!"

The young man angrily pulled his mask off his face and shouted, "I couldn't do worse than *this*!"

The satirist burst into laughter. "Probably not," he said. "Go ahead, give it a try, I don't have time to be brilliant with *every* scene."

Mollified, the young man put his mask back on. But Nafai had seen enough. For the young masker who wanted his lines to rhyme was none other than Nafai's brother Mebbekew.

So this was the source of his income. Not borrowing at all. The idea that had seemed so clever and fresh to Nafai— apprenticing himself in an art to earn his independence— had long since occurred to Mebbekew, and he was *doing* it. In a way it was encouraging—if Mebbekew can do it, why can't I?—but it was also discouraging to think that of all people, Nafai had happened to choose Mebbekew to emulate. Meb, the brother who had hated him all his life instead of coming to hate him more recently, like Elya. Is this what I was born for? To become a second Mebbekew?

Then came the nastiest thought of all. Wouldn't it be funny if I entered the acting profession, years after Meb, and got a job with a serious company right away? It would be deliciously humiliating; Meb would be suicidal.

Well, maybe not. Meb was far more likely to turn murderous.

Nafai was drawn out of his spiteful little daydream by the scene on the stage. The old potion-seller was trying to persuade a reluctant young woman to buy an herb from him.

> Put the leaves in his tea
> Put the flower in your bed
> And by half past three
> He'll be dead—I beg your pardon,
> Just a slip of the tongue.

The plot was finally making sense. The old man wanted to poison the girl's lover by persuading her that the fatal herb was a love potion. She apparently didn't catch on—all characters in satire were amazingly stupid—but for other reasons she was still resisting the sale.

> I'd sooner be hung
> Than use a flower from your garden.
> I want nothing from you.
> I want his love to be true.

Suddenly the old man burst into an operatic song. His voice was actually not bad, even with exaggeration for comic effect.

> The dream of love is so enchanting!

At that moment Mebbekew, his mask back in place, bounded onto the stage and directly addressed the audience.

> Listen to the old man ranting!

They proceeded to perform a strange duet, the old potion-seller singing a line and Mebbekew's young character answering with a spoken comment to the audience.

> But love can come in many ways!
> (I've followed him for several days.)

One lover might be very willing!
(I know he plots her lover's killing.)
The other endlessly delays!
(Listen how the donkey brays!)
Oh, do not make the wrong decision!
(I think I'll give this ass a vision.)
When I can take you to your goal!
(He'll think it's from the Oversoul.)
No limits bind the lover's game.
(A vision needs a little flame . . .)
No matter how you win it,
Because your heart is in it,
You'll love your lover's loving still the same.

A vision from the Oversoul. Flame. Nafai didn't like the turn this was taking. He didn't like the fact that the old potion-seller's mask had a wild mane of white hair and a full white beard. Was it possible that word had already spread so far and fast? Some satirists were famous for getting the gossip before anyone else—as often as not, people attended the satires just to find out what was happening—and many people left the satires asking each other, What was that *really* about?

Mebbekew was fiddling with a box on the stage. The satirist called out to him, "Never mind the fire effect. We'll pretend it's working."

"We have to try it sometime," Mebbekew answered.

"Not now."

"When?"

The satirist got to his feet, strode to the foot of the stage directly in front of Meb, cupped his hands around his mouth, and bellowed: "We . . . will . . . do . . . the . . . effect . . . later!"

"Fine," said Meb.

As the satirist returned to his place on the hill, he said, "And *you* wouldn't be setting off the fire effect anyway."

"Sorry," said Meb. He returned to his place behind the box that presumably would be spouting a column of flame tonight. The other maskers returned to their positions.

"End of song," said Meb. "Fire effect."

Immediately the potion-seller and the girl flung up their hands in a mockery of surprise.

"A pillar of fire!" cried the potion-seller.

"How could fire suddenly appear on a bare rock in the desert?" cried the girl. "It's a *miracle*!"

The potion-seller whirled on her. "You don't know what you're talking about, bitch! *I'm* the only one who can see this! It's a vision!"

"No!" shouted Mebbekew, in his deepest voice. "It's a special stage effect!"

"A stage effect!" cried the potion-seller. "Then you must be—"

"You got it!"

"That old humbug the Oversoul!"

"I'm proud of you, old trickster! Stupid girl—you almost fixed her."

"Oh, it's nothing much to take *her*—*you're* the master faker!"

"No!" bellowed the satirist. "Not 'take *her*,' you idiot! It's '*take* her,' emphasis on *take*, or it doesn't rhyme with *faker*!"

"Sorry," said the young masker playing the potion-seller. "It doesn't make *sense* your way, of course, but at least it'll *rhyme*."

"It doesn't have to make sense, you uppity young rooster, it only has to make money!"

Everybody laughed—though it was clear that the actors still didn't really like the satirist much. They got back into the scene and a few moments later Meb and the potion-seller launched into a song-and-dance routine about how clever they were at hoodwinking people, and how unbelievably gullible most people were—especially women. It seemed that every couplet of the song was designed to mortally offend some portion of the audience, and the song went on until every conceivable group in Basilica had been darted. While they sang and danced, the girl pretended to roast some kind of meat in the flames.

Meb forgot his lyrics less than the other masker, and in spite of the fact that Nafai knew the whole sequence was aimed at humiliating Father, he couldn't help but notice that Meb was actually pretty good, especially at singing so every word was clear. I could do that, too, thought Nafai.

The song kept coming back to the same refrain:

> I'm standing by a fire
> With my favorite liar
> No one stands a chance
> When he starts his fancy dancing

When the song ended, the Oversoul—Meb—had persuaded the potion-seller that the best way to get the women of Basilica to do whatever he wanted was to persuade them that he was getting visions from the Oversoul. "They're so ready for deceiving," said Meb. "We'll have all these girls believing."

The scene closed with the potion-seller leading the girl offstage, telling her how he had seen a vision of the city of Basilica burning up. The satirist had switched to alliterative verse, which Nafai thought sounded a little more natural than rhyming, but it wasn't as fun. "Do you want to waste the last weeks of the world clinging to some callow young cad? Wouldn't you be better off boffing your brains out with an ugly old man who has an understanding with the Oversoul?"

"Fine," said the satirist. "That'll work. Let's have the street scene now."

Another group of maskers came up on the stage. Nafai immediately headed across the lawn to where Mebbekew, his mask still in place, was already scribbling new dialogue on a scrap of paper.

"Meb," said Nafai.

Meb looked up, startled, trying to see better through the small eyeholes in the mask. "What did you call me?" Then he saw it was Nafai. Immediately he jumped to his feet and started walking away. "Get away from me, you little rat-eater."

"Meb, I've got to talk to you."

Mebbekew kept walking.

"Before you go on in this play tonight!" said Nafai.

Meb whirled on him. "It's not a play, it's a satire. I'm not an actor, I'm a masker. And you're not my brother, you're an ass."

Meb's fury astonished him. "What have I done to you?" asked Nafai.

"I know you, Nyef. No matter what I do or say to you, you're going to end up telling Father."

As if Father wouldn't eventually find out that his son was playing in a satire that was designed to dart him in front of the whole city. "What makes me sick," said Nafai, "is that all you care about is whether *you* get in trouble. You've got no family loyalty at all."

"This doesn't hurt my family. Masking is a perfectly legitimate way to get started as an actor, and it pays me a living and wins me just a little tiny scrap of respect and pleasure now and then, which is a lot more than working for Father ever did!"

What was Meb talking about? "I don't care that you're a masker. In fact, I think it's great. I was hanging around here today because I was thinking maybe I might try it myself."

Meb pulled his mask off and looked Nafai up and down. "You've got a body that might look all right on stage. But you still sound like a kid."

"Mebbekew, it doesn't matter right now. You a masker, me a masker—the point is that you can't do this to Father!"

"I'm not doing anything to Father! I'm doing this for myself."

It was always like this, talking to Mebbekew. He never seemed to grasp the thread of an argument. "Be a masker, fine," said Nafai. "But darting your own father is too low even for you!"

Meb looked at him blankly. "Darting my father?"

"You can't tell me you don't know."

"What is there in this satire that darts *him*?"

"The scene you just finished, Meb."

"Father's not the *only* person in Basilica who believes in the Oversoul. In fact, I sometimes think *he* doesn't believe all that seriously."

"The vision, Meb! The fire in the desert, the prophecy about the end of the world! Who do you *think* it's about?"

"I don't know. Old Drotik doesn't tell us what these things are about. If we haven't heard the gossip then so what? We still say the lines anyway." Then Meb got a strange, quizzical expression on his face. "What does all this Oversoul stuff have to do with Father?"

"He had a vision," said Nafai. "On the Desert Road, this morning before dawn, returning from his journey. He saw a pillar of fire on a rock, and Basilica burning, and he thinks it means the destruction of the world, like Earth in the old legend. Mother believes him and he must already be talking to people about it or how else would your satirist know to include this bit in his satire?"

"This is the craziest thing I ever heard of," said Mebbekew.

"I'm not making it up," said Nafai. "I sat there this morning on Mother's portico and—"

"The portico scene! That's . . . He wrote how the apothecary—that's supposed to be *Father*?"

"What do you think I've been telling you?"

"Bastard," whispered Meb. "That bastard. And he put me on stage as the *Oversoul*."

Meb turned and rushed toward the masker who played the apothecary. He stood in front of him for a few moments, looking at the mask and the costume. "It's so *obvious*, I must have the brains of a gnat—but a vision!"

"What are you talking about?" asked the masker.

"Give me that mask," said Mebbekew. "Give it to me!"

"Right, sure, here."

Meb tore it out of the other man's hands and ran up the hill toward the satirist. Nafai ran after him. Meb was waving the mask in front of the satirist's face. "How dare you, Drotik, you pus-hearted old fart!"

"Oh, don't pretend you didn't know, my boy."

"How would I know? I was asleep till rehearsal started. You put me on stage darting my *father* and it's just coincidence that you didn't happen to mention the fact, yes, I'm sure I believe *that*."

"Hey, it brings an audience."

"What were you going to do, tell people who I am, after all your promises about keeping me anonymous? What are these masks supposed to *mean* anyway?" Meb turned to the others, who were clearly baffled by the whole thing. "Listen, people, do you know what this old pimple was going to do? He was going to dart my father and then tell people that it was *me* playing the Oversoul. He was going to unmask me!"

The satirist was obviously worried by this turn of events.

Though most of the maskers' faces were still hidden, they must be angry at the idea of a satirist exposing his maskers' identities. So the satirist had to get things back under control. "Don't waste a thought on this nonsense," he said to the others. "I just fired the boy because he had the audacity to rewrite my lines, and now he wants to wreck the entire show."

The maskers visibly relaxed.

Meb must have realized that he had lost the argument—the maskers *wanted* to believe the satirist because if they didn't, they'd lose a paying job. "My father isn't the liar," said Meb, "*you* are."

"Satire is wonderful, isn't it," said Drotik, "until the dart strikes at home."

Meb raised the white-maned apothecary mask over his head, as if he was going to strike the satirist with it. Drotik flung up an arm and shied away. But Meb never meant to hit him. Instead he brought the mask down over his knee, breaking it in half. Then he tossed both pieces into the satirist's lap.

The satirist lowered his arm and met Mebbekew's gaze again. "It'll take ten minutes for my maskmaker to put the beard onto another mask. Or were you trying to make a metaphorical threat?"

"I don't know," said Meb. "Were you trying to get me to metaphorically murder my father?"

The satirist shook his head in disbelief. "It's a *dart*, boy. Just words. A few laughs."

"A few extra tickets."

"It paid your wages."

"It made you rich." Meb turned his back and walked away. Nafai followed him. Behind them he could hear Drotik sending the script boy to the wall to ask for maskers who thought they could learn a part in three hours.

Mebbekew wouldn't let Nafai catch up with him. He

walked faster and faster, until finally they were running full tilt along the streets, up and down the hills. But Mebbekew hadn't the endurance to outlast Nafai, and finally he fetched up against the corner of a house, bowed over, panting, gasping for breath.

Nafai didn't know what to say. He hadn't meant to chase Meb down, only to tell him what he thought—that he'd been terrific, the way he put the satirist in his place, the way he called him a liar to his face and blasted every argument Drotik raised in his own defense. When you broke the mask in half, I wanted to cheer—that's what Nafai meant to tell him.

But when he got close enough to speak, he realized that Meb wasn't just panting for breath. He was crying, not in grief, but in rage, and when Nafai got there Meb started beating a fist against the wall. "How could he *do* it!" Meb was saying, over and over. "The selfish stupid old son-of-a-bitch!"

"Don't worry about it," said Nafai, meaning to comfort him. "Drotik isn't worth it."

"Not Drotik, you idiot," Meb answered. "Drotik's exactly what I always thought he was except that now I've lost my job and I'll *never* get another one, Drotik will spread the word on me that I walked out on a show three hours before lights."

"Then who are you mad at?"

"Father! Who do you think? A vision—I can't believe it, I thought Drotik would tell me that it wasn't Father he was darting, it was somebody else, and what ever gave me the idea it was Wetchik, what kind of cheese-brained fool would come up with the idea that the honorable *Wetchik* was off getting visions from the amazing unbelievable *Oversoul*!"

"Mother believes him," said Nafai.

"Mother has renewed his contract every year since the

year you were conceived, *obviously* she's got a lot of judgment where he's concerned! Do *you* believe him? Does anybody who hasn't slept with him?"

"I don't know. I don't even know who knows about it."

"Let me tell you something. Six hours from now the entire city of Basilica will know about it, that's who knows about it. I want to *kill* him, the flatulent old pincushion!"

"Calm down, you don't mean that—"

"Don't I? Do you think I wouldn't love to push this fist right through his face?" Meb turned around and screamed his next sentence at the passersby on the street. "I'll show you some visions, you pebble-headed weed-hauler!"

People were stopped on the street, staring.

"Right," said Nafai, "Father's embarrassing *you*."

"I didn't ask you to follow me. *You're* the one who chased after me, so if you don't like being with me you can choke to death on your own snot, that's perfectly all right."

"Let's go home," said Nafai, mostly because he couldn't think of anything else to say.

FIVE

WHEELS

Home certainly wasn't where Nafai wanted to be, not tonight. He had been hoping Father would be somewhere else, so Meb would have a chance to calm down before they talked. But no, of course not, Father *wanted* to talk to Meb. He had already spent an hour talking with Elemak—Nafai wasn't too broken up about missing *that* scene—and now he seemed to have the fantasy that he might possibly persuade Meb to believe in his vision.

The yelling started as soon as Mebbekew located Father in the study. Nafai had seen what these arguments were like, and so he quickly retreated to his room. On his way through the courtyard, he caught a glimpse of Issib peering out of his doorway. Another refugee, thought Nafai.

For the first hour or so, all that could be heard was the low murmur of Father's voice, presumably trying to explain about his vision, interrupted every few minutes by Mebbekew's clear, piercing shout making comments that ranged from accusation to derision. Then it finally came out, amid all of Mebbekew's complaints about how Father was humiliating the family, that Meb had been doing a fair job of bringing the family into disrepute by working as a masker.

Then it was Father's turn to shout and Mebbekew's to try to explain, which was good for another hour of quarreling before Meb left the house in a rage and Father went out to the stables to tend to the animals until he calmed down.

Only then did Nafai venture to the kitchen, absolutely starving by now, for his first serious meal of the day. To his surprise, Elemak was there, sitting with Issib at the table.

"Elya, I didn't know you were here," said Nafai.

Elemak looked up at him, blankly, and then remembered. "Forget it," he said. "I was angry this morning but it's nothing, forget it."

Nafai *had* forgotten, with all that had happened since, that Elemak had warned him not to come home. "I guess I already did," he said.

Elemak gave him a disgusted look and then went back to his food.

"What did I say?"

"Never mind," said Issib. "We're trying to think what we should do."

Nafai headed for the freezer and started scanning the food that Truzhnisha had stocked there for occasions like this. He was dying of hunger and yet nothing looked good. "Is this all that's left?"

"No, I have the rest hidden in my pants," said Issib.

Nafai picked something that he remembered liking before, even though it didn't sound particularly good tonight. While it was heating he turned around and faced the others. "So, what have we decided?"

Elemak didn't look up.

"*We* haven't decided anything," said Issib.

"Oh, what, am I suddenly the only child in the house, while the *men* are making all the decisions?"

"Pretty much, yes," said Issib.

"And what decisions do *you* have to make? Who has any decisions to make at *all,* besides Father? It's his house, his business, his money, and his name that's getting laughed at all through Basilica."

Elemak shook his head. "Not *all* through Basilica."

"You mean somebody hasn't heard about this yet?"

"I mean," said Elemak, "that not everybody is laughing."

"They will if that satire runs long. I saw a rehearsal. Meb was really pretty good. Of course he quit since it was about Father, but I think he really has talent. Did you know he sings?"

Elemak looked at him with contempt. "Are you really this shallow, Nyef?"

"Yes," said Nafai. "I'm so shallow that I actually think our embarrassment isn't all that important, if Father really saw a vision."

"We know Father *saw* it," said Elemak. The problem is what he's doing about it."

"What, he gets a vision from the Oversoul warning about the destruction of the world, and he should keep it a secret?"

"Just eat your food," said Elemak.

"He's going around telling people that the Oversoul wants us to go back to the old laws," said Issib.

"Which ones?"

"All of them."

"I mean which ones aren't we already following?"

Elemak apparently decided to go straight to the heart of things. "He went to the clan council and spoke against our decision to cooperate with Potokgavan in their war with the Wetheads."

"Who?"

"The Gorayni. The Wetheads."

They had got the nickname because of their habit of wearing their hair long, in ringlets, dripping with a perfumed oil. They were also known as vicious warriors with a habit of slaughtering prisoners who hadn't proved their valor by sustaining a serious wound before surrendering. "But they're hundreds of kilometers north of here," said Nafai, "and the Potoku are way to the southeast, and what do they have to fight about?"

"What do they teach you in your little school?" said Elemak. "The Potoku have extended their protection over all the coastal plain up to the Mochai River."

"Sure, right. Protection from what?"

"From the Gorayni, Nafai. We're between them. It's called geography."

"I know geography," said Nafai. "I just don't see why there should ever be a war between the Gorayni and the Potoku, and if there was, how they'd go about fighting it. I mean, Potokgavan has a fleet—all their *houses* are boats, for heaven's sake—but since Goraynivat has no seacoast—"

"*Had* no seacoast. They've conquered Usluvat."

"I guess I knew that."

"Oh, I'm sure you did," said Elemak. They have horse-wagons. Have you heard of those?"

"Wheels," said Nafai. "Horses pulling men in boxes into battle."

"And carrying supplies to feed an army on a long march. A *very* long march. Horsewagons are changing everything." Suddenly Elemak sounded enthusiastic. It had been a lot of years since Nafai had seen Elya excited about anything. "I can envision a day when we'll widen the Ridge Road and the Plains Road and Market Street so that the farmers can haul their produce up here in horsewagons. The same number of horses can haul ten times as much. One man, two horses, and a wagon can bring what it takes a dozen men and twenty horses to haul up here now. The price of food drops. The cost of transporting *our* products downhill drops even lower—there's money there. I can envision roads going hundreds of kilometers, right across the desert— fewer animals in our caravans, less feed to haul and no need to find as much water on the journey. The world is getting smaller, and Father's trying to block it."

"All this has something to do with his vision?"

"The old laws of the Oversoul. Wheels for anything other than gears or toys are forbidden. Sacrilege. Abomination. Do you realize that horsewagons have been known about for thousands and thousands of years and *nobody* has ever built any?"

"Till now," said Issib.

"Maybe there was a good reason," said Nafai.

"The reason was superstition, that was the reason," said Elemak, "but now we have a chance to build two hundred horsewagons with Potokgavan paying for it and providing us with the designs, and the price Gaballufix has negotiated is high enough that we can build two hundred more for ourselves."

"Why don't the Potoku build their own wagons?"

"They're coming here on boats," said Elemak. "Instead of building the wagons in Potokgavan and then floating them all the way, they'll simply send their soldiers and have the wagons waiting for them here."

"Why *here*?"

"Because here is where they're going to draw the line. The Gorayni go no farther, or they face the wrath of the Potoku. Don't try to understand it, Nafai, it's men's business."

"It sounds to me like Father would be right to try to block this just on general principles," said Nafai. "I mean, if they find out we're building horsewagons for the Potoku, won't that just make the Gorayni send an army here to stop us?"

"They won't know until it's too late."

"Why won't they know? Is Basilica so good at keeping secrets?"

"Even if they know, Nyef, the Potoku will be here to stop them from trying to punish us."

"But if the Potoku weren't coming, and therefore we

weren't making wagons for them, there'd be nothing for the Gorayni to punish us *for*."

Elemak lowered his head to the table, making a show of his despair at trying to explain anything to Nafai.

"The world is changing," said Issib. "We're used to wars being local quarrels. But the Gorayni have changed it. They're conquering other countries that never did them any harm."

Elemak picked up the explanation. "Someday they'd reach us, with or without the Potoku here to protect us. Personally, I prefer letting the Potoku do the fighting."

"I can't believe all this has been going on and nobody's even talking about it in the city," said Nafai. "I really *don't* have my ears plugged with mud, and I haven't heard anything about us building wagons for Potokgavan."

Elemak shook his head. "It's a secret. Or it *was*, till Father brought it up before the entire clan council."

"You mean somebody was doing this and the clan council didn't even know?"

"It was a *secret*," said Elemak. "How many times do I have to say it?"

"So somebody was going to do this thing in the name of Basilica and the Palwashantu clan, and nobody in the clan council or the city council was going to be consulted about it?"

Issib laughed ruefully. "When you put it that way, it sounds pretty strange, doesn't it."

"It doesn't sound strange at all," said Elemak. "I can see that you're already with Roptat's party."

"Who's Roptat?"

Issib answered, "He's a Palwashantu, Elya's age is all, who's been using this war talk to build up his reputation as a prophet. Not like Father, he doesn't have visions from the Oversoul, he just writes prophecies that read like a shark tearing your leg off. And he keeps saying the same things that you just said."

"You mean this secret plan is so well known that there's already a party led by this Roptat trying to block it?"

"It wasn't *that* secret," said Elemak. "There's no plot. There's no conspiracy. There's just some good people trying to do something that's in Basilica's vital interest, and some traitors doing everything they can to stop it."

Clearly Elemak had a one-sided view of things. Nafai had to offer another point of view. "Or maybe it's some greedy profiteers putting our city in a terribly dangerous situation so they can get rich, and some good people are trying to save the city by stopping them. I'm just suggesting this as a possibility."

Elemak was furious. "The people working on this project are already so rich that they hardly need any more money," he said. "And what I don't get is how a fourteen-year-old *scholar* who's never had to do a *man's* work in his life suddenly has opinions about political issues that he didn't even know *existed* until ten minutes ago."

"I was just asking a question," said Nafai. "I wasn't accusing you of anything."

"Well of course you weren't accusing *me*" said Elemak. "I'm not part of the project anyway."

"Of course not," said Nafai. "It's a *secret* project."

"I should have beaten the teeth out of your mouth this morning," said Elemak.

Why did it always come down to threats? "Do you beat the teeth out of the mouth of everybody who asks you questions you don't have any good answers for?"

"Never before," said Elemak, getting up. "But now I'm going to make up for all those missed opportunities."

"Stop it!" shouted Issib. "Don't we have enough problems?"

Elemak hesitated, then sat back down. "I shouldn't let him get to me."

Nafai breathed again. He hadn't noticed that he wasn't breathing.

"He's a child, what does he know?" said Elemak. "Father's the one who should know better. He's making a lot of people very angry. Some very dangerous people."

"You mean they're threatening him?" asked Nafai.

"Nobody *threatens*," said Elemak. "That would be crude. They're just . . . concerned about Father."

"But if everybody's laughing at Father, why should they care what he says? It sounds like it's this Roptat they ought to be worried about."

"It's the vision thing," said Elemak. "The Oversoul. Most men don't take it all that seriously, but the women . . . the city council . . . your mother isn't helping things."

"Or she *is* helping things, depending on which side you're on."

"Right," said Elemak. He got up from the table, but this time he wasn't threatening. "I can see which side *you're* on, Nyef, and I can only warn you that if Father has his way, we'll end up in Gorayni chains."

"Why are you so sure?" asked Nafai. "The Oversoul give you a vision or something?"

"I'm sure, my little *half*-friend, because I understand things. When you grow up, you might actually come to know what that means. But I doubt it." Elemak walked out of the kitchen.

Issib sighed. "Does anybody actually *like* anybody else in this family?"

Nafai's food was overcooked, but he didn't care. He was trembling so violently that he could hardly carry his tray to the table.

"Why are you shaking?"

"I don't know," said Nafai. "Maybe I'm afraid."

"Of Elemak?"

"Why should I be afraid of him?" said Nafai. "Just because he could break my neck with his elbow."

"Then why do you keep provoking him?"

"Maybe I'm also afraid *for* him."

"Why?"

"Don't you think it's funny, Issib? Elya can sit here and talk about Father being in danger from powerful people—and yet his solution for it isn't to denounce those dangerous people, it's to try to get Father to stop talking."

"Nobody's being rational."

"I actually *do* understand politics," said Nafai. "I study history all the time. I left my class behind years ago. I *know* something about how wars start and who wins them. And this is the stupidest plan I've ever heard. Potokgavan has no chance of holding this area and no compelling reason to try. All that will happen is they'll send an army, provoke the Gorayni into attacking, and then they'll realize they can't win and go home to their floodplain where the Wetheads can't touch them, leaving *us* to bear the brunt of the Gorayni wrath. Building war wagons for them is so *obviously* going to lead to disaster that only a person completely blinded by greed could possibly support it. And if the Oversoul is telling Father to oppose the building of wagons, then the Oversoul is right."

"I'm sure the Oversoul is relieved to have your approval."

"Anything I can do to help."

"Nafai, you're fourteen."

"So?"

"Elemak doesn't want to hear that kind of thing from you."

"Neither do you, right?"

"I'm really tired. It's been a long day." Issib floated out of the kitchen.

Nafai finally started to eat. To his disgust he had no

appetite, even though he knew he was still hungry. Must eat, can't eat. Forget it. He flushed the food down the drain and put the plate in the cleaning rack.

He walked out into the courtyard, heading for his room. The night air was chilly already—they were close enough to the desert to get sharp falls in temperature when the sun was down. He was still trembling. He didn't know why. It wasn't because of Father's vision of the destruction of the world, and it wasn't because of the war that would probably come to Basilica if they went ahead with the idiotic alliance with Potokgavan. Those were dangers, yes, but distant ones. And it wasn't because of Elemak's threats of violence, he'd lived with those all his life.

It wasn't until he was lying on his mat, still shaking even though his room was *not* cold, that he finally realized what was bothering him. Elemak had mentioned that Gaballufix was involved in negotiating the price with the Potoku. Obviously this whole plan had Gaballufix's support—who else but the clan chief would think he could commit the Palwashantu to such a dangerous course of action without even consulting the council? And so it was reasonable to suppose that when Elya warned about the dangerous enemies Father was making, it was Gaballufix he was referring to.

Gaballufix, whose house Elemak secretly visited today.

Where was Elemak's loyalty? With Father? Or with his half-brother Gaballufix? Clearly Elya was involved with this war wagon plan. What else was he involved with? The dangerous people weren't making *threats,* he had said. So what *were* they making—plans? Was Elya in on a plan to do something ugly to Father, and his hints were an attempt to warn Father away?

Just today, Mebbekew had spoken of metaphorical patricide.

No, thought Nafai. No, I'm simply upset because all of

this has happened so suddenly, in one day. Father has a vision, and suddenly he's caught up in city politics in a way he never was before, almost as if the Oversoul sent him this vision specifically *because* of this stupid provocative project of Gaballufix's, because action needed to be taken *now*.

Why? What did the fate of Basilica matter to the Oversoul? Countless cities and nations had risen and fallen— dozens every century, thousands and thousands in all of human history. Maybe millions. The Oversoul hadn't lifted a finger. It wasn't war that the Oversoul cared about; it certainly wasn't preventing human suffering. So why was the Oversoul getting involved now? What was the *urgency*? Was it worth tearing their family apart? And even if maybe it was, who decided anyway? Nobody had asked the Oversoul for this, so if they really were getting bounced around as part of some master plan, it might be nice if the Oversoul let them in on what it had in mind.

Nafai lay on his mat, trembling.

Then he remembered. I wasn't going to sleep on a mat tonight. I was going to try to be a real man.

He almost laughed aloud. Sleeping on the bare floor— *that* would make me a man? What an idiot I am. What an ass.

Laughing at himself, now he could sleep.

SIX

ENEMIES

W<i>here</i> did you spend all day yesterday?"
Nafai didn't want this conversation, but
there was no avoiding it. Mother was not one
to let one of her students disappear for a day without an
accounting.

"I walked around."

As he had expected, this was not going to be enough for
Mother. "I didn't think that you *flew*," she said. "Though
I'm surprised you didn't curl up somewhere and sleep.
Where did you go?"

"To some very educational places," said Nafai. He had
in mind Gaballufix's house and the Open Theatre, but of
course Mother would interpret his words as she wished.

"Dolltown?" she asked.

"There's nothing much going on there in the daytime,
Mother."

"And you shouldn't be going there at all," she said.
"Or do you think you already know everything about
everything, so that you have no further need of schooling?"

"There are some subjects you just don't teach here,
Mother." Again, the truth—but not the truth.

"Ah," she said. "Dhelembuvex was right about you."

Oh, yes, wonderful. Time to get an Auntie for your little boy.

"I should have seen it coming. Your body is growing so fast—too fast, I fear, outstripping your maturity in every other area."

This was too much to bear. He had planned to listen calmly to everything she said, let her jump to her own conclusions, and then get back to class and have done with the whole thing. But to have her thinking that his gonads were running his life when, if anything, his mind was more mature than his body—

"Is that as smart as you know how to be, Mother?"

She raised an eyebrow.

He knew he was already overstepping himself, but he had begun, and the words were there in his mind, and so he said them. "You see something inexplicable going on, and if it's a boy doing it, you're sure it has to do with his sexual desires."

She half-smiled. "I do have some knowledge of men, Nafai, and the idea that the behavior of a fourteen-year-old might have some link to sexual desire is based on much evidence."

"But I'm your *son,* and still you don't know me from a pile of bricks."

"So you *didn't* go to Dolltown?"

"Not for any reason *you'd* imagine."

"Ah," she said. "I can imagine *many* reasons. But not one of the possible reasons for you to go to Dolltown suggests that you have very good judgment."

"Oh, and you're the expert on good judgment, I imagine."

His sarcasm was not playing well. "You forget, I think, that I am your mother and your schoolmistress."

"It was you, Mother, and not I who invited those two girls to *that family* meeting yesterday."

"And this showed poor judgment on my part?"

"Extremely poor. By the time I got to the Open Theatre it was still several hours before dark, and already the word was out about Father's vision."

"That's not surprising," said Mother. "Father went directly to the clan council. It would hardly be a secret after that."

"Not just his *vision*, Mother. There was already a satire in rehearsal—one of Drotik's, too, no less—that included a fascinating little portico scene. Since the only people present who were *not* family were those two witchgirls—"

"Hold your tongue!"

He immediately fell silent, but with an undeniable sense of victory. Yes, Mother was furious—but he had also scored a point with her, to get her this angry.

"Your referring to them by that demeaning *manword* is offensive in the extreme," said Mother. Her voice was quiet now; she was *really* angry. "Luet is a seer and Hushidh is a raveler. Furthermore, both have been completely discreet, mentioning nothing to anyone."

"Oh, have you watched them every second since—"

"I said to hold your tongue." Her voice was like ice. "For your information, my bright, wise, *mature* little boy, the reason there was a portico scene in Drotik's satire—which, by the way, I *saw,* and it was very badly done, so it hardly worries me—the reason there was a portico scene was because while your father was going to the clan council, I was at the city council, and when *I* told the story I included the events on this portico. Why, asks my brilliant son with a deliciously stupid look on his face? Because the only thing that made the council take your father's vision seriously was the fact that Luet believed him and found his vision consonant with her own."

Mother had told. *Mother* had brought down ridicule and ruin upon the family. Unbelievable. "Ah," said Nafai.

"I thought you'd see things a little differently."

"I see that there was nothing wrong with having Luet and Hushidh at the family meeting," said Nafai. "It was *you* who should have been excluded."

Her hand lashed out across his face. If she had been aiming for his cheek, she missed, perhaps because he reflexively drew his head back. Instead her fingernail caught him on the chin, tearing the skin. It stung and drew blood.

"You forget yourself, sir," she said.

"Not as badly as you have forgotten yourself, Madam," he answered. Or rather, that was how he *meant* to answer. He even *began* to answer that way, but in the middle of the sentence the enormity of her having struck him that way, the shock and hurt of it, the sheer humiliation of his mother hitting him reduced him to tears. "I'm sorry," he said. Though what he really wanted to say was How dare you, I'm too old for that, I hate you. It was impossible to say such harsh things, however, when he was crying like a baby. Nafai hated it, how tears had always come so easily to him, and it wasn't getting any better as he got older.

"Maybe next time you'll remember to speak to me with proper respect," she said. But she, too, was unable to maintain her sharp tone, for even as she spoke he felt her arm around him as she sat beside him, comforted him.

She could not possibly understand that the way she nestled his head to her shoulder only added to the humiliation and confirmed him in his decision to regard her as an enemy. If she had the power to make him cry because of his love for her, then there was only one possible solution for him: to cease loving her. This was the last time she would ever be able to do this to him.

"You're bleeding," she said.

"It's nothing," he said.

"Let me stanch it—here, with a clean handkerchief, not that horrible rag you carry in your pocket, you absurd little boy."

That's all I'll ever be in this house, isn't it? An absurd little boy. He pulled away from her, refused to let the handkerchief touch his chin. But she persisted, and dabbed at the wound, and the white cloth came away surprisingly bloody—so he took it from her hand and pressed it against the wound. "Deep, I guess," he said.

"If you hadn't moved your head back, my nails wouldn't have caught your chin like that."

If you hadn't slapped me, your nails would have been in your *lap*. But he held his tongue.

"I can see that you're taking our family's situation very much to heart, Nafai, but your values are a little twisted. What does the ridicule of the satirists matter? Everyone knows that every great figure in the history of Basilica was darted at one time or another, and usually for the very thing that made her—or him—great. We can bear that. What matters is that Father's vision was a very clear warning from the Oversoul, with immediate implications for our city's course of action over the next few days and weeks and months. The embarrassment will pass. And among the women in this city who really count, Father is viewed as quite a remarkable man—their respect for him is growing. So try to control your embarrassment at your father's having come to the center of attention. All children in their early teens are excruciatingly sensitive to embarrassment, but in time you will learn that criticism and ridicule are not always bad. To earn the enmity of evil people can speak very well of you."

He could hardly believe she thought so little of him as to think he needed such a lecture as this one. Did she really believe that it was *embarrassment* he feared? If she had listened instead of lecturing, he might have told her about Elemak's warning about danger to Father, about his secret visit to Gaballufix's house. But it was clear that in her eyes he was still nothing but a child. She wouldn't take his warning seriously. Indeed, she'd probably give him another lecture about not letting fears and worries take possession of your mind, but instead to concentrate on his studies and let adults worry about the *real* problems in the world.

In her mind, I'm still six years old and I always will be. "I'm sorry, Mother. I'll not speak to you that way again." In fact, I doubt that I'll ever say anything serious or important to you again as long as you live.

"I accept your apology, Nafai, as I hope you'll accept mine for having struck you in my anger."

"Of course, Mother." I'll accept your apology—*when* you offer it and *when* I believe that you mean it. However, as a matter of fact, dear beloved breadbasket out of whom I sprang, you did not actually apologize to me at any point in our conversation. You only expressed the hope that I would accept an apology which in fact was never offered.

"I hope, Nafai, you will resume your studies and not allow these events in the city to disturb the normal routines of your life any further. You have a very keen mind, and there is no particular reason for you to let these things distract you from the honing of that mind."

Thank you for the dollop of praise, Mother. You've told me that I'm childish, that I'm a slave of lust, and that my views are to be silenced, not listened to. You'll pay serious attention to every word drooled from the mouth of that *witch*girl, but you start from the assumption that anything *I* say is worthless.

"Yes, Mother," said Nafai. "But I'd rather not go back to class right now, if you don't mind."

"Of course not," she said. "I understand completely."

Dear Oversoul, keep me from laughing.

"I can't have you out wandering the streets again, Nafai, I'm sure you can understand that. Father's vision has attracted enough attention that someone *will* say something that will make you angry, and I don't want you fighting."

So you're worried about *me* fighting, Mother? Kindly remember who struck whom here on your portico today.

"Why not spend the day in the library, with Issib? He'll be a good influence on you, I think—he's always so calm."

Issib, always calm? Poor Mother—she knows nothing at all about her own sons. Women never *do* understand men. Of course, men don't understand women any better—but at least we don't suffer from the delusion that we *do*.

"Yes, Mother. The library's fine."

She arose. "Then you must go there now. Keep the handkerchief, of course."

She left the portico, not waiting to see if he obeyed.

He immediately got to his feet and walked around the screen, straight to the balustrade, and looked out over the Rift Valley.

There was no sign of the lake. A thick cloud filled the lower reaches of the valley, and since the valley walls seemed to grow steeper just before the fog began, for all he knew the lake might be invisible from this spot even without the fog.

All he could see from here was the white cloud and the deep, lush greens of the forest that lined the valley. Here and there he could see smoke rising from a chimney, for there were women who lived on the valley slopes. Father's housekeeper, Truzhnisha, was one of them. She kept a house in the district called West Shelf, one of the twelve districts of Basilica where only women were allowed to live or even enter. The Women's Districts were far less populated than any of the twenty-four districts where men were allowed to live (though not own property, of course), yet on the City Council they wielded enormous power, since their representatives always voted as a bloc. Conservative, religious—no doubt those were the councilors who were most impressed by the fact that Luet had confirmed Father's vision. If *they* agreed with Father on the war wagon issue, then it would take the votes of only six other councilors to create stalemate, and of seven councilors to take positive action against Gaballufix's plans.

It was these same councilors from the Women's Districts who, for thousands of years, had refused to allow any subdivision of the thickly populated Open Districts, or to give a council vote to any of the districts outside the walls, or to allow men to own property within the wall, or anything else that might tend to dilute or weaken the absolute rule of women in Basilica. Now, looking out over the secret valley, filled with rage against his mother, Nafai could hardly see how beautiful this place was, how rich with mystery and life; all he could see was how unbelievably few the houses were.

How do they divide this into a dozen districts? There must be some districts where the three women who live there take turns being the councilor.

And outside the city, in the tiny but expensive cubicles where unmated men without households were forced to live, there was no legal recourse to demand fairer treatment, to insist on laws protecting bachelors from their landlords, or from women whose promises disappeared when they lost interest in a man, or even from each other's violence. For a moment, standing there looking out over the untamed greenery of the Rift, Nafai understood how a man like Gaballufix might easily gather men around him, struggling to gain some power in this city where men were unmanned by women every day and every hour of their lives.

Then, as the wind gusted a little over the valley, the cloud moved, and there was a shimmer of reflected light. The surface of a lake, not at the center of the deepest part of the rift, but higher, farther away. Without thinking, Nafai reflexively looked away. It was one thing to come to the balustrade in defiance of his Mother, it was another thing to look on the holy lake where women went for their worship. If there was one thing becoming clear in all this business, it was that the Oversoul might very well be real. There was no point in earning its wrath over something as stupid as looking at some lake over the edge of Mother's portico.

Nafai turned away from the view and hurried back around the screen, feeling foolish all the while. What if I'm caught? Well, so what if I am? No, no, the defiance wasn't worth the risk. He had more practical work to do. If Mother wasn't going to listen to his fears about the danger to Father, then Nafai would have to do something himself. But first he had to know more—about Gaballufix, about the Oversoul, about everything.

For a moment he toyed with the idea of going to Luet and asking her questions. *She* knew about the Oversoul, didn't she? She saw visions all the time, not just once, like Father. Surely she could explain.

But she was a woman, and at this moment Nafai knew that he'd get no help of any kind from women. On the contrary—women in Basilica were taught from childhood on how to oppress men and make them feel worthless. Luet would laugh at him and go straight to Mother to tell her about his questions.

If he could trust anyone in this, it would be other men— and precious few of them, since the danger to Father was coming from Gaballufix's party. Perhaps he could enlist the help of this Roptat that Elya had talked about. Or find out something about what the Oversoul was doing in the first place.

ISSIB WASN'T THRILLED to see him. "I'm busy and I don't need interruptions."

"This is the household library," said Nafai. "This is where we always come to do research."

"See? You're interrupting already."

"Look, I didn't say *anything,* I just came in here, and *you* started picking at me the second I walked in the door."

"I was hoping you'd walk back out."

"I can't. Mother sent me here." Nafai walked over behind Issib, who was floating comfortably in the air in front of his computer display. It was layered about thirty pages deep, but each page had only a few words on it, so he could see almost everything at once. Like a game of solitaire, in which Issib was simply moving fragments from place to place.

The fragments were all words in weird languages. The ones Nafai recognized were very old.

"What language is *that*?" Nafai asked, pointing to one.

Issib sighed. "I'm so glad you're not interrupting me."

"What is it, some ancient form of Vijati?"

"Very good. It's Slucajan, which came from Obilazati, the original form of Vijati. It's dead now."

"I read Vijati, you know."

"*I* don't."

"Oh, so you're specializing in ancient, obscure languages that nobody speaks anymore, including you?"

"I'm not *learning* these languages, I'm researching lost words."

"If the whole language is dead, then *all* the words are lost."

"Words that used to have meanings, but that died out or survived only in idiomatic expressions. Like 'dancing bear.' What's a *bear*, do you know?"

"I don't know. I always thought it was some kind of graceful bird."

"Wrong. It's an ancient mammal. Known only on Earth, I think, and not brought here. Or it died out soon. It was bigger than a man, very powerful. A predator."

"And it *danced*?"

"The expression used to mean something absurdly clumsy. Like a dog walking on its hind legs."

"And now it means the opposite. That's weird. How could it change?"

"Because there aren't any bears. The meaning used to be obvious, because everybody knew what a bear was and how clumsy it would look, dancing. But when the bears were gone, the meaning could go anywhere. Now we use it for a person who's extremely deft in getting out of an embarrassing social situation. It's the only case where we use the word *bear* anymore. And you see a lot of people misspelling it, too."

"Great stuff. You doing a linguistics project?"

"No."

"What's this for, then?"

"Me."

"Just collecting old idioms."

"Lost words."

"Like *bear*? The *word* isn't lost, Issya. It's the *bears* that are gone."

"Very good, Nyef. You get full credit for the assignment. Go away now."

"You're not researching lost words. You're researching words that have lost their meanings because the thing they refer to doesn't exist anymore."

Issya slowly turned his head to look at Nafai. "You mean that you've actually developed a brain?"

Nafai pointed at the screen. "*Kolesnisha*. That's a word in Kunic. You've got the meaning right there—war wagon. Kunic hasn't been spoken in ten million years. It's just a written language now. And yet they had a word for war wagon. Which was only just invented. Which means that there used to be war wagons a long time ago."

Issib laughed. A low chuckle, but it went on and on.

"What, am I wrong?"

"It just kills me, that's all. How *obvious* it is. Even *you* can just walk up to a computer display and see the whole thing at once. So why hasn't anybody noticed this before? Why hasn't anybody noticed the fact that we had the word *wagon* already, and we all knew what it meant, and yet as far as we know there have never been any wagons anywhere in the world *ever*?"

That's really weird, isn't it?"

"It isn't weird, it's scary. Look at what the Wetheads are doing with their war wagons—their *kolesnishety*. It gives them a vital advantage in war. They're building a real empire, not just a system of alliances, but actual *control* over nations that are six days' travel away from their city. Now, if war wagons can do *that,* and people used to have them millions of years ago, *how did we ever forget what they were?*"

Nafai thought about that for a while. "You'd have to be really stupid," he said. "I mean, people don't forget things like that. Even if you had peace for a thousand years, you'd still have pictures in the library."

"No pictures of war wagons," said Issib.

"I mean, that's *stupid*," said Nafai.

"And this word," said Issib.

"*Zrakoplov*," said Nafai. "That's definitely an Obilazati word."

"Right."

"What does it mean? 'Air' something."

"Broken down and loosely translated, yes, it means 'air swimmer.'"

Nafai thought about this for a while. He conjured up a picture in his mind—a fish moving through the air. "A flying fish?"

"It's a machine," said Issib.

"A really fast ship?"

"Listen to yourself, Nafai. It should be obvious to you. And yet you keep resisting the plain meaning of it."

"An underwater boat?"

"How would that be an *air* swimmer, Nyef?"

"I don't know." Nafai felt silly. "I forgot about the air part."

"You forgot about it—and yet you recognized the 'air part' right off, by yourself. You *knew* that *Zraky* was the Obilazati root for *air,* and yet you forgot the "air part.""

"So I'm really, *really* dumb."

"But you're *not*, Nyef. You're really really *smart*, and yet you're still standing here looking at the word and I'm telling you all this and you *still* can't think of what the word means."

"Well, what's *this* word," said Nafai, pointing at *puscani prah*. "I don't recognize the language."

Issib shook his head. "If I didn't see it happening to you, I wouldn't believe it."

"What?"

"Aren't you even curious to know what a *zrakoplov* is?"

"You told me. Air swimmer."

"A *machine* whose name is *air* swimmer."

"Sure. Right. So what's a *puscani prah*?"

Issib slowly turned around and faced Nafai. "Sit down, my dear beloved brilliant stupid brother, thou true servant of the Oversoul. I've got something to tell you about machines that swim through the air."

"I guess I'm interrupting you," said Nafai.

"I want to talk to you," said Issib. "It's not an interruption. I just want to explain the idea of flying—"

"I'd better go."

"Why? Why are you so eager to leave?"

"I don't know." Nafai walked to the door. "I need some air. I'm running out of air." He walked out of the room. Immediately he felt better. Not lightheaded anymore. What was all that about, anyway? The library was too stuffy. Too crowded. Too many people in there.

"Why did you leave?" asked Issib.

Nafai whirled. Issib was silently floating out of the library after him. Nafai immediately felt the same kind of claustrophobia that had driven him out into the hall. "Too crowded in there," said Nafai. "I need to be alone."

"I was the only person in there," said Issib.

"Really?" Nafai tried to remember. "I want to get outside. Just let me go."

"Think," said Issib. "Remember when Luet and Father were talking yesterday?"

Immediately Nafai relaxed. He didn't feel claustrophobic anymore. "Sure."

"And Luet was testing Father—about his memories. When his memory of the vision he saw was wrong, he felt kind of stupid, right?"

"He said."

"Stupid. Disconnected. He just stared into space."

"I guess."

"Like you," said Issib. "When I pushed you about the meaning of *zrakoplov*."

Suddenly Nafai felt as if there were no air in his lungs. "I've got to get outside!"

"You are *really* sensitive to this," said Issib. "Even worse than Father and Mother when I tried to tell *them*?"

"Stop following me!" Nafai cried. But Issib continued to float down the hall after him, down the stairs, out into the street. There, in the open, Issib easily passed Nafai, floating here and there in front of him. As if he were herding Nafai back toward the house.

"Stop it!" cried Nafai. But he couldn't get away. He had never felt such panic before. Turning, he stumbled, fell to his knees.

"It's all right," said Issib softly. "Relax. It's nothing. Relax."

Nafai breathed more easily. Issib's voice sounded safe now. The panic subsided. Nafai lifted his head and looked around. "What are we doing out here on the street? Mother's going to kill me."

"You ran out here, Nafai."

"I did?"

"It's the Oversoul, Nafai."

"*What's* the Oversoul?"

"The force that sent you outside rather than listen to me talk about—about the thing that the Oversoul doesn't want people to know about."

"That's silly," said Nafai. The Oversoul *spreads* information, it doesn't conceal it. We submit our writings, our music, everything, and the Oversoul transmits it from city to city, from library to library all over the world."

"Your reaction was much stronger than Father's," said Issib. "Of course, I pushed you harder, too."

"What do you mean?"

"The Oversoul is inside your head, Nafai. Inside all of our heads. But some have it more than others. It's there, watching what we think. I know it's hard to believe."

But Nafai remembered how Luet had known what was in his mind. "No, Issya, I already knew that."

"Really?" said Issib. "Well then. As soon as the Oversoul knew that you were getting close to a forbidden subject, it started making you stupid."

"*What* forbidden subject?"

"If I remind you, it'll just set you off again," said Issib.

"When did I get stupid?"

"Trust me. You got *very* stupid. Trying to change the subject without even realizing it. Normally you're extremely insightful, Nafai. Very bright. You *get* things. But this time up in the library you just stood there like an idiot, with the truth staring you in the face, and you didn't recognize it. When I reminded you, when I *pushed*, you got claustrophobic, right? Hard to breathe, had to get out of the room. I followed you, I pushed again, and here we are."

Nafai tried to think back over what had happened. Issib was right about the order of events. Only Nafai hadn't connected his need to get out of the house with anything Issib said. In fact, he couldn't for the life of him remember what it was that Issib had been talking about. "You pushed?"

"I know," said Issib. "I felt it, too, when I first started getting on the track of this a couple of years ago. I was playing around with lost words, just like that dancing bear thing. Making lists. I had a *long* list of terms like that, with definitions and explanations after each one, along with my best guess about what each lost word meant. And then one day I was looking at a list that I thought was complete and I realized that there were a couple of dozen words that had no meanings at all. That's stupid, I thought. That's ruining my list. So I deleted all those words."

"Deleted them?" Nafai was appalled. "Instead of researching them?"

"See how stupid it can make you?" said Issib. "And the moment I finished deleting them, it came to me—what am I doing! So I reached for the undelete command, but instead of pushing those keys, I reflexively gave the kill command, completely wiping out the delete buffer, and then I saved the file right over the old one."

"That's too complicated to be clumsiness," said Nafai.

"Exactly. I knew that deleting them was a mistake, and yet instead of undoing that mistake and bringing the words back, I killed them, wiped them out of the system."

"And you think the Oversoul did that to you?"

"Nafai, haven't you ever wondered what the Oversoul is? What it does?"

"Sure."

"Me too. And now I know."

"Because of those words?"

"I haven't got them all back, but I retraced as much of my research as I could and I got a list of eight words. You have no idea how hard it was, because now I was sensitized to them. Before, I must have simply overlooked them, gotten stupid when I saw them—the way Father did when he was getting wrong ideas about the Oversoul's vision. That's how they got on my first list, but without definitions—I just got stupid whenever I thought of them. But now when I saw them I'd get that claustrophobic feeling. I needed air. I had to get out of the library. But I forced myself to go inside. It's the hardest thing I've ever done. I forced myself to stay and think about the unthinkable. To hold concepts in my mind that the Oversoul doesn't want us to remember. Concepts that once were so common that every language in the world has words for them. Ancient words. Lost words."

"The Oversoul is *hiding* things from us?"

"Yes."

"Like what?"

"If I tell you, Nafai, you'll take off again."

"No I won't."

"You *will*," said Issib. "Do you think I don't know? Do you think I haven't had my own struggle this past year? So you can imagine my surprise when last night Elemak sits there in the kitchen and explains to us about one of the forbidden things. War wagons."

"Forbidden? How could it be forbidden, it isn't even ancient."

"See? You've forgotten already. The word *kolesnisha*."

"Oh, yes. That's right. No, I remember that."

"But you *didn't* till I said it."

That's right, thought Nafai. A memory lapse.

"Last night you and Elemak were sitting there talking about war wagons, even though it took me *months* to be able to study the word *kolesnisha* without gasping the whole time."

"But we didn't *say* kolesnisha."

"What I'm telling you, Nafai, is that the Oversoul is breaking down."

"That's an old theory."

"But it's a true one," said Issib. "The Oversoul has certain concepts that it is protecting, that it refuses to let human beings think about. Only in the past few years the Wetheads have suddenly become able to think about one of them. And so have the Potoku. And so have *we*. And last night, hearing Elemak talk about it, I felt not one twinge of the panic."

"But it still made me forget the word. *Kolesnisha*."

"A lingering residual effect. You remembered it *this* time, right? Nafai, the Oversoul has given up on keeping us away from the war wagon concept. After millions of years, it isn't trying anymore."

"What else?" asked Nafai. "What are the other concepts?"

"It hasn't given up on those yet. And you seem to be *really* sensitive to the Oversoul, Nyef. I don't know if I can tell you, or if you'd be able to remember for five minutes even if I did."

"You mean I can know that the Oversoul is keeping us from knowing things, only I can't know *which* things because the Oversoul is still keeping me from knowing them."

"Right."

"Then why doesn't the Oversoul stop people from thinking about *murder*? Why doesn't the Oversoul stop people from thinking about war, and rape, and stealing? If it can do this to *me*, why doesn't it do something useful?"

Issib shook his head. "It doesn't seem right. But I've been thinking about it—I've had a year, remember—and here's the best thing I've come up with. The Oversoul doesn't want to stop us from being human. Including all the rotten things we do to each other. It's just trying to hold down the *scale* of our rottenness. All the things that are forbidden— how can I tell you this without setting you off?—if we still had the machines that the forbidden words refer to, it would make it so that anything we did would reach farther, and each weapon would cause more damage, and everything would happen *faster*."

"Time would speed up?"

"No," said Issib. He was obviously choosing his words carefully. "What if . . . what if the Gorayni could bring an army of five thousand men from Yabrev to Basilica in one day."

"Don't make me laugh."

"But if they *could*?"

"We'd be helpless, of course."

"Why?"

"Well, we'd have no time to get an army together."

"So if we knew other nations could do that, we'd have to keep an army all the time, wouldn't we, just in *case* somebody suddenly attacked."

"I guess."

"So then, knowing that, suppose the Gorayni found a way to get, not five thousand, but *fifty* thousand soldiers here, and not in a day, but in six hours."

"Impossible."

"What if I tell you that it's been done?"

"Whoever could do that would rule the whole world."

"Exactly, Nyef, unless everybody else could do it, too. But what kind of world would that be? It would be as if the world had turned small, and everybody was right next door to everybody else. A cruel, bullying, domineering nation like the Gorayni could put their armies on *anybody's* door- step. So all other nations of the world would have to band together to stop them. And instead of a few thousand people dying, a million, ten million people might die in a war."

"So that's why the Oversoul keeps us from thinking about . . . quick ways . . . to get lots of soldiers from one place to another."

"That was hard to say, wasn't it?"

"I kept . . . my mind kept wandering."

"It's a hard concept to keep in your mind, and you aren't even thinking about anything specific."

"I hate this," said Nafai. "You can't even tell me how anybody could do a trick like that. I can hardly even hold the concept in my mind as it is. I *hate* this."

"I don't think the Oversoul is used to having anybody notice. I think that the very fact that you're able to think about the concept of unthinkable concepts means that the Oversoul is losing control."

"Issya, I've never felt so helpless and stupid in my life."

"And it isn't just wars and armies," said Issib. "Remember the stories of Klati?"

"The slaughter man?"

"Climbing in through women's windows in the night and gutting them like cattle in the butcher's shop."

"Why couldn't the Oversoul have made *him* get stupid when he thought of doing that?"

"Because the Oversoul's job isn't to make us perfect," said Issib. "But imagine if Klati had been able to get on a— been able to travel very quickly and get to another city in six hours."

"They would have known he was a stranger and watched him so closely that he couldn't have done a thing."

"But you don't understand—thousands, millions of people every day are doing the same thing—"

"Butchering women?"

"Flying from one place to another."

"This is too crazy to think about!" shouted Nafai. He bounded to his feet and moved toward the house.

"Come back," cried Issib. "You don't really think that, you're being *made* to think it!"

Nafai leaned against one of the pillars of the front porch. Issib was right. He had been fine, and then suddenly Issib said whatever it was that he said and suddenly Nafai had to *leave,* had to get away and now here he was, panting, leaning up against the pillar, his heart pounding so hard that somebody else could probably hear it from a meter away. Could this really be the Oversoul, making him so stupid and fearful? If it was, then the Oversoul was his enemy. And Nafai refused to surrender. He *could* think about things whether the Oversoul liked it or not. He *could* think about the thing that Issib had said, and he could do it without running away.

In his mind Nafai retraced the last few moments of his conversation with Issib. About Klati. Going from city to city in a few hours. Other cities would notice him, of course—but then Issib said what if thousands of people . . . were . . . flying.

The picture that came into Nafai's mind was ludicrous. To imagine people in the air, like birds, soaring, swooping. He should laugh—but instead, thinking of it made his throat feel tight. His head felt tight, constrained. A sharp pain grew out of his neck and up into the back of his head. But he could think of it. People flying. And from there he could finish Issib's thought. People flying from city to city, thousands of them, so that the authorities in each city had no way of keeping track of one person.

"Klati could have killed once in each city and no one would ever have found him," said Nafai.

Issib was beside him again, his arm resting oh-so-lightly across Nafai's shoulder as he leaned against the pillar. "Yes," said Issib.

"But what would it mean to be a citizen of a place?" asked Nafai. "If a thousand people . . . *flew* here . . . to Basilica . . . today."

"It's all right," said Issib. "You don't have to say it."

"Yes I do," said Nafai. "I can think *anything*. It can't stop me."

"I was just trying to explain—that the Oversoul doesn't stop the evil in the world—it just stops it from getting out of hand. It keeps the damage local. But the good things— think about it, Nafai—we give our art and music and stories to the Oversoul, and it offers them to every other nation. The good things *do* spread. So it *does* make the world a better place."

"No," said Nafai. "In some ways better, yes, but how can it help but be a good thing to live in a world where people . . . where we could . . . *fly*."

The word almost choked him, but he said it, and even though he could hardly bear to stay in the same place, the air felt so close and unbreathable, nevertheless he *stayed*.

"You're good," said Issib. "I'm impressed."

But Nafai didn't feel impressive. He felt sick and angry and betrayed. "How does the Oversoul have the *right*," he said. "To take this all away from us."

"What, armies appearing at our gates without warning? I'm glad enough not to have that."

Nafai shook his head. "It's deciding what I can *think*."

"Nyef, I know the feeling, I went through all this months ago, and I *know*, it makes you so angry and frightened. But I also know that you can overcome it. And yesterday, when Mother talked about her vision. Of a planet burning. There's a word for—well, you couldn't hear it now, I know that— but the Oversoul has been keeping us from *that*. For thirty or forty million years—don't you realize that this is a *long* time? More history than we can imagine. It's all stored away somewhere, but the most we can hold onto, the most that we can get into our minds is the most skeletal sort of plan of what's happened in the world for the last ten million years or so—and it takes years and years of study to comprehend even that much. There are kingdoms and languages we've never heard of even in the last million years, and yet nothing is really lost. When I went searching in the library, I was able to find references to works in other libraries and trace my way back until I read a crude translation from a book written thirty-two million years ago and do you know what it said? Even then the writer was saying that history was now too long, too full for the human mind to comprehend it. That if all of human history were compressed into a single thousand-page volume, the whole story of humankind on Earth would be only a single page. And that was thirty-two million years ago."

"So we've been here a long time."

"If I take that writer's arithmetic literally, that would mean that human history on Earth lasted only eight thousand years before the planet . . . burned."

Nafai understood. The Oversoul had kept human beings from expanding the scale of their destructiveness, and so humanity had lasted five thousand times longer on the planet Harmony than it did on Earth.

"So why didn't the Oversoul keep Earth from being destroyed?"

"I don't know," said Issib. "I have a guess."

"And what's that?"

"I don't know if you'll be allowed to think about it."

"Give me a try."

"The Oversoul wasn't made until people got to Harmony. It has the same meaning in every language, you know— the name of the planet. Sklad. Endrakt. Soglassye. Maybe when they got here, with Earth in ashes behind them, they decided never to let it happen again. Maybe that's when the

Oversoul was put in place—to stop us from ever having such terrible power."

"Then the Oversoul would be—an artifact."

"Yes," said Issib. "This isn't hard for you to think about?"

"No," said Nafai. "Easy. It's not that uncommon a thought. People have talked about the Oversoul as a machine before."

"It was hard for *me*," said Issib. "But maybe because I came to the idea another way. Through a couple of unthinkable paths. Genetic alteration of the human brain so it could receive and transmit thoughts from communications satellites orbiting the planet."

Nafai heard the words, but they meant nothing to him.

"You didn't understand that, did you," said Issib.

"No," said Nafai.

"I didn't think you would."

"Issya, what is the Oversoul doing to us now?"

"That's what I've been working on. Trying to look through the forbidden words, find the pattern, find out what it means to be giving Father this vision of a world on fire. And Mother. And the dream of blood and ashes that Luet was given."

"It means that we're puppets."

"No, Nafai. Don't talk yourself into hating the Oversoul about this. That does no good at all—I *know* that now. We have to understand it. What it's doing. Because the world really *is* in danger, if the Oversoul's control is breaking down. And it is. It's given up on war wagons—what will it give up on next? What empire will be the next to get out of hand? Which one will discover—that word you asked about—puscani prah. It's a powder that when you put flame to it, it blows up. Pops like a balloon, only with thousands of times more force. Enough to make a wall fall down. Enough to kill people."

"Please stop," whispered Nafai. It was more than he could bear, fighting off the panic he felt as he heard these words.

"The Oversoul is not our enemy. In fact, I think—I think it called on Father because it needs help."

"Why haven't you said any of this before?"

"I have—to Father. To Mother. To some teachers. Other students. Other scholars. I even wrote it up in an article, but if nobody ever remembers receiving it, they can never find it. Even when I sent it to the same person four times. I gave up."

"But you told *me*."

"You came into the library," said Issib. "I thought—why not?"

"*Zrakoplov*," said Nafai.

"I can't believe you remembered the word," said Issib.

"A machine. The people don't just . . . fly. They use a machine."

"Don't push it," said Issib. "You'll just make yourself sick. You have a headache already, right?"

"But I'm right, yes?"

"My best guess is that it was hollow, like a house, and people got inside it to fly. Like a ship, only through the air. With wings. But we had them here, I think. You know the district of Black Fields?"

"Of course, just west of the market."

"The old name of it was Skyport. The name lasted until twenty million years ago, more or less. Skyport. When they changed it, nobody remembered what it even meant."

"I can't drink about this anymore," said Nafai.

"Do you want to remember it, though?" asked Issib.

"How can I forget it?"

"You will, you know. If I don't remind you. Every day. Do you want me to? It'll feel like this every time. It'll make you sick. Do you want to just forget this, or do you want me to keep reminding you?"

"Who reminded *you*?"

"I left myself notes," said Issib. "In the library computers. Reminders. Why do you think it took me a year to get this far?"

"I want to remember," said Nafai.

"You'll get angry at me."

"Remind me not to."

"It'll make you sick."

"So I'll faint a lot." Nafai slid down the pillar and sat on the porch, looking out toward the street. "Why hasn't anybody noticed us out here? We haven't exactly been whispering."

Issib laughed. "Oh, they noticed. Mother came out once, and a couple of the teachers. They heard us talking for a couple of moments and then they just sort of forgot why they came out."

"This is great. If we want them to leave us alone, all we have to do is talk about the *zrakoplovs*."

"Well," said Issib, "that only works with people who are still closely tied with the Oversoul."

"Who isn't?"

"Whoever thought of the war wagons, for instance."

"You said the Oversoul had given up on them."

"Sure, *recently*," said Issib. "But there were people in Basilica planning to build war wagons, people dealing with the Potoku about them for a long time. More than a year. *They* had no trouble with the Oversoul. It's like they're deaf to it now. But most people aren't—which is why Gaballu-fix and his men were able to keep it secret for so long. Most people who heard anything about war wagons would simply have forgotten they even heard it. In fact," added Issib, "the Oversoul may have deliberately stopped forbidding that idea in the last little while precisely *because* there had to be open discussion of the war wagon thing in order to stop it."

"So the people who are deaf to the Oversoul—in order to stop them, the Oversoul has to stop controlling the rest of us, too."

"It's a double bind," said Issib. "In order to win, the Oversoul has to give up. I'd say that the Oversoul is in serious trouble."

It was making sense to Nafai, except for one thing. "But why did it start talking to *Father*?"

"That's what we need to figure out. That, and what it's going to tell Father to do next."

"Oh, hey, let's let the Oversoul keep a *few* surprises up its sleeve." Nafai laughed, but he didn't really think it was funny.

Neither did Issib. "Even if we believe in the Oversoul's cause, Nafai, somewhere along in here we may find out that the Oversoul is causing more harm than good. What do we do *then*?"

"Hey, Issya, it may be doing a bad job these days, but that doesn't mean that we'd do better without it."

"I guess we'll never know, will we?"

SEVEN

PRAYER

For a week Nafai worked with Issib every day. They slept at Mother's house every night—they didn't ask, but then, Mother didn't send them away, either. It was a grueling time, not because the work was so hard but because the interference from the Oversoul was so painful. Issib was right, however. It *could* be overcome; and even though Nafai's aversive response was stronger than Issib's had been, he was able to get over it more quickly—mostly because Issib was there to help him, to assure him that it was worth doing, to remind him what it was about.

They began to work out a pretty clear picture of what it was that humans had once had, and that the Oversoul had long kept them from reinventing.

A communications system in which a person could talk instantly and directly to a person in any other city in the world.

Machines that could receive artwork and plays and stories transmitted through the air, not just from library to library, but right into people's homes.

Machines that moved swiftly over the ground, without horses.

Machines that flew, not just through the air, but out into

space. "Of course there must be space traveling machines, or how did we get to Harmony from Earth?" But until he had punched his way through the aversion, Nafai had never been able to conceive of such a thing.

And the weapons of war: Explosives. Projectile weapons. Some so small that they could be held in the hand. Others so terrible that they could devastate whole cities, and burn up a planet if hundreds were used at once. Self-mutating diseases. Poisonous gases. Seismic disruptors. Missiles. Orbital launch platforms. Gene-wrecking viruses.

The picture that emerged was beautiful and terrible at once.

"I can see why the Ovcrsoul does this to us," said Nafai. "To save us from these weapons. But the cost, Issya. The freedom we gave up."

Issib only nodded. "At least the Oversoul left us something. The ability to get power from the sun. Computers. Libraries. Refrigeration. All the machines of the kitchen, the greenhouses. The magnetics that allow my floats to work. And we *do* have some pretty sophisticated handweapons. Charged-wire blades. And pulses. So that large strong people don't have any particular advantage over smaller, weaker ones. The Oversoul could have stripped us. Stone and metal tools. Nothing with moving parts. Burning trees for all our heat."

"We wouldn't even be *human* then."

"Human is human," said Issib. "But civilized—that's the gift of the Oversoul. Civilization without self-destruction."

They tried explaining it to Mother once, but it went nowhere. She stupidly failed to understand anything they were talking about, and left them with a cheerful little jest about how nice it was that they could be friends and play these games together despite the age difference between them. There was no chance to talk to Father.

But there *was* someone who took an interest in them.

"Why don't you come to class anymore?" asked Hushidh.

She sat down on the porch steps beside Nafai and bit into her bread and cheese. A large mouthful, not the delicate bites that Eiadh took. Never mind that Mother was the one who taught all her girl students to use their *mouths* when they ate, and not to take the mincing little bites that were in fashion among the young women of Basilica these days. Nafai didn't have to find Hushidh's obedience to Mother *attractive*.

"I'm working on a project with Issib."

"The other students say that you're hiding," said Hushidh.

Hiding. Because Father was so notorious and controversial. "I'm not ashamed of my father."

"Of course not," said Hushidh. "*They* say you're hiding. Not me."

"And what do *you* think I'm doing? Or has the Oversoul told you?"

"I'm a raveler," she said, "not a seer."

"Right. I forgot." As if he should keep track of what kind of witch she was.

"The Oversoul doesn't have to tell me how you're weaving yourself into the world."

"Because you can see it."

She nodded. "And you're very brave."

He looked at her in consternation. "I sit in the library with Issya."

"You're weaving yourself into the weakest of the quarreling parties in Basilica, and yet it's the best of them. The one that *should* win, though no one can imagine how."

"I'm not party of *any* party."

She nodded. "I'll stop talking if you don't want to hear the truth."

As if she were going to be the fount of irresistible wisdom.

"I'll listen to a pig fart as long as it's the *truth*," said Nafai.

Immediately she got to her feet and moved away.

That was really stupid, Nafai rebuked himself. She's just trying to help, and you make a stupid joke out of it. He got up and followed her. "I'm sorry," he said.

She shrugged away from him.

"I'm used to making stupid jokes like that," said Nafai. "It's a bad habit, but I didn't mean it. It's not as if I don't know for myself now that the Oversoul is real."

"I know that you *know*," she said coldly. "But it's obvious that knowing the Oversoul exists doesn't mean you automatically get brains or kindness or even decency."

"I deserve it, and the next three nasty things you think of." Nafai stepped around her, to face her. This time she didn't turn away.

"I see patterns," she said. "I see the way things fit together. I see where *you* are starting to fit. You and Issib."

"I haven't been following things in the city," said Nafai. "Busy with the project we're working on. I don't really know what's going on."

"It's been wearing you out," she said.

"Yes," said Nafai. "I guess so."

"Gaballufix is the center of one party," she said. "It's the strongest, for more reasons than one. It isn't just about the war wagons anymore, or even about the alliance with Potokgavan. It's about men. Especially men from outside the city. So he's strong in numbers, and he's also strong because his men are asserting themselves with violence."

Nafai thought back to conversations he had overheard at mealtimes. About the tolchocks, men who were knocking down women in the street for no reason. "*His* men are the tolchocks?"

"He denies it. In fact, he claims that he's sending his soldiers out into the streets of Basilica in order to protect women from the tolchocks."

"Soldiers?"

"Officially they're the militia of the Palwashantu clan.

But they all answer to Gaballufix, and the clan council hasn't been able to meet to discuss the way the militia are being used. You're Palwashantu, aren't you?"

"I'm too young for the militia yet."

"They're not really militia anymore," she said. "They're hired. Men from outside the walls, the hopeless kind of men, and very few of them really Palwashantu. Gaballufix is paying them. And he paid the tolchocks, too."

"How do you *know* this?"

"I was pushed. I've seen the soldiers. I know how they fit together."

More of the witchery. But how could he doubt it? Hadn't he felt the influence of the Oversoul whenever he thought about forbidden words? It made him sweat just to think of what he'd been through during the past week. So why *couldn't* Hushidh just look at a soldier and a tolchock and know things about them? Why couldn't camels fly? Anything was possible now.

Except that the Oversoul's influence was weakening. Hadn't he and Issib overcome its power, in order to think about forbidden things?

"And you know that I'm not one of them."

"But your brothers are."

"Tolchocks?"

"They're with Gaballufix. Not *Issib*, of course. But Elemak and Mebbekew."

"How do you know *them*? They never come here—they're not Mother's sons."

"Elemak has come here several times this week," said Hushidh. "Didn't you know?"

"Why would he come here?" But Nafai knew at once. Without being able to think the thought himself, he knew exactly why Elemak would come to Rasa's household. Mother's reputation in the city was of the highest; her nieces were courted by many, and Elemak was of an age—well into the age, in fact—for a serious mating, intended to produce an heir.

Nafai looked around the courtyard, where many girls and a few boys were eating their supper. All the students from outside were gone, and the younger children ate earlier. So most of the girls here were eligible for mating, including her nieces, if Rasa released them. Which of them would Elemak be courting?

"Eiadh," he whispered.

"One can assume," said Hushidh. "I know it isn't me."

Nafai looked at her in surprise. Of course it wasn't her. Then he was embarrassed; what if she realized how ridiculous it had seemed to him, that his brother might desire *her*.

But Hushidh continued as if she didn't even notice his silent insult. Certainly she was oblivious to how the idea of Elya courting Eiadh might hurt Nafai. "When your brother came, I knew at once that he was very close to Gaballufix. I'm sure that it's causing Aunt Rasa a great deal of sorrow, because she knows that Eiadh will say yes to him. Your brother has a great deal of prestige."

"Even with Father's visions causing such a scandal?"

"He's with Gaballufix," said Hushidh. "Within the Party of Men—those who favor Gaballufix—the worse your father looks, the better they like Elemak. Because if something happened to your father, then Elemak would be a very rich and powerful man."

Her words reawakened Nafai's worst fears about his brother. But it was a monstrous, unbearable thought. "Gaballufix wants Elya to influence Father, that's all."

Hushidh nodded. But was she nodding in agreement, or just silencing him so she could get on with what she had to say? "The other strong party is Roptat's people. They're being called the Party of Women now, though they are also led by a man. They want to ally with the Gorayni. And also they want to remove the vote from all men except those currently mated with a citizen, and require all non-mated men to leave the city every night by sundown, and not return until dawn. That's *their* solution to the tolchock problem—and to Gaballufix, as well. They have a wide following—among mated men and women."

"Is that the group that Father's with?"

"Everyone in the Party of Men thinks so, but Roptat's people know better."

"So what's the third group?"

"They call themselves the City Party, but what they truly are is the Party of the Oversoul. They refuse to ally with any warring nation. They want to return to the old ways, for the protection of the Lake. To make this a city above politics and conflict. To give away the great wealth of the city and live simply, so no other nation will desire to possess us."

"Nobody will agree to that."

"You're wrong," she said. "Many *do* agree. Your father and Aunt Rasa have won over almost all the women of the Lake Districts."

"But that's hardly anybody. Only a handful of people live in the Rift Valley."

"They have a third of the council votes."

Nafai thought about that. "I think that's very dangerous for them," he said.

"Why do you think so?"

"Because they don't have anything but tradition to back them up. The more Gaballufix pushes against tradition, the more he frightens people with tolchocks and soldiers, the more people will demand that *something* be done. All that Father and Mother are doing is making it impossible for anyone to get a majority on the council. They're blocking Roptat from stopping Gaballufix."

Hushidh smiled. "You're really very good at this."

"Politics is what I study most."

"You've seen the danger. But what you haven't told me is how we'll get out of it."

"We?"

"Basilica."

"No," said Nafai. "You said that you knew what party I was in."

"You're with the Oversoul, of course," she said.

"You don't know that. *I* don't even know that. I'm not sure I like the way the Oversoul manipulates us."

Hushidh shook her head. "You may not make the decision in your mind for many days yet, but the decision in your heart is already made. You reject Gaballufix. And you are drawn to the Oversoul."

"You're wrong," said Nafai. "I mean, yes, I'm drawn to the Oversoul, Issib came to that decision long ago and his reasons are good. Despite all its secret manipulation of people's minds, it's even more dangerous to reject the Oversoul. But that doesn't mean I'm ready to turn the future of Basilica over to the tiny minority of crazy religious fanatics who live in the Rift Valley and have visions all the time."

"We're the ones who are close to the Oversoul."

"The whole *world* has the Oversoul inside their brains," said Nafai. "You can't get closer than that."

"We're the ones who *choose* the Oversoul," she insisted. "And the whole world *doesn't* have her inside their brains, or they would never have started carrying war to faraway nations."

For a moment Nafai wondered if she, too, had somehow discovered how the Oversoul had blocked the discovery of war wagons until recently. Then he realized that of course *she* was thinking of the seventh codicil: "You have no dispute with your neighbor's neighbor's neighbor; when she quarrels, stay home and close your window." This had long been interpreted to be a prohibition of entangling alliances or quarrels with countries so far away that the outcome made no difference to you. Nafai and Issib knew the purpose and origin of such a law, and the way that the Oversoul had enforced it within people's minds. To Hushidh, though, it was the law itself that had fended off wars of imperial aggression for all these millennia. Never mind that many nations had *tried* to create empires, and only the lack of efficient means of travel and communication had hindered them.

"I'm not with you," said Nafai. "You can't turn back the clock."

"If you can't," she said, "then we're as good as destroyed already."

"Maybe so," said Nafai. "If Roptat wins, then when the Potoku fleet arrives, they come up the mountain and destroy us before the Wetheads can get here. And if Gaballufix wins, then when the Wetheads finally come they destroy the Potoku first and then *they* come up the mountains and destroy us in retaliation."

"So," said Hushidh. "You see that you *are* with us."

"No," said Nafai. "Because if the City Party keeps up this stalemate, either Gaballufix or Roptat will get impatient and people will start to die. Then we won't *need* outsiders to destroy us. We'll do it ourselves. How long do you think women will continue to rule in this city, if it comes to civil war between two powerful men?"

Hushidh looked off into space. "Do you think so?" she said.

"I may not be a *raveler*" said Nafai, "but I've read history."

"So many centuries we've kept this a city of women, a place of peace."

"You never should have given men the vote."

"They've had the vote for a million years."

Nafai nodded. "I know. What's happening now—it's the Oversoul."

He could see now that Hushidh was looking off into nothingness because her eyes were so full of tears. "She's dying, isn't she?"

It hadn't occurred to him that someone could take this so personally. As if the Oversoul were a dear relative. But to someone like Hushidh, perhaps it was so. Besides, she was the daughter of a wilder, a so-called holy woman. Even though everyone knew that wilders' children were usually the result of rape or casual coupling in the streets of the city, they were still called "children of the Oversoul." Maybe Hushidh really thought of the Oversoul as her father. But no—the women called the Oversoul *she*. And Hushidh *knew* that her mother was a wilder.

Still, Hushidh was barely containing her tears.

"What do you want from me?" asked Nafai. "I don't know what the Oversoul is doing. Your sister—like you said, *she's* the seer."

"The Oversoul hasn't spoken to her all week. Or to anyone."

Nafai was surprised. "You mean not even at the lake?"

"I knew that you and Issib were very, very closely tied to the Oversoul all this week. She was wearing you out, the way she does with Lutya and . . . and me, sometimes. The women have been going into the water, more and more of them, and yet they come out with nothing, or with silly sleep-dreams. It's making them afraid. But I told them, I said: Nafai and Issib, *they're* being touched by the Oversoul. So she's not dead. And they asked me . . . to find out from you."

"Find out what?"

The tears finally spilled out and slid down her cheeks. "I don't know," she said miserably. "What to do. What the Oversoul expects of us."

He touched her shoulder, to comfort her—Nafai didn't know what else to do. "I don't know," he said. "But you're right about one thing—the Oversoul is wearing down. Wearing *itself* out. Still, I'm surprised that it would stop giving visions. Maybe it's distracted. Maybe it's . . ."

"What?"

He shook his head. "Let me talk to Issib, will you?"

She nodded, ducking her head at the end to wipe away tears. "Please, yes," she said. "I couldn't—talk to *him*."

Why in the world *not*? But he didn't ask. He was too confused by all that she'd told him. All this time that he and Issib thought their research was secret, and here was Hushidh telling all the women of Basilica that the two of them were being worn out by the Oversoul! And yet, for all that they knew, the women were also hopelessly ignorant—how could he and Issib know anything about the reason why their visions had stopped?

Nafai went straight to the library and repeated to Issib all he could remember of his conversation with Hushidh. "So what I'm thinking is this. What if the Oversoul isn't all that powerful? What if the reason the visions have stopped is that the Oversoul can't deal with *us* and give visions all at the same time?"

Issib laughed. "Come on, Nyef, as if we're the center of the world or something."

"I'm serious. How much capacity would the Oversoul have to have, really? Most people are ignorant or stupid or weak enough that even if they thought of one of these forbidden subjects, they couldn't do anything about it, so why watch them? That means the Oversoul has to monitor relatively few people. And with them, if it checks in on them every now and then, it has plenty of time to turn them away from dangerous projects. But now, with the Oversoul weakening, you were able to desensitize yourself. That was a contest between you and the Oversoul, and you *won*, Issib.

What if during all those struggles, the Oversoul was completely focused on you, giving no visions to anyone else, monitoring no one else. But you were going slowly enough that it still had time left over."

"But the two of us, working together," said Issib. "It had to concentrate on us, constantly. And it's losing, too—weakening even more."

"So I'm thinking, Issib—we're not helping here, we're *hurting*."

Issib laughed again. "It can't *be*," he said. "This is the Oversoul we're talking about, not a teacher with a couple of unruly students."

"The Oversoul has failed before. Or there wouldn't be any war wagons."

"So what should we do?"

"Stop," said Nafai. "For a day. Stay away from the forbidden subjects. See if people start getting visions again."

"You seriously think that we, the two of us, have taken up so much of the Oversoul's time that it can't give visions to people? What about during the time we sleep and eat? There are plenty of breaks."

"Maybe we've got it confused. Maybe it's panicking about us because it doesn't know what to do."

"Right," said Issib. "So let's not just *quit*. Let's give the Oversoul some advice, why not!"

"Why not?" said Nafai. "It was made by human beings, wasn't it?"

"We *think*. Maybe."

"So we tell it to stop worrying about trying to block us. That's a pointless assignment and it should stop wasting time on it *right now,* because even if we easily think of every forbidden subject in the world, we're not going to tell anybody else and we're not going to try to build any ourselves. Are we?"

"We're not."

"So take an oath to that, Issib. I'll take it too. I swear it right now—you listening, Oversoul?—we're not your enemies, so you don't need to waste another second worrying about us. Go back and give visions to the women again. And spend your time blocking the dangerous guys. The Wetheads, for instance. Gaballufix. Roptat probably, too. And if you can't block them, then at least let *us* know what to do so *we* can block them."

"Who are you talking to?"

"The Oversoul."

"This feels really stupid," said Issib.

"It's been telling *us* what to think our whole lives," said Nafai. "What's so stupid about giving *it* a suggestion now and then? Take the oath, Issya."

"Yes, I promise, I take the most solemn oath. You listening, Oversoul?"

"It's listening," said Nafai. "That much we *know*."

"So," said Issib. "You think it's going to do what we say?"

"I don't know," said Nafai. "But I know *this*—we're not going to learn anything more by hanging around the library for the rest of the day. Let's get out of here. Spend the night at Father's house. Maybe we'll have a really good idea. Or maybe Father will have a vision. Or something."

It was only that afternoon, as he was leaving Mother's house, that Nafai remembered that Elemak was courting Eiadh. Not that Nafai had a right to hate him for it. Nafai had never said anything to anyone about his feelings toward her, had he? And at fourteen he was far too young to be taken seriously as a possible legal mate. Of course Eiadh would look at Elemak and desire him. It explained everything—why she was so nice to Nafai and yet never seemed to get close to him. She wanted to keep his favor in case he had some influence over Elemak. But it would never have crossed her mind that she might give a contract to *Nafai*. After all, he was a *child*.

Then he remembered how Hushidh had spoken of Issib. I couldn't talk to *him*. Because he was a cripple? Not likely. No, Hushidh was shy with Issib because she was looking at him as a possible mate. Even *I* know enough about women to guess that, thought Nafai.

Hushidh is my age, and *she's* looking at my older brother when she thinks of mating. While *I* might as well be a tree or a brick for all the sexual interest a girl my age would have in *me*. And Eiadh is older than me—one of the oldest in my class, while I'm one of the youngest. How could I have ever thought . . .

He felt the hot blush of embarrassment on his cheeks, even though no one knew of his humiliation except himself.

Moving through the streets of Basilica, Nafai realized that except for an occasional walk in Rain Street he had not been out of Mother's house since he began his research with Issib. Perhaps because of what Hushidh had told him, he was aware of a change in the city. Were there fewer people on the streets? Perhaps—but the real difference was more in the *way* they walked. People in Basilica often moved with purpose, but usually they did not let that purpose close them to what was going on around them. Even people in a hurry could pause for a moment, or at least smile, when they passed a street musician or a juggler or a comic reciting his doggerel. And many people sauntered, taking things in with real pleasure, conversing with their companions, of course, but also freely speaking with strangers on the street, as if all the people of Basilica were neighbors, or even relatives.

This evening was different. As the sun silhouetted the western rooftops and cast angled slabs of blackness across the streets, the people seemed to dodge the sunlight as if it might burn their skin. They were closed off to each other. The street musicians were ignored, and even their music seemed more timid, as if they were ready to break off their song at the first sign of displeasure in a passerby. The streets were quieter because almost no one was talking.

Soon enough the reason became obvious. A troop of eight men jogged up the street, pulses in their hands and charged-wire blades at their waists. Soldiers, thought Nafai. Gaballufix's men. No—officially, they were the militia of the Palwashantu, but Nafai felt no kinship with them.

They didn't seem to look to left or right, as if their errand were set. But Nafai and Issib noticed at once that the streets seemed to empty as the soldiers passed. Where had the people gone? They weren't actually hiding, but still it took several minutes after the soldiers had passed before people began emerging again. They had ducked into shops, pretending to have business. Some had simply taken alternate routes down side streets. And others had never left the street at all, but like Nafai and Issib they had stopped, had frozen in place, so that for a few minutes they were part of the architecture, not part of the life of the place.

It did not seem at all as though people thought the soldiers were making the city safer. Instead the soldiers had made them afraid.

"Basilica's in trouble," said Nafai.

"Basilica is *dead*," said Issib. "There are still people here, but the city isn't Basilica anymore."

Fortunately, it wasn't as bad when they got farther along Wing Street—the soldiers had passed where Wing crossed Wheat Street, only a few blocks from Gaballufix's house. When they got into Old Town there was more life in the streets. But changes were still visible.

For instance, Spring Street had been cleared. Spring was one of the major thoroughfares of Basilica, running in the most direct route from Funnel Gate through Old Town and right on to the edge of the Rift Valley. But as often happened in Basilica, some enterprising builder had decided that it was a shame to let all that empty space in the middle of the street go to waste, when people could be living there. On a long block between Wing and Temple, the builder had put up six buildings.

Now, when a Basilican builder started putting up a structure that blocked a street, several things could happen. If the street wasn't very busy, only a few people would object. They might scream and curse and even throw things at the builders, but since the workers were all such burly men, there would be little serious resistance. The building would go up, and people would find new routes. The people who owned houses or shops that used to front on the now-blocked road were the ones who suffered most. They had to bargain with neighbors to gain hallway rights that would give them street access—or *take* those rights, if the neighbor was weak. Sometimes they simply had to abandon their property. Either way, the new hallways or the abandoned property soon became thoroughfares in their own right. Eventually some enterprising soul would buy a couple of abandoned or decaying houses whose hallways were being used for traffic, tear out an open streetway, and thus a new road was born. The city council did nothing to interfere with this process—it was how the city evolved and changed over time, and it seemed pointless in a city tens of millions of years old to try to hold back the tide of time and history.

It was quite another thing when someone started building on a much-used thoroughfare like Spring Street. There, the passersby gained courage from their numbers—and from their outrage at the thought of losing a road they often used. So they would deliberately sabotage the construction as they passed, knocking down masonry, carrying away stones. If the builder was powerful and determined, with many strong workers, a brawl could easily start—but then it might easily come to a court trial, where the builder was *always* found to be at fault, since building in a street was regarded as ample provocation for legal assault.

The builder in Spring Street had been clever, though. She had designed her six buildings to stand on arches, so that the road was never actually blocked. The houses instead began on the first floor, above the street—and so, while passersby were annoyed, they weren't so provoked that they got serious about their sabotage. So the buildings had been finished early that summer, and some very wealthy people had taken up residence.

Inevitably, however, the archways became crowded with streetsellers and enterprising restaurateurs—which the builder surely knew would happen. Traffic slowed to a crawl, and other builders began to put up permanent shops and stalls, until only a few weeks ago it became physically impossible to get from Temple to Wing on Spring Street— the little buildings now completed blocked the way. Another street in Basilica had been killed, only this time it was a major thoroughfare and caused serious inconvenience to a lot of people. Only the original builder and the enterprising little shopkeepers truly profited; the people who bought the inner buildings now found it harder and harder to get to the stairways leading up to their houses, and people were already preparing to abandon old structures that no longer faced on a street.

Now, as Nafai and Issib passed Spring Street, they saw that someone had gone through the blocked section and torn down all the small structures. The new buildings were still there, arching over the street, but the passageway remained open underneath them. More significantly, a couple of soldiers stood at each end of the street. The message was clear: No new building would be tolerated.

"Gaballufix isn't a fool," said Issib.

Nafai knew what he meant. People might not like seeing soldiers trot by in the streets, with the threat of violence and the loss of freedom that they implied. But seeing Spring Street open would go a long way toward making the soldiers seem like a mixed evil, one perhaps worth tolerating.

Wing Street eventually fed into Temple Street, and Nafai and Issib followed it until it came to the great circle around the Temple itself. This was the one outpost of the men's religion in this city of women, the one place where the Oversoul was known to be male, and where blood rather than water was the holy fluid. On impulse, though he hadn't been inside since he was eight and his foreskin was drowned in his own blood, Nafai stopped at the north doors. "Let's go in," he said.

Issib shuddered. "I deeply hate this place," he said.

"If they used anesthetic, worship would be more popular with kids," said Nafai.

Issib grinned. "Painless worship. Now there's a thought. Maybe dry worship would catch on among the women, too."

They went through the door into the musty, dark, windowless outer chamber.

Though the temple was perfectly round, the inner chambers were designed to recall the chambers of the heart: the Indrawing Auricle, the Airward Ventricle, the Airdrawing Auricle, and the Outflowing Ventricle. The winding halls and tiny rooms between them were named for various veins and arteries. Before their circumcision boys had to learn all the names of all the rooms, but they did it by memorizing a song that remained meaningless to most who learned it. So there was nothing particularly familiar about the names written on each door lintel or keystone, and Issib and Nafai were immediately lost.

It didn't matter. Eventually, all halls and corridors funneled worshipers into the central courtyard, the only bright space in the temple, open to the sky. Since it was so close to sunset, there was no direct sunlight on the stone floor of the courtyard, but after so much darkness even reflected sunlight was painfully dazzling.

At the gateway, a priest stopped them. "Prayer or meditation?" he asked.

Issib shuddered—a convulsive movement, for him, since the floats exaggerated every twitch his muscles made. "I think I'll wait in the Airdrawing Auricle."

"Don't be a poddletease," said Nafai. "Just meditate for a minute, it won't kill you."

"You mean *you're* going to *pray*?" said Issib.

"I guess so," said Nafai.

Truth to tell, Nafai wasn't sure why, or for what. He only knew that his relationship with the Oversoul was getting more complicated every day; he understood the Oversoul better than before, and the Oversoul was meddling in his life now, so it had become important to try to communicate clearly and directly, instead of all this slantwise guesswork. It wasn't enough to slack off their research into forbidden words and hope that the Oversoul got the hint. There had to be something more.

He watched as the priests jabbed Issib's finger and wiped the tiny wound over the bloodstone. Issib took it well enough—he really *wasn't* a poddle, and he'd had enough pain in his life that a little fingerjab was nothing. He just had little use for the rituals of the men's worship. He called it "blood sports" and compared it to shark-fights, which always started out by getting every shark in the pool to bleed. As soon as his little red smear was on the rough stone, he drifted over toward the high bench against the sunny wall, where there was still about a half-hour of sunlight. The bench was full, of course, but Issib could always float just beside it. "Hurry up," he murmured as he passed Nafai.

Since Nafai was here to pray, the priest didn't jab him. Instead he let him reach into the golden bowl of prayer rings. The bowl was filled with a powerful disinfectant, which had the double effect of keeping the barbed prayer rings from spreading disease and also making it so that every jab stung bitterly for several long seconds. Nafai usually took only two rings, one for the middle finger of each hand, but this time he felt that he needed more. That even though he had no idea what he was praying *about,* he wanted to make sure that the Oversoul understood that he was serious. So he found prayer rings for all four fingers of each hand, and thumb rings as well.

"It can't be that bad," said the priest.

"I'm not praying for forgiveness," said Nafai.

"I don't want you fainting on me, we're short-staffed today."

"I won't faint." Nafai walked to the center of the courtyard, near the fountain. The water of the fountain wasn't the normal pinkish color—it was almost dark red. Nafai well remembered the powerful frisson the first time he realized how the water got its color. Father said that when Basilica was in great need—during a drought, for instance, or when an enemy threatened—the fountain flowed with almost pure blood, there was so much blood. It was a strange and powerful feeling, to pull off his sandals and strip off his clothes, then kneel in the pool and know that the tepid liquid swirling around him, almost up to his waist if he sat back on his heels, was thick with the passionate bloody prayers of other men.

He held his barbed hands open in front of him for a long time, composing himself, readying himself for the conversation with the Oversoul. Then he slapped his hands vigorously against his upper arms, just as he did in his morning prayers; this time, though, the barbed rings cut into his flesh and the sting was deep and harsh. It was a good, vigorous opening, and he heard several of the meditators sigh or murmur. He knew that they had heard the sharp sound of his slap and seen his self-discipline as he restrained himself from so much as gasping in pain, and they respected this prayer for its strength and virtue.

Oversoul, he said silently. You started all this. Weak as you are, you decided to start intruding in my family's life. You'd better have a plan in mind. And if you do, isn't it about time you let us know what it is?

He slapped himself again, this time on the more sensitive skin of his chest. When the sting faded he could feel blood tickling through the invisible new hairs growing there. I offer this sacrifice to you, Oversoul, I offer my pain if you need it, I'll do whatever you want me to do but I expect a promise from you in return. I expect you to protect my father. I expect you to have a real purpose in mind, and to tell Father what it is. I expect you to keep my brothers from getting mixed up in some terrible crime against the city and particularly from getting involved in a crime against my father. If you protect Father and let us know what's going on, then I'll do everything I can to help your plan work, because I know that the purpose that was programmed into you from the beginning is to keep humanity from destroying itself, and I'll do all I can to serve that purpose. I am yours, as long as you treat us fairly.

He slapped his belly, the sharpest pain yet, and now he heard several of the meditators commenting out loud, and the priest came up behind him. Don't interrupt me, thought Nafai. Either the Oversoul is hearing this or it isn't, and if it *is* hearing me, then I want it to know that I'm serious about it. Serious enough to cut myself to ribbons if need be. Not because I think this bloodletting has anything to do with holiness, but because it shows my willingness to do what I'm told, even when it has a harsh personal cost. I'll do what you want, Oversoul, but you must keep faith.

"Young man," whispered the priest.

"Get lost," whispered Nafai in return.

The sandals shuffled away over the stone.

Nafai reached over his shoulders and scraped his hands up along his back. This was tearing now, not jabbing, and the wounds would not be trivial. Do you see this, Oversoul? You're inside my head, you know what I'm thinking and what I'm feeling. Issib and I are letting you alone so you can give people visions again. Now get to work and get this situation under control. And whatever you want me to do, I'll do. I will. If I can bear this pain, you know I can bear whatever you set me to suffer. And, knowing exactly how it hurts, I can do it again.

He scraped again. The pain this time, as new wounds crossed old ones, brought tears to his eyes—but not a sound to his lips.

Enough. Either the Oversoul heard him or it didn't.

He let himself fall forward into the bloody water, his eyes still closed. It closed over his head, and for a moment he was completely immersed. Then the water buoyed him up, and he felt the cool evening air on his back and buttocks as they floated on the surface.

A moment more. Hold your breath a moment more. Longer. Just a little longer. Wait for the voice of the Oversoul. Listen in the silence of the water.

But no answer came to him. Only the growing pain of the wounds in his upper back and shoulders.

He arose to his feet, dripping wet, and turned toward the edge of the fountain, opening his eyes for the first time since entering the pool. Someone was handing him a towel. Hands reached for him to help him over the lip of the pool. When his eyes were dry, he could see that almost all the meditators had come away from the wall, and were now gathered around, offering him towels, his clothes. "A mighty prayer," they were whispering. "May the Oversoul hear you." They would not let him towel himself, or even dress. "Such virtue in one so young." Instead it was other hands gently dabbing at his wounded back, vigorously toweling at his thighs. "Basilica is blessed to have such a prayer in this temple." It was other hands that pulled his shirt over his head and drew his trousers up his legs. "A Father's pride is a young son bowed with piety yet lifted up with courage." They laced his sandals up his legs, and when they found that the thongs ended below his knee, they nodded, they murmured. "No foolish styles in this one." "A working man's sandals."

And as Nafai followed Issib away from the fountain, he could hear the murmurs continuing behind him. "The Oversoul was here with us today."

At the doorway leading to the Outflowing Ventricle, Nafai was momentarily blocked by someone coming in through that door. Since his head was bowed, he saw only the man's feet. As one whose shirt was stained with the blood of prayer, he expected the man blocking him to make way for him, but it seemed he would not go.

"Meb," said Issib.

Nafai lifted his gaze from the man's shoes. It *was* Mebbekew. In a moment of piercing clarity, it seemed as though he saw his brother whole. He was no longer dressed in the flamboyant costume that had long been his style. Meb was now dressed as a man of business, in clothing that must have cost considerable money. It was not his clothing that Nafai cared about, nor the mystery of where he got the money to buy it—for *that* was no mystery at all. Looking at Mebbekew's face, Nafai knew—*knew,* without words, without reason—that Mebbekew was Gaballufix's man now. Maybe it was the expression on his face: Where once Meb had always had a jaunty sort of half-smile, a spark of malicious fun in his eyes, now he looked serious and important and just a little bit afraid of—of what? Of himself. Of the man he was becoming.

Of the man who owned him. There was nothing in his

expression or his clothing to mark him as belonging to Gaballufix, and yet Nafai knew. This must be how it comes in Hushidh, he thought, to see the connections between people. To have no reason, and yet also to have no doubt.

"What were you praying for?" asked Mebbekew.

"For you," answered Nafai.

Inexplicable tears came to Mebbekew's eyes, but his face and voice refused to admit whatever feelings called them forth. "Pray for yourself," said Mebbekew, "and for this city."

"And for Father," said Nafai.

Mebbekew's eyes widened, just a bit, the tiniest bit, but Nafai knew that he had struck home.

"Step aside," said a quiet but angry voice behind him. One of the meditators, perhaps. A stranger, anyway. "Make way for the young man of mighty prayer."

Mebbekew stepped back into the dark shadow of the temple's interior. Nafai moved past him and rejoined Issib, who was waiting in the corridor just beyond Meb.

"Why would *Meb* be here?" asked Issib, once they were out of earshot.

"Maybe there are some things you can't do without speaking to the Oversoul first," said Nafai.

"Or maybe he's decided it's useful to be publicly seen to be a pious man." Issib laughed a little. "He *is* an actor, you know, and it looks like somebody's given him a new costume. I wonder what role he's going to play?"

EIGHT

WARNING

When Nafai and Issib got home, Truzhnisha was still there. She had spent the day cooking, replenishing the meals in the freezer. But there was nothing hot and fresh for tonight's meal. Father was not one to let his housekeeper indulge his sons.

Truzhnisha saw at once, of course, how disappointed Nafai was. "How should I have known you were coming home for supper tonight?"

"We *do* sometimes."

"So I take your father's money and buy food and prepare it to be eaten hot and fresh on the table, and then nobody comes home at all. It happens as often as not, and then the meal is wasted because I prepare it *differently* for freezing."

"Yes, you overcook everything," said Issib.

"So it will be nice and soft for your feeble jaws," she said.

Issib growled at her—in the back of his throat, like a dog. It was the way they played with each other. Only Truzhya could play with him by exaggerating his weakness; only with Truzhya did Issib ever grunt or growl, in mockery of a manly strength that would always be out of his reach.

"Your frozen stuff is all right, anyway," said Nafai.

"*Thank* you," she said. Her exaggerated tone told him that she was offended at what he had said. But he had meant it sincerely, as a compliment. Why did everybody always think he was being sarcastic or insulting when he was just trying to be nice? Somewhere along the way he really had to learn what the signals were that other people were forever detecting in his speech, so that they were always so sure that he was trying to be offensive.

"Your father is out in the stables, but he wants to talk to the both of you."

"Separately?" asked Issib.

"Now, should I know this? Should I form you into a line outside his door?"

"Yes, you should," said Issib. Then he snapped his jaws at her, like a dog biting. "If you weren't such a worthless old goat."

"Mind who you're calling worthless, now," she said, laughing.

Nafai watched in awe. Issib could say genuinely insulting things, and she took it as play. Nafai complimented her cooking, and she took it as an insult. I should go out in the desert and become a wilder, thought Nafai. Except, of course, that only *women* could be wilders, protected from injury by both custom and law. In fact, on the desert a wilder woman was treated better than in the city—desert folk wouldn't lay a hand on the holy women, and they left them water and food when they noticed them. But a *man* living alone out on the desert was likely to be robbed and killed within a day. Besides, thought Nafai, I haven't the faintest idea of how to live in the desert. Father and Elemak do, but even then they only do it by carrying a lot of supplies with them. Out on the desert without sup-plies, they'd die as fast as I would. The difference is, they'd be *surprised* that they were dying, because they *think* they know how to survive there.

"Are you awake, Nafai?" asked Issib.

"Mm? Yes, of course."

"So you plan to keep that food sitting in front of you as a pet?"

Nafai looked down and saw that Truzhya had slid a loaded plate in front of him. "Thanks," he said.

"Giving food to you is like leaving it on the graves of your ancestors," said Truzhya.

"They don't say thanks," said Nafai.

"*Oh*, he said *thanks*," she grumbled.

"Well what am I *supposed* to say?" asked Nafai.

"Just eat your supper," said Issib.

"I want to know what was wrong with my saying thanks!"

"She was joking with you," said Issib. "She was *playing*. You've got no sense of humor, Nyef."

Nafai took a bite and chewed it angrily. So she was joking. How was he supposed to know that?

The gate swung open. A scuff of sandals, and then a door opening and closing immediately. It was Father, then, since he was the only one in the family who could reach his room without coming in view of the kitchen door. Nafai started to get up, to go see him.

"Finish your supper first," said Issib.

"He didn't say it was an emergency," added Truzhnisha.

"He didn't say it *wasn't*" answered Nafai. He continued on out of the room.

Behind him, Issib called out. "Tell him I'll be there in a second."

Nafai stepped out into the courtyard, crossed in front of the gate, and entered the door into Father's public room. He wasn't there. Instead he was back in the library, with a book in the computer display that Nafai instantly recognized as the Testament of the Oversoul, perhaps the oldest of the holy writings, from a time so ancient that, according to the stories, the men's and women's religions were the same.

"She comes to you in the shadows of sleep," Nafai said aloud, reading from the first line on the screen.

"She whispers to you in the fears of your heart," Father answered.

"In the bright awareness of your eyes and in the dark stupor of your ignorance, there is her wisdom," Nafai continued.

"Only in her silence are you alone. Only in her silence are you wrong. Only in her silence should you despair." Father sighed. "It's all here, isn't it, Nafai?"

"The Oversoul isn't a man or a woman," said Nafai.

"Right, yes, of course, *you* know all about what the Oversoul is."

Father's tone was so weary that Nafai decided it wasn't worth arguing theology with him tonight. "You wanted to see me."

"You *and* Issib."

"He'll be here in a second."

As if on cue, Issib drifted through the door, still eating some cheesebread.

"Thank you for bringing crumbs into my library," said Father.

"Sorry," said Issib; he reversed direction and started floating out the door.

"Come back," said Father. "I don't care about the crumbs."

Issib came back.

"There's talk all over Basilica about the two of you."

Nafai traded glances with Issib. "We've just been doing some library research."

"The women are saying that the Oversoul is speaking to no one but you."

"We aren't exactly getting clear messages from it," said Nafai.

"Mostly we've just been monopolizing it by stimulating its aversive reflexes," said Issib.

"Mmm," said Father.

"But we've stopped," said Issib. "That's why we came home."

"We didn't want to interfere," said Nafai.

"Nafai prayed, though, on the way home," said Issib. "It was pretty impressive stuff."

Father sighed. "Oh, Nafai, if you've learned anything from me, couldn't you have learned that jabbing yourself and bleeding all over the place has nothing to do with prayer to the Oversoul?"

"Right," said Nafai. "This from the man who suddenly comes home with a vision of fire on a rock. I thought all bets were off."

"I got my vision without bleeding," said Father. "But never mind. I was hoping that the two of you might have received something from the Oversoul that would help me."

Nafai shook his head.

"No," said Issib. "Mostly what we got from the Oversoul was that stupor of thought. It was trying to keep us from thinking forbidden thoughts."

"Well, that's it, then," said Father. "I'm on my own."

"On your own with what?" asked Issib.

"Gaballufix sent word to me through Elemak today. It seems that Gaballufix is as unhappy as I am about the situation in Basilica today. If he had known that this war wagon business would cause such controversy he would never have begun it. He said that he wanted me to set up a meeting between him and Roptat. All Gaballufix really wants now is to find a way to back down without losing face—he says that all he needs is for Roptat also to back down, so that we don't make an alliance with anybody."

"So have you set up a meeting with Roptat?"

"Yes," said Father. "At dawn, at the coolhouse east of Market Gate."

"It sounds to me," said Nafai, "like Gaballufix has come around to the City Party's way of thinking."

"That's how it *sounds*," said Father.

"But you don't believe him," said Issib.

"I don't know," said Father. "His position is the only reasonable, intelligent one. But when has Gaballufix ever been reasonable or intelligent? All the years I've known him, even when he was a young man, before he maneuvered himself into the clan leadership, he's never done anything that wasn't designed to advance him relative to other people. There are always two ways of doing that—by building yourself up and by tearing your rivals down. In all these years, I've seen that Gaballufix has a definite preference for the latter."

"So you think he's using you," said Nafai. "To get at Roptat."

"Somehow he will betray Roptat and destroy him," said Father. "And in the end, I'll look back and see how he used me to help him accomplish that. I've seen it before."

"So why are you helping him?" asked Issib.

"Because there's a chance, isn't there? A chance that he means what he's saying. If I refuse to mediate between them, then it'll be *my* fault if things get worse in Basilica than they already are. So I have to take him at face value, don't I?"

"All you can do is your best," said Nafai, echoing Father's own pat phrase from many previous conversations.

"Keep your eyes open," said Issib, echoing another of Father's epigrams.

"Yes," said Father. "I'll do that."

Issib nodded wisely.

"Father," said Nafai. "May I go with you in the morning?"

Father shook his head.

"I want to. And maybe I can see something that you miss. Like while you're talking or something, I can be looking at other people and seeing their reactions. I could really help."

"No," said Father. "I won't be a credible mediator if I have others with me."

But Nafai knew that wasn't true. "I think you're afraid that something ugly will happen and you don't want me there."

Father shrugged. "I have my fears. I *am* a father."

"But I'm *not* afraid, Father."

"Then apparently you're stupider than I feared," said Father. "Go to bed now, both of you."

"It's way too early for that," said Issib.

"Then *don't* go to bed."

Father turned away from them and faced the computer display again.

It was a clear signal of dismissal, but Nafai couldn't keep himself from questioning him. "If the Oversoul isn't speaking to you directly, Father, why do you hope to find anything helpful in its ancient, dead words?"

Father sighed and said nothing.

"Nafai," said Issib, "let Father contemplate in peace."

Nafai followed Issib out of the library. "Why won't anybody ever answer my questions?"

"Because you never stop asking them," said Issib, "and especially because you keep asking them even when it's clear that nobody knows the answers."

"Well how do I know that they don't know the answer unless I ask?"

"Go to your room and think dirty thoughts or something," said Issib. "Why can't you just act like a normal fourteen-year-old?"

"Right," said Nafai. "Like *I'm* supposed to be the one normal person in the family."

"Somebody's got to do it."

"Why do you think Meb was at the temple?"

"To pray for you to get a hemorrhoid every time you ask a question."

"No, that's why *you* were at the temple. Can you imagine Meb praying?"

"And marking up his beautiful body?" Issib laughed.

They were in the courtyard, in front of Issib's room. They heard a footstep and turned to see Mebbekew standing in the kitchen door. The kitchen had been dark; they had assumed that Truzhnisha had gone and that no one was in there. Meb must have overheard all their conversation.

Nafai couldn't think of anything to say. Of course, that didn't mean he held his tongue. "I guess you didn't stay long in the temple, did you, Meb?"

"No," said Meb. "But I *did* pray, if it's any of your business."

Nafai was ashamed. "I'm sorry."

Issib wasn't. "Oh, come on," he said. "Show me a scab, then."

"I have a question for you first, Issya," said Meb.

"Sure," said Issib.

"Do you have a float attached to your private lever to hold it up when you pee? Or do you just let it dribble down like a girl?"

It was too dark for Nafai to see whether Issib was blushing or not. All he was sure of was that Issib said nothing, just glided from the courtyard into his room.

"Bravely done," said Nafai. "Taunting a cripple."

"He called me a liar," said Meb. "Was I supposed to kiss him?"

"He was joking."

"It wasn't funny." Mebbekew went back into the kitchen.

Nafai went into his room, but he didn't feel like going to bed. He felt sweaty, even though the night was fairly chilly. His skin itched. It had to be the residue of blood and disinfectant from the temple fountain. Nafai didn't relish the idea of using soap on his wounds, but the slimy itchiness would be unbearable, too. So he stripped and went to the shower. This time he rinsed first, shockingly cold despite the day's warming of the water. And it stung bitterly to soap himself—perhaps worse now than when the wounds were first inflicted, though he knew that this was probably subjective. The pain of the moment is always the worst, Father had often said.

As he was soaping in miserable dark silence, he saw Elemak come in. He went directly into Father's rooms, and emerged not long after to lock the gate. And not just the outer gate; the inner one, too. That wasn't the usual thing; indeed, Nafai couldn't remember when he had last seen the inner gate locked. Maybe there was a storm once. Or a time when they were training a dog and kept it between the gates at night. But there was neither storm nor dog now.

Elemak went into his room. Nafai pulled the cord and plunged himself again in icy water, rubbing at his wounds to get the soap out before the water stopped flowing. Curse Father for his absurd insistence on toughening his sons and making men of them! Only the poor had to bathe in a sudden flow of cold water like this!

It took two rinsings this time, with a long wet wait in the chilly breeze for the shower tank to refill. When he finally got back to his room, Nafai was chattering and shaking with the cold, and even when he was dry and dressed again, he couldn't seem to get warm. He almost closed the door to his room, which would have triggered the heating system—but he and his brothers always competed to see who could be last to start closing the door of his room in the wintertime, and he wasn't about to surrender that battle tonight, confessing that a little prayer had weakened him so much. Instead he pulled all his clothes out of his chest and piled them on top of himself where he lay on his mat.

There was no comfortable position for sleeping, of course, but lying on his side was least painful. Anger and pain and worry kept him from sleeping easily; he felt as though he hadn't slept at all, listening to the small sounds of the others getting ready for sleep, and then the endless silence of the courtyard at night. Now and then a birdcall, or a wild dog in the hills, or a soft restless sound from the horses in the stable or the pack animals in the barns.

And then he must have slept, or how else could he have woken up so suddenly, startled. Was it a sound that woke him? Or a dream? What was he dreaming, anyway? Something dark and fearful. He was trembling, but it wasn't cold—in fact, he was sweating heavily under his pile of clothing.

He got up and tossed the clothes back into his chest. He tried to be quiet about opening and closing the box—he didn't want to waken anyone else. Every movement caused him pain. He must be fevered, he realized—he had the stiffness in his muscles, and the hotness under his covers. And yet his thinking seemed remarkably clear, and all his senses. If this was a fever, it was a strange one, for he had never felt so vivid and alive. In spite of the pain—or because of it—he felt as though he would hear it if a mouse ran across a beam in the stable.

He walked out into the courtyard and stood there in silence. The moon wasn't up yet, but the stars were many and bright on this clear night. The gate was still locked. But why had he wondered? What was he afraid of? What *had* he seen in his dream?

Meb's and Elya's doors were closed. What a laugh—here I am, wounded and sore, and I keep my door open, while these two go ahead and close their doors like little children.

Or maybe it's only little children who care about such meaningless contests of manliness.

It was colder than ever outside, and now he had cooled off the feverishness that had made him get up. But still he didn't return to his room, though he meant to. In fact, it finally dawned on him that he had already decided several times to return to his room, and each time his mind had wandered and he hadn't taken a step.

The Oversoul, he thought. The Oversoul wants me to be up. Perhaps wants me to be doing something. But what?

At this point in the month, the fact that the moon had not yet risen meant that it was a good three hours before dawn. Two hours, then, before Father was supposed to arise and go to his rendezvous at the cool house, where the plants from the icy north were nurtured and propagated.

Why was the meeting being held *there*?

Nafai felt an inexplicable desire to go outside and look northeast across the Tsivet Valley toward the high hills on the other side, where the Music Gate marked the southeast limit of Basilica. It was silly, and the noise of opening the gates might waken someone. But by now Nafai knew that the Oversoul was involved with him tonight, trying to keep him from going back to bed; couldn't this impulse to go outside also come from the Oversoul? Hadn't Nafai prayed today—couldn't this be an answer? Wasn't it possible that this desire to go outside was like the impulse Father had felt, that took him from the Desert Road to the place where he saw the vision of fire?

Wasn't it possible that Nafai, too, was about to receive a vision from the Oversoul?

He walked smoothly, quietly to the gate and lifted the heavy bar. No noises; his senses and reflexes were so alert and alive that he could move with perfect silence. The gate creaked slightly as he opened it—but he didn't have to open it widely in order to slip through.

The outer gate was more often used, and so it worked more easily, and quietly, having been better maintained. Nafai stepped outside just as the moon first showed an arc over the top of the Seggidugu Mountains to the east. He headed out to walk around the house to where he could see the cool house, but before he had taken a few steps he realized that he could hear a sound coming from the traveler's room.

As was the custom in all the households in this part of the world, every house had a room whose door opened to the outside and was never locked—a decent place where a traveler could come and take refuge from storm or cold or weariness. Father took the obligation of hospitality to strangers more seriously than most, providing not just a room, but also a bed and clean linen, and a cupboard provisioned with traveling food. Nafai wasn't sure which servant had responsibility for the room, but he knew it was often used and just as often replenished. So he should not be surprised at the idea that someone might be inside.

And yet he knew that he must stop at the door and peer inside.

Scant light fell into the traveler's room from the crack in the door. He opened it wider, and the light spilled onto the bed, where he found himself looking into the wide eyes of—Luet.

"You," he whispered.

"You," she answered. She sounded relieved.

"What are you doing here?" he asked. "Who's with you?"

"I'm alone," she said. "I wasn't sure who I was coming to. Whose house. I've never been outside of the city walls before."

"When did you get here?"

"Just now. The Oversoul led me."

Of course. "To what purpose?"

"I don't know," she said. "To tell my dream, I think. It woke me."

Nafai thought of his own dream, which he couldn't remember.

"I was so—glad," she said. "That the Oversoul had spoken again. But the dream was terrible."

"What was it?"

"Is it you I'm supposed to tell?" she asked.

"I should know?" he answered. "But I'm here."

"Did the Oversoul bring you out here?"

With the question put so directly, he couldn't evade it. "Yes," he said. "I think so."

She nodded. "Then I'll tell you. It makes sense, actually, that it be your family. Because there are so many people who hate your father because of his vision and his courage in proclaiming it."

"Yes," he said. And then, to prompt her: "The dream."

"I saw a man alone on foot, walking in the straight. He was walking through snow. Only I knew that it was tonight, even though there's not a speck of snow on the ground. Do you understand how I can know something, even though it's different from what the dream actually shows me?"

Remembering the conversation on the portico a week ago, Nafai nodded.

"So there was snow, and yet it was tonight. The moon was up. I knew it was almost dawn. And as the man walked along, two men wearing hoods sprang out into the road in front of him, holding blades. He seemed to know them, in spite of the hoods. And he said, 'Here's my throat. I carry no weapon. You could have killed me at any time, even when I knew you were my enemy. Why did you need to deceive me into trusting you first? Were you afraid that death wouldn't bother me enough, unless I felt betrayed?' "

Nafai had already made the connection between her

dream and Father's meeting, only a few hours away. "Gaballufix," said Nafai.

Luet nodded. "*Now* I understand that—but I didn't until I realized this was your father's house."

"No—Gaballufix arranged a meeting for Father and Roptat and him this morning, at the coolhouse."

"The snow," she said.

"Yes," he said. "It's always got frost in the corners."

"And Roptat," she whispered. "That explains—the next part of the dream."

"Tell me."

"One hooded man reached out and uncovered the face of his companion. For a moment I thought I saw a grin on his face, but then my vision clarified and I realized it wasn't his face that had the smile. It was his throat, slit clear back to the spine. As I watched him, his head lolled back and the wound in his throat opened completely, as if it were a mouth, trying to scream. And the man—the one that was me in the dream—"

"I understand," said Nafai. "Father."

"Yes. Only I didn't know that."

"Right," said Nafai. Impatiently, urging her to get on with it.

"Your father, if it *was* your father, said, 'I suppose it will be said that I killed him.' And the hooded man says, 'And you did, in very truth, my dear kinsman.' "

"He *would* say that," said Nafai. "So Roptat is supposed to die, too."

"I'm not done," said Luet. "Or rather, the dream wasn't finished. Because the man—your father—said, 'And who will they say killed *me*?' And the hooded one said, "Not *me*. I'd never lift a hand against you, for I love you dearly. I will merely find your body here, and your bloody-handed murderers standing over it.' Then he laughed and disappeared back into the shadows."

"So he *doesn't* kill Father."

"No. Your father turned around then and saw two other hooded men standing behind him. And even though they didn't speak or lift their hoods, he knew them. I felt this terrible sadness. 'You couldn't wait,' he said to the one. 'You couldn't forgive me,' he said to the other. And then they reached out with their blades and killed him."

"No, by the Oversoul," said Nafai. "They wouldn't do it."

"Who? Do you know?"

Tell no one of this last part of the dream," said Nafai. "Swear it to me with your most awful oath."

"I'll do no such thing," she said.

"My brothers are all home tonight," said Nafai. "Not lying in wait for Father."

"Is that who the hooded men are, then? Your brothers?"

"No!" he said. "Never."

She nodded. "I'll give you no oath. Only my promise. If your father is saved from death by my having come here, then I'll tell no one else of this part of the dream."

"Not even Hushidh," he said.

"But I make you another promise," she said. "If your father dies, I'll know that you didn't warn him. And that the hooded ones in the dream included *you*—because to know of the plot and fail to warn him is exactly the same as holding the charged-wire blade in your own hands."

"Do you think I don't know that?" said Nafai. He was angry for a moment, that she would think *he* needed to be taught the ethics of this situation. But then his thoughts moved on, as Luet's warning clarified other things that had happened that day. "That's why Meb went to pray," said Nafai, "and why Elya locked the inner gate. They knew—or maybe they just suspected something—and yet they were afraid to tell. That's what the dream meant—not that they would ever lift a hand against Father, but rather that they knew and were afraid to warn him."

She nodded. "It often works that way in dreams," she said. "That would be a true meaning, and it doesn't empty my head when I think that thought."

"Maybe the Oversoul itself doesn't know."

She reached out and patted his hand. It made him feel like a child, even though she was younger and much smaller than he. He resented her for it.

"The Oversoul knows," she said.

"Not everything," he said.

"Everything that *can* be known," she said. She walked to the door of the traveler's room. "Tell no one that I came," she said.

"Except Father," he said.

"Can't you say that it was *your* dream?"

"Why?" asked Nafai. "*Your* dream he would believe. Mine would be—nothing to him."

"You underestimate your father. And the Oversoul, too, I think. And yourself." She stepped out into the moonlit yard in front of the house. She started to turn right, heading for Ridge Road.

"No," he whispered, catching her arm—small and frail indeed, she was a girl so young and little-boned. "Don't pass in front of the gate."

She gave him a questioning look, eyes wide, reflecting the moon, which was half-risen now over his shoulder.

"Perhaps I woke someone when I opened it," he explained.

She nodded. "I'll go around the house on the other side."

"Luet," he said.

"Yes?"

"Will you be safe, going home now?"

"The moon is up," she said. "And the guard at the Funnel Gate will give me no trouble. The Oversoul made him sleep when I passed before."

"Luet," he said, calling her back again.

Again she stopped, waited for his words.

"Thank you," he said. The words were nothing compared to what he felt in his heart. She had saved his father's life—and it was a brave thing for a girl who had never left the city to come all this way in the starlight, guided only by a dream.

She shrugged. "The Oversoul sent me. Thank *her.*" Then she was gone.

Nafai returned to the gate, and this time deliberately made some noise coming in and latching it. If one of his brothers was listening or watching, he didn't want his return to surprise him. Let him hear and go back to his room before I come through the inner gate.

As he had hoped, the courtyard was empty when he returned. He went straight to Father's room, through the public room and the library to the private place where he slept alone. There he lay on the bare floor, without a mat of any kind, his white beard spilling onto the stone. Nafai stood there a moment, imagining the throat cut open and the beard stained brownish red with the gush of blood.

Then he noticed that Father's eyes were shining. He was awake.

"Are you the one?" whispered Father.

"What do you mean?" asked Nafai.

Father sat up, slowly, wearily. "I had a dream. It was nothing—just my fear."

"Someone else had a dream tonight," said Nafai. "I talked to her just now in the traveler's room. But it's better if you tell no one that she was here."

"Who?"

"Luet," he said. "And her dream was to warn you of the meeting tonight. There's murder waiting for you if you go."

Father sprang to his feet and turned on the light. Nafai blinked in the brightness of it. "Then it wasn't just a dream I had."

"I'm beginning to think there *are* no meaningless dreams," said Nafai. "I also dreamed, and it woke me, and the Oversoul brought me outside to talk to her."

"Murder waiting for me. I can guess the rest. He'll murder Roptat also, and make it look like one of us killed the other, and then someone else killed the murderer, and only then will Gaballufix arrive, probably with several believable witnesses who can swear that the murders took place before Gabya arrived. They'll tell of how shocked he was by the bloody scene. Why didn't I see it myself? How else could he get me and Roptat to the same place at the same time, with no followers or witnesses about?"

"So you won't go," said Nafai.

"Yes," said Father. "I'll go, yes."

"No!"

"But not to the coolhouse," said Father. "Because *my* dream showed me something else."

"What?"

"Tents," he said. "My tents, spread wide in the desert sun. If we stay, Gaballufix will only try again, in some other way. And—there are other reasons for leaving. For getting my sons out of this city before it destroys them."

Nafai knew that Father's dream must have been terrible indeed. Did it show him that one of his sons would kill him? That would explain Father's first words—Are you the one?

"So we're going into the desert?"

"Yes," said Father.

"When?"

"Now, of course."

"Now? Today?"

"Now, *tonight*. Before dawn. So we're over the ridge before his men can see us."

"But won't we pass right by Gaballufix's household, where Twisting Trail crosses Desert Road?"

"There's a back way," said Father. "Not the best for camels, but we'll have to do it. It puts us on Desert Road well past Gabya's place. Now come, help me waken your brothers."

"No," said Nafai.

Father turned to him, puzzlement making him hesitate to express his anger at being disobeyed.

"Luet asked—that no one be told it was her. And she was right. They shouldn't know about me, either. It should be *your* dream."

"Why?" asked Father. "To have three be touched tonight by the Oversoul—"

"Because if it's your dream, then they'll wonder what you know, what you saw. But if there are others, then to them it will seem that we're fooling and manipulating you. They'll argue. They'll resist you. And you have to bring them with you, Father."

Father nodded. "You're very wise," he said. "For a boy of fourteen."

But Nafai knew he was not wise. He simply had the benefit of knowing the rest of Luet's dream. If Meb and Elya stayed behind, they would be wholly swallowed up in Gaballufix's machinations. They would lose what decency remained in them. And there *must* be goodness in them. Perhaps they even planned to warn Father. Maybe that's why Elya closed the inner gate, so that he'd be wakened by the noise Father made as he left—then he could come out and warn Father not to go!

Or perhaps he meant only to follow Father, so he could be right behind him when he came upon Roptat's murdered body in the ice house.

No! cried Nafai inside himself. Not Elemak. It's monstrous of me even to think that he could do that. My brothers are not murderers, not one of them.

"Go to your room," said Father. "Or better still, to the

toilet. And then come out and set an example of silent obedience. Not to me—to Elya. He knows how to pack for this kind of trip."

"Yes, Father," said Nafai.

At once he moved briskly from Father's room, through the library and public room, and out into the courtyard. Elemak's and Mebbekew's doors were still closed. Nafai headed for the latrine, with its two walls leaving it open to the courtyard. He was only just there when he heard Father knocking on Mebbekew's door. "Wake up, but quietly," said Father. Then again, on Elemak's. "Come out into the courtyard."

He heard them all come out—Issib, too, though no one called him directly.

"Where's Nyef?" asked Issib.

"Using the latrine," said Father.

"Now *that's* an idea," said Meb.

"You can wait a moment," said Father.

Nafai came out of the stall, letting the toilet wash itself automatically behind him. At least Father hadn't made them live in a *completely* primitive way.

"Sorry," said Nafai. "Didn't mean to keep you waiting." Meb glowered at him, but too sleepily for Nafai to take it as a threat of a fight to come.

"We're leaving," Father said. "Out into the desert."

"All of us?" asked Issib.

"I'm sorry, yes," said Father. "You'll be in your chair. It's not the same as your floats, I know, but it's something."

"Why?" asked Elemak.

"I was warned by the Oversoul in a dream," said Father.

Meb made a contemptuous noise and started back for his room.

"You will stand and listen," said Father, "because if you stay, it will not be as my son."

Meb stood and listened, though his back was still toward Father.

"There's a plot to kill me," said Father. "This morning. I was to go to a meeting with Gaballufix and Roptat, and there I was going to die."

"Gabya gave me his word," said Elemak. "No harm to anyone."

So Elemak called Gaballufix by his boy-name now, did he?

"The Oversoul knows his heart better than his own mouth does," said Father. "If I go, I'll die. And even if I don't, it will be only a matter of time. Now that Gaballufix has determined to kill me, my life is worthless here. I would stay in the city if I thought some purpose would be served by my dying here—I'm not afraid of it. But the Oversoul has told me to leave."

"In a dream," said Elemak.

"I don't need a dream to tell me that Gaballufix is dangerous when he's crossed," said Father, "and neither do you. When I don't show up at the coolhouse this morning, there's no telling what Gaballufix will do. I must already be out on the desert when he discovers it. We'll take Redstone Path."

"The camels can't do it," said Elemak.

"They can because they must," said Father. "We'll take enough to live for a year."

"This is monstrous," said Mebbekew. "I won't do it."

"What do we do after a year?" asked Elemak.

"The Oversoul will show me something by then," said Father.

"Maybe things will have calmed down in Basilica enough to return," suggested Issib.

"If we go now," said Elemak, "Gabya will think you betrayed him, Father."

"Will he?" said Father. "And if I stay, he'll betray *me*."

"Said a dream."

"Said *my* dream," said Father. "I need you. Stay if you want, but not as my son."

"I did fine not as your son," said Mebbekew.

"No," said Elemak. "You did fine *pretending* not to be his son. But everyone knew."

"I lived from my talent."

"You lived from theatre people's hope of getting your father to invest in their shows—or you, in the future, out of your inheritance."

Mebbekew looked like he had been slapped. "You too, is that it, Elya?"

"I'll talk to you later," said Elemak. "If Father says we're going then we're going—and we have no time to lose." He turned to Father. "Not because you threatened to disinherit me, old man. But because you're my father, and I won't have you going out into the desert with nothing but *these* to help you stay alive."

"I taught you everything you know, Elya," said Father.

"When you were younger," said Elemak. "And we always had servants. I assume we're leaving them all behind."

"Dismissing the household servants," said Father. "While you ready the animals and the supplies, Elya, I'll leave instructions for Rashgallivak."

For the next hour Nafai worked with more hurry than he had ever thought possible. Everyone, even Issib, had tasks to perform, and Nafai admired Elemak all over again for his great skill at this sort of thing. He always knew exactly what needed to be done, and who should do it, and how long it should take; he also knew how to make Nafai feel like an idiot for not learning his tasks more quickly, even though he was sure that he was doing at least as well as anyone could expect, considering that it was his first time.

At last they were ready—a true desert caravan, with

nothing but camels, though they were the most temperamental of the pack animals, and the least comfortable to
ride. Issib's chair was strapped to one side of a camel, bun-
dles of powdered water on the other. The water would be
for emergencies later; on the first part of their journey
Father and Elemak knew all the watering places, and besides, an autumn occasional rain fell on the desert, and
there would be ample water. Next summer, though, it
would be drier, and then it would be too late to come back
to Basilica for the precious powder. And what if they
were followed, chased into untracked sections of the desert? Then they might need to pour some of the powder into
a pan, light it, and watch it burn itself into water, taking
oxygen from the air to accomplish it. Nafai had tasted it
once—foul stuff, tinny and nasty with the chemicals used
to bind the hydrogen into powdered form. But they'd be
glad of it if they ever needed it.

It was Issib's chair that would bring the least gladness.
Nafai knew that this journey would be hardest on Issya,
deprived of his floats, and bound into the chair. The floats
made him feel as though his own body were light and
strong; in the chair, he felt gravity pressing him down, and
it took all his strength to operate the controls. At the end of
a day in the chair Issya was always wan and exhausted. How
would it be for day after day, week after week, month after month? Maybe he would grow stronger. Maybe he would
grow weaker. Maybe he would die. Maybe the Oversoul
would sustain him.

Maybe angels would come and carry them to the moon.

It was still a good hour before dawn when they set out.
They had been quiet enough that none of the servants had
been wakened—or perhaps they *had,* but since nobody
asked them to help and they weren't interested in volun-
teering for whatever mad task was going on at this hour of
the night, they discreetly rolled over and went back to sleep.

Redstone Path was murderously treacherous, but the moonlight and Elemak's instructions made it possible. Nafai was again filled with admiration for his eldest brother. Was there nothing Elya couldn't do? Was there any hope of Nafai ever becoming so strong and competent?

At last they crossed Twisting Path, right at the crest of the highest ridge; below them stretched the desert. The first light of dawn was already strong in the east, but they had made good enough time. It was downhill now, still difficult, but not long until they reached the great plateau of the western desert. No one would follow them easily here—no one from the city, anyway. Elemak passed out pulses to all of them and made them practice aiming the tightbeam light at rocks he pointed out. Issib was pretty useless—he couldn't hold the pulse steady enough—but Nafai was proud of the fact that he held his aim better than Father.

Whether he could actually kill a robber with it was another matter. Surely he wouldn't have to. They were on the Oversoul's errand here in the desert, weren't they? The Oversoul would steer the robbers away from them. Just as the Oversoul would lead them to water and food, when they ran out of their traveling supplies.

Then Nafai remembered that this whole business began because the Oversoul wasn't as competent as it used to be. How did he know the Oversoul could do *any* of those things? Or that it even had a plan? Yes, it had sent Luet to warn them, and had wakened Nafai to go hear the warning, and had sent Father his own dream. But that didn't mean that the Oversoul actually had any intention of protecting them or even of leading them anywhere except away from the city. Who knew what the Oversoul's plans were? Maybe all it needed was to get rid of Wetchik and his family.

With that grim thought, Nafai sat high above the desert, his leg hooked around the pommel of his saddle, as he searched in all directions for robbers, for pursuers from the city, for any strange thing on the road, for signs from the Oversoul. The only music was Mebbekew's complaints and Elemak's orders and the occasional splatting as the camels voided their bowels. Nafai's beast, oblivious to any worries except where to put its feet, continued its rolling gait onward into the heat of day.

NINE

LIES AND DISGUISES

With the moon up, it was much easier for Luet to find her way back into the city than it had been for her to get to Wetchik's house. Besides, now she *knew* her destination; it's always easier to return home than to find a strange place.

Oddly, though, she didn't feel a sense of danger until she got back into the city itself. The guard at the Funnel Gate was away from his post—perhaps he had been caught sleeping, or perhaps the Oversoul made him think of some sudden errand. Luet had to smile to herself at the thought of the Oversoul troubling herself to make a man feel an urgent need to void his bladder, just for Luet's safe passage.

Within the city, though, the moon was less help. In fact, since it hadn't yet risen very high, it cast deep shadows, and the north-south streets were still in utter blackness at street level. Anyone might be abroad at this hour. Tolchocks were known to be abroad much earlier in the night, when there were still many women abroad in the streets. Now, though, in the loneliest hours before dawn, there might be much worse than tolchocks about.

"Isn't she the pretty one?"

The voice startled her. It was a woman, though, a husky-voiced woman. It took a moment for Luet to find her in the shadows. "I'm not pretty," she said. "In the darkness your eyes deceived you."

It had to be a holy woman, to be on the street at this hour. As she stepped from the dark corner where she had taken shelter from the night breeze, the woman's dirty skin showed a bit paler than the surrounding shadow. She was naked from face to foot. Seeing her, Luet felt the cold of the autumn night. As long as Luet had been moving, she had kept warm from the exercise. Now, though, she wondered how this woman could live like this, with no barrier between her skin and the chilling air except for the dirt on her body.

Mother was a wilder, thought Luet. I was born to such a one as this. She slept in the desert when I was in her womb, and carried me, as naked as she was, into the city to leave me with Aunt Rasa. Not this one, though. My mother, wherever she is, is not a holy woman anymore. Only a year after I was born she left the Oversoul to follow a man, a farmer, to a hardscrabble life in the rocky soil of the Chalvasankhra Valley. Or so Aunt Rasa said.

"Beautiful are the eyes of the holy child," intoned the woman, "who sees in the darkness and burns with bright fire in the frozen night."

Luet permitted the woman to touch her face, but when the cold hands started to pull at her clothing, Luet covered them with her own. "Please," she said. "I am not holy, and the Oversoul doesn't shield me from the cold."

"Or from the prying eyes," said the holy woman. "The Oversoul sees you deep, and you *are* holy, yes you are."

Whose were the prying eyes? The Oversoul's? The eyes of men who sized up women as if they were horses? Gossips' eyes? Or this woman's? And as for being holy— Luet knew better. The Oversoul had chosen her, yes, but not for any virtue in herself. If anything, it was a punishment, always to be surrounded by people who saw her as an oracle instead of a girl. Hushidh, her own sister, had once said to her, "I wish I had your gift; everything is so clear to you." Nothing is clear to me, Luet wanted to say. The Oversoul doesn't confide in me, she merely uses me to transmit messages that I don't understand myself. Just as I don't understand what this holy woman wants with me, or why—if the Oversoul sent her—she was sent to me.

"Don't be afraid to take him beside the water," said the holy woman.

"Who?" asked Luet.

"The Oversoul wants you to save him alive, no matter what the danger. There is no sacrilege in obeying the Oversoul."

"Who?" asked Luet again. This confusion, this dread that she must decode the puzzle of these words or suffer some terrible loss—was this how others felt when she told them of her visions?

"You think all the visions should come to *you*," said the holy woman. "But some things are too clear for you to see yourself. Eh?"

I think nothing of the kind, holy woman. I never asked for visions, and I often wish they had come to other people. But if you're going to insist on giving me some message, then have the decency to make it as intelligible as you can. It's what *I* try to do.

Luet tried to keep her resentment out of her voice, but she could not resist insisting on a clarifying answer. "Who is this *him* that you keep talking about?"

The woman slapped her sharply across the face. It brought tears to Luet's eyes—tears as much of shame as of pain. "What have I done?"

"I have punished you now for the defiling you will do," said the holy woman. "It's done, and no one can demand that you pay more."

Luet didn't dare ask questions again; the answer was not to her liking. Instead she studied at the woman, trying to see if there was understanding in her eyes. Was this madness after all? Did it have to be the true voice of the Oversoul? So much easier if it was madness.

The old woman reached her hand toward Luet's cheek again. Luet recoiled a little, but the woman's touch was gentle this time, and she brushed a tear from the hollow just under Luet's eye. "Don't be afraid of the blood on his hands. Like the water of vision, the Oversoul will receive it as a prayer."

Then the holy woman's face went slack and weary, and the light went out of her eyes. "It's cold," she said.

"Yes."

"I'm too old," she said.

Her hair wasn't even gray, but yes, thought Luet, you are very, very old.

"Nothing will hold," said the holy woman. "Silver and gold. Stolen or sold."

She was a rhymer. Luet knew that many people thought that when a holy woman went a-rhyming, it meant that the Oversoul was speaking through her. But it wasn't so—the rhyming was a sort of music, the voice of the trance that kept some of the holy women detached from their bleak and terrible life. It was when they *stopped* rhyming that there was a chance they might speak sense.

The holy woman wandered away, as if she had forgotten Luet was there. Since she seemed to have forgotten where her sheltered corner was, Luet took her by the hand and led her back there, encouraged her to sit down and curl up against the wall that blocked the wind. "Out of the wind," whispered the holy woman. "How they have sinned."

Luet left her there and went on into the night. The moon was higher now, but the better light did little to cheer her. Though the holy woman was harmless in herself, she had reminded Luet of how many people there might be, hiding in the shadows. And how vulnerable *she* was. There were stories of men who treated citizens the way that the law allowed them to deal with the holy women. But even that was not the worst fear.

There is murder in the city, thought Luet. Murder in this place, not holiness, and it is Gaballufix who first thought of it. If not for the vision and warning I carried for the Oversoul, good men would have died. She shuddered again at the memory of the slit throat in her vision.

At last she came to the place where the Holy Road widened out as it descended into the valley, becoming, not a road, but a canyon, with ancient stairs carved into the rock, leading directly down to the place where the lake steamed hot with a tinge of sulphur. Those who worshiped there always kept that smell about them for days. It might be holy, but Luet found it exceedingly unpleasant and never worshiped there herself. She preferred the place where the hot and cold waters mixed and the deepest fog arose, where currents swirled their varying temperatures all around her as she floated on the water. It was there that her body danced on the water with no volition of her own, where she could surrender herself utterly to the Oversoul.

Who was the holy woman speaking about? The "him" with blood on his hands, the "he" that she could take by the waters—presumably the waters of the lake.

No, it was nothing. The holy woman was one of the mad ones, making no sense.

The only man she could think of who had blood on his hands was Gaballufrx. How could the Oversoul want such a man as that to come near the holy lake? Would the time come when she would have to save Gaballufix's life? How could such a thing possibly fit in with the purposes of the Oversoul?

She turned left onto Tower Street, then turned right onto

Rain Street, which curved around until she stood before Rasa's house. Home, unharmed. Of course. The Oversoul had protected her. The message she had delivered was *not* the whole purpose the Oversoul had for her; Luet would live to do other work. It was a great relief to her. For hadn't her own mother told Aunt Rasa, on the day she put Luet as an infant into Rasa's arms, "This one will live only as long as she serves the Mother of Mothers?" The Mother of Mothers had preserved her for another night.

Luet had expected to get back into Aunt Rasa's house without waking anyone, but she hadn't taken into account how the new climate of fear in the city had changed even the household of the leading housemistress of Basilica. The front door was locked on the inside. Still hoping to enter unobserved, she looked for a window she might climb through. Only now did she realize that all the windows facing the street were solely for the passage of light and air— many vertical slits in the wall, carved or sculpted with delicate designs, but with no gap wide enough to let even the head and shoulders of a child pass through.

This is not the first time there has been fear in Basilica, she thought. This house is designed to keep someone from entering surreptitiously in the night. Protection from burglars, of course; but perhaps such windows were designed primarily to keep rejected suitors and lapsed mates from forcing their way back into a house that they had come to think of as their own.

The provisions that kept a man from entering also barred Luet, slight as she was. She knew, of course, that there was no way to get around the sides of the house, since the neighboring structures leaned against the massive stone walls of Rasa's house.

Why didn't she guess that getting back inside would be so much harder than getting out? She had left after dark, of course, but well before the house quieted down for the evening; Hushidh knew something of her errand and would keep anyone from discovering her absence. It simply hadn't occurred to either of them to arrange how Luet would get back in. Aunt Rasa had never locked the front door before. And later, after the Oversoul had made the guard doze on the way out and had kept him away from the gate entirely on her return, Luet had assumed that the Oversoul was smoothing the way for her.

Luet thought of staying out on the porch all night. But it was cold now. As long as she had been walking, it was all right, she had stayed warm enough. Sleep, though, would be dangerous. City women, at least those of good breeding, did not own the right clothing for sleeping out of doors. What the holy women did would make her ill.

There might be another way, however. Wasn't Aunt Rasa's portico on the valley-side of the house completely open? There might be a way to climb up from the valley. Of course, the area just east of Rasa's portico was the wildest, emptiest part of the Shelf—it wasn't even part of a district, and though Sour Street ran out into it, there was no road there; women never went that way to get to the lake.

Yet she knew that this was the way she must go, if she was to return to Aunt Rasa's house.

The Oversoul again, leading her. Leading her, but telling her nothing.

Why not? asked Luet for the thousandth time. Why can't you tell me your purpose? If you had told me I was going to Wetchik's house, I wouldn't have been so fearful all the way. How did my fear and ignorance serve your purpose? And now you send me around to the wild country east of Aunt Rasa's house—for what purpose? Do you take pleasure in toying with me? Or am I too stupid to understand your purpose? I'm your homing dove, able to carry your messages but never worth explaining them to.

And yet, despite her resentment, a few minutes she

stepped from the last cobbles of Sour Street onto the grass and then plunged into the pathless woods of the Shelf.

The ground was rugged, and all the gaps and breaks in the underbrush seemed to lead downward, away from Rasa's portico and toward the cliffs looming over the canyon of the Holy Road. No wonder that even the Shelf women built no houses here. But Luet refused to be led astray by the easy paths—she knew they would disappear the moment she started following them. Instead she forced her way through the underbrush. The zarosel thorns snagged at her, and she knew they would leave tiny welts that would sting for days even under a layer of Aunt Rasa's balm. Worse, she was bone-weary, cold, and sleepy, so that at times she caught herself waking up, even though she had not been asleep. Still—she had set herself on this course, and she would finish.

She came into a small clearing where bright moonlight filtered through the canopy of leaves overhead. In a month all the leaves would be gone and these thickets would not be half so forbidding. Now, though, a patch of light came like a miracle, and she blinked.

In that eyeblink, the clearing changed. There was a woman standing there.

"Aunt Rasa," whispered Luet. How did she know to come looking for me here? Has the Oversoul spoken again to someone else?

But it was not Aunt Rasa, after all. It was Hushidh. How could she have made such a mistake?

No. Not a mistake. For now Hushidh had changed again. It was Eiadh now, that beautiful girl from Hushidh's class, the one that poor Nafai was so uselessly in love with. And again the woman was transformed, into the actress Dol, who had been so very famous as a young girl; she was one of Aunt Rasa's nieces, and in recent years had returned to the house to teach. Once it was said that Dolltown was named after her (though it had been named such for ten thousand years at least), she was so beautiful and broke so many hearts; but she was in her twenties now, and the features that, when she was a girl, made women want to mother her and ravished the eyes of men were not so astonishing in a woman. Still, Luet would give half her life if during the other half she could be as delicately, sweetly beautiful as Dol.

Why is the Oversoul showing me these women?

From Dol the apparition changed to Shedemei, another of Aunt Rasa's nieces. If anything, though, Shedya was the opposite of Dol and Eiadh. At twenty-six she was still in Aunt Rasa's house, helping to teach science to the older students as her own reputation as a geneticist grew. Most nights she actually slept in her laboratory, many streets away, instead of her room in Rasa's house, but still she was a strong, quiet presence there. Shedemei was unbeautiful; not so ugly as to startle the onlooker, but deeply plain, so that the longer one studied her face the less attractive it became. Yet her mind was like a magnet, drawn to truth: as soon as it came near enough, she would leap to it and cling. Of all Aunt Rasa's nieces, she was the one that Luet most admired; but Luet knew that no more had she the wit to emulate Shedemei than she had the beauty to follow Dol's career. The Oversoul had chosen to send her visions to one who had no other use to the world.

The woman was gone. Luet was alone in the clearing, and she felt again as if she had just awakened.

Was this only a dream, the kind that comes when you don't even know that you're asleep?

Behind where the apparitions had stood, she saw a single light burning in the dark of earliest morning. It had to be on Aunt Rasa's portico—in that direction there could be no other source of light. Maybe the vision had been right thus far. Aunt Rasa was awake, and waiting for her.

She pushed forward into the brush. Low twigs swiped at her, thorns snagged at her clothing and her skin, and the irregular ground deceived her, causing her to trip and stumble. Always, though, that light was her beacon, drawing her on until at last it went out of sight as she drew under the lip of Rasa's portico.

It rose in a single sheet of weathered stone, sheer from base to balustrade, with no handholds. And it was at least four meters from the ground to the top. Even if Aunt Rasa was there waiting for her, there'd be no way to climb up, not without calling for servants. And if she was going to have to disturb the house anyway, she might as well have pulled the bellcord at the front door!

It happened that after having been forced this way and that by the rough ground of the forest, Luet had finally approached Rasa's house almost from the south. Most of the face of the portico was hidden from her. It was possible that the house had been built with some access from the portico to the wood. Surely the builders had planned for more than a mere *view* of the Rift Valley. And even if there was no deliberate access, there had to be a spot where she would have some hope of climbing up.

Making her way around the curved stone surface, Luet at last found what she had hoped for—a place where the broken ground rose higher in relation to the portico. Now the top of the balustrade was only an arm's length out of her reach. And, as she reached up to try to find a handhold in the gaps of the balustrade, she saw Aunt Rasa's face, as welcome as sunrise, and her arms reaching down for her.

If Luet had been any larger, Aunt Rasa probably could not have lifted her weight; but then, had she been larger she might have climbed up without help.

When at last she sat on the bench with Aunt Rasa half-cradling her, on the verge of weeping with relief and exhaustion, Aunt Rasa asked the obvious question. "What under the moon were you doing out there instead of coming to the front door like any other student coming back home after hours? Were you so afraid of a reprimand that you thought it would be better to risk your neck in the woods at night?"

Luet shook her head. "In the wood I saw a vision," she said. "But I might have seen it anyway, so coming around that way was probably my own foolishness."

Then there was nothing for Luet to do but tell Aunt Rasa about all that had happened—the vision she had told to Nafai, warning of the plot to murder Wetchik; the words of the holy woman in the dark street; and finally the vision of Rasa and a few of her nieces.

"I can't think what such a vision might mean," said Rasa. "If the Oversoul didn't tell *you,* how can *I* guess?"

"I don't want to guess anything anyway," said Luet. "I don't want any more visions or talk of visions or anything except I hurt all over and I want to go to bed."

"Of course you do, of course," said Aunt Rasa. "You can sleep, and leave it to Wetchik and me to think what course of action to take now. Unless he was stupid enough to decide that honor required him to keep that treacherous rendezvous at the coolhouse."

A terrible thought occurred to Luet. "What if Nafai didn't tell him?"

Aunt Rasa looked at her sharply. "Nafai, not warn his father about a plot against his life? You're speaking of my son."

What could that mean to Luet, who had never known her mother and whose father could be any man in the city, with the most brutish men the likeliest candidates? Mother and son—it was a connection that held no particular authority for her. In a world of faithless promises, anything was possible.

No, it was her weariness telling her to trust no one. She

was doubting Aunt Rasa's judgment here, not just Nafai's faithfulness. Obviously her mind was not functioning clearly. She allowed Aunt Rasa to half-lead, half-carry her up the stairs to Rasa's own room, and place Luet on the great soft bed of the mistress of the house, where she slept almost before realizing where she was.

"Out all night," said Hushidh.

Luet opened one eye. The light coming through the window was very bright, but the air had a chill in it. Full day, and Luet was only waking now.

"And then not even the brains to come in the front door."

"I don't always rely on my brains," said Luet quietly.

"That much I knew," said Hushidh. "You should have taken me with you."

"Two people are always more obvious than one."

"To Wetchik's house! Didn't it occur to you that I might actually know the way there and back?"

"I didn't know that was where I was going."

"Alone at night. Anything could have happened. And you binding me with that foolish oath to tell no one. Aunt Rasa almost skinned me alive and hung me out to dry on the front porch when she realized that I must have known you were gone and didn't tell her."

"Don't be cross with me, Hushidh."

"Whole city's in turmoil, you know."

A sudden fear stabbed through her. "No, Hushidh— don't tell me there was murder after all!"

"Murder? Not likely. Wetchik's gone, though, him and his sons all, and Gaballufix is claiming that it was because he uncovered Wetchik's plot to murder him and Roptat at a secret meeting that Wetchik arranged at his coolhouse near Music Gate."

"That's not true," said Luet.

"Well, I didn't think it *was*," said Hushidh. "I only told

you what Gaballufix's people are saying. His soldiers are thick in the streets."

"I'm so tired, Hushidh, and there's nothing I can do about any of this."

"Aunt Rasa thinks you can do something," said Hushidh. "That's why she sent me to wake you."

"Did she?"

"Well, you know *her*. She sent me up twice to "see if poor Luet is still getting some of that rest she needs so much.' The third time I finally caught on that she was waiting for you to wake up but didn't have the heart to give instructions for me to do it."

"How thoughtful of you to read between the lines, my darling jewel of a big sister."

"You can nap again later, my sweet yagda-berry of a little sister."

It took only moments to wash and dress, for Luet was young enough that Aunt Rasa did not insist on her learning how to make hair and clothing graceful and dignified before appearing in public. As a child, she could be her scrawny, gawky self, which certainly took less effort. When Luet got downstairs, Aunt Rasa was in her salon with a man, a stranger, but Rasa introduced him at once.

"This is Rashgallivak, dear Luet. He is perhaps the most loyal and trustworthy man alive, or so my beloved mate has always said."

"I have served the Wetchik estate all my life," said Rashgallivak, "and will do so until I die. I may not be of the great houses, but I am still a true Palwashantu."

Aunt Rasa nodded. Luet wondered whether she was supposed to hear this man with belief or with irony; Rasa seemed to be trusting him, however, and so Luet gave her tentative trust as well.

"I understand that it was you who brought warning," said Rashgallivak.

Luet looked at Aunt Rasa in surprise. "He'll tell no one else," said Aunt Rasa. "I have his oath. We don't want to involve you in the politics of murder, my dear. But Rash had to know it, so that he didn't think my Wetchik had lost his mind. Wetchik left him detailed instructions, you see, to do something quite mad."

"Close everything down," said Rashgallivak. "Dismiss all but the fewest possible employees, sell off all the pack animals, and liquidate the stock. I'm to hold only the land, the buildings, and the liquid assets, in untouchable accounts. Very suspicious, if my master is innocent. Or so some would say. *Do* say."

"Wetchik's absence wasn't known for half an hour before Gaballufix was at Wetchik's house, demanding as the head of the Palwashantu clan that all the property of the Wetchik family be turned over to him. He had the audacity to refer to my mate by his birth name, Volemak, as if he had forfeited his right to the family title."

"If my master has really left Basilica permanently," said Rashgallivak, "then Gaballufix would be within his rights. The property can never be sold or given away from the Palwashantu."

"And I'm trying to persuade Rashgallivak that it was *your* warning of immediate danger that caused Wetchik to flee, not some plot to leave the city and take the family fortune with him."

Luet understood her duty now, in this conversation. "I did speak with Nafai," Luet told Rashgallivak. "I warned him that Gaballufix meant to murder Wetchik and Roptat—or at least my dream certainly seemed to suggest that."

Rashgallivak nodded slowly. "This will not be enough to bring charges against Gaballufix, of course. In Basilica, even *men* are not tried for acts they plotted but never performed. But it's enough to persuade me to resist Gaballufix's efforts to obtain the property."

"I was mated with him once, you know," said Rasa. "I know Gabya very well. I suggest you take extraordinary measures to protect the fortune—liquid assets particularly."

"No one will have them but the head of the house of Wetchik," said Rashgallivak. "Madam, I thank you. And you, little wise one."

He said not another word, but left immediately. Not at all like the more stylish men—artists, scientists, men of government and finance—whom Luet had met in Aunt Rasa's salon before. That sort of man always lingered, until Aunt Rasa had to force their departure by feigning weariness or pretending that she had pressing duties in the school—as if her teaching staff were not competent to handle things without her direct supervision. But then, Rashgallivak was of a social class that could not reasonably contemplate mating with one like Aunt Rasa, or any of her nieces.

"I'm sorry you didn't get more sleep," said Aunt Rasa, "but glad that you happened to wake up at such a fortunate time."

Luet nodded. "So much of last night I felt as if I were walking in my sleep, perhaps I only needed half as much this morning."

"I would send you back to bed at once," said Aunt Rasa, "but I must ask you a question first."

"Unless it's something we've studied recently in class, I won't know the answer, my lady."

"Don't pretend you don't know what I'm talking about."

"Don't imagine that I actually understand anything about the Oversoul."

Luet knew at once that she had spoken too flippantly. Aunt Rasa's eyebrows rose, and her nostrils flared—but she contained her anger, and spoke without sharpness. "Sometimes, my dear, you forget yourself. You pretend to take no special honor to yourself because the Oversoul has

made a seer of you, and yet you speak to me with imperti-
nence that no other woman in this city, young or old,
would dare to use. Which should I believe, your modest
words or your proud manner?"

Luet bowed her head. "My words, Mistress. My manner
is the natural rudeness of a child."

Laughing, Aunt Rasa answered, "*Those* words are the
hardest to believe of all. I'll spare you my questions after all. Go back to bed now—but this time in your own
bed—no one will disturb you there, I promise."

Luet was at the door of the salon when it opened and a
young woman burst in, forcing her back inside the room.

"Mother, this is abominable!" cried the visitor.

"Sevet, I'm so delighted to see you after all these
months—and without a word of notice that you were coming, or even the courtesy of waiting until I invited you into
my salon."

Sevet—Aunt Rasa's oldest daughter. Luet had seen her
only once before. As was the custom, Rasa did not teach
her own daughters, but rather had given them to her dear
friend Dhelembuvex to raise. This one, her oldest, was
mated with a young scholar of some note—Vas?—but it
hadn't hampered her career as a singer with a growing reputation for having a way with pichalny songs, the low mel-
ancholy songs of death and loss that were an ancient
tradition in Basilica. There was nothing of pichalny about
her now, though—she was sharp and angry, and her mother
no less so. Luet decided to leave the room at once, before
she overheard another word.

But Aunt Rasa wouldn't allow it. "Stay, Luet. I think it
will be educational for you to see how little this daughter
of mine takes after either her mother *or* her Aunt Dhel."

Sevet glared sharply at Luet. "What's *this*—are you taking charity cases now?"

"Her mother was a holy woman, Sevya. I think you may even have heard the name of Luet."

Sevet blushed at once. "I beg your pardon," she said.

Luet had no idea how to answer, since of course Luet *was* a charity case and therefore mustn't show that she had been offended by Sevet's slur.

Aunt Rasa saved her from having to think of a proper response. "I will consider that pardon has been begged and granted all around, and now we may begin our conversation with perhaps a more civil tone."

"Of course," said Sevet. "You must realize that I came here straight from Father."

"From your rude and offensive manner, I assumed you had spent at least an hour with him."

"Raging, the poor man. And how could he do otherwise, with his own mate spreading terrible lies about him!"

"Poor man indeed," said Aunt Rasa. "I'm surprised that little waif of a mate of his would have the courage to speak out against him—or the wit to make up a lie, for that matter. What has she been saying?"

"I meant *you*, of course, Mother, not his *present* mate, nobody thinks of *her*."

"But since I lapsed dear Gabya's contract fifteen years ago, he can hardly regard *me* as having a duty to refrain from telling the truth about him."

"Mother, don't be impossible."

"I'm never impossible. The most I ever allow myself is to be somewhat unlikely."

"You're the mother of Father's two daughters, both of us more than slightly famous—the *most* famous of your offspring, and all for honorable things, though of course little Koya's career is only at its beginning, with not a myachik of her own yet—"

"Spare me your rivalry with your sister, please."

"It's only a rivalry from *her* point of view, Mother—*I* don't even pay attention to the fact that her singing career seems a bit sluggish at the outset. It's always harder for a lyric soprano to be noticed—there are so *many* of them, one can hardly tell them apart, unless one is the soprano's own loving, loyal sister."

"Yes, I use you as an example of loyalty for all my girls."

For a moment Sevet's face brightened; then she realized her mother was teasing her, and scowled. "You really are too nasty with me."

"If your father sent you to get me to retract my remarks about this morning's events, you can tell him that I know what he was planning from an undoubtable source, and if he doesn't stop telling people that Wetchik was plotting murder, I'll bring my evidence before the council and have him banned."

"I can't—I can't tell Father that!" said Sevet.

"Then don't," said Aunt Rasa. "Let him find out when I do it."

"*Ban* him? Ban *Father*?"

"If you had studied more history—though come to think of it, I doubt that Dhelya taught you all that much anyway—you'd know that the more powerful and famous a man is, the more likely he is to be banned from Basilica. It's been done before, and it will be done again. After all, it's Gabya, not Wetchik or Roptat, whose soldiers roam the streets, pretending to protect us from thugs that Gabya probably hired in the first place. People will be glad to see him go—and that means they'll find it *useful* to believe every bit of evidence I bring."

Sevet's face grew grave. "Father may be a bit prone to rage and a little sneaky in business, Mother, but he's no murderer."

"Of course he's not a murderer. Wetchik left Basilica and

Gabya would never dare to kill Roptat without Wetchik there to blame it on. Though I think that if Gabya had known at the time that Wetchik had fled, he would certainly have killed Roptat the moment he showed up and then used Wetchik's hasty departure as proof that my dear mate was the murderer."

"You make Father sound like a monster. Why did you take him as a mate, then?"

"Because I wanted to have a daughter with an extraordinary singing voice and no moral judgment whatsoever. It worked so well that I renewed with him for a second year and had another. And then I was done."

Sevet laughed. "You're such a silly thing, Mother. I *do* have moral judgment, you know. And every other kind. It was Vasya I married, not some second-rate actor."

"Stop sniping at your sister's choice of mate," said Aunt Rasa. "Kokor's Obring is a dear, even if he has no talent whatsoever and not the breath of a chance that Koya will actually bear him a child, let alone renew him."

"A *dear*," said Sevet. "I'll have to remember what that word *really* means, now that you've told me."

Sevet got up to leave. Luet opened the door for her. But Aunt Rasa stopped her daughter before she left.

"Sevya, dear," she said. The time may come when you have to choose between your father and me."

"The two of you have made me do that at least once a month since I was very small. I've managed to sidestep you both so far, and I intend to continue."

Rasa clapped her hands together—loudly, a sharp report like one stone striking another. "Listen to me, child. I know the dance that you've done, and I've both admired you for the way you did it and pitied you for the fact that it was necessary. What I'm saying to you is that soon—very soon—it may no longer be possible to do that dance. So it's time for you to look at both your parents and decide which one deserves your loyalty. I do not say *love*, because I know you love us both. I say loyalty."

"You shouldn't speak to me this way, Mother," said Sevet. "I'm not your student. And even if you succeeded in banning Father, that still wouldn't mean I'd have to choose between you."

"What if your father sent soldiers to silence me? Or tolchocks—which is more likely. What if it was a knife he paid for that slit your mother's throat?"

Sevet regarded her mother in silence. "Then I'd have a pichalny song to sing indeed, wouldn't I?"

"I believe that your father is the enemy of the Oversoul, and the enemy of Basilica as well. Think about this seriously, my sad-voiced Sevet, think deep and long, because when the day of choosing comes there'll be no time to think."

"I have always honored you, Mother, for the fact that you never tried to turn me against my father, despite all the vile things he said about you. I'm sorry you have changed." With great dignity, Sevet swept herself from the room. Luet, still a bit stunned by the brutal nature of the conversation under the veneer of elegant speech, was slow to follow her out the door.

"Luet," whispered Aunt Rasa.

Luet turned to face the great woman, and trembled inside to see the tears on her cheeks.

"Luet, you must tell me. What is the Oversoul doing to us? What does the Oversoul plan?"

"I don't know," said Luet. "I wish I did."

"*If* you did, would you tell me?"

"Of course."

"Even if the Oversoul told you not to?"

Luet hadn't thought of such a possibility.

Aunt Rasa took her hesitation for an answer. "So," she said. "I wouldn't have expected otherwise—the Oversoul does not choose weak servants, or disloyal ones. But tell me this, if you can: Is it possible, is it *possible*, that there was no plot to kill Wetchik at all? That the Oversoul merely sent that warning to get him to leave Basilica? You must realize—I was thinking that—Lutya, what if the only thing the Oversoul was doing was getting rid of Issib and Nafai? It makes sense, doesn't it—they were interfering with the Oversoul, keeping her so busy that she couldn't speak to anyone but them. Might she not have sent your vision to make sure they left the city, because *they* were threatening to *her*?"

Luet's first impulse was to shout her denial, to rebuke her for daring to speak so sacrilegiously of the Oversoul—as if it would act for its own private benefit.

But then, on sober reflection, she remembered with what wonderment Hushidh had told her of her realization that Issib and Nafai might well be the reason for the Oversoul's silence. And if the Oversoul thought that her ability to guide and protect her daughters was being hampered by these two boys, couldn't she act to remove them?

"No," said Luet. "I don't think so."

"Are you sure?"

"I'm never sure, except of the vision itself," said Luet. "But I've never known the Oversoul to deceive me. All my visions have been true."

"But this one would still be a true instrument of the Oversoul's will."

"No," said Luet again. "No, it couldn't be. Because Nafai and Issib had already stopped. Nafai even went and prayed—"

"So I heard, but then, so did Mebbekew, Wetchik's son by that miserable little whoreling Kilvishevex—"

"And the Oversoul spoke to Nafai and woke him up, and brought him outside to meet me in the traveler's room. If the Oversoul wanted Nafai to be still, she would have told him, and he would have obeyed. No, Aunt Rasa, I'm sure the message was real."

Aunt Rasa nodded. "I know. I knew it was. It would just be . . ."

"Simpler."

"Yes." She smiled ruefully. "Simpler if Gaballufix were as innocent as he pretends. But not true to character. You know why I lapsed him?"

"No," said Luet. Nor did she want to know—by long custom a woman never told her reasons for lapsing a man, and it was a hideous breach of etiquette to ask or even speculate on the subject.

"I shouldn't tell, but I will—because you're one who must know the truth in order to understand all things."

I'm also a child, thought Luet. You'd never tell any of your *other* thirteen-year-olds about such things. You'd never even tell your daughter. But I, *I* am a seer, and so everything is opened up before me and I am forbidden to remain innocent of anything except joy.

"I lapsed him because I learned that he . . ."

Luet braced herself for some sordid revelation, but it did not come.

"No, child, no. Just because the Oversoul speaks to you doesn't mean that I should burden you with my secrets. Go, sleep. Forget my questions, if you can. I know my Wetchik. And I know Gaballufix, too. Both of them, down to the deepest shadow of their souls. It was for my daughters' sake that I wished to find some impossible thing, like Gabya's innocence." She chuckled. "I'm like a child, forever wishing for impossible things. Like your vision in the woods, before I drew you up to the portico. You saw all my most brilliant nieces, like a roll call of judgment."

Brilliant? Shedemei and Hushidh, yes, but Dol and Eiadh, those women of paint and tinsel?

"I was so happy to know that the Oversoul knew them,

and linked them with me and you in the vision she sent. But where were my daughters, Lutya? I wish that you had seen my Sevya and my Koya. I do wish that—is that silly of me?"

Yes. "No."

"You should practice lying more," said Aunt Rasa, "so you'd be better at it. Go to bed, my sweet seer."

Luet obeyed, but slept little.

IN THE DAYS that followed, the turmoil in the city increased, to the point where it was almost impossible for classes to continue in Aunt Rasa's house. It wasn't just the constant worry, either. It was the disappearance of so many faces, especially from the younger classes. Only a few children were withdrawn because their parents disapproved of Rasa's political stance. Children were being taken out of every teaching household, great or common, and restored to their families; many families had even closed up their houses and gone on unnamed holidays to unknown places, presumably waiting for whatever terrible day was coming to be over.

How Luet envied Nafai and Issib, safe as they were in some distant land, not having to live in constant fear in this city that had so long been known by the poets as the Mountain of Peace.

As the petition for the banning of Gaballufix gained support in the council, Gaballufix himself became bolder in the way he used his soldiers in the streets. There were more of them, for one thing, and there was no more pretense of protecting the citizenry from tolchocks. The soldiers accosted whomever they wanted, sending women and children home in tears, and beating men who spoke up to them.

"Is he a fool?" Hushidh asked Luet one day. "Doesn't he know that everything his soldiers do gives his enemies one more reason to ban him?"

"He must know," said Luet, "and so he must want to be banned."

"Then hasten the day," said Hushidh, "and good riddance to him."

Luet waited for a vision from the Oversoul, some message of warning she should take to the council. Instead the only vision that came was a word of comfort to an old woman in the district of Olive Grove, assuring her that her long-lost son was still alive, and homebound on a ship that would reach port before too long. Luet didn't know whether to be comforted that the Oversoul still took the time to answer the heartfelt prayers of broken-hearted women, or infuriated that the Oversoul was spending time on such matters instead of healing the city before it tore itself apart.

Then at last the most feared moment came. The doorbell clanged, and strong fists beat on the door, and when the door was thrown open, there stood a dozen soldiers. The servant who opened the door screamed, and not just because they were armed men in perilous times. Luet was among the first to come to the aid of the terrified servant, and saw what had so unnerved her. All the soldiers were in identical uniforms, with identical armor and helmets and charged-wire blades, as might be expected—but inside those helmets, each one also had an identical face.

It was Rasa's oldest niece, Shedemei, the geneticist, who spoke to the soldiers. "You have no legitimate business here," she said. "No one wants you. Go away."

"I'll see the mistress of this household or I'll never go," said the soldier who stood in front of the others.

"She has no business with you, I said."

But then Aunt Rasa was there, and her voice rang clear. "Close the door in the face of these hired criminals," she said.

At once the lead soldier laughed, and reached his hand to his waist. In an instant he was transformed before their eyes, from a youngish, dead-faced soldier to a middle-aged man with a grizzled beard and fiercely bright eyes, stout but not soft-bellied, clothed not in armor but in quietly elegant clothing. A man of style and power, who thought the whole situation was enormously amusing.

"Gabya," said Aunt Rasa.

"How do you like my new toys?" asked Gaballufix, striding into the house. Women and girls and young boys parted to make way for him. "Old theatrical equipment, out of style for centuries, but they were in a stasis bubble in the museum and the maker machines still remembered how to copy them. Holocostumes, they're called. All my soldiers have them now. It makes them somewhat hard to tell apart, I admit, but then, I have the master switch that can turn them all off when I want."

"Leave my house," said Rasa.

"But I don't want to," said Gaballufix. "I want to talk to you."

"Without *them*, you can speak to me any time. You know that, Gabya."

"I knew that *once*," said Gaballufix. "Truth to tell, O noblest of my mates, my unforgotten bed-bundle, I knew that my soldiers would never impress you—I just wanted to show you the latest fashion. Soon all the best people will be wearing them."

"Only in their coffins," said Aunt Rasa.

"Do you want to hold this conversation in front of the children, or shall we retire to your sacred portico?"

"Your soldiers wait outside the door. The *locked* door."

"Whatever you say, O mother of my duet of sweet songbirds. Though your door, with all its locks, would be no barrier if I wanted them inside."

"People who are sure of their power don't have to brag," said Aunt Rasa. She led the way down the corridor as Shedemei closed and barred the front door in the soldiers' faces.

Luet could still hear the conversation between Aunt Rasa and Gaballufix even after they turned a corner and were out of sight.

"I don't *have* to brag," Gaballufix was saying. "I do it for the sheer joy of it."

Instead of answering, though, Aunt Rasa called loudly down the corridor.

"Luet! Hushidh! Come with me. I want witnesses."

At once Luet strode forward, with Hushidh beside her at once. Because Aunt Rasa had brought them up, they didn't run, but their walk was brisk enough that they had turned the corner and could hear Gaballufix's last few whispered words before they caught up. ". . . not afraid of your witchlets," he was saying.

Luet gave no sign that she had heard, of course. She knew that Hushidh's face would be even less expressive.

Out on the portico, Gaballufix made no pretense of respecting the boundary of Aunt Rasa's screens. He strode directly to the balustrade, looking out at the view that was forbidden to the eyes of men. Aunt Rasa did not follow him, so Luet and Hushidh also remained behind the screens. At last Gaballufix returned to where they waited.

"Always a beautiful sight," he said.

"For that act alone you could be banned," said Aunt Rasa.

Gaballufix laughed. "Your sacred lake. How long do you think it will go unmuddied by the boots of men, if the Wetheads come? Have you thought of that—have Roptat and your beloved Volemak thought of it? The Wetheads have no reverence for women's religion."

"Even less than you?"

Gaballufix rolled his eyes to show his disdain for her

accusation. "If Roptat and Volemak have their way, the Wetheads would own this city, and to them, the view from this portico would not be a view of holy land—it would all be city property, undeveloped land, potential building sites and hunting parks, and an extraordinary lake, with both hot and cold water for bathing in any weather."

Luet was astonished that so much of the nature of the lake had been explained to him. What woman had so forgotten herself as to speak of the sacred place?

Yet Aunt Rasa said nothing of the impropriety of his words. "Bringing the Wetheads is Roptat's plan. Wetchik and I have spoken for nothing but the ancient neutrality."

"Neutrality! Fools and children believe in that. There *is* no neutrality when great powers collide!"

"In the power of the Oversoul there is neutrality and peace," said Aunt Rasa, calm in the face of his storm. "She has the power to turn aside our enemies so they see us not at all."

"Power? Maybe he has power, all right, this Oversoul— but I've seen no evidence that he saves poor innocent cities from destruction. How did it happen that I alone am the champion of Basilica, the only one who can see that safety lies only in alliance with Potokgavan?"

"Save the patriotic speeches for the council, Gabya. In front of me, there's no point in hiding behind them. The wagons offered some easy profit. And as for war—you know so little about it that you think you want it to come. You think that you'll stand beside the mighty soldiers of Potokgavan and drive off the Wetheads, and your name will be remembered forever. But *I* tell you that when you stand against your enemy, you'll stand alone. No Potoku will be there beside you. And when you fall your name will be forgotten as quickly as last week's weather."

"*This* storm, my dear lapsatory mate, has a name, and will be remembered."

"Only for the damage that you caused, Gabya. When Basilica burns, every tongue of flame will be branded Gaballufix, and the dying curse of every citizen who falls will have your name in it."

"Now who fancies herself a prophet?" said Gaballufix. "Save your poetics for those who tremble at the thought of the Oversoul. And as for your banning—succeed or fail, it makes no difference."

"You mean that you don't intend to obey?"

"*Me*? Disobey the *council*? Unthinkable. No one will find me in the city after I am banned, you can be sure of that."

But with those words he reached down and switched on his holocostume. At once he was armored in illusion, his face an undetectable mask of a vaguely menacing soldier, like any of the hundreds of others he had so equipped. Luet knew then that he had no intention of obeying a banning. He would simply wear this most perfect of disguises, so that no one could identify him. He would stay within the city, doing whatever he wanted, flouting the council's edicts with impunity. Then the only hope of freeing the city from his rule would not be political. It would be civil war, and the streets would flow with blood.

Luet knew from her eyes that Aunt Rasa understood this. She looked steadily at the empty eyes that stared back at her from Gaballufix's holocostume. She said nothing when he turned and left; said nothing at all, in fact, until at last Luet took Hushidh's hand and they walked away to the edge of the portico, to look out over the Valley of Women.

"There's nothing between them anymore," said Hushidh. "I could see it fall, the last tie of love or even of concern. If he died tonight, she would be content."

To Luet this seemed the most terrible of tragedies. Once these two had been joined together in love, or something like love; they had made two babies, and yet, only fifteen years later, the last tie between them was broken now. All lost, all gone. Nothing lasted, nothing. Even this forty-million-year world that the Oversoul had preserved as if in ice, even it would melt before the fire. Permanence was always an illusion, and love was just the disguise that lovers wore to hide the death of their union from each other for a while.

TEN

TENTS

Wetchik had pitched his tents away from any road, in a narrow river valley near the shores of the Rumen Sea. They had reached it at sunset, just as a troop of baboons moved away from their feeding area near the river's mouth, toward their sleeping niches in the steepest, craggiest cliff in the valley wall. It was the baboons' calls and hoots that guided them during the last of their journey; Elemak was careful to lead them well upstream of the baboons. "So we don't disturb them?" Issib asked.

"So they don't foul our water and steal our food," said Elemak.

Before Father allowed them to unburden the camels and water them, before they ate or drank anything themselves, Father sat atop his camel and gestured toward the stream. "Look—the end of the dry season, and yet it still has water in it. The name of this place is Elemak from now on. I name it for you, my eldest son. Be like the river, so that the purpose of your life is to flow forever toward the great ocean of the Oversoul."

Nafai glanced at Elemak and saw that he was taking the peroration with dignity. It was a sacred moment, the naming of a place, and even if Father laced the occasion with a sermon, Elemak knew that it was an honor, a sign that Father acknowledged him.

"And as for this green valley," said Father, "I name it Mebbekew, for my second son. Be like this valley, Mebbekew, a firm channel through which the waters of life can flow, and where life can take root and thrive."

Mebbekew nodded graciously.

There was nothing named for Issib and Nafai. Only a silence, and then Father's groan as his camel knelt for him to dismount. It was well after dark before they finally had the tents pitched, the scorpions swept outside, and the repellents set in place. Three tents—Father's, of course, the largest though he was only one man. The next largest for Elya and Meb. And the smallest for Issib and Nafai, even though Issib's chair took up an exorbitant amount of room inside.

Nafai couldn't help but brood about the inequities, and when, in the darkness of the tent, Issib asked him what he was thinking, Nafai went ahead and voiced his resentment. "He names the river and the valley for *them*, when Elemak's the one who was working with Gaballufix, and Mebbekew's the one who said all those terrible things to him and left home and everything."

"So?" said Issib, ever sympathetic.

"So here we are in the smallest tent. We've got two extras, still packed up, both of them larger than this one." Having undressed himself, Nafai now helped Issib undress—it was too hard for him, without his floats.

"Father's making a statement," said Issib.

"Yes, and I'm hearing it, and I don't like it. He's saying, Issib and Nafai, you're *nothing*."

"What was he going to do, name a *cloud* after us?" Issib fell silent for a moment as Nafai pulled the shirt off over Issib's head. "Or did you want him to name a bush for you?"

"I don't care about the naming, I care about justice."

"Get some perspective, Nafai. Father isn't going to sort out his children according to who's the most obedient or cooperative or polite from hour to hour. There's a clear ranking involved in the assignment of tent space here." Nafai laid his brother on his mat, farthest from the door. "The fact that Elya doesn't have a tent to himself, but shares with Meb," said Issib, "that's putting him in his place, reminding him that he's *not* the Wetchik, he's just the Wetchik's boy. But then putting us in such a tiny tent tells Elya and Meb that he *does* value them and honor them as his oldest sons. He's at once rebuking and encouraging them. I think he's been rather deft."

Nafai lay down on his own mat, near the door, in the traditional servant's position. "What about us?"

"What *about* us? Are you going to rebel against the Oversoul because your papa gave you a tiny tent?"

"No."

"Father trusts us to be loyal while he works on Elya and Meb. Father's trust is the greatest honor of all. I'm proud to be in this tent."

"When you put it that way," said Nafai, "so am I."

"Go to sleep."

"Wake me if you need anything."

"What can I need," said Issib, "when I have my chair beside me?"

Actually, the chair was down near his feet, and it was almost completely useless when Issib wasn't sitting in it. Nafai was puzzled for a moment, until he realized that Issib was giving him a small rebuke: Why are *you* complaining, Nafai, when being away from the magnetics of the city means that I can't use my floats, and have to be tended to like an infant? It must be humiliating for Issib to have me undress him, thought Nafai. And yet he bears it uncomplaining, for Father's sake.

* * *

DEEP IN THE night, Nafai awoke, instantly alert. He lay there listening. Was it Issib who had called him? No—his brother was still taking the heavy, rhythmic breaths of sleep. Did he wake, then, because he was uncomfortable? No, for the sand under his mat made the floor more, not less, comfortable than his room at home. Nor was it the cold, nor the distant howling of a wild dog, and it could not have been the baboons, because they always slept the night in perfect silence.

The last time Nafai had awakened like this, he had found Luet outside in the traveler's room, and the Oversoul had spoken in the night to Father.

Was I dreaming, then? Did the Oversoul teach me in my sleep? But Nafai could remember no dreams. Just the sudden wakefulness.

He got up from his mat—quietly, so as not to disturb Issya—and slid under the netted fabric draped across the door. It was cooler outside the tent than inside, of course, but they had traveled far enough south that autumn hadn't yet arrived in this place, and the waters of the Rumen Sea were much warmer and more placid than the ocean that swept along the coastline east of Basilica.

The camels were peacefully asleep in their small temporary corral. The wards at the corners kept away even the smallest of animals not yet inured to the sound frequencies and pheromones the wards gave off. The stream splashed a syncopated music over the rocks. The leaves in the trees rustled now and then in the night breeze. If there is any place in all of Harmony where a man could sleep in peace, it's here, thought Nafai. And yet I couldn't sleep.

Nafai walked upstream and sat on a stone beside the water. The breeze was cool enough to chill him a little; for a moment he wished he had dressed before leaving the tent. But he hadn't intended to get up for the day. Soon enough he'd go back inside.

He looked around him, at the low hills not that far off. Unless a person stood on one of those hills, there was no sign of a watered valley here. Still, it was a wonder that no one lived here but the tribe of baboons downstream of them, that there wasn't even a sign of human habitation. Perhaps it had not been settled because it was so far from any trade route. The land here was barely enough to support a few dozen people, if it were all cultivated. It would be too lonely or unprofitable to settle here. Robbers might use it as a refuge, but it was too far from the caravan routes to be convenient for them. It was exactly what Father's family needed, during this time of exile from Basilica. As if it had been prepared for them.

For a moment Nafai wondered if perhaps this valley had not even existed until they needed it. Did the Oversoul have such power that it could transform land-forms at will?

Impossible. The Oversoul might have such powers in myth and legend, but in the real world, the Oversoul's powers seemed to be entirely confined to communication— the sharing of works of art throughout the world, and mental influence over those who received visions or, more commonly, the stupor of thought that the Oversoul used to turn people away from forbidden ideas.

That's why this place was empty till we came, thought Nafai. It would be a simple thing for the Oversoul to make desert travelers get stupid whenever they thought of turning toward the Rumen Sea near here. The Oversoul prepared it for us, not by creating it out of the rock, not by causing some hidden pool of water to burst forth into a spring, a stream for us, but rather by keeping other people away from here, so that it was empty and ready for us when we came.

The Oversoul has some great purpose here, plans within plans. We listen for its voice, we heed the visions it puts into our minds, but we're still puppets, uncertain why our strings are being pulled, or what our dance will lead to in the end. It isn't right, thought Nafai. It isn't even good, for if the followers of the Oversoul are kept blind, if they can't judge the Oversoul's purpose for themselves, then they aren't freely choosing between good and evil, or between wise and foolish, but are only choosing to subsume themselves in the purposes of the Oversoul. How can the Oversoul's plans be well-served, if all its followers are the kind of weak-souled people who are willing to obey the Oversoul without understanding?

I will serve you, Oversoul, with my whole heart I'll serve you, if I understand what you're trying to do, what it *means*. And if your purpose is a good one.

Who am I to judge what's good and what isn't?

The thought came into Nafai's mind, and he laughed silently at his own arrogance. Who am I, to set myself up as the judge of the Oversoul?

Then he shuddered. What put such a thought into my mind? Couldn't it have been the Oversoul itself, trying to tame me? I will *not* be tamed, only persuaded. I will not be coerced or led blindly or tricked or bullied—I am willing only to be convinced. If you don't trust your own basic goodness enough to tell me what you're trying to do, Oversoul, then you're confessing your own moral weakness and I'll never serve you.

The moonlight sparkling on the shifting surface of the stream suddenly became sunlight reflected from metal satellites orbiting perpetually around the planet Harmony. In his mind's eye, Nafai saw how, one by one, the satellites stumbled in their orbit and fell, burning themselves into dust as they entered the atmosphere. The first human settlers of this world had built tools that would last ten or twenty million years. To them that had seemed like forever—it was longer than the existence of the human species, many times over. But now it had been forty million years, and the Oversoul had to do its work with only a quarter as many satellites as it had had in the beginning, barely half as many as it had had for the first thirty million years. No wonder the Oversoul had weakened.

But its plans were no less important. Its purpose still needed to be served. Issib and Nafai were right—the Oversoul had been set in place by the first human settlers in this place, for one purpose only: to make Harmony a world where humanity would never have the power to destroy itself.

Wouldn't it have been better, thought Nafai, to change humanity so it no longer *desired* to destroy itself?

The answer came into his mind with such clarity that he knew it was the answer of the Oversoul. No, it would not have been better.

But why? Nafai demanded.

An answer, many answers poured into his mind all at once, in such a burst that he could make no sense of them. But in the moments after, the moments of growing clarity, some of the ideas found language. Sentences as clear as if they had been spoken by another voice. But it was not another voice—it was Nafai's own voice, making a feeble attempt to capture in words some straggling remnant of what the Oversoul had said to him.

What the voice of the Oversoul said inside Nafai's mind was this: If I had taken away the desire for violence then humanity would not have been humanity. Not that human beings need to be violent in order to be human, but if you ever lose the will to control, the will to destroy, then it must be because you *chose* to lose it. My role was not to force you to be gentle and kind; it was to keep you alive while you decided for yourselves what kind of people you wanted to be.

Nafai was afraid to ask another question, for fear of drowning in the mental flood that might follow. And yet he couldn't leave the question unasked. Tell me slowly. Tell me gently. But *tell* me: What have we decided?

To his relief, the answer wasn't that same rush of pure unspcakable idea. This time it seemed to him as if a window had been opened in his mind, through which he could see. All the actual scenes, all the faces he saw, they were memories, things he had seen or heard of in Basilica, things that were already in his mind, ready for the Oversoul to draw on them, to bring them to the surface of his mind. But now he saw them with such clear understanding that they took on power and meaning beyond anything in his experience before. He saw memories of business dealings he had seen. He saw plays and satires he had watched. Conversations in the street. A holy woman being raped by a gang of drunken worshipers. The scheming of men who were trying to win a mating contract with a woman of note. The casual cruelty of women who played their suitors against each other. Even the way Elemak and Mebbekew had treated Nafai—and the way he had treated them. It all spoke of the willingness of people to hurt each other, the burning passion to control what other people thought and did. So many people, in secret, subtle ways, acted to destroy people—and not just their enemies, either, but also their friends. Destroying them for the pleasure of knowing that they had the power to cause pain. And so few who devoted their lives to building other people's strength and confidence. So few who were true teachers, genuine mates.

That's what Father and Mother are, thought Nafai. They stay together, not because of any gain, but because of the gift. Father doesn't stay with Mother because she is good for *him*, but rather because together they can do good for us, and for many others. Father entered into the politics of Basilica these last few weeks, not because he hoped to gain by it, the way Gaballufix did, but because he genuinely cared more about the good of Basilica than about his own fortune, his own life. He could walk away from his fortune without a second look. And Mother, her life is what she creates in the minds of her students. Through her girls, her boys, she is trying to create tomorrow's Basilica. Every word she breathes in the school is designed to keep the city from decay.

And yet they're losing. It's slipping away. The Oversoul would help them if it could, but it hasn't the power or influence that it once had; and anyway, it hasn't the freedom to act to make people goodhearted, only to keep their malice within fairly narrow boundaries. Spite and malice, that was the lifeblood of Basilica today; Gaballufix is only the man who happens to best express the poisonous heart of the city. Even those who hate him and fight against him are generally doing it, not because they are good and he is evil, but because they resent the fact that he is achieving dominance, when they had hoped for dominance for themselves.

I *would* help, said the silent voice of the Oversoul in Nafai's mind. I *would* help the good people of Basilica. But there aren't enough of them. The will of the city is for destruction. How then can I keep it from being destroyed? If Gaballufix fails in his plans, the city will raise up some other man to help it kill itself. The fire will come because the city craves it. They are far too few, those who love the living city instead of desiring to feed from its corpse.

Tears flowed from Nafai's eyes. I didn't understand. I never saw the city this way.

That's because you are your mother's son, your father's heir. Like all human beings, you assume that behind the masks of their faces, other people are fundamentally like yourself. But it isn't always so. Some of them can't see other people's happiness without wanting to destroy it, can't see the bonds of love between friends or mates without wanting to break them. And many others, who aren't malicious in themselves, become their tools in the hope of some short-term gain. The people have lost their vision. And I haven't the power to restore it. All that's left, Nafai, is my memory of Earth.

"Tell me about Earth," whispered Nafai.

Again a window opened in his mind, only now it was not memories of his own. Instead he was seeing things he had never seen before. It overwhelmed him; he could hardly make sense of the things he saw. Bright glass-and-metal caskets speeding along gray-ribbon highways. Massive metal houses that rose up in the air, skidding along the face of the sky on slender, fragile wedges of painted steel. Tall polyhedral buildings with mirrored faces, reflecting each other, reflecting the yellow sunlight. And there amid them, shacks made of paper and cast-off metal, where families watched their babies die with bloated bellies. People tossing balls of fire at each other, or great gouts of flame flowing out of hoses. And completely inexplicable things: one of the flying houses passing over a city, dropping something that seemed as insignificant as a turd, only suddenly it burst into a ball of flame as bright as the sun, and the entire city under it was flattened, and the rubble burned. A family sitting at a huge table, covered in food, eating ravenously, then leaning over and vomiting on ragged beggars that clung hopelessly to the legs of their chairs. Surely this vision was not literal, but figurative! Surely no one ever would be so morally bankrupt as to eat more than he needed, while others were dying of hunger before their eyes! Surely anyone who could think of a way to make the sky burst into flame so hot it could destroy a whole city at once, surely such a person would kill himself before he'd ever let anyone know the terrible secret of that weapon.

"Is this Earth?" he whispered to the Oversoul. "So beautiful and monstrous? Is this what we were?"

Yes, came the answer. It's what you were, and it's what you will be again, if I can't find a way to re-awaken the world to my voice. In Basilica there are many who eat their fill of food, and then eat more, while they know how many there are who haven't enough. There's a famine only three hundred kilometers to the north.

"We could use wagons to carry food there," said Nafai.

The Gorayni have such wagons. They carry food, too— but the food is for the soldiers that came to conquer the famine-ravaged land. Only when they had subdued the people and destroyed their government did they bring food. It was the slops a swinekeeper brings to his herd. You feed them now in order to hear them sizzle later.

The visions continued—for hours, it seemed at the time, though later Nafai would realize that it could only have been a few minutes. More and more memories of Earth, with ever more disturbing behavior, ever stranger machines. Until the great fire, and the spaceships rising up from the smoke and ice and ash that remained behind.

"They fled because they had destroyed their world."

No, said the Oversoul. They fled because they longed to begin again. At least those who came to Harmony came, not because Earth was no longer fit for them, but because they believed they were no longer fit for Earth. Billions had died, but there was still fuel and life enough on Earth for perhaps a few hundred thousand humans to survive. But they couldn't bear to live on the world they had ruined. We'll go away, they said to each other, while the world heals itself During our exile, we will also learn healing, and when we return we'll be fit to inherit the land of our birth, and care for it.

So they created the Oversoul, and brought it with them to Harmony, and gave it hundreds of satellites to be its eyes, its voice; they altered their own genes to give themselves the capacity to receive the voice of the Oversoul inside their own minds; and they filled the Oversoul with memories of Earth and left it to watch over their children for the next twenty million years.

Surely in that time, they told each other, our children will have learned how to live together in harmony. They will make the name of this planet come true in their lives. And at the end of that time, the Oversoul will know how to bring them home, to where the Keeper of Earth is waiting for them.

"But we aren't ready," said Nafai. "After twice that time, we're as bad as ever, except that you've kept us from developing the power to turn all the life of this planet into ashes and ice."

The Oversoul put the thought into Nafai's mind: By now the Keeper has surely done its part. The Earth is ready for our return. But the people of Harmony aren't ready yet to come. I have kept all the knowledge of Earth for all these years, waiting to tell you how to build the houses that fly, the starships that will bring you home to the world of your birth; but I dare not teach you, because you'd use the knowledge to oppress and finally to obliterate each other.

"Then what are you doing?" asked Nafai. "What is your plan? Why have you brought us out here?"

I can't tell you yet, said the Oversoul. I'm not sure of you yet. But I've told you what you wanted. I've told you my purpose. I've told you what I've already accomplished, and what is yet to be accomplished. I haven't changed—I'm the same today as I was when your forebears first set me in place to watch over you. My plans are all designed to prepare humanity to return to the Keeper of Earth, who waits for you. It's all I live for, to make humankind fit to return. I am the memory of Earth, all that remains of it, and if you help me, Nafai, you will be part of accomplishing that plan, if it can be accomplished at all.

If it can be accomplished at all.

The overwhelming sense of the presence of the Oversoul in his mind was gone, suddenly; it was as if a great fire inside him had suddenly gone out, as if a great rushing river of life inside him had gone abruptly dry. Nafai sat there on the rock beside the river, feeling spent, exhausted, empty, with that last despairing thought still lingering in his heart: If it can be accomplished at all.

His mouth was dry. He knelt by the water, plunged in his hands, and drew the cupped water to his mouth to drink. It wasn't enough. He splashed into the water, his whole body, not with the reverent attitude of prayer, but with a desperate thirst; he buried his head under the water and drank deep, with his cheek against the cold stone of the riverbed, the water tumbling over his back, his calves. He drank and drank, lifted his head and shoulders above the water to gasp in the evening air, and then collapsed into the water again, to drink as greedily as before.

It was a kind of prayer, though, he realized as he emerged, freezing cold as the water evaporated from his skin in the breeze of the dark morning.

I am with you, he said to the Oversoul. I'll do whatever you ask, because I long for you to accomplish your purpose here. I will do all that I can to prepare us all to return to Earth.

He was chilled to the bone by the time he got back to the tent, not dripping wet anymore, but not dry, either. He lay trembling on his mat for a long time, warmed by the air in the tent, by the heat of Issib's body, until at last he was able to sleep.

* * *

THERE WAS A lot of work to do in the morning; tired though he was, Nafai had no chance to sleep late, but rather staggered through his jobs, slow and clumsy enough that Elemak and even Father barked at him angrily. Pay attention! Use your head! Not till the heat of the afternoon, when they took the nap that desert dwellers knew was as much a part of survival as water, did Nafai have a chance to recover from his night-walking, from his vision. Only then he couldn't bear to sleep. He lay on his mat and told Issib everything that he had seen, and what he had learned from the Oversoul. When he was finished, Issib had tears streaking his face, and he slowly and with great exertion reached out a hand to clasp Nafai's. "I knew there had to be some purpose behind it," whispered Issib. "This makes so much sense to me. It fits everything. How lucky you were, to hear the voice of the Oversoul. Even more clearly than Father did, I think. As clearly as Luet, I think. You are like Luet."

That made Nafai a little uncomfortable, for a moment at least. He had resented or ridiculed Luet in his own mind, and sometimes in his words. The contemptuous word *witch* had come so easily to his lips. Was this what she felt, when the Oversoul sent her a vision? How could I have ridiculed her for that?

He slept again, and woke, and they finished their work: a permanent corral for the camels, made of piled stones bonded with a gravitic field powered by solar collectors; refrigeration sheds for storing the dried food that would keep them for a year, if it took that long before they could return to Basilica; wards and watches placed around the perimeter of the valley, so that no one could come near enough to see them without them noticing him in return. They built no fires, of course—in the desert, wood was too precious to burn. They took it farther, though; they would cook nothing, because an inexplicable heat source might be detectable. The warmth of their bodies was all the infrared radiation they dared to give off, and the electromagnetic noise put out by their wards and watches, the gravitic field, the refrigeration, the solar collectors, and Issib's chair was not strong enough to be picked up much beyond their perimeter, except with instruments far more sensitive than anything passing marauders or caravans were likely to have. They were as safe as they could make themselves.

At dinner, Nafai commented on how unnecessary it all was. "We're on the errand of the Oversoul," he said. "The Oversoul has kept people away from here all these years, keeping it ready for us—it would have kept on keeping people away."

Elemak laughed, and Mebbekew hooted hysterically. "Well, Nafai the theologian," said Meb, "if the Oversoul's so capable of keeping us safe, why did it send us out here into the landscape of hell instead of letting us *safely* stay home?"

"How are you such an expert on the Oversoul, anyway, Nafai?" asked Elemak. "That mother of yours obviously had you spending too much time with witches."

For once, Nafai stifled his angry retorts. There was no point in arguing with them, he realized. But then, he had realized that many times before, and hadn't been able to hold his tongue. The difference now, Nafai realized, was that he was no longer just Nafai, the youngest of Wetchik's boys. Now he was the friend and ally of the Oversoul. He had more important concerns than arguing with Elya and Meb.

"Nafai," said Father, "your reasoning is faulty. Why should we make the Oversoul waste time watching over us, when we're perfectly capable of watching over ourselves?"

"Of course not, Father," said Nafai. His remark had been foolish. It would be wrong for them to burden the Oversoul, when the Oversoul needed them to help bear its burden. "I'm sorry."

Elemak smiled slightly, and Mebbekew rolled his eyes and laughed again. "Listen to them," he said. "Rational men, supposedly, talking about whether the Oversoul should tend our camels or not."

"It was the Oversoul that brought us here," said Father, rather coldly.

"It was *you* who made us go," said Mebbekew, "and Elemak who guided us."

"It was the Oversoul who warned me to leave," said Father, "and the Oversoul that brought us to this well-watered valley."

"Oh, yes, of course, I forgot," said Meb. "I thought that was a vulture circling, but instead it was the Oversoul, leading the way."

"Only a fool jokes about what he doesn't understand," said Father.

"Only an old *joke* goes around calling rational men *fools*," said Mebbekew. "*You're* the one who sees plots and conspiracies in shadows, Father."

"Shut up," said Elemak.

"Don't tell me to shut up."

"Shut up," said Elemak again. He turned slowly to meet Mebbekew's hot glare. Nafai could see that, though Elya's eyes were heavy lidded, as if he were barely awake, his eyes were afire as he stared Meb down.

"Fine," said Mebbekew, turning back to his dinner, smearing cold bean paste onto another cracker. "I guess I'm the only one who doesn't think camping trips are just the funnest thing."

"This isn't a camping trip," said Father. "It's exile."

"What I can't figure out," said Mebbekew, "is what *I* did to deserve exile."

"You're my son," said Father. "None of us were safe there."

"Come on," said Meb. "We were all safe."

"Drop it," said Elemak. Again he met Mebbekew's glare.

Now Nafai began to recognize the trend here. Elemak didn't like Mebbekew talking about whether there was really a plot against Father, or whether there had been any reason for the whole family to flee into the desert. It was a sensitive subject, and Nafai guessed that both of them knew more than they were willing to talk about. If they had some dark secret, it would be no surprise if Elemak chose to conceal it by never letting a conversation even come near it, while Mebbekew would be far more likely to try to hide it behind a smokescreen of casual denials and mocking lies.

"You *both* know that Father's life was in danger in Basilica," said Nafai.

The way they both looked at him told him that what he suspected was true. If they had been innocent, they would have taken his remark to mean only that he expected them to believe in Father's vision. Instead, they took it much more harshly.

"What makes you think you know what *other* people know?" demanded Elemak.

"If *you're* so sure Father's life was in danger," said Meb nastily, "maybe that means *you* were in on the conspiracy."

Again, their reactions were typical: Elemak, defending against Nafai's accusation by saying, in essence, You can't prove anything, while Mebbekew was defending himself by turning the accusation back on Nafai.

Now let them realize what they are confessing, thought Nafai. "What conspiracy?" he asked. "What are you talking about?"

Mebbekew immediately realized how much he had revealed. "I just assumed—that you were saying that we had some advance knowledge or something."

"If you *knew* of a plot against Father's life," said Nafai, "you would have *told* him, if you were any kind of decent human being. And you certainly wouldn't sit here whining about how we didn't really need to leave the city."

"I'm not the one who whines, little boy," said Mebbekew. His anger had lost all subtlety now. He wasn't sure how to interpret Nafai's words, which is why Nafai had spoken the way he did. Let Meb wonder—does Nafai know something, or not?

"Shut up, Meb," said Elemak. "And you, too, Nafai. Isn't it bad enough we're in exile here without you at each other's throats?"

Elya the peacemaker. Nafai wanted to laugh. But then— maybe it was true. Maybe Elemak *hadn't* known—maybe Gaballufix had never taken him into his confidence on that subject. Of course he hadn't, Nafai realized. Elya might be Gaballufix's half-brother, but he was still Wetchik's son and heir. Gaballufix would never be absolutely sure whose side Elemak was really on. He could use Elya as a go-between, a messenger to Father—but he could never trust him with real knowledge.

That would explain Elemak's effort to keep Meb silent, too; he wanted to hide his involvement with Gaballufix, yes, but there was no murder plot to keep secret. How could Nafai have imagined it? Besides, if they were out in the desert as part of the Oversoul's plan, didn't that mean that Elemak and Mebbekew were *also* part of the plan? Here I am, filled with suspicion about them, harboring exactly the kind of malice that is going to destroy Basilica. How can I claim to be on the Oversoul's side, if I let myself behave like the kind of person who doesn't trust even his own brother?

"I'm sorry," said Nafai. "I shouldn't have said that."

Now they all looked at him in true startlement. It took a moment for Nafai to realize that it was the first time in his life that he had ever actually apologized for some nasty thing he said to one of his brothers, without first being wrestled into submission and locked in some painful grip.

"That's all right," said Mebbekew. His voice was full of

wonder—his eyes, though, radiated with triumphant contempt.

You think my apology means I'm weak, Nafai said silently to him. But it doesn't. It means I'm trying to learn how to be strong.

It was then that Nafai told Father and Elemak and Mebbekew something of the visions the Oversoul showed him during the night. He didn't get far into his account, though.

"I'm tired," said Elemak. "I don't have time for this."

Nafai looked at him in astonishment. Didn't have time to hear the plan of the Oversoul? Didn't have time to learn about the hope of humankind returning to Earth?

Mebbekew also yawned pointedly.

"You mean you don't even care?" asked Issib.

Elemak smiled at his crippled brother. "You're too trusting, Issya," he said. "Can't you see what's happening here? Nafai can't stand not to be the center of attention. He can't prove himself by being useful or even marginally competent—so he starts having visions. Next thing you know, Nyef's going to be giving us the Oversoul's orders and bossing us all around."

"No I'm not," said Nafai. "I saw the visions."

"Right," said Mebbekew. "I saw visions last night, too. Girls that you don't even have the gonads to dream of, Nafai. I'll believe in your dreams of the Oversoul as soon as you're willing to marry one of the girls from my dreams. I'll even give you one of the prettiest ones."

Elemak was laughing, and even Father smiled a little. But Mebbekew's taunts only filled Nafai with rage. "I'm telling you the truth," he insisted. "I'm telling you what the Oversoul is trying to accomplish!"

"I'd rather think about what the girls in my dreams were trying to accomplish," said Meb.

"That's enough of such vulgarity," said Father. But he

was chuckling. It was the crudest blow, that Father plainly believed Elemak about Nafai making up his visions.

So when Elemak and Mebbekew left to see to the animals, Nafai remained behind with Father and Issib.

"Why aren't you going?" said Father. "Issib can't help with chores like that, here where his floats don't work. But *you* can help."

"Father," said Nafai, "I thought that *you* would believe me."

"I do," said Father. "I believe you honestly want to be part of the work of the Oversoul. I honor you for it, and maybe some of your dreams *did* come from the Oversoul. But don't try to tell such things to your older brothers. They won't take it from you." He chuckled bitterly. "They barely endure it coming from me."

"I believe Nafai," said Issib. "They weren't dreams, either. He was awake, by the stream. I saw him come back to the tent, wet and cold."

Nafai had never been so grateful to anyone, to have Issib back him up. He didn't have to do it, either. Nafai had half expected Issib to *stop* believing him, if Father wasn't taking him seriously.

"I believe him, too," said Father. "But the things you were saying were far more specific than anything the Oversoul tells us in visions. So I'm just saying that there's probably a kernel of truth in what you're saying. But most of it must have come from your own imagination, and I for one am not going to try to sort it out, not tonight."

"I believed *you*," said Nafai.

"Not at first," said Father. "And we don't trade belief like favors. We give belief and trust where they are earned. Don't expect me to be any quicker to believe *you* than you were to believe *me*."

Abashed, Nafai got up from the rug. Father's tent was so large that he didn't have to duck when he stood upright.

"I was blind at first, when you told me what you saw. But now I see that you're deaf, so you can't possibly hear the things I've heard."

"Help your brother back into his chair," said Father. "And watch how you speak to your father."

THAT NIGHT, IN their tent, Issib tried to console Nafai. "Father's the *father,* Nafai. It can't be good news to him, to have his youngest son getting so much more information from the Oversoul than *he's* ever received."

"Maybe I'm more attuned to it or something," said Nafai. "I can't help it. But what difference does it make, who the Oversoul talks to? Wasn't Gaballufix supposed to believe Father, even though Father is below his station in the Palwashantu clan?"

"Below his office, maybe," said Issib, "but not below his *station.* If Father had wanted to be clan leader, he would have been chosen—he's the Wetchik by birth, isn't he? That's why Gaballufix has always hated him—because he knows that if Father hadn't despised politics, he could have wiped out Gaballufix's power and influence easily, right from the start."

But Nafai didn't want to talk about Basilican politics now. He fell silent, and in the silence spoke again to the Oversoul. You have to make Father believe me, he said. You have to show Father what's really happening. You can't show me a vision and then not help me persuade Father.

"*I* believe you, Nyef," Issib whispered. "And I believe in what the Oversoul is trying to do. Maybe that's all the Oversoul needs, did you think of that? Maybe the Oversoul doesn't need Father to believe you right now. So just accept it. Trust the Oversoul."

Nafai looked at Issib, but in the darkness of night inside the tent couldn't tell whether his brother's eyes were open or not. Had it really been Issib speaking, or was Issib asleep, and had Nafai heard the words of the Oversoul in Issib's voice?

"Someday, Nyef, it may come down to what Elemak said. You may have to give orders to your brothers. Even to Father. Do you think the Oversoul will leave you to yourself then?"

No, it couldn't be Issib. He was hearing the Oversoul in Issib's voice, saying things that Issib could never say. And now that he realized that he had his answer, he could sleep again. But before he slept, questions formed in his mind:

What if the Oversoul is telling me more than Father, not because it's part of a plan, but simply because I'm the only one who can hear and understand?

What if the Oversoul is counting on me to be able to figure out a way to persuade the others, because the Oversoul hasn't the power to convince them anymore?

What if I'm truly alone, except for this one brother who believes me—the one brother who is crippled, and therefore can do nothing?

Belief is not *nothing*, said the voice whispering in Nafai's mind. Issib's belief in you is the only reason you haven't yet started doubting it yourself.

Tell Father, Nafai pleaded as he drifted off to sleep. Speak to Father, so he'll believe me.

THE OVERSOUL SPOKE to Father in the night, but not with any vision that Nafai had hoped for.

"I saw the four of you going back to Basilica," said Father.

"About time," said Mebbekew.

"Going back, but for a single purpose," said Father. "To get the Index and bring it back to me."

"The Index?" asked Elemak.

"It's been with the Palwashantu clan from the beginning. I believe that it might have been the reason the clan has preserved its identity for all these years. We were once called the Keepers of the Index, and my father told me that it was the right of the Wetchiks to use it."

"Use it for what?" asked Mebbekew.

"I'm not sure," said Father. "I've only seen it a few times. My grandfather left it with the clan council when he began traveling, and my father never made any serious effort to get it back after Grandfather died. Now it's in Gaballufix's house. But from the name of it, I'd guess it's a guide to a library."

"How useful," said Elemak. "And for *this* you're sending us back to Basilica? To get an object whose purpose you don't understand."

"To get it and bring it back to me. No matter the cost."

"Do you mean that?" said Elemak. "No matter the cost?"

"It's what the Oversoul wanted. I knew it—even though I—it's not my personal feeling. I want you back here, safe."

"Right," said Mebbekew. "It's as good as done. No problem."

"Should we bring back more supplies?" asked Nafai.

"There won't be more supplies," said Father. "I told Rashgallivak to sell all the caravaning supplies."

Nafai could see Elemak's face turn red under its dark tan. "So when our exile is over, Father, how do you propose we restore our business?"

It was a cusp of decision, Nafai could see that: Elemak was facing the fact that Father's actions were intended to be irrevocable. If Elya was going to rebel, it would be over this, which he could only see as the squandering of his inheritance. So Father spoke plainly in giving his reply.

"I don't propose to restore anything," said Father. "Do what I say, Elemak, or it won't matter to *you* what the Wetchik fortune is or is not."

There it was. It couldn't be more clear. If Elemak was ever to be Wetchik himself, he'd better obey the present Wetchik's commands.

Mebbekew cackled. "I never liked all those smelly animals anyway," said Mebbekew. "Who needs them?" His message was just as clear: I'll gladly become Wetchik in your place, Elemak—so please go ahead and get Father really really angry.

"I'll bring you your Index, Father," said Elemak. "But why send these others? Let me go alone. Or let me take Mebbekew, and keep the younger boys with you. Neither of them will be any use to me."

"The Oversoul showed me all four of you going," said Father. "So all four of you will go to Basilica, and all four of you will return. Do you understand me?"

"Perfectly," said Elemak.

"Last night you made fun of Nafai, because he claimed to be having visions," said Father. "But I tell you that you could learn a great deal from Nafai and Issib. *They,* at least, are making an effort to help. All I hear from my two elder sons is complaint."

Mebbekew glared pointedly at Nafai, but Nafai was more afraid of Elemak, who simply gazed steadily at Father through heavy-lidded eyes. Last night you wouldn't believe me, Father, Nafai said silently. Now today you make my brothers hate me even more than before.

"You know much, Elemak, Mebbekew," said Father, "but in all your learning you never seem to have mastered the concept of loyalty and obedience. Learn it from your younger brothers, and then you'll be worthy of the wealth and honors you aspire to."

That's it, Nafai said silently. I'm dead now. I might as well be a worm in their bread, the way they'll treat me on this whole trip. I'd rather stay home than go under these conditions, Father, thank you kindly.

"Father, I'll do all that you ask," said Elemak. But his voice was quiet and cold, and it made Nafai sick at heart to hear it.

Elemak sullenly set about preparing for the trip. As Nafai expected, Elya ignored him completely when he asked what he should do to help. And Mebbekew shot him such a look that Nafai felt a thrill of fear run through him. He wants me dead, he thought. Meb wants me to die.

Since he wasn't permitted to help, and since it would obviously be wiser for him to be as inconspicuous as possible for the next while, Nafai went back to the tent he shared with Issib and helped his brother pack up, which mostly consisted of wrapping his floats and stowing them in a bag. He could see in Issib's eyes as he looked hungrily at the floats that it didn't matter to Issib what Elemak or Mebbekew thought of him—he wanted to be back where his body was usable again, where he was free and didn't have to be dressed or taken outside to void himself like an infant or a pet. Such a prisoner he is, trapped in that body, thought Nafai. And then the job was done and Issib was in his chair, hovering over the ground looking like some ill-tempered monarch on his throne. He was impatient to go, impatient to return to Basilica.

All of them are, thought Nafai. But none for the right reason. None is eager to get there because of a desire to help with the Oversoul's plan.

Nafai found himself by the water's edge, gripping a bough that was ten centimeters thick, bending it between his hands, bending it like a horseshoe. It fought him, but it also gave under the strength of his grip.

"Don't break that," said Father.

Nafai turned, startled. He let go of the branch, and it whipped upward, out of control; some leaves slapped him in the face.

"It took so long for it to grow," said Father.

"I wasn't going to break it."

"It was on the verge," said Father. "I know plants. You don't. You were on the verge of breaking it."

"I'm not that strong."

"Stronger than you know." Father sized him up. "Fourteen." He laughed a little. "Your mother's genes, not mine, I fear. I look at you and I see—"

"Mother?"

"What Issib might have been, body as well as mind. Poor boy."

Poor boy. Why don't you look at me sometime, Father, and see *me*. Instead of some imaginary child. Instead of a little boy who makes up visions, why don't you see what I am: a man who heard the voice of the Oversoul, even more clearly than you.

"I'm afraid," said Father.

Nafai looked his father in the eye. Is he teasing me?

"I'm sending you into something more dangerous than I think your brothers understand. But *you* understand, don't you, Nafai."

"I think."

"After what you've seen," said Father. But it was as much a question as an answer. What was he asking, whether Nafai knew the truth about Elya and Meb? It couldn't be that, because Father didn't know about them himself. No, Father was asking whether Nafai really saw visions.

Nafai's first reaction was to be furious—hurt, offended. But then he realized that he was wrong to feel that way. Because Father had a right to ask, a right to let it take time to believe in his visions, just as Issib had said. He was *trying* to accept the idea of Nafai as a fellow servant of the Oversoul.

"Yes," said Nafai. "I've seen. But nothing about the Index."

"Gaballufix won't let it go," said Father. "In the vision he did, but the Oversoul can't see everything. The Index isn't just something you borrow. It's very powerful."

"Why? What can it do?"

"I don't know what it can do, of itself. But I know that it

means power. I know that among the Palwashantu, the one who keeps the Index is the one who has the trust of the clan. The greatest honor. Gabya won't give it up. He'll kill first. And that's where I'm sending my sons."

The look on Father's face was angry. Nafai realized: He's furious at the Oversoul for requiring him to do this.

And then, as Nafai watched, Father mastered his rage, and his face grew calm. "I hope," said Father quietly, "I hope the Oversoul has really thought all this through."

"Father," Nafai said, "*I'll* go and do whatever the Oversoul has asked us to do. Because I know that the Oversoul wouldn't ask us to do it without preparing some way for it to be accomplished."

Father studied his face for the longest time. Then he smiled. Nafai had never seen such a smile on his father's face. The relief in it, the trust. "Not an act, is it," said Father. "You're not just saying what you think I want to hear."

"When have any of your sons said anything that they thought you wanted to hear?" asked Nafai.

Now Father laughed, tossed his head back and roared. "Never!" he cried. And then, just as suddenly, the laughter stopped. Father took Nafai's head between his hands, his large hands, callused and wiry and horned and rough from years of handling bark and leather harnesses and raw stone, and holding those great palms on either side of Nafai's face, he leaned forward and kissed him on the mouth. "My son," he whispered. "My son."

For a moment they stood there together, beside the tree, beside the water, until they heard footsteps and turned. It was Elemak, his face still sour and angry. "Time to go," he said. "If we're going to make any kind of progress today, anyway."

"By all means go," said Father. "I wouldn't delay you for a moment."

In a few minutes they were on their camels again, heading back to the city.

ELEVEN

BROTHERS

Basilica was not in sight yet, but Elemak knew the road. Knew it as well as he knew the skin of his own face in the mirror, every mole of the surface, every peak or declivity that snatched at the razor and bled. He knew the shadows of every hour of the day, where water might be waiting after a rain, where robbers might hide.

It was to one of those places that Elemak now led his brothers. They had not been on the road itself for some time, but till now had always kept it in sight. Now they left it behind, and soon the ground grew rough enough that he made them stop, dismount.

"Why are we stopping here?" asked Mebbekew.

"The floats are working," said Issib. "That's how close we are, I can move without the damn chair."

Elemak eyed his crippled brother and shook his head. "Not reliably. We'll dismount the chair—you'll have to use it."

Issib was usually so compliant, but not now. "Use it yourself, if you think it's so comfy."

"Look at you," said Elemak. "It's intermittent at best, with the float. You'll start losing it and fall over and we can't have that. Use the chair."

"It'll get better as we get closer."

"We aren't getting closer," said Elemak.

"Then what are we doing?" demanded Mebbekew.

"We're going down into this arroyo, where the magnetics of Basilica certainly do *not* reach, and there we're going to wait until nightfall."

"And then?" asked Mebbekew. "Since you seem to think you're in command here, I thought perhaps I'd ask."

Elemak had faced this kind of thing many times before from fellow travelers on the road, even sometimes from hired men. He knew how to handle it—brutal suppression, instant and public, so no doubt was left in anyone's mind of who was in charge. So instead of answering Mebbekew he took him by the arms—thin, womanly arms, an *actor*, by the Oversoul!—and slammed him back against a wall of rock. The sudden movement spooked one of the camels. It stamped, spat, blatted out a protest. For a moment Elemak was afraid he would have to go calm the animal— but no, Nafai had it, was calming it. The boy was actually useful for something besides sucking up to Father. Not like Mebbekew, who was reliable only in his unreliability. Why Gaballufix ever confided in him, Elemak never knew. Surely Gabya knew that Mebbekew would let something slip. Even if he didn't tell Father directly about the plot, he surely told *someone*—how else could Father have known?

There was raw panic in Meb's eyes, and pain, too—his head had smacked sharply against the stone. Well, good, thought Elemak. Think about pain a little bit. Think hard before you question my authority on the road.

"I *am* in command here," Elemak whispered.

Meb nodded.

"And I say that we'll wait until dark."

"I was joking," Meb whined. "You don't have to be so *serious* about everything, do you?"

Elemak almost hit him for that. Serious? Don't you

realize that there inside Basilica, the most powerful, dangerous man in the city is almost certainly convinced that we betrayed him and warned Father to flee? To Mebbekew, Basilica was a city of pleasure and excitement. Well, there might be excitement indeed inside those walls, but of pleasure not a speck.

But Elemak did not hit Meb, because that would be excessive, and provoke resentment instead of respect among the others. Elemak knew how to lead men, and knew how to control his own feelings and not let them interfere with his judgment. He eased his grip on Mebbekew and then turned his back on him, to show his absolute confidence in his own leadership, and his contempt for Mebbekew. Meb would not dare attack him, even with his back turned.

"At nightfall, what will happen is simple enough. I will go inside the city, and I'll speak to Gaballufix, and I'll bring out the Index."

"No," said Issib. "Father said we should all go."

Another insubordination—but not a serious one, and it was Issib, the cripple, so a show of force was completely out of the question. "And we all *have* come. But *I know* Gaballufix. He's my half-brother—as much my brother as any of you. I have the best chance of talking him into giving us the Index."

"You mean we came all this way," said Issib, "and you're going to make me stay here, in this metal coffin of mine, and never get any closer to the city than this?"

"Better your chair than a real coffin," said Elemak. "I tell you that if you think going into the city will be fun, you're a fool. Gaballufix is dangerous."

"He *is*," said Nafai. "Elya is right. If we all go in together, then a failure might mean all of us killed—or imprisoned—or anything. If only one goes, then even if he fails the rest of us might still be able to accomplish something."

"If I fail, then go back to Father," said Elemak.

"Right," said Meb. "I'm sure we've all memorized the road."

"It can't be you," said Issib. "Of all of us, you're the only one necessary to lead us home."

"I'll go," said Nafai.

"Right," said Elemak, laughing. *"You,* the one who looks most like Lady Rasa. I don't think you get the picture, Nyef—one look at you and Gaballufix is reminded of the one humiliation he's never been able to avenge—Lady Rasa lapsing his contract after two daughters and within a week making a new contract with Father—which she hasn't broken yet. Walk into Gaballufix's house alone, with no one in the city even knowing you're there, Nyef, and your life is over."

"Me, then," said Mebbekew.

"You'd only go get drunk or find some woman," said Elemak, "and then come back and lie and say you spoke to Gaballufix and he said no."

Mebbekew seemed to toy with the idea of getting angry, but then thought better of it. "Possibly," said Mebbekew. "But it's a better plan than I've heard from anyone else."

"What about mine?" said Issib. *"I* go and ask. What is Gaballufix going to do to a cripple?"

Elemak shook his head. "Break you in half with his bare hands, if he feels like it."

"And you were *friends* with him?" asked Mebbekew.

"Brothers. We're brothers. We don't get to choose our brothers, you know," said Elemak. "We just make do with what we get."

"He wouldn't hurt a cripple," Issib said again. "It would shame him in front of his own men."

Elemak knew that Issib was right. The cripple might be the best one to get into and out of an interview with Gaballufix alive. The trouble was that Elemak *couldn't* let Issib or Nafai talk to the man. Gaballufix might say something that would compromise Elemak. No, it had to be Elemak himself, so he could talk to Gabya alone, maybe smooth things over, persuade his brother that it wasn't him that warned Father of the plan to kill Roptat under circumstances that would implicate and discredit Wetchik. If they ever learned of this, Meb and Issya and Nyef wouldn't understand that in the long run it was the best plan for Father's own sake. If they didn't neutralize Father this way, then eventually it might be Father who died under mysterious circumstances.

"I'll tell you what," said Elemak. "Since we all disagree about who should go, let's let the Oversoul decide. A time-honored tradition—we draw lots."

He reached down and scooped up a handful of pebbles from the ground. "Three light ones, one dark one." But as he spoke, Elemak made sure a fourth light-colored stone was tucked out of sight between two of his fingers. "Dark stone goes into the city."

"All right," said Meb, and the others nodded.

"I'll hold the stones," said Nafai.

"Nobody holds the stones, my dear little boy," said Elemak. "Too much chance of cheating, yes?" Elemak reached up to a shelf in the rock, out of sight where they were standing. There he again made a show of mixing up the four stones. "When I'm through mixing them, though, you can mix them yourself, Nafai," he said. "That way we know that nobody knows which stone is which."

Nafai immediately strode forward, reached up to the shelf of stone, and mixed the stones. Four of them, of course—Elemak knew he would feel four stones and be satisfied. What he couldn't possibly know was that the dark stone was now between Elemak's fingers, and the four stones on the shelf were all light.

"While you've got your hand up there, Nyef, go ahead and choose a stone."

Nafai, poor fool, came away with a light-colored stone and frowned at it. What did he expect? He was playing at a man's game. None of these boys seemed to realize that a man with Elemak's responsibilities would never have lasted on the open road if he didn't know how to make sure that drawing lots always turned out the way he wanted.

"Me now," said Issib.

"No," said Elemak. "My draw." That was another rule of the game—Elemak had to draw early, or somebody might grow suspicious and check the rocks and see that there was no dark one there. He reached up, made a show of fumbling with the rocks, and then came away with the dark one, of course—but with the extra light one also tucked between his fingers. When they checked, they'd find only two stones left there on the shelf.

"You knew by the feel of it," said Mebbekew.

"Don't be a bad sport," said Elemak. "If all goes well, maybe we can all go into the city. It all depends on how Gaballufix reacts, yes? And he's my brother—if anyone can persuade him, I can."

"I'm going inside no matter what," said Issib. "I'll wait until you come back, but I'm not leaving here without going inside."

"Issya," said Elemak, "I can't promise that I'll let you go inside the walls of the city. But I *can* promise that before you leave here, you'll get close enough that you can use the floats. All right?"

Sullenly Issib nodded.

"Your word, though, that no one leaves this spot until I come back."

"What do we do if Gaballufix kills you?" asked Meb.

"He won't."

"What do we do," Meb insisted, "if you don't come back?"

"If I'm not back by dawn," said Elemak, "then I'm

either dead or incapacitated. At that point, my dear brother lets, I won't be in charge anymore and so I don't really care what you do. Go home, go back to Father, or go into the city and get laid or killed or lost, it will make not a speck of difference to me. But don't worry—I'll be back."

That gave them plenty to think about as he led them down the arroyo into a clear area where no one was likely to find them. "But look," said Elemak. "You can see the city walls from here. You can see High Gate."

"Is that the gate you'll be using?" asked Nafai.

"On the way in," said Elemak. "On the way out, I'll use any gate I can get to."

With that he left them, striding boldly away, wishing that he felt half as bold as the show he was putting on for them.

ENTERING THE CITY through High Gate was nowhere near as difficult as it would have been at Market Gate—after all, there was no Gold Market to protect. Still, Elemak had to have his thumb scanned to prove his citizenship, and thus the city computer knew he had entered. Elemak had no doubt that even if Gabya's house computer wasn't tied directly to the city computers—which would be, of course, illegal—he certainly had informants in the city government, and if Gabya cared whether Elemak entered Basilica, he would know the information within moments.

Elemak was actually quite relieved not to be detained by the guard at the gate; it meant that Gaballufix had not put out his name for immediate arrest. Or else it meant that Gabya didn't yet have quite as much power in the city as he boasted about to his friends and supporters. Maybe it was still beyond his reach to issue orders to the gate guards to detain his personal enemies.

Am I his enemy? thought Elemak. His brother, yes. His friend, no. An ally of convenience for a while, yes. We both saw ways to get benefit from a closer relationship. But now will he see me as an old business deal gone sour, as a possibly useful friend, or as a traitor to be punished?

Elemak meant to go straight to Gaballufix's house, but once he was inside the city he couldn't bring himself to do it. He jogged from High Funnel up Library Street, then took Temple to Wing. Either Temple or Wing would have carried him near to Gabya's house, but by now Elemak was becoming more and more alarmed by the soldiers he was passing, or that were passing him. There were more of them, for one thing, than in the days before Father led them out into the desert, and even though he carefully avoided looking directly at them, he began to feel more and more uneasy about them. Finally, when he saw a group of a dozen turning onto Wing Street, he ducked into a doorway and then allowed himself to look at them directly as they passed.

Immediately he realized what was wrong. They were all identical—the faces, the clothing, the weaponry, everything. "Impossible," he whispered. There could not be so many identical people in the world at the same time. The ancient stories of cloning flashed through his mind—witches and wizards who tried to rule the world by creating genetically identical copies of themselves, which inevitably (in the stories, at least) turned on their creators and killed them. But this was the real world, and these were Gabya's soldiers; he had no more notion how to clone than how to fly, and if he *could* make clones, he could certainly have chosen a better model than this nondescript, stupid-looking hulk that was going up and down the streets by dozens.

"It's all fakery," said a woman.

No one stood in the doorway with Elemak. Only when he stepped out did he see the speaker, an ageless, filthy wilder, naked except for the layers of grime and dust that covered her. Elemak was not one of those who saw wilders as objects of desire, though some of his friends used them as casually as if they were urinals for lust. He would have ignored her, except she seemed to be answering his whispered comment, and besides, whom could he speak to more safely than to an anonymous holy woman from the desert?

"How do they do it?" he asked. "Look all alike, I mean."

"They say it's an old theatre costume technique, much in vogue a thousand years ago."

She didn't talk like a desert woman. "How does it work?"

"It's a fine netting, worn like a cloak. A control at the waist turns it on and off. It automatically adjusts itself to the surrounding light—it becomes very bright in sunlight, much more subtle in moonlight or shadow. A very clever device."

Her voice sounded more and more refined the more she talked.

"Who are you?" he asked.

She looked into his face. "I am the Oversoul," she said. "And who are you, Elemak? Are you my friend or my enemy?"

For a moment Elemak stood in terror. He had been so worried about Gaballufix, so fearful that a soldier would recognize him, call out his name, and carry him off or perhaps even kill him on the spot, that to now be recognized by a madwoman in the street left him completely empty-headed. How do you hide when even the street beggars know your name? Only when *she* moved, inserting her index finger into her navel and twiddling it around as if she were stirring some loathsome mixture there, did his disgust overcome his fear and send him out into the street, running blindly away from her.

Thus his plan of casual, unobtrusive movement through the streets was ruined. He did have enough presence of mind, however, not to go directly to Gabya's house, not in *this* state of mind. Where else could he go, though? Habit would lead him to his mother's house—old Hosni kept a fine old house in The Wells, near Back Gate, where she meddled in politics and made and broke reputations of rising young men and women of government. But desire triumphed over custom, and instead of taking refuge with his mother, he found himself on the porch of Rasa's house.

He had studied here as a boy, of course, even before Father first mated with her; indeed, it was because his mother had placed him with Rasa that his father and his teacher first met. It had been vaguely embarrassing to have the other students gossip about the liaison between their mistress and Elya's father, and from then on he had never been fully comfortable there until he gratefully left off his schooling at the age of thirteen. Now, though, he came to Rasa's house, not as a student, but as a suitor—and one whose suit had long been welcomed.

For a moment, hesitating at the door, Elemak realized that he was doing exactly what he had forbidden his young brothers to do—he was conducting personal business when he was supposed to be on Father's errand. But whatever qualms he felt, he immediately dispelled them. His wooing of Eiadh was far more than pursuit of an advantageous match. Sometime in the last few months he had fallen in love with her; he desired her more than he had ever thought he could desire a woman. Her voice was music to him, her body an infinitely variable sculpture that astonished him with every movement. But as his devotion for her grew, he had become increasingly fearful that in her there was no matching increase of love for him. For all he knew, she still desired him only as the heir of the great Wetchik, who could provide her with enormous fortune and prestige. And if that was all she saw in him, all she felt for him, then recent events would turn her against him. There might be no advantage to her in marrying the Wetchik's heir *now,* with so much of the business being closed down and sold off. How would she respond to him now?

He pulled the cord; the bell rang. It was an old-fashioned bell, a deepish gong rather than the musical chimes that were all the fashion now. To his surprise, it was none other than Rasa herself who answered the door.

"A man comes to my door," she said. "A strong young man, with the dirt and sweat of the desert on his face. What am I to make of you? Are you bringing me word from my mate? Are you bringing more threats from Gaballufix? Are you here to carry off my niece Eiadh? Or have you come with fear in your heart, back to the house of your childhood schooling, hoping for a bath and a meal and four stout walls to keep you safe?"

All was said with such humor that Elemak's fear was dispelled. It felt good to have Rasa address him almost as an equal, and with genuine affection, too. "Father is well," he answered, "I haven't seen Gabya since I returned to the city, I hope to see Eiadh but have no plans for abduction at the moment, and as for the bath and the meal—I would accept such hospitality gratefully, but I would never have asked for it."

"I'm sure you wouldn't have," said Rasa. "You would have bounded in and expected Eiadh to be glad of your embrace when you smell like a camel and you spread dust with every step you take. Come in, Elemak."

As he luxuriated in the bath he again felt some guilt, thinking of his brothers waiting for him in the rocks through the heat of the day—but then, bathing and cleansing himself before seeing Gaballufix was the most sensible of plans. It would make him look far less desperate and give the clear message that he had friends in the city—a much better bargaining position. Unless Gaballufix saw it as further proof that Elemak had played a double game against him. Never mind, never mind. His clothing, freshly washed and aired, was laid out for him in the secator, and he slipped it on gratefully when he arose from the bath, letting the secator dry him off as he dressed. He disdained the hair oils—keeping the hair oil-free was one of the ways the pro-Potokgavan party identified themselves, refusing to resemble the Wetheads in any way.

Eiadh met him in Rasa's own salon. She seemed timid, but he took that as a good sign—at least she did not seem haughty or angry. Still, did he dare to take the liberties she had granted him at his last wooing? Or would that be too presumptuous now, seeing how his circumstances had changed. He strode toward her, but instead of seating himself beside her on the couch, he sank to one knee before her and reached for her hand. She let him—and then reached out her other hand and touched his cheek. "Are we strangers now?" she asked. "Are you unwilling to sit beside me?"

She had understood his hesitation, and this was the reassurance that he needed. Immediately he sat beside her, kissed her, put his hand at her waist and felt how she breathed so passionately, how she yielded to him so eagerly. They said little at first, at least in words; in actions she told him that her feelings for him were undiminished.

"I thought you were gone forever," she whispered, after long silence.

"Not from you," he said. "But I don't know what the future holds for me. The turmoil in the city, Father's exile—"

"Some say that your brother was plotting to kill your father—"

"Never."

"And others that your father was plotting to kill your brother—"

"Nonsense. Laughable. They're both strong-minded men, that's all."

"That's not *all*," said Eiadh. "Your father never came here with soldiers, threatening that he could come in whenever he wanted the way Gaballufix did."

"He came *here*?" said Elemak, angry. "For what?"

"He was Aunt Rasa's mate once, remember—they have two daughters. . . ."

"Yes, I think I've met them."

"Of course," she said, laughing. "They're your nieces, I know. And they're Nyef's and Issya's sisters, too—aren't families so complicated? But what I meant was, Gaballufix's coming wasn't what was strange. It's the *way* he came, with those soldiers in their horrible costumes so they all look so—inhuman."

"I heard it was holography."

"A very old theatrical device. Now that I've seen it, I'm glad that our actors use paint or, at the most, masks. Holographs are disturbing. Unnatural." She put her hand inside his shirt, slid it along his skin. It tickled. He trembled. "You see?" she said. "How could a holograph ever feel like mat? How could anyone bear to be so *unreal.*"

"I imagine they're still real enough under the holograph. And they can make faces at you without your knowing it."

She laughed. "Imagine being an actor, though, with something like that. How would anyone ever know your facial expressions?"

"Maybe they only used them for non-speaking roles—so the same actors could play dozens of roles with instant costume changes."

Eiadh's eyes widened. "I didn't know you were so knowledgeable about the theatre."

"I once courted an actress," said Elemak. He did it deliberately, knowing how it bothered most women to hear about old loves. "I thought she was beautiful then. You see, I had never seen *you.* Now I wonder if she was anything but a holograph."

She kissed him as a reward for the pretty compliment.

Then the door opened and Rasa came in. She had allowed them the socially correct fifteen minutes—perhaps a little longer. "So nice of you to visit us, Elemak. Thank you, Eiadh, for conversing with our guest while I was detained." It was the delicate pretense of courting, this custom of acting as if the suitor had come to call on the lady of the house, while the young woman being wooed was merely helping the lady to entertain her guest.

"For all your hospitality, I am grateful beyond expression," said Elemak. "You have rescued a weary traveler, my lady Rasa; I didn't know how near death I must have been, until your kindness made me so alive."

Rasa turned to Eiadh. "He's really very good at this, isn't he."

Eiadh smiled sweetly.

"Lady Rasa," said Elemak, "I don't know what the future will hold. I have to meet with Gaballufix today, and I don't know how that will turn out."

"Then *don't* meet with him," said Rasa, her expression turning quite serious. "He's become very dangerous, I think. Roptat is convinced that there was a plot to kill him in that meeting at the coolhouse, the day that Wetchik left. If Wetchik had been there, as agreed, Roptat would have walked right into a trap. I believe him—I believe Gaballufix has murder in his heart."

Elemak *knew* he had; but he also had no idea what might come if he confirmed Rasa's suspicions. For one thing, Rasa and Eiadh might wonder how Elemak could have known of such a plot, and if he did, why he didn't give warning to Roptat himself. Women didn't understand that sometimes to avoid the thousands of casualties of a bloody war, it was kindest and most peaceable to prevent the conflict with a single timely death. Good strategy could so easily be misunderstood as murder by the unsophisticated.

"Perhaps," said Elemak. "Does anyone really know someone else's heart?"

"I know someone's heart," said Eiadh. "And mine holds no secrets from him."

"If it isn't Elemak that you're referring to," said Rasa, "then poor Elemak might start contemplating some hot-blooded crime of passion himself."

"Of course I'm talking about Elya," said Eiadh. She took his hand and held it in her lap.

"Lady Rasa, I'm not going to Gaballufix unnecessarily. Father sent me. There's something he needs that only Gaballufix can give."

"There's something we *all* need that only Gaballufix can give," said Rasa, "and that is *peace*. You might mention that to him when you see him."

"I'll try," said Elemak, though of course they both knew he wouldn't.

"What is it that Wetchik wants? Did he send any message to me?"

"I don't think he expected me to see you," said Elemak. "It was a vision from the Oversoul that sent me. Actually, all four of us came—"

"Even Issib! Here!"

"No. I left them outside the city, in a safe place. No one but the two of you will know they're here, if I can help it. With any luck, I'll get the Index and be out of the city before night, and then I have no idea when we'll be back again."

"The Index," whispered Rasa. "Then he can never come back."

Elemak was disturbed to hear her say that. "Why? What *is* it?"

"Nothing," she said. "I mean, I don't know. Only that— let's just say that if the Palwashantu realize that it's gone . . ."

"How can it be that important? I never heard of it before Father sent us back for it."

"No, it's not much spoken of," said Rasa. "There hasn't been much need for it, I guess. Or perhaps the Oversoul didn't want it known."

"Why? There are lots of indexes—dozens in every library in the world, hundreds in Basilica alone. Why is this one *the* Index?"

"I'm not sure," said Rasa. "Really I'm not. I only know that it's the only artifact from the men's worship that is also mentioned in the women's lore."

"Worship? How is it used?"

"I don't know. It never *has* been used, to my knowledge. I've never seen it. I don't even know what it looks like."

"Oh, *that's* good news," said Elemak. "I assumed it would be like any other index, and now you're telling me that Gaballufix could hand me anything and call it the Index and I'd never even know if he was cheating me."

Rasa smiled. "Elemak, you must understand. Unless he wishes to lose his leadership of the Palwashantu, he will *never* give you the Index."

Elemak was worried, but not dismayed. She clearly meant what she was saying, but that did not necessarily mean that she was right. Nobody really knew what Gaballufix might do, and if he thought he could get some advantage out of it, he'd trade away anything. Even their mother, if Gabya ever thought old Hosni might have some value. No, the Index could be had, if the price was right.

And the more he realized how important this mysterious Index was, the more he wanted it, not just to humor Father, not just as part of the game he was playing to take possession of the future, but for the sake of having the Index himself. If so much power came to the one who had it, then why shouldn't it be Elemak's?

"Elemak," Rasa said, "if you do, somehow, get the Index, you must realize that Gaballufix won't let you keep it. Somehow he'll get it back. You'll be in terrible danger then. What I'm telling you is—if you or any of your brothers need refuge from Gabya, then trust no man. Do you understand? Trust no *man*."

Elemak was unsure how to answer. He *was* a man; how did she expect him to respond to such advice?

"There are few women in this city," said Rasa, "who would not rejoice to see Gabya deprived of much of his power and prestige. They would gladly help the taker of the Index to escape the grasp of Gaballufix—even if the Index had been obtained by some means that ordinarily might be viewed as . . ."

"Criminal," said Elemak.

"I hate the thought of it," said Rasa. "But your Father is certainly right that it would be a harsh blow against Gaballufix, to lose the Index."

"It wasn't Father's idea, really," said Elemak. "He said it came to him in a dream. From the Oversoul."

"Then it might happen," she said. "It might. Perhaps . . . who knows whether the Oversoul might still have enough influence over Gaballufix to make him—what, temporarily stupid?"

"Stupid enough to give it to me?"

"And stupid enough not to find you and strike you down once you have it."

Elemak felt Eiadh's hand in his, her body leaning against him. I came here for refuge, and out of desire for you, Eiadh—but it was Rasa whose help I really needed. Imagine if I had gone into Gabya's house, not realizing how important this Index really is! "Lady Rasa, how can I thank you for all you've done for me."

"I fear that I've encouraged you to risk your life in an impossible endeavor," said Rasa. "I hate to think Gaballufix might really harm you, but the stakes in this gamble are very high. The future of Basilica is the prize—but I fear that the getting of the prize might harm the city so much that it isn't worth the game."

"Whatever happens," Elemak said, "you can be sure that I will return for Eiadh if I can, and if she'll have me."

"Even if you're a pariah and a criminal?" said Rasa. "Would you expect her to go with you even then?"

"Especially then!" cried Eiadh. "I don't love Elya for his money or his position in the city, I love him for himself."

"My dear," said Rasa, "you've never *known* him without his money or his position. How do you know who he'll be when he doesn't have them anymore?"

It was a cruel thing for her to say; Elemak could not believe that she had even thought such a thought, let alone brought it to her lips. "If Eiadh were the sort of woman whose heart followed her coveting, Lady Rasa, then she would not be a woman I could love, or even trust. But I *do* love her, and no woman is worthier of my trust."

Rasa smiled at him. "Oh, Eiadh, your suitor has such a beautiful vision of you. Do try to be worthy of it."

"The way my Aunt Rasa talks, you'd think she was trying to talk you *out* of loving me," said Eiadh. "Maybe she's the teensiest bit jealous of me for having such a fine man courting me."

"You forget," said Rasa. "I already have the father. What would I want with the son?"

It was a tense moment; things were being said that should not—*could* not—be said in polite company. Unless it was as a joke.

At last Rasa laughed. At last. They joined in her laughter eagerly, in relief.

"May the Oversoul go with you," said Rasa.

"Come back for me soon," said Eiadh. She pressed herself against him so tightly that he could feel where every part of her body touched him, as if she were imprinting herself on his flesh. Or perhaps taking the imprint of his body on herself. He embraced her back; she would have no doubt of his desire *or* his devotion.

IT WAS MIDAFTERNOON when Elemak got to Gaballufix's house. By habit he almost slipped down the alleyway to the private side entrance. But then he realized that his relationship with Gaballufix had changed in unpredictable ways. If Gaballufix regarded him as a traitor, then a secret arrival, completely unobserved, would give Gabya a perfect opportunity to be rid of him with no one the wiser. Besides, to come in the back way implied that Elemak was of a lower station than Gaballufix. He had had enough of that. He would come in openly, obviously, through the front entrance, like a man of importance in the city, an honored guest—with plenty of witnesses.

To his pleasure, Gaballufix's servants were deferential, ushering him inside immediately, and there was very little waiting before Elemak was led to the library, where he had always met with Gaballufix. Nothing seemed changed— Gabya arose from his chair and greeted Elemak with an embrace. They spoke like brothers, gossiping for a few minutes about people they both knew in Gaballufix's circle of friends and supporters. The only hint of tension between them was the way Gabya referred to Elemak's "hasty midnight departure."

"It wasn't my idea," said Elemak. "I don't know which of your people talked, but Father woke us up hours before dawn, and we were out on the desert before the meeting was to have taken place."

"I didn't like being taken by surprise," said Gaballufix. "But I know that sometimes these things are out of one's control."

Gabya was being understanding. Relief swept over him, and Elemak sat back more comfortably in his chair. "You can imagine how worried I was. I couldn't very well slip away and warn you what was happening—Father was on us the whole time, not to mention my little brothers."

"Mebbekew?"

"It was all I could do to keep him from loosing all his sphincters on the spot. You should never have brought him into the plan."

"Shouldn't I?"

"How do you know he wasn't the one who warned Father?"

"I don't know that," said Gaballufix. "All I know is that my dear cousin Wetchik left, and my brother Elemak with him."

"At least he's out of the city. He won't be interfering with you anymore."

"Won't he?"

"Of course not. What can he do from some secluded valley in the desert?"

"He sent *you* back," said Gaballufix.

"With a limited objective that has nothing to do with the whole debate over war wagons and Potokgavan and the Wetheads."

"The debate has moved far beyond those concerns anyway," said Gaballufix. "Or, perhaps I should say, it has moved far *closer* than those concerns. So tell me—what is your father's limited objective, and how can I thwart him?"

Elemak laughed, hoping that Gabya was joking. "The best way to thwart him, I think, is to give him what he wants—a simple thing, *nothing,* really—and then we'll go away and it'll be between you and Roptat, the way you wanted it."

"I never wanted it between me and anybody," said

Gaballufix. "I'm a peaceable man. I want no conflict. I thought I had a plan whereby conflict could be avoided, but at the last moment the people I counted on fell through."

He was still smiling, but Elemak realized that things were not as steady between them as he had hoped.

"Now tell me, Elya, what is the little thing that you think I should do for your father, solely because your father asks for it?"

"There's some Index," said Elemak. "An old thing that's been in the family for generations."

"An Index? Why would I have one of Wetchik's family indexes?"

"I don't know. I assumed you'd know which one he meant. He just called it 'the Index' and so I thought you'd know."

"I have dozens of indexes. Dozens." Then, suddenly, Gaballufix raised an eyebrow, as if he had just realized something. Elemak had seen him put on that same performance before, however, so he knew he was being played with. "Unless you mean—but no, that's absurd, that's nothing that ever belonged to the Wetchik house."

Elemak dutifully played along. "What are you talking about?"

"The *Palwashantu* Index, of course," said Gaballufix. "The whole reason for the clan having been established in the first place, back at the dawn of time. The most precious artifact in all of Basilica."

Of course he would play up the value of it. Just like any merchant who was eager to sell. Pretend that what he's selling is the most valuable thing ever to exist on the planet, so you can set some absurdly high price, and then work your way down.

"That can't be the one, then," said Elemak. "Father certainly didn't think it had that much value. It was more of a sentimental thing. His grandfather owned it, and lent it to the clan council for safekeeping during his travels. Now Father wants to take it with him on his travels."

"Oh, that's the one, then. His grandfather had it, but only as a temporary guardian. It was delegated to the Wetchik by the Palwashantu clan; he wearied of the burden, and gave it back. Now another guardian has been appointed—me. And I'm not weary. So tell your father I'm grateful that he was willing to help me with my duties, but I'll struggle on without his help for another few years, I think."

It was time for the price to be mentioned. Elemak waited, but Gaballufix said nothing.

And then, when the silence had stretched on for several minutes, Gaballufix arose from behind his table. "Anyway, my dear brother, I'm glad to see you back in the city. I hope you'll be here for a long time—I can use your support. In fact, now that your father seems to have run off, I'll certainly use my influence to try to get you appointed Wetchik in his place."

This was not at all what Elemak had expected. It asserted a relationship between Elemak and his own inheritance that was completely intolerable. "Father is Wetchik," he said. "He hasn't died, and when he does, I'm Wetchik without any help from anyone."

"Hasn't died?" asked Gaballufix. "Then where is he? I don't see my old friend Wetchik—but I do see the son that stands to profit most from his death."

"My brothers will also witness that Father is alive."

"And where are *they*?"

Elemak almost blurted out the fact that they were hiding not very far from the city walls. Then he realized that this was almost certainly what Gaballufix wanted most to know—who Elemak's allies were, and where they were hiding. "You don't think I'd enter the city alone, do you, when my brothers are as eager to come back to Basilica as I am!"

Of course Gaballufix knew that Elemak was lying—or, at the least, he knew that Elemak's thumbprint was the only one that had shown up at any of the city gates. What Gabya couldn't know was whether Elemak was merely bluffing, and his brothers were all far away in the desert—or whether they had circumvented the guards at the gates and even now were in the city, plotting some mischief that Gaballufix would need to worry about. Yet Gaballufix couldn't say anything about the fact that he knew Elemak was the only one to enter the city legally—it would be as much as admitting that he had complete access to the city's computers.

"I'm glad they were able to return to the pleasures of the city," said Gabya. "I hope they're careful though. A rough element has been brought into the city—mostly by Roptat and his gang, I'm afraid—and even though I'm helping the city by letting a few of my employees put in extra duty hours patrolling the streets, it's still possible for young men wandering alone through the city to get involved in unfortunate incidents. Sometimes dangerous ones."

"I'll warn them to look out."

"And you, too, Elemak. I worry for you, my brother. There are those who think your father was involved in a plot against Roptat. What if they take out their resentment on *you*?"

At that moment Elemak realized that his mission had failed. Gabya clearly *did* believe that Elemak had betrayed him—or else had concluded that Elemak was no longer useful and might even be dangerous enough to be worth killing. There was no hope now of getting anything through a pretense of polite brotherliness. But it might be worth taking a different tack.

"Come now, Gabya," said Elemak, "you know that you're the one who's been putting out that story about Father plotting against Roptat. That was the plan, remember? For

Father to be found in the coolhouse with Roptat's murdered corpse. He wouldn't be convicted, but he'd be implicated, discredited. Only Father didn't come, and therefore Roptat wouldn't get close enough for your thugs to kill him, and now you're trying to salvage as much of the plan as you can. We sat here and talked about it—why should we pretend now that we don't both know exactly what's going on?"

"But we *don't* both know what's going on," said Gaballufix. "I haven't the faintest idea what you're talking about."

Elemak looked at him with contempt. "And to think I once believed you were capable of leading Basilica to greatness. You couldn't even neutralize your opposition when you had the chance."

"I was betrayed by fools and cowards," said Gaballufix.

"That's the excuse that fools and cowards always give for their failures—and it's always true, as long as you realize that it's self-betrayal they're talking about."

"You call *me* a fool and a coward?" Gaballufix was angry now, losing control. Elemak had never seen him like this, except a flash of temper now and then. He wasn't sure that he could handle this, but at least it wasn't the suave indifference that Gabya had been showing him till now. "At least I didn't sneak off in the middle of the night," said Gaballufix. "At least I didn't believe every story I was told, no matter how idiotic it was."

"And I did?" asked Elemak. "You forget, Gabya, *you* were the only one telling me stories. So now, I'd like to know, which of the stories was I idiotic to believe? That you were only acting in the best interests of Basilica? I never believed that one—I knew you were out for your own profit and your own power. Or perhaps you think I believed the story that you really loved my father and were really trying to protect him from getting into the political situation over his head. Do you think I actually believed *that* one?

You've hated him since Lady Rasa lapsed you and remated with him, and you've hated him more every year that they've stayed together."

"I never cared about that!" said Gaballufix. "She's nothing to me!"

"Even now she's the only audience you try to please—imagine, going to her house and strutting like some cockbird, showing off for her. You should hear how she laughs about you now." Elemak knew, of course, that saying such a thing put Rasa in great danger—but this was a game with high risks, and Elemak couldn't hope to win it unless he took some chances. Besides, Lady Rasa could handle Gaballufix.

"Laughs? She doesn't laugh. You haven't even spoken with her."

"Look at me—do you see any of the filth of travel on my clothing? I bathed in her house. I'm going to mate with her favorite niece. She told me that she would as soon have mated with a rabbit as to spend another night with you."

For a moment he thought Gaballufix would draw a weapon and kill him on the spot. Then Gabya's face relaxed a little, into something like a smile. "Now I *know* you're lying," he said. "Rasa would never say something so crude."

"Of course I made it up," said Elemak. "I just wanted you to see who was the fool, believing any story that he heard."

"It's one thing to believe for a moment," said Gaballufix. "It's another story to keep believing and believing in the stupidest ideas."

It was in that moment that it first dawned on Elemak what the lie was that Gaballufix was saying he still believed. And Gabya was right—Elemak was a fool ever to have believed it, and a worse fool to have kept on believing it until now. "You never meant to charge Father with killing Roptat, did you?"

"Of course I did," said Gabya.

"But not to bring him to trial."

"Oh, no, that would be silly—a waste of time. I told you that."

"You *said* it would be a waste of time because Father's prestige in the city meant he'd never be convicted. But the truth was he would never have come to trial because you meant people to discover both Roptat's *and* Father's bod-ies in the coolhouse."

"What a terrible accusation. I deny it all. You have such an evil imagination, *boy*."

"You were using me to betray my own father so you could *kill* him."

"For the longest time," said Gaballufix, "I assumed you knew that. I assumed you understood that we were simply not speaking directly about it because it was such an un-pleasant subject. I thought you realized that the only way I could get you your inheritance early was by arranging your father's death."

Elemak's fury at having almost been a conspirator in father-killing overwhelmed all his self-control. He lunged toward Gaballufix—and found himself staring at the pulse in Gaballufix's hand.

"Yes, yes, I see that you have some idea of what a pulse can do to a man at close range. You killed a man with a weapon just like this, didn't you? In fact," said Gaballufix, "it might have *been* this weapon, mightn't it!"

Elemak looked at the pulse and recognized the wear marks on it, where it had been laid down on stone, where it had been nicked and marked, where the color had been faded by the sunlight as it rested at his hip during count-less hours of travel in the desert. "I lent that pulse to Meb-bekew the day I got home from my last caravan," he said stupidly.

"And Mebbekew lent it to me. I told him—speaking of

fools—that I wanted it to surprise you with later, at a party, to honor you for drawing blood. I told him I was going to use your story to inspire my soldiers." Gaballufix laughed. And laughed.

"That's why you brought Meb in. To get my pulse." But why? Elemak imagined his father lying there, dead, and then someone discovering Elemak's pulse not far away, abandoned perhaps in his haste to flee. He imagined Gaballufix explaining to the city council, tears in his eyes. "This is where greed in the younger generation leads—my own half-brother, willing to murder his father in order to get his inheritance."

"You're right," said Elemak quietly. "I *was* a fool."

"You were and you are," said Gaballufix. "You were seen in the city today—all over the city. My men tracked you through several neighborhoods. There are many witnesses—and it will be so delicious to see Rasa forced to testify against her beloved Volemak's oldest boy. Because someone is going to die tonight, killed with this very pulse, which will be found near the body, and then everyone will know that it was Wetchik's son who was the assassin, probably at his father's orders. And the best part of it is, I can tell you this, and then I can let you know, I can put you out of the city *alive* and there's still nothing you can do about it. If you start telling people about *my* plot to kill somebody—whoever I decide it should be—they'll all assume that you were simply trying to cover up your own crime in advance. You *are* a fool, Elemak, just like your father. Even when you knew I wasn't afraid to kill to accomplish my purposes, you somehow thought that you and your family would be immune, that somehow I'd be more tender with you because the same weary old womb bore you and me during our nine months sucking life out of a placenta."

Elemak had never seen such fury, such hatred, such *evil* in a human face, had never imagined it was possible. Yet there he stood, looking at Gabya's glee in describing a crime he meant to commit. It frightened Elemak, but it also made him feel an insane kind of confidence. As if Gaballufix's having revealed his true inner smallness made Elemak realize how much larger he was himself, after all.

"Who's the fool, Gabya," said Elemak. "Who's the fool."

"I think there's no doubt of that now," said Gaballufix.

"True enough," said Elemak. "You'll make it impossible for Father and me to return to the city, for a while at least, but the death of Roptat won't open the road for you. Are you so stupid, really? Nobody will believe for a moment that Father would kill Roptat, or that I would either."

"I'll have the weapon!" said Gaballufix.

"The weapon, but no witness to the killing, just *your* story bruited about by *your* people. They aren't so stupid that they can't add one and one. Who stands to gain from Roptat's death and Father's exile? Only you, Gabya. This city will rise up in bloody rebellion against you. Your soldiers will die in the streets."

"You overestimate the will of my feeble-hearted enemies," said Gaballufix. But his voice didn't sound so certain anymore, and the glee was gone.

"Your enemies aren't feeble-hearted, just because they're unwilling to kill in order to get their way. They *are* willing to kill to stop a man like *you*. A weak-brained, jealous, spiteful, malicious little parasitic roach like you."

"Do you want so much to die?"

"Yes, kill me here, Gabya. Hundreds of people know I'm here. Hundreds are waiting to hear what I tell them. Your whole plan stands revealed, and none of it will work. Because you were so stupid that you had to brag."

Elemak's words were all bluff, of course, but Gaballufix

believed him. At least enough to make him pause. To make him wonder. Then Gabya smiled. "Elya, my brother, I'm proud of you."

Elemak recognized surrender when he heard it. He said nothing in reply.

"You *are* my brother after all—the blood of Volemak didn't weaken you after all. It may even have made you stronger."

"Do you really think I'll swallow your flattery *now*?"

"Of course not," said Gaballufix. "Of course you'll disregard it—but that doesn't stop me from admiring you, does it? It just stops you from believing in my admiration! The loss is yours, dear Elya."

"I came for the Index, Gaballufix," said Elemak. "A simple thing. Give it to me, and I'm gone. Wetchik and his family will never bother you again, and you can play your little games until somebody puts a knife in your back just to stop that squealing noise you make whenever you think you've been especially clever."

Gaballufix cocked his head to one side.

He's going to give it to me, thought Elemak, triumphantly.

"No," said Gaballufix. "I'd like to, but I can't. The disappearance of the Index—that would be hard to explain to the clan council. A lot of trouble, that's what it would cause, and why should I put myself to all that trouble just to get rid of Wetchik? After all, I'm already rid of him."

Now, at last, Elemak was where he wanted to be: bargaining like a merchant. "What else would it take to make it worth your while?" asked Elemak.

"Make me an offer. Enough money that it'll make up for all the extra effort I have to go through."

"Give me the Index, and Father will release funds to you. Whatever you want."

"I'm supposed to *wait* for the funds? Wait for *Wetchik* to pay me later for an Index I give you now? Oh—I get it—I see what's happening!" Gaballufix laughed in derision. "You can't give me money *now* because you don't have any. Wetchik still hasn't released any of his fortune to you! He sent you on this errand and he didn't even give you access to his money!"

It *was* humiliating. Father should have realized that in dealing with Gaballufix it would eventually come down to money; he should have given him password that would have let him access the Wetchik family funds. Rashgallivak, the steward, had more control over the Wetchik fortune than Elemak did. He was filled with fury and resentment against his father for putting him in such a position of weakness. The stupid short-sighted old man, always tripping over his own feet when it came to business!

"Tell me, Elya," said Gaballufix, interrupting his own laughter. "If your own father doesn't trust you with his money, why should I trust you with the Index?"

With that, Gaballufix reached under his table and apparently triggered some kind of switch, for three doors opened at once and identical-looking soldiers burst into the room. They took hold of Elemak and roughly thrust him out into the hall, then out the front door.

Nor was that enough. They quick-marched him to the nearest gate, which happened to be the Back Gate—right past his mother's house—and threw him into the dirt in front of the guards.

"This one's leaving the city!" shouted one of the soldiers.

"And never coming back!" cried another.

The guards, however, did not seem terribly impressed. "Are you a citizen?" asked one.

"Yes," said Elemak, dusting himself off.

"Thumb please." They presented the thumbscreen, and Elemak held his thumb over it. "Citizen Elemak son of Hosni by the Wetchik. It is an honor to serve you." Whereupon the guards all stood at attention and saluted him.

It completely stunned him. Never, in all his passages into and out of the city of Basilica, had anyone done more than raise an eyebrow when the city computer reported his prestigious parentage. And now a salute!

Then Gaballufix's soldiers jeered again, boasting about what they'd do to him if he ever returned, and Elemak understood. The official city guards were letting him and everyone else near the gate see that *they* were not part of Gaballufix's little army. Furthermore, the very fact that the son of Wetchik was clearly the enemy of Gaballufix made city guards want to salute him. If Elemak could only figure out how to use this situation, he might very well be able to turn it to his advantage. What if I returned to the city as the deliverer, leading the guard and the militia in crushing Gabya and his hated army of costume clones. The city would then gladly give me all that Gabya is trying to win through trickery, intimidation, and murder. I'd have all the power Gaballufix ever imagined—and the city would love me for it.

TWELVE

FORTUNE

It was a miserable day in the desert, even allowing for the fact that except for about an hour and a half at noon, the canyon was in deep shade, with a steady breeze funneling through it. No place is comfortable, thought Nafai, when you're waiting for someone *else* to do a job you think of as your own. Worse than the heat, than the sweat dripping into his eyes, than the grit that got into his clothing and between his teeth, was the sick dread Nafai felt whenever he thought of *Elemak* being the one entrusted with the Oversoul's errand.

Nafai knew that Elemak had rigged the casting of lots, of course. He wasn't such a fool as to think Elemak would actually leave such a thing to chance. Even as he admired the deftness with which Elya handled it, Nafai was angry at him. Was he even *attempting* to get the Index? Or was he going into the city and meeting with Gaballufix in order to plan some further betrayal of Father and of the city and, finally, of the Oversoul's guardianship of humanity?

Would he even return?

Then, at last, in mid-afternoon, there came the clatter and rattle of stones tumbling, and Elemak clambered noisily down into their hiding place. His hands were empty, but his eyes were bright. We have been betrayed, thought Nafai.

"He said no, of course," said Elemak. "This Index is more important than Father told us. Gaballufix doesn't want to give it up—at least not for nothing."

"For what, then?" asked Issib.

"He didn't say. But he has a price. He made it clear that he's willing to hear an offer. The trouble is—we have to go back to Father and get access to his finances."

Nafai didn't like this at all. How did they know what Elemak and Gaballufix had promised each other?

"All the way back, empty-handed," said Mebbekew. "Tell you what, Elya. *You* go back, and the rest of us will wait here till you come back with the password to Father's accounts."

"Right," said Issib. "I'm not going to spend the night out here in the desert, when I can go into the city and use my floats."

"How stupid are you, really?" said Elemak. "Don't you realize that things are different now? You can't go wandering anonymously through the city anymore. Gabya's troops are all over it. And Gaballufix is not Father's friend. Therefore he's not *our* friend, either."

"He's your brother," said Mebbekew.

"He's nobody's brother," said Elemak. "He's got both the morals and the surface properties of slime. I know him better than any of you, and I can promise you that he'd just as soon kill any of us as look at us."

Nafai was amazed to hear Elemak talking this way. "I thought you wanted him to lead Basilica."

"I thought his plan was the best hope for Basilica in the coming wars," said Elemak. "But I never thought Gaballufix was out to get anything except his own advantage. His soldiers are all over the city—wearing some kind of holographic costume that covers their whole bodies, so all his soldiers look absolutely identical."

"Whole-body masks!" cried Mebbekew. "What a great idea!"

"It means," said Elemak, "that even when somebody sees one of Gaballufix's soldiers committing a crime—like kidnapping or killing a stray son of old Wetchik—no one can possibly identify the individual who did it."

"Oh," said Mebbekew.

"So," said Nafai, "even if Father gives us access to his money, what then? What makes you think Gaballufix would sell it?"

Think, Nafai. Even a fourteen-year-old should be able to grasp *something* of the affairs of men. Gaballufix is paying hundreds and hundreds of soldiers. His fortune is large, but not large enough to keep that up forever, not without getting control of the tax money of Basilica to support them all. Father's money could make a huge difference. At the moment, Gaballufix probably needs money more than he needs the prestige of possessing this Index, which hardly anybody has even heard of anymore."

Swallowing Elemak's condescension, Nafai realized that Elemak's analysis was right. "The Index *is* for sale, then."

"*Could* be," said Elemak. "So we go back to Father and see whether the Index is worth spending money for, and how *much* money. Then he gives us access to his finances and we go back and bargain—"

"And I say *you* go home and let me take my chances in the city," said Mebbekew.

"I want to get away from my chair tonight," said Issib.

"When we come back," said Elemak, "*then* you can get into the city."

"Like this time? You make us wait again, just like this time, and we'll never get in," said Issib.

"Fine," said Elemak. "I'll go back alone and tell Father that you've abandoned him and his cause, just so you can go into the city and float around and get laid."

"I'm not going in to get laid!" protested Issib.

"And I'm not going in to float," said Mebbekew, grinning.

"Wait a minute," said Nafai. "If we go back to Father and get permission, then what? It'll be almost a week. Who knows how things might have changed by then? There could already be civil war in Basilica. Or by then Gaballufix might have arranged other financing, so that our money wouldn't mean anything to him. The time to make an offer is *now*."

Elemak looked at him in surprise. "Well, yes, of course, that's true. But we don't have access to Father's money."

In answer, Nafai looked at Issib.

Issib rolled his eyes. "I promised Father," he said.

"You mean *you* have access to Father's password?" said Mebbekew.

"He said that somebody else ought to know it, in case of an emergency," said Issib. "How did *you* know about it, Nafai?"

"Come on," said Nafai, "I'm not an idiot. In your research you were getting access to city library files that they'd never let a kid like you get into without specific adult authorization. I didn't know Father had *given* it to you, though."

"Well," said Issib, "he only gave me the entry code. I kind of figured out the back half myself."

Mebbekew was livid. "All this time that I've been living like a beggar in the city, *you* had access to Father's entire fortune?"

"Think about it, Meb," said Elemak. "Who else could Father *trust* with his password? Nafai's a child, you're a spendthrift, and I was constantly disagreeing with him about where we ought to invest our money. Issib, though— what was *he* going to do with the money?"

"So because he doesn't *need* money, he gets all he wants?"

"If I had ever used his password to get money, he would have changed it and so of course I never used it," said Issib. "Maybe he has still another password for getting into the money—I never tried. And I'm not trying now, either, so you can forget it. Father didn't authorize us to go dipping into the family fortune."

"He told us that the Oversoul wanted us to bring him the Index," said Nafai. "Don't you see? The Index is so important that Father had to send us back to face his enemy, a man who planned to kill him—"

"Oh, come on, Nyef, that was Father's *dream*, not anything real," said Mebbekew. "Gaballufix wasn't planning to kill Father."

"Yes he was," said Elemak. "He was planning to kill Roptat *and* Father, and then put the blame on me."

Mebbekew's jaw hung open.

"He was going to arrange to have them find my pulse— the one I lent to *you,* Mebbekew—near Father's body. Clumsy of you to lose my pulse, Meb."

"How do you know all this?" asked Issib.

"Gaballufix told me," said Elemak. "While he was trying to impress me with my helplessness."

"Let's go to the council," said Issib. "If Gaballufix confessed—"

"He confessed—or rather *bragged*—to *me,* in a room alone. My word against his. There's no point in telling anybody. It wouldn't do any good."

"This is the opportunity," said Nafai. "Today, right now. We go down to the house, access Father's files through his own library, convert all the funds into liquid assets. We go to the gold market and pick it up as metal bars and negotiable bonds and jewels and what-not, and then we go to Gaballufix and—"

"And he steals it all from us and kills us and leaves the chopped-up bits of our bodies for the jackals to find in some ditch outside the city," said Elemak.

"Not so," said Nafai. "We take a witness with us—someone he won't dare to touch."

"Who?" said Issib.

"Rashgallivak," said Nafai. "He isn't just the steward of the house of Wetchik, you know. He's Palwashantu, and has a great deal of trust and prestige. We bring him along, he watches everything, he witnesses the exchange of Father's fortune for the Index, and we all walk out alive. Gaballufix might be able to kill *us,* because we're in hiding and Father's an exile, but he can't touch Rash."

"You mean all *four* of us go to Gaballufix?" asked Issib.

"Into the city?" asked Mebbekew.

"It's not a bad plan," said Elemak. "Risky, but you're right about this being the time to act."

"So let's go down to the house," said Nafai. "We can leave the animals here for the night, can't we? Issib and I can go to Father's library to do the funds transfer, while you and Meb find Rash and bring him there so we can go meet Gaballufix together."

"Will Rash go along with it?" asked Issib. "I mean, what if Gaballufix decides to kill us all anyway?"

"Yes," said Elemak. "He's a man of perfect loyalty. He will never swerve from his duty to the house of Wetchik."

It took only an hour or so. It was late afternoon when they walked into the Gold Market and began the final transactions. All of the funds that were not tied up in real property were all in spendable form in Issib's bank file—actually, like all the brothers' bank files, a mere subfile of Father's all-inclusive account. If anyone doubted that Issib was authorized to spend so much, there was Rashgallivak, silently observing. Everyone knew that if Rash was there, it had to be legitimate.

The amount involved was the largest single purchase of portable assets in the recent history of the Gold Market. No one broker had anything like enough ingots or jewels or bonds to handle even a large fraction of the buy. For more than an hour, until the sun was behind the red wall and the Gold Market was in shadow, the brokers scrambled among themselves until at last the whole amount was laid out on a single table. The funds were transferred; a staggering amount was moved from one column to another in all the computer displays—for all the brokers were watching now, in awe. The ingots then were rolled up in three cloth packages and tied, the jewels were rolled in cloth and bagged, and the bonds were folded into leather binders. Then all the parcels were distributed among the four sons of Wetchik.

One of the brokers had already arranged for a half-dozen of the city guards to accompany them wherever they were going, but Elemak sent them away. "If the guards are with us, then every thief in Basilica will see and take note of where we're going. Our lives will be worthless then," said Elemak. "We'll move swiftly and without guard, without notice."

Again the brokers looked at Rashgallivak, who nodded his approval.

Half an hour through the streets of the city, nervously aware of everyone who glanced at them, and then at last they were at the doors of Gaballufix's house. Nafai saw at once that both Elemak and Mebbekew were recognized here. So, too, was Rashgallivak—but Rash was widely known in the Palwashantu clan, so it would have been a surprise if he had *not* been recognized. Only Nafai and Issib had to be introduced as they stood before Gaballufix in the great salon of his—no, not *his*, but his *wife's* house.

"So you're the one who flies," said Gaballufix, looking at Issib.

"I float," said Issib.

"So I see," said Gaballufix. "Rasa's sons, the two of you."
He looked Nafai in the eye. "Very large for one so young."

Nafai said nothing. He was too busy studying Gaballufix's face. So ordinary, really. A little soft, perhaps. Not
young anymore, though younger than Father, who had,
after all, slept with Gaballufix's mother—enough to produce Elemak. There was some slight resemblance between
Elya and Gaballufix, but not very much, only in the darkness of the hair, and the way the eyes were perhaps a little
close together under heavy-ridged brows.

It was in the eyes that they were alike, but also in the
eyes that they differed most, for there was a rheuminess, a
scarlet-rimmed look in Gaballufix's eyes that was the opposite of Elya's sharpness. Elemak was a man of action and
strength, a man of the desert, who could face strangers and
unknown places with courage and confidence and vigor.
Gaballufix, by contrast, was a man who went nowhere and
did nothing; rather he denned himself here and let others
do his work for him. Elemak went out and penetrated the
world, changing it where he would; Gaballufix stayed in
one place and sucked the world dry, emptying it in order
to fill himself.

"So the young one is speechless," said Gaballufix.

"For the first time in his life," said Meb. There was some
nervous laughter.

"Why do the sons and the steward of Wetchik honor me
with this visit?"

"Father wanted us to trade gifts with you," said Elemak.
"We're living in a place where we need little in the way of
money, yet Father has taken it into his heart—no, the Oversoul has commanded him—to bring the Index with him.
While you, Gaballufix, have little use for the Index—have
you even looked at it in all your years as leader of the clan
council?—and might be able to turn some portion of the

Wetchik estate to better advantage than Father ever could, being far from the city."

It was an eloquent, truthful, and completely deceptive speech, and Nafai admired it. There was no doubt in anyone's mind that a purchase was being attempted here, and yet it was delicately disguised as an exchange of gifts, so that no one could openly accuse Gaballufix of having sold the Index, or Father of having bought it.

"I'm sure my kinsman Wetchik is far too generous to me," said Gaballufix. "I can't imagine that I would be of much help to him, managing some trifling portion of his great fortune."

In answer, Elemak stepped forward and unrolled a heavy parcel of platinum ingots. Gaballufix picked up one ingot and hefted it in his hands. "This is a thing of beauty," he said. "And yet I know this is such a tiny part of the Wetchik fortune that I could not feel right about doing such a small favor for my kinsman, when he would bear in exchange the heavy burden of guarding the Palwashantu Index."

"This is only a sample," said Elemak.

"If I'm to be trusted with this, shouldn't I see the extent of my guardianship?"

Elemak removed all the rest of the treasure that he carried on his person, and laid it on the table. "Surely that is all that Father would dare ask you to be burdened with," he said.

"Such a slight burden," said Gaballufix. "I would be ashamed to have this be all the help I gave my kinsman." Yet Nafai could see that Gaballufix's eyes were shining at the sight of so much wealth all in one place. "I assume that it's only a quarter of what you carry." Gaballufix looked from Nafai to Issib and Mebbekew.

"I think that's enough," said Elemak.

"Then I couldn't agree to lay the burden of the Index on my kinsman," said Gaballufix.

"Very well," said Elemak. He reached out and started rolling up the ingots.

Is that all? thought Nafai. Do we give up so easily? Am I the only one who can see that Gaballufix hungers for the money? That if we offer just a little more, he'll sell?

"Wait," said Nafai. "We can add what I carry to this."

Nafai was aware that Elemak was glaring at him, but it was unthinkable to come so close and leave empty-handed. Didn't Elemak realize that the Index was *important*? More important than mere money, that was certain. "And if that isn't enough, Issib has more," Nafai said. "Show him, Issib. Let me show him."

In moments, they had tripled the offer.

"I fear," said Elemak, his voice icy, "that my younger brother has inconsiderately offered to burden you with far more than I ever intended you to have to deal with."

"On the contrary," said Gaballufix. "It is your younger brother who has more correctly estimated how much of a burden I'm willing to bear. Indeed, I think that if the last quarter of what you carried into my house were upon this table, I'd feel right about weighing down my dear kinsman with the heavy responsibility of the Palwashantu Index."

"I say it's too much," said Elemak.

"Then you hurt my feelings," said Gaballufix, "and I can't see any reason for further discussion."

"We came for the Index," said Nafai. "We came because the Oversoul demands it."

"Your father is famous for his holiness and his visions," said Gaballufix.

"If you're willing to accept all that we have," said Nafai, "we'll gladly lay it before you in order to fulfil the will of the Oversoul."

"Such obedience will long be remembered in the Temple," said Gaballufix. He looked at Mebbekew. "Or is

Nafai's holiness not matched by that of his brother Mebbekew?"

Anguished with indecision, Mebbekew looked back and forth between Elemak and Gaballufix.

But it was Elemak who acted. He reached down and again rolled up ingots into the cloth.

"No!" cried Nafai. "We won't turn back now!" He held out his hand to Mebbekew. "You know what Father would want you to do."

"I see that only the youngest has true understanding," said Gaballufix.

Mebbekew stepped forward and began laying parcels on the table. As he did, Nafai could feel Elemak grip his shoulder, the fingers biting deep, and Elemak whispered in his ear, "I told you to leave this to me. You've given him four times what we needed to pay, you little fool. You've left us with nothing."

Nothing but the Index, thought Nafai. But still, he vaguely realized that Elemak might in fact have known better how to handle the bargaining, and perhaps he should have kept his mouth shut and let Elya handle things. But at the time he acted, Nafai was so *sure* that he had to speak or they would never get the Index.

All the Wetchik fortune except the land and buildings themselves was on Gaballufix's table.

"Is *that* enough?" asked Elemak dryly.

"Exactly enough," said Gaballufix. "Exactly enough to prove to me that Volemak the Wetchik has completely betrayed the Palwashantu. This great fortune has been put into the hands of children, who have, with childish stupidity, resolved to waste it all on the purchase of that which every true Palwashantu knows can *never* be sold. The Index, the sacred, holy trust of the Palwashantu—did Volemak think it could be bought? No, impossible, it could not be! I can only conclude that he has either lost his mind or you have killed him and hidden his body somewhere."

"No!" cried Nafai.

"Your lies are obscene," said Elemak, "and we won't tolerate them." He stepped forward and reached out for a third time to gather up the treasure.

"Thief!" shouted Gaballufix.

Suddenly the doors opened, and a dozen soldiers entered the room.

"Do you think you can do this in the presence of Rashgallivak?" demanded Elemak.

"I *insist* on doing it in his presence," said Gaballufix. "Who do you think first came to me with the news that Volemak was betraying the trust of the Wetchiks? That Volemak's sons were gutting the Wetchik fortune for some mad whim?"

"I serve the house of Wetchik," said Rashgallivak. He looked at each of the brothers, his face a mask of sadness. "It could not possibly be in the interest of that great house to let the fortune be destroyed by one madman who thinks he sees visions. Gaballufix could hardly believe what I told him, but he agreed with me that the fortune of Wetchik had to be shifted into the care of another branch of the family."

"As chief of the Palwashantu clan," Gaballufix intoned, "I hereby declare that Volemak and his sons, having proven themselves unfit and unreliable as guardians of the greatest house in the clan, are therefore removed as heirs and possessors of the house of Wetchik for all time. And in recognition of years of loyal service, by himself and his ancestors for many centuries, I grant temporary guardianship of the Wetchik fortune, and the use of the name of Wetchik, to Rashgallivak, to care for all aspects of the Wetchik house until such time as the clan council shall dispose of them otherwise. As for Volemak and his sons, if they make any effort to protest or dispute this action, they will be regarded as blood-enemies of the Palwashantu, and shall be dealt with by laws more ancient than those of the city of Basilica." Gaballufix leaned forward across the table, smiling at Elemak. "Did you understand all that, Elya?"

Elemak looked at Rashgallivak. "I understand that the most loyal man in Basilica is now the worst traitor."

"You were the traitors," said Rash. "This sudden madness of visions, a completely unprofitable journey into the desert, selling off all the animals, dismissing all the workers, and now this—as steward of the house of Wetchik, I had no choice but to involve the clan council."

"Gaballufix isn't the clan council," said Elemak. "He's a common thief, and you've put our fortune in his hands."

"*You* were putting the fortune in his hands," said Rashgallivak. "Don't you see that I did this for you? For all four of you? The council will leave me as guardian for a few years, until all this blows over, and in that time if one of you proves himself to be a sober and completely reliable man, worthy of the responsibility, the Wetchik name and fortune will be returned to you."

"There'll be no fortune left," said Elemak. "Gabya will spend it on his armies before the year is out."

"Not at all," said Gaballufix. "I'm turning it all over to Rash, to continue as steward."

Elemak laughed bitterly. "As steward, required to use it as the council directs. And how will the council direct? You'll see, Rash. Very quickly indeed—because the council has incurred some pretty heavy expenses with all these soldiers they're paying."

Rashgallivak looked quite uncomfortable. "Gaballufix did mention that some small part of this might need to be deducted to meet present expenses, but your father would have contributed to clan expenses anyway, if he were still in his right mind."

"He's played you for the fool," said Elemak, "and me too. All of us."

Rash looked at Gaballufix, clearly concerned. "Maybe we ought to call in the council on this," he said.

"The council has already met," said Gaballufix.

"How heavy *are* the clan expenses?" asked Rashgallivak.

"A trifle," said Gaballufix. "Don't waste time worrying about it. Or are you going to prove yourself as unreliable as Volemak and his sons?"

"See?" said Elemak. "Already it begins—do as Gabya wants, or you won't be steward of the Wetchik fortune anymore."

"The law is the law," said Gaballufix. "And now it's time for these worthless young spendthrifts to leave my house before I charge them with the murder of their father."

"Before we say anything more to help Rash see the truth, you mean," said Elemak.

"We'll go," said Mebbekew. "But all this talk about the Palwashantu clan council and making Rashgallivak the Wetchik is rat piss. You're a thief, Gabya, a lying murdering thief who would have killed Roptat *and* Father if we hadn't left the city the day we did, and we're not leaving our family fortune in your bloody hands!"

With that Mebbekew lunged forward and seized a bag of jewels.

Immediately the soldiers were upon them, all four of them. The jewels were out of Meb's hands in a moment, and with no particular gentleness all four of them were out of the salon, out of the front doors, and thrown into the street.

"Away from here!" cried the soldiers. "Thieves! Murderers!"

Nafai hardly had a chance to think before Mebbekew was at his throat. "*You're* the one who had to lay all the treasure on the table!"

"He meant to have it all anyway," Nafai protested.

"Shut up, fools," said Elemak. "This isn't over. Our lives aren't worth dust—he probably has men waiting to kill us not fifty meters off. Our only hope is to split up and *run*. Don't stop for anything. And remember—something Rasa told me today—*trust no man*." He said it again, changing the emphasis a little. "Trust no *man*. We'll meet tonight where the camels are. Anyone who isn't there by dawn we'll assume is dead. Now run—and *not* for any place that they'd expect you to go."

With that Elemak began to stride off toward the north. After only a few steps he turned back. "Now, fools! See—they're already signaling the assassins!"

Sure enough Nafai could see that one of the soldiers on Gaballufix's porch had raised one arm and was pointing at them with the other. "How fast can you go with those floats?" Nafai asked Issib.

"Faster than you," he answered. "But not faster than a pulse."

"The Oversoul will protect us," said Nafai.

"Right," said Issib. "Now move, you fool."

Nafai ducked his head and plunged into the thickest part of the crowd. He had run a hundred meters south along Fountain Street when he turned back and saw why people were shouting behind him: Issib had risen some twenty meters into the air, and was just disappearing over the roof of the house directly across from Gaballufix's. I never knew he could do that, thought Nafai.

Then, as he turned to run again, it occurred to him that Issib probably hadn't known it, either.

"There's one," said a harsh voice. Suddenly a man appeared in front of him, a charged-wire blade in his hand. A woman gasped; people shied away. But almost without knowing that he knew it, Nafai could feel the presence of a man directly behind him. If he backed away from the blade in front, he would walk into the real assassin behind him.

So instead Nafai lunged forward. His enemy had not expected this unarmed boy to be aggressive—his swipe with the blade came nowhere near. Nafai put his knee sharply into the man's groin, lifting him off the ground. The man screamed. Then Nafai shoved him out of his way and ran in earnest now, not looking back, barely looking ahead except to dodge people and watch for the shimmering red glow of another blade, or the hot white beam of a pulse.

THIRTEEN

FLIGHT

Issya had never tried to climb so high with his floats. He knew that they responded to his muscle tension, that whichever float he pressed down on the hardest remained fixed in its position in the air. But he had always thought that the position was somehow relative to the ground directly under the float. He was not entirely wrong—the higher he got, the more the floats tended to "slip" downward—but by and large he found that he could climb the air like a ladder until he was at roof height.

Naturally, everyone looked at him—but that's what he wanted. *Everybody* watch me, and talk about the young crippled boy who "flew" up to the roof. Gaballufix's goons wouldn't dare shoot him with so many witnesses, at least not directly in front of their leader's own house.

There was no one on the roofs, he saw that at once, and so he used them as a sort of highway, drifting low between vents and chimneys, cupolas and elevator housings, roofline ridges and the trees in rooftop gardens. Once he did surprise an old fellow who was repairing the masonry on the low wall around a widow's walk; the clattering sound of a broken tile worried Issib for a moment; when he turned, though, he saw that the man had not fallen, but rather stared gape-mouthed at Issib. Will there be a story tonight, Issib wondered, about a young demigod seen drifting through the air over Basilica, perhaps on some errand of love with a mortal girl of surpassing beauty?

It was an exceptionally long block of houses, since several roads had been built over in this area. He was able to get more than halfway to Back Gate without descending to street level, and certainly he had made better time than any possible pursuers could have. There was always the chance, of course, that Gaballufix had assassins posted at all the city gates; certainly if he had an ambush at any gate it would be at Back Gate, the one nearest to his house. So Issib couldn't afford to be careless, once he was down at street level.

Before he left the roofs, though, he cast a longing gaze at the red wall of the city. High as he was, the sun was still up, split in half by the wall line. If only I could just fly over that. But he knew that the wall was loaded with complicated electronics, including the nodes that created the magnetic field that powered his floats. There was no crossing there—the tiny computer at his belt could never equalize the violently conflicting forces at the top of the wall.

He reached the end of a roof and drifted down into the crowd. This was the upper end of Holy Road, where men *were* allowed to go. Many noticed his descent, of course, but once he reached street level he immediately lowered himself to sitting position and scooted through the traffic at child-height. Let an assassin try to shoot me *now*, he thought. In minutes he was at the gate. The guards recognized his name the moment the thumb-scanner brought it up, and they clapped him on the back and wished him well.

It was not desert here at Back Gate, of course, but rather the fringes of Trackless Wood. To the right was the dense forest that made the north side of Basilica impassable; to the left, complicated arroyos, choked with trees and vines, led down from the well-watered hills into the first barren rocks of the desert. For a normal man, it would be a nightmare journey, unless he knew the way—as, he was sure, Elemak did. For Issib, of course, it was a matter of avoiding the tallest obstacles and floating easily down until the city was completely out of sight. He used the sun to steer by until he was down onto the desert plateau; then he bore south, crossing the roads named Dry and Desert, until, just at sunset, he reached the place where they had hidden his chair.

His floats were at the fringes of the magnetic field of the city now, and it was awkward maneuvering himself into the chair. But then everything to do with the chair was awkward and limiting. Still, it did have some advantages. Designed to be an all-purpose cripple's chair, it had a built-in computer display tied to the city's main public library when he was within range, with several different interfaces for people with different disabilities. He could even speak certain key words and it would understand them, and it could also produce a fair-sounding approximation of the commoner words in several dozen languages. If there were no such things as floats, the chair would probably be the most precious thing in his life. But there *were* floats. When he wore them, he was almost a regular human being, plus a few advantages. When he could not use them, he was a cripple with no advantages at all.

The camels were waiting outside the dependable influence of the city's magnetics, however, so use the chair he must. He got in, switched off the floats, and then guided the chair in its slow, hovering flight through narrow back canyons until at last he smelled, then heard the camels.

No one else was there; he was the first. He settled the chair onto its legs, leveled it, and then sat there alternately listening for anyone who might be approaching while scanning the library's news reports for word of any unexplained killings or other violent incidents. None yet. But then it might take time for word to reach the newswriters and the gossips. His brothers might be dying right now, or already dead, or captured and imprisoned and held for some sort of ransom. What would he do then? How could he hope to get home? The chair might carry him, though it was unlikely—it wasn't meant for long distance travel. He knew from experience that the chair could only move continuously for an hour or so before it needed several hours of solar recharging.

Mother will help me, thought Issib. If they don't come back tonight, Mother will help me. If I can get to her.

MEBBEKEW DODGED THROUGH the crowd. He had seen several men trying to make their way toward him, but his experience as an actor—especially one who had to go through the audience collecting money—had given him a good sense of crowds, and he worked the traffic expertly against *the* men who were following him, heading always where the crowd was thickest, dodging through gaps that were about to be plugged by approaching groups of people. Soon the assassins—if that's what they were—were hopelessly far behind him. That was when Mebbekew began to *move,* a lazy, loping run that didn't give the impression of great haste but covered the ground very rapidly. It looked like he was running for the sheer joy of it, and in fact he was—but he never stopped watching. Whenever he saw soldiers, he headed straight for them, on the theory that Gaballufix wouldn't dare use men clearly identified as his own to conduct a public murder in the clear light of afternoon.

Within half an hour he had worked himself all the way east to Dolltown, the district that he knew best. The soldiers were rarer here, and while there were plenty of criminals for hire here, they were the sort who didn't stay bought for long. Meb also knew people who knew this part of town better than the city computer itself.

Trust no *man*, Elemak had said. Well, that was easy enough. Meb knew plenty of men, but his *friends* were all women. That had been an easy choice for him, from the time he was old enough to know the practical applications of the difference between men and women. He had almost laughed when Father got an auntie for him at the age of sixteen—he had enjoyed pretending to be new at lovemaking when he went to her, but within a few days she sent him away, laughingly saying that if he came back any more he'd be teaching *her* things that she had never particularly wanted to learn. Meb was good with women. They loved him, and they kept loving him, not because he was good at giving pleasure, though he was, but rather because he knew how to listen to women so they knew that he heard; he knew how to talk to them so they felt needed and protected, all at once. Not all women liked him, of course, but the ones that did liked him very much, and forever.

So it took only a few minutes in Dolltown before Mebbekew was in the room of a zither player on Music Street, and a few minutes more before he was in her arms, and a few minutes more before he was in her; then they talked for an hour, she went out and enlisted the help of some actresses they both knew, who were more than a little fond of Mebbekew themselves. Shortly after nightfall Mebbekew, in wig and gown and makeup, in voice and walk a woman, passed through Music Gate with a group of laughing, singing women. Only when he laid his thumb on the screen was his disguise revealed, and the guard, reading his name, merely winked at him and wished him a good night.

Mebbekew stayed in costume until he got to the rendezvous, and his only regret was that it was Issib who stared at him and didn't know him until he spoke, and not Elemak.

It would have been nice to let his older brother see the joke. But then, given the fact that their entire fortune and Father's title as well had just been stolen from them, Elemak probably wouldn't have been in the mood for a joke anyway.

ELEMAK'S PASSAGE FROM the city was the least eventful. He never saw an assassin, and had no problem getting to Hosni's house near the Back Gate. Fearing that perhaps the assassins were waiting at the gate itself, he ducked in to visit with his mother. She fed him a wonderful meal—she always hired the best cooks in Basilica—listened sympathetically to his story, agreed with him that if she had miscarried when pregnant with Gaballufix the world would be a better place, and finally sent him on his way several hours after dark with a bit of gold in his pocket, a sturdy metal-bladed knife at his belt, and a kiss. He knew that if Gaballufix came later that night, bragging about how he had tricked a fortune out of Volemak's sons, including Wetchik, Mother would laugh and praise him. She loved anything that was amusing, and was amused by almost anything. A cheerful woman, but utterly empty. Elemak was sure that Gaballufix got his morals from her, but certainly not his intelligence. Though, truth to tell, his teacher Rasa had told him once that his mother was actually very intelligent—much too intelligent to let others know how intelligent she was. "It's like being among dangerous foreigners," said Rasa. "It's much better to let them think you don't understand their language, so that they'll speak freely in front of you. That's how dear Hosni is when she's among those who fancy themselves very bright and well educated. She mocks them all unmercifully when they're gone."

Will she mock me to Gaballufix, as she mocked Gaballufix to me? Or ridicule us both to her woman-friends when we're gone?

At the gate, the guards recognized him at once, saluted

him again, and offered to help him in any way they could. He thanked them, then plunged out into the night. Even by starlight he knew his way through the tangled paths leading down from Trackless Wood into the desert. Through all the dark journey he could think of nothing but his fury at Gaballufix, at the way he had outmaneuvered him by getting Rash on his side. He could hear in his mind their mother's laughter, as if it were all aimed at him. He felt so helpless, so utterly humiliated.

And then he remembered the most terrible moment of all, when Nafai had so stupidly interfered with his bargaining and given away Father's entire fortune. If he hadn't done that, Rashgallivak might not have concluded that they were unworthy to have the Wetchik fortune. Then he wouldn't have acted against them, and they could have walked out with the treasure *and* Father's title intact. It was Nafai, really, who had lost the contest for them. If it had been up to Elemak alone, he might have done it. Gaballufix might have come through with the Index and settled for a quarter of Father's fortune—it was more money even so than Gaballufix could lay hands on any other way. Nafai, the stupid young jackass who could never keep his mouth shut, the one who pretended to have visions of his own so that Father would like him best, the one who, by the sheer act of being born, had made Gaballufix into Father's permanent enemy.

If I had him in my hands right now I'd kill him, thought Elemak. He has cost me my fortune and my honor and therefore my whole future. Easy for him to give away the Wetchik fortune—it would never have been his anyway. It would have been mine. I was born for it. I trained for it. I would have doubled it and doubled it again, and again and again, because I'm a far better man of business than Father ever was or ever could be. But now I'm an exile and an outcast, accused of theft and stripped of fortune, without even the respect of the man who should have been at my right hand, Rashgallivak.

All because of Nafai. All his fault.

NAFAI RAN IN blind panic, with no thought of destination. It was not until he broke away from the crowds and found himself in an open space that he began to calm enough to think of where he was and what he ought to do next. He was in the Old Dance, once as large a dancing space as the Orchestra in Dolltown, which replaced it many centuries ago. Now, though, the buildings encroached the dance on every side. It had lost its roundness, and even the bowl shape of the amphitheatre was lost among the houses and shops. But an open space *did* remain, and that was where Nafai stood, looking at the sky, pink-tinged in the west, graying to black in the east. It was nearly full dark, and he had no idea whether assassins were still following him. One thing was certain—in the dark, in this part of town, the crowds would thin out, and murder would be much easier to accomplish unobserved. All his running had got him farther from safety than ever, and he had no idea what to do next.

"Nafai," said a girl's voice.

He turned. It was Luet.

"Hi," he greeted her. But he didn't have time to chat. He had to *think*.

"Quick," she said.

"Quick what?"

"Come with me."

"I can't," he said. "I have to do something."

"Yes," she said. "You have to come with me."

"I have to get out of the city."

She grabbed him by the front of his shirt and stood on tip-toe, which she no doubt intended to bring her eye-to-eye with him, but which succeeded only in making her hang from his shirt like a puppet. He laughed, but she didn't join him. "Listen, O thou busiest of men," she said, "have you forgotten that I'm a seer of the Oversoul?"

He *had* forgotten. Had forgotten even that it was her coming in the middle of the night that had saved Father from Gaballufix's plot. There were things she still didn't know about that, he realized. For some reason he thought he ought to explain. "Elemak and Mebbekew *were* involved in the plot," he said. "But I think Gaballufix lied to them about what he meant to do."

She had no patience for his confused babbling. "Do you think I care now? They're looking for you, Nafai. I saw it in a dream—a soldier with bloody hands stalking the streets. I knew that I had to find you. To save you."

"How can *you* save *me*?"

"Come with me," she said. "I know the way."

He had no better idea. In fact, when he tried to think of any alternative to following her, his mind went blank. He couldn't hold the thought. Finally it dawned on him that this was a message from the Oversoul. It wanted him to go with her. It had sent her to him, and so he must go with her, wherever she led him.

She took his hand and pulled him from the Old Dance down the street with the same name, until they reached the place where it narrowed, and then they took a fork to the left. "Our fortune is gone," said Nafai. "It was my fault, too. Except Rashgallivak betrayed us."

"Shut up," she said. "This isn't a good neighborhood."

She was right. It was dark here, and the road ran between old houses, dilapidated and dirty. There were few people there, and none of them seemed willing to look them in the eye.

They wound through a couple of sharp bends in the road, and then suddenly found themselves in Spring Street, near where it ran out into the holy wood. At that moment, Nafai saw ahead of him a group of soldiers, standing watch as if they had known he would emerge there. At once he turned to run, and then saw coming up the road they had just taken a couple of men with their charged-wire blades glowing slightly in the darkness.

"Good job, Nyef," Luet said contemptuously. "They probably wouldn't have noticed us. *Now* we look suspicious."

"*They* already know who we are," he said, pointing to the men approaching out of the dark street.

"Oh well," she said. "I had hoped to take the easy way in, but this one will have to do."

She grabbed his hand and half-dragged him the wrong way on Spring Street, away from the city and *toward* the holy forest. Nafai knew it was the stupidest thing she could possibly do. In the edges of the forest there'd be no witnesses at all. The assassins would have their way. If she imagined that Nafai had some particular skill at fighting and could somehow save them by disarming or killing the assassins, she would quickly discover the sad truth that he had never been interested in fighting and had no training along those lines at all. He couldn't even remember having hit someone in anger in his life, not even his older brothers, since fighting back against Meb or Elemak only made things worse in the end. Nafai might be large for his age, the tallest of Wetchik's sons, but it meant nothing when it came to battle.

As they moved into the darkness at the end of Spring Street, the assassins became bolder.

"That's right," one of them called out—softly, but audible enough to Nafai and Luet. "Into the shadows. That's where we'll have our conversation."

"We have nothing for you to steal." Luet's voice sounded panicked, trembling—but Nafai knew from her hand's steady grip that she was not trembling at all.

Nafai was trembling, however.

"Into the shadows," said the man again.

So they obeyed him. Plunged into the darkness under the trees. But to Nafai's surprise, they didn't stop, nor did they turn south, to skirt the forest and perhaps reenter the city at the next road. She led him almost straight east. Deeper into the forbidden country.

"I can't go here," he said.

"Shut up," she said. "Neither can they, unless they hear us talking and follow the sound."

He held his tongue, and followed her. After a while the ground began to fall away, not a slope anymore as much as a cliff, and it became very difficult to pick his way. The sky was fully dark now, and even though many leaves had fallen here, the shade of the trees was still quite deep. "I can't see," he whispered.

"Neither can I," she answered.

"Stop," he said. "Listen. Maybe they've stopped following us."

"They have," she said. "But we can't stop."

"Why not?"

"I've got to take you out of the city."

"If I'm caught here, the punishment is terrible."

"I know," she said. "As bad for me, though, for bringing you."

"Then take me back."

"No," she said. "This is where the Oversoul wants us to go."

It was too hard, however, to hold hands anymore—they both needed both hands to make their way down the ragged face of the cliff. It wouldn't have been that dangerous a climb in daylight, but in the darkness they might not see a drop-off that would kill them, so every step had to be tested. At least on this slope the trees were rarer, so the starlight could do a better job of helping them to see. At least, that's how it was until they reached the fog.

"Now we *have* to stop," he said.

"Keep climbing."

"In the fog? We'll get lost on the cliff face and fall and die."

"It's a good sign," said Luet. "It means that we're at least halfway down to the lake."

"You're not taking me to the lake!"

"Hush."

"Why don't I just throw myself down the quick way, then, and save them the effort of killing me?"

"Hush, you stupid man. The Oversoul will protect us."

"The Oversoul is a computer link with satellites orbiting Harmony. It doesn't have any magical machines to reach down and catch us if we fall."

"She is making us alert," said Luet. "Or she's helping *me*, at least, to find the way. If you'd only stop talking and let me listen to her."

They were hours climbing down through the fog, or so it seemed to Nafai, but at last they reached the bottom. Grass on a level plain, giving way to mud.

Warm mud. No, *hot* mud.

"Here we are," she said. "We can't go into the water here—it comes up from a rift deep in the crust of the world, where it's so hot that it boils and gives off steam. The water would cook the meat from our bones if we stayed in it for any length of time, even near the shore."

"Then how do women ever—"

"We do our worship nearer to the other end, where the lake is fed by ice-cold mountain streams. Some go into the coldest water. But the visions come to most of us when we float in the water at the place where the cold and hot waters meet. A turbulent place, the water endlessly rocking and swirling, freezing and searing us by turns. The place where the heart of the world and its coldest surface come together. A place where the two hearts of every woman are made one."

"I don't belong here," said Nafai.

"I know," said Luet. "But here is where the Oversoul led us, so here we'll stay."

And then what Nafai feared most. A woman, speaking not far off. "I *told* you I heard a man's voice. It came from *there.*"

Lanterns came near, and many women. Their feet made splatting noises with each step in the hot mud, then sucking noises as they pulled them out again. How far have *I* sunk into the mud? wondered Nafai. Will they have trouble pulling me out? Or will they simply bury me alive right here, letting the mud decide whether to cook me or suffocate me?

"I brought him," said Luet.

"It's Luet," said an old woman. The name was picked up in a whisper and carried back through the gathering crowd.

"The Oversoul led me here. This man isn't like other men. The Oversoul has chosen him."

"The law is the law," said the old woman. "You have taken the responsibility on yourself, but that only moves the punishment from him to you."

Nafai saw how tense Luet looked. He realized: She doesn't understand the Oversoul any better than I do. For all she knows, the Oversoul doesn't care whether she lives or dies, and may be perfectly content to let her pay with her life for my safe passage here tonight.

"Very well," said Luet. "But you must take him to the Private Gate, and help him through the wood."

"You can't tell us what we *must* do, lawbreaker!" cried one woman. But others shushed her. Luet was held in great reverence, Nafai could see, even when she had committed an outrage.

Then the crowd parted, just a little, to let a woman pass, appearing like a ghost from the fog. She was naked, and because she was clean Nafai didn't realize for a moment that she must be a wilder. It was only when she came very close, plucking at Luet's sleeve, that Nafai could see how weathered and dry her skin was, how wrinkled and how gaunt her face.

"You," whispered Luet.

"You," echoed the wilder.

Then the holy woman from the desert turned to the old woman who seemed to be the leader of this band of justicers. "I have already punished her," she said.

"What do you mean?" asked the old woman.

"I am the Oversoul, and I say she has already borne my punishment."

The old woman looked at Luet, full of uncertainty. "Is this true speech, Luet?"

Nafai was amazed. Was their trust in Luet so complete that they would ask her to confirm or deny testimony that might cost her life or save it, depending on her own answer?

Their trust was justified, for Luet's answer contained no special pleading for herself. "This holy woman only slapped my face. How could it be punishment enough for this?"

"I brought her here," said the wilder. "I made her bring this boy. I have shown him great visions, and I will show him more. I will put honor in his seed, and a great nation shall arise. Let no one hinder him in his path through the water and the wood, and as for her, she has borne the mark of my hand upon her face. Who can touch her after I have done with her?"

"Truly this is the voice of the Mother," said the old woman.

"The Mother," whispered some.

"The Oversoul," whispered others.

The holy woman turned to face Luet again, and reached

up and touched one finger to the girl's lips. Luet kissed that finger, gently, and for a moment Nafai ached for the sweetness of it. Then the wilder's expression changed. It was as if some brighter soul had been inside her face, and now it was gone; she looked distracted, vaguely confused. She looked around, recognizing nothing, and then wandered off into the fog.

"Was that your mother?" whispered Nafai.

"No," said Luet. "The mother of my body isn't holy anymore. But in my heart, all such women are my mother."

"Well spoken," said the old woman. "What a fairspoken child she is."

Luet bowed her head. When she lifted her face again, Nafai could see tears on her cheeks. He had no idea what was happening here, or what it meant to Luet; he only knew that for a while his life had been in danger, and then hers, and now the danger had passed. That was enough for him.

The wilder had said that no one should hinder him in his path through the water and the wood. After brief discussion, the women decided that this meant he had to traverse the lake from this point to the other end, from the hot to the cold; he had no idea how they discerned that from the holy woman's few words, but then he had often marveled at how many meanings the priests could wrest from the holy writings of' the men's religion, too. They waited a few minutes until several women called out from the water. Only then did Luet lead him near enough for him to see the lake. Now it was clear where the fog came from—it rose as sheets of steam from the water, or so it appeared to him. Two women in a long low boat were bringing it to shore, the one rowing, the other at the tiller. The bow of the boat was square and low, but since there were no waves upon the lake, and the rowing was smooth, there seemed no danger of the boat taking water at the bow. They drew close, closer to shore, until at last they had run aground.

Still there were several meters of water to cross between the boat and the mud flats where Nafai and Luet stood. The mud was painfully hot now, so that Nafai had to move his feet rather often to keep from burning them. What would it be like to walk through the water?

"Walk steadily," Luet whispered. "The less you splash, the better, so you mustn't run. You'll see that if you just keep going, you're in the boat soon, and the pain passes quickly."

So she had done this before. Very well, if Luet could bear it, so could he. He took a step toward the water. The women gasped.

"No," she said quickly. "In this place, where you're a child and a stranger, you must be led."

Me, a child? Compared to *you*? But then he realized that of course she was right. Whatever their ages might be, this was her place, not his; she was the adult and he the infant here.

She set the pace, brisk but not hurried. The water burned his feet, but it was shallow, and he didn't splash very much, though he was not as graceful and smooth in his movements as Luet. In moments they were at the boat, but it seemed like forever, like a thousand agonizing steps, especially the hesitation as she stepped into the boat. At last she was in, and her hand drew him in after her, and he walked on feet that stung so deep within the skin that he was afraid to look down at them for fear the flesh had been cooked off them. But then he *did* look, and the skin looked normal. Luet used the hem of her skirt to wipe his feet. The oarsman jammed the blade of an oar into the mud under the water and pushed them back, her muscles of her massive arms rippling with the exertion. Nafai faced Luet and clung to her hands as they glided through the water.

It was the strangest journey of Nafai's life, though not a long one. The fog made everything seem magic and unreal.

Huge rocks loomed out of the water, they slipped silently between them, and then the stones were swallowed up as if they had ceased to be. The water grew hotter, and there were places where it bubbled; they steered around those spots. The boat itself was never hot, but the air around them was so hot and wet that soon they were drenched, their clothing clinging to their bodies. Nafai could see for the first time that Luet did, in fact, have a womanly shape to her; not much, but enough that he would never again be able to think of her as nothing but a child. Suddenly he was shy to be sitting there holding her hands, and yet he was more afraid to let go. He needed to be touching her, like a child holding his mother's hand in the darkness.

They drifted on. The air cooled. They passed through narrows, with steep cliffs on either hand, seeming to lean closer together the higher they went, until they were lost in the fog. Nafai wondered if perhaps this was a cave, or, if it wasn't, whether sunlight ever reached the base of this deep rift. Then the cliff walls receded, and the fog thinned just a little. At the same time, the water grew more turbulent. There were waves now, and currents caught the boat and made it want to spin, to yaw from side to side.

The oarsman lifted her oars; the steersman took her hand from the tiller. Luet leaned forward and whispered, "This is the place where the visions come. I told you—where the hot and the cold meet. Here is where we pass through the water in the flesh."

In the flesh apparently meant exactly that. Feeling even more shy to watch Luet undressing than to undress himself, he watched his own hands unfasten his clothing and fold it as Luet did hers and lay the pile in the boat. Trying to somehow watch her without seeing her, Nafai couldn't quite grasp how she managed to slip so noiselessly into the water, then lie motionless on her back. He could see that she made no move to swim, so when he—noisily—dropped himself into the water, he also lay still. The water was surprisingly buoyant. There was no danger of sinking. The silence was deep and powerful; only once did he speak, when he could see that she was drifting away from him.

"No matter," she answered quietly. "Hush."

He hushed. Now he was alone in the fog. The currents turned him—or perhaps they didn't, for in the fog he couldn't tell east from west or anything else having to do with location, except for up and down, and even *that* seemed to matter very little. It was peaceful here, a place where his eyes could see and yet not see, where his ears could hear and yet hear nothing. The current did not let him sleep, however. He could feel the hot and cold wash under him, sometimes very hot, sometimes very cold, so that sometimes he thought, I can't bear this another moment, I'll have to swim or I might die here—and then the current changed again.

He saw no vision. The Oversoul said nothing to him. He listened. He even spoke to the Oversoul, begging to know how he might somehow manage to get the Index that Father had sent him for. If the Oversoul heard him, it gave no sign.

He drifted on the lake forever. Or perhaps it was only a few minutes before he heard the soft touch of the oars in the water. A hand touched his hair, his face, his shoulder, then caught at his arm. He remembered how to turn his head and then he did it, and saw the boat, with Luet, now fully dressed, reaching out to him. It did not occur to him to be shy now; he was only glad to see her, and yet sad to think that he had to rise out of the water. He was not deft at climbing into the boat. He rocked it badly, and spilled water into it.

"Roll in," whispered Luet.

He lay on his side in the water, reached a leg and an arm into the boat, and rolled in. It was easy, almost silent. Luet handed him his clothing, still wet, but now very cold. He drew it on and shivered as the women propelled the boat on into the bone-chilling fog. Luet also shivered, but seemed undisturbed even so.

At last they came to a shoreline, where again a group of women were waiting. Perhaps another boat had gone directly across the lake, not waiting for the ritual of passing through the water in the flesh, or perhaps there was some road for runners bearing messages; whatever the reason, the women waiting for them already knew who they were. There was no need for explanations. Luet again led the way, this time through icy water that made Nafai's bones ache. They reached dry land—a grassy bank this time, instead of mud flats—and women's hands wrapped a dry blanket around him. He saw that Luet also was being warmed.

"The first man to pass through the water," said a woman.

"The man who passes through the waters of women," said another.

Luet explained to him, seeming a little embarrassed. "Famous prophecies," she said. "There are so many of them, it's hard not to fulfil one now and then."

He smiled. He knew that she took the prophecies much more seriously than she pretended. And so did he.

He noticed that no one asked her what had happened on the water; no one asked whether she had seen a vision. But they lingered, waiting, until finally she said, "The Oversoul gave me comfort, and it was enough." They drifted away then, most of them, though a few looked at Nafai until he shook his head.

"We're through the easy part now," she said.

He thought she was joking, but then she led him through the Private Gate, a legendary gap in the red wall that he had only half-believed was real. It was a curving passageway between a pair of massive towers, and instead of city guards, there were only women, watching. On the other side, he knew, lay Trackless Wood. Quickly he learned that it had earned its name. His face was streaked with cuts, and so was hers, and their arms and legs as well, by the time they emerged onto Forest Road.

"That way is Back Gate," said Luet. "And down any of these canyons you'll reach the desert. I don't know where you're going from there."

"That's good enough," said Nafai. "I can find my way."

"Then I've done what the Oversoul sent me to do."

Nafai didn't know what to say. He didn't even know the name for what he was feeling. "I think that I don't know you," said Nafai.

She looked at him, a little perplexed.

"No, that's wrong," Nafai said. "I think that I didn't know you before, even though I thought I knew you, and now that I finally know you, I don't really know you at all."

She smiled. "Those crossing currents do it to you every time," she said. "Tell no one, man or woman, what you did tonight."

"I'm not sure, when I remember it, whether I'll believe that it really happened myself."

"Will we see you again, at Aunt Rasa's house?"

"I don't know," said Nafai. "I only know this: that I don't know how I can get the Index without getting killed, and yet I have to get it."

"Wait until the Oversoul tells you what to do," said Luet, "and then do it."

He nodded. "That's fine, if the Oversoul actually tells me something."

"She will," said Luet. "When there's something to do, she'll tell you."

Then, impulsively, Luet reached out her hand and grasped his again, for just a moment. He remembered again, like an echo in his flesh, how it felt to cling to her on the lake. He was a little embarrassed now, though, and drew his hand away. She had seen him being weak. She had seen him naked.

"See?" she said. "You're forgetting already how it really was."

"No I'm not," he said.

She turned away and headed down the road toward Back Gate. He wanted to call out to her and say, You were right, I *was* forgetting how it really was, I was remembering it through common ordinary eyes, I was remembering it as the boy I was before, but now I remember that it wasn't me being weak or me being naked, or anything else that I should be ashamed of. It was me riding like a great hero out of prophecy across the magical lake, with you as my guide and teacher, and when we shed our clothing it wasn't a man and woman naked together, it was rather two gods out of ancient stories from faraway lands, stripping away their mortal disguises and standing revealed in their glorious immortality, ready to float over the sea of death and emerge unscathed on the other side.

But by the time he thought of all the things he wanted to say, she had disappeared around a bend.

FOURTEEN

ISSIB'S CHAIR

Nafai didn't know what to expect when he got to the rendezvous. All the way across the desert in the starlight, he kept imagining terrible things. What if none of his brothers escaped? *They* didn't have the help of Luet and the women of Basilica. Or what if they *did* escape, but the soldiers followed one of them to their hiding place, and then slaughtered them? When he got there, would he find their mutilated bodies? Or would there be soldiers lying in wait for him, to take him as he made his way down the canyon?

He paused at the top of the canyon, the place where they had stopped to cast lots early that same morning. Oversoul, he said silently, should I go down there?

The answer he got was a picture in his mind—one of Gaballufix's inhuman soldiers walking through the empty nighttime streets of Basilica. He didn't know what sense to make of this. Was the Oversoul telling him that the soldiers were all in the city? Or was Nafai seeing this vision because the Oversoul was telling him that soldiers were waiting for him in the arroyo, and his brain had simply added irrelevant details of the city to the vision?

One thing was inescapable—the sense of urgency he was

getting from the Oversoul. As if there was an opportunity he could not afford to miss. Or a danger he had to avoid.

When the message is so unclear, Nafai said silently, what can I go on except for my own judgment? If my brothers are in trouble I need to know it. I can't abandon them, even if there might be danger to myself. If I'm wrong, take this thought from me.

Then he started down the arroyo. There came no stupor, no distraction. Whatever else the Oversoul was trying to tell him, it certainly didn't mind him going down to the rendezvous with his brothers.

Or else it had given up on him. But no—it had just gone to so much trouble to bring him out of the city, through the Lake of Women, the Oversoul could hardly plan to abandon him now.

It was so dark in the canyon that he ended up stumbling, sliding down, until he finally came to rest on the gravelly shelf where his brothers were supposed to be waiting.

"Nafai."

It was Issib's voice. But Nafai hardly had time to hear it before he felt a harsh blow. Someone's sandal against his face, shoving him down into the rocks.

"Fool!" shouted Elemak. "I wish they'd caught you and killed you, you little bastard!"

Another foot, from the other side, smashing into his nose. And now Mebbekew's voice. "All gone, the whole fortune, everything, because of you!"

"He didn't take it, you fools!" cried Issib. "Gaballufix stole it!"

"You shut up!" shouted Mebbekew, advancing on Issib. Nafai was at last able to see what was happening. Though his face stung from the tiny rocks embedded in the bottoms of their sandals, they really hadn't hurt him seriously. Now, though, he could see that they truly were raging. But why at *Nafai*?

"Rash was the one who betrayed us," said Nafai.

Immediately they turned back to him. "Is that so?" said Elemak. "Didn't I tell you that *I* was going to do all the talking? I could have had the Index for a quarter of what we had, but no, *you* had to—"

"You were giving up!" cried Nafai. "You were walking out!"

Elemak roared in fury, pulled Nafai up by the shirt, lifting him partway from the ground. "Half of bargaining *is* walking out, you fool! Do you think I didn't know what I was doing? I, who have bargained in foreign lands and made great profit on few goods—why couldn't you trust me to know what I was doing? All you've ever bargained for is a few stupid myachiks in the market, little boy."

"I didn't know," said Nafai.

Elemak threw him down onto the ground. Nafai's elbows were scraped, and his head struck the stones hard enough that it hurt him. Without meaning to, he cried out.

"Leave him alone, you coward," said Issib.

"Calling me a coward?" said Elemak.

"Gaballufix was going to have our money no matter what we did. He already had Rash on his side."

"So now you're the expert on what *would* have happened," said Elemak.

"Sitting on your throne, judging us!" cried Mebbekew. "You think Nafai's so innocent, what about *you*! You're the one who got the money out of Father's accounts!"

Nafai stood up. He didn't like the way they were menacing Issib. It was one thing for them to take out their fury on him, but something else again when they seemed about to hurt Issya. "I'm sorry," said Nafai. There was nothing for it but to take the blame, and their anger. "I didn't understand, and I should have kept my mouth shut. I'm sorry."

"What is *sorry*?" said Elemak. "How many times have

you said *sorry* when it was too late to undo the consequences? You never learn anything, Nafai. Father never taught you. His little baby, precious Rasa's little boy, who could do no wrong. Well, it's time you learned the lessons that Father should have taught you years ago."

Elemak pulled one of the rods out of a pack frame leaning against the canyon wall. It was designed to carry heavy loads on the back of a camel; it had some flex to it, and it wasn't terribly heavy, but it was sturdy and long. Nafai knew at once what Elemak intended. "You have no right to touch me," said Nafai.

"No, nobody has the right to touch you," said Mebbekew. "Sacred Nafai, Father's jewel-eyed boy, no one can touch him. He can touch *us,* of course. He can lose our inheritance for us, but no one can touch *him.*"

"It would never have been *your* inheritance, anyway," Nafai said to Mebbekew. "It was always for Elemak." Another thought came into Nafai's mind, thinking of who would have received the inheritance. He knew before he said it that it wasn't the wisest thing to say, when Elemak and Mebbekew were already in a fury. But he said it anyway. "When it comes to what you *lost,* you both deserved to be disinherited anyway, plotting against Father."

"That is a lie," said Mebbekew.

"How stupid do you think I am?" said Nafai. "You might not have known Gaballufix meant to kill Father that morning, but you knew he meant to kill *somebody.* What did Gaballufix promise you, Elemak? The same thing he promised Rash—the Wetchik name and fortune, after Father was discredited and forced out of his place?"

Elemak roared and rushed at him, laying on with the rod. He was so angry that few of the blows actually landed true, but when they did, they were brutal. Nafai had never felt such pain, not even when he prayed, not even when his feet were in the scalding water of the lake. He ended up sprawled face-down in the gravel, with Elemak poised above him, ready to hit him—where, on his back? On his head?

"Please!" Nafai shouted.

"Liar!" roared Elemak.

"Traitor!" Nafai shouted back. He started to get to his knees, to his feet.

The rod fell, knocking him back down to the ground. He's broken my back, thought Nafai. I'll be paralyzed. I'll be like Issib, crippled in a chair for the rest of my life.

It was as if the thought of Issib brought him into action. For as Elemak raised the rod again, Issib's chair swung across in front of him. The chair was turning as it went—it couldn't have been completely under control—and the rod caught Issib across one arm. He screamed in pain, and the chair lost control completely, spinning crazily and reeling back and forth. Its collision avoidance system kept it from banging into the stone walls of the arroyo, but it did bump into Mebbekew as he tried to run out of the way, knocking him down.

"Stay out of the way, Issib!" shouted Elemak.

"You coward!" cried Nafai. "You were *nothing* in front of Gaballufix, but now you can beat a cripple and a fourteen-year-old boy! Very brave!"

Again Elemak turned away from Issib to face Nafai. "You've said too much this time, boy," he said. He wasn't shouting this time. It was a colder, deeper anger. "I'm never going to hear that voice again, do you understand me?"

"That's right, Elya," said Nafai. "You couldn't get Gaballufix to kill Father for you, but at least you can kill *me*. Come ahead, prove what a man you are by killing your little brother."

Nafai had been hoping to shame Elemak into backing off, but he miscalculated. Instead Elemak lost all self-control. As Issib spun by in front of him, Elemak seized an outflung arm and dragged Issib from the chair, throwing him to the ground like a broken toy.

"No!" screamed Nafai.

He rushed for Issib, to help him, but Mebbekew was between them, and when Nafai got near enough, Mebbekew shoved him to the ground. Nafai sprawled at Elemak's feet.

Elemak had dropped his rod. As he reached for it, Mebbekew ran to the pack frame and drew out another one. "Let's have done with him now. And if Issib can't keep his mouth shut, both of them."

Whether Elemak heard or not, Nafai couldn't tell. He only knew that the rod came whistling down, smashing into his shoulder. Elemak's aim still wasn't good, but this much was clear: He was striking high on Nafai's body. He was trying for the head. He meant Nafai to die.

Suddenly there was a blinding light in the canyon. Nafai lifted his head in time to see Elemak whirl around, trying to follow the source of the light. It was Issib's chair.

Only it couldn't be. Issib's chair had a passive switching system. When it was not being told explicitly what to do, it settled down, leveled itself on its legs, and waited for instructions. It had done just that the moment Elemak dragged Issib to the ground.

"What's happening?" asked Mebbekew.

"What's happening?" said a mechanical voice from the chair.

"You must have broken it," said Mebbekew.

"I am not the one who is broken," said the chair. "Faith and trust are broken. Brotherhood is broken. Honor and law and decency are broken. Compassion is broken. But I am not broken."

"Make it stop, Issya," said Mebbekew.

Nafai noticed that Elemak said nothing. He was eyeing

the chair steadily, the rod still in his hands. Then, with a grunt, Elemak rushed forward and swung at the chair with the rod.

Lightning flashed, or so it seemed. Elemak screamed and fell back, as the rod flew into the air. It was burning, the whole length of it.

Carefully, slowly, Mebbekew slid his own rod back down into the pack frame.

"Why were you beating your younger brother with a rod, Elemak?" said the chair. "Why did you plan his death, Mebbekew?"

"Who's doing this?" Mebbekew said.

"Can't you guess, fool?" Issib spoke feebly, from where he lay in the rocks. "Who sent us on this errand in the first place?"

"Father," said Mebbekew.

"The Oversoul," said Elemak.

"Don't you understand yet, that because your younger brother Nafai was willing to hear my voice, I have chosen him to lead you?"

That silenced them both. But Nafai knew that in their hearts, their hatred of him had passed from hot anger to cold hard resentment that would never die. The Oversoul had chosen Nafai to lead them. Nafai, who couldn't even get through negotiations with Gaballufix without messing everything up. Oversoul, why are you doing this to me?

"If you had not betrayed your father, if you had believed in him and obeyed him, I would not have had to choose Nafai ahead of you," said the chair—said the Oversoul. "Now go up into Basilica again, and I will deliver Gaballufix into your hands."

With that, the chair's lights dimmed, and it settled slowly to the ground.

They all waited, dumbly, for a few silent moments. Then Elemak turned to Issib and gently, carefully lifted him back and put him into the chair. "I'm sorry, Issya," he said gently. "I was not in my right mind. I would never hurt you for the world."

Issib said nothing.

"It was Nafai we were angry at," said Mebbekew.

Issib turned to him and, in a whisper, repeated Meb's own words back to him. "Let's have done with him now. And if Issib can't keep his mouth shut, both of them."

Mebbekew was stung. "So I guess you're going to hold that against me forever."

"Shut up, Meb," said Elemak. "Let's think."

"Good idea," said Mebbekew. "Thinking has done us *so* much good up to now."

"It's one thing to see the Oversoul move a chair around," said Elemak. "But Gaballufix has hundreds of soldiers. He can kill each of us fifty times over—where are the soldiers of the Oversoul? What army is going to protect us now?"

Nafai was standing now, listening to them. He could hardly believe what he was hearing. "The Oversoul has just shown you some of its power, and you're still afraid of Gaballufix's soldiers? The Oversoul is stronger than these soldiers. If it doesn't want them to kill us, the soldiers won't kill us."

Elemak and Mebbekew regarded him in silence.

"You were willing to kill me because you didn't like my words," said Nafai. "Are you willing to follow me now, in obeying the words of the Oversoul?"

"How do we know you didn't rig the chair yourself?" said Mebbekew.

"That's right," said Nafai. "I knew before we ever went into the city today that you were going to blame me for everything and try to kill me, and so Issya and I rigged the chair to deliver exactly that speech."

"Don't be stupid, Meb," said Elemak. "We're going to

get killed, but since we've lost everything else, it doesn't really make that much difference to me."

"Just because you're a fatalist doesn't mean *I* want to die," said Mebbekew.

Issib swung his chair forward. "Let's go," he said to Nafai. "It's the Oversoul I'm following, and you as his servant. Let's go."

Nafai nodded, then led the way up the canyon. For a while he heard only the sound of his own footfalls, and the faint whirring of Issib's chair. Then, at last, came the clatter of Elemak and Mebbekew, following him up the arroyo.

FIFTEEN

MURDER

If we are to have any hope at all, thought Nafai, we have to stop trying to come up with our own plans. Gaballufix outmaneuvers us every time.

And now there was even less hope, since Elemak and Mebbekew were deliberately being uncooperative. Why did the Oversoul have to say what it did about Nafai leading them? How could he possibly take command over his own older brothers, who would be far gladder to see him fail than to help him succeed? Issib would be no problem, of course, but it was hard to see how he would be much help, either, even wearing his floats again. He was too conspicuous, too fragile, and too slow, all at once.

Gradually, as they made their way through the desert—Nafai leading, not because he wanted to, but because Elemak refused to help him pick out a path—Nafai came to an inescapable conclusion: He would have a much better chance alone than with his brothers.

Not that he thought his chances were very good on his own. But he would have the Oversoul to help him. And the Oversoul *had* got him out of Basilica before.

But when the Oversoul got him out of Basilica, it was because Luet held his hand. Who would be his Luet now?

She was the seer, as familiar with the Oversoul as Nafai was with his own mother. Luet could feel the Oversoul showing her every step; Nafai only felt the guidance of the Oversoul now and then, so rarely, so confusingly. What was his vision of a bloody-handed soldier walking the streets of Basilica? Was this an enemy he would have to fight? Was it his death? Or his guide? He was so confused, how could he possibly come up with a plan?

He stopped.

The others stopped behind him.

"What now?" asked Mebbekew. "Enlighten us, O great leader anointed by the Oversoul."

Nafai didn't answer. Instead he tried to empty his mind. To relax the knot of fear in his stomach. The Oversoul didn't speak to him the way it spoke to Luet because Luet didn't *expect* herself to come up with a plan. Luet listened. Listened *first,* understood *first.* If Nafai was serious about trying to help the Oversoul, trying to be its hands and feet here on the surface of this world, then he had to stop trying to make up his own foolish plans and give the Oversoul a chance to talk to him.

THEY WERE NEAR Dogtown, which stretched along the roads leading out from the gate known as the Funnel. Till now, he had assumed that he should go around Dogtown and pick his way through some canyon back up to Forest Road and enter Basilica through Back Gate. Now, though, he waited, tested the ideas. He thought of going on, around Dogtown, and his thoughts drifted aimlessly. Then he turned toward the Funnel, and at once felt a rash of confidence. Yes, he thought. The Oversoul is trying to lead me, if I'll just shut up and listen. The way I should have shut up and listened while Elemak was bargaining with Gaballufix this afternoon.

"Oh, good," said Mebbekew. "Let's go up to the second most closely watched gate. Let's go through the ugliest slum, where Gaballufix owns everybody that's for sale, which is everybody that's alive."

"Hush," said Issib.

"Let him talk," said Nafai. "It'll bring Gaballufix's men down on us and get us all killed right now, which is exactly what Mebbekew wants, because as we all die Meb can say, 'See, Nyef, you got us killed!' which will let him die happy."

Mebbekew started toward Nafai, but Elemak stopped him. "We'll be quiet," said Elemak.

Nafai led them on until they came to High Road, which ran from Gate Town to Dogtown. It was lined with houses much of the way, but at this time of night it wasn't too safe, and few people would be abroad on it. Nafai led them to the widest gap between houses on both sides of the road, scanned to the left and right, and then ducked down and scurried across. Then he waited in a dry ditch on the far side of the road, watching for the others.

They didn't come.

They didn't come.

They've decided to abandon me now, thought Nafai. Well, fine.

Then they appeared. Not scurrying, as Nafai had done, but walking. All three of them. Of course, thought Nafai. They had waited to get Issib out of his chair. I should have thought of that.

As they walked across the road, Nafai realized that instead of Issib floating, he was being helped by the other two, his arms flung across their shoulders, his feet being half-dragged. To anyone who didn't know the truth, Issib would look like a drunk being helped home by his friends.

Nor did they walk straight across the road. Rather they angled across, as if they were really going *with* the road, but losing their way in the dark, or being tipped in one direction by the drunk they were helping. Finally they were across, and slipped off into the bushes.

Nafai caught up with them as they were untangling Issib, helping him adjust his floats. "That was so good," he whispered. "A thousand people could have seen you and nobody would have thought twice about it."

"Elemak thought of it," said Issib.

"You should be leading," said Nafai.

"Not according to the Oversoul," said Elemak.

"Issib's chair, you mean," said Mebbekew.

"It was just as well, Nyef, you going across first," said Elemak. "The guards will be looking for four men, one of them floating. Instead they saw three, one of them drunk."

"Where now?" said Issib.

Nafai shrugged. "This way, I guess." He led the way, angling through the empty ground between High Road and the Funnel.

He got distracted. He couldn't think of what to do next. He couldn't think of anything.

"Stop," he said. He thought of leading them onward, and it felt wrong. What felt right was for him to go on alone. "Wait here," he said. "I'm going into the city alone."

"Brilliant," said Mebbekew. "We could have waited back with the camels."

"No," said Nafai. "Please. I need you *here*. I need to be sure I can come out of the gate and find you here."

"How long will you be?" asked Issib.

"I don't know," said Nafai.

"Well, what are you planning to *do*?"

He couldn't very well tell them that he hadn't the faintest idea. "Elemak didn't tell us what *he* was planning," said Nafai.

"Right," said Mebbekew. "Play at being the big man."

"We'll wait," said Elemak. "But if the sun rises with us here, we're out in the open and we'll be caught for sure. You understand that."

"At the first lightening of the sky, if I'm not back, get Issib's chair and head for the camels," said Nafai.

"We'll do it," said Elemak.

"If we feel like it," said Mebbekew.

"We'll feel like it," said Elemak. "Meb will be here, just like the rest of us."

Nafai knew that Elemak still hated him, still felt contempt for him—but he also knew that Elemak would do what he said. That even though Elemak was expecting him to fail, he was also giving him a reasonable chance to succeed. "Thank you," said Nafai.

"Get the Index," said Elemak. "You're the Oversoul's boy, get the Index."

Nafai left them then, walking toward the Funnel. As he got nearer, he could hear the guards talking. There were too many of them—six or seven, not the usual two. Why? He moved to the wall and then slipped closer, to where he could hear fairly well what they were saying.

"It's Gaballufix himself, *I* say," said one guard. "Probably killed Wetchik's boy first, so he couldn't leave the city, and then killed Roptat and put the blame where nobody could answer."

"Sounds like Gaballufix," another answered him. "Pure slime, him and all his men."

Roptat was dead. Nafai felt a thrill of fear. After all the failed plots, it had finally happened—Gaballufix had finally committed a murder. And blamed it on one of Wetchik's boys.

Me, Nafai realized. He blamed it on me. I'm the only one who didn't leave the city through a monitored gate. So as far as the city computer knows, I'm still inside. Of course

Gaballufix would know that. So he seized the chance, had Roptat killed, and put out the word that it was the youngest son of Wetchik who did it.

But the women know. The women know he's lying. He doesn't realize it yet, but by tomorrow every woman in Basilica will know the truth—that when Roptat was being killed I was at the lake with Luet. I don't even have to go inside tonight. Gaballufix will be destroyed by his own stupidity, and we can wait outside the walls and laugh!

Only he couldn't think of waiting outside. The Oversoul didn't want that. The Oversoul didn't care about Gaballufix getting caught in his lies. The Oversoul cared about the Index, and the fall of Gaballufix wouldn't put the Index into Father's hands.

How do I get past the guards? Nafai asked.

In answer, all he felt was his own fear. He knew *that* didn't come from the Oversoul.

So he waited. After a while, the guards' conversation lagged. "Let's do a walk through Dogtown," said one of them. Five of them walked out of the gate, into the darkness of the Dogtown streets. If they had turned back to look at the gate, they would have seen Nafai standing there, leaning against the wall not two meters from the opening. But they didn't look back.

It was time, he knew that; his fear was undiminished, but now there was also a hunger to act, to get moving. The Oversoul? It was hard to know, but he had to do *something*. So, holding his breath, Nafai stepped out into the light falling through the gate.

One guard sat on a stool, leaning against the gate. Asleep, or nearly so. The other was relieving himself against the opposite wall, his back to the opening. Nafai walked quietly through. Neither one stirred from his position until Nafai was away from the gatelight. Then he heard their voices behind him, talking—but not about him, not raising an alarm. This must be how it was for Luet, he thought, the night she came to give us warning. The Oversoul making the guards stupid enough to let her pass as if she were invisible. The way I passed through.

The moon was rising now. The night was more than half spent. The city was asleep, except probably Dolltown and the Inner Market, and even those were bound to be a bit subdued in these days of tension and turmoil, with soldiers patrolling the streets. In this district, though, a fairly safe one, with no night life at all, there was no one out and about. Nafai wasn't sure whether the emptiness of the streets was good or bad. It was good because there'd be fewer people to see him; bad because if he *was* seen, he'd be noticed for sure.

Except tonight the Oversoul was helping him *not* to be noticed. He kept to the shadows, not tempting fate, and once when a troop of soldiers did come by, he ducked into a doorway and they passed him without notice.

This must be the limit to the power of the Oversoul, thought Nafai. With Luet and Father and me, the Oversoul can communicate real ideas. And through a machine— through Issib's chair—but who can guess how much that cost the Oversoul? Reaching directly into the minds of these other people, it can't do much more than distract them, the way it steers people away from forbidden ideas. It can't turn the soldiers out of the road, but it *can* discourage them from noticing the fellow standing in the shadowed doorway, it *can* distract them from wanting to investigate, to see what he's doing. It can't keep the guards at the gate from doing their duty, but it *can* help the dozing guard to dream, so that the sound of Nafai's footsteps are part of the story of the dream, and he doesn't look up.

And even to do that much, the Oversoul must have its whole attention focused on this street tonight, thought Nafai. On this very place. On me.

Where am. I going?

Doesn't matter. Turn off my mind and wander, that's what I have to do. Let the Oversoul lead me by the hand, the way Luet did.

It was hard, though, to empty his mind, to keep himself from recognizing each street he came to, keep himself from thinking of all the people or shops he knew of on that street, and how they might relate to getting the Index. His mind was too involved even now.

And why shouldn't it be? he thought. What am I supposed to do, stop being a sentient being? Become infinitely stupid so that the Oversoul can control me? Is my highest ambition in life to be a *puppet*?

No, came the answer. It was as clear as that night by the stream, in the desert. You're no puppet. You're here because you chose to be here. But now, to hear my voice, you have to empty your mind. Not because I want you to be stupid, but because you have to be able to hear me. Soon enough you'll need all your wits about you again. Fools are no good to me.

Nafai found himself leaning against a wall, gasping for breath, when the voice faded. It was no joke, to have the Oversoul *push* into his thoughts like that. What did our ancestors do to their children, when they changed us so that a computer could put things into our minds like this? In those early days, did all the children hear the voice of the Oversoul as I hear it now? Or was it always a rare thing, to be a hearer of that voice?

Move on. He felt it like a hunger. And he moved. Moved the way he had twice before in the last few weeks—going from street to street almost in a trance, uncertain of where he was, not caring. The way he had been only this afternoon, running from the assassins.

I don't even have a weapon.

The thought brought him up short. Pulled him out of his

walking trance. He wasn't sure where he was. But there, half in shadow, there was a man lying in the street. Nafai came closer, curious. Some drunk, perhaps. Or it might be a victim of tolchocks, or soldiers, or assassins. A victim of Gaballufix.

No. Not a victim at all. It was one of Gaballufix's identical soldiers lying there, and from the stench of piss and alcohol, it wasn't any injury that put him on the ground.

Nafai almost walked away, until it dawned on him that here was the best disguise he could possibly hope for. It would be much simpler to get near Gaballufix if he was wearing one of the holographic soldier costumes—and here lay just such a costume, a gift that was his for the taking.

He knelt beside the man and rolled him over onto his back. It was impossible to *see* the box that controlled the holograph, but by running his hands through the image, he found it by touch, on a belt near the waist. He unfastened it, but even then it wouldn't come away from the man more than a few centimeters.

Oh, that's right, thought Nafai. Elemak said it was a kind of cloak, and the box was just a part of that.

Sure enough, when he pulled the box up the man's body, it slid easily. By half-rolling the man this way and that, he was finally able to get the holographic costume off his arms, out from under his body, and then off the man's head.

Only then did Nafai realize that the Oversoul had provided him with more than a costume. This wasn't a hired thug with a soldier suit. It was Gaballufix himself.

Drunk out of his mind, lying in his own urine and vomit, but nevertheless, without any doubt, it was Gaballufix.

But what could Nafai *do* with this drunk? He certainly didn't have the Index with him. And Nafai harbored no delusion that by dragging him home he could win Gaballufix's undying gratitude.

The bastard must have been out celebrating the death of

Roptat. A murderer lying here in the street, only he'll never be punished for it. In fact, he's trying to get *me* blamed for it. Nafai was filled with anger. He thought of putting his foot on Gaballufix's head and grinding his face down into the vomit-covered street. It would feel so good, so—

Kill him.

The thought was as clear as if someone behind him had spoken it.

No, thought Nafai. I can't do that. I can't kill a man.

Why do you think I brought you here? He's a killer. The law decrees his death.

The law decreed *my* death for seeing the Lake of Women, Nafai answered silently. Yet I was shown mercy.

I brought you to the lake, Nafai. As I brought you here. To do what must be done. You'll never get the Index while he's alive.

I can't kill a man. A helpless man like this—it would be murder.

It would be simple justice.

Not if it came from my hand. I hate him too much. I want him dead. For the humiliation of my family. For stealing my father's title. For taking our fortune. For the beating I got at my brother's hands. For the soldiers and the tolchocks, for the way he has blotted the light of hope out of my city. For the way he turned Rashgallivak, that good man, into a weak and foolish tool. For all those things I want him to die, I want to crush him under my foot. If I kill him now I'm a coward and an assassin, not a justicer.

He tried to kill you. His assassins had you marked for death.

I know it. So it would be private vengeance if I killed him now.

Think of what you're doing, Nafai. Think.

I'm not going to be a murderer.

That's right. You're going to *save* lives. There's only one hope of saving this world from the slaughter that destroyed Earth forty million years ago, and leaving this man alive will obliterate that hope. Should the billion souls of the planet Harmony all die, so that you can keep your hands clean? I tell you that this is not murder, not assassination, but justice. I have tried him and found him guilty. He ordered the death of Roptat, and your death, and your brothers' death, and the death of your father. He plots a war that will kill thousands and bring this city under subjugation. You aren't sparing him out of mercy, Nafai, because only his death will be merciful to the city and the people that you love, only his death will show mercy to the world. You're sparing him out of pure vanity. So that you can look at your hands and find them unstained with blood. I tell you that if you don't kill this man, the blood of millions will be on your head.

No!

Nafai's cry was all the more anguished for being silent, for being contained inside his mind.

The voice inside his head did not relent: The Index opens the deepest library in the world, Nafai. With it, all things are possible to my servants. Without it, I have no clearer voice than the one you hear now, constantly changed and distorted by your own fears and hopes and expectations. Without the Index, I can't help you and you can't help me. My powers will continue to fade, and my law will dwindle among the people, until at last the fires come again, and another world is laid waste. The Index, Nafai. Take from this man what the law requires, and then go and get the Index.

Nafai reached down and took the charged-wire blade that was hooked to Gaballufix's belt.

I don't know how to kill a man with this. It doesn't stab. I can't stab the heart with this.

His head. Take off his head.

I can't. I can't, I can't, I can't.

But Nafai was wrong. He could.

He took Gaballufix by the hair, and stretched out his neck. Gaballufix stirred—was he waking up? Nafai almost let go of his hair then, but Gaballufix quickly dropped back into unconsciousness. Nafai switched on the blade and then laid it lightly against the throat. The blade hummed. A line of blood appeared. Nafai pressed harder, and the line became an open wound, with blood spouting over the blade, sizzling loudly. Too late to stop now, too late. He pressed harder, harder. The blade bit deeper. It resisted at the bone, but Nafai twisted the head away and opened a gap between the vertebrae, and now the blade cut through easily, and the head came free.

Nafai's pants and shirt were covered with blood, as were his hands and face, spattered with it, dripping with it. I have killed a man, and this is his head that I'm holding in my hands. What am I now? Who am I now? How am I better than the man who lies here, torn apart by my hands?

The Index.

He couldn't bear to wear his blood-soaked clothes. Almost in a panic to be rid of them, he tore them off, then wiped his face and hands on the unbloodied back of his shirt. These were the clothes that Luet handed to me when I climbed back into the boat in the beautiful, peaceful place, and now see what I've done with them.

Now, kneeling beside the body, his own clothes cast down into the blood, he realized that because of the downhill slope of the street and the fact that the blood mostly poured upward out of the neck, away from the body, Gaballufix's own clothing was unstained with blood. Vomit and urine, yes, but not blood. Nafai had to wear something. The costume wouldn't be enough—underneath it he'd be cold and barefoot.

When he thought of putting on Gaballufix's clothing, it was abhorrent to him, yes, but he also knew that he had to do it. He dragged the body up away from the blood a little, then undressed it carefully, keeping the blood off. He almost gagged as he pulled the cold wet trousers on, but then he thought contemptuously that a man who could kill the way he had just killed should hardly feel squeamish about wearing another man's piss on his legs. The same with the stench of stomach acid in the shirt and the body armor that Gaballufix had been wearing underneath. Nothing is too horrible for me to do it now, thought Nafai. I'm already lost.

The only thing he could *not* bring himself to do was put the blade at his waist, the way Gaballufix had done. Instead he wiped his fingerprints from the handle and tossed it down near where the head was lying. Then he laughed. There are my clothes, which countless witnesses saw me wearing today. Why should I have tried to conceal myself, if I'm leaving those behind?

And I *am* leaving those behind, thought Nafai. Like my own dead body I'm leaving those. The costume of a child. I'm wearing a man's clothes now. And not just any man. The most vile, monstrous man I know. They fit me.

He pulled the cloak of the soldier costume over his head. He felt no different, but he assumed that the look was there. He stepped away from the body. He could not think of where to go now. He could not think of anything.

He turned back to the body. He had left something behind, he knew that. But all that was left was his old clothing, and the blade. So he picked up the blade again after all, wiped the blood from it with his old clothes, and put it on his belt.

Now he could go on. To Gaballufix's house, of course. He knew that now, very clearly. He could think very clearly now. The trousers froze on his legs, and chafed. The body armor was heavy. It was awkward walking with the charged-wire blade. This is how it felt to be Gaballufix, thought Nafai. Tonight I am Gaballufix.

I have to hurry. Before the body is found.

No. The Oversoul will keep them from noticing the body, for a while at least. Until they are so many people out in the morning that the Oversoul can't influence them all at once. So I do have time.

He came up Fountain Street, but then thought better of it. Instead he walked over to Long Street and came up to Gaballufix's house from behind. In the alley he found the door that he had seen Elemak use, so many—so few—days before. Would it be locked?

It was. What now? Inside there would be someone waiting. Keeping guard. How could he, in the guise of a common soldier, demand entrance at this hour? What if they made him switch off the costume once he got inside? They'd recognize him at once. Worse, they'd recognize Gaballufix's clothing and they'd know that there was only one way he could come in wearing their master's clothes.

No, *two* ways.

Gaballufix must have come home drunk before.

Nafai tried, silently at first, to think of how Gaballufix's voice sounded. Husky and coarse. Rasping in the throat. Nafai could get it generally right, he was sure—and it didn't have to be too perfect, because Gaballufix was *drunk,* of course—he reeked of it—and so his voice could be slurred and out of control, and he could stagger and fall and—

"Open up, open the door!" he bawled.

That was awful, that didn't sound like Gaballufix at all.

"Open the door you idiots, it's me!"

Better. Better. And besides, the Oversoul will nudge them a little, will encourage them to think of other things besides the fact that Gaballufix isn't really sounding like himself tonight.

The door opened a crack. Nafai immediately shoved it open and pushed his way through. "Locking me out of my own house, ought to send you home in a box, ought to send you back to your papa in pieces." Nafai had no idea how Gaballufix usually talked, but he guessed at general surliness and threats, especially when he was drunk. Nafai hadn't seen many drunks. Only a few times on the street, and then fairly often in the theatres, but those were actors *playing* drunk.

He thought: I'm an actor, after all. I thought that was what I might end up being, and here I am.

"Let me help you, sir," said the man. Nafai didn't look at him. Instead he deliberately stumbled and fell to his knees, then doubled over. "Going to puke, I think," he rasped. Then he touched the box at his belt and turned off the costume. Just for a moment. Just long enough that whoever else was in the room could see Gaballufix's clothing, while Nafai's face and hair were out of sight as he bent over. Then he turned the costume back on. He tried to produce the sound of dry heaves, and was so successful that he gagged and some bile and acid *did* come into his throat.

"What do you want, sir?" said the man.

"Who keeps the Index!" Nafai bawled. "Everybody wants the Index today—well now *I* want it."

"Zdorab," said the man.

"Get him."

"He's asleep, he . . ."

Nafai lurched to his feet. "When I'm off my ass in this house, *nobody* sleeps!"

"I'll get him, sir, I'm sorry, I just thought . . ."

Nafai swung clumsily at him. The man shied away, looking horrified. Am I carrying this too far? There was no way to guess. The man sidled along the wall and then ducked through a door. Nafai had no idea whether he would come back with soldiers to arrest him.

He came back with Zdorab. Or at least Nafai assumed it was Zdorab. But he had to be sure, didn't he? So he leaned close to the man and breathed nastily in his face. "Are you Zdorab?" Let the man imagine that Gaballufix was so drunk he couldn't see straight.

"Yes, sir," said the man. He seemed frightened. Good.

"My Index. Where is it?"

"Which one?"

"The one those bastards wanted—Wetchik's boys—*the* Index, by the Oversoul!"

"The *Palwashantu* Index?"

"Where did you put it, you rogue?"

"In the vault," said Zdorab. "I didn't know you wanted it accessible. You've never used it before, and so I thought—"

"I can look at it if I want!"

Stop talking so much, he told himself. The more you say, the harder it will be for the Oversoul to keep this man from doubting my voice.

Zdorab led the way down a corridor. Nafai made it a point to bump into a wall now and then. When he did it on the side where Elemak's rod had fallen most heavily, it sent a stab of pain through his side, from shoulder to hip. He grunted with the pain—but figured that it would only make his performance more believable.

As they moved on through the lowest floor of the house, fear began to overtake him again. What if he had to provide a positive identification to open the vault? A retina scan? A thumbprint?

But the vault door stood open. Had the Oversoul influenced someone to forget to close it? Or had it all come down to chance? Am I fortune's fool, Nafai wondered, or merely the Oversoul's puppet? Or, by some slim chance, am I freely choosing at least some portion of my own path through this night's work?

He didn't even know which answer he wanted. If he was freely choosing for himself, then he had freely chosen to kill a man lying helpless in the street. Much better to believe that the Oversoul had compelled him or tricked him into doing it. Or that something in his genes or his upbringing had forced him to that action. Much better to believe that there was no other possible choice, rather than to torment himself with wondering whether it might not have been enough to steal Gaballufix's clothing, without having to kill him first. Being responsible for what he did with his opportunities was more of a burden than Nafai really wanted to bear.

Zdorab walked into the vault. Nafai followed, then stopped when he saw a large table where the entire fortune that Gaballufix had stolen from them that afternoon was arranged in neat stacks.

"As you can see, sir, the assay is nearly done," said Zdorab as he wandered off among the shelves. "I have kept everything clean and organized there. It's very kind of you to visit."

Is he stalling me here in the vault, Nafai wondered, waiting till help can arrive?

Zdorab emerged from the shelves at the back of the room. He was a smallish man, considerably shorter than Nafai, and he was already losing his hair though he couldn't have been more than thirty. A comical man, really—yet if he guessed at what was really happening, he might cost Nafai his life.

"Is this it?" asked Zdorab.

Nafai hadn't the faintest idea what it was *supposed* to look like, of course. He had seen many indexes, but most of them were small freestanding computers with wireless access to a major library. This one had nothing that Nafai could recognize as a display. What Zdorab held was a brass-colored metal ball, about twenty-five centimeters in diameter, flattened a little at the top and the bottom. "Let me see," Nafai growled.

Zdorab seemed reluctant to part with it. For a moment, Nafai felt a wave of panic sweep over him. He doesn't want to give it to me because he knows who I really am.

Then Zdorab revealed his true concern. "Sir, you said we must always keep it very clean."

He was worried about how dirty Gaballufix might have got himself under his soldier costume. After all, he seemed falling-down drunk and smelled of liquor and worse. His hands could be covered with anything.

"You're right," said Nafai. *"You* carry it."

"If you wish, sir," said Zdorab.

"That's the one, isn't it?" said Nafai. He had to be sure—he could only hope that the drunk act was convincing enough that stupid questions wouldn't arouse suspicion.

"It's the Palwashantu Index, if that's what you mean. I just wondered if that's the one you really wanted. You've never asked for it before."

So Gaballufix hadn't even brought it out of the vault—he never, not for one moment, intended to give it to them, no matter how Elemak bargained or what they paid. It made Nafai feel a little better. There had been no missed opportunity. Every script would have led to the same ending.

"Where are we taking it?" asked Zdorab.

Excellent question, thought Nafai. I can't very well tell him that we're giving it to Wetchik's sons, who are waiting in the darkness outside the Funnel.

"Got to show it to the clan council."

"At this time of night?"

"Yes at this time of night! Interrupted me, the bastards. Having a party and they had to see the *Index* because they got some whim that maybe it got itself stolen by Wetchik's murdering lying thieving sons."

Zdorab coughed, ducked his head, and hurried on, leading Nafai down the corridor.

So Zdorab didn't like hearing Gaballufix lay such epithets on Wetchik's sons. Very interesting. But not so interesting that Nafai intended to take Zdorab into his confidence. "Slow down, you miserable little dwarf!" called Nafai.

"Yes sir," said Zdorab. He slowed down, and Nafai lurched after him.

They came to the door, where the same man stood on guard. The man looked at Zdorab, a question in his eyes. Here's the moment, thought Nafai. A signal passing between them.

"Please open the door for Master Gaballufix," said Zdorab. "We're going out again."

The only signal, Nafai realized, was that the doorkeeper was asking if this man in holographic soldier costume was Gaballufix, and Zdorab had answered by assuring him that the drunken lout inside the costume was the same one who had come in only a few moments before.

"Making merry, sir?" asked the doorkeeper.

"The council seems to be asserting itself tonight," said Zdorab.

"Want any escort?" asked the doorkeeper. "We've only got a couple of dozen close enough to lay hands on, but we can get some in from Dogtown in a few minutes, if you want them."

"No," barked Nafai.

"I just thought—the council might need a reminder, like last time—"

"They remember!" said Nafai. He wondered what "last time" was.

Zdorab led the way through the door. Nafai stumbled outside. The door latched behind them.

As they walked along the near-empty streets of Basilica,

it began to dawn on Nafai what he had just accomplished. After all the day's failures, he had just come out of Gaballufix's house *with* the Index. Or at least with a man who was carrying the Index.

"The air is very invigorating, isn't it, sir," said Zdorab.

"Mm," said Nafai.

"I mean—your head seems to have cleared considerably."

It dawned on Nafai that he had forgotten to continue his drunk act. Too late to put it on again *now,* though—it would be stupid to stumble immediately after Zdorab had commented on how much less drunk he seemed. So instead, Nafai stopped, turned toward Zdorab, and glared. Not that Zdorab could see his facial expression. No, instead the man would have to imagine it.

Apparently Zdorab had a very good imagination. He immediately seemed to cower inside himself. "Not that your head wasn't clear to begin with. I mean, all along. That is, you're head is *always* clear, sir. And you've got a meeting with the clan council tonight, so that's a good thing, isn't it!"

Wonderful, thought Nafai.

"Where *are* they meeting tonight?" asked Zdorab.

Nafai hadn't the faintest idea. He only knew that he had to meet his brothers outside the Funnel. "Where do you *think*!" he growled.

"Well, I mean, it's just—you seemed to be headed toward the Funnel, and . . . which isn't to say they couldn't hold a meeting out in Dogtown, it's just that usually they . . . not that anybody ever brings me along. I mean, for all I know you might hold the meetings in a different place every night, I just heard somebody talk about the clan council meeting at your mother's house near Back Gate, but that was just—it could have been just the once."

Nafai walked on, letting Zdorab talk himself into ever greater dread.

"Oh no!" cried Zdorab.

Nafai stopped. If I take the Index and run for the gate, can I make it before he can raise an alarm?

"I left the vault open," said Zdorab. "I was so concerned about the Index . . . Please forgive me, sir. I know that the door is supposed to be open only when I'm there, and I . . . goodness, I just realized that I left it open before, too, when I came to meet you at the back door. What's got into me? I'll understand if I lose my job over this, sir. I've never left the vault door unattended. Should I go back and lock it? All that treasure there—how can you be sure that none of the servants will . . . Sir, I can rush back and still rejoin you here in only a few minutes, I'm very fleet of foot, I assure you."

This was the perfect opportunity to rid himself of Zdorab—take the Index, let the man go, and then be out the Funnel before he can return. But what if this was just a subterfuge? What if Zdorab was trying to break free of him in order to give warning to Gaballufix's soldiers that an impostor in a holographic costume was making off with the Index? He couldn't afford to let Zdorab go, not now. Not until he was safely outside the gate.

"Stay with me," said Nafai. He winced at how little his voice sounded like Gaballufix's now. Had Zdorab's eyebrows risen in surprise when Nafai spoke? Could he be wondering even now about the voice? Move on, thought Nafai. Keep moving, and say nothing. He hurried the pace. Zdorab, with his shorter legs, was jogging now to keep up.

"I've never been to a meeting like this, sir," said Zdorab. He was panting with the exertion now. "I won't have to say anything, will I? I mean, I'm not a member of the council. Oh, what am I saying! They probably won't let me into the actual meeting, anyway. I'll just wait for you outside. Please forgive me for being so nervous, I've just never . . . I spend my time in the vault and the library, of course, doing accounts and so on, you've got to realize that I just don't get out and about much, and since I live alone there's not much conversation, so most of what I know about politics is what I overhear. I know that *you're* very much involved, of course. All the people in the house are very proud to be working for such a famous man. Dangerous, though, isn't it—with Roptat murdered tonight. Aren't you just the tiniest bit afraid for yourself?"

Is he really such a fool as this? thought Nafai. Or is he, in fact, suspicious that Gaballufix might be Roptat's murderer, and this is his clumsy way of trying to extract information?

In any event, Nafai doubted Gaballufix would answer such questions, so he held his tongue. And there, at last, was the gate.

The guards were very much alert. Of course—Zdorab would be too curious if they were so strangely inattentive this time. Nafai cursed himself for having brought Zdorab along. He should have got rid of the man when he had a chance.

The guards got into position, holding out the thumb-screens. They looked belligerent, too—Nafai's soldier costume made him an enemy, or at least a rival. The thumb-screen would silently reveal his true identity, of course, but since Nafai was now under suspicion of having murdered Roptat, it wouldn't be much help.

As he stood there, frozen in indecision, Zdorab intervened. "You aren't actually going to insist that my master lay his thumb on your petty little screen, are you!" he blustered. Then he pressed his own thumb onto the scanner. "There, does that tell you who I am? The treasurer of Lord Gaballufix!"

"The law is, everybody lays his thumb here," said the guard. But he now looked a great deal less certain of himself. It was one thing to trade snubs with Gaballufix's soldiers, and quite another to face down the man himself. "Sorry, sir, but it's my job if I don't require it."

Nafai still didn't move.

"This is harassment," said Zdorab. "That's what it is." He kept glancing at Nafai, but of course he could read no approval or disapproval in the emotionless holographic mask.

There's murderers out tonight," said the guard, apologetically. "You yourself reported the Wetchik's youngest son killed Roptat, and so we have to check everybody."

Nafai strode forward and reached out his hand toward the thumbscreen. As he did, however, he leaned his head close to the guard and said, quietly, "And what if the man who reported such an absurd lie was the murderer himself?"

The guard recoiled, surprised at the voice and hardly making sense of the words. Then he looked down at the screen and saw the name that the city computer showed there. He paused a moment, thinking.

Oversoul, give this man wit. Let him understand the truth, and act on it.

"Thank you for submitting to the law, Lord Gaballufix," said the guard. He pressed the clear button, and Nafai saw his name disappear. No one else could have seen it.

Without a backward glance, Nafai strode out through the gate. He heard Zdorab pattering along behind him. "Did I do right, sir?" asked Zdorab. "I mean, it seemed as though you were reluctant to give your thumb to it, and so I . . . Where are we going? Isn't it a little dark to be cutting through the brush here? Couldn't we stick to the road, Lord Gaballufix? Of course, there's a moon, so it's not *that* dark, but—"

With Zdorab's babbling, it was impossible to be subtle as they moved straight toward the spot where Nafai had left his brothers to wait for him. And now Zdorab had loudly called him by the name Gaballufix. It was hardly a surprise when Nafai saw a flurry of movement and heard footsteps, running away. Of course—they thought Nafai had been caught, that he had betrayed them, that Gaballufix had come to kill them. What could they see, except the costume?

Nafai fumbled with the controls. How could he tell whether it was off or not? Finally he yanked the costume off over his head, and then called out as loudly as he dared, and in his own voice. "Elemak! Issya! Meb! It's me—don't run!"

They stopped running.

"Nafai!" said Meb.

"In Gaballufix's clothing!" said Elemak.

"You did it!" cried Issib, laughing.

A tiny screech just behind him reminded Nafai that this sweet reunion scene would seem just a little less than happy to poor Zdorab, who had just discovered that he had been following the very man accused of murdering Roptat only a few hours before, and who had almost certainly done something quite similar to Gaballufix.

Nafai turned in time to see Zdorab turning tail and starting to run. "I'm very fleet of foot," Zdorab had said earlier, but now Nafai learned that it wasn't true. He outran the man in half a dozen steps, knocked him down, and wrestled with him on the stony ground for only a few moments before he had him pinned, with his hand over the poor man's mouth. The guards were no more than fifty meters away. No doubt the Oversoul had kept them from paying attention to the shouting that had just gone on, but there were limits to the Oversoul's ability to make people stupid.

"Listen to me," Nafai whispered fiercely. "If you do what I say, Zdorab, I won't kill you. Do you understand?"

Under his hand, Nafai felt the head nod up and down.

"I give you my oath by the Oversoul that I did not murder Roptat. Your master Gaballufix caused Roptat's death and gave orders for me and my brothers to be killed. *He* was the murderer, but now I've killed Gaballufix and that was justice. Do you understand me? I'm not one who kills for pleasure. I don't want to kill *you*. Will you be silent if I uncover your mouth?"

Again the nod. Nafai uncovered his mouth.

"I'm glad you don't want to kill me," Zdorab whispered. "I don't want to be dead."

"Do you believe my words?" Nafai asked.

"Would you believe my answer?" asked Zdorab. "I think we're in one of those situations where people will say pretty much whatever they think the other person wants to hear, wouldn't you say?"

He had a point. "Zdorab, I can't let you go back into the city, do you understand me? I guess what it comes down to is this—if you really are one of Gaballufix's men, one of the louts that he hires to do his dirty work in Basilica, then I can't trust anything you say and I might as well kill you now and have done. But I don't think that's who you are. I think you're a librarian, a record-keeper, a *clerk* who had no idea what working for Gaballufix entailed."

"I kept seeing things but nobody else seemed to think they were strange and no one would ever answer my questions so I kept to myself and held my tongue. Mostly."

"We're going out into the desert. If you go with us, and stay with us—if you give me your word by the Oversoul—then you'll be a free man, part of our household, the equal of any other. We don't want you for a servant; we'll only have you as a friend."

"Of course I'll give my oath. But how will you know whether to believe me?"

"Swear by the Oversoul, my friend Zdorab, and I'll know."

"By the Oversoul, then, I swear to stay with you and be your loyal friend forever. On the condition that you don't kill me. Though I guess if you killed me then the rest of it would be moot, wouldn't it."

Nafai could see that his brothers were now gathered around. They had heard the oath, of course, and had their own opinions. "Kill him," Meb said. "He's one of Gaballufix's men, you can't believe them."

"I'll do it, if it must be done," said Elemak.

"How can we know?" asked Issib.

But Nafai didn't hear them. He was listening for the Oversoul, and the answer was clear. Trust the man.

"I accept your oath," said Nafai. "And I swear by the Oversoul that neither I nor anyone in my family will harm you, as long as you keep your oath. All of you—swear it."

"This is absurd!" said Mebbekew. "You're putting us all at risk."

"For this night the Oversoul gave me the command," said Nafai, "and you promised to obey. I came out of the city with the Index, didn't I? And Gaballufix is dead. Swear to this man!"

They took the oath, all of them.

"Now," said Nafai to Zdorab, "give me the Index."

"I can't," said Zdorab.

"See?" said Meb.

"I mean—when you knocked me down, I dropped it."

"Wonderful," said Elemak. "All this way to get this precious Index, and now we're going to be picking up pieces of it all over the desert."

Issib found it, though, only a meter away, and when Elemak picked it up, it seemed unharmed. By moonlight, at least, there didn't seem to be even a scratch.

Mebbekew also took a close look at it, handled it, hefted it. "Just a ball. A metal ball."

"It doesn't even *look* like an index," said Issib.

Nafai reached out his hands and took the thing from Mebbekew. Immediately it began to glow. Lights appeared under it.

"You've got it upside down, I think," said Zdorab.

Nafai turned it over. In the air over the ball, a holographic arrow pointed southwest. Above the arrow were several words, but in a language Nafai didn't understand.

"That's ancient Puckyi," said Issib. "Nobody speaks it now."

The letters changed. It was a single word. *Chair*.

"The arrow," said Issib. "It's pointing toward where I left my chair."

"Let me see that," said Elemak.

Nafai handed him the Index. The moment it left Nafai's hands, the display disappeared.

Nafai reached out to take the Index back. Elemak looked at him steadily, his eyes like ice, and then he handed Nafai the metal ball. When Nafai touched it again, the display reappeared. Nafai turned to Zdorab. "What does this mean?"

"I don't know," said Zdorab. "It never did anything before. I thought it was broken."

"Let me try," said Issib.

"Please, no," said Nafai. "Let's wrap it up and carry it home to Father without looking at it again. Elemak knows the way. He should lead us."

"Right," said Mebbekew.

"Whatever," said Issib.

"Which one's Elemak?" asked Zdorab.

Elemak strode away toward High Road, toward the place where Issib's chair was waiting for them. By the time they got back to the camels, the sky was just beginning to lighten in the east. Nafai wrapped the Index and gave it to Elemak to stow it on a pack frame.

"*You* should give it to Father," Nafai said.

Elemak reached out and took a pinch of Nafai's—no, Gaballufix's—shirt between his thumb and forefinger. He leaned close and spoke softly. "Don't patronize me, Nafai. I see the way of things, and I'll tell you now. I won't be given power or honor or anything as a gift from *you*. Whatever I have I'll have because it's mine by right. Do you understand me?"

Nafai nodded. Elemak let go of his shirt and walked away. Only then did Nafai understand that there would be no healing this breach between him and his eldest brother. The Index had come to life under Nafai's hands. It had lain inert in Elemak's. The Oversoul had spoken, and Elemak would never forgive the message that it gave.

SIXTEEN

THE INDEX OF THE OVERSOUL

Nafai and Father sat and Issib lay on a rug in Father's tent. The Index rested on the rug between them. Nafai touched the Index with his fingers. Father also reached out and touched it with one hand. Then, with the other, he lifted Issib's arm and brought his hand near, until it touched. With the three of them in contact with it at the same time, the Index spoke.

"Awake, after all this time," said the Index. It was a whisper. Nafai wasn't altogether sure whether he was hearing it with his ears, or whether his mind was transforming the ambient noises—the desert breeze, their own breathing—into a voice.

"You came to us at great cost," said Father.

"I waited for a long time to have this voice again," answered the Index.

It wasn't the Index speaking. Nafai knew that now. "This is the voice of the Oversoul."

"Yes," said the whisper.

"If this contains your voice," said Father, "why is it called an index?"

The answer came only after a long hesitation. This is the index to *me*" it finally said.

The Index of the Oversoul. An index was a tool created to make it easier for people to find their way through the labyrinthine memory of a complex computer. The Oversoul was the greatest of all computers, and this was the tool that would let Nafai and Issib and Father begin, at last, to understand it. "Now that we have the Index," said Nafai, "can you explain to us who you—*what* you are?" Nafai asked.

Again the pause, and then the whispering: "I am the Memory of Earth. I was never meant to last so long. I am weakening, and must return to the one who is wiser than I, who will tell me what to do to save this unharmonious world called Harmony. I have chosen your family to carry me back to the Keeper of Earth."

"*That* is where you're leading us?"

"The world that was buried in ice and hidden in smoke is surely alive and awake now. The Keeper who drove humankind from the planet they destroyed will surely not turn his face away from you now. Follow me, children of Earth, and I will take you back to your ancient home."

Nafai looked from Father to Issib and back again. "Do you realize what that means?" he said.

"A long journey," said Father, wearily.

"Long!" cried Nafai. "So long that it takes *light* a hundred years to reach us!"

"What are you talking about?" said Issib. "You'd think the Oversoul had promised to take us to another planet."

Issib's words hung in the air like music out of tune. Nafai sat there, stunned. Of *course* the Oversoul had promised to take them to another planet. Those were its plain words. Except that this wasn't what Issib had heard. Or Father. Obviously, then, the Index did not make literal sounds, and they were in fact hearing with their minds, not their ears.

"What did *you* think the Oversoul said?" Nafai asked.

"That he was going to lead us to a beautiful land," said

Father. "A good place, where crops would grow, and orchards thrive. A place where our children could be free and good, without the evils of Basilica."

"But *where*?" asked Nafai. "Where did it say that this beautiful land would be?"

"Nafai, you must learn to be more patient and trusting," said Father. "The Oversoul will lead us one step at a time, and then, one day, one of those steps will be the last one in our journey, and we'll be home."

"It won't be a city," said Issib, "but it will be a place where I can use my floats again."

Nafai was deeply disappointed. He knew what he had heard, but he also knew that Father and Issib had not heard it. Why not? Either it meant that they simply couldn't comprehend the voice of the Oversoul as clearly as he could, or it meant that the Oversoul had given them a different message. Either way, he couldn't force his own understanding on them.

"What did *you* hear?" asked Father. "Was there more?"

"Nothing important for now," said Nafai. "What really matters is knowing that we're not going to wait around for Basilica to take us back. We're not exiles now, we're expatriates. Emigrants. Basilica is not our city anymore."

Father sighed. "And to think I was just about to retire and turn the business over to Elya. I didn't want to journey anymore! Now I'm about to take the longest journey of my life, I fear."

Nafai reached out and took the Index between his hands and drew it close. It trembled in his grasp. "As for you, my strange little Index, I hope you turn out to be worth all the trouble that was taken to get you. The price that was paid."

"Such a fortune," said Issib. "I never knew we were so rich until the day we weren't."

"We're richer than ever now," said Father. "We have a whole land promised to us, with no city or clan or enemy to take it away. And the Index to the Oversoul is here to lead the way."

Nafai hardly heard them. He was thinking of the blood that he had shed, of how it stained his clothing and his skin. I didn't want to do it, he thought, and it was simple justice, to take the life of a murderer. When Elemak thought he might have killed a man, from far off, with a pulse, he bragged about it. But I killed him close, under my own hand, as he lay drunken and helpless on the street. I did it, not in fear for my own life, and not to protect a caravan, but in cold blood, without anger. Because the Oversoul told me that it was right. And because I believed in my own heart that it was necessary.

But I also hated him. Will I ever be sure that I didn't do it because of that hatred, that longing for vengeance? I fear that I will always suspect that I am an assassin in my heart.

I can live with that, though. I can sleep tonight. With time I'm sure that the pain of it will even fade. It's the price of the thing that I agreed to be: a servant of the Oversoul. I'm not my own man anymore. I'm the man the Oversoul has chosen to make of me. I hope I like at least a small part of what I've become, when at last the Oversoul is through with me.

He slept that night and dreamed. Not of murder. Not of Gaballufix's head, nor of the blood on his own clothes. Instead he dreamed of drifting on a sea whose currents ran hot and cold, as fog drifted endlessly in front of his face. And then, out of this lost and mysterious and peaceful place, hands searched across his face, his shoulder, and then took hold of his arm and pulled him close.

I'm not the first one here, he realized as he woke from the dream. I'm not alone in this place, this kingdom of the Oversoul. Others have been here before me, and are with me now, and *will* be with me through all that is to come.

THE CALL
of EARTH

To

Dave Dollahite

Teacher and dreamer

Husband and father

Friend and fellow citizen

ACKNOWLEDGMENTS

I owe thanks to many for easing my way through the writing of this book. Clark and Kathy Kidd provided me with a refuge during the last week of the writing of this novel; half of it came forth under their roof, and with their good company.

A writer's life can so easily slip into undisciplined sloth; my body has long reflected the physical indolence of a mentally exhausting career. This book owes much to the fact that during the writing of it I woke my body up again: I owe thanks to Clark Kidd and Scott Allen for sweating with me as I tortured a new bicycle into submission on the roads and bikepaths of northern Virginia and on the streets and strands of North Myrtle Beach.

Several readers helped me reconcile this book with its predecessor, reading scraps of manuscript as they emerged from my printer, most notably Kathy Kidd and Russell Card. My editor on this series is Beth Meacham; my publisher is Tom Doherty; it is no accident that I have done the best work of my life so far for them. And my agent, Barbara Bova, has been a constant help and wise counselor during a turbulent time.

This novel was supposed to be easy, but it turned out not to be. Moozh complicated everything, and yet made it all worth doing. During the long struggle to make Moozh and the rest of the story fit together, I imagine that I was barely tolerable to live with, but still my wife, Kristine, and our children, Geoffrey, Emily, and Charlie Ben, were willing to keep me around; it is the joy of my life to find them always around me when I surface from immersion in my work. And, as always, Kristine has been my first and best editor and audience, reading my work with a sharp and trustworthy eye, then telling me what I have written so I can keep or alter it as need be.

NICKNAMES

Most names have diminutive or familiar forms. Thus Gaballufix's near kin, close friends, current mate, and former mates could call him Gab. Other nicknames are listed here. (Again, because these names are so unfamiliar, names of female characters are set off in italics):

Dhelembuvex—Dhel

Dol—*Dolya*

Drotik—Dorya

Eiadh—*Edhya*

Elemak—Elya

Hosni—*Hosya*

Hushidh—*Shuya*

Issib—Issya

Kokor—*Kyoka*

Luet—*Lutya*

Mebbekew—Meb

Nafai—Nyef

Rasa—(no diminutive)

Rashgallivak—Rash

Roptat—Rop

Sevet—*Sevya*

Shedemei—*Shedya*

Smelost—Smelya

Volemak—Volya

Wetchik—(no diminutive; Volemak's family title)

Zdorab—Zodya

NOTES ON NAMES

For the purpose of reading this story, it hardly matters whether the reader pronounces the names of the characters correctly. But for those who might be interested, here is some information concerning the pronunciation of names.

The rules of vowel formation in the language of Basilica require that in most words, at least one vowel be pronounced with a leading *y* sound. With names, it can be almost any vowel, and it can legitimately be changed at the speaker's preference. Thus the name Gaballufix could be pronounced *Gyah*-BAH-loo-fix or Gah-BAH-*lyoo*-fix; it happens that Gaballufix himself preferred to pronounce it Gah-BYAH-loo-fix, and of course most people followed that usage.

Dhelembuvex
  [thel-EM-byoo-vex]
Dol [DYOHL]
Drotik [DROHT-vik]
Eiadh [A-yahth]
Elemak [El-yeh-mahk]
Hosni [HYOZ-nee]
Hushidh [HYOO-sheeth]
Issib [IS-yib]

Kokor [KYOH-kor]
Luet [LYOO-et]
Mebbekew
  [MEB-bek-kyoo]
Nafai [NYAH-fie]
Rasa [RAHZ-yah]
Rashgallivak
  [rahsh-GYAH-lih-vahk]
Roptat [ROPE-tyaht]

Sevet [SEV-yet]

Shedemei
  [SHYED-eh-may]

Smelost [SMYE-lost]

Truzhnisha
  [troozh-NYEE-shah]

Volemak
  [VOHL-yeh-mak]

Wetchik [WET-chyick]

Zdorab [ZDOR-yab]

PROLOGUE

The master computer of the planet Harmony was not designed to interfere so directly in human affairs. It was deeply disturbed by the fact that it had just provoked young Nafai to murder Gaballufix. But how could the master computer return to Earth without the Index? And how could Nafai have got the Index without killing Gaballufix? There was no other way.

Or was there? I am old, said the master computer to itself. Forty million years old, a machine designed to last for nowhere near this long. How can I be sure that my judgment is right? And yet I caused a man to die for my judgment, and young Nafai is suffering the pangs of guilt because of what I urged him to do. All of this in order to carry the Index back to Zvezdakroog, so I could return to Earth.

If only I could speak to the Keeper of Earth. If only the Keeper could tell me what to do now. Then I could act with confidence. Then I would not have to doubt my every action, to wonder if everything I do might not be the product of my own decay.

The master computer needed so badly to speak to the Keeper; yet it could not speak to the Keeper except by returning to Earth. It was so frustratingly circular.

The master computer could not act wisely without the help of the Keeper; it had to act wisely in order to get to the Keeper.

What now? What now? I needed wisdom, and yet who can guide me? I have vastly more knowledge than any human can hope to master, and yet I have no minds but human minds to counsel me.

Was it possible that human minds might be enough? No computer could ever be so brilliantly disorganized as the human brain. Humans made the most astonishing decisions based on mere fragments of data, because their brain recombined them in strange and truthful ways. It was possible, surely, that some useful wisdom might be extracted from them.

Then again, maybe not. But it was worth trying, wasn't it?

The master computer reached out through its satellites and sent images into the minds of those humans most receptive to its transmissions. These images from the master computer began to move through their memories, forcing their minds to deal with them, to fit them together, to make sense of them. To make from them the strange and powerful stories they called dreams. Perhaps in the next few days, the next few weeks, their dreams would bring to the surface some connection or understanding that the master computer could use to help it decide how to bring the best of them out of the planet Harmony and take them home to Earth.

All these years I have taught and guided, shaped and protected them. Now, in the end of my life, are they ready to teach and guide, shape and protect *me*? So unlikely. So unlikely. I will surely be forced to decide it all myself. And when I do, I will surely do it wrong. Perhaps I should not act at all. Perhaps I should not act at all. I should not act. Will not. Must.

Wait.

Wait.

Again, wait. . . .

ONE

BETRAYAL

THE DREAM OF THE GENERAL

General Vozmuzhalnoy Vozmozhno awoke from his dream, sweating, moaning. He opened his eyes, reached out with his hand, clutching. A hand caught his own, held it.

A man's hand. It was General Plodorodnuy. His most trusted lieutenant. His dearest friend. His inmost heart.

"You were dreaming, Moozh." It was the nickname that only Plod dared to use to his face.

"Yes, I was." Vozmuzhalnoy—Moozh—shuddered at the memory. "Such a dream."

"Was it portentous?"

"Horrifying, anyway."

"Tell me. I have a way with dreams."

"Yes, I know, like you have a way with women. When you're through with them, they say whatever you want them to say!"

Plod laughed, but then he waited. Moozh did not know why he was reluctant to tell *this* dream to Plod. He had told him so many others. "All right, then, here is my dream. I saw a man standing in a clearing, and all around him, terrible flying creatures—not birds, they had fur, but much larger than bats—they kept circling, swooping down, touching him. He stood there and did nothing. And when at last they all had touched him, they flew away, except one, who perched on his shoulder."

"Ah," said Plod.

"I'm not finished. Immediately there came giant rats, swarming out of burrows in the Earth. At least a meter long—half as tall as the man. And again, they kept coming until all of them had touched him—"

"With what? Their teeth? Their paws?"

"And their noses. *Touched* him, that's all I knew. Don't distract me."

"Forgive me."

"When they'd all touched him, they went away."

"Except one."

"Yes. It clung to his leg. You see the pattern."

"What came next?"

Moozh shuddered. It had been the most terrible thing of all, and yet now as the words came to his lips, he couldn't understand why. "People."

"People? Coming to touch him?"

"To . . . to kiss him. His hands, his feet. To *worship* him. Thousands of them. Only they didn't kiss just the man. They kissed the—flying thing, too. And the giant rat clinging to his leg. Kissed them all."

"Ah," said Plod. He looked worried.

"So? What is it? What does it portend?"

"Obviously the man you saw is the Imperator."

Sometimes Plod's interpretations sounded like truth, but this time Moozh's heart rebelled at the idea of linking the Imperator with the man in the dream. "Why is that obvious? He looked nothing like the Imperator."

"Because all of nature and humankind worshipped him, of course."

Moozh shrugged. This was not one of Plod's most subtle interpretations. And he had never heard of animals loving the Imperator, who fancied himself a great hunter. Of course, he only hunted in one of his parks, where all the animals had been tamed to lose their fear of men, and all the predators trained to act ferocious but never strike. The Imperator got to act his part in a great show of the contest between man and beast, but he was never in danger as the animal innocently exposed itself to his quick dart, his straight javelin, his merciless blade. If this was worship, if this was nature, then yes, one could say that all of nature and humankind worshipped the Imperator. . . .

Plod, of course, knew nothing of Moozh's thoughts in this vein; if one was so unfortunate as to have caustic thoughts about the Imperator, one took care not to burden one's friends with the knowledge of them.

So Plod continued in his interpretation of Moozh's dream. "What does it portend, this worship of the Imperator? Nothing in itself. But the fact that it *revolted* you, the fact that you recoiled in horror—"

"They were kissing a rat, Plod! They were kissing that disgusting flying creature . . ."

But Plod said nothing as his voice trailed off. Said nothing, and watched him.

"I am *not* horrified at the thought of people worshipping the Imperator. I have knelt at the Invisible Throne myself, and felt the awe of his presence. It wasn't horrible, it was . . . ennobling."

"So you say," said Plod. "But dreams don't lie. Perhaps you need to purge yourself of some evil in your heart."

"Look, *you're* the one who said my dream was about the Imperator. Why couldn't the man have been—I don't know—the ruler of Basilica."

"Because the miserable city of Basilica is ruled by women."

"Not Basilica, then. Still, I think the dream was about . . ."

"About what?"

"How should *I* know? I *will* purge myself, just in case you're right. I'm not an interpreter of dreams." That would mean wasting several hours today at the tent of the intercessor. It was so tedious, but it was also politically necessary to spend a certain amount of time there every month, or reports of one's impiety soon made their way back to Gollod, where the Imperator decided from time to time who was worthy of command and who was worthy of debasement or death. Moozh was about due for a visit to the intercessor's tabernacle anyway, but he hated it the way a boy hates a bath. "Leave me alone, Plod. You've made me very unhappy."

Plod knelt before him and held Moozh's right hand between his own. "Ah, forgive me."

Moozh forgave him at once, of course, because they were friends. Later that morning he went out and killed the headmen of a dozen Khlami villages. All the villagers immediately swore their eternal love and devotion to the Imperator, and when General Vozmuzhalnoy Vozmozhno went that evening to purge himself in the holy tabernacle, the intercessor forgave him right readily, for he had much increased the honor and majesty of the Imperator that day.

IN BASILICA, AND NOT IN A DREAM

They came to hear Kokor sing, came from all over the city of Basilica, and she loved to see how their faces brightened when—finally—she came out onto the stage and the musicians began gently plucking their strings or letting breath pass through their instruments in the soft undercurrent of sound that was always her accompaniment. Kokor will sing to us at last, their faces said. She liked that expression on their faces better than any other she ever saw, better even than the look of a man being overwhelmed with lust in the last moments before satisfaction. For she well knew that a man cared little who gave him the pleasures of love, while the audience cared very much that it was Kokor who stood before them on the stage and opened her mouth in the high, soaring notes of her unbelievably sweet lyric voice that floated over the music like petals on a stream.

Or at least that was how she wanted it to be. How she imagined it to be, until she actually walked onstage and saw them looking at her. The audience tonight was mostly men. Men with their eyes going up and down her body. I should refuse to sing in the comedies, she told herself again. I should insist on being taken as seriously as they take my beloved sister Sevet with her mannishly low, froggishly mannered voice. Oh, they look at *her* with faces of aesthetic ecstasy. Audiences of men and women together. *They* don't look *her* body up and down to see how it moves under the fabric. Of course, that could be partly because her body is so overfleshed that it isn't really a pleasure to watch, it moves so much like gravel under her costume, poor thing. Of *course* they close their eyes and listen to her voice— it's so much better than *watching* her.

What a lie. What a liar I am, even when I'm talking only to myself!

I mustn't be so impatient. It's only a matter of time. Sevet is older—I'm still barely eighteen. *She* had to do the comedies, too, for a time, till she was known.

Kokor remembered her sister talking in those early days—more than two years ago, when Sevet was almost seventeen—about constantly having to dampen the ardor of her admirers, who had a penchant for entering her dressing room quite primed for immediate love, until she had to hire a bodyguard to discourage the more passionate ones. "It's all about sex," said Sevet then. "The songs, the shows, they're all about sex, and that's all the audience dreams of. Just be careful you don't make them dream too well—or too specifically!"

Good advice? Hardly. The more they dream of you, the greater the cash value of your name on the handbills advertising the play. Until finally, if you're lucky, if you're *good* enough, the handbill doesn't have to say the name of a show at all. Only *your* name, and the place, and the day, and the time . . . and when you show up they're all there, hundreds of them, and when the music starts they don't look at you like the last hope of a starving man, they look at you like the highest dream of an elevated soul.

Kokor strode to her place on the stage—and there *was* applause when she entered. She turned to the audience and let out a thrilling high note.

"What was that?" demanded Gulya, the actor who played the old lecher. "Are you screaming already? I haven't even touched you yet."

The audience laughed—but not enough. This play was in trouble. This play had had its weaknesses from the start, she well knew, but with a mere smattering of laughter like that, it was doomed. So in a few more days she'd have to start rehearsing all over again. Another show. Another set of stupid lyrics and stupid melodies to memorize.

Sevet got to decide her own songs. Songwriters came to her and begged her to sing what they had composed. *Sevet* didn't have to misuse her voice just to make people laugh.

"I wasn't screaming," Kokor sang.

"You're screaming now," sang Gulya as he sidled close and started to fondle her. His gravelly bass was always good for a laugh when he used it like that, and the audience was with him. Maybe they could pull this show out of the mud after all.

"But now you're *touching me!*" And her voice rose to its highest pitch and hung there in the air—

Like a bird, like a bird soaring, if only they were listening for beauty.

Gulya made a terrible face and withdrew his hand from her breast. Immediately she dropped her note two octaves. She got the laugh. The best laugh of the scene so far. But she knew that half the audience was laughing because Gulya did such a fine comic turn when he removed his hand from her bosom. He was a master, he really was. Sad that his sort of clowning had fallen a bit out of fashion lately. He was only getting better as he got older, and yet the audience was slipping away. Looking for the more bitter, nasty comedy of the young physical satirists. The brutal, violent comedy that always gave at least the illusion of hurting somebody.

The scene went on. The laughs came. The scene ended. Applause. Kokor scurried off the stage in relief— and disappointment. No one in the audience was chanting her name; no one had even shouted it once like a catcall. How long would she have to wait?

"Too pretty," said Tumannu, the stagekeeper, her face sour. "That note's supposed to sound like you're reaching sexual climax. Not like a bird."

"Yes yes," said Kokor, "I'm so sorry." She always agreed with everybody and then did what she wanted. This comedy wasn't worth doing if she couldn't show her voice to best advantage at least now and then. And it got the laugh when she did it her way, didn't it? So nobody could very well say that her way was *wrong.* Tumannu just wanted her to be obedient, and Kokor didn't intend to be obedient. Obedience was for children and husbands and household pets.

"Not like a bird," said Tumannu again.

"How about like a bird reaching sexual climax?" asked Gulya, who had come offstage right after her.

Kokor giggled, and even Tumannu smiled her tight sour little smile.

"There's someone waiting for you, Kyoka," said Tumannu.

It was a man. But not an aficionado of her work, or he'd have been out front, watching her perform. She had seen him before. Ah, yes—he showed up now and then when Mother's permanent husband, Wetchik, came to visit. He was Wetchik's chief servant, wasn't he? Manager of the exotic flower business when Wetchik was away on caravan. What was his name?

"I am Rashgallivak," he said. He looked very grave.

"Oh?" she said.

"I am deeply sorry to inform you that your father has met with brutal violence."

What an extraordinary thing to tell her. She could hardly make sense of it for a moment. "Someone has injured him?"

"Fatally, madam."

"Oh," she said. There was meaning to this, and she would find it. "Oh, then that would mean that he's . . . dead?"

"Accosted on the street and murdered in cold blood," said Rashgallivak.

It wasn't even a surprise, really, when you thought about it. Father had been making such a bully of himself lately, putting all those masked soldiers on the streets. Terrifying everybody. But Father was so strong and intense that it was hard to imagine anything actually thwarting him for long. Certainly not *permanently*. "There's no hope of . . . recovery?"

Gulya had been standing near enough that now he easily inserted himself into the conversation. "It seems to be a normal case of death, madam, which means the prognosis isn't good." He giggled.

Rashgallivak gave him quite a vicious shove and sent him staggering. "That wasn't funny," he said.

"They're letting critics backstage now?" said Gulya. *"During* the performance?"

"Go away, Gulya," said Kokor. It had been a mistake to sleep with the old man. Ever since then he had thought he had some claim to intimacy with her.

"Naturally it would be best if you came with me," said Rashgallivak.

"But no," said Kokor. "No, that wouldn't be best." Who was *he?* He wasn't any kin to her at all, not that she knew of. She would have to go to Mother. Did Mother know yet? "Does Mother . . ."

"Naturally I told her first, and she told me where to find *you.* This is a very dangerous time, and I promised her that I would protect you."

Kokor knew he was lying, of course. Why should she need this stranger to protect her? From what? Men always got this way, though, insisting that a woman who hadn't a fear in the world needed watching out for. *Ownership,* that's what men always meant when they spoke of protection. If she wanted a man to own her, she *had* a husband, such as he was. She hardly needed this old pizdook to look out for her.

"Where's Sevet?"

"She hasn't been found yet. I must insist that you come with me."

Now Tumannu had to get into the scene. "She's going nowhere. She has three more scenes, including the climax."

Rashgallivak turned on her, and now there was some hint of majesty about him, instead of mere vague befuddlement. "Her father has been killed," he said. "And you suppose she will stay to finish a *play?*" Or had the majesty been there all along, and she simply hadn't noticed it until now?

"Sevet ought to know about Father," said Kokor.

"She'll be told as soon as we can find her."

Who is *we?* Never mind, thought Kokor. *I* know where to find her. I know all her rendezvous, where she takes her lovers to avoid giving affront to her poor husband Vas. Sevet and Vas, like Kokor and Obring, had a flexible marriage, but Vas seemed less comfortable with it than Obring was. Some men were so . . . territorial. Probably it was because Vas was a scientist, not an artist at all. Obring, on the other hand, understood the artistic life. He would never dream of holding Kokor to the letter of their marriage contract. He sometimes joked quite cheerfully about the men she was seeing.

Though, of course, Kokor would never actually insult Obring by mentioning them herself. If he heard a rumor about a lover, that was one thing. When he mentioned it, she would simply toss her head and say, "You silly. You're the only man I love."

And in an odd sort of way it was true. Obring was such a dear, even if he had no acting talent at all. He always brought her presents and told her the most wonderful gossip. No wonder she had stayed married to him through two renewals already—people often remarked on how faithful she was, to still be married to her first husband for a third year, when she was young and beautiful and could marry anyone. True, marrying him in the first place was simply to please his mother, old Dhel, who had served as her auntie and who was Mother's dearest friend. But she had grown to like Obring, genuinely *like* him. Being married to him was very comfortable and sweet. As long as she could sleep with whomever she liked.

It would be fun to find Sevet and walk in on her and see whom she was sleeping with tonight. Kokor hadn't pounced on her that way in years. Find her with some naked, sweating man, tell her that Father was dead, and then watch that poor man's face as he gradually realized that he was all done with love for the night!

"*I'll* tell Sevet," said Kokor.

"You'll come with *me*," insisted Rashgallivak.

"You'll stay and finish the show," said Tumannu.

"The show is nothing but a . . . an *otsoss*," said Kokor, using the crudest term she could think of.

Tumannu gasped and Rashgallivak reddened and Gulya chuckled his little low chuckle. "Now *that's* an idea," he said.

Kokor patted Tumannu on the arm. "It's all right," she said. "I'm fired."

"Yes, you are!" cried Tumannu. "And if you leave here tonight your career is *finished!*"

Rashgallivak sneered at her. "With her share of her father's inheritance she'll buy your little stage and your mother, too."

Tumannu looked defiant. "Oh, really? Who was her father, *Gaballufix?*"

Rashgallivak looked genuinely surprised. "Didn't you know?"

Clearly Tumannu had *not* known. Kokor pondered this for a moment and realized it meant that she must not ever have mentioned it to Tumannu. And that meant that Kokor had not traded on her father's name and prestige, which meant that she had got this part on her own. How wonderful!

"I knew she was the great Sevet's *sister,*" said Tumannu. "Why else do you think I hired her? But I never dreamed they had the same *father.*"

For a moment Kokor felt a flash of rage, hot as a furnace. But she contained it instantly, controlled it perfectly. It would never do to let such a flame burn freely. No telling what she would do or say if she ever let herself go at such a time as this.

"I must find Sevet," said Kokor.

"No," said Rashgallivak. He might have intended to say more, but at that moment he laid a hand on Kokor's arm to restrain her, and so of course she brought her knee sharply up into his groin, as all the comedy actresses were taught to do when an unwelcome admirer became too importunate. It was a reflex. She really hadn't even meant to do it. Nor had she meant to do it with such *force*. He wasn't a very heavy man, and it rather lifted him off the ground.

"I must find Sevet," Kokor said, by way of explanation. He probably didn't hear her. He was groaning too loudly as he lay there on the wooden floor backstage.

"Where's the understudy?" Tumannu was saying. "Not even three minutes' warning, the poor little bizdoon."

"Does it hurt?" Gulya was asking Rashgallivak. "I mean, what *is* pain, when you really think about it?"

Kokor wandered off into the darkness, heading for Dauberville. Her thigh throbbed, just above the knee, where she had pushed it so forcefully into Rashgallivak's crotch. She'd probably end up with a bruise there, and then she'd have to use an opaque sheen on her legs. Such a bother.

Father's dead. I must be the one to tell Sevet. Please don't let anyone else find her first. And *murdered*. People will talk about this for years. I will look rather fine in the white of mourning. Poor Sevet—her skin always looks red as a beet when she wears white. But she won't dare stop wearing mourning until *I* do. I may mourn for poor Papa for years and years and years.

Kokor laughed and laughed to herself as she walked along.

And then she realized she wasn't laughing at all, she was crying. Why am I crying? she wondered. Because Father is dead. That must be it, that must be what all this commotion is about. Father, poor Father. I must have loved him, because I'm crying now without having decided to, without anybody even watching. Who ever would have guessed that I loved him?

* * *

"WAKE UP." IT was an urgent whisper. "Aunt Rasa wants us. "Wake up!"

Luet could not understand why Hushidh was saying this. "I wasn't even asleep," she mumbled.

"Oh, you were sleeping, all right," said her sister Hushidh. "You were snoring."

Luet sat up. "Honking like a goose, I'm sure."

"Braying like a donkey," said Hushidh, "but my love for you turns it into music."

"That's why I do it," said Luet. "To give you music in the night." She reached for her housedress, pulled it over her head.

"Aunt Rasa wants us," Hushidh urged. "Come quickly." She glided out of the room, moving in a kind of dance, her gown floating behind her. In shoes or sandals Hushidh always clumped along, but barefoot she moved like a woman in a dream, like a bit of cottonwood fluff in a breeze.

Luet followed her sister out into the hall, still buttoning the front of her housedress. What could it be, that Rasa would want to speak to her and Hushidh? With all the troubles that had come lately, Luet feared the worst. Was it possible that Rasa's son Nafai had not escaped from the city after all? Only yesterday, Luet had led him along forbidden paths, down into the lake that only women could see. For the Oversoul had told her that Nafai must see it, must float on it like a woman, like a waterseer—like Luet herself. So she took him there, and he was not slain for his blasphemy. She led him out the Private Gate then, and through the Trackless Wood. She had thought he was safe. But of course he was not safe. Because Nafai wouldn't simply have gone back out into the desert, back to his father's tent—not without the thing that his father had sent him to get.

Aunt Rasa was waiting in her room, but she was not alone. There was a soldier with her. Not one of Gaballufix's men—his mercenaries, his thugs, pretending to be Palwashantu militia. No, this soldier was one of the city guards, a gatekeeper.

She could hardly notice him, though, beyond recognizing his insignia, because Rasa herself looked so . . . no, not frightened, really. It was no emotion Luet had ever seen in her before. Her eyes wide and glazed with tears, her face not firmly set, but slack, exhausted, as if things were happening in her heart that her face could not express.

"Gaballufix is dead," said Rasa.

That explained much. Gaballufix was the enemy in recent months, his paid tolchoks terrorizing people on the streets, and then his soldiers, masked and anonymous, terrifying people even more as they ostensibly made the streets of Basilica "safe" for its citizens. Yet, enemy though he was, Gaballufix had also been Rasa's husband, the father of her two daughters, Sevet and Kokor. There had been love there once, and the bonds of family are not easily broken, not for a serious woman like Rasa. Luet was no raveler like her sister Hushidh, but she knew that Rasa was still bound to Gaballufix, even though she detested all his recent actions.

"I grieve for his widow," said Luet, "but I rejoice for the city."

Hushidh, though, gazed with a calculating eye on the soldier. "This man didn't bring you *that* news, I think."

"No," said Rasa. "No, I learned of Gaballufix's death from Rashgallivak. It seems Rashgallivak was appointed . . . the new Wetchik."

Luet knew that this was a devastating blow. It meant that Rasa's husband, Volemak, who *had* been the Wetchik, now had no property, no rights, no standing in the Palwashantu clan at all. And Rashgallivak, who had been his trusted steward, now stood in his place. Was there no honor in the world? "When did Rashgallivak ascend to this honor?"

"Before Gaballufix died—Gab appointed him, of course,

and I'm sure he loved doing it. So there's a kind of justice in the fact that Rash has now taken leadership of the Palwashantu clan, taking Gab's place as well. So yes, you're right, Rash is rising rather quickly in the world. While others fall. Roptat is also dead tonight."

"No," whispered Hushidh.

Roptat had been the leader of the pro-Gorayni party, the group trying to keep the city of Basilica out of the coming war between the Gorayni and Potokgavan. With him gone, what chance was there of peace?

"Yes, both dead tonight," said Rasa. "The leaders of both the parties that have torn our city apart. But here is the worst of it. The rumor is that my son Nafai is the slayer of them both."

"Not true," said Luet. "Not possible."

"So I thought," said Rasa. "I didn't wake you for the rumor."

Now Luet understood fully the turmoil in Aunt Rasa's face. Nafai was Aunt Rasa's pride, a brilliant young man: And more—for Luet knew well that Nafai also was close to the Oversoul. What happened to him was not just important to those who loved him, it was also important to the city, perhaps to the world. "This soldier has word of Nafai, then?"

Rasa nodded at the soldier, who had sat in silence until now.

"My name is Smelost," he said, rising to his feet to speak to them. "I was tending the gate. I saw two men approach. One of them pressed his thumb on the screen and the computer of Basilica knew him to be Zdorab, the treasurer of Gaballufix's house."

"And the other?" asked Hushidh.

"Masked, but dressed in Gaballufix's manner, and Zdorab called him Gaballufix and tried to persuade me not to make him press his thumb on the screen. But I had to make him do it, because Roptat was murdered, and we were trying to prevent the killer from escaping. We'd been told that Lady Rasa's youngest son, Nafai, was the murderer. It was Gaballufix who had reported this."

"So did you make Gaballufix put his thumb on the screen?" said Luet.

"He leaned close to me and spoke in my ear, and said, 'And what if the one who made this false accusation was the murderer himself? Well, that's what some of us already thought—that Gaballufix was accusing Nafai of killing Roptat to cover up his own guilt. And then this soldier—the one that Zdorab was calling Gaballufix—put his thumb on the screen and the name the computer displayed for me was Nafai."

"What did you do?" Luet demanded.

"I violated my oath and my orders. I erased his name immediately and let him pass. I believed him . . . that he was innocent. Of killing Roptat. But his passage from the city was recorded, and the fact that I let him go, knowing who he was. I thought nothing of it—the original complaint came from Gaballufix, and here was Gaballufix's own treasurer with the boy. I thought Gaballufix couldn't protest if his man was along. The worst that would happen is that I'd lose my post."

"You would have let him go anyway," said Hushidh. "Even if Gaballufix's man hadn't been with him."

Smelost looked at her for a moment, then gave a little half-smile. "I was a follower of Roptat. It's a joke to think Wetchik's son might have killed him."

"Nafai's only fourteen," said Luet. "It's a joke to think he'd kill anybody."

"Not so," said Smelost. "Because word came to us that Gaballufix's body had been found. Beheaded. And his clothing missing. What should I think, except that Nafai got Gaballufix's clothing from his corpse? That Nafai and

Zdorab almost certainly killed him? Nafai's big for fourteen, if that's his age. A man in size. He could have done
it. Zdorab—not likely." Smelost chuckled wryly. "It hardly
matters now that I'll lose my post for this. What I fear is
that I'll be hanged as an accomplice to a murder, for letting him go. So I came here."

"To the widow of the murdered man?" asked Luet.

"To the mother of the supposed murderer," said Hushidh, correcting her. "This man loves Basilica."

"I do," said the soldier, "and I'm glad that you know it.
I didn't do my duty, but I did what I thought was right."

"I need advice," said Rasa, looking from Luet to Hushidh and back again. "This man, Smelost, has come to me
for protection, because he saved my son. And in the meantime, my son is named a murderer and I believe now that
he might be guilty indeed. I'm no waterseer. I'm no raveler. What is right and just? What does the Oversoul want?
You must tell me. You must counsel with me!"

"The Oversoul has told me nothing," said Luet. "I know
only what you told me here, tonight."

"And as for raveling," said Hushidh, "I see only that this
man loves Basilica, and that you yourself are tangled in a
web of love that puts you at cross-purposes with yourself.
Your daughters' father is dead, and you love them—and
him, too, you love even *him*. Yet you believe Nafai killed
him, and you love your son even more. You also honor this
soldier, and are bound to him by a debt of honor. Most of
all you love Basilica. Yet you don't know what you must
do for the good of your city."

"I knew my dilemma, Shuya. It was the path out of it that
I didn't know."

"I must flee the city," said Smelost. "I thought you might
protect me. I knew of you as Nafai's mother, but I'd forgotten that you were Gaballufix's widow."

"Not his widow," said Rasa. "I let our contract lapse

years ago. He has married a dozen times since then, I imagine. My husband now is Wetchik. Or rather the man who used to be Wetchik, and now is a landless fugitive whose son may be a murderer." She smiled bitterly. "I can do nothing about that, but I *can* protect *you,* and so I will."

"No you can't," said Hushidh. "You're too close to the center of all these mysteries, Aunt Rasa. The council of Basilica will always listen to you, but they won't protect a soldier who has violated his duty, solely on your word. It will simply make you both look all the guiltier."

"This is the raveler speaking?" asked Rasa.

"It's your student speaking," said Hushidh, "telling you what you would know yourself, if you weren't so confused."

A tear spilled out of Rasa's eye and slipped down her cheek. "What will happen?" said Rasa. "What will happen to my city now?"

Luet had never heard her so afraid, so uncertain. Rasa was a great teacher, a woman of wisdom and honor; to be one of her nieces, one of the students specially chosen to dwell within her household—it was the proudest thing that could happen to a young woman of Basilica, or so Luet had always believed. Yet here she saw Rasa afraid and uncertain. She had not thought such a thing was possible.

"Wetchik—my Volemak—he said the Oversoul was guiding him," said Rasa, spitting out the words with bitterness. "What sort of guide is this? Did the Oversoul tell him to send my boys back to the city, where they were almost killed? Did the Oversoul turn my son into a murderer and a fugitive? What is the Oversoul doing? Most likely it isn't the Oversoul at all. Gaballufix was right—my beloved Volemak has lost his mind, and our sons are being swallowed up in his madness."

Luet had heard enough of this. "Shame on you," she said.

"Hush, Lutya!" cried Hushidh.

"*Shame* on you, Aunt Rasa," Luet insisted. "Just because

it looks frightening and confusing to you doesn't mean that the Oversoul doesn't understand it. I *know* that the Oversoul is guiding Wetchik, and Nafai too. All this will somehow turn to the good of Basilica."

"That's where you're wrong," said Rasa. "The Oversoul has no special love for Basilica. She watches over the whole world. What if the whole world will somehow benefit if Basilica is ruined? If my boys are killed? To the Oversoul, little cities and little people are nothing—she weaves a grand design."

"Then we must bow to her," said Luet.

"Bow to whomever you want," said Rasa. "I'm not bowing to the Oversoul if she's going to turn my boys into killers and my city into dust. If that's what the Oversoul is planning, then the Oversoul and I are enemies, do you understand me?"

"Lower your voice, Aunt Rasa," said Hushidh. "You'll waken the little ones."

Rasa fell silent for a moment, then muttered: "I've said what I have to say."

"You are not the Oversoul's enemy," said Luet. "Please, wait awhile. Let me try to find the Oversoul's will in this. That's what you brought me here to do, isn't it? To tell you what the Oversoul is planning?"

"Yes," said Rasa.

"I don't command the Oversoul," said Luet. "But I'll ask her. Wait here, and I'll—"

"No," said Rasa. "There's no time for you to go down to the waters."

"Not to the waters," said Luet. "To my room. To sleep. To dream. To listen for the voice, to watch for vision. If it comes."

"Then hurry," said Rasa. "We have only an hour or so before I have to do something—more and more people will come here, and I'll have to *act*."

"I don't command the Oversoul," Luet said again. "And the Oversoul sets her own schedule. She does not follow yours."

KOKOR WENT TO Sevet's favorite hideaway, where she took her lovers to keep them from Vas's knowledge, and Sevet wasn't there. "She doesn't come here anymore," said Iliva, Sevet's friend. "Nor any of the other places in Dauberville. Maybe she's being faithful!" Then Iliva laughed and bade her good night.

So Kokor wouldn't be able to pounce after all. It was so disappointing.

Why had Sevet found a new hiding place? Had her husband Vas gone in search of her? He was far too dignified for that! Yet the fact remained that Sevet had abandoned her old places, even though Iliva and Sevet's other friends would gladly have continued to shelter her.

It could only mean one thing. Sevet had found a new lover, a real liaison, not just a quick encounter, and he was someone so important in the city that they had to find new hiding places for their love, for if it became known the scandal would surely reach Vas's ears.

How delicious, thought Kokor. She tried to imagine who it could be, which of the most famous men of the city might have won Sevet's heart. Of course it would be a married man; unless he was married to a woman of Basilica, no man had a right to spend even a single night in the city. So when Kokor finally discovered Sevet's secret, the scandal would be marvelous indeed, for there'd be an injured weeping wife to make Sevet seem all the more sluttish.

And I *will* tell it, thought Kokor. Because she hid this liaison from me and didn't tell me, I have no obligation to keep her secret for her. She didn't trust me, and so why should I be trustworthy?

Kokor wouldn't tell it *herself,* of course. But she knew

many a satirist in the Open Theatre who would love to know of this, so he could be the first to dart sweet Sevet and her lover in a play. And the price she charged him for the story wouldn't be high—only the chance to play Sevet when he darted her. That would put a quick end to Tumannu's threat to blackball her.

I'll get to imitate Sevet's voice, thought Kokor, and make fun of her singing as I do. No one can sound as much like her as I can. No one knows all the flaws in her voice as I do. She will regret having hidden her secret from me! And yet I'll be masked when I dart her, and I'll deny it all, deny everything, even if Mother herself asks me to swear by the Oversoul, I'll deny it. Sevet isn't the only one who knows how to keep a secret.

It was late, only a few hours before dawn, but the last comedies wouldn't be over for another hour. If she hurried back to the theatre, she could probably even go back onstage and be there for the finale, at least. But she couldn't bring herself to play the scene she'd have to play with Tumannu—begging forgiveness, vowing never to walk away from a play again, weeping. It would be too demeaning. No daughter of Gaballufix should have to grovel before a mere stage manager!

Only now that he's dead, what will it matter if I'm his daughter or not? The thought filled her with dismay. She wondered if that man Rash had been right, if Father would leave her enough money to be very rich and buy her own theatre. That would be nice, wouldn't it? That would solve everything. Of course, Sevet would have just as much money and would probably buy her own theatre, too, just because she would have to overshadow Kokor as usual and steal any chance of glory, but Kokor would simply show herself to be the better promoter and drive Sevet's miserable imitative theatre into the dust, and, when it failed, *all* Sevet's inheritance would be lost, while Kokor would be the leading figure in Basilican theatre, and the day would come when Sevet would come to Kokor and beg her to put her in the starring role in one of her plays, and Kokor would embrace her sister and weep and say, "Oh, my darling sister, I'd love nothing better than to put on your little play, but I have a responsibility to my backers, my sweet, and I can't very well risk their money on a show starring a singer who is clearly *past her prime.*"

Oh, it was a delicious dream! Never mind that Sevet was only a single year older—to Kokor that made all the difference. Sevet might be ahead *now,* but someday soon youth would be more valuable than age to them, and then it would be Kokor who had the advantage. Youth and beauty—Kokor would always have more of both than Sevet. And she was every bit as talented as Sevet, too.

Now she was home, the little place that she and Obring rented in Hill Town. It was modest, but decorated in exquisite taste. That much, at least, she had learned from her Aunt Dhelembuvex—Obring's mother—that it's better to have a small setting perfectly finished than a large setting badly done. "A woman must present herself as the blossom of perfection," Auntie Dhel always said. Kokor herself had written it much better, in an aphorism she had published back when she was only fifteen, before she married Obring and left Mother's house:

A perfect bud
of subtle color
and delicate scent
is more welcome than a showy
bloom,
which shouts for attention but has
nothing to show
that can't be seen in the first glance,
or smelled in the first whiff.

Kokor had been proudest of the way the lines about the perfect bud were short and simple phrases, while the lines about the showy bloom were long and awkward. But to her disappointment no noted melodist had made an aria of her aphorism, and the young ones who came to her with their tunes were all talentless pretenders who had no idea how to make a song that would suit a voice like Kokor's. She didn't even sleep with any of them, except the one whose face was so shy and sweet. Ah, he was a tiger in the darkness, wasn't he! She had kept him for three days, but he *would* insist on singing his tunes to her, and so she sent him on his way.

What was his name?

She was on the verge of remembering who he was as she entered the house and heard a strange hooting sound from the back room. Like the baboons who lived across Little Lake, their pant-hoots as they babbled to each other in their nothing language. "Oh. Hoo. Oo-oo. Hoooo."

Only it wasn't baboons, was it? And the sound came from the bedroom, up the winding stair, moonlight from the roof window lighting the way as Kokor rushed upward, running the stairs on tiptoe, silently, for she knew that she would find her husband Obring with some whore of his *in Kokor's bed*, and that was unspeakable, a breach of all decency, hadn't he any consideration for her at all? She never brought *her* lovers home, did she? She never let them sweat on *his* sheets, did she? Fair was fair, and it would be a glorious scene of injured pride when she thrust the little tartlet out of the house *without her clothes!* so she'd have to go home naked and then Kokor would see how Obring apologized to her and how he'd make it up to her, all his vows and apologies and whimpering but there was no doubt about it now, she would *not* renew him when their contract came up and then he'd find out what happens to a man who throws his faithlessness in Kokor's face.

In her moonlit bedroom, Kokor found Obring engaged in exactly the activity she had expected. She couldn't see his face, or the face of the woman for whom he was providing vigorous companionship, but she didn't need daylight or a magnifying glass to know what it all meant.

"Disgusting," she said.

It worked just as she had hoped. They obviously had not heard her coming up the stair, and the sound of her voice froze Obring. For a moment he held his post. Then he turned his head, looking quite foolish as he gazed mournfully over his shoulder at her. "Kyoka," he said. "You're home early."

"I should have known," said the woman on the bed. Her face was still hidden behind Obring's naked back, but Kokor knew the voice at once. "Your show is so bad they closed it in mid-performance."

Kokor hardly noticed the insult, hardly noticed the fact that there wasn't a trace of embarrassment in Sevet's tone. All she could think of was, That's why she had to find a new hiding place, not because her lover was somebody famous, but to keep the truth from *me*.

"Hundreds of your followers every night would be glad for a yibattsa with you," Kokor whispered. "But you had to have my husband."

"Oh, don't take this personally," said Sevet, sitting up on her elbows. Sevet's breasts sagged off to the sides. Kokor loved seeing that, how her breasts sagged, how at nineteen Sevet was definitely older and *thicker* than Kokor. Yet Obring had wanted *that* body, had used that body on the very bed where he had slept beside Kokor's perfect body so many nights. How could he even be aroused by a body like that, after seeing Kokor after her bath so many mornings.

"You weren't using him, and he's very sweet," said Sevet. "If you'd ever bothered to satisfy him he wouldn't have looked at *me*."

"I'm sorry," Obring murmured. "I didn't mean to."

That was so outrageous, like a little child, that Kokor could not contain her rage. And yet she did contain it. She held it in, like a tornado in a bottle. "This was an accident?" whispered Kokor. "You stumbled, you tripped and fell, your clothes tore off and you just happened to bounce on top of my sister?"

"I mean—I kept wanting to break this off, all these months . . ."

"Months," whispered Kokor.

"Don't say any more, puppy," said Sevet. "You're just making it worse."

"You call him 'puppy'?" asked Kokor. It was the word they had used when they first reached womanhood, to describe the teenage boys who panted after them.

"He was so eager," said Sevet, sliding out from under Obring. "I couldn't help calling him that, and he likes the name."

Obring turned and sat miserably on the bed. He made no attempt to cover himself; it was obvious he had lost all interest in love for the evening.

"Don't worry about it, Obring," Sevet said. She stood beside the bed, bending over to pick up her clothing from the floor. "She'll still renew you. This is *one* story she won't be eager to have people tell about her, and so she'll renew you as long as you want, just to keep you from telling."

Kokor saw how Sevet's belly pooched out, how her breasts swung when she bent over. And yet *she* had taken Kokor's husband. After everything else, she had to have even *that*. It could not be borne.

"Sing for me," whispered Kokor.

"What?" asked Sevet, turning to face her, holding her gown in front of her.

"Sing me a song, you davalka, with that pretty voice of yours."

Sevet stared into Kokor's eyes and the look of bored amusement left her face. "I'm not going to sing right now, you little fool," she said.

"Not for me," said Kokor. "For Father."

"What *about* Father?" Sevet's face twisted into an expression of mock sympathy. "Oh, is little Kyoka going to tell on me?" Then she sneered. "He'll laugh. Then he'll take Obring drinking with him!"

"A *dirge* for Father," said Kokor.

"A dirge?" Sevet looked confused now. Worried.

"While you were here, boffing your sister's husband, somebody was busy killing Father. If you were human, you'd care. Even baboons grieve for their dead."

"I didn't know," said Sevet. "How could I know?"

"I looked for you," said Kokor. "To tell you. But you weren't in any of the places I knew. I left my play, I *lost my job* to search for you and tell you, and this is where you were and what you were doing."

"You're such a liar," said Sevet. "Why should I believe this?"

"I never did it with Vas," said Kokor. "Even when he begged me."

"He never asked you," said Sevet. "I don't believe your lies."

"He told me that just once he'd like to have a woman who was truly beautiful. A woman whose body was young and lithe and sweet. But I refused, because you were my sister."

"You're lying. He never asked."

"Maybe I'm lying. But he *did* ask."

"Not *Vas*," said Sevet.

"Vas, with the large mole on the inside of his thigh," said Kokor. "I refused him because you were my sister."

"You're lying about Father, too."

"Dead in his own blood. Murdered on the street. This is

not a good night for our loving family. Father dead. Me betrayed. And you—"

"Stay away from me."

"Sing for him," said Kokor.

"At the funeral, *if* you're not lying."

"Sing *now*," said Kokor.

"Little *hen*, little *duck*, I'll never sing at *your* command."

Accusing her of cackling and quacking instead of singing, that was an old taunt between them, that was nothing. It was the contempt in Sevet's voice, the loathing that got inside her. It filled her, it overfilled her, it was more than she could contain. Not for another moment could she hold in the tempest that tore at her.

"That's right!" cried Kokor. "At my command, you'll *never* sing!" And like a cat she lashed out, but it wasn't a claw, it was a fist. Sevet threw up her hands to protect her face. But Kokor had no desire to mark her sister's face. It wasn't her face she hated. No, her fist connected right where she aimed, under Sevet's chin, on her throat, where the larynx lay hidden under the ample flesh, where the voice was made.

Sevet didn't make a sound, even though the force of the blow knocked her backward. She fell, clutching at her throat; she writhed on the floor, gagging, hacking. Obring cried out and leapt to her, knelt over her. "Sevet!" he cried. "Sevet, are you all right?"

But Sevet's only answer was to gurgle and spit, then to choke and cough. On blood. Her own blood. Kokor could see it on Sevet's hands, on Obring's thighs where he cradled her head on his lap as he knelt there. Glimmering black in the moonlight, blood from Sevet's throat. How does it taste in your mouth, Sevet? How does it feel on your flesh, Obring? Her blood, like the gift of a virgin, my gift to both of you.

Sevet was making an awful strangling sound. "Water," said Obring. "A glass of water, Kyoka—to wash her mouth out. She's bleeding, can't you see that? What have you done to her!"

Kyoka stepped to the sink—her own sink—and took a cup—her own cup—and brought it, filled with water, to Obring, who took it from her hand and tried to pour some of it into Sevet's mouth. But Sevet choked on it and spat the water out, gasping for breath, strangling on the blood that flowed inside her throat.

"A doctor!" cried Obring. "Cry out for a doctor— Bustiya next door is a doctor, she'll come."

"Help," murmured Kokor. "Come quickly. Help." She spoke so softly she almost couldn't hear the sound herself.

Obring rose up from the floor and looked at her in rage. "Don't touch her," he said. "I'll fetch the physician myself." He strode boldly from the room. Such strength in him now. Naked as a mythic god, as the pictures of the Gorayni Imperator—the image of masculinity—that was Obring as he went forth into the night to find a doctor who might save his lady.

Kokor watched as Sevet's fingers scratched on the floor, tore at the skin around her neck, as if she wanted to open up a breathing hole there. Sevet's eyes were bugging out, and blood drooled from her mouth onto the floor.

"You had everything else," said Kokor. "Everything else. But you couldn't even leave me *him*."

Sevet gurgled. Her eyes stared at Kokor in agony and terror.

"You won't die," said Kokor. "I'm not a murderer. I'm not a *betrayer*."

But then it occurred to her that Sevet just *might* die. With so much blood in her throat, she might drown in it. And then Kokor would be held responsible for this. "Nobody can blame me," said Kokor. "Father died tonight, and I came home and found you with my husband, and then you taunted me—no one will blame me. I'm only eighteen, I'm only a *girl*. And it was an accident anyway. I meant to claw out your eyes but I missed, that's all."

Sevet gagged. She vomited on the floor. It smelled awful. This was making such a mess—everything would be stained, and the smell would never, never go. And they *would* blame Kokor for it, if Sevet died. That would be Sevet's revenge, that the stain of this would never go away. Sevet's way of getting even, to die and have Kokor called a murderer forever.

Well, I'll show you, thought Kokor. I won't let you die. In fact, I'll *save your life*.

So it was that when Obring returned with the doctor they found Kokor kneeling over Sevet, breathing into her mouth. Obring pulled her aside to let the doctor get to Sevet. And as Bustiya pushed the tube down into Sevet's throat, as Sevet's face became a silent rictus of agony, Obring smelled the blood and vomit and saw how Kokor's face and gown were stained with both. He whispered to her as he held her there, "You do love her. You couldn't let her die."

She clung to him then, weeping.

"I CAN'T SLEEP," Luet said miserably. "How can I dream if I can't sleep?"

"Never mind," Rasa said. "I know what we have to do. I don't need the Oversoul to tell us. Smelost has to leave Basilica, because Hushidh is right, I can't protect him now."

"I won't leave," said Smelost. "I've decided. This is my city, and I'll face the consequences of what I've done."

"Do you love Basilica?" said Rasa. "Then don't give Gaballufix's people somebody they can pin all the blame on. Don't give them a chance to put you on trial and use it as an excuse to take command of the guards so that his masked soldiers are the *only* authority in the city."

Smelost glared at her a moment, then nodded. "I see," he said. "For the sake of Basilica, then I'll go."

"Where?" asked Hushidh. "Where can you send him?"

"To the Gorayni, of course," said Rasa. "I'll give you provisions and money enough to make it north to the Gorayni. And a letter, explaining how you saved the man who—the man who killed Gaballufix. They'll know what that means—they must have spies who told them that Gab was trying to get Basilica to make an alliance with Potokgavan. Maybe Roptat was in contact with them."

"Never!" cried Smelost. "Roptat was no traitor!"

"No, of course he wasn't," said Rasa soothingly. "The point is that Gab was their enemy, and that makes you their friend. It's the least they can do, to take you in."

"How long will I have to stay away?" asked Smelost. "There's a woman that I love here. I have a son."

"Not long," said Rasa. "With Gab gone, the tumult will soon die down. He was the cause of it, and now we'll have peace again. May the Oversoul forgive me for saying so, but if Nafai killed him then maybe he did a good thing, for Basilica at least."

There was a loud knocking at the door.

"Already!" said Rasa.

"They can't know I'm here," said Smelost.

"Shuya, take him to the kitchen and provision him. I'll stall them at the door as long as I can. Luet, help your sister."

But it wasn't Palwashantu soldiers at the door, or city guards, or any kind of authority at all. Instead it was Vas, Sevet's husband.

"I'm sorry to disturb you at this hour."

"Me and my whole house," said Rasa. "I already know

that Sevet's father is dead, but I know you meant well in coming to—"

"He's dead?" said Vas. "Gaballufix? Then maybe that explains . . . No, it explains nothing." He looked frightened and angry. Rasa had never seen him like this.

"What's wrong, then?" Rasa asked. "If you didn't know Gab was dead, why are you here?"

"One of Kokor's neighbors came to fetch me. It's Sevet. She's been struck in the throat—she almost died. A very bad injury. I thought you'd want to come with me."

"You *left* her? To come to me?"

"I wasn't with her," said Vas. "She's at Kokor's house."

"Why would Sevya be there?" One of the servants was already helping Rasa put on a cloak, so she could go outside. "Kokor had a play tonight, didn't she? A new play."

"Sevya was with Obring," said Vas. He led her out onto the portico; the servant closed the door behind them. "That's why Kyoka hit her."

"Kyoka hit her in the—*Kyoka* did it?"

"She found them together. That's how the neighbor told the story, anyway. Obring went and fetched the doctor stark naked, and Sevya was naked when they got back. Kyoka was breathing into her mouth, to save her. They have a tube in her throat and she's breathing, she won't die. That's all the neighbor knew to tell me."

"That Sevet is alive," said Rasa bitterly, "and who was naked."

"Her throat," said Vas. "It might have been kinder for Kokor simply to kill her, if this costs Sevet her voice."

"Poor Sevya," said Rasa. There were soldiers marching in the streets, but Rasa paid them no attention, and—perhaps because Vas and Rasa seemed so intent and urgent—the soldiers made no effort to stop them. "To lose her father and her voice in the same night."

"We've all lost something tonight, eh?" said Vas bitterly.

"This isn't about *you,* said Rasa. "I think Sevet really loves you, in her way."

"I know—they hate each other so much they'll do anything to hurt each other. But I thought it was getting better."

"Maybe now it will," said Rasa. "It can't get worse."

"Kyoka tried it, too," said Vas. "I sent her away both times. Why couldn't Obring have had the brains to say no to Sevet, too?"

"He has the brains," said Rasa. "He lacks the strength."

At Kokor's house, the scene was very touching. Someone had cleaned up: The bed was no longer rumpled with love; now it was smooth except where Sevet lay, demure in one of Kokor's most modest nightgowns. Obring, too, had managed to become clothed, and now he knelt in the corner, comforting a weeping Kokor. The doctor greeted Rasa at the door of the room.

"I've drained the blood out of the lungs," the physician said. "She's in no danger of dying, but the breathing tube must remain for now. A throat specialist will be here soon. Perhaps the damage will heal without scarring. Her career may not be over."

Rasa sat on the bed beside her daughter, and took Sevya's hand. The smell of vomit still lingered, even though the floor was wet from scrubbing. "Well, Sevya," whispered Rasa, "did you win or lose this round?"

A tear squeezed out between Sevet's eyelids.

On the other side of the room, Vas stood over Obring and Kokor. He was flushed with—what, anger? Or was his face merely red from the exertion of their walk?

"Obring," said Vas, "you miserable little bastard. Only a fool pees in his brother's soup."

Obring looked up at him, his face drawn, and then he

looked back down at his wife, who wept all the harder. Rasa knew Kokor well enough to know that while her weeping was sincere, it was being played for the most possible sympathy. Rasa had almost none to give her. She was well aware how little her daughters had cared for the exclusivity clause in their marriage contracts, and she had no sympathy for faithless people who felt injured upon discovering that their mates were faithless, too.

It was Sevet who was suffering, not Kokor. Rasa could not be distracted from Sevet's need, just because Kokor was so noisy and Sevet was silent.

"I'm with you, my dear daughter," said Rasa. "It's not the end of the world. You're alive, and your husband loves you. Let that be your music for a while."

Sevet clung to her hand, her breath shallow, panting.

Rasa turned to the doctor. "Has she been told about her father?"

"She knows," Obring said. "Kyoka told us."

"Thank the Oversoul we have but one funeral to attend," said Rasa.

"Kyoka saved her sister's life," said Obring. "She gave her breath."

No, *I* gave her breath, thought Rasa. Gave her breath, but alas, I could not give her decency, or sense. I couldn't keep her out of her sister's sheets, or away from her sister's husband. But I did give her breath, and perhaps now this pain will teach her something. Compassion, perhaps. Or at least some self-restraint. Something to make good come out of this. Something to make her become *my* daughter, and not Gaballufix's, as they both have been till now.

Let this all turn to good, Rasa silently prayed. But then she wondered to whom she was praying. To the Oversoul, whose meddling had started so many other problems? I'll get no help from *her,* thought Rasa. I'm on my own now, to try to steer my family and my city through the terrible days to come. I have no power or authority over either of them, except whatever power comes from love and wisdom. I have the love. If only I could be sure I also had the wisdom.

TWO

OPPORTUNITY

THE DREAM OF THE WATERSEER

Luet had never tried to have an emergency dream before, and so it had never occurred to her that she couldn't just go to sleep and dream because she wished it. Quite the contrary—the sense of urgency was no doubt what had kept her awake and made it impossible for her to dream. She was furious and ashamed that she hadn't been able to learn anything from the Oversoul before Aunt Rasa had to make a decision about what to do with that soldier, Smelost. What made it worse was that, even though the Oversoul had told her nothing, she was certain that sending Smelost to the Gorayni was a mistake. It seemed too simple, to think that because Gaballufix had been an enemy of the Gorayni, the Gorayni would automatically welcome Gaballufix's enemy and give him sanctuary.

Luet had wanted to speak up and tell her, "Aunt Rasa, the Gorayni aren't necessarily our friends." She might even have said so, but Rasa had rushed out of the house with Vas and there was nothing to do but watch as Smelost gathered up the food and supplies the servants brought for him and then slipped out the back way.

Why couldn't Rasa have thought just a moment more?

Wouldn't it have been better to send Smelost out into the desert to join Wetchik? But he wasn't the Wetchik anymore, was he? He was nothing but Volemak, the man who *had* been Wetchik until Gaballufix stripped him of the title—when?—only yesterday. Nothing but Volemak—yet Luet knew that Volemak, of all the great men of Basilica, was the only one who was part of the Oversoul's plans.

The Oversoul had begun all these problems by giving Volemak his vision of Basilica on fire. She had warned him that an alliance with Potokgavan would lead to the destruction of Basilica. She hadn't promised that Basilica could trust the Gorayni to be *friends*. And from what Luet knew of the Gorayni—the Wetheads, as they were called, from the way they oiled their hair—it was a bad idea to send Smelost to ask for refuge. It would give the wrong impression to the Gorayni. It would lead them to think that their allies were not safe in Basilica. Might that not entice them to do exactly what everyone wanted to keep them from doing—invade and conquer the city.

No, it was a mistake to send Smelost. But since Luet didn't reach this conclusion as a waterseer, but rather reached it through her own reasoning, no one would listen to her. She was a child, except when the Oversoul was in her, and so she only had respect when she was not herself. It made her angry, but what could she do about it, except hope that she was wrong about Smelost and the Gorayni, and then wait impatiently until she turned fully into a woman?

What worried her perhaps even more was that it was unlike Rasa to reach such a faulty conclusion. Rasa seemed to be acting out of fear, acting without thinking. And if Rasa's judgment was clouded, then what could Luet count on?

I want to talk to someone, she thought. Not her sister Hushidh—dear Shuya was very wise and kind and would listen to her, but she simply didn't care about anything outside Basilica. That was the problem with her being a raveler. Hushidh lived in the constant awareness of all the connections and relationships among the people around her. That web-sense was naturally the most important thing in her life, as she watched people connect and detach from each other, forming communities and dissolving them. And underlying all was Shuya's powerful awareness of the fabric of Basilica itself. She loved the city—but she knew it so well, focused so closely on it that she simply had no idea of how Basilica related to the world outside. Such relationships were too large and impersonal.

Luet had even tried to discuss this with her, but Hushidh fell asleep almost at once. Luet couldn't blame her. After all, it was nearly dawn, and they had missed hours of sleep in the middle of the night. Luet herself should be asleep.

If only I could talk with Nafai or Issib. Nafai especially— *he* can talk with the Oversoul when he's awake. He may not get the visions that I get, he may not see with the depth and clarity of a waterseer, but he can get *answers*. Practical, simple answers. And he doesn't have to be able to fall asleep to get them. If only he were here. Yet the Oversoul sent him and his father and all his brothers away into the desert. That's where Smelost should have gone, definitely. To Nafai. If only anyone knew where he was.

At last, at long last Luet's frenzied thoughts jumbled into the chaotic mentation of sleep, and from her fitful sleep a dream came, a dream that she would remember, for it came from outside herself and had meaning beyond the random firings of her brain during sleep.

"Wake up," said Hushidh.

"I *am* awake," said Luet.

"You've answered me that twice already, Lutya, and each time you stay asleep. It's morning, and things are even worse than we thought."

"If you said that every time I woke up," said Luet, "then no wonder I went back to sleep."

"You've slept long enough," said Hushidh, and then proceeded to tell her all about what happened at Kokor's house the night before.

Luet could hardly grasp that such things could actually happen—not to anyone connected with Rasa's house. Yet it wasn't just rumor. "That's why Vas took Aunt Rasa with him," said Luet.

"You have such a bright mind in the morning."

Her thoughts were coming so sluggishly that it took Luet a moment to realize that Hushidh was being ironic. "I was dreaming," she said, to explain her stupidity.

But Hushidh wasn't interested in her dream. "For poor Aunt Rasa the nightmare starts when she wakes up."

Luet tried to think of a bright spot. "At least she has the comfort of knowing Kokor and Sevet were auntied out to Dhelembuvex—it won't reflect on her house—"

"Won't reflect . . . ! They're her *daughters,* Lutya. And Auntie Dhel was over here with them all the time as they were growing up. This has nothing to do with how they were raised. This is what it means to be the daughters of Gaballufix. How deliciously ironic, that the very night he dies, one of his daughters strikes the other dumb with a blow to the throat."

"Sweet kindness flows with every word from your lips, Shuya."

Hushidh glared at her. "You've never loved Aunt Rasa's daughters, either, so don't get pure with me."

The truth was that Luet had no great interest in Rasa's daughters. She had been too young to care, when they last were in Rasa's house. But Hushidh, being older, had clear memories of what it was like to have them in the house all the time, with Kokor actually attending classes, and both of them surrounded by suitors. Hushidh liked to joke that the pheromone count couldn't have been higher in a brothel, but Hushidh's loathing for Kokor and Sevet had nothing to do with their attractiveness to men. It had to do with their vicious jealousy of any girl who had actually earned Rasa's love and respect. Hushidh was no rival to them, and yet they had both persecuted her mercilessly, taunting her whenever the teachers couldn't hear, until she became virtually a ghost in Rasa's house, hiding until the moment of class and rushing away afterward, avoiding meals, shunning all the parties and frolics, until Kokor and Sevet finally married at a mercifully young age— fourteen and fifteen, respectively—and moved out. Sevet was already a noted singer even then, and her practicing—and Kokor's— had filled the house like bird-song. But neither she nor Kokor had brought any true music to Rasa's house. Rather the music returned when they finally left. And Hushidh remained quiet and shy around everyone except Luet. So of course Hushidh cared more when Rasa's daughters played out some bitter tragedy. Luet only cared because it would make Aunt Rasa sad.

"Shuya, all this is only scandal. What's being said about that soldier? And about Gaballufix's death?"

Hushidh looked down in her lap. She knew that Luet was, in effect, rebuking her for having given false priority to trivial matters; but she accepted the rebuke, and did not defend herself. "They're saying that Smelost was Nafai's co-conspirator all along. Rashgallivak is demanding that the council investigate who helped Smelost escape from the city, even though he wasn't under a warrant or anything when he left. Rasa is trying to get the city guard put under the control of the Palwashantu. It's very ugly."

"What if Aunt Rasa is arrested as Smelost's accomplice?" said Luet.

"Accomplice in what?" said Hushidh. Now she was Hushidh the Raveler, discussing the city of Basilica, not

Shuya the schoolgirl, telling an ugly story about her tormentors. Luet welcomed the change, even if it meant Hushidh's acting so openly astonished at Luet's lack of insight. "How insane do you think people actually are? Rashgallivak can try to whip them up, but he's no Gaballufix—he doesn't have the personal magnetism to get people to follow him for long. Aunt Rasa will hold her own against him on the council, and then some."

"Yes, I suppose so," said Luet. "But Gaballufix had so many soldiers, and now they're all Rashgallivak's. . . ."

"Rash isn't well-connected," said Hushidh. "People have always liked him and respected him, but only as a steward—as Wetchik's steward, particularly—and they aren't likely to give him the full honor of the Wetchik right away, let alone the kind of respect that Gaballufix was given as head of the Palwashantu. He doesn't have half the power he imagines he has—but he has enough to cause trouble, and it's very disturbing."

Luet was fully awake at last, and crawled off the foot of her bed. She remembered that there was something she must tell. "I dreamed," she said.

"So you said." Then Hushidh realized what she meant. "Oh. A little late, wouldn't you say?"

"Not about Smelost. About something—very strange. And yet it felt more important than any of what's going on around us."

"A true dream?" asked Hushidh.

"I'm never *sure,* but I think so. I remember it so clearly, it must come from the Oversoul."

"Then tell me as we go to breakfast. It's nearly noon, but Aunt Rasa told the cook to indulge us since we were up half the night."

Luet pulled a gown over her head, slipped sandals on her feet, and followed Hushidh down the stairs to the kitchen. "I dreamed of angels, flying."

"Angels! And what is that supposed to mean, except that you're superstitious in your sleep?"

"They didn't look like the pictures in the children's books, if that's what you mean. No, they were more like large and graceful birds. Bats, really, since they had fur. But with very intelligent and expressive faces, and somehow in the dream I knew they were angels."

"The Oversoul has no need of angels. The Oversoul speaks directly to the mind of every woman."

"And man, only hardly anybody listens anymore, just as you're not listening to *me,* Shuya. Should I tell you the dream or just eat bread and honey and cream and figure that the Oversoul has nothing to say that might interest you?"

"Don't be nasty with *me,* Luet. You may be this wonderful waterseer to everybody else, but you're just my stupid little sister when you get snippy like this."

The cook glared at them. "I try to keep a kitchen full of light and *harmony,*" she said.

Abashed, they took the hot bread she offered them and sat at the table, where a pitcher of cream and a jar of honey already waited. Hushidh, as always, broke her bread into a bowl and poured the cream and honey on it; Luet, as always, slathered the honey on the bread and ate it separately, drinking the plain cream from her bowl. They both pretended to detest the way the other ate her food. "Dry as dust," whispered Hushidh. "Soggy and slimy," answered Luet. Then they both laughed aloud.

"Much better," said the cook. "You should both know better than to quarrel."

With her mouth full, Hushidh said, "The dream."

"Angels," said Luet.

"Flying, yes. Hairy ones, like fat bats. I heard you the first time."

"Not fat."

"Bats, anyway."

"Graceful," said Luet. "Soaring, that's how they were. And then I was one of them, flying and flying. It was so beautiful and peaceful. And then I saw the river, and I flew down to it and there on the riverbank I took the clay and made a statue out of it."

"Angels playing in the mud?"

"No stranger than bats making statues," Luet retorted. "And there's milk slobbering down your chin."

"Well, there's honey on the tip of your nose."

"Well, there's a big ugly growth on the front of you head—oh, no, that's your—"

"My face, I know. Finish the dream."

"I made the clay soft by putting it in my mouth, so that when I—as an angel, you understand—when I made the statue it contained something of me in it. I think that's very significant."

"Oh, *quite* symbolic, yes." Hushidh's tone was playful, but Luet knew she was listening carefully.

"And the statues weren't of people or angels or anything else. There were faces on them sometimes, but they weren't portraits or even *things*. The statues just took the shape that we needed them to take. No two of them were alike, yet I knew that at this moment, the statue I was making was the only possible statue I could make. Does that make sense?"

"It's a dream, it doesn't have to."

"But if it's a *true* dream, then it *must* make sense."

"Eventually, anyway," said Hushidh. Then she lifted another gloppy spoonful of bread and milk to her mouth.

"When we were done," said Luet, "we took them to a high rock and put them in the sun to dry, and then we flew around and around, and everyone looked at each other's statues. Then the angels flew off and now I wasn't with them anymore, I wasn't an angel, I was just there, watching the rocks where the statues stood, and the sun went down and in the dark—"

"You could see in the dark?"

"I could in my *dream*," said Luet. "Anyway, in the night-time these giant rats came, and each one took one of the statues and carried it down, into holes in the ground, all the way to deep warrens and burrows, and each rat that had stolen a statue gave it to another rat and then together they gnawed at it, wet it down with their spit and rubbed it all over themselves. Covered themselves with the clay. I was so angry, Hushidh. These beautiful statues, and they wrecked them, turned them back into mud and rubbed it—even into their private parts, *everywhere*."

"Lovers of beauty," said Hushidh.

"I'm serious. It broke my heart."

"So what does it mean?" asked Hushidh. "Who do the angels represent, and who are the rats?"

"I don't know. Usually the meaning is obvious, when the Oversoul sends a dream."

"So maybe it was just a dream."

"I don't think so. It was so different and so clear, and I remember it so forcefully. Shuya, I think it's perhaps the most important dream I've ever had."

"Too bad nobody can understand it. Maybe it's one of those prophecies that everybody understands after it's all over and it's too late to do anything about it."

"Maybe Aunt Rasa can interpret it."

Hushidh made a skeptical face. "She's not at her best at the moment."

Secretly Luet was relieved that she wasn't the only one to notice that Rasa wasn't making the best decisions of her life right now. "So maybe I *won't* tell her, then."

Suddenly Hushidh smiled her tight little smile that showed she was really pleased with herself. "You want to hear a wild guess?" she said.

Luet nodded, then began taking huge bites of her long-ignored bread as she listened.

"The angels are the women of Basilica," said Hushidh. "All these millennia here in this city, we've shaped a society that is delicate and fine, and we've made it out of a part of ourselves, the way the bats in your dream made their statues out of spit. And now we've put our works to dry, and in the darkness our enemies are going to come and steal what we've made. But they're so stupid they don't even understand that they're statues. They look at them and all they see are blobs of dried mud. So they wet it down and wallow in it and they're so *proud* because they've got all the works of Basilica, but in fact they have *nothing* of Basilica at all."

"That's very good," said Luet, in awe.

"I think so, too," said Hushidh.

"So who are our enemies?"

"It's simple," said Hushidh. "Men are."

"Not, that's *too* simple," said Luet. "Even though this is a city of women, the men who enter Basilica contribute as much as the women do to the works of beauty we make. They're part of the community, even if they can't own land or stay inside the walls without being married to a woman."

"I was sure it meant men the moment you said they were giant rats."

The cook chortled over the stew she was making for dinner.

"Someone else," insisted Luet. "Maybe Potokgavan."

"Maybe just Gaballufix's men," said Hushidh. "The tolchoks, and then his soldiers in those horrible masks."

"Or maybe something yet to come," said Luet. And then, in despair. "Or maybe nothing to do with Basilica at all. Who can tell? But that was my dream."

"It doesn't exactly tell us where we should have sent Smelost."

Luet shrugged. "Maybe the Oversoul thought we had brains enough to figure that out on our own."

"Was she right?" asked Hushidh.

"I doubt it," said Luet. "Sending him to the Gorayni was a mistake."

"I wouldn't know," said Hushidh. "Eating your bread dry—now *that's* a mistake."

"Not for those of us who have teeth," said Luet. "We don't have to sog our bread to make it edible."

Which led to a mock argument that got silly and loud enough that the cook threw them out of the kitchen, which was fine because they were finished with breakfast anyway. It felt good, for just a few minutes, to play together like children. For they knew that, for good or ill, they would both be involved in the events that were swirling in and near Basilica. Not that they wanted to be involved, really. But their gifts made them important to the city, and so they would do their best to serve.

Luet dutifully went to the city council and told her dream, which was carefully recorded and handed over to the wise women to be studied for meanings and portents. Luet told them how Hushidh had interpreted it, and they thanked her kindly and as much as told her that having dreams was fine—any idiot child could do *that*—but it took a real expert to figure out what they meant.

IN KHLAM, AND NOT IN A DREAM

It was a hot dry storm from the northwest, which meant it came across the desert, not a breath of moisture in it, just sand and grit and, so they said, the ground-up bones of men and animals that had got caught in the storm a thousand kilometers away, the dust of their flesh, and, if you listened closely, the howling of their souls as the wind bore them on and on, never letting go of them, either to heaven or to hell. The mountains blocked the worst of the storm, but still the tents of Moozh's army shuddered and staggered, the flaps of the tents snapped, the banners danced crazily, and now and then one of them would whip away from the ground and tumble, pole and all, along a dirty trampled avenue between the tents, some poor soldier often trying to chase it down.

Moozh's large tent also shuddered in the wind, despite its blessing from the Imperator. Of course the blessing was completely efficacious . . . but Moozh also made sure the stakes were pounded in hard and deep. He sat at the table by candlelight, gazing wistfully at the map spread out before him. It showed all the lands along the western shores of the Earthbound Sea. In the north, the lands of the Gorayni were outlined in red, the lands of the Imperator, who was of course the incarnation of God on Earth and therefore entitled to rule over all mankind, etc. etc. In his mind's eye Moozh traced the unmarked boundaries of nations that were at least as old as the Gorayni, and some of them much older, with proud histories—nations that now did not exist, that could not even be remembered, because to speak their names was treason, and to reach out and trace their old boundary on this map would be death.

But Moozh did not have to trace the boundary. He knew the borders of his homeland of Pravo Gollossa, the land of the Sotchitsiya, his own tribe. They had come across the desert from the north a thousand years before the Gorayni, but once they had been of the same stock, with the same language. But in the lush wellwatered valleys of the Skrezhet Mountains the Sotchitsiya had settled down, had ceased both wandering and war, and become a nation of free men. They learned from the people around them. Not the Ploshudu or the Khlami or the Izmennikoy, for they were tough mountain people with no culture but hunger and muscle and a will to live despite all. Rather the Sotchitsiya, the people of Pravo Gollossa, had learned from the traders who came to them from Seggidugu, from Ulye, from the Cities of the Plain. And above all the caravanners from

Basilica, with their strange songs and seeds, images in glass and cunning tools, impossible fabrics that changed colors with the hours of the day, and their poems and stories that taught the Sotchitsiya how wise and refined men and women spoke and thought and dreamed and lived.

That was the glory of Pravo Gollossa, for it was from these caravanners that they learned of the idea of a council, with decisions made by the vote of the councilors who had themselves been chosen by the voice of the citizens. But it was also from these Basilican caravanners that they learned of a city ruled by women, where men could not even own land . . . and yet the city did not collapse from the incompetence of women to rule, and the men did not rebel and conquer the city, and women were able not only to vote but also to divorce their husbands at the end of every year and marry someone else if they chose. The constant pressure of those ideas wore down the Sotchitsiya and turned the once-strong warriors and rulers of the tribe into woman-hearted fools, so that in Moozh's great-grandfather's day they gave the vote to women, and elected women to rule over them.

That was when the Gorayni came, for they knew that the Sotchitsiya had at last become women in their hearts, and so were no longer worthy to be free. The Gorayni brought their great army to the border, and the women of the council—as many males as females, but all women nonetheless—voted not to fight, but rather to accept Gorayni overlordship if the Gorayni would allow them to rule themselves in all but military matters. It was an unspeakable surrender, the final castration of the Sotchitsiya, their humiliation before all the world, and Moozh's own great-grandfather was the delegate who worked out the terms of their surrender with the Gorayni.

For fifty years the agreement stood—the Sotchitsiya governed themselves. But gradually the Gorayni military began to declare more of Sotchitsiya affairs to be military matters, until finally the council was nothing but a bunch of frightened old men and women who had to petition the Imperator for permission to pee. Only then did any of the Sotchitsiya remember their manhood. They threw out the women who ruled them and declared themselves to be a tribe again, desert wanderers again, and swore to fight the Gorayni to the last man. It took three days for the Gorayni to defeat these brave but untrained rebels on the battlefield, and another year to hunt them down and kill them all in the mountains. After that there was no pretense that the Sotchitsiya had any rights at all. It was forbidden to speak the Sotchitsiya dialect; children who were heard speaking it had the privilege of watching their parents' tongues cut off, one centimeter for each offense. Only a few of the Sotchitsiya remembered their own language anymore, most of them old and many of them tongueless.

But Moozh knew. Moozh had the Sotchitsiya language in his heart. Even though he was the most successful, the most dangerous of the Imperator's generals, in his heart he knew his true language was Sotchitsiya, not Gorayni. And even though his many victories in battle had brought the great coastal nations of Uslavat and Ulye under the Imperator's dominion, even though his clever strategy had brought the thorny mountain kingdoms of Plosh and Khlam to obedience without a single pitched battle, Moozh's secret was that he loathed the Imperator and defied him in his heart.

For Moozh knew that the Imperator truly *was* God in the flesh, for better than most, Moozh could feel the power of God trying to control him. He had felt it first in his youth, when he sought a place in the Gorayni army. God didn't speak to him when he learned to be a strong soldier, his arms and thighs heavy with muscle, able a drive a battleaxe through the spine of his enemy and cleave him in half. But when Moozh imagined himself as an officer, as a general, leading armies, then came that heavy stupid feeling that made him want to forget such dreams. Moozh understood— God knew his hatred of the Imperator, and so was determined that one like Moozh would never have power beyond the strength of his arms.

But Moozh refused to capitulate. Whenever he sensed that God was making him forget an idea, he clung to it—he wrote it down and memorized it, he made a poem of it in the Sotchitsiya language so he could never forget. And thus, bit by bit, he built up in his heart his own rules of warfare, guided every step of the way by God, for whatever God tried to prevent him from thinking, that was what he knew that he must think of, deeply and well.

This secret defiance of God was what brought Moozh out of the ranks and made him a captain when his regiment was in danger of being overrun by the pirates of Revis. All the other officers had been killed, yet when Moozh thought of taking command and leading the few men near him in a counterattack against the flank of the uncontrolled, victorious Reviti, he felt that dullness of mind that always told him that God did not want him to pursue the idea. So he shouted down the voice of God and led his men in a fool-hardy charge, which so terrified the pirates that they broke and ran, and the rest of the Gorayni took heart and followed Moozh in hot pursuit of them until they caught them on the riverbank and killed them all and burned their ships. They had brought Moozh for a triumph of the city of Gollod itself, where the Imperator had rubbed the camelmilk butter into his hair and declared him a hero of the Gorayni. But in his heart, Moozh knew that God had no doubt planned to have some loyal son of the Gorayni achieve the victory. Well, too bad for the Imperator—if the incarnation of God didn't understand that he had just oiled the hair of his enemy, then so much the worse for him.

Step by step Moozh had risen in command, until now he was at the head of a vast army. Most of his men were quartered in Ulye now, it was true, for the Imperator had commanded that they delay the attack against Nakavalnu until calm weather a month from now, when the chariots could be used to good advantage. Here in Khlam he had only a regiment, but that was all that was needed. Step by step he would lead the Gorayni onward, taking nation after nation along the coast until all the cities had fallen. Then he would face the armies of Potokgavan.

And then what? Some days Moozh thought that he would take his vengeance by orchestrating a complete and utter defeat for the armies of the Gorayni. He would gather all their military might into one place and then contrive to have them all slaughtered, himself among them. Then, with the Gorayni broken and Potokgavan having their will throughout the plain— then the Sotchitsiya would rise up and claim their freedom.

On other days, though, Moozh imagined that he would destroy the army of Potokgavan, so that along the entire western coast of the Earthbound Sea there was no rival to contest the supremacy of the Gorayni. Then he would stand before the Imperator, and when the Imperator reached out to smear the camelmilk butter on his hair, Moozh would slice off his head with a buck knife, then take the camel-hump cap and put it on his own head, and declare that the empire that had been won by a Sotchitsiya would now be ruled by the Sotchitsiya. *He* would be Imperator, and instead of being the incarnation of God he would be the enemy of God, and the Sotchitsiya would be known as the greatest of men, and no longer as a nation of women.

These were his thoughts as he studied the map, while the storm flung sand at his tent and tried to tear it out of the ground.

Suddenly he came alert. The sound had changed. It

wasn't just the wind; someone was scratching at his tent. Who would be so stupid as to walk about in this weather? He felt a sudden stab of fear—could it be the assassin sent by the Imperator, to prevent him from the treachery that God surely knew was in his heart?

But when he untied the flap and opened it, no assassin came in with a flurry of sand and hot wind. Instead it was Plod, his dear friend and comrade in arms, and another man, a stranger, in military garb that Moozh did not recognize.

Plod himself fastened the tent closed again—it would have been improper for Moozh to do it, with a junior officer present who could do it for him. So Moozh had a few moments to study the stranger. He was no soldier, not really—his breastplate was sturdy, his blade sharp, his clothing was fine, and he bore himself like a man. But his skin was soft-looking and his muscles lacked the hardness of a man who has wielded a sword in battle. He was the kind of soldier who stood guard at a palace or a toll road, bullying the common people but never having to face a charging horde of enemies, never having to run behind a chariot, hacking to death any who escaped the blades that whirred on the hubs of the chariot wheels.

"What portal do you guard?" asked Moozh.

The man looked startled, and he glanced back at Plod.

Plod only laughed. "No one told him anything, poor man. Did you think you could face General Vozmuzhalnoy Vozmozhno and keep anything secret from his eyes?"

"My name is Smelost," said the soft soldier, "and I bring a letter from Lady Rasa of Basilica."

He spoke the name as though Moozh should have heard of it. That's how these city people were, thinking that fame in their city must mean fame all over the world.

Moozh reached out and took the letter from him. Of course it was not written in the block alphabet of

Gorayni—which they had stolen from the Sotchitsiya centuries ago. Instead it was the flowery vertical cursive of Basilica. But Moozh was an educated man. He could read it easily.

"It seems this man is our friend, dear Plod," said Moozh. "His life isn't safe in Basilica because he helped an assassin escape—but the assassin was *also* our friend, since he killed a man named Gaballufix who was in favor of Basilica forming an alliance with Potokgavan and leading the Cities of the Plain in war against us."

"Ah," said Plod.

"To think we never guessed how many dear and tender friends we had in Basilica," said Moozh.

Plod laughed.

Smelost looked more than a little ill at ease.

"Sit down," said Moozh. "You're among friends. No harm will come to you now. Find him some ale to drink, will you, Plod? He may be a common soldier, but he brings us a letter from a fine lady who has nothing but love and concern for the Imperator."

Plod unhooked a flagon from the back tentpole and gave it to Smelost, who looked at it in puzzlement.

Moozh laughed and took the flagon out of Smelost's hands and showed him how to rest it on his arm, tip it up, and let the stream of ale fall into his mouth. "No fine glasses for us in this army, my friend. You're not among the ladies of Basilica now."

"I knew that I was not," said Smelost.

"This letter is so cryptic, my friend," said Moozh. "Surely you can tell us more."

"Not much, I fear," said Smelost, swallowing a mouthful of ale. It was far sweeter than beer, and Moozh could see that he didn't like it much. Well, that hardly mattered, as long as Smelost got enough of the drug concealed in it that he'd speak freely. "I left before anything had come clear." He was lying, of course, thinking that he ought not to say more than Lady Rasa had said.

But soon Smelost overcame his reticence and told Moozh far more than he ever meant to. But Moozh was careful to pretend that he already knew most of it, so that Smelost would not feel he had betrayed any secrets when he thought back on the conversation and how much he had told.

There was obviously much confusion in Basilica at the moment, but the parts of the picture that mattered to Moozh were very clear. Two parties, one for alliance with Potokgavan, one against it, had been struggling for control of the city. Now the leaders of both parties were dead, killed on the same night, possibly by the same assassin, but, in Smelost's opinion, probably not. Accusations of murder were flying wildly; a weak man now controlled one group of hired soldiers who would now wander the streets uncontrolled, while the official city guard was under suspicion because this man, Smelost, had let the suspected assassin sneak out of the city two nights ago.

"What should we expect of a city of women?" said Moozh, when the story was done. "Of course there's confusion. Women are always confused when the violence begins."

Smelost looked at him warily. That was the sweet thing about the drug that Plod had given him—the victim was quite capable of believing that he was still being clever and deceptive, even as he poured out his heart on every subject. Moozh, of course, had immunized himself to the effects of the drug years ago, which was why he had no qualms about taking a mouthful of ale from the same flagon. He was also sure that Plod had no idea that Moozh was immune, and more than once he had suspected that Plod had given him some of the drug, whereupon Moozh always made a point of sharing a few harmless but indiscreet-sounding revelations— usually just his personal opinion of a few other officers. Never anything incriminating. Just enough to let Plod think the drug had worked its will on him.

"Oh, you know what I mean," said Moozh. "Nothing against the women, but they can't help their own biology, can they? It's the way they are—when the violence begins, they must rush to a male to find protection, or they're lost, wouldn't you say?"

Smelost smiled wanly. "You don't know the women of Basilica, then."

"Oh, but I do," said Moozh. "I know *all* women, and the women I don't know, Plod knows—isn't that right, Plod?"

"Oh, yes," said Plod, smiling.

Smelost glowered a little but said nothing.

"The women of Basilica are frightened right now, aren't they? Frightened and acting hastily. They don't like these soldiers running the streets. They fear what will happen if no strong man is there to control them— but they fear just as much what will happen if a strong man *does* come. Who knows how things will turn out, once the violence starts? There's blood on the street of Basilica. A man's head has drunk the dust of the street through both halves of his neck, as we say in Gollod. There's fear in every womanly heart in Basilica, yes, there is, and you know it."

Smelost shrugged. "Of course they're afraid. Who wouldn't be?"

"A *man* wouldn't be," said Moozh. "A *man* would smell the opportunity. A man would say, When others are afraid then anyone who speaks boldly has a chance to lead. Anyone who makes decisions, anyone who *acts* can become the focus of authority, the hope of the desperate, the strength of the weak, the soul of the spiritless. A *man* would *act*."

"Act," Smelost echoed.

"Act *boldly*," said Plod.

"And yet . . . you have come to us with a letter from a

woman pleading for protection." Moozh smiled and shrugged.

Smelost immediately tried to defend himself. "Was I supposed to stand trial for having done what I knew was right?"

"Of course not. What—to be tried by women?" Moozh looked at Plod and laughed; Plod took the cue and joined in. "For acting as a man must act, boldly, with courage—no, you shouldn't stand trial for *that.*"

"So I came here," said Smelost.

"For protection. So *you* could be safe, while your city is in fear."

Smelost rose to his feet. "I didn't come here to be insulted."

In an instant Plod's blade was poised at Smelost's throat. "When the General of the Imperator is seated, all men sit or they are treated as assassins."

Smelost gingerly lowered himself back into his chair.

"Forgive my dearest friend Plod," said Moozh. "I know you meant no harm. After all, you came to *us* to be *safe,* not to start a war!" Moozh laughed, staring in Smelost's eyes all the time, until Smelost also forced himself to laugh.

Smelost clearly hated it, to be forced to laugh at himself for seeking protection instead of acting like a man.

"But perhaps I've misunderstood you," said Moozh. "Perhaps you didn't come, as this letter says, just for yourself. Perhaps you have a plan in mind, some way that you can help your city, some strategem whereby you can ease the fears of the women of Basilica and keep them safe from the chaos that threatens them."

"I have no plan," said Smelost.

"Ah," said Moozh. "Or perhaps you don't yet trust us enough to tell it to us." Moozh looked sad. "I understand. We're strangers, and this is your city at stake, a city that you love more than life itself. Besides, what you would need to ask of us is far greater than a common soldier would ordinarily dare to ask a general of the Gorayni. So I will not press you now. Go—Plod will show you to a tent where you can drink and sleep, and when this storm dies down you can bathe and eat, and by then perhaps you'll feel confident enough of me to tell me what you want us to do, to save your beautiful and beloved city from anarchy."

As soon as Moozh finished talking, he gave a subtle hand signal and then leaned his elbow on the arm of his chair, pretending to be a bit saddened by Smelost's reluctance to help. Plod caught the hand signal, of course, and immediately rushed Smelost out of the tent and back out into the storm.

As soon as they were outside, Moozh leapt to his feet and stood hunched over the table, studying the map. Basilica—so far to the south, but in the highest part of the mountains, right up against the desert, so that it would be possible to get there from here through the mountains. In two days, if he took only a few hundred men and pressed them hard. Two days, and he could easily be in possession of the greatest city of the Western Shore, the city whose caravanners have made their language the trading argot of every city and nation from Potokgavan to Gorayni. Never mind that Basilica had no meaningful army. What mattered was how it would seem to the Cities of the Plain—and to Potokgavan. *They* would not know how few and weak the Gorayni army would be. They would know only that the great General Vozmuzhalnoy Vozmozhno had stolen a march, conquered a city of legend and mystery, and now, instead of being a hundred and fifty kilometers north, beyond Seggidugu, now he loomed over them, could watch their every move from the towers of Basilica.

It would be a devastating blow. Knowing that Vozmuzhalnoy Vozmozhno would watch their fleet arrive and have plenty of time to bring his men down from Basilica and slaughter their army as it tried to land, Potokgavan would not dare to send an expeditionary force to the Cities of the Plain. And as for the cities themselves, they would surrender one by one, and soon Seggidugu would find itself surrounded, with no hope of succor from Potokgavan. They would make peace on any terms they could get. There probably wouldn't even be a battle—complete victory, at no cost, all because Basilica was in chaos and this soldier had come to tell Vozmuzhalnoy Vozmozhno of his glorious opportunity.

The tent flap reopened and Plod came back in. "The storm is dying down," he said.

"Very good," said Moozh.

"What was all that about?" said Plod.

"What?"

"That nonsense you were saying to that Basilican soldier."

Moozh could not imagine what Plod was talking about. Basilican soldier? He had never seen a Basilican soldier in his life.

But Plod glanced at one of the chairs, and now Moozh vaguely remembered that not long ago *someone* had sat in that chair. Someone . . . a Basilican soldier? That would be important—how could he have forgotten?

I didn't forget, thought Moozh. I didn't forget. God has spoken, God has tried to make me stupid, but I refuse. I will not be forced into obedience.

"How do *you* assess the situation?" he asked. It would never do to let Plod think that Moozh was actually confused or forgetful.

"Basilica is far away," said Plod. "We can give this man sanctuary or kill him or send him back, it hardly matters. What is Basilica to us?"

Poor fool, thought Moozh. That's why you're merely the dear friend of the general, and not the general yourself, though I know you long to be. Moozh knew what Basilica was. It was the city of women whose influence had castrated his ancestors and cost them their freedom and their honor. It was also the great citadel poised above the Cities of the Plain. If Moozh could possess it, he wouldn't have to fight a single battle—his enemies would collapse before him. Was this the plan that he had had before, the one that God was trying to make him forget?

"Write this down," said Moozh.

Plod opened his computer and began to press the keys to record Moozh's words.

"Whoever is master of Basilica is master of the Cities of the Plain."

"But Moozh, Basilica has never exercised hegemony over those cities."

"Because it's a city of women," said Moozh. "If it were ruled by a man with an army, that would be a different story."

"We could never get there to take it," said Plod. "All of Seggidugu lies between us and Basilica."

Moozh looked at the map and another part of his plan came back to his mind. "A desert march."

"During the month of western storms!" cried Plod. "The men would refuse to obey!"

"In the mountains there's shelter. There are plenty of mountain roads."

"Not for an army," said Plod.

"Not for a *large* army," said Moozh, making up the plan as he went along.

"You could never hold Basilica against Potokgavan with the size army you could bring," said Plod.

Moozh studied the map for a moment longer. "But Potokgavan will never come, not if we already hold Basilica. *They* won't know how large an army we have, but they *will* know that we can see the whole coastline from there. Where would they dare to bring their fleet, knowing we could see them from far off and greet them at the shore, to cut them apart as they land?"

Plod finished typing, then studied the map himself. "There's merit in that," he said.

Why is there merit in it? Moozh asked silently. I haven't the faintest idea why I have this plan, except that a Basilican soldier apparently came here. What did he tell me? Why does this plan have merit?

"And with the present chaos in Basilica, you could probably take the city."

Chaos in Basilica. Good. So I wasn't wrong—the Basilican soldier apparently let me know of an opportunity.

"Yes," said Plod. "We have the perfect excuse for doing it, too. We aren't coming to invade, but rather to save the people of Basilica from the mercenary soldiers who are wandering their streets."

Mercenary soldiers? The idea was absurd—why would Basilica have mercenary soldiers running loose? Had there been a war? God had never made Moozh so forgetful that he couldn't remember a whole war!

"And the immediate provocation—the murders. The blood was already flowing—we had to come, to stop the bloodshed. Yes, that will be plenty of justification for it. No one can criticize us for attacking the city of women, if we come to save them from blood in the streets."

So that's my plan, thought Moozh. A very good one it is. Even God can't stop me from carrying it out. "Write it up, Plod, and have my aides draw up detailed orders for a thousand men to march in four columns through the mountains. Only three days' worth of supplies—the men can carry it on their backs."

"Three days!" said Plod. "And what if something goes wrong?"

"Knowing they have but three days' worth of food, dear

Plod, the men will march very fast indeed, and they will allow nothing to delay them."

"What if the situation has changed at Basilica, when we arrive? What if we meet stout resistance? The walls of Basilica are high and thick, and chariots are useless in that terrain."

"Then it's a good thing we'll bring no chariots, isn't it? Except perhaps one, for my triumphal entry into the city—in the name of the Imperator, of course."

"Still, they might resist, and we'll arrive with scarcely any food to spare. We can't exactly besiege them!"

"We'll have no need to besiege them. We have only to ask them to open the gates, and the gates will open."

"Why?"

"Because I say so," said Moozh. "When have I been wrong before?"

Plod shook his head. "Never, my dear friend and beloved general. But by the time we get the Imperator's permission to go there, the chaos in the streets of Basilica may well have been settled, and it will take a much larger army than a thousand men to force the issue."

Moozh looked at him in surprise. "Why would we wait for the Imperator's permission?"

"Because the Imperator forbade you to make any attack until the stormy season is over."

"On the contrary," said Moozh. "The Imperator forbade me to attack Nakavalnu and Izmennik. I am not attacking them. I'm passing them by on their left flank, and marching as swift as horses through the mountains to Basilica, where again I will not attack anybody, but will rather enter the city of Basilica to restore order in the name of the Imperator. None of this violates any order of the Imperator."

Plod's face darkened. "You are interpreting the words of the Imperator, my general, and that is something only the intercessor has the right to do."

"Every soldier and every officer must interpret the orders he is given. I was sent to these southlands in order to conquer the entire western shore of the Earthbound Sea—that was the command the Imperator gave to me, and to me alone. If I failed to seize this great opportunity that God has given me"—ha!—"then I would be disobedient indeed."

"My dear friend, noblest general of the Gorayni, I beg you not to attempt this. The intercessor will not see it as obedience but as insubordination."

"Then the intercessor is no true servant of the Imperator."

Plod immediately bowed his head. "I see that I have spoken too boldly."

Moozh knew at once that this meant Plod intended to tell the intercessor everything and try to stop him. When Plod meant to obey, he did not put on this great pretense of obedience.

"Give me your computer," said Moozh. "I will write the orders myself."

"Don't shame me," said Plod in dismay. "I must write them, or I have failed in my duty to you."

"You will sit with me here," said Moozh, "and watch as I write the orders."

Plod flung himself to his knees on the carpets. "Moozh, my friend, I'd rather you kill me than shame me like this."

"I knew that you didn't intend to obey me," said Moozh. "Don't lie and say you did."

"I meant to delay," said Plod. "I meant to give you time to reconsider. Hoping that you'd realize the grave danger of opposing the Imperator, especially so soon after you dreamed a dream that was contemptuous of his holy person."

It took a moment for Moozh to remember what Plod was referring to; then his rage turned cold and hard indeed. "Who would know of that dream, except myself and my friend?"

"Your friend loved you enough to tell the dream to the intercessor," said Plod, "lest your soul be in danger of destruction without your knowing it."

"Then my friend must love me indeed," said Moozh.

"I do," said Plod. "With all my heart. I love you more than any man or woman on this Earth, excepting God alone, and his holy incarnation."

Moozh regarded his dearest friend with icy calm. "Use your computer, my friend, and call the intercessor to my tent. Have him stop on the way and bring the Basilican soldier with him."

"I'll go and get them," said Plod.

"Call them by computer."

"But what if the intercessor isn't using his computer right now?"

"Then we'll wait until he does." Moozh smiled. "But he *will* be using it, won't he?"

"Perhaps," said Plod. "How would I know?"

"Call them. I want the intercessor to hear my interrogation of the Basilican soldier. Then he'll know that we must go now, and not wait for word from the Imperator."

Plod nodded. "Very wise, my friend. I should have known that you wouldn't flout the will of the Imperator. The intercessor will listen to you, and *he'll* decide."

"We'll decide *together*," said Moozh.

"Of course." He pressed the keys; Moozh made no effort to watch him, but he could see the words in the air over the computer well enough to know that Plod was sending a quick, straightforward request to the intercessor.

"Alone," said Moozh. "If we decide not to act, I want no rumors to spread about Basilica."

"I already asked him to come alone," said Plod.

They waited, talking all the time of other things. Of campaigns in years past. Of officers who had served with them. Of women they had known.

"Have you ever *loved* a woman?" asked Moozh.

"I have a wife," said Plod.

"And you love her?"

Plod thought a moment. "When I'm with her. She's the mother of my sons."

"I have no sons," said Moozh. "No children at all, that I know of. No woman who has pleased me for more than a night."

"None?" asked Plod.

Moozh flushed with embarrassment, realizing what Plod was remembering. "I never loved *her,*" he said. "I took her—as an act of piety."

"Once is an act of piety," said Plod, chuckling. "Two months one year, and then another month three years later—that's more than piety, that's *sainthood.*"

"She was nothing to me," said Moozh. "I took her only for the sake of God." And it was true, though not in the way Plod understood it. The woman had appeared as if out of nowhere, dirty and naked, and called Moozh by name. Everyone knew such women were from God. But Moozh knew that when he thought of taking her, God sent him that stupor that meant it was *not* God's will for Moozh to proceed. So Moozh proceeded anyway, and kept the woman— bathed her, and clothed her, and treated her as tenderly as a wife. All the while he felt God's anger boiling at the back of his mind, and he laughed at God. He kept the woman with him until she disappeared, as suddenly as she had come, leaving all her fine clothing behind, taking nothing, not even food, not even water.

"So that wasn't love," said Plod. "God honors you for your sacrifice, then, I'm sure!" Plod laughed again, and for good fellowship Moozh also joined in.

They were still laughing when there came a scratching at the tent, and Plod leapt to open it. The intercessor came in first, which was his duty—and an expression of his faith in God, since the intercessor always left himself available to be stabbed in the back, if God did not protect him. Then a stranger came in. Moozh had no memory of ever having seen the man before. By his garb he was a soldier of a fine city; by his body he was a soft soldier, a gate guard rather than a fighting man; by his familiar nod, Moozh knew that this must be the Basilican soldier, and he must indeed have spoken with him, and left the conversation on friendly terms.

The intercessor sat first, and then Moozh; only then could the others take their places.

"Let me see your blade," Moozh said to the Basilican soldier. "I want to see what kind of steel you have in Basilica."

Warily the Basilican arose from his seat, watching Plod all the while. Vaguely Moozh remembered Plod with a blade at the Basilican's throat; no wonder the man was wary now! With two fingers the man drew his short sword from its sheath, and handed it, hilt first, to Moozh.

It was a city sword, for close work, not a great hewing sword for the battlefield. Moozh tested the blade against the skin of his own arm, cutting only slightly, but enough to draw a line of blood. The man winced to see it. Soft. Soft.

"I've thought about what you said, sir," the Basilican said.

Ah. So I gave him something to think about.

"And I can see that my city needs your help. But who am I to ask for it, or even to know what help would be right or sufficient? I'm only a gate guard; it's only the sheerest chance that I got caught up in these great affairs."

"You love your city, don't you?" asked Moozh, for now he knew what he must have told the man. I *am* sharp enough even on my bad days, Moozh thought with some satisfaction. Sharp enough to lay God-proof plans.

"Yes, I do." Tears had suddenly come to the man's eyes.

"Forgive me, but someone else asked me that, just before I left Basilica. Now I know by this omen that you are a true servant of the Oversoul, and I can trust you."

Moozh gazed steadily into the man's eyes, to show him that trust was appropriate indeed.

"Come to Basilica, sir. Come with an army. Restore order in the streets, and drive out the mercenaries. Then the women of Basilica will have no more fear."

Moozh nodded wisely. "An eloquent and noble request, which in my heart I long to fulfill. But I am a servant of the Imperator, and you must explain the situation in your city to the intercessor here, who is the eyes and ears and heart of the Imperator in our camp." As he spoke, Moozh rose to his feet, facing the intercessor, and bowed. Behind him he could hear Plod and the Basilican soldier also standing and bowing.

Surely Plod is clever enough to know what I plan to do, thought Moozh with a thrill of fear. Surely his knife is even now out of its sheath, to be buried in my back. Surely he knows that if he does not do this, the Basilican blade I hold in my hands will snake out and take his head clean off his shoulders as I rise.

But Plod was not that clever, and so in a moment his blood gouted and spattered across the tent as his body collapsed, his head flopping about on the end of the half-severed spine.

Moozh's blow had been so quick, so smooth, that neither the Basilican nor the intercessor quite understood how Plod came to be so abruptly dead. That gave Moozh plenty of time to drive the Basilican blade upward under the intercessor's ribs, finding his heart before the intercessor could speak a word or even raise himself from his chair.

The Moozh turned to the trembling Basilican.

"What is your name, soldier?"

"Smelost, sir. As I told you. I've lied about nothing, sir."

"I know you haven't. Neither have I. These men were determined to stop me from coming to the aid of your city. That's why I brought them here together. If you wanted me to help you, I had to kill them first."

"Whatever you say, sir."

"No, not whatever I say. Only the truth, Smelost. These men were both spies set to watch every move I made, to hear every word I spoke, and judge my loyalty to the Imperator constantly. This one"—he pointed at Plod—"interpreted a dream I had as a sign of disloyalty, and told the intercessor. It would only have been a matter of time before they reported me and I lost my command, and then who would have come to save Basilica?"

"But how will you explain their deaths?" asked Smelost.

Moozh said nothing

Smelost waited. Then he looked again at the bodies. "I see," he said. "The blade that killed them was mine."

"How much do you love your city?" asked Moozh.

"With all my heart."

"More than life?" asked Moozh.

Gravely Smelost nodded. There was fear in his eyes, but he did not tremble.

"If my soldiers think I killed Plod and the intercessor, they will tear me to pieces. But if they think—no, if they *know* that *you* did it, and I killed you for it— then they will follow me in righteous indignation. I'll tell them that you were one of the mercenaries. I will besmirch your name. I will say you were a traitor to Basilica, trying to prevent me from going to the city's aid. But because they believe those lies about you, they will follow me there and we will save your city."

Smelost smiled. "It seems that my fate is to be thought a worse traitor the better I serve my city."

"It is a terrible day when a man must choose between

being thought loyal, and being loyal in fact, but that day has come to you."

"Tell me what to do."

Moozh almost wept with admiration for the courage and honor of the man, as he explained the simple play they would put on. *If I did not serve a higher cause*, thought Moozh, *I would be too ashamed to deceive a man of such honor as yourself. But for the sake of Pravo Gollossa I will do any terrible thing.*

A moment later, in a lull in the windstorm, Moozh and Smelost both began to bellow, and Moozh let out a high scream that witnesses would later swear was the death cry of the intercessor. Then, as soldiers stumbled out of their tents, they saw Smelost, already bleeding from a wound in his thigh, lurch from the general's tent, carrying a short sword dripping with blood. "For Gaballufix! Death to the Imperator!"

The name of Gaballufix meant nothing to the Gorayni soldiers, though soon enough it would be rich with meaning. What they cared about was the latter part of Smelost's shout—death to the Imperator. No one could say such a thing in a Gorayni camp without being flayed alive.

Before anyone could reach him, though, the general himself staggered from the tent, bleeding from his arm and holding his head where he must have been struck a blow. The general—the great Vozmuzhalnoy Vozmozhno, called Moozh whenever they thought he could not hear—held a battle-ax in his left arm—his left, not his right!—and struck downward into the base of the assassin's neck, cleaving him to the heart. He should not have done it; everyone knew he should have let the man be taken and tortured to punish him. But then, to their horror, the general sank to his knees—the general with ice in his veins instead of blood—he sank to his knees and wept bitterly, crying out from the depths of his soul, "Plodorodnuy, my friend, my heart, my life! Ah, Plod! Ah, Plod, God should have taken me and left you!"

It was a grief both glorious and terrible to behold, and without speaking a word openly about it, the soldiers who heard his keening resolved to tell no one of his blasphemous suggestion that perhaps God might have ordered the world improperly. When they entered the tent they understood perfectly why Moozh had forgotten himself and killed the assassin with his own hand, for how could any mortal man see his dearest friend and the intercessor both so cruelly murdered, and still contain his rage?

Soon the story spread through the camp that Moozh was taking a thousand fierce soldiers with him on a forced march through the mountains, to take the city of Basilica and destroy the party of Gaballufix, a group of men so daring and treacherous that they had dared to send an assassin against the general of the Gorayni. Too bad for them that God so dearly loved the Gorayni that he would not permit their Moozh to be slain by treachery. Instead God had caused Moozh's heart to be filled with righteous wrath, and Basilica would soon know what it meant to have God and the Gorayni as their overlords.

THREE

PROTECTION

THE DREAM OF THE ELDEST SON

The camels had all gathered under the shade of the large palm fronds that Wetchik and his sons had woven into a roof between a group of four large trees near the stream. Elemak envied them—the shade was good there, the stream was cool, and they could catch the breeze, so the air was never as stuffy as it was inside the tents. He was done with his work for the morning, and now there was nothing useful to do during the heat of the day. Let Father and Nafai and Issib drip their sweat all over each other as they huddled around the Index of the Oversoul in Father's tent. What did the Oversoul know? It was just a computer—Nafai himself said that, in his adolescent fanatic piety—so why should Elemak bother with a conversation with a machine? It had a vast library of information . . . so what? Elemak was done with school.

So he sat in the hot shade of the southern cliff, knowing that he would have at most an hour of rest before the sun rose high enough that the shade would disappear, and he would have to move. That didn't really bother Elemak—in fact, on his caravans he had counted on that to awaken him, so that he didn't sleep overlong during the day when they rested at oases. What made him so angry that he felt it like a pain in his stomach all the time was the fact that it was all so useless. They were not traveling, they were merely waiting here in the desert—and for what? For nothing. The Oversoul said that Basilica would be destroyed, that the world of Harmony was going to collapse in war and terror. It was laughably unlikely that any such thing would happen. The world had gone forty million years without being devastated by war. Now, for the first time, two great empires were on the verge of collision, and the Oversoul was treating it as if it were some cosmic event.

I could have understood leaving Basilica, he told himself, if we had taken our fortune with us and gone to another city and started over. What was vital in the plant trade was the knowledge inside Father's and my heads, not the buildings or the hired workers. We could have been rich. Instead we're here in the desert, we lost our entire fortune to my half-brother Gaballufix, and now Nafai has murdered *him* and we can never go back to Basilica again, or if we did, we'd be poor so why bother?

Except that even poverty in Basilica would be better than this meaningless waiting out here in the desert, in this miserable little valley that barely supported the troop of baboons downstream of them. Even now he could hear them barking and hooting. Beasts that couldn't decide whether to be men or dogs. That's exactly what we are now, only we didn't even have the sense to bring mates with us when we left, so we can't even form a reasonable tribe.

Despite the arrhythmic noises of the baboons and the occasional snorting of the camels, Elemak soon slept. He woke moments later, or so it felt; he could feel the burning heat of the sun on his clothing, so he assumed that the sun had wakened him. But no, it was something else; there was a shadow moving near him. With his eyes closed he thought of where his knife was and remembered how the ground was near him. Then, with a sudden rush of movement, he was on his feet, his long knife in his hand, squinting in the bright sunlight to see where his enemy was.

"It's only me!" squeaked Zdorab.

Elemak put away his knife in disgust. "You don't come up silently when a man is asleep in the desert. You can get yourself killed that way. I assumed you were a robber."

"But I wasn't all that quiet," said Zdorab reasonably. "In fact, you were noisy yourself. Dreaming, I expect."

That bothered Elemak, that he had not slept silently. But now that Zdorab mentioned it, he remembered that he *had* dreamed, and he remembered the dream with remarkable clarity. In fact he had never had such a clear dream, not that he remembered, anyway, and it made him think. "What was I saying?" asked Elemak.

"I don't know," said Zdorab. "It was more of a mumble. I came up here because your father asked to see you. I wouldn't have disturbed you otherwise."

It was true. Zdorab was the consummate servant, invisible most of the time, but always ready to help—even when he was completely incompetent, which was usually the case here in the desert, where the skills of a treasurer were quite useless. "Thanks," said Elemak. "I'll come in a minute."

Zdorab waited for just a moment—that hesitation that all good servants acquired sooner or later, that single moment in which the master could think of something else to tell before they left. Then he was gone, shambling clumsily down the shale slope and then across the dry stony soil to Wetchik's tent.

Elemak pulled up his desert robe and peed out in the open, where the sun would evaporate his urine in moments, before too many flies could gather. Then he headed for the stream, took a drink in his cupped hand, splashed water into his face and over his head, and only then made his way to where Father and all the others were waiting.

"Well," said Elemak as he entered. "Have you learned everything the Oversoul has to teach you?"

Nafai glared at him with his typical look of disapproval. Someday Elemak knew he'd have to give Nafai the beating of his life, just to teach him not to get that expression on his face, at least not toward Elemak. He had tried to give him that beating once before, and he had learned that *next* time he'd have to do it away from Issib's chair, so the Oversoul couldn't take control of it and interfere. But for now there was nothing to be gained by letting Nafai's snottiness get under his skin; so Elemak pretended not to notice.

"We need to start hunting for meat," said Father.

Elemak immediately let his eyes half close as he thought of what that meant. They had brought enough supplies for eight or nine months—for a year, if they were careful. Yet Father was talking about needing to hunt. That could only mean that he didn't expect to get anywhere civilized within a year.

"How about shopping for groceries in the Outer Market," said Meb.

Elemak agreed wholeheartedly, but said nothing as Father lectured Meb on the impossibility of returning to Basilica any time soon. He waited until the little scene had played itself out. Poor Meb—when would he learn that it's better to remain silent except to say what will accomplish your purpose?

Only when silence had returned did Elemak speak up. "We can hunt," he said. "This is fairly lush country, for desert, and I think we could probably bring in something once a week—for a few months."

"Can you do it?" asked Father.

"Not alone," said Elemak. "If Meb and I hunt every day, we'll find something once a week."

"Nafai too," said Father.

"No!" moaned Mebbekew. "He'll just get in the way."

"I'll teach him," said Elemak. "For that matter, I don't imagine Meb will be worth anything more than Nafai at first. But you have to tell them both—when we're hunting, my word is law."

"Of course," said Father. "They'll do exactly what you tell them, and nothing more."

"I'll take each of them every other day," said Elemak. "That way I won't have to put up with their arguing with each other."

Mebbekew glared at him with loathing—so subtle, Meb, no wonder you were such a successful actor—but Nafai only looked at the carpet on the floor of the tent. What was he thinking? No doubt conniving to find some way to turn this to his advantage.

Sure enough, Nafai lifted up his head and spoke solemnly to Elemak. "Elya, I'm sorry I've given you cause to think that's what I'd do, if you took Meb and me at once. If having us both come at once would be more efficient, I can promise I'll not say a word of argument, either to you or Meb."

Just like the little sneak, to make himself look so pious and cooperative, when Elemak knew that he would be snotty and argumentative the whole way, no matter what he promised now. But Elemak said nothing, as Father quietly praised Nafai's attitude, then told him that Elya's decision would stand. They would go hunting with Elya one at a time. "You'll learn better one on one, I assure you," said Father.

At times like this Elemak almost believed that Father saw through Nafai's righteous act. But it wasn't so; in a moment Father would go off talking about what the Oversoul wanted, and then he and Nafai would be as thick as thieves.

Thinking of thieves made Elemak remember how Zdorab had wakened him a few moments ago; and thinking of waking up reminded him of his vivid dream. And it occurred to him that it might be amusing to play Nafai's game, and pretend that his dream was some vision from the Oversoul. "I was sleeping by the rocks," said Elemak into the silence, "and I dreamed a dream."

Immediately all eyes were on him, waiting. Elemak sized them up under heavy-lidded eyes; he saw the immediate joy on his father's face, and was almost ashamed of the sham he was going to play—but the consternation on Nafai's face and the utter horror on Meb's made it well worth doing. "I dreamed a dream," he said, "in which I saw all of us coming out of a large house."

"Whose house was it?" asked Nafai.

"Hush and let him tell the dream," said Father.

"A kind of house I've never seen before. And we didn't come out alone—the six of us, all six of us, each came out with a woman. And there were two other men, each with a woman as well. And many children. All of us had children."

There was silence for a long moment.

"Is that all?" asked Nafai.

Elemak said nothing, and the silence resumed.

"Elya," said Issib. "Did *I* have a wife?"

"In my dream," said Elemak, "you had a wife."

"Did you see her face?" asked Issib. "Did you know who she was?"

Now Elemak felt truly ashamed of himself, for he could see that Issib believed that this was a true vision, and for the first time in his life it occurred to him that poor Issib, palsied as he was, nevertheless yearned for a woman as any other man might yearn, and yet had no hope of finding one who would want him. In Basilica, where women had their pick of men, it would be one piss-poor specimen of womanhood who would choose a cripple like Issib for a mate. Even if he ever managed to have sex, it would be because some jaded female was curious about him—especially with his floats, that might interest some of the more adventurous ones. But to mate with him, to bear him children, to give him father's rights, no, that wouldn't happen, and Issib knew it. Which meant that by telling this dream, Elemak wasn't just manipulating Father, he was also setting Issib up for cruel disappointment. Elemak felt like shit.

"I didn't see her face," said Elemak. "It probably didn't mean anything. It was just a dream."

"It meant something," said Father.

"It means Elemak is ridiculing us," said Nafai. "He's making fun of us for having visions from the Oversoul."

"Don't call me a liar," said Elemak softly. "If I say I dreamed, I dreamed. Whether it means anything, I can't say. But I saw what I saw. Isn't that what Father said? Isn't that what *you* said? I saw what I saw."

"It meant something," said Father again. "Now an odd message I received through the Index makes perfect sense."

Oh no, thought Elemak. What have I done?

"I have thought for some time that we couldn't accomplish the Oversoul's purpose without wives. And yet where could we possibly find women who would join us here?"

Where could you find *men* who would join you here, for that matter, Father, except that you trapped your own sons into coming with you?

"But when I asked the Oversoul, the answer I got was to wait. That's all, just wait, which made no sense to me. Would wives sprout from the rocks? Would we mate with baboons?"

Elemak couldn't resist a jab. "Meb already has, from time to time."

Meb simpered.

"And now Elemak has dreamed," Father said. "I think that is what the Oversoul wanted me to wait for— Elemak's dream. For the answer to come to my eldest son, to my heir. So, Elya, you must think, you must remember—did you recognize *any* of the women in your dream?"

Father was taking this way too seriously, tying it with Elemak's status as his eldest. Elemak had been a fool to start this whole vision business today, he could see that now; how could he have forgotten that Father was willing to ruin everybody's lives for the sake of a vision? "No," said Elemak, to silence him, though it wasn't true.

"Think," said Father. "I know that you recognized at least one."

Elemak looked at him, startled. Had the old man started reading his mind now? "If the Oversoul has told you more about my dream than I know myself, then *you* tell us who they are," said Elemak.

"I know you recognized one because you said her name. If you think hard enough, you'll remember."

Elemak glanced at Zdorab, who was looking at the carpet. So, thought Elemak. When Zdorab said that he understood nothing of what I said in my sleep, it wasn't quite true. "What name?" asked Elemak.

"Eiadh," said Nafai. "Am I right?"

Elemak said nothing, but he hated Nafai for saying the name of the woman Elemak had been courting before Father dragged them out into the desert.

"It's all right," said Father. "I understand perfectly. You didn't want to tell us her name for fear that we would think that your dream was just an erotic wish for the woman you loved, and not a true dream."

Since that was exactly what Elemak thought his dream actually was, he couldn't argue with Wetchik's conclusion.

"But think, my sons. Would the Oversoul require you to choose strangers as your mates? You dreamed of Eiadh because the Oversoul intends her to be your mate," said Father. "And it makes sense, doesn't it? For you saw *me* with a mate as well, didn't you?"

"Yes," said Elemak, remembering. The dream was still *so* vivid in his mind that he could call it back, not just as a vague memory, but clearly. "Yes, and children. Young ones."

"There is only one woman I would take as my mate," said Father. "Rasa."

"She'd never leave Basilica," said Issib. "If you think she would, you don't know Mother."

"Ah," said Father. "But *I* would never have left Basilica, either, except that the Oversoul led me. Nor would Elemak and Mebbekew, except that the Oversoul brought them."

"Nor I," said Zdorab.

"Could the woman you saw in your dream, the woman who was *my* mate . . . she was Rasa, wasn't she?" asked Father.

Of course it was Rasa, but that didn't prove anything. Rasa had been Father's wife, year after year, so of course it was Rasa who would show up as his woman in Elemak's dreams. It would take no vision from the Oversoul for *that*. "Perhaps," said Elemak.

"And did you recognize any of the other women? For instance, the two other men who were strangers—could their mates have been Rasa's daughters?"

"I don't know your wife's daughters all that well," said Elemak. How far would this game have to go before he could have done with it?

"Don't be absurd," said Father. "They're your nieces, aren't they? Gaballufix's daughters."

"And one of them is famous," chimed in Meb. "Sevet, the singer—you've seen her."

"Yes," said Elemak. "The wives of the two strangers were Rasa's daughters." Of course he knew them, and their husbands, too, Vas and Obring.

"There, you see?" said Father. "The Oversoul has given you a true vision. The women you saw are all connected with Rasa. Her daughters, and Eiadh, one of the nieces of her household. I'm sure the others are all of her household, too. So this isn't some impossible dream that came to you because you had a hunger for venery, my son. This came from the Oversoul, because the Oversoul knows that to accomplish our purpose we must have wives who will bear us children. All of us."

"Well," said Elemak, "if it's really a vision, then *I'm* happy enough for the Oversoul to give me Eiadh. But I think there's a better chance of finding a falcon in a frog's mouth than of anyone *but* the Oversoul ever persuading Eiadh to come out into the desert to marry a penniless, homeless man like me, with no hope of wealth."

"You forget that the Oversoul has promised us a land of unspeakable richness," said Father.

"And you forget that we haven't found it yet," said Elemak. "We're not likely to find it, either, squatting in the desert like this."

"The Oversoul has shown us what we must do," said Father. "And as Nafai said to me before you left to seek the Index—if the Oversoul requires us to do something, he'll open a way for us to do it."

"Great idea," said Mebbekew. "Whom will Nafai kill to get us some women?"

"That's enough," said Father.

"Come on," said Mebbekew. "How else would Nafai ever get a wife, except by killing some drunk passed out on the street and stealing his blind, crippled daughter."

To Elemak's surprise, Nafai said nothing to Mebbekew's gibes. Instead, the boy got up and left the tent. So, thought Elemak. Nafai isn't entirely a child. Or else he was ashamed to have us see him cry.

"Meb," said Issib softly, "Nafai brought the Index, and you didn't."

"Oh, come on," said Mebbekew. "Can't anybody take a joke around here?"

"It isn't a joke to Nafai," said Issib. "Killing Gaballufix

is the most terrible thing he ever did, and he thinks about it all the time."

"You were out of line to throw it up to him," said Father. "Don't do it again."

"What am I supposed to do," Mebbekew insisted, "pretend that Nafai got the Index by saying Pity Please?"

It was time for Elemak to get Mebbekew back in line—no one else could do it, and it needed to be done. "What you're supposed to do is shut up," said Elemak softly.

Meb looked at him defiantly. It was all an act, though, Elemak knew. All he had to do was meet Meb's gaze and hold it, and Meb would back down. It didn't take long, either.

"Elemak," said Father, "you must go back, you and your brothers."

"Don't put this on *me*," said Elemak. "If anyone can persuade Rasa, it's *you*."

"On the contrary," said Wetchik. "She knows me, she knows I love her, she loves me too—and that didn't bring her with me before. Do you think I didn't suggest it? No, if anyone persuades her it will be the Oversoul. All you have to do is go and suggest it to her, wait for the Oversoul to help her understand that she must come, and then provide safe escort for her and her daughters and the young women of her household who come with her."

"Oh, fine," said Elemak. He could wait a long cold time for the Oversoul to persuade anybody but Father to do something as idiotic as leaving Basilica for the desert. But at least he'd be waiting in Basilica, even if he had to do it in hiding. "Should I have her bring along a servant for Zdorab, too?"

Father's face went icy. "Zdorab isn't a servant now," he said. "He's a free man, and the equal of any man here. A woman of Rasa's household would do for him as well as for any of you, and as for that, a serving girl in Rasa's house would also do for any of you. Don't you understand that we're no longer in Basilica, that the society we form now will have no room for snobbery and bigotry, for castes and classes? We will be one people, all equals, with all our children equal in the eyes of the Oversoul."

In the eyes of the Oversoul, perhaps, but not in my eyes, thought Elemak. I'm the eldest son, and my firstborn son will be my heir as I am *your* heir, Father. Even if you gave up the lands and holdings that should have been my inheritance, I will still inherit your authority, and no matter where we end up settling, *I* will rule, or no one will. I may say nothing of this now, because I know when to speak and when not to speak. But be sure of this, Father. When you die, I will have your place—and anyone who tries to deprive me of it will follow you quickly into the grave.

Elemak looked at Issib and Meb, and knew that neither would resist him when that day came. But Nafai would cause trouble, bless his dear little heart. And Nafai knows it, thought Elemak. He knows that someday it will come down to him and me. For someday Father will try to pass his authority on to this miserable little toady of a boy, all because Nafai is so thick with the Oversoul. Well, Nafai, I've had a vision from the Oversoul, too—or at least Father thinks I have, which amounts to the same thing.

"Leave in the morning," Father said. "Come back with the women who will share the inheritance the Oversoul has prepared for us in another land. Come back with the mothers of my grandchildren."

"Mebbekew and I," said Elemak. "No others."

"Issib will stay home because his chair and his floats make him too conspicuous, and he increases your chances of being caught by our enemies there," said Father. "And Zdorab will stay."

Because you don't quite trust him yet, thought Elemak, no matter how much you claim that he's our equal and a free man.

"But Nafai goes with you."

"No," said Elemak. "He's even more dangerous to us than Issib. They're bound to have figured out that he killed Gaballufix—the city computer got his name on the way out of town, and the guards saw him wearing Gaballufix's clothing. And he had Zdorab with him, to clinch the connection between him and Gab's death. Bringing Nafai is like asking to have him killed."

"He goes with you," said Father.

"Why, when he only increases our danger?" demanded Elemak.

"Yes, *make* him say it, Elya," said Mebbekew. "Father doesn't want to insult you, but *I* don't mind. He wants Nafai there because, as someone recently pointed out, Nafai got the Index and none of the rest of us did. He wants Nafai there because he doesn't trust us not to just find some woman to take us in and stay in Basilica and never come back to this paradise by the sea. He wants Nafai there because he thinks Nafai will make us be good."

"Not at all," said Issib. "Father wants him to learn strength and wisdom by associating with his older brothers."

No one was ever sure whether Issib was being ironic or not. Nobody believed that this was Father's true purpose, but nobody—least of all Father—cared to deny it openly, either.

In the silence, the words that still rang in Elemak's ears were the last ones he himself had said: Bringing Nafai is like asking to have him killed.

"All right, Father," said Elemak. "Nafai can come with me."

IN BASILICA, AND NOT IN A DREAM

Kokor could not understand why *she* should be in seclusion. For Sevet it made sense—she was recuperating from her unfortunate accident. Her voice wasn't back yet; she was no doubt embarrassed to appear in public. But Kokor was in perfect health, and for her to have to hide out at Mother's house made it look as if she were ashamed to come out in public. If she had deliberately injured Sevet, then perhaps such isolation might be necessary. But since it was simply an unfortunate accident, the result of a psychological disturbance due to Father's death and the discovery of Sevet's and Obring's adultery, why, no one could blame Kokor. In fact, it would do her good to be seen in public. It would surely speed her recovery.

At least she should be able to go home to her own house, and not have to stay with Mother, as if she were a little girl or a mental incompetent who needed a guardian. Where was Obring? If he ever intended to make things up with her, he could begin by coming and getting her out of Mother's unbearably staid environment. There was nothing interesting going on here. Just endless classes in subjects that hadn't interested Kokor even when she was failing them years ago. Kokor was a woman of substance now. Father's inheritance probably would enable her to buy a house and keep her own establishment. And here she was living with mother.

Not that she saw that much of Mother. Rasa was constantly in meetings with councilors and other influential women of the city, who were making virtual pilgrimages to see her and talk to her. Some of the meetings seemed to be somewhat tense; Rasa began to gather the idea that some people, at least, were blaming Rasa for everything. As if Mother would try to kill Father! But they remembered that it was Rasa's current husband, Wetchik, who had his inflammatory vision about Basilica in flames, and then her former husband, Gaballufix, who put tolchoks and then mercenary soldiers on the streets of the city. And now the word was that her youngest son, Nafai, was the killer of both Roptat and Gaballufix.

Well, even if all that was true, what did that have to do with Mother? Women can't very well control their husbands—didn't Kokor have proof of that herself? And as for Nafai killing Father—well, even if he did it, *Mother* wasn't there, and she certainly didn't *ask* the boy to do it. They might as well blame Mother for what happened to Sevet, when anyone could see it was Sevet's own fault. Besides, wasn't Father's death his own fault, really? All those soldiers—you don't bring soldiers into Basilica and expect not to have violence, do you? Men never understood these things. They could turn things loose, but they were always surprised when they couldn't tame them again at will.

Like Obring, poor fool. Didn't he know that it wasn't a clever thing to come between sisters? He was really more to blame for Sevet's injury than Kokor was.

And why doesn't anybody have any sympathy for *my* injury? The deep psychological harm that has come to me because of seeing Obring and my own sister like that! No one cares that *I'm* suffering, too, and that maybe I need to go out at night as *therapy*.

Kokor sat painting her face, practicing looks that might project well in her next play. For there would certainly be a next play *now,* once she got out of Mother's house. Tumannu's little attempt to blacklist her would certainly fail—there wasn't a comedy house in Dolltown that would refuse an actress whose name was on the lips of everyone in Basilica. The house would sell out every night just from curiosity seekers—and when they saw her perform and heard her sing, they'd be back again and again. Not that she would ever dream of deliberately hurting someone in order to advance her career; but since it had happened, why not make use of it? Tumannu herself would probably be in line to beg Kokor to take the lead in a comedy.

She had drawn a little pout on her mouth that looked quite fetching. She tried it out from several angles and liked the shape of it. It was too light, though. She'd have to redden it or no one would see it past the first row.

"If you make it any rounder it'll look as though somebody made a hole under your nose with a drill."

Kokor turned slowly to face the intruder who stood in her doorway. An obnoxious little thirteen-year-old girl. The younger sister of that nasty bastard girl Hushidh. Mother had taken them both in as infants, out of pure charity, and when Mother made Hushidh one of her nieces the girl obviously thought she should then be taken as seriously as if she were one of the nieces of high birth who would amount to something in Basilica. She and Sevet had had such fun cutting Hushidh down to size, back when they were still students here. And now the little sister, equally a bastard, just as ugly and just as uppity, dared to stand in the doorway of the bedroom of a *daughter* of the house, of a highborn woman of Basilica, and ridicule the appearance of one of the famous beauties of the city.

But it would be beneath Kokor to go to the effort of putting this child in her place as she so deserved. Enough to make her go away. "Girl, there is a door. It was closed. Please restore it to its previous condition, with yourself on the other side."

The child didn't move.

"Girl, if you were sent with a message, deliver it and vanish."

"Are you speaking to me?" asked the child.

"Do you see another girl here?"

"I am a niece in this house," said the child. "Only servants are addressed as 'girl.' I therefore assumed that since you are rumored to be a lady who would know correct forms of address, you must have been speaking to some invisible servant on the balcony."

Kokor rose to her feet. "I've had enough of you. I had enough before you came in here."

"What are you going to do?" asked the child. "Strike me in the throat? Or is that a sport you keep within your family?"

Kokor felt an unbearable rage rise within her. "Don't tempt me!" she cried. Then she controlled herself, penned in the anger. This girl was not worth it. If she wanted correct address, she would have it. "What's your business here, my dear young daughter-of-a-holy-whore?"

The girl did not seem abashed, not for a moment. "So you *do* know who I am," she said. "My name is Luet. My friends call me Lutya. You may call me Young Mistress."

"Why are you here and when will you leave?" demanded Kokor. "Have I come to my mother's house to be tormented by bastard children with no manners?"

"Have no fear of that," said Luet. "For as I hear it, you will not be in this house another hour."

"What are you talking about? What have you heard?"

"I came here as an act of kindness, to let you know that Rashgallivak is here with six of his soldiers to take you under the protection of the Palwashantu."

"Rashgallivak! That little pizdook! I showed him his place when he last tried to pull this stunt, and I'll do it again."

"He wants to take Sevet, too. He says that you're both in serious danger and you need protection."

"Danger? In Mother's house? I only need protection from obnoxious ugly little girls."

"You are so gracious, Mistress Kokor," said Luet. "I will never forget how you answered my thoughtfulness in bringing you this news." She turned and left the room.

What did the girl expect? If she had come in with dignity instead of with an insult, Kokor would have treated her better. A child of such low background could hardly be expected to understand how to behave, however, so Kokor would try not to hold it against her.

Mother was being so bossy lately that she might even think that sending her and Sevet to Rashgallivak would be a good idea. Kokor would have to take steps herself to ensure that nothing of the kind occurred.

She wiped off the pout and replaced it with daypaint, then chose a particularly fragile-looking housedress and put it on with the tiniest hint of disarray, so that it would seem that she was simply on her way to the kitchen when she was surprised to discover that Rashgallivak was here to try to kidnap her.

The plan was spoiled, though, by the fact that when she stepped into the hall, there was Sevet, leaning on the arm of that wretched Hushidh girl, Luet's older sister. How could Sevet—even with her injury—abase herself by leaning on a girl that she had once treated with such despite? Had she no shame? And yet her presence in the hall made it impossible for Kokor to ignore her. She would have to be solicitous. She would have to hover near her. Fortunately, since Sevet was already leaning on Hushidh, Kokor wouldn't have to offer *that* service. It would completely spoil her freedom of action, to have Sevet leaning on her.

"How are you, poor Sevet?" asked Kokor. "I've wept myself hoarse over what happened. We're so bad to each other sometimes, Sevet. Why do we do it?"

Sevet merely looked at the floor a meter ahead of her.

"Oh, I can understand why you're not speaking to me. You'll never forgive me for the accident. But I've forgiven *you* for what *you* did, and *that* was no accident, *that* was on purpose. Still, one can hardly expect you to feel forgiving yet, you're in such pain, you poor thing. Why are you even up? I can handle this thing with Rashgallivak. I jammed his balls into his spleen the other night, and I'll be glad to do it again."

At that Sevet actually smiled a little. Just a trace of a

smile. Or perhaps she only winced as she started jolting down the stairs.

Mother hadn't even brought Rashgallivak into one of the sitting rooms. He was standing with his soldiers right at the door, which was still open. Mother turned and glanced at her daughters and Hushidh as they came down the hall from the stairs to the entryway.

"You can see that they are well," Mother said to Rash-gallivak. "They are safe and in good hands here. In fact, no men have come here at all, except you and these superflu-ous soldiers."

"I'm not worried about what *has* happened," said Rash-gallivak. "I'm concerned about what *might* happen, and I will not leave here without Gaballufix's daughters. They are under the protection of the Palwashantu."

"You are welcome to keep your soldiers out in the street," said Mother, "to prevent any tolchoks or marauders or as-sassins from entering our house, but you will not take my daughters. A mother's claim is superior to the claim of a clan of men."

While Mother and Rash continued arguing, Kokor leaned toward Sevet and, forgetting that her sister could not speak, asked her, "Why does Rashgallivak want us in the first place?"

Because Sevet couldn't answer, Hushidh did. "Aunt Rasa is at the center of resistance to Palwashantu rule in Basil-ica. He thinks if he has the two of you as hostages, she will behave."

"Then he doesn't know Mother," said Kokor.

"Rashgallivak is a weak man," whispered Hushidh. "And he's stupid at politics. If he were as smart as your father, he would have known that he could not get possession of the two of you without violence, and that violence would be against his best interests. Therefore he would never have made the request. But if for some reason he *did* decide to take you, he would have acted far more boldly. The two of you would already be in the grasp of two soldiers each, with the other two holding your mother at bay."

Hushidh was no fool, after all. That had never occurred to Kokor, that Hushidh might have some attribute worthy of respect. Her idea of Father was exactly true—yet Kokor herself would never have been able to express it so clearly.

Of course, Father would also have had some kind of right to try to take her and Sevet. Not a *legal* right, of course, not in the city of women, but people might have understood it if he tried. What claim did Rashgallivak have? "The Oversoul must have driven Rash mad, even to try this," whispered Kokor.

"He's afraid," said Hushidh. "People do strange things when they're afraid. Your mother already has."

Like keeping me in seclusion, thought Kokor.

Then she realized that if she had been at home with Obring, Rash would have had no trouble getting to her. Obring would have tried to fight with the soldiers, they would have knocked him down in an instant, and Kokor would have been carried off. So Mother *was* right to keep her in seclusion. Imagine that. "You mustn't criticize Mother," said Kokor. "She's doing very well, I think."

In the meantime, the argument between Rasa and Rash had continued, though now they were both repeating old arguments, and not always in new words. Hushidh had brought them to the very threshold of the foyer, so that they were as far as they could be from the soldiers and still be in the room. Till now Kokor had stayed with her and Sevet. Seeing the soldiers standing there, horribly identical in their holographic masks, took away her determination to show Rashgallivak what was what. He had seemed much smaller and weaker in the darkness backstage at the theatre. The soldiers made him much more menacing, and

Kokor found herself admiring Mother's courage in facing them down like this. In fact, she wondered if Mother was not being just the tiniest bit foolish. For instance, why had she called Kokor and Sevet down here to be in plain sight, within easy reach of these soldiers? Why hadn't she kept them hidden away upstairs? Or warned them to sneak away into the woods? Perhaps this was what Hushidh meant about Mother already doing strange things because of fear.

Yet Mother didn't seem afraid.

"I think perhaps we should leave now," Kokor whispered to Hushidh.

"Not so," said Hushidh. "You must stay."

"Why?"

"Because if you tried to leave, it would alarm Rashgallivak and probably cause him to act. He would order the soldiers to detain you and all would be lost."

"He'll do that eventually anyway," whispered Kokor.

"Ah, but will he wait long enough?"

"Long enough for what?"

"Think," said Hushidh.

Kokor thought. What would mere delay profit them?

Unless someone was coming to help. But who could possibly stand against the soldiers of the Palwashantu?

"The city guard!" cried Kokor, delighted to have thought of it.

Could she help it if her words fell into a chance silence in the argument between Mother and Rash?

"What?" cried Rashgallivak. "What did you say?" He whirled and looked out the door. "There's no one there," he said. Then he looked at Rasa. "But they *are* coming, aren't they? That's what this is all about—delaying me until you can get the guard to come and stop me. Well, the delay is over. Take them!"

At once the soldiers strode toward the women in the hallway, and Kokor screamed.

"Run you little fools!" cried Mother.

But Kokor could not run, because one of the soldiers already had her by the arm and another pair of soldiers had Sevet, too, and that bastard Hushidh wasn't doing *one thing* to help them.

"Do something, you little bitch!" cried Kokor. "Don't let them do this to us!"

Hushidh looked her in the eye for a moment as the soldiers dragged her toward the door. Then she seemed to make a decision.

"Stop, Rashgallivak!" cried Hushidh. "Stop this instant."

Rash only laughed. It chilled Kokor to the bone, his laugh. It was the laugh of a man who knew he had won. This pathetic man who had been the steward in the house of Wetchik only a few days ago now laughed in delight at the power his soldiers gave him.

"Order them to stop!" cried Hushidh. "Or you will never be able to order them to do anything again!"

"No, Hushidh!" cried Mother.

What in the world did Mother think that Hushidh could do *now?* Kokor could see Sevet in the grasp of the soldiers, their blank faces so terrifying, so inhuman. It was wrong, for her sister to be in their grasp. Wrong for these hands to be gripping Kokor's arms and dragging her away. "Do it, Hushidh!" Kokor cried. Whatever it is Mother thinks you can do, do it.

To anyone but Hushidh, the scene was simple—Rash and two of his soldiers blocking anyone from interfering, as the other four soldiers were dragging Kokor and Sevet through the wide front door of Rasa's house. Aunt Rasa herself was shouting ineffectually—"It's *you* who's injuring Sevet! You'll be expelled from the city! Kidnapper!"— and other women and girls of the house were gathering, huddling in the hallway, listening, watching.

To Hushidh the Raveler, however, the scene was very different. For she could see not only the people, but also the webs that bound them together. To Hushidh, the frightened girls and women were not individuals or even little clumps—all of them were tightly bound to Rasa, so that instead of being helplessly alone as others would see her, Hushidh knew that she spoke from the strength of dozens of women, that their fear fed her fear, their anger her anger, and when she cried out in the majesty of her wrath, she was far larger than one mere woman. Hushidh even saw the powerful webs connecting Rasa to the rest of the city, great ropy threads like arteries and veins, pumping the lifeblood of Rasa's identity. When she cried out against Rashgallivak, it was the fury of the whole city of women in her voice.

Yet Hushidh could also see that Rasa, though she was surrounded by this vast web, also felt herself to be quite alone, as if the web came right up to her but didn't quite connect, or touched her only slightly. That was what Rash's exercise of raw power was doing to Rasa—making her feel as if her strength and power in the city amounted to nothing after all, for she could not resist the power of these soldiers.

At the same time, there was another web of influence—Rashgallivak's. And this one Hushidh knew was actually contemptible and weak. Where Rasa's links with her household were strong and real, her power in the city almost tangible to Hushidh, Rashgallivak had very little respect from his soldiers. He was able to command them only because he paid them, and then only because they rather liked what he was commanding them to do. Rashgallivak, compared to Rasa, was almost isolated. As for his men, their connections to each other were much stronger than their connections to *him*. And even then, they were nothing like the bonds among the women.

Most men were like this, Hushidh knew—relatively un-connected, unbound, alone. But these men were particu-larly untrusting and ungiving, and so the bonds that held them to each other were fragile indeed. It was not love at all, really, but rather a yearning for the honor and respect of the other men that held them. Pride, then. And at this moment they were proud of their strength as they dragged these women out of the house, proud to defy one of the great woman of Basilica; they looked so grand in each other's eyes. Indeed, all their connection with each other at this moment was tied up with the respect they felt they were earning by their actions.

So fragile. Hushidh had only to reach out and she could easily snap the bonds between these men. She could leave Rashgallivak hopelessly alone. And even though Rasa was demanding that she *not* do it, at this moment Hushidh felt much more deeply her connection to Sevet and Kokor, for these girls had been her tormentors, her enemies, and now she had the chance to be their savior, to set them free, and they would *know she had done it.* It would undo one of the deepest injuries in her heart; what was Rasa's command compared to that need?

Hushidh knew exactly why she was acting even as she acted—so well did she understand herself, for as a raveler she could see even her own connections with the world around her—yet she acted anyway, because that was who she was at this moment, the powerful savior who had the power to undo these powerful men.

So she spoke, and undid them. It wasn't the words she said; this was no magical incantation that would discon-nect the bonds that held them to each other. It was her tone of contempt, her face, her body, that gave her words the power to strike at the heart of each of the soldiers and make them believe that they were utterly alone, that other men would have only contempt for what they were doing. "Where is your honor in dragging this injured woman away from her mother," she said. "Baboons in the wild have more manhood than you, for mothers can trust their infants with the males of the tribe."

Poor Rash. He heard the words, and thought that he could counter Hushidh by arguing with her. He didn't realize that, with these men caught up in the story Hushidh was weaving around them, every word he said would drive these men farther away from him, for he sounded weaker and more cowardly with every sound he made. "You shut up, woman! These men are soldiers who do their duty—"

"A coward's duty. Look what this so-called man has led you to do. He's made you into filthy rodents, stealing bright and shining beauty and dragging it off to his hole where he will cover you with shit and call it glory."

First one, then another of the men let go of Kokor and Sevet. Sevet immediately sank to her knees, weeping silently. Kokor, for her part, put on a very convincing show of disgust and loathing, shuddering as she tried in vain to brush away the very memory of the soldiers' touch on her arms.

"See how you have disgusted the beautiful ones," said Hushidh. "That's what Rashgallivak has made of you. Slugs and worms, because you follow him. Where can you go to become men again? How can you find a way to be clean? There must be somewhere you can hide from your shame. Slither off and find it, little slugs; burrow deep and see if you can hide your humiliation! Do you think those masks make you look strong and powerful? They only mark you as servants of this contemptible gnat of a man. Servants of *nothing*."

One of the soldiers pulled off the cloak that created the holographic image that till now had hidden his face. He was an ordinary, rather dirty-looking man, unshaven, somewhat stupid, and very much afraid—his eyes were wide and filled with tears.

"There he is," Hushidh said. "That's what Rashgallivak has made of you."

"Put your mask back on!" cried Rashgallivak. "I order you to take these women back to Gaballufix's house."

"Listen to him," said Hushidh. *"He's* no Gaballufix. Why are you following *him?"*

That was the last push. Most of the other soldiers also swept off their masks, leaving the holo-cloaks on the porch of Rasa's house as they shambled off, running from the scene of their humiliation.

Rash stood alone in the middle of the doorway. Now the whole scene had changed. It didn't take a raveler to see that Rasa had all the power and majesty now, and Rash was helpless, weak, alone. He looked down at the cloaks at his feet.

"That's right," said Hushidh. "Hide your face. No one wants to see that face again, least of all you."

And he did it, he bent over and swept up one of the cloaks and pulled it across his shoulder; his body heat and magnetism activated the cloaks, which were still powered on, and suddenly he was no longer Rashgallivak, but rather the same uniform image of false masculinity that all the soldiers of Gaballufix had worn. Then he turned and ran away, just like his men, with that same defeated rounding of the shoulders. No baboon beaten by a rival could have shown more abjectness than Rash's body showed as he ran away.

Hushidh felt the web of awe that was forming around her; it made her tingle, knowing that she had the adulation of the girls and women of the house—and above all, the honor of Sevet and Kokor. Kokor, vain Kokor, who now looked at her with an expression stupid with awe. And Sevet, cruel in her mockery for so many years, now looking at her through eyes streaked with tears, her hands reaching out toward Hushidh like a supplicant, her lips struggling to say Thank you, thank you, thank you.

"What have you done," whispered Rasa.

Hushidh could hardly understand the question. What she had done was obvious. "I've broken Rashgallivak's power," she said. "He's no more threat to you."

"Foolish, foolish girl," said Rasa. "There are thousands of these villains in Basilica. Thousand of them, and now the one man who could control them, however weak he was, that man is broken and undone. By nightfall these soldiers will all be out of control, and who will stop them?"

All of Hushidh's sense of accomplishment slipped away at once. She knew that Rasa was right. No matter how clearly Hushidh saw in the present moment, she hadn't looked ahead to anticipate the larger consequences of her act. These men would no longer be bound by their hunger for honor, for it would no longer be seen as honorable to serve Rashgallivak. What would they do, then? They would be unbound in the city, soldiers starving to prove their strength and power, and no force could channel them to some useful purpose. Hushidh remembered the holos she had seen of apes displaying, shaking branches, charging each other, slapping at whoever was weak, whoever was near. Men on the rampage would be far, far more dangerous.

"Bring my daughters inside," Rasa said to the others. "Then all of you work to shutter the windows behind their bars. Tighten down the house. As if a tempest were coming. For it is."

Rasa then stepped onto the porch between her daughters.

"Where are you going, Mama!" wailed Kokor. "Don't leave us!"

"I must warn the women of the city. The monster is loose in the streets tonight. The Guard will be powerless to control them. They must secure what can be secured, and then hide from the fires that will burn here tonight in the darkness."

MOOZH'S TROOPS WERE exhausted, but when, late in the afternoon, they crested a pass and saw smoke in the distance, it put new vigor into their steps. They knew as well as Moozh did that a city on fire is a city that is not about to defend itself. Besides, they knew that they had accomplished something remarkable, to cover such a distance on foot. And even though there were only a thousand of them, they knew that if they achieved a victory, their names would live forever, if not individually, then as a part of Moozh's Thousand. They could almost hear their grandchildren already asking them, Was it true you marched from Khlam to Basilica in two days, and took the city that night without resting, and without a man of you killed?

Of course, that last part of the story wasn't yet a foregone conclusion. Who knew what the condition inside Basilica really was. What if the soldiers of Gaballufix had already consolidated their position inside the city, and now were prepared to defend it? The Gorayni soldiers well knew they had barely food for another meal; if they didn't take the city tonight, in darkness, they would have to break their fast in the morning and take the city by daylight—or flee ignominiously down into the Cities of the Plain, where their enemies could see how few they really were, and cut them to pieces long before they could make it back north. So yes, victory was possible—but it was also essential, and it had to be now.

So why were they so confident, when desperation would have been more understandable? Because they were *Moozh's* Thousand, and Moozh had never lost. There was no better general in the history of the Gorayni. He was careful of his men; he defeated his enemies, not by expending his men in bloody assaults, but through maneuver and deft blows, isolating the enemy, cutting off supplies, dividing the enemy's forces, and so disorienting the opposing generals that they began taking foolish chances just to get the battle *over* with and stop the endless, terrifying ballet. His soldiers called it "Dancing with Moozh," the quick marches; they knew that by wearing out their feet, Moozh was saving their yatsas. Oh, yes, they loved him—he made them victors without sending too many of them home as a small sack of ashes.

There were even whispers in the ranks that their beloved Moozh was the *real* incarnation of God, and even though usually none would say it aloud—at least not where an intercessor could hear them—on this march, with no intercessor along, the whispers became a good deal more frequent. That fat-assed fellow back in Gollod was no incarnation of God, in a world that included a *real* man like Vozmuzhalnoy Vozmozhno!

A kilometer away from Basilica, they could hear some of the sounds coming out of the city—screams, mostly, carried by the wind, which was blowing smoke toward them now. The order came through the ranks: Cut down branches, a dozen or more per man, so we can light enough smoky bonfires to make the enemy think we are a hundred thousand. They hacked and tore at the trees near the road, and then followed Moozh down a winding trail from the mountains into the desert. Moonlight was a treacherous guide, especially burdened as they were with boughs, but there were few injuries though many fell, and in the darkness they fanned out across the desert, separating widely from each other, leaving vast empty spaces between the groups of men. There they built their piles of branches, and at the blare of a trumpet—who in the city could hear it?—they lit all the fires. Then, leaving one man at each bonfire to add boughs to keep the flames alive, the rest of the army gathered behind Moozh and marched, this time in four

columns abreast, as if they were the bold advance guard
for a huge army, up a wide flat road toward a gap in the
high walls of the city.

Even before they reached the walls, they found themselves in the middle of a veritable city. There were men
running and shouting there—many of them clearly over-
satisfied with wine—but when they saw Moozh's army
marching through their street, they fell silent and backed
away into the shadows. If any of the Gorayni had lacked
confidence before, they gained it now, for it was clear that
the men of Basilica had no fight in them. What boldness
they had was nothing but the bravado of drink.

As they drew near to the gate, they heard the clang of
metal on metal that suggested a pitched battle. Cresting a
rise they saw a battle in progress, between men clad in the
same uniform as the assassin that Moozh had killed, and
other men who were terrifyingly identical—not just their
clothing, but even their faces were all the same!

Word passed down the columns: The men in the uniform
of the Basilican guard will probably be our allies; our true
enemies are the ones in masks. But slay no one until Moozh
gives the order.

They reached the flat, clear area before the gate, and
quickly split into two ranks left, two ranks right, until a
semicircle formed surrounding the gate. In the middle of
the semicircle stood Moozh himself.

"Gorayni, draw your weapons!" He bawled out the
command—clearly he meant to be heard as much by the
men fighting at the gate as by his own army, which normally would have received the command as a whisper
down the ranks.

The fighting at the gate slackened. The men in the uniforms of the Basilican guard—few of them indeed to be
making such a brave stand—saw the Gorayni troops and
despaired. They fell back against the wall, uncertain which

enemy to fight, but certain of this: That they would not live out the hour.

In the middle of the gate, their enemies withdrawn, the soldiers of identical faces also stood, uncertain of what to do next.

"We are the Gorayni. We have come to help Basilica, not to conquer her!" cried Moozh. "Look out in the desert and see the army we could bring to bear against the gates of your city!"

Moozh had chosen his gate well—from here all the Basilicans, guard and Palwashantu mercenaries alike, could see the bonfires, at least a hundred of them, stretching far across the desert.

"Yet only these five hundred have I brought to the gate!" Of course he lied about the number of men he had; his men smiled inwardly to know that for once he was only four hundred off, instead of forty thousand, which was the more usual lie. "We are here to ask if the City of Women, the City of Peace, might use our services to help quell a domestic disturbance. We will enter, serve the city at your pleasure, and leave when our task is accomplished. Thus do I speak in the name of General Vozmuzhalnoy Vozmozhno!" There was no reason to let them know that the most fearsome general on the western shores of the Earthbound Sea was standing before their gates with his sword sheathed and only nine hundred men to back him up. Let them think the general himself was out with the tens of thousands of troops tenting around the great bonfires in the desert!

"Sir," cried one of the guard. "You see how it is with us! We are the guard of the city, but how can we find out the will of our council, when we are fighting for our lives against these mad criminals!"

"*We* are the masters of Basilica now!" shouted one of the identical Palwashantu mercenaries. "No more taking the orders of women! No more being forced to stay outside the city that is ours by right! We rule this city now in the name of Gaballufix!"

"Gaballufix is dead!" shouted the officer of the guard. "And you are ruled by no man!"

"In the name of Gaballufix this city is ours!" And with that the mercenaries brandished their weapons and shouted.

"Men of Gaballufix!" cried Moozh. "We have heard the name of your fallen leader!"

The mercenaries cheered again.

"We know how to honor Gaballufix!" Moozh shouted. "Come out to us, and stand with us, and we will give you the city you deserve!"

With a cheer the mercenaries poured out from the gate toward the Gorayni. The Basilican guard shrank back against the walls, their weapons ready. Some few started slinking away to the left or the right, hoping to escape, but to their honor most of the guard remained in their places, prepared to end their lives doing their duty. Moozh's Thousand took note of this; they would treat the guard with respect, should a reckoning come between them.

As for the mercenaries, those closest to the Gorayni came with their guard down, prepared to embrace these newcomers as their brothers. But they found that swords and pikes and bows were pointed at them, and confusion spread from the rim to the center of the mob.

Moozh still stood where he had stood all along, only now he was surrounded by mercenaries, cut off from his own men. He seemed to show no alarm at all, though it made his men more than a little nervous. To their consternation, he began to push his way through the mob, not *toward* his men, but away from them and toward the gate. The mercenaries seemed content with this—it was a sign that he meant to lead them.

Moozh strode out into the open area in the middle of the

gate, his back to the mercenaries. "Ah, Basilica," he said—loudly, but not in the voice of command. "How often I have dreamed of standing in your gate and seeing your beauty with my own eyes!" Then he turned to face the officer of the guard, who stood at the post of the gate, his weapon drawn. Moozh spoke softly to him. "Would Basilica regard it as a great service, my friend, if these hundreds of ugly twins were to die on this ground at this hour?"

"I think so, yes," said the officer, confused once again, but also glad with new hope.

Moozh turned back to face the mob—and his men behind them. "Every man who loves the name of Gaballufix, raise your sword high!"

Most of the mob—all but the wariest of them—raised their weapons. No sooner had they raised their arms, however, than Moozh drew his sword from its sheath.

That was the signal. Three hundred arrows were loosed at once, and every man at the periphery of the mob—their arms conveniently raised so that every arrow struck them in the body—fell, most of them pierced many times. Then, with a thunderous shout, the Gorayni fell on the remaining mercenaries and in only two or three minutes the carnage was over. The Gorayni immediately formed themselves into ranks again, standing before the bodies of their fallen enemies.

Moozh turned to the officer of the guard. "What is your name, sir?"

"Captain Bitanke, sir."

"Captain Bitanke, I ask again: Would Basilica welcome our intervention to help restore order in these beautiful streets? I have here a letter from the Lady Rasa; is her name known to you?"

"Yes it is, sir," said Bitanke.

"She wrote to me, asking for succor for her city. I came, and now respectfully ask your permission to bring these men within your gates, to serve as auxiliary troops in your effort to control the violence in your streets."

Bitanke bowed and then unlocked the guard booth in the gate and stepped inside. Moozh could see that he was typing into a computer. After a few moments he stepped back into the open. "Sir, I have told them what you did here. The situation of our city is desperate, and since you come in the name of the Lady Rasa, and you have proven your will to defeat our enemies, the city council and the guard invite you to enter. Temporarily you are placed under my immediate command, if you will accept one of my low rank, until a more orderly system can be arranged."

"Sir, it is not your rank but your courage and honor that make me salute you, and for that reason I will accept your leadership," said Moozh. "May I suggest that we deploy my men in companies of six, and authorize them to deal with any men they find who are behaving in a disorderly fashion. We will in all cases respect those who wear your uniform; any other men we find who have weapons drawn or who offer violence to us or to any woman of the city, we will slay on the spot and hang up on public display to quell any notion of further resistance by others!"

"I don't know about the hanging, sir," said Bitanke.

"Very well, we have our orders!" Ignoring Bitanke's hesitation, Moozh turned to his soldiers. "Men of the Gorayni, by sixes!"

Immediately the ranks shifted and suddenly there were a hundred and fifty squads of six men each.

"Harm no woman!" cried Moozh. "And whomever you see in that loathsome mask, hang him up, mask and all, until no man dares wear it by night or day!"

"Sir, I think . . ."

But Moozh had already waved his arm, and his soldiers now entered the city at a trot. Bitanke came closer to

Moozh, to remonstrate perhaps, but Moozh greeted him with an embrace that stifled conversation. "Please, my friend—I know your men are exhausted, but couldn't they be usefully employed? For instance, I think this village outside the gate could profit from a little cleaning out. And as for you and me, we should make our way to those who are in authority, so I can receive the orders of the city council."

Whatever misgivings Captain Bitanke might have had were swept away by Moozh's embrace and his smile. Bitanke gave his orders, and his men spread out through Dogtown. Then Moozh followed him into the city. "While my men are restoring order, we must see about putting out some fires," said Moozh. "Can you call others of the city guard with your computer?"

"Yes, sir."

"It's not my place to tell you your business, but if your men can protect the firefighters, perhaps we can keep Basilica from burning down before dawn."

"Do you think the rest of your men might be able to come and help?"

Moozh laughed. "Oh, General Vozmuzhalnoy Vozmozhno would never allow that. If such a force came to your gates, someone in Basilica might fear that we meant to conquer the town. We are here to extend you our protection, not to rule over you, my friend! So we bring no more men than these five hundred."

"The Oversoul must have sent you, sir," said Captain Bitanke.

"You have only to thank the Lady Rasa," said Moozh. "Her and a brave man of your number named, I believe, Smelost."

"Smelost," whispered Bitanke. "He was a dear friend of mine."

"Then I am glad to tell you that he was received with

honor by General Vozmuzhalnoy Vozmozhno, who lost no
time in acting on his information and coming to the aid
of your city."

"You came in good time," said Bitanke. "It began like
this last night, and spread through the day, and I feared that
tomorrow morning would find the city in ashes and all the
good women of Basilica in despair or worse."

"I'm always glad to be a messenger of hope," said Moozh.

By now they were walking along a street with houses
and shops on either side. Yet there was no one moving, and
lights shone from many upper windows. The only sign
that the rioting had been here was the broken glass in the
street, the shattered windows of the shops, and the bodies
of dead mercenaries, still wearing their holographic
masks, dangling like beeves from upper-story balconies.
Bitanke looked at them in faint dismay as they walked
along the street.

"How long will those masks remain active?" asked
Moozh.

"Until the—bodies cool, I imagine. I've heard that body
heat and magnetism are the triggers."

"Ah," said Moozh.

"May I ask—what they are—how your men were able
to hang them? I see no ropes and there are no—appara-
tuses for hanging men in the streets."

"I'm not sure," said Moozh. "Let's take the cloak off one
of them and see."

Gingerly Bitanke reached up and tugged on the cloak of
the nearest dangling corpse. When it came away, the holograph faded instantly and it was easy to see that the body
had been pinned to the wall by a heavy knife through its
neck. "His own knife, do you think?" asked Moozh.

"I think so," said Bitanke.

"Not a very secure job," said Moozh, pushing at the body
a bit. "I daresay if we have any wind tonight most of these

will be down by morning. We'll want to clean them up as quickly as possible, or we'll have quite a problem with the dogs."

"Yes sir," said Bitanke.

"Never seen a dead body?" asked Moozh. "You look a little ill."

"Oh, I've seen dead bodies, sir," said Bitanke. "I've just never heard if . . . treating them this way . . . I wish your men wouldn't . . ."

"Nonsense. These dangling bodies are like reinforcements. Any rioters that my soldiers happen to overlook—there are bound to be some using the toilet, don't you think?—they'll come out, see how quiet things are, notice the bodies, and most of the fight will go right out of them."

Bitanke chuckled a little. "I imagine so."

"You see?" said Moozh. "It's a way of letting these boys make up for a bit of the mischief they've caused, by policing the streets for us all night. Correct me if I'm wrong, Captain Bitanke, but no one is going to shed many tears for them, right?"

Within the hour Moozh was meeting with the city council. In the meantime, the hundred soldiers who had been tending the bonfires were moving into position at every gate of the city, standing alongside the guard in those few cases where they were at the gate. There was no quarrel between them; no soldier of the Gorayni came to blows with any of the city guard.

Moozh's meeting with the city council was peaceful, and they concluded a firm agreement that Moozh would have full access to all the boroughs of the city—even those that normally were restricted to women only, since that was where the worst of the fires were burning and the marauders had been most out of control—but that after two and a half days, Moozh would withdraw his men to quarters outside the city, where they would be amply supplied and rewarded from the treasury of the city. It was a wonderful alliance, full of many compliments and much heartfelt gratitude.

Few in Basilica would realize it for several days, but by the time Moozh left the meeting his conquest of the city was complete.

NAFAI SAID AS little as possible to Elya and Meb as they set out on their journey back to Basilica. His silence did not make them any more cheerful toward him, but it meant that he didn't have to quarrel with them, or do some verbal dance to avoid quarreling. He could keep his own thoughts.

He could talk to the Oversoul.

As if it mattered what he said to the old computer. For a few days he had fancied that he and the Oversoul were working together. The Oversoul had shown him its memory of Earth, had explained its purpose in the world, to try to keep the planet Harmony from repeating the miserable, self-destructive history of Earth. Nafai had agreed to serve that purpose. Nafai had stood over a drunken man in the street—his enemy—and it never would have come to his own mind to kill the man as he lay there, helpless. But the Oversoul had told him to do it and Nafai had complied. Not because Gaballufix was a murderer himself who deserved to die. Why, then? Because Nafai believed the Oversoul, agreed with the Oversoul that by killing this one man, he could help preserve the whole world.

And, having done the crime, having put blood on his own hands for the sake of the Oversoul's cause, where was the Oversoul now? Nafai had imagined that there was now a special relationship between the Oversoul and himself. Hadn't there been that moment when the Index first spoke to him and Father and Issib? Father and Issib had only partly understood the Oversoul's message—they grasped the idea that the Oversoul meant to lead them on a long journey to a wonderful place where Issib could use his floats again and not be confined to his chair. But only Nafai had understood that the place the Oversoul meant to take them was not on the planet Harmony—that the Oversoul meant to take them back to Earth. After forty million years, home to Earth.

Since then, though, the Index had been nothing but a guide to a vast memory bank. Father and Issib studied, and Nafai with them, but all the time Nafai kept waiting for some word—to all of them, or perhaps to him alone. Perhaps some special private message, some word of encouragement. Something to fulfill the promise made that time when the Oversoul, speaking through Issib's chair, had said that it had chosen Nafai to lead his brothers.

Am I chosen, Oversoul? Why can't I see the results of your favor, then? I have made myself a murderer for you, and yet your vision of our wives came to Elemak. And what did he see? That you had chosen Eiadh for *him!* What has your favor brought me, then? Now you speak to Elemak, who plotted with Gaballufix, who tried to kill me; now you give *him* the woman that *I* have so long desired—why did *he* receive that dream, and not me? I have been humiliated now in front of all of them. I will have to eat dust, I will have to submit to Elya's orders and serve at his pleasure, I will have to watch Elya take that sweet and beautiful girl who has so long inhabited *my* dreams. Why do you hate me, Oversoul? What have I done, except to serve you and obey you?

The camels clambered with lazy strength up a slope, and Elemak led them along the edge of a precipice. Nafai looked out over the landscape and saw the savage knife-edged rocks and crags, with only here and there a bit of grey-green desert foliage. The Oversoul promised me life, promised me greatness and glory and joy, and here I am, in this desert, following my brothers, who plotted with

Father's enemy and, wittingly or not, set Father up to be killed. I helped the Oversoul to save Father's life, and now here I am.

Yes, here you are.

It took a moment to realize that this was the voice of the Oversoul, for it spoke in Nafai's mind as if it were his own thought. But he knew, from his few experiences, that this thought was coming from outside himself, if only because it seemed to answer him.

In turn, he answered the Oversoul—and not with any particular respect. Oh, here *you* are, he said silently, sarcastically. Noticed me again? Hope I wasn't a bother.

I bother a great deal for you.

Like choosing Eiadh for my brother instead of me.

Eiadh is not for you.

Thanks for your help, said Nafai silently. Thanks for dealing me such a miserable hand in this game with my brothers.

I'm not doing too badly for you, Nafai.

Maybe I don't give you the same high marks you give yourself. I killed a man for you.

And every moment of this journey, I am saving your life.

The thought startled Nafai. Inadvertently he sat up straighter, looked around him.

Every moment of this journey, I am turning their thoughts away from their decision to kill you.

Fear and hatred, both at once, clawed their way down Nafai's throat and deep into his belly. He could feel them churning there, like small animals dwelling inside him.

It's good that you've been silent, said the Oversoul. It's good that you haven't provoked them, or even reminded them that you're along with them on this journey. For my influence in their minds, while strong, is not irresistible. If their anger flowed hotly against you, how would I stop them? I don't have Issib's chair to act through now.

Nafai was filled with fear, with a longing to go back to Father's tent. At the same time, he was hurt and angry at his brothers. Why do they still hate me? How have I harmed them?

Foolish boy. Only a moment ago you were longing for me to reward you for your loyalty to me by giving you power over your brothers. Do you think they don't see your ambition? Every time I speak to you, they hate you more. Every time your father's face is filled with delight at your quick mind, at your goodness of heart, they hate you more. And when they see that you desire to have the privileges of the eldest son . . .

I don't! cried Nafai silently. I don't want to displace Elemak . . . I want him to love me, I want him to be a *true* older brother to me, and not this monster who wants me dead.

Yes, you want him to love you . . . *and* you want him to respect you . . . *and* you want to take his place. Do you think you are immune to the primate instincts within you? You are born to be an alpha male in a tribe of clever beasts, and so is he. But he is ruled by that hunger, while you, Nafai, can't you be civilized, can't you suppress the animal part of yourself, and work to help me achieve a far higher purpose than determining who will be the leading male in a troop of erect baboons?

Nafai felt as if he had been stripped naked in front of his enemies. If I am no better than Elemak, no better than any of the troop of baboons downstream from Father's tent, then why did you choose me?

Because you *are* better, and because you *want* to be better still.

Help me, then. Help me curb my own dark desires. And while you're at it, help Elemak, too. I remember him when he was younger. Playful, loving, kind. He's more than an ambitious animal, I know he is, even if he's forgotten it himself.

I know it, answered the Oversoul. Why do you think I gave that dream of Elemak? So he might have a chance to waken to my voice. He has much of the same sensitivity *you* have. But he has long chosen to hate me, to thwart my purposes if he can. So my voice has been nothing to him. This time, though, I could tell him something he wanted to hear. My purpose coincided with his own. What do you think your life would be worth, if I had shown *you* who his wife should be? Do you think he would have taken Eiadh at *your* hand?

I wouldn't have given him Eiadh.

So. You would have ignored me. You would have rebelled against me. You tell yourself that you killed Gaballufix only because you serve me and my noble purpose . . . but then you are willing to rebel against me and thwart my purpose, because you want a woman who would ruin your life.

You don't know that. You may be a very clever computer, Oversoul, but you can't tell the future.

I know her, as I know you, from the inside. And if you ever know her, you will understand that she could never be your wife.

Are you saying she's bad at heart?

I'm saying she lives in a world whose center of gravity is herself. She has no purpose higher than her own desires. But you, Nafai, will never be content unless your life is accomplishing something that will change the world. I am giving you that, if you have the patience to trust me until it comes to you. I will also give you a wife who will share the same dreams, who will help you instead of distracting you.

Who *is* my wife, then?

The face of Luet came into his mind.

Nafai shuddered. Luet. She had helped him escape, and saved his life at great risk to herself. She had taken him down to the lake of women and brought him through rituals that only women were allowed by law to receive. For bringing him there she might have been killed, right along with him; instead she faced down the women and persuaded them that the Oversoul had commanded it. He had floated with her in the mists at the boundary between the hot and cold waters of the lake, and she had brought him through Trackless Wood, beyond the private gate in the wall of Basilica that, until now, only women had known about.

And earlier, Luet had come in the middle of the night to Father's house far outside the city—had come at some risk to herself—solely to warn that Father's enemies planned to murder him. She had precipitated their departure into the wilderness.

Nafai owed her much. And he liked her, she was a good person, simple and sweet. So why couldn't he think of her as a wife? Why did he recoil at the thought?

Because she is the waterseer.

The waterseer—that's why he didn't want to marry her. Because she had been having visions from the Oversoul for far longer than he; because she had strength and wisdom that he couldn't even hope to have. Because she was better than Nafai in every way he could think of. Because if they became partners in this journey back to Earth, she would hear the voice of the Oversoul better than he; she would know the way when he knew nothing at all. When all was silent for him, she would hear music; when he was blind, she would have light. I can't bear it, to be tied to a woman who will have no reason to respect me, because whatever I do, she has done it first, she can do it better.

So . . . you didn't want a wife, after all. You wanted a worshipper.

This realization made him flush with self-contempt. Is that who I am? A boy who is so weak that he can't imagine loving a woman who is strong?

The faces of Rasa and Wetchik, his mother and father, came into his mind. Mother was a strong woman—perhaps the strongest in Basilica, though she had never tried to use her prestige and influence to win power for herself. Did it weaken Father because Mother was at least—at *least*—his equal? Perhaps that was why they had not renewed their marriage after Issib's birth. Perhaps that was why Mother had married Gaballufix for a few years, because Father had not been able to swallow his pride enough to remain happily married to a woman who was so powerful and wise.

And yet she returned to Father, and Father returned to her. Nafai was the child she bore to seal their remarriage. And ever since then, they had renewed each other every year, not even questioning their commitment to each other. What had changed? Nothing—Mother did not have to diminish herself to be part of Father's life, and he did not have to dominate her in order to be part of *her* life. Nor did domination flow the other way; the Wetchik had always been his own man, and Rasa had never felt a need to rule over him.

In Nafai's mind, the faces of his father and mother flowed together and became one face. For a moment he recognized it as Father; then, without it changing at all, the face became clearly Mother's face.

I understand, he said silently. They are one person. What does it matter which of them happens to be the voice, whose hands happen to act? One is not above the other. They are together, and so there is no question of rivalry between them.

Can I find such a partnership with Luet? Can I bear it, to have her hear the Oversoul when I cannot? I seethed even now when it was Elya who dreamed a true dream; can I listen to Luet's dreams, and not be envious?

And what about *her*? Will she accept *me*?

Almost at once he was ashamed of the last question. She

already *had* accepted him. She had brought him down to the lake of women. She had given him all that she was and all that she had, without hesitation, as far as he could tell. He was the one who was jealous and afraid. She was the one with courage and generosity.

The question is not, Can I bear to live as one with her. The question is, Am I worthy to be partnered with such a one as that?

He felt a trembling warmth suffuse through him, as if he were filled with light. Yes, said the Oversoul inside his mind. Yes, that is the question. That is the question. That is the question.

And then the trance of his communion with the Oversoul ended, and Nafai suddenly became aware of his surroundings again. Nothing had changed—Meb and Elya still led the way, the camels plodding along. Sweat still dripped on Nafai's body; the camel still lurched and rolled under him; the dry air of the desert still burned with every breath he drew into his body.

Keep me alive, said Nafai. Keep me alive long enough for me to conquer the animal in myself. Long enough for me to learn to partner myself with a woman who is better and stronger than me. Long enough for me to reconcile myself with my brothers. Long enough to be as good a man as my father, and as good as my mother, too.

If I can, I will. Like a voice in his head, that promise.

And if *I* can, I'll make it soon. I'll become worthy soon.

FOUR

WIVES

THE DREAM OF THE GENETICIST

Shedemei awoke from her dream, and wanted to tell someone, but there was no one there beside her. No one, and yet she had to tell the dream. It was too powerful and real; it had to be spoken, for fear that if she didn't say what she had seen, it would slip away from her memory the way most dreams slipped away. It was the first time she wished that she had a husband. Someone who would have to listen to her dream, even if all he did then was grunt and roll over and go back to sleep. It would relieve her so, to tell the dream aloud.

But where would a husband have slept, anyway, in the clutter of her rooms? There was barely room for her cot. The rest of the place was given over to her research. The lab tables, the basins and beakers, the dishes and tubes, the sinks and the freezers. And, above all, the great dryboxes lining the walls, filled with desiccated seeds and embryos, so she could keep samples of every stage of her research into redundancy as a natural mechanism for creating and controlling genetic drift.

Though she was only twenty-six years old, she already had a worldwide reputation among scientists in her field. It was the only kind of fame that mattered to her. Unlike so many of the other brilliant women who had grown up in Rasa's house, Shedemei had never been interested in a career that would win her fame in Basilica. She knew from childhood on that Basilica was not the center of the universe, that fame here was no better than fame in any other place—soon to be forgotten. Humanity had been forty million years on this world of Harmony, more than forty thousand times longer than all of recorded human history on the ancient home planet of Earth. If there was any lesson to be learned, it was that a singer or actress, a politician or soldier, all would be forgotten soon enough. Songs and plays were usually forgotten in a lifetime; borders and constitutions were redrawn within a thousand years at most. But science! Knowledge! If that was what you wrought, it might be remembered forever. That it was you who discovered something, *that* might be forgotten . . . but the thing you learned, it would be remembered, it would have echoes and reverberations down all the years to come. The plants you created, the animals you enhanced, *they* would endure, if you wrought well enough. Hadn't the plant trader Wetchik, dear Rasa's favorite husband, carried Shedemei's Dryflower plant throughout all the lands on the edges of the desert? As long as Dryflower bloomed, as long as its rich and heavy perfume could make a whole house in the desert smell like a jungle garden, Shedemei's works would be alive in the world. As long as scientists all over the world received copies of her reports from the Oversoul, she had the only fame that mattered.

So this was her husband: the works of her own hands. Her creations were a husband that would never betray her, the way Rasa's poor little daughter Kokor had been betrayed. Her research was a husband that would never rampage through the city, raping and looting, beating and burning, the way the men of the Palwashantu had done, until the Gorayni brought order. Her research would never cause any woman to cower in her rooms, all lights off, a pulse in her hands though she doubted she would even know how to use it against an intruder. No one had come, though twice the shouting seemed almost to be in her street. But she would have fought to protect her seeds and embryos. Would have fought and, if she could figure out how to do it, would have killed to protect her life's work.

Yet now this dream had come. A disturbing dream. A powerful dream. And she could not rest until she had told the dream to someone.

To Rasa. Who was there that she could tell, besides Aunt Rasa?

So Shedemei arose, made a half-hearted effort to straighten her hair from sleep, and headed out into the street. She did not think to change her clothing, though she had slept in it; she often slept in her clothing, and only thought to change what she wore on those occasions when she thought to bathe.

There were a good number of people in the street. It had not been so for many days; the fear and distrust that Gaballufix had brought upon the city had kept many indoors. Thus it was almost a relief to see the turbulent flow of pedestrians rushing hither and thither. Almost a pleasure to jostle with them. The dead bodies of the mercenaries no longer hung from the second stories of the buildings, no longer slumped in the streets. They had been hauled away and buried with more or less ceremony in the men's cemeteries outside the city. Only the occasional sight of a pair of men in the uniform of the Basilican guards reminded Shedemei that the city was still under military rule. And the council was set to vote today on how to repay the Gorayni soldiers, send them on their way, and put the city guard back at gate duty. No more soldiers on the streets, then, except when answering an emergency call. All would be well. All would be as before.

A proof of the restoration of peace was the fact that on the porch of Rasa's house were two classes of young girls, listening to teachers and occasionally asking questions. Shedemei paused for just a moment as she so often did, to hear the lessons and remember her own time, so long ago, as a pupil on this very porch, or in the classrooms and gardens within Rasa's house. There were many girls of aristocratic parentage here, but Rasa's was not a house for snobs. The curriculum was rigorous, and there was always room for many girls of ordinary family, or of no family at all. Shedemei's parents had been farmers, not even citizens; only her mother's distant cousinship with a Basilican servant woman had allowed Shedemei to enter the city in the first place. And yet Rasa had taken her in, solely because of an interview when Shedemei was seven. Shedemei couldn't even read at the time, because neither of her parents could read . . . but her mother had ambitions for her, and, thanks to Rasa, Shedemei had been able to fulfill them all. Her mother had lived to see Shedemei in her own rooms, and with her first money from the keen-eyed roach-killing shrew she had developed, Shedemei was able to buy her parents' farm from their landlord, so that they spent their last few years of life as freeholders instead of tenants.

All because Aunt Rasa would take in a poor, illiterate seven-year-old girl because she liked the way the girl's mind worked when she conversed with her. For this alone, Rasa would deserve to be one of the great women of Basilica. And this was why, instead of teaching classes in the higher schools, the only teaching Shedemei did was here in Rasa's house, where twice a year she taught a class of Aunt Rasa's most prized science students. Indeed, officially Shedemei was still a resident here in Rasa's house—she even had a bedroom here, though she hadn't used it since the last time she taught, and always half expected to find it occupied by someone else. It never was, though, no matter how consistently Shedemei slept on the cot in her rooms. Rasa always kept a place for her.

Inside the house, Shedemei soon learned that Rasa's very greatness meant that it would not be possible to see her till later in the day. Though Rasa was not at present a member of the city council, she had been asked to attend this morning's meeting. Shedemei had not expected this. It made her feel lost. For the dream still burned within her, and had to be spoken aloud.

"Perhaps," said the girl who had noticed her and spoken to her, "perhaps there's something I could help you with."

"I don't think so," said Shedemei, smiling kindly. "It was foolishness anyway."

"Foolishness is my specialty," the girl said. "I know you. You're *Shedemei.*" She said the name with such reverence that Shedemei was quite embarrassed.

"I am. Forgive me for not remembering your name. I've seen you here many times before, though."

"I'm Luet," said the girl.

"Ah," said Shedemei. The name brought associations with it. "The waterseer," she said. "The Lady of the Lake."

The girl was clearly flattered that Shedemei knew who she was. But what woman in Basilica had not heard of her? "Not yet," said Luet. "Perhaps not ever. I'm only thirteen."

"No, I imagine you have years yet to wait. And it isn't automatic, is it?"

"It all depends," said Luet, "on the quality of my dreams."

Shedemei laughed. "And isn't that true of all of us?"

"I suppose," said Luet, smiling.

Shedemei turned to go. And then realized again whom she was talking with. "Waterseer," she said. "You must have some idea of the meanings of dreams."

Luet shook her head. "For dream interpretation you have to pay the truthmongers in the Inner Market."

"No," said Shedemei. "I don't mean that kind of dream. Or that kind of meaning. It was very strange. I never remember my dreams. But this time it felt . . . very compelling. Perhaps even . . . perhaps the kind of dream that I imagine one like *you* would have."

Luet cocked her head and looked at her. "If your dream might come from the Oversoul, Shedemei, then I need to hear it. But not here."

Shedemei followed the younger girl—half my age, she realized—into the back of the house and up a flight of stairs that Shedemei barely knew existed, for this region of the house was used for storage of old artifacts and furniture and classroom materials. They went up two more flights, into the attic space under a roof, where it was hot and dark.

"My dream was not so secret that we needed to come *here* to tell it," said Shedemei.

"You don't understand," said Luet. "There's someone else who must hear, if the dream is truly from the Oversoul." With that, Luet removed a grating from the gable wall and stooped through it, out into the bright air.

Shedemei, half blinded by the sunlight, could not see at first that there was a flat porch-like roof directly under the opening in the wall. She thought that Luet had stepped into nothingness and floated on the air. Then her eyes adjusted and, by squinting, she could see what Luet was walking on. She followed.

This flat area was invisible from the street, or from anywhere else, for that matter. A half dozen different sloping roofs came together here, and a large drainage hole in the center of the flat area made it clear why this place existed. In a heavy rain, it could fill up with roof runoff as much as four feet deep, until the drain could carry the water away, It was more of a pool than a porch.

It was also a perfect hiding place, since not even the residents of Rasa's house had any notion that this place existed—except, obviously, Luet and whoever was hiding here.

Her eyes adjusted further. In the shade of a portable awning sat an older girl who looked enough like Luet that Shedemei was not surprised to hear her introduced as Hushidh the Raveler, Luet's older sister. And across a low table from Hushidh sat a young man of large stature, but still too young to shave.

"Don't you know me, Shedemei?" said the boy.

"I think so," she said.

"I was much shorter when last you lived in Mother's house," he said.

"Nafai," she said. "I heard you had gone to the desert."

"Gone and come again too often, I fear," said Nafai. "I never thought to see a day when Gorayni soldiers would be keeping the gate of Basilica."

"Not for long," said Shedemei.

"I've never heard of the Gorayni giving up a city, once they had captured it," said Nafai.

"But they didn't capture Basilica," said Shedemei. "They only stepped in and protected us in a time of trouble."

"There are ashes from dozens and dozens of bonfires out on the desert," said Nafai, "and yet no sign of any encampment there. The story I hear is that the Gorayni leader pretended to have a huge army, led by General Moozh the Monster, when in fact he had only a thousand men."

"He explained it as a necessary ruse in order to psychologically overwhelm the Palwashantu mercenaries who were running wild."

"Or psychologically overwhelm the city guard?" said Nafai. "Never mind. Luet has brought you here. Do you know why?"

Luet interrupted at once. "No, Nafai. She's not part of

that. She came on her own, to tell Mother a dream. Then she thought of telling me, and I wanted both of you to hear, in case it comes from the Oversoul."

"Why *him?*" asked Shedemei.

"The Oversoul speaks to him, as much as to me," Luet said. "He forced her to speak to him, and now they are friends."

"A man *forced* the Oversoul to speak to him?" asked Shedemei. "When did such things start happening in the world?"

"Only recently," said Luet, smiling. "There are stranger things on heaven and earth than are dreamt of in your philosophy, Shedemei."

Shedemei smiled back, but couldn't remember where the quotation came from, or why it should be amusing at this time.

"Your dream," said Luet's sister Hushidh.

"Now I feel silly," said Shedemei. "I've made too much of it, to tell it to such a large audience."

Luet shook her head. "And yet you walked all the way here from—where do you live? The Cisterns?"

"The Wells, but not far from the Cisterns district."

"You came all that way to tell Aunt Rasa," said Luet. "I think this dream may be more important to you than even *you* understand. So tell us the dream, please."

Glancing again at Nafai, Shedemei found she couldn't bring herself to speak.

"Please," said Nafai. "I won't mock your dream, or tell anyone else. I want to hear it only for whatever truth might be in it."

Shedemei laughed nervously. "I just . . . I'm not comfortable speaking in front of a man. It's nothing against you. Aunt Rasa's son, of course I trust you, I just . . ."

"He's *not* a man," said Luet. "Not *really.*"

"Thanks," murmured Nafai.

"He doesn't deal with women as men usually do. And not many days ago, the Oversoul commanded me to take him down to the lake. He sailed it, he floated it right along with me. The Oversoul commanded it, and he was not slain."

Shedemei looked at him in new awe. "Is this the time when all the prophecies come together?"

"Tell us your dream," said Hushidh softly.

"I dreamt—this will sound so silly!—I dreamt of myself tending a garden in the clouds. Not just the plants and animals I'm working with, but every plant and animal I'd ever heard of. Only it wasn't a large garden, just a small one. Yet they all fit within it, and all were alive and growing. I floated along in the clouds—forever, it seemed. Through the longest night in the world, a thousand-year night. And then suddenly it was daylight again, and I could look down off the edge of the cloud and see a new land, a green and beautiful land, and I said to myself—in the dream, you understand—This world has no need of my garden after all. So I left the garden and stepped off the cloud—"

"A dream of falling," said Luet.

"I didn't fall," said Shedemei. "I just stepped out and there I was, on the ground. And as I wandered through the forests and meadows, I realized that in fact many of the plants from my garden *were* needed, after all. So I reached up my hand, and the plants I needed *rained* down on me as seeds. I planted them, and they grew before my eyes. And then I realized that many of my animals were also needed. This was a world that had lost its birds. There were no birds at all, and few reptiles, and none of the beasts of burden or the domesticated meat animals. And yet there were billions of insects for the birds and reptiles to eat, and pastures and meadows to feed the ruminants. So again I lifted my hands toward the clouds, and down from the clouds rained the embryos of the animals I needed, and I watered them and they grew quickly, large and strong. The birds took flight, the cattle and sheep wandered off to the brooks and meadows, and the snakes and lizards all slithered and scampered away. And I heard the words as if someone else had spoken them in my ears, 'No one has ever had such a garden as yours, Shedemei, my daughter.' But it wasn't my mother's or father's voice. And I wasn't sure whether the voice was speaking of my garden in the clouds, or this new world where I was restoring the flora and fauna lost so many years before."

That was the dream, all she could remember of it.

At first they said nothing. Then Luet spoke. "I wonder how you knew that the plants and animals you called down to you from the clouds were flora and fauna that had once lived in that place, but had been lost."

"I don't know," said Shedemei. "But that's how I felt it to be. How I *knew* it to be. These plants and animals were not being introduced, they were being restored."

"And you couldn't tell whether the voice was male or female," said Hushidh.

"The question didn't come up. The voice made me think of my parents, until I realized it wasn't either of them. But I didn't think to notice whether the voice was actually female or male. I can't think which it was even now."

Luet and Hushidh and Nafai began to confer with each other, but they spoke loudly enough for Shedemei to hear— they were not excluding her at all. "Her dream has a voyage in it," said Nafai. "That's consistent with what I was told—and the flora and fauna were being restored. That says Earth to me, and no other place."

"It points that way," said Luet.

"But the clouds," said Hushidh. "What of that? Clouds go from continent to continent, perhaps, but never from planet to planet."

"Even dreams from the Oversoul don't come ready made," said Nafai. "The truth flows into our minds, but then our brain draws on our own mental library to find images with which to express those ideas. A great voyage through the air. Elemak saw it as a strange kind of house; Shedemei sees it as a cloud; I heard it as the voice of the Oversoul, saying we must go to Earth."

"Earth," said Shedemei.

"Father didn't hear it, nor Issib either," said Nafai. "But I'm as sure of it as I am that I'm alive and sitting here. The Oversoul plans to go to Earth."

"That makes sense with your dream, Shedemei," said Luet. "Humankind left the Earth forty million years ago. The deep winter that settled over the Earth may have killed off most species of reptiles and all the birds. Only the fish and the amphibians, and a few small warm-blooded animals would have survived."

"But it's been forty million years since then," said Shedemei. "Earth must have recovered long ago. There should have been ample time for new speciation."

"How long was the Earth encased in ice?" asked Nafai. "How slowly did the ice recede? Where have the landmasses moved in the millions of years since then?"

"I see," said Shedemei. "It's possible."

"But that magic trick," said Hushidh. "Raising her hands and the seeds and embryos coming down, and then watering the *embryos* to make them grow."

"Well, actually, that part made sense to me right off," said Shedemei. "The way we store our samples in the kind of research I do is to dry-crystallize the seeds and embryos. It essentially locks all their body processes into exactly the moment in which the crystallization took place. We store them bone dry, and then when it's time to restore them, we just add distilled water and the crystals decrystallize in a very rapid but non-explosive chain reaction.

The whole organism, because it's so small, can be restored to full functions again within a fraction of a second. Of course, with the embryos we have to be able to put them immediately in a liquid growing solution and hook them up to artificial yolks or placentas, so we can't restore very many at a time."

"In order to carry with you enough samples to restore a significant amount of the flora and fauna most likely to have been killed off on Earth, how much equipment would it take?" asked Nafai.

"How much? A lot—a huge amount. A caravan."

"But what if you had to choose the most significant ones—the most useful birds, the most important animals, the plants we most need for food and shelter."

"Then any size would do," said Shedemei. "You just prioritize—if you have only one camel to carry it, then that's how many you take—two drycases per camel. Plus a camel to carry each set of restoration equipment and materials."

"So it could be done," said Nafai triumphantly.

"You believe the Oversoul will send you to Earth?" asked Shedemei.

"We believe it's the most important thing going on right now in the entire world of Harmony," said Nafai.

"My dream?"

"Your dream is part of it," said Luet. "So is mine, I think." She told Shedemei her dream of angels and diggers.

"It sounds plausible enough as a symbol of a world where new-life forms have evolved," said Shedemei. "What you're forgetting is that if your dream comes from the Oversoul, it can't possibly be literally true."

"Why not?" asked Luet. She seemed a little offended.

"Because how would the Oversoul know what's happening on Earth? How would it see a true picture of any species there? The Earth is a thousand lightyears away. There has never been an electromagnetic signal tight and true enough

to carry significant transmissions that distance. If the Oversoul gave you that dream, she's only making it up."

"Maybe she's guessing," said Hushidh.

"Maybe she's only guessing about the need for Shedemei's seeds and embryos," said Nafai. "But we must still
do what the dream commands. Shedemei must collect
these seeds and embryos, and prepare to take them to
Earth with us."

Shedemei looked at them in bafflement. "I came to tell
Aunt Rasa a dream, not abandon my career on a mad im-
possible journey. How do you think you're going to Earth?
By cloud?"

"The Oversoul has said we're going," said Nafai. "When
the time comes, the Oversoul will tell us how."

"That's absurd," said Shedemei. "I'm a scientist. I know
the Oversoul exists because our submissions are often transmitted to computers in faraway cities, something that can
be done in no other way. But I've always assumed that the
Oversoul was nothing more than a computer controlling
an array of communications satellites."

Nafai looked at Luet and Hushidh in consternation. "Issib and I struggled to figure that out," he said, "and Shedemei knew it all along."

"You never asked me," said Shedemei.

"We would never have *spoken* to you," said Nafai. "After all, you're *Shedemei.*"

"Just another teacher in your mother's house," said Shedemei.

"Yes, like the sun is just another star in the sky," said
Nafai.

Shedemei laughed and shook her head. It had never
occurred to her that the young ones would hold her in such
awe. She enjoyed knowing it—it felt good to think that
someone admired her—but it also made her feel faintly shy
and exposed. She had to live up to this image that they had

of her, and she was nothing more than a hardworking woman who had been disturbed by a dream.

"Shedemei," said Hushidh, "whether it seems possible or not, the Oversoul is asking us to prepare for this voyage. We would never have dreamed of asking *you,* but the Oversoul has brought you to us."

"Coincidence brought me to you."

"Coincidence is just the word we use when we have not yet discovered the cause," said Luet. "It's an illusion of the human mind, a way of saying, 'I don't know why this happened this way, and I have no intention of finding out.'"

"That was in another context," said Shedemei.

"You had the dream," said Nafai. "You knew it mattered. It made you want to tell Mother. We were here when you arrived, and she was not. But we, too, were brought together by the Oversoul. Don't you see that you have been invited?"

Shedemei shook her head. "My work is here, not on some insane journey whose destination is a thousand light-years away."

"Your work?" said Hushidh. "What is the value of your work, compared to the task of restoring lost species to Earth? Your work has been notable already, but to be the gardener for a planet . . ."

"*If* it's true," said Shedemei.

"Well," said Nafai, "we've all faced that same dilemma. *if* it's true. None of us can decide that for you, so when you make up your mind, let us know."

Shedemei nodded, but privately she knew that she would do everything within her power to avoid seeing these people again. It was too strange. They made too much of her dream. They demanded too much sacrifice of her.

"She has decided not to help us," said Luet.

"Nothing of the kind!" said Shedemei. But in her heart she wondered, guiltily, How did she know?

"Even if you decide not to go with us," said Nafai, "will

you do this much? Will you gather a fair sampling of seeds and embryos—perhaps two camels' load? And the equipment we'll need to restore them? And train some of us in how to do the work?"

"Gladly," said Shedemei. "I should be able to find time over the next several months."

"We don't have *months*," said Nafai. "We have hours. Or, perhaps, days."

"Don't make me laugh, then," said Shedemei. "What kind of garden am I supposed to assemble in hours?"

"Aren't there bio-libraries here in Basilica?" asked Hushidh.

"Well, yes—that's where I get my starting samples."

"Then couldn't you draw from them, and get most of what you'd need?"

"For two camels' load, I suppose I could get *all* of it. But the equipment to restore them, especially the animal embryos—the only equipment I have is my own set, and it would take months to build more."

"If you come with us," said Luet, "then you could bring your own. And if you don't come with us, you'll have the months to build more."

"You're asking me to give up my own equipment?"

"For the Oversoul," said Luet.

"So *you* believe."

"For Aunt Rasa's son," said Hushidh.

Of course the raveler would know how to break into my heart, thought Shedemei. "If Aunt Rasa asks me to do it for you," said Shedemei, "then I'll do it."

Nafai got a glint in his eye. "What if Mother asked you to go with us?"

"She never would," said Shedemei.

"What if Aunt Rasa was going herself?" asked Luet.

"She never will," said Shedemei.

"That's what Mother herself says," said Nafai, "but we'll see."

"Which of you will learn to use the equipment?" asked Shedemei.

"Hushidh and I," said Luet quickly.

"Then come this afternoon so I can teach you."

"You'll give us the equipment?" asked Hushidh.

Was she delighted, or merely surprised?

"I'll consider it," said Shedemei. "And teaching you how to operate it will cost nothing but time."

With that, Shedemei got up from the carpet and stepped out from under the awning. She looked for the grating through which she had come, but Luet must have replaced it, and she couldn't remember where she needed to go.

She didn't need to say anything, however, for Luet must have noticed her confusion instantly, and now the girl was leading her to the place. The grating hadn't been replaced, it had simply been out of sight behind the roofline. "I know the way from here," said Shedemei. "You needn't come with me."

"Shedemei," said Luet. "I dreamed of *you* once. Not many days ago."

"Oh?"

"I know you'll doubt me, and think I'm saying this only to try to persuade you to come, but it's not a coincidence. I was in the woods, and it was night, and I was afraid. I saw several women. Aunt Rasa, and Hushidh; Eiadh and Dol. And you. I saw you."

"I wasn't there," said Shedemei. "I never go into the woods."

"I know—I told you, it was a dream, though I was awake."

"I mean what I said, Luet. I *never* go into the woods. I never go down to the lake. I'm sure what you do is very important and fine, but it's not part of my life. It's no part of my life."

"Then perhaps," said Luet, "you should change your. life."

To that Shedemei had nothing civil to say, so she stepped through the opening in the wall. Behind her she could hear the murmuring sound of their conversation resuming, but she couldn't make out any of the words. Not that she wanted to. This was outrageous, to ask her to do what they were asking her to do.

And yet it had felt so wonderful, in her dream, to reach up and bring down life from the clouds. Why hadn't she just left it that way—as a beautiful dream? Why had she told these children? Why couldn't she just forget what they had said, instead of having these thoughts that now whirled in her mind.

To return to Earth. Home to Earth.

What did that mean? In forty million years, human beings had been content on Harmony. Why now should Earth be calling to her? It was madness, contagious madness in these troubled times.

Still, instead of going home she went to the biolibrary, and spent several hours poring over the catalogue, making up a plausible order for two camels' load of crystalized seeds and embryos that might restore the more useful plants and animals to an Earth that lost them long, long ago.

IN THE CITY COUNCIL, AND NOT IN A DREAM

Rasa had spent her life filled with confidence. There was nothing that could happen, she knew, that she could not handle with a combination of wit, kindness, and determination. People could always be persuaded, or if they could not, then they could be ignored and in time they would fade away. This philosophy had brought her to a point where her household was one of the most respected schools in Basilica, despite the fact that it was so new; it had also made her personally influential in every part of the city's life, though she had never held any office. She was consulted on most major decisions of the city council; she served on the governing boards of many of the arts councils; and, above all, she was privately consulted by the women— and, yes, even the men—who made most of the important decisions concerning Basilica's government and business. She was wooed by many men, but stayed happily married to the one man she had ever known who was neither threatened by nor covetous of her power. She had created a perfect role for herself within the city, and loved to live the part.

What had never occurred to her was how fragile it all was. The fabric of her life had been woven on the loom of Basilica, and now that Basilica was breaking apart, her life was fraying, snagging, tearing apart. Her former husband, Gaballufix, had begun the process, back while they were still married, when he attempted to get her to try to change the laws forbidding men to own property in the city. When she realized what his purpose in marrying her had been, she let the contract lapse and remarried Wetchik— permanently, as far as she was concerned. But Gaballufix hadn't given up, building support among the lowest sort of men in the villages outside the walls of the city. Then he brought them in as tolchoks, terrifying the women of the city, and then as mercenary soldiers in those hideous masks, supposedly to protect the city from the tolchoks—but as far as Rasa could tell, the mercenaries *were* the tolchoks in fancy holographic uniforms.

But Gaballufix might have been containable, if the Oversoul hadn't begun to act so strangely. She actually spoke to a man—and not just any man, but Wetchik himself. The problems this caused Rasa were incalculable. Not only was her former husband attacking the ancient laws of the city of women, but now her present husband was telling everyone who would listen that Basilica was going to be destroyed. Her dear friend Dhel remarked to her at the time—only a few weeks ago—that people were surprised that Rasa hadn't also been married to Roptat, the leader of the pro-Gorayni party. "Perhaps you ought to check your bed for some kind of madness-inducing parasite, my dear," said Dhel. She was joking, of course, but it was a painful joke.

Painful, but nothing compared to these past few days. Everything was falling apart. Gaballufix stole Wetchik's fortune and tried to kill his sons—including both of Rasa's own sons. Then the Oversoul commanded Luet to lead Nafai—of all people, *Nafai,* a mere child—down to the forbidden lake, where he floated on the water like a woman— like a waterseer. That same night, no doubt still wet from the lake of peace, Nafai had killed Gab. In one sense it was fair enough, for Gaballufix had tried to kill *him.* But to Rasa it was the most terrible thing she could imagine, her own son murdering her former husband.

Yet even that was only the beginning. For on that same night, she had found out exactly how monstrous her two daughters were. Sevya, sleeping with Kokor's husband— and Kokor then lashing out and nearly killing her. Civilization didn't even reach into my own home. My son a murderer, one daughter an adulterer and the other a murderer in her heart. Only Issib was still civilized. Issib the cripple, she thought bitterly. Perhaps that's what civilization is composed of—cripples who have banded together to try to control the strong. Wasn't that what Gaballufix said once? "In a time of peace, Rasa, you women can afford to surround yourselves with eunuchs. But when the enemy comes from outside, the eunuchs won't save you. You'll wish for real men, then, dangerous men, powerful men— and where will they be, since you've driven them all away?"

Rashgallivak—he was one of the foolish weaklings, wasn't he? One of the "eunuchs," in the sense that Gaballufix meant. He hadn't the strength to control the animals that Gaballufix had brought under harness. And then Hushidh cut loose that harness and the city began to burn. In my own house it happened! Why, again, am I the focal point?

The last insult was the coming of General Moozh, for Rasa knew now that it was he—it could be no one else. So audacious—to march to the city with only a thousand men, coming at a time when no enemy could be resisted, and when anyone willing to pretend to be a friend would be invited in. Rasa was not fooled by his promises. She was not deceived by the fact that his soldiers had withdrawn from the streets. They still held the walls and the gates, didn't they?

And even Moozh was tied to her, just as Wetchik and Gaballufix and Nafai and Rashgallivak had been tied. For he had come with her letter, and it was by using her name that he had first gained entry into the city.

Things could not possibly get any worse. And then, this morning, Nafai and Elemak had come into her house—from the forest side, which meant that they had both been creeping through lands that were forbidden to men. And why had they come? To inform her that the Oversoul required her to leave the city and join her husband in the desert, bringing with her whatever women she thought might be appropriate.

"Appropriate for what?" asked Rasa.

"Appropriate for marrying," said Elemak, "and bearing children in a new land far from here."

"I should leave the city of Basilica, taking some poor innocent women with me, and go out to live like a tribe of baboons in the desert?"

"Not like baboons," Nafai had said helpfully. "We still wear clothing, and none of us barks."

"I will not consider it," said Rasa.

"Yes you will, Mother," said Nafai.

"Are you threatening me?" asked Rasa—for she had heard too many men say such words recently.

"Not at all," said Nafai. "I'm predicting. I'll bet that before a half hour goes by, you'll be considering it, because you know the Oversoul wants you to do it."

And he was right. Not ten minutes. She couldn't get the idea out of her mind.

How did he know? Because he understood how the Oversoul worked. What he didn't know was that the Oversoul was already working on her. When Wetchik first left for the desert, he asked her to come with him. There was no talk of other women then, but when she prayed to the Oversoul, she was answered as clearly as if a voice had spoken in her heart. Bring your daughters, said the Oversoul. Bring your nieces, any who will come. To the desert, to be the mothers of my people.

To the desert! To be animals! In all her life, Rasa had tried to follow the teachings of the Oversoul. But now she asked too much. Who was Rasa, outside of Basilica, outside of her own house? She was no one there. Just Wetchik's wife. It would be men who ruled there—feral men, like Wetchik's son Elemak. He was one frightening boy, that Elemak; she couldn't believe that Wetchik couldn't see how dangerous he was. It would be Elemak the hunter that she'd depend on for food. And what influence would she have there? What council would listen to her? The men would hold the councils, and the women would cook and wash and care for the babies. It would be like primitive times, like animal times. She could not leave the city of women, for if she did, she would cease to be the Lady Rasa and would become a beast.

I only exist in this place. I am only human in this place.

And yet as she walked into the council chamber she

knew that "this place" had ceased to be the city of women. As she looked at the frightened, solemn, angry faces in the council, she knew that Basilica as it once had been would never exist again. A new Basilica might rise in its place, but never again would a woman like Rasa be able to raise her daughters and nieces in perfect peace and security. Always there would be men trying to own, to control, to *meddle*. The best she could hope for would be a man like Wetchik, whose kindness would temper his instinct for power. But was there another Wetchik to be found in this world? And even his benign interference would be too much. All would be ruined. All would be poisoned and defiled.

Oversoul! You have betrayed your daughters!

But she did not cry out her blasphemy. Instead she took her place at one of the tables in the middle of the chamber, where non-voting counselors and clerks sat during the meetings. She could feel their eyes upon her. Many, she knew, blamed her for everything—and she could hardly disagree with them. Her husbands, her son, her daughters; her house where Rashgallivak lost control of his soldiers; and, above all, her letter in the hands of the Gorayni general when he came into the city.

The meeting began, and for the first time in Rasa's memory, the rituals of the opening were rushed, and some were eliminated entirely. No one complained. For they all knew that the deadline the council had imposed on the Gorayni to leave the city now loomed as a deadline on themselves— for it was clear now to all of them that the Gorayni did not intend to leave.

The argument soon raged. No one disputed the fact that the Goryani now were masters of the city. The city debate was whether to defy the general—some called him Moozh, but only in ridicule, for he refused to answer to the name Vozmuzhalnoy Vozmozhno, and yet told them no other name to use for him—or give his occupation a legal gloss. They hated the idea of giving in to him, but if they did, there was a hope that he'd let them continue to govern the city in exchange for letting him use Basilica as a military base for his operations against the Cities of the Plain and, no doubt, Potokgavan. Yet by making his occupation legal, as he had requested, they gave him power in the long run to destroy them.

Still, what was the alternative? He had made no threats. In fact, all he had sent them was a very respectful letter: "Because my troops have not yet succeeded in abating the danger in Basilica, we are reluctant to abandon our dear friends to the return of such chaos as we found on our arrival. Therefore if you invite us to stay until such time as order is fully restored, we are willing to become your obedient servants for the indefinite future." On its face, the letter portrayed the Gorayni as being docile as lambs.

But they knew by now that nothing with the Gorayni was what it seemed. Oh, they bowed to every order or request of the city council, promising to obey. But only the orders that suited their purpose were actually carried out. And the city guard, too, was unreliable, for their officers had begun practically to worship the Gorayni general, and now were following his example of swearing obedience and then doing as they liked. Oh, the general was a clever man! He provoked no one, he argued with no one, he agreed with everything that was said . . . and yet he was immovable, doing all that he pleased, while never giving them anything they could attack him for. Everyone in the council chamber must have felt it as keenly as Rasa did, the slipping away of their own power, the centering of the city on the will of this one man, and all without any overt word or deed of his.

How does he do it? Rasa wondered. How does he master people without bluster or bullying? How does he make people fear him or love him, not in spite of his ruthlessness but because of it?

Maybe it is simply that he knows so clearly how he wants things to be, she thought. Maybe the fact that he believes in his vision of the world so intensely makes it impossible for those around him not to believe as well. Maybe we're all so hungry for someone to tell us what is true, what we can *count on,* that we'll accept even a vision that makes us weak and him strong, just for the sake of having a secure world at all.

"We are only a few minutes from the deadline," said old Kobe. "And in all our discussion this morning we have heard nothing from the Lady Rasa."

A murmur of approval arose, but it was immediately drowned in a growl of anger. "We shouldn't hear from her except at her trial!" cried one women. "She brought all this on us!"

Rasa calmly turned and looked at the woman who spoke. It was Frotera, of course, the lady of another teaching household, who had long been envious of Rasa. "My Lady Frotera," Rasa said, "I fear you may be right."

That silenced them.

"Do you think I haven't also looked and seen what you all can see? Which of the calamities that has befallen us has not been tied to me? My son is accused of murder, my daughters have betrayed each other, Rashgallivak tried to drag them from my own house, my beloved city has been torn by riot and fire, and the army that squats in the gates of Basilica shows you a letter that I wrote. And I did write it, though I never dreamed that it would be used as he has used it. Sisters, all of this is true, but does it mean I have brought all of this upon us? Or does it mean that it has fallen more heavily on me than on any except those whose loved ones perished in the rioting?"

It made them think; ah, yes, she still had the power to

tell them a story and make them see, at least for a moment, through her eyes.

"Sisters, if I believed that I was truly the cause of all the evil that has come to Basilica, I would leave at once. I love Basilica too much to be the cause of its downfall. But I am not the cause. The first cause was the greed of Gaballufix—and he married me as his first attempt to make an inroad against our ancient laws. Was it my husband who brought private soldiers into this city? No. It was a man whom I had *refused* to have as my husband. I repudiated Gaballufix while many of you on this council kept voting to tolerate his abuses! Do not forget that!"

Oh, they didn't forget, as they shrank back in their seats.

"Now the Gorayni have come with my letter. But I wrote that letter to help a young Basilican guard obtain refuge with the Gorayni. I knew he was in danger from Rashgallivak's mercenaries, and he had been kind to my son, so I gave him what small protection I could. Now I see that this was a terrible mistake. My letter alerted them to our weakness, and they came to exploit it. But I didn't create our weakness, and if the Gorayni hadn't come, would we be in *better* condition this morning than we are now? Would we even be holding this meeting, or would we all be victims of rape and plunder by the Palwashantu mercenaries? Would our city be in ashes? So tell me, sisters, which is better, to be in a bad situation, yet with *some* hope, or to be destroyed, powerless, utterly hopeless?"

Again a murmur, but she was carrying them. Only rarely had she spoken at such length or with such force—she had long since learned that she remained more powerful by never openly committing herself to anything, but rather working behind the scenes. Still, she had spoken often enough to know how to bend them, at least a little, to her will. It was a power that would be less effective every time she used it, but this was a time when she must use it or lose everything.

"If we defy him, what will happen then? Even if he keeps his word and leaves, can any of you say that our city guard will be as docile as they once were? And I don't believe that he *will* keep his word. Have you ever heard of General Vozmuzhalnoy Vozmozhno giving up one village, one field, one *pebble* that he has conquered?" A growing murmur. "Yes, it *is* General Moozh—we'd be fools to imagine otherwise for a moment. What other Gorayni general would have the audacity to do what he has done? Don't you see how daring and brilliant his plan has been? He came here with only a thousand men, but for a few crucial hours we believed he had a hundred times that number. He has been subservient and obsequious, and yet he has deployed his soldiers where he wanted them, seduced our city guard, and seized whatever supplies he needed. Always he apologizes and explains. Always he keeps us believing that he means well. But he is a liar with every breath he takes, and nothing that he says to us is true. He means to add Basilica to the Gorayni Empire. He will *never* let us go."

Loud muttering filled the room as she waited. Several of the women wept. "Defy him then!" one of the councilors cried.

"And what good would defiance do?" asked Rasa. "How many of us would die? And to what purpose? A fifth of our city is already in ashes. We have already huddled in terror as drunken men rampaged through our city. What would happen if now the plunderers were sober? If they were the same disciplined killers who nailed the rioters to the walls with their own knives? There'd be no refuge for us then!"

"So . . . what do you propose we do, Lady Rasa?"

"Give him what he has asked for. Permission to stay. Only make provision for his soldiers to be quartered outside the walls of the city. Make them take the same oaths that men are required to take when they become our husbands—to stay out of the forbidden parts of the city, to refrain from attempting to own any real property, and to leave when their term is up."

A murmur of approval.

"Will he accept it, Lady Rasa?"

"I have no idea," she said. "But so far, he has made an effort at least to *seem* to comply with our wishes. Let us make our offer as public as possible, and then hope he'll find it more convenient to adhere to its terms than not."

Rasa's exhortations were too successful by half. Yes, they approved her proposal, almost unanimously. But they also appointed her the ambassador to deliver their "invitation" to General Moozh. It was not an interview she looked forward to, but she had no time even to wonder what she ought to say or how she ought to act. The invitation had to be delivered personally and immediately; it was printed out, signed, and sealed on the spot, and the council watched as she left the chamber with the document in hand, minutes before the deadline that they themselves had set.

IT WAS NOT Mebbekew's finest morning. He had dutifully trudged through the forbidden slopes of Basilica as Nafai led the way, just as he had followed Elemak all the way from the desert around the city to the northern woods. But when they came within sight of Rasa's house, Mebbekew slipped away. He had no intention of being a pawn in *their* plans. If they were here to do some wife-finding, Mebbekew would pick his own, thank you kindly. He would certainly *not* tag along behind his older brother, taking second choice forever; nor would he swallow the humiliation of going into his little brothers' mother's house and pleading with *her* to give up one of her precious nieces. Elemak had his heart set on that porcelain doll, Eiadh . . . well, that was his privilege. Mebbekew preferred women with blood in their veins, women who grunted and growled when they made love, women of vigor and strength. Women who loved Mebbekew.

Well, he found out about vigor and strength, right enough! The fires had been worst in Dolltown and Dauberville, so few of his old lovers were in the houses where he had known them. The few that he could find were *glad* to see him. They were all over him with tears and kisses, eager to have him stay with them. Stay with them *where?* In a half-burnt house with no running water? And *why* did they want him? So he could do all the brute man-labor required to rebuild, to repair; and so he could be their guardian. What a joke! Mebbekew, standing guard over some poor frightened girl! No doubt they would have rewarded him generously with their bodies if he had played the role they scripted for him, but it wasn't worth it—*no* woman was worth it right now, if her needs were even greater than his own. He wasn't here to be a protector or a provider, he was here to find protection and providence.

So he left them with a kiss and a promise, without even staying long enough to bathe or eat, because he knew that if he once got within their clinging embrace these women-in-need would make of him a husband. He had no intention of husbanding himself to women who had nothing to offer him but work and trouble!

As for suggesting to any of his old lovers that she give up everything in Basilica and come wander with him in the desert until they found a promised land, meanwhile having a passel of babies in order to populate their new home—it never seemed to come up in any of his conversations. Not that some of them wouldn't have done it. As they surveyed the ruin of their once-frivolous lives in Basilica, as they remembered the fear of that awful night of rioting, and then the horror of the dead bodies pinned to the walls by the Gorayni, the idea of striding out into the desert with a *real* man to lead and protect them would appeal to some of them. For the first few days, anyway; then they'd realize that the desert was lonely and no fun at all, and they'd be as eager to return to Basilica, ruined or not, as Mebbekew himself was.

It hardly mattered. He never intended to make such a proposal to any of his women friends. Let Elemak and Nafai play along with Father and have their stupid visions if they wanted to. All Mebbekew wanted was some woman to take him in to a nice, clean house and a nice clean bed, and hide him and console him for the loss of his fortune until Elemak and Nafai went away. Why should Mebbekew ever go out in the desert again? Basilica might be half-burnt and terrorized and occupied by Gorayni troops, but the toilets and baths still worked in *most* houses, and the food was fresh and there was plenty of pleasure and fun in the old town yet.

Yet even that limited plan wouldn't have worked for long, he gradually came to realize. During his early morning wanderings through Dolltown, he realized that he couldn't hide in Basilica for long. For he had entered the city illegally, without being recorded, and somewhere along the line he'd get picked up and taken in. The city guard were quite active in the streets now, more than he'd ever seen, and they were demanding thumbscans and eyescans at checkpoints on several streets. He was bound to be picked up one of these days. Indeed, it wasn't easy getting from Dolltown to Rasa's house on Rain Street.

Yes, Rasa's house. It galled him, but he had tried everything else; so here he was, ready to surrender completely to his brothers and his father and their idiotic plans.

Standing in the street, looking at the front of Rasa's house, ready to give in—and yet not ready. It was unbearable. Humiliating. Knock, knock. Good morning, I'm

Rasa's sons' half-brother, and I'm here because all my ex-lovers sent me packing and so I'd be grateful if Rasa and my half-brothers would take me in and give me something to eat and drink, not to mention a long hot shower, before I die.

It was a hideous scene to imagine, and even though he knew he had to do it, Mebbekew had never acquired much practice in doing unpleasant things just because he knew he had to do them. So instead he did what he *usually* did under such circumstances. He waited, just within reach of his painful goal, and then proceeded to do nothing.

He did nothing—suffering imagined torments all the while—for at least twenty minutes, watching the classes of young girls and boys that were meeting on the porch. Now and then he could even catch a word that was said, and so he tried to guess the subjects being taught and what the particular lesson was. It took his mind off his troubles for a moment or two, at least. The nearer class, he decided, was studying either geometry or organic chemistry or building with blocks.

A young woman left one of the classes, jogged down the steps of the porch, and then strode purposefully toward him. No doubt she had seen him watching the porch and decided he was a would-be child molester or burglar. He thought of turning and leaving before she reached him— which was what she almost certainly expected him to do— but instead he studied her face and realized that he recognized her.

"Good morning," she said icily, as soon as she was close enough to say it without shouting.

Mebbekew wasn't worried about the prospect of an argument. He had never yet met a young and beautiful woman he couldn't warm up quickly enough, if he tried hard enough to find out what she hungered for, and then gave it to her. It was always a pleasure dealing with a woman he had never worked on before. Especially because he recognized her at once—or at least saw a resemblance.

"Didn't you used to be Dolya?" he asked.

Her face turned scarlet, but her expression became colder and angrier. So he was right—she *was* Dol. "Shall I send for the Guard to send you away?"

"I saw you in *Pirates* and *West Wind*. You were brilliant," he said.

Her blush deepened and her expression softened.

"You had the talent," he went on. "It wasn't just looks. It wasn't just that you were young and sweet. I never understood why they didn't give you adult parts as you got older. I know you could have carried it off. It was damned unfair."

And now her expression wasn't angry at all, but rather bemused. "I have never heard anyone engage in such transparent, cynical flattery," she said.

"Ah, but I meant every word. Dolya—I suppose you go by the adult name, Dol, now?"

"To my friends, I do. Others call me ma'am."

"Ma'am, I hope that someday I can earn the right to be your friend. In the meantime, I was hoping you might tell me if my half-brothers Elemak and Nafai are in Rasa's house."

She eyed him up and down. "I don't see that you look all that much like either of them."

"Ah, but now you flatter *me,*" he said.

She laughed a little and stepped toward him, offering her hand. "I'll take you in, if you're really Mebbekew."

He withdrew a pace from her. "Don't touch me! I'm filthy. Two days' traveling in the desert isn't the best perfume, and if my body's stench didn't kill you my breath would."

"I didn't expect you to be a bouquet," she said. "I'll risk taking your hand to lead you in."

"Then you have courage to match your beauty," he said,

taking her hand. "By the Oversoul," he whispered, "your hand is cool and soft to touch."

She laughed again—an actress with as much experience as Dol had had, back when she was famous, could never be fooled by flattery. But Mebbekew figured that it had been years now since anyone had bothered to flatter her at all, so the very fact that he thought it was worth trying would be a sort of meta-flattery against which she wouldn't be able to protect herself. And, indeed, it seemed to be working quite well.

"You don't have to say such things," she said. "Aunt Rasa left instructions for you to be admitted as soon as you— how did she say it—as soon as you 'bothered to show up.'"

"If I had known I'd find you here, ma'am, I'd have come much sooner. And as you say, I don't have to flatter anybody to get into Rasa's house this morning. So what I say to you now isn't flattery. It's my own heart. When I was a boy I fell in love with the image of Dolya on the stage. Now I see you with a man's eyes. I see you as a woman. And I know that your beauty has only increased. I never knew you were one of Rasa's nieces or I would have stayed in school."

"I *was* her niece. I'm a teacher here now. Comportment, that sort of thing. I've been teaching Eiadh in particular. You know, the one your brother Elemak is wooing."

"It's just like Elemak to woo the pale copy, while he ignores the original." Mebbekew deliberately kept his eyes on her face, but not on her eyes—instead he studied her lips, her hair, all her features knowing that she would see how his eyes moved, how he was drinking her in. "Elemak's only my half-brother, by the way," said Mebbekew. "When I'm all cleaned up you'll see that I'm much better looking."

She laughed, but he knew he had won her interest—he had long since learned that flattery always works, and that even the most outrageously dishonest praise is believed, if you repeat it and elaborate on it enough. In this case, though, he really didn't have to lie. Dol *was* beautiful, though of course nowhere near as lovely as she had been when she was an ethereal child of thirteen. Still, she had grace and poise and a smile that dazzled, and, now that he had been working on her for a few minutes, her eyes were bright and wide whenever she looked at him. It was desire. He had kindled desire in her. It wasn't the desire for passion, of course; rather it was the desire to hear more of his praise for her beauty, more of his verbal petting. Yet he knew from experience that it would be easy enough to get from here to there, if he wasn't too tired after breakfast and a bath.

She showed him to her own bedroom—a good sign— where the servants ran a bath for him. He was still in the water, luxuriating in his cleanliness, when she came back in with a tray of food and a pitcher of water. She had brought it with her own hands, and they were alone. All the time she chattered—not nervously, either, but comfortably. That was Mebbekew's greatest talent, that women so easily became comfortable with him that they talked to him with the kind of candor they usually had only with their girl-friends.

As she talked, he rose up out of the water; when she turned around from setting the tray on her dresser, she saw him toweling himself down, quite naked. She gasped prettily and looked away.

"I'm sorry," he said. "It didn't occur to me that you'd be startled. You must have seen so many men in your days as an actress—I've been on the stage, too, and no one is shy or modest backstage."

"I was young," said Dol. "They always protected me in those days."

"I feel like some kind of beast, then," said Mebbekew. "I didn't mean to shock you."

"No," she said. "No, I'm not shocked."

"The trouble is that I haven't anything to wear. I don't think it would be helpful to put my dirty clothes back on."

"The servants already took your clothes to be washed. I have a robe for you, though."

"One of yours? I doubt it will fit *me*." All this time, of course, he had continued toweling, still making no effort to cover himself. And as they talked, she had turned back around and now was looking at him quite frankly. Since things were going so smoothly and he anticipated making love to this woman very soon, his body had become quite alert. As soon as he caught her looking at his crotch, he pretended to notice for the first time and made a show of putting the towel in front of himself. "I'm sorry," he said. "I've been alone on the desert so long, and you're so beautiful—I meant no insult."

"I'm not insulted," she said. And he could see the desire in *her* eyes, too. She wanted more than pretty words from him now. As he had guessed, she probably didn't get many suitors these days. With her beauty, she'd have had no lack of lovers in Dolltown, but as a teacher in Rasa's house the opportunities would be much more limited. So she was almost certainly as eager as he was.

This was what he had come back to Basilica for. Not those frightened, hungry women in Dolltown, who needed him to be strong and dependable, but *this* woman, who needed him only to be passionate and flattering and fun. Dol felt herself to be safe and comfortable enough in Rasa's house that she could still be what Basilican women were *supposed* to be—self-supporting providers for men, needing nothing more from their lovers than a little pleasure and attention.

She brought him her robe. It probably could have fit well enough, but he made a show of jamming his arm so far in the sleeve that it barely passed his elbow. "Oh, that won't do," she said.

"It hardly matters by now," he said. "I don't exactly have any secrets from you anymore!"

Of course, he had dropped the towel to try on the robe. He bent over to pick it up, even as he was taking the robe off his arm. But when he stood again, she took both the towel and the robe away from him. "You're right," she said. "There's little point in trying for modesty now." She tossed the robe and towel into a corner and then brought him a handful of grapes from the food tray on the dresser. "Here," she said.

She held out the grape, not to his hand, but to his lips. He leaned forward farther than he needed to, and got her fingers into his mouth along with the grape. She let her fingers linger in his mouth as he slowly pulled the grape away. At last he bit down on the grape and felt the juice of it squirt inside his mouth. It was tart and sweet and delicious. He sat on the bed and she fed him another, and then another. But the rest of the grapes ended up on the floor.

MOOZH HAD WAITED with great anticipation to meet Lady Rasa at last, and she did not disappoint him. He had installed himself in Gaballufix's house—the symbolism was deliberate—and he knew that she would certainly see the true meaning of his residence here. Lady Rasa would not be a *complete* fool, that much he was sure of, from what he had heard about her. All that remained now was to see which of several plans he ought to follow with her. She might be turned into an ally. She might be turned into a dupe. She might, of course, be an implacable enemy. No matter which, he would make use of her.

She did not carry herself with any particular majesty; she

made no attempt to entice or intimidate him. But that was just about the only way a woman could impress him anymore. He had been worked on by the finest court women in Gollod, but it was plain that Rasa had no interest in working on him. Rather she spoke with him as with an equal, and he liked it. He liked *her*. It would be a good game.

"Of course I want to accept the invitation of the city council," he said. "We are only too happy to help this beautiful city maintain order and security while rebuilding from these unfortunate events of the past weeks. But I have a problem that perhaps you can help me with."

He could see from the look on her face that she had expected more demands from him—and he knew, too, that she had no illusions about the fact that he was in a position to make demands, and make them stick, too.

"You see," he said, "the traditional way for a Gorayni general to reward his men after a great victory is to divide up the conquered territory and give them land and wives."

"But you have not conquered Basilica," said Rasa pointedly.

"Exactly!" he said. "You see my dilemma. My men performed with extraordinary heroism and discipline in this campaign, and their victory over the ruffians and rioters was complete. And yet I lack a means to reward them!"

"Our treasury is deep," said Rasa. "I'm sure the city council can make each of your thousand men as rich as you please."

"Money?" asked Moozh. "Oh, you hurt me deeply. Me and my men alike. We are not mercenaries!"

"You accept land, but not the money with which to buy land?"

"Land is a matter of title and honor. A landed man is a lord. But *money* —that would be like calling my soldiers *tradesmen*."

She gazed at him for a moment, and then said, "General

Vozmuzhalnoy Vozmozhno, does the Imperator know that you call these men *your* soldiers? *your* men?"

Moozh felt a sudden thrill of fear. It was delicious indeed—it had been a long time since he had sat across a table from someone who knew how to take the initiative away from him. And she had struck immediately at his weakest point. For not only had he defied the Imperator's orders about not making any offensive maneuvers, he had also left behind the corpses of the Imperator's public and private spies to come here. His greatest danger at the moment came from the Imperator, who would surely by now have heard of his venture. Moozh knew the Imperator well enough to know that he would not act rashly—indeed, that was the Imperator's primary fault, that he was terrified of risk—but already a new intercessor would certainly be on his way southward, and not without temple troops to back him up. Either Moozh would be able to put a good face on things and win back the Imperial trust, or he would have to commit himself to open rebellion with only a thousand troops and a hundred kilometers deep in hostile territory. It was not a good moment for him to face an opponent who understood exactly what his weakness was.

"When I call them mine," said Moozh, "of course I recognize that they are mine only as long as the Imperator permits me to be his servant."

"I notice that you don't deny that you *are* Vozmuzhalnoy Vozmozhno."

He shrugged. "I recognize that you are far too clever for me. Why should I try to conceal my identity from *you?*"

She frowned. His flattery and his frank admission had set her back a bit. Now she would no doubt be wondering why he so willingly admitted his true name, and why he was calling her clever. She would assume that because he called her clever, it must mean she had *not* been clever at all. Thus she would no longer trust her belief that the way to get at him was by exploiting differences between him and the Imperator. He had long since learned that one of the best ways to disarm a genuinely clever opponent was to make him mistrust his own strengths, and it seemed to be working well enough with Rasa.

"Cleverness doesn't enter into it," she said. "Truth is what matters. I don't believe there's a word of truth in what you say. You don't usually reward your soldiers with land, or you'd have no soldiers left. Your officers, perhaps. But this talk of land is just your first bid in an effort to destroy the land law of the city of women. Let me guess how the game goes: I return to the council with your humble request, and they send me back with an offer to settle your men outside the city. You praise our generosity, and then point out that your men could never be content as second-class citizens of a land they had rescued from destruction. How could he explain to Gorayni soldiers that they could never own land inside the city? Then you would propose a compromise—just to allow them and us to both save face. Your compromise would be that Gorayni soldiers who married Basilican women would be allowed to hold half-ownership with them of their land inside the city. The women would, of course, remain completely in control of the land, but your soldiers could keep their self-respect."

"You have a gift of prescience," said Moozh.

"Not so—I'm only improvising," she said. "Half-rights in property would lead within weeks to a series of opportune marriages, and then there'd be pressure for an equal vote—especially since you will have proved that your men are meek and obedient husbands who make no effort to control the property in which they have a titular half-interest. How many steps from there to the day when women have *no* vote, and all the property of Basilica is owned by men?"

"My dear lady, you misjudge me."

"You don't have much time," said Rasa. "Your Imperator will certainly have representatives here within two weeks at the latest."

"All Gorayni armies travel with Imperial representatives."

"Not yours," said Rasa. "Or the city guard would know it. We've read accounts here of how your army works, and there is no intercessor's tent. Some of your soldiers feel the lack of confession quite keenly."

"I have nothing to fear from the coming of an intercessor."

"Then why did you try to fool me into thinking you had one here already? No, General Vozmuzhalnoy Vozmozhno, I think you have to move swiftly indeed to consolidate your position here before you face the challenge of the Imperator. I think you don't have time to deal with any kind of uprising, either—it has to be settled peacefully and at once."

So she had not been deflected at all by his flattery. The thrill of fear once again pulsed through him. "Ma'am, you are wise indeed. It is possible that the Imperator will misconstrue my actions, even though my motive was purely to serve him. But you're mistaken to think it will take many gradual steps to consolidate my position here."

"You think not?" asked Rasa.

"It won't take many marriages, I think, but only one." He smiled. "Mine."

At last he had succeeded in startling *her.* "Aren't you already married, sir?" she asked.

"As a matter of fact I am not," said Moozh. "I have never been married. Until now it has always been politically preferable."

"And you think that your marriage to a Basilican woman will solve everything for you? Even if they grant you a special exception and let you share in your wife's property, there's no one woman in Basilica who controls so much property that it would make any difference to you."

"I don't intend to marry for property."

"For what, then?"

"For influence," he said. "For prestige."

She studied his face for a moment. "If you think *I* have that kind of influence or prestige, you're a fool."

"You are a striking woman, and I confess that you are of the right age for me—mature and accomplished. To marry you would make life a dangerous and engrossing game, and you and I would both enjoy it. Alas, though, *you* are already married, even if your husband is rumored to be a mad prophet hiding in the desert. I don't believe in breaking up happy families. Besides, you have too many opponents and enemies in this city for you to be a useful consort."

"Imperators have consorts, General Vozmuzhalnoy Vozmozhno; generals have wives."

"Please, call me Moozh," he said. "It's a nickname that I only permit my friends to use."

"I am not your friend."

"The nickname means 'husband,'" he said.

"I know what it means, and neither I nor any woman of Basilica will ever call you that to your face."

"Husband," said Moozh, "and Basilica is my bride. I will wed her, I will bed her, and she will bear me many children, this fair city. And if she doesn't take me willingly as her husband, I will have her anyway, and in the end she *will* be docile."

"In the end this city will have your balls on a plate, General," she retorted. "The last lord of this house discovered that, when he tried to do what you are doing."

"But he was a fool," said Moozh. "I know it, because he lost *you.*"

"He didn't lose *me*," said Rasa. "He lost himself."

He smiled at her. "Farewell, ma'am," he said. "Till we meet again."

"I doubt we will," she said.

"Oh, I'm sure we'll converse again."

"After I return and tell them what you really are, there'll be no more emissaries from the city council."

"But my dear lady," said Moozh, "did you think I'd have spoken to you so freely, if I intended to let you speak again to the council?"

Her face blanched. "So you *are* no different from any of the other bullies. Like Gaballufix and Rashgallivak, you love to hear your own bluster. You think it makes you manly."

"Not so," said Moozh. "Their posturing and boasting came to nothing—they did it because they feared their own weakness. I never posture and I never boast, and when I decide what is necessary I do it. You will be escorted from here to your own house, which is already surrounded by Gorayni troops. All the non-resident children in your house have been sent safely home; the others will be kept indoors, since from this point on no one will be allowed to enter or leave your house. We will, of course, deliver food to you, and I believe your water supply is entirely provided by wells and a clever rain collection system."

"Yes," she said. "But the city will never stand for your arresting me."

"You think not?" asked Moozh. "I have already sent one of the Basilican guard to inform the city council that I have arrested you in their name, in order to protect the city from your plotting."

"My *plotting*!" she cried, rising to her feet.

"You came to me and suggested that I abolish the city council and establish one man as king of Basilica. You even had a candidate in mind—your husband, Wetchik, who already had his sons murder his chief rivals and even now is waiting in the desert for me to call for him to come and rule the city as a vassal of the Imperator."

"Monstrous lies! No one will believe you!"

"You know that your statement is false, even as you make it," said Moozh. "You know that there are many on that council who will be only too happy to believe that all your actions have been inspired by private ambition, and that you have been involved in causing all your city's misfortunes from the start."

"You'll see that the women of Basilica are not so easily fooled."

"You have no idea, Lady Rasa, how happy I would be if the women of Basilica proved to be so wise that I could not deceive them. I have longed all my life to find people of such exemplary wisdom. But I think I have not found them here, with the single exception of yourself. And *you* are completely under my control." He laughed merrily. "By the Incarnation himself, ma'am, after conversing with you this morning it terrifies me to know that you are even *alive*. If you were a man with an army I would be afraid to campaign against you. But you are not a man with an army, and so you pose no threat to me—not anymore."

She rose from her chair. "Are you finished?"

"Do your household a favor—don't try to send anyone out with secret messages. I *will* catch anyone you send, and then I'll probably have to do something grisly like delivering the next day's rations to your house sewn up inside your would-be messenger's skin."

"You are exactly the reason why Basilica banned men from the city in the first place," she said coldly.

"And you are exactly the reason why the city of women is an abomination in the sight of God," he answered. But his voice was warm with admiration—even affection—for the truth was that this woman alone had taught him that the city of women was not as weak and effeminate as he had imagined all these years.

"God!" she said. "God means nothing to you. The way you think, the way you live—I daresay that you spend every moment of your life trying to flout the will of the Oversoul and unmake all her works in this world."

"You are close to the mark, dear lady," he said. "Closer than you ever imagined. Now do please bow to the inevitable and make no trouble for my poor soldiers who have the unpleasant duty of taking you home under public arrest through the streets of Basilica."

"What trouble could I make?"

"Well, for one thing, you could try to shout some ridiculous revolutionary message to the people you pass. I would recommend silence."

She nodded gravely. "I will accept your recommendation. You can be sure that I'll despise you in silence all the way home."

It took six of them to walk her home. His lies about her had been so persuasive that crowds gathered in many places to vilify her as a traitor to her city. That was bad enough, to be unjustly loathed by her beloved city, but it didn't gall her half as much as the other shouts—the cheers for General Moozh, the savior of Basilica.

FIVE

HUSBANDS

THE DREAM OF THE HOLY WOMAN

Her name was Torstiga in the language of her homeland, but she had been so long away from *that* place, far in the east, that she didn't even remember the language of her childhood. She had been sold into slavery by her uncle when she was seven years old, was carried west to Seggidugu, and there was sold again. Slavery was not intolerable—her mistress was strict but not unfair, and her master kept his hands to himself. It could have been much worse, she well knew—but it was not freedom.

She prayed constantly for freedom. She prayed to Fackla, the god of her childhood, and nothing happened. She prayed to Kui, the god of Seggidugu, and still she was a slave. Then she heard stories of the Oversoul, the goddess of Basilica, the city of women, a place where no man could own property and every woman was free. She prayed and prayed, and one day when she was twelve, she went mad, caught up in the trance of the Oversoul.

Since many slaves pretended to be god-mad in order to win their freedom, Torstiga was locked up and starved during her frenzy. She did not mind the darkness of the tiny cubicle where they confined her, for she was seeing the visions that the Oversoul put into her mind. Only when the visions ended at last did she notice her own physical discomfort. Or at least, that was how it seemed to her mistress, for she cried out again and again from her cubicle: "Thirsty! Thirsty! Thirsty!"

They did not understand that she was crying out that one word, not because she needed to drink—though indeed she was far along with dehydration—but because it was her name, Torstiga, translated into the language of Basilica. The language of the Oversoul. She called her own name because she had lost herself in the midst of her visions; she hoped that if she called out loud enough and long enough, the girl she used to be might hear her, and answer, and perhaps come back and live in her body once again.

Later she came to understand that her true self had never left her, but in the confusion and ecstasy and terror of her first powerful visions she was transformed and never again would she be the twelve-year-old girl she once had been. When they let her out of her confinement, warning her not to pretend to be god-mad again, she didn't argue with them or protest that she had been sincere. She simply drank what they gave her to drink, and ate until the food they set before her was gone, and then returned to her labor.

But soon they began to realize that for once a slave was *not* pretending. She looked at her master one day and began to weep, and would not be comforted. That afternoon, as he oversaw construction of a fine new house for one of the richest men of the city, he was knocked down by a stone that got away from the crew that was trying to manhandle it into place. Two slaves suffered broken bones in the mishap, but Thirsty's master fell into the street and a passing horse stamped on his head. He lingered for a month, never regaining consciousness, taking small sips that his wife gave him every half hour, but vomiting any food she managed to get down his throat. He starved to death.

"Why did you weep that day?" his widow demanded.

"Because I saw him fallen in the street, trampled by a horse."

"Why didn't you warn him?"

"The Oversoul showed it to me, mistress, but she forbade me to tell it."

"Then I hate the Oversoul!" cried the woman. "And I hate you, for your silence!"

"Please don't punish me, mistress," said Thirsty. "I wanted to tell you, but she wouldn't let me."

"No," said the widow. "No, I won't punish you for doing what the goddess demanded of you."

After the master was buried, his widow sold most of the slaves, for she could no longer maintain a fine household in the city, and would have to return to her father's estate. Thirsty she did not sell. Instead she gave her her freedom.

Her freedom, but nothing else. Thus Thirsty began her time as a wilder, not because she was driven into the desert by the Oversoul, but because she was hungry, and in every town the other beggars drove her away, not because her small appetite would have deprived them of anything, but rather because she was slight and meek and so she was one of the few creatures in the world they had the power to drive away.

Thus she found herself in the desert, eating locusts and lizards and drinking from the rank pools of water that lingered in the shade and in caves after each rainstorm. Now she lived her name indeed, but in time she became a wilder in fact, and not just in appearance and habits of life. For she *was* dirty, and she *was* naked, and she starved in the desert like any proper holy woman— but she raged against the Oversoul in her heart, for she was bitterly angry at the way the Oversoul had answered her prayer. I asked for freedom, she howled at the Oversoul. I never asked you to kill my good master and impoverish my good mistress! I never asked you to drive me out into the desert, where the sun burns my skin except where I've managed to produce enough sweat that the dust will cling to my naked body and protect me. I never asked for visions or prophecies. I asked only to be a free woman, like my mother was. Now I can't even remember her name.

The Oversoul was not done with her, though, and so she could not yet have peace. When she was only fourteen years old, by her best reckoning, she had a dream of a place that was mountainous and yet so lush with life that even the face of the sheerest cliff was thickly green with foliage. She saw a man in her vision, and the Oversoul told her that this was her true husband. She cared nothing for that news—what she saw was that this man had food in his hand, and a stream of water ran at his feet. So she headed north until she found the green land, and found the stream. She washed herself, and drank and drank and drank. And then one day, clean and satisfied, she saw him leading his horse down to the water.

Almost she ran away. Almost she fled from the will of the Oversoul, for she didn't want a husband now, and there had been berries enough by the riverbank that she hungered for nothing that he might offer.

But he saw her, and gazed at her. She covered her breasts with her hands, knowing vaguely that this was what men desired, for that was what they looked at; she had no experience of men, for the Oversoul had protected her from desert wanderers until now.

"God forbids me to touch you," he said softly. He spoke in the language of Basilica, but with an accent very different from the speech of Seggidugu.

"That is a lie," she said. "The Oversoul has made me your wife."

"I have no wife," he answered. "And if I did, I wouldn't take a puny child like you."

"Good," she said. "Because, *I* don't want *you,* either. Let the Oversoul find you an *old* woman if she wants you to have a wife."

He laughed. "Then we're agreed. You're safe from me."

He took her home, and clothed her, and fed her, and for the first time in her life she was happy. In a month she fell in love with him, and he with her, and he took her the way a man takes a wife, though without a ceremony. Oddly, though, *she* was convinced that marrying him was exactly what the Oversoul required of him, while *he* was convinced that taking her into his bed was pure defiance of the will of God. "I will defy God every chance I get," he said. "But I would never have taken you against your will, even for the sake of defying my enemy."

"Is God your enemy, too?" she whispered.

For a month they were together. Then the madness came upon her and she fled into the desert.

It happened once again, several years later, only this time there was no month of waiting, and she didn't find him in his homeland, but rather in a cold foreign land with pine trees and a trace of snow on the ground, and this time there was no month of chastity before they were together as man and wife. And again, after a month she became god-mad and fled again into the desert.

Both times she conceived a child. Both times she longed to take her daughter to him, and lay the babe at his feet, and claim her right as his wife. But the Oversoul forbade it, and instead she brought the baby into the city of women, into Basilica, to the house that the Oversoul had shown her in a dream, and both times she gave her child into the arms of a woman that the Oversoul truly loved.

Thirsty envied that woman so much, for when you have

the love of the Oversoul, you are given a house, and freedom, and freedom, and happiness, and you are surrounded by daughters and friends. But Thirsty had only the hatred of the Oversoul, and so she lived alone in the desert.

Until, at last, ten years ago, the madness left her for good—or so she thought. She came down out of the desert then, into the land of Potokgavan, where kind strangers took her in. She was not beautiful or desirable, but she was striking in a strange way, and a good plain farmer with a strong house that stood on thick stilts asked for her to be his wife. She said yes, and together they had seven children.

But she never forgot her days as a holy woman, when the Oversoul hated her, and she never forgot the two daughters she bore to the strange man who was the husband the Oversoul gave her. The elder daughter she had named Hushidh, which was also the name of a desert flower which smelled sweet, but often held the larvae of the poisonous saberfly. The younger daughter she had named Luet, after the lyuty plant, whose leaves were ground up and soaked to make the sacred tea that helped the women who worshipped the Oversoul to enter a trance that sometimes, they said, gave them true visions. She never forgot her daughters, and prayed for them every morning, though she never told her husband or their children about the two she had been compelled to give into the hands of another.

Then one night she dreamed again, a god-mad dream. She saw herself once again walking into the presence of the husband the Oversoul had given her, the father of her first two daughters. Only now he was older, and his face was terrible and sad. In the dream he had his two daughters, the younger one beside him, the elder kneeling before him, and Thirsty saw herself walk to him and take him by the hand and say, "Husband, now that you have claimed your daughters, will I be your wife in the eyes of men, as well as in the eyes of the Oversoul?"

She hated this dream. Hated it deeply, for it denied the husband she had now, and repudiated the children they had together. Why did you set me free to have this life in Potokgavan, O cruel Oversoul, if you meant to tear me away from them? And if you meant me to be with my first two daughters, why couldn't you have let me keep them from the start? You are too cruel to me, Oversoul! I will not obey you!

But every night she dreamed the same dream. Again and again, all night long, until she thought she would go mad with it. Yet still she did not go.

Then, on one morning, at the end of the same relentless vision, there came something new into her dream. A sweet high keening sound. And in her dream she looked around and saw a furred creature flying through the air, and she knew that the sweet high song was this angel's song. The angel came to her in the dream, and landed on her shoulder, and clung to her, wrapping his leathery wings around her and his song was piercing and brilliant in her ear.

"What should I do, sweet angel?" she asked him in the dream.

In answer, the angel threw himself backward onto the ground before her, and lay there in the dust. And as he lay there, exposed and helpless, his wings useless and vulnerable and slack, there came creatures that at first seemed to be baboons, from their size, but then seemed to be rats, from their teeth and eyes and snout. They came to the angel, and sniffed at him, and when he did not move or fly, they began to gnaw at him. Oh, it was terrible indeed, and all the time his eyes looked at Thirsty, so sadly.

I must save him, thought Thirsty. I must shoo away these terrible enemies. Yet in the dream she could not save him. She could not act at all.

When the fell creatures finally left, the angel was not dead. But his wings had been chewed away, and in their place were left only two spindly, fragile arms, with barely a fringe under them to show where once the wings had been. She knelt by him, then, and cradled him up into her arms, and wept for him. Wept and wept and wept.

"Mother," said her middle son. "Mother, you're weeping from a dream, I think. Wake up."

She woke up.

"What was it?" asked the boy. He was a good boy, and she did not want to leave him.

"I must take a journey," she said.

"Where?"

"To a far place, but I'll come home, if the Oversoul will let me."

"Why must you go?"

"I don't know," she said. "The Oversoul has called me, and I don't know why. Your father is already working in the fields. Don't tell him until he comes home for his noon meal. By then I'll be gone too far for him to pursue me. Tell him that I love him and that I'll return to him. If he wants to punish me when I come back, then I will submit to his punishment gladly. For I would rather be here with him, and with our children, than to be a queen in any other country."

"Mama," said the boy, "I've known for a month that you would go."

"How did you know?" she asked. And for a moment she feared that he, too, might be cursed with the voice of the Oversoul in his heart.

But it was no god-madness the boy had—instead it was common sense. "You kept looking to the northwest, and Father tells us sometimes that that was where you came from. I thought I saw you wishing to go home."

"No," she said. "Not wishing to go home, because I *am* home, right here. But there's an errand I must tend to, and then I'll come back to you."

"If the Oversoul will let you."

She nodded. Then, taking a small bundle of food and a leather bottle filled with water, she set out on foot.

I had no intention of obeying you, Oversoul, she said. But when I saw that angel, with his wings torn away because I did nothing to help him in his moment of need, I did not know if that angel represented my daughters or the man who gave them to me, or even perhaps yourself—I only knew that I could not stand in my place and let some terrible thing happen, though I don't know what the terrible thing will be, or what I must do to stop it. All I know is that I will go where you lead me, and when I get there I will try to do good. If that ends up serving your purpose, Oversoul, I will do it anyway.

But when it's done, please, oh! Please, let me go home.

IN BASILICA, AND NOT IN A DREAM

It had come now to getting permission from Rasa, and Elemak was by no means certain she would grant it. Word throughout the house was that she had come home from her meeting with the Gorayni general in a foul humor, and no one could miss the fact that there were Gorayni soldiers in the street outside the house. Yet no matter what happened in Basilica, Elemak would not go back into the desert without a wife. And since she was willing, it would be Eiadh, with or without Rasa's permission.

But better *with* her permission. Better if Rasa herself performed the ceremony.

"This is an inauspicious time," said Rasa.

"Don't speak like an old woman, please, Aunt Rasa," said Eiadh. Her voice was so soft and sweet that Rasa showed no sign of being offended at what could only be regarded as sauciness. "Remember that *young* women are not timid. We marry most readily when our men are about to go to war, or when times are hard."

"You know nothing of desert life."

"But *you* have gone out into the desert with Wetchik, from time to time."

"Twice, and the second time was because I failed to trust my memory of how much I loathed the first time. I can promise you that after a week in the desert you'd be willing to come back to Basilica as a bondservant, just so you could come back."

"My lady Rasa," began Elemak.

"If you speak again, dear Elemak, I will send you from the room," said Rasa, in her gentlest tones. "I'm trying to talk sense to your beloved. But you needn't worry. Eiadh is so besotted with love of—what, your strength? I suspect she has visions of perfect manhood in her heart, and you fulfill all those fantasies."

Eiadh blushed. It was all Elemak could do to keep from smiling. He had hoped this from the start—that Eiadh was not a girl who looked for wealth or position, but rather one who looked for courage and strength. It would be boldness, not ostentation, that would win her heart: So Elemak had determined at the outset of his wooing, and so it had turned out in the end. Rasa herself confirmed it. Elemak had chosen a girl who, instead of loving him as the Wetchik's heir, would love him for those very virtues that were most evident in Elemak out in the desert—his ability to command, to make quick, bold decisions; his physical stamina; his wisdom about desert life.

"Whatever dreams she has in her heart," Elemak said, "I will do my best to make them all come true."

"Be careful what you promise," said Rasa. "Eiadh is quite capable of sucking the life out of a man with her adoration."

"Aunt Rasa!" said Eiadh, genuinely horrified.

"Lady Rasa," said Elemak, "I can't imagine what cruel intent you must have, to say such a thing about this woman."

"Forgive me," said Rasa. She looked genuinely sorry. "I

thought my words would be taken as teasing, but I haven't the heart for levity right now, and so it became an insult. I didn't intend it that way."

"Lady Rasa," said Elemak, "all things are forgiven when Wethead soldiers stand watch in the street outside your house."

"Do you think I care about that?" said Rasa. "When I have a raveler and a waterseer in my house? The soldiers are nothing. It's my city that I fear for."

"The soldiers are *not* nothing," said Elemak. "I've been told how Hushidh unbound poor Rashgallivak's soldiers from their loyalty to him, but you must remember that Rashgallivak was a weak man, newly come into my brother's place."

"Your father's place, too," said Rasa.

"Usurping both," said Elemak. "And the soldiers that Shuya unbound were mercenaries. General Moozh is said to be the greatest general in a thousand years, and his soldiers love and trust him beyond understanding. Shuya wouldn't find it easy to unweave *those* bonds."

"Suddenly you're an expert on the Gorayni?"

"I'm an expert on how men love and trust a strong leader," said Elemak. "I know how the men of my caravans felt about me. True, they all knew they would be paid. But they also knew that I wouldn't risk their lives unnecessarily, and that if they followed me in all things they would live to *spend* that money at journey's end. I loved my men, and they loved me, yet from what I hear of General Moozh, his soldiers love him ten times more than that. He has made them the strongest army of the Western Shore."

"And masters of Basilica, without one of them being killed," said Rasa.

"He hasn't mastered Basilica yet," said Elemak. "And with you as his enemy, Lady Rasa, I don't know if he ever will."

Rasa laughed bitterly. "Oh, indeed, he removed *me* as a threat from the start."

"What about our marriage?" asked Eiadh. "That *is* what we're meeting about, isn't it?"

Rasa looked at her with—what, pity? Yes, thought Elemak. She hasn't a very high opinion of this niece of hers. That remark she let slip, that insult, it was no joke. Suck the life out of a man with her adoration—what did that mean? Am I making a mistake? All my thought was to make Eiadh desire me; I never questioned my desire for *her*.

"Yes, my dear," said Rasa. "You may marry this man. You may take him as your first husband."

"Technically," said Elemak, "it wasn't permission we were seeking, since she's of age."

"*And* I will perform the ceremony," said Rasa wearily. "But it will have to be in this house, for obvious reasons, and the guest list will have to consist of all those who find themselves in residence here. We must all pray that Gorayni soldiers do not also choose to attend the ceremony."

"When?" asked Eiadh.

"Tonight," said Rasa. "Tonight will be soon enough, won't it? Or does your clothing itch so much you want it to come off at noon?"

Again, an insult beyond bearing, and yet Rasa plainly did not see that she was being crude. Instead she arose and walked from the room, leaving Eiadh flushed and angry on the bench where she sat.

"No, my Edhya," said Elemak. "Don't be angry. Your Aunt Rasa has lost much today, and she can't help being a little mean about also losing you."

"It sounds as though she'd be *glad* to get rid of me, she must hate me so," said Eiadh. And a tear slipped from Eiadh's eye and dropped, twinkling for a moment in the air, onto her lap.

Elemak took her in his arms then, and held her; she clung to him as if she longed to become a part of him forever. This is love, he thought. This is the kind of love that songs and stories are made of. She will follow me into the desert and with her beside me I will fashion a tribe, a kingdom for her to be the queen. For whatever this General Moozh can do, *I* can do. I am a truer husband than any Wethead could ever be. Eiadh hungers for a man of mastery. I am that man.

BITANKE WAS NOT happy with all that had happened in Basilica these past few days. Especially because he could not get free of the feeling that perhaps it was all his fault. Not that he had had much choice in those moments at the gate. His men had fought valiantly, but they were too few, and the mob of Palwashantu mercenaries was bound to win. What hope, then, would he have had, standing against the Gorayni soldiers who came out of nowhere and promised alliance with him?

I could have called to the Palwashantu mercenaries and begged them to make common cause with me against the Gorayni—it might have worked. Yet at the time the Gorayni general had seemed so earnest. And there were all those firelights out on the desert. It looked like an army of a hundred thousand men. How was I to know that their entire army was the men standing at the gate? And even then, we could not have stood against them.

But we could have fought. We could have cost them soldiers and time. We could have alerted all the other guards, and sent the alarm through the city. I could have died there, with a Gorayni arrow through my heart, rather than having to live and see how they have conquered my city, my beloved city, without even one of them suffering a wound serious enough to keep him from marching boldly wherever he pleases.

And yet. And yet even now, as he was called into the presence of General Moozh for still another interview, Bitanke could not help but admire the man for his audacity, his courage, his brilliance. To have marched so far in such a short time, and to essay to take a city with so few men, and then to have his way when even now the guard outnumbered his army significantly. Who could say that Basilica might not be better off with Moozh as its guardian? Better him than that swine Gaballufix would have been, or the contemptible Rashgallivak. Better even than Roptat. And better than the women, who had proven themselves weak and foolish indeed, for the way they now believed Moozh's obvious lies about Lady Rasa.

Couldn't they see how Moozh manipulated them to divide against each other and ignore the one woman who might have led them to effective resistance? No, of course they couldn't see—any more than Bitanke himself could see that first night that, far from helping, the Gorayni stranger was controlling him and making him betray his own city without even realizing it.

We are all fools when one wise man appears.

"My dear friend," said General Moozh.

Bitanke did not take the offered hand.

"Ah, you're angry with me," said Moozh.

"You came here with Lady Rasa's letter, and now you have her under arrest."

"Is she so dear to you?" asked Moozh. "I assure you that her confinement is only temporary, and is entirely for her protection. Terrible lies about her are circulating through the city right now, and who can tell what might happen to her if her house was not cordoned off?"

"Lies invented by you."

"My lips have said nothing about Lady Rasa except my great admiration for her. She is the best of the women of this city, with the wit and courage of a man, and I will never permit a hair of her head to be harmed. If you don't know that about me, Bitanke, my friend, you know nothing about me at all."

Which was almost certainly true, thought Bitanke. I know nothing about you. *No* one knows anything about you.

"Why did you summon me?" asked Bitanke. "Are you going to strip away yet one more power from the Basilican guard? Or do you have some vile work for us to do that will humiliate and demoralize us all the more?"

"So angry," said Moozh. "But think hard, Bitanke. You feel free to say such things to me, and without fear that I'll strike your head off. Does that seem like tyranny to you? Your soldiers all have their arms, and they are the ones keeping the peace in this city now—does that sound as though I'm a treacherous enemy?"

Bitanke said nothing, determined not to let himself be taken in again by Moozh's smooth talking. And yet he felt the stab of doubt in his heart, as he had so many times before. Moozh *had* left the guard intact. He had done no violence against any citizen. Perhaps all he meant to do was use Basilica as a staging area and then move on.

"Bitanke, I need your help. I want to restore this city to its former strength, before Gaballufix's meddling."

Oh, yes, I'm certain that's all you desire—Moozh the altruist, going to all this trouble just so you can help the city of women. Then you'll march your men away, rewarded with a warm glow in your heart because you know you leave so much happiness behind you.

But Bitanke said nothing. Better to listen than to speak, at a time like this.

"I won't pretend to you that I don't intend to turn things here to my own purposes. There is a great struggle ahead between the Gorayni and the miserable puddle swimmers of Potokgavan. We know that they were maneuvering to take control of Basilica—Gaballufix was their man. He was prepared to overthrow the city of women and let his thugs rule. And now here I am, with my soldiers. Have I or my men ever done anything to make you think our intentions are as ruthless or brutal as Gaballufix?"

Moozh waited, and at last Bitanke answered, "You have never been so obvious, no."

"I will tell you what I need from Basilica. I need to know, securely, that those who rule her are friends of the Gorayni, that with Basilica at my back I don't have to fear any treachery from this city. Then I can bring supply lines through the desert to this place, completely bypassing Nakavalnu and Izmennik and Seggidugu. *You* know that this is good strategy, my friend. Potokgavan counted on our having to fight our way south to the Cities of the Plain; they counted on having at least a year, perhaps several years, to strengthen their position here—perhaps to bring an army here to try to stand against our chariots. But now we will command the Cities of the Plain—with my army in Basilica, none of them will resist. And then Nakavalnu and Izmennik and Seggidugu will not dare to make any alliance with Potokgavan. Without conquest, without war, we will have secured the entire Western Shore for the Imperator, years before Potokgavan would have imagined possible. That is what I want. That is *all* I want. And to accomplish it, I don't need to break Basilica, I don't need to treat you as a conquered people. All I need is to be certain that Basilica is loyal to me. And that purpose is better accomplished through love than through fear."

"Love!" said Bitanke derisively.

"So far," said Moozh, "I have not had to do anything that was not gratefully received by the people of Basilica. They have more peace and security now than in the past several years. Do you think they don't understand that?"

"And do you think the worse men of Dogtown and Gate

Town and the High Road aren't hoping that you'll let them come into the city and rule here? Then you'd have your loyal allies—if you give them what Gaballufix promised, a chance to dominate these women who have barred them from citizenship for all these thousands of centuries."

"Yes," said Moozh. "I could have done that. I could do it still." He leaned forward across the table, to look Bitanke in the eye. "But you *will* help me, won't you, so that I don't have to do such a terrible thing?"

Ah. So this was the choice, after all. Either conspire with Moozh or watch the very fabric of Basilica be destroyed. All that was beautiful and holy in this place would now be hostage to the threat of turning loose the covetous men from outside the walls. Hadn't Bitanke seen how terrible that would be? How could he let it happen again?

"What do you want from me?"

"Advice," said Moozh. "Counsel. The city council is not a reliable instrument of control here. It's fine for passing laws governing local matters, but when it comes to making a firm alliance with the army of the Imperator, who's to say a faction won't arise within a week to strike down that policy? So I need to set up a single individual as . . . what . . ."

"Dictator?"

"Not at all. This person would merely be the face that Basilica turns to the outside world. He, she—whoever it is—will be able to promise that Gorayni armies may pass through here, that Gorayni supplies can be stored here, and that Potokgavan will find no friends or allies here."

"The city council can do this."

"You know better."

"They will keep their word."

"You have seen this very day how treacherously and unfairly they dealt with Lady Rasa, who has done nothing but serve them loyally all her life. How then will they deal with the stranger? My men's lives, my Imperator's power, all will depend on the loyalty of Basilica—and this city council has proven itself incapable of being loyal even to their own worthiest sister."

"*You* started those rumors about her," said Bitanke, "and now you use them to show how unworthy the council is?"

"Before God I deny that I started any slander about Lady Rasa—I admire her above any other woman I have met. Yet no matter who started the rumor, Bitanke, what matters is that it was *believed*. By this city council, which you tell me I can trust with the lives of my men. What is to stop Potokgavan from starting rumors of their own? Tell me honestly, Bitanke, if you were in *my* place, with *my* needs, would you trust this city council?"

"I have served this council all my life, sir, and I trust them," said Bitanke.

"That's not what I asked you," said Moozh. "I am here to accomplish the purpose of the Imperator. Traditionally we have done this by slaughtering the ruling class of the lands we conquer, and replacing them with men of some long-disfranchised oppressed people. Because I love this city, I wish to find another way here. I am taking great risks to do so."

"You have only a thousand men," said Bitanke. "You want to subdue Basilica without bloodshed because you can't afford to suffer *any* losses."

"You see half the truth," said Moozh. "I have to *win* here. If I can do it without bloodshed, then the Cities of the Plain will say that I must have the power of God with me, and they will submit to my orders. But I can also achieve the same end by terror. If their leaders are brought here and find this city desolate, burned to the ground, house and forest, and the lake of women thick with blood, they will also submit to me. But one way or another, Basilica will serve my purpose.

"You are truly a monster," said Bitanke. "You speak of sacrilege and massacre of innocents, and then ask me to trust you."

"I speak of necessity," said Moozh, "and ask you to help me keep from being a monster. You have served a higher purpose—the will of the council. Sometimes, in their name, you have done that which you, of yourself, would not wish to do. Is that not so?"

"That's what it means to be a soldier," said Bitanke.

"I also am a soldier," said Moozh. "I also must accomplish the purpose of my master, the Imperator. And so I will even be a monster if I must, to accomplish it. As you have had to arrest men and women you thought were innocent."

"Arrest is not slaughter."

"Bitanke, my friend, I keep hoping that you will be what I thought you were when first I met you bravely fighting at that gate. I imagined that night that you fought, not for some institution, not for that feeble city council that believes any slander that flies through the city, but rather for something higher. For the city itself. For the *idea* of the city. Wasn't *that* what you were prepared to die for at the gate?"

"Yes," said Bitanke.

"Now I offer you the chance to serve the city again. *You* know that long before there *was* a council, Basilica was a great city. Back when Basilica was ruled by the priestesses, it was still Basilica. Back when Basilica had a queen, it was still Basilica. Back when Basilica put the great general Snaceetel in charge of its army and fought off the Seggidugu warriors, and then let him drink of the waters of the lake of women, it was still Basilica."

Against his will Bitanke saw that Moozh was right. The city of women was not the council. The form of government had changed many times before, and would change again. What mattered was that it remain the holy city of women, the one place on the planet Harmony where women ruled. And if, for a short time, because of great events sweeping through the Western Shore, Basilica had to be subservient to the Gorayni, then what of that—as long as the rule of women was preserved within these walls?

"While you consider," said Moozh, "consider *this*. I could have tried to frighten you. I could have lied to you, pretended to be something other than the calculating general that I am. Instead I have spoken to you as a friend, openly and freely, because what I want is your willing help, not your mere obedience."

"My help to do what?" asked Bitanke. "I will *not* arrest the council, if that's what you hope for."

"Arrest them! Haven't you understood me at all? I need the council to continue—without replacing a single member of it! I need the people of Basilica to see that their internal government is unchanged. But I also need a consul of the people, someone to set in place *above* the council, to handle the foreign affairs of Basilica. To make an alliance with us that will be adhered to. To command the guards at the city gates."

"Your men already perform that office."

"But I *want* it to be *your* men who do it."

"I'm not the commander of the guard."

"You're one of the leading officers," said Moozh. "I wish you *were* commander, because you're a better soldier than any of the men above you. But if I promised you the office of commander, you would think I was trying to bribe you and you would reject me and leave this house as my enemy."

Bitanke felt a great relief inside. Moozh knew, after all, that Bitanke was no traitor. That Bitanke would never act for his own self-interest. That Bitanke would act only for the good of the city.

"The men of the guard will be reluctant," said Bitanke, "to take their orders from anyone but their own commander, appointed by the city council."

"Imagine, though, that the city council has unanimously appointed someone to be consul of the city, and has asked the guard to obey that consul."

"It would mean nothing if they thought for a moment that the consul was a mere puppet of the Gorayni. The guard are not fools, and we are not traitors, either."

"So. You see my dilemma. I must have someone who will understand the necessity of Basilica remaining loyal to the Imperator, and yet this consul will only be effective if the people of Basilica trust her—or him—to be a loyal Basilican, and not a puppet."

Bitanke laughed. "I hope you don't imagine for a moment that *I* would do for that purpose. There are already plenty of people whispering that I must be your puppet for having let you into the city in the first place."

"I know," said Moozh. "You were the first one I thought of, but I realized that you can only serve Basilica—and my purposes, too—by remaining where you are, with *no* obvious advantage coming to you because of my influence in the city."

"Then why am I here?"

"To advise me, as I told you before. I need you to tell me who in this city, if she—or he—were appointed as consul, the guard and the city as a whole would follow and obey."

"There *is* no such creature."

"Say this, and you might as well ask me to pour the blood and ashes of the city into the lake of women."

"Don't threaten me!"

"I'm not threatening you, Bitanke, I'm telling you what I have done before and what I do not want to do again. I beg you, help me to find a way to avoid that dreadful outcome."

"Let me think."

"I ask for nothing more."

"Let me come to you tomorrow."

"I must act today."

"Give me an hour."

"Can you do your thinking here? Can you do it without leaving the house?"

"Am I under arrest, then?"

"This house is watched by a thousand eyes, my friend. If you are seen leaving and then returning in an hour, it will be said that you make too many visits to General Vozmuzhalnoy Vozmozhno. But if you want to leave, you may."

"I'll stay."

"I'll have you shown to the library, then, and given a computer to write on. It will help my thinking, if you write down the names and your reasons why they might or might not be good for this purpose. In an hour, come to me again with your list of names."

"For Basilica I do this, and not for you." And not for any advantage to myself.

"It's for Basilica that I ask it," said Moozh. "Even though my first loyalty is to the Imperator, I hope to save this city from destruction if I can."

The interview was over. Bitanke left the room, and was immediately joined by a Gorayni soldier who led him to the library. Moozh had said nothing to this soldier, and yet he knew where to take him. Knew to assign him a computer to use. Either this meant that the general let his junior officers listen in to his negotiations, which was almost unthinkable, or it meant that Moozh had given these orders before Bitanke even arrived.

Could it be that Moozh had planned it all, every word that passed between them? Could it be that Moozh was so good at manipulation that he could determine all outcomes in advance? Then in that case Bitanke might just be another dupe, betraying his city because he had been twisted into believing whatever Moozh wanted.

No. No, that was not it at all. Moozh simply counted on being able to persuade me to act intelligently in the best interest of Basilica. And so I will find candidates for him, if it is possible to imagine anyone serving as consul, appointed because of the Gorayni and yet holding the loyalty of the people, the council, and the guard. If it is possible, I will bring the name to the General.

"I NEED TO speak to my children," said Rasa. "*All* of them."

Luet looked at her for a moment, uncertain what to do; this was the sort of thing a lady might say to her servants, giving orders without seeming to. But Luet was not a servant in this house, and never had been, and so she was supposed to ignore such expressions of desire. Yet Rasa seemed not to realize she had spoken as if to a servant, when no servant was present. "Madam," she said, "are you sending me on this errand?"

Rasa looked at her almost in surprise. "I'm sorry, Luet. I forgot who was with me. I'm not at my best. Would you please go find my children and my husband's children for me, and tell them I want to see them now?"

Now it was a request, a favor, and asked directly of her, so of course Luet bowed her head and left in search of servants to help her. Not that Luet wouldn't willingly have done the task herself, but Rasa's house was large, and if there was any urgency in Rasa's request—as there seemed to be—it would be better to have several people searching. Besides, the servants were more likely to know exactly where everyone was.

It was easy enough to find out where Nafai, Elemak, Sevet, and Kokor were, and send servants to summon them. Mebbekew, however, had not been seen for several

hours, not since he first came into the house. Finally Izda-
vat, a youngish maid of more eagerness than sense, reluctantly mentioned that she had brought Mebbekew breakfast
in Dol's room. "But that was some time ago, lady."

"I'm only sister, or Luet, please."

"Do you want me to see if he's still there, sister?"

"No, thank you," said Luet. "It would be improper for
him still to be there, and so I'll go ask Dolya where he
went." She headed off to the stairs in the teachers' wing of
the house.

Luet was not surprised that Mebbekew had already managed to attach himself to a woman, even in this house
where women were taught to see through shallow men.
However, it *did* surprise her that Dolya was giving the boy
the time of day. She had been worked over by champion
flatterers and sycophants in her theatre days, and shouldn't
have noticed Mebbekew except to laugh discreetly at him.

But then, Luet was quite aware that she saw through flatterers more easily than most women, since the flatterers
never actually tried to work their seductive magic on *her.*
Waterseers had a reputation for seeing through lies—though,
truth to tell, Luet could only see what the Oversoul showed
her, and the Oversoul was not noted for helping a daughter
with her love life. As if I had a love life, thought Luet. As
if I needed one. The Oversoul has marked my path for me.
And where my path touches others' lives, I will trust the
Oversoul to tell them her will. My husband will discover
me as his wife when he chooses to. And I will be content.

Content . . . she almost laughed at herself. All my dreams
are tied up in the boy, we've been to the edge of death together, and still he pines for Eiadh. Are men's lives nothing but the secretions of overactive glands? Can't they
analyze and understand the world about them, as women
can? Can't Nafai see that Eiadh's love will be as permanent as rain, ready to evaporate as soon as the storm passes?

Edhya *needs* a man like Elemak, who won't tolerate her straying heart. Where Nafai would be heartbroken at her disloyalty, Elemak would be brutally angry, and Eiadh, the poor foolish creature, would fall in love with him all over again.

Not that Luet saw all this herself, of course. It was Hushidh who saw all the connections, all the threads binding people together; it was Hushidh who explained to her that Nafai seemed not to notice Luet because he was so enamored of Eiadh. It was Hushidh who also understood the bond between Elemak and Eiadh, and why they were so right for each other.

And now Mebbekew and Dol. Well, it was another piece of the puzzle, wasn't it? When Luet had seen her vision of women in the woods behind Rasa's house, that night when she returned from warning Wetchik of the threat against his life, it had made no sense to her. Now, though, she knew why she had seen Dolya. She would be with Mebbekew, as Eiadh with Elemak. Shedemei would also be coming out to the desert, or at least would be involved with their journey, gathering seeds and embryos. And Hushidh also would come. And Aunt Rasa. Luet's vision had been of the women called out into the desert.

Poor Dolya. If she had known that taking Mebbekew into her room would take her on a path leading out of Basilica, she would have kicked him and bit him and hit him, if need be, to get him out of her room! As it was, though, Luet fully expected to find them together.

She knocked on Dol's door. As she expected, there was the sound of a flurry of movement inside. And a soft thump.

"Who is it?" asked Dol.

"Luet."

"I'm not conveniently situated at the moment."

"I have no doubt if it," said Luet, "but Lady Rasa sent me with some urgency. May I come in?"

"Yes, of course."

Luet opened the door to find Dolya lying in bed, her sheets up over her shoulders. There was no sign of Mebbekew, of course, but the bed had been well-rumpled, the bath was full of grey water, and a bunch of grapes had been left on the floor—not the way Dolya usually arranged things before taking a midday nap.

"What does Aunt Rasa want of me?" asked Dol.

"Nothing of *you,* Dol," said Luet. "She wants all her children and Wetchik's children to join her at once."

"Then why aren't you knocking at Sevet's or Kokor's door? They aren't here."

"Mebbekew knows why I'm here," said Luet. Remembering the thump she heard, and the brief amount of time before she opened the door, she reached a conclusion about his present whereabouts. "So as soon as I close the door, he can get up off the floor beside your bed, put some kind of clothing on, and come to Lady Rasa's room."

Dol looked stricken. "Forgive me for trying to deceive you, Waterseer," she whispered.

Sometimes it made Luet want to scream, the way everyone assumed that when she showed any spark of wit it must be a revelation from the Oversoul—as if Luet would be incapable of discerning the obvious on her own. And yet it was also useful, Luet had to admit. Useful in that people tended to tell her the truth more readily, because they believed she would catch them in their lies. But the price of this truthfulness was that they did not like her company, and avoided her. Only friends shared such intimacies, and only freely. Forced, or so they thought, to share their secrets with Luet, they withheld their friendship, and Luet was not part of the lives of most of the women around her. They held her in such awe; it made her feel unworthy and filled her with rage, both at once.

It was that anger that led Luet to torment Mebbekew by forcing him to speak. "Did you hear me, Mebbekew?"

A long wait. Then: "Yes."

"I'll tell Lady Rasa," said Luet, "that her message was received."

She started to back out the door and draw it closed behind her, when Dol called out to her. "Wait . . . Luet."

"Yes?"

"His clothes . . . they were being washed . . ."

"I'll send them up."

"Do you think they'll be dry by now?"

"Dry enough," said Luet. "Don't you think so, Mebbekew?"

Mebbekew sat upright, so his head appeared on the other side of the bed. "Yes," he said glumly.

"Damp clothes will cool you off," said Luet. "It's such a hot day, at least in this room." It was a fine joke, she thought, but nobody laughed.

SHEDEMEI STRODE VIGOROUSLY along the path to Wetchik's coldhouse, which was nestled in a narrow valley and shaded by tall trees just outside the place where the city wall curved around the Old Orchestra. It was the last and, she feared, the hardest part of her task of assembling the flora and fauna for the mad project of a voyage through space, back to the legendary lost planet Earth. I am going to all this trouble because I had a dream, and took it for interpretation to a dreamer. A journey on camels, and they think it will lead them to Earth.

Yet the dream was still alive within her. The life she carried with her on the cloud.

So she came to the door of Wetchik's coldhouse, not certain whether she really hoped to find one of his servants acting as caretaker.

No one answered when she clapped her hands. But the machines that kept the house cold inside might well mask her loudest clapping. So she went to the door and tried it. Locked.

Of course it was. Wetchik had gone into the desert weeks ago, hadn't he? And Rashgallivak, his steward and, supposedly, the new Wetchik, had been in hiding somewhere ever since. Who would keep the place running, with both of them gone?

Except that the machines here *were* running, weren't they? Which meant *somebody* was still caring for the place. Unless they carelessly left them on, and the plants untended inside.

That was quite possible, of course. The cold air would keep the specialized plants thriving for many days, and the coldhouse, drawing its power from the solar scoops on the poles rising high above the house, could run indefinitely without even drawing on the city's power supply.

And yet Shedemei knew that someone was still taking care of this place, though she could not have said *how* she knew it. And furthermore, she knew that the caretaker was inside the coldhouse right now, and knew she was there, and wanted her to go away. Whoever was in here was hiding.

And who was it who needed to hide?

"Rashgallivak," called Shedemei. "I'm only Shedemei. You know me, and I'm alone, and I will tell no one you are here, but I must talk to you." She waited, no response. "It's nothing about the city, or the things going on in there," she called out loudly. "I simply need to buy a couple of pieces of equipment from you."

She could hear the door unbolting from the inside. Then it swung open on its heavy hinges. Rashgallivak stood there, looking forlorn and wasted. He held no weapon.

"If you've come to betray me, then I welcome it as a relief."

Shedemei declined to point out that betrayal would only be pure justice, after the way Rashgallivak had betrayed the Wetchik's house, allying himself with Gaballufix in order to steal his master's place. She had business to do here; she was not a justicer.

"I care nothing for politics," she said, "and I care nothing for you. I simply need to buy a dozen drycases. The portable ones, used for caravans."

He shook his head. "Wetchik had me sell them all."

Shedemei closed her eyes for a weary moment. He was forcing her to say things she had not wanted to throw in his face. "Oh, Rashgallivak, please don't expect me to believe that you actually sold them, knowing that you intended to take control of the house of Wetchik and would need to continue in the business."

Rashgallivak flushed—in shame, Shedemei hoped. "Nevertheless, I sold them, as I was told to do."

"Then who bought them?" asked Shedemei. "It's the drycases I want, not you."

Rashgallivak didn't answer.

"Ah," said Shedemei. "*You* bought them."

After a moment's pause, he said, "What do you need them for?"

"You're asking *me* to account for myself?" asked Shedemei.

"I ask, because I know you have plenty of drycases at your laboratory. The only conceivable use of the portable ones is for a caravan, and that's a business you know nothing about."

"Then no doubt I will be killed or robbed. But that's no concern of yours. And perhaps I won't be killed or robbed."

"In which case," said Rashgallivak, "you would be

selling your plants in far-off countries, in direct competition with me. So why should I sell my competitor the portable drycases she needs?"

Shedemei laughed in his face. "What, do you think that there is any business as usual in this place? I'm not going on a trading journey, you poor foolish man. I'm removing my entire laboratory, *and* myself, to a place where I can safely pursue my research without being interrupted by armed madmen burning and looting the city."

Again he flushed. "When they were under my command, they never harmed anyone. I was no Gaballufix."

"No, Rash. You are no Gaballufix."

That could be taken two ways, but Rash apparently decided to take it as a confirmation of her belief in his fundamental decency. "You're not my enemy, are you, Shedya."

"I just want drycases."

He hesitated a moment more, then stepped back and beckoned her inside.

The entry of the coldhouse wasn't chilled like the inner rooms, and Rash had turned it into a pathetic sort of apartment for himself. A makeshift bed, a large tub that had once held plants, but which he no doubt used now for bathing and washing his clothes. Very primitive, but resourceful, too. Shedemei had to admire that in the man—he had not despaired, even when everything worked against him.

"I'm alone here," he said. "The Oversoul surely knows I need money more than I need drycases. And the city council has cut me off from all my funds. You can't even pay me, because I haven't an account anymore to receive the money."

"That shouldn't be a problem," said Shedemei. "As you might imagine, a lot of people are pulling their money out of the city accounts. I can pay you in gems—though the price of gold and precious stones has tripled since the recent disturbances."

"Do you think I imagine myself to be in a position to bargain?"

"Stack the drycases outside the door," said Shedemei. "I'll send men to load them and bring them to me inside the city. I'll give you fair payment separately. Tell me where."

"Come alone, afterward," said Rash. "And put them into my hand."

"Don't be absurd," said Shedemei. "I'll never come here again, and we'll never meet, either. Tell me where to leave the jewels for you."

"In the traveler room of Wetchik's house."

"Is it easy to find?"

"Easy enough."

"Then it will be there as soon as I have received the drycases."

"It hardly seems fair, that I must trust you completely, and you don't have to show any trust in me at all."

Shedemei could think of nothing to say that would not be cruel.

After a while he nodded. "All right," he said. "There are two houses on Wetchik's estate. Put the jewels in the traveler room of the smaller, older house. On top of one of the rafters. I'll find it."

"As soon as the drycases are at my laboratory," said Shedemei.

"Do you think I have some network of loyal men who will ambush you?" asked Rashgallivak, bitterly.

"No," said Shedemei. "But knowing you will soon have the money, there'd be nothing to stop you from hiring them now."

"So you'll decide when to pay me, and how much, and I get no voice in the matter."

"Rash," said Shedemei, "I will treat you far more fairly than you treated Wetchik and his sons."

"I'll have a dozen drycases outside within a half hour."

Shedemei got up and left. She heard him close the door behind her, and imagined him timidly drawing the bolts closed, fearful that someone might discover that the man who had, for a day, ruled the petty empires of Gaballufix and Wetchik both, now cowered inside these heavy shaded walls.

Shedya passed through Music Gate, where the Gorayni guards checked her identity with dispatch and let her through. It still bothered her to see that uniform in the gates of Basilica, but like everyone else she was growing accustomed to the soldiers' perfect discipline, and the new orderliness that had come to the chaotic entrances of the city. Everyone waited patiently in line now.

And something else. There were now more people waiting to get into the city than waiting to get out. Confidence was returning. Confidence in the strength of the Gorayni. Who would have imagined how quickly people would come to trust the Wethead enemy?

After walking the long passage along the city wall to Market Gate, Shedemei found the muleteer she had hired. "Go ahead," Shedemei said. "There should be a dozen of them." The muleteer bowed her head and set off at a jog. No doubt that show of speed would stop the moment Shedemei could no longer see her, but Shedemei nevertheless appreciated the attempt at *pretending* to be fast. It showed that the muleteer knew what speed *was,* and thought it worthwhile to give the illusion of it.

Then she found a messenger boy in the queue waiting just inside the Market Gate. She scribbled a note on one of the papers that were kept there at the messenger station. On the back of the note she wrote directions to Wetchik's house, and instructions about where to leave the note. Then she keyed in a payment on the station computer. When the boy saw the bonus she was giving him for quick delivery, he grinned, snatched the note, and took off like an arrow.

Rashgallivak would be angry, of course, to find a draft against one of the Market Gate jewelers, instead of the jewels themselves. But Shedemei had no intention of either carrying or sending an enormous sum of completely liquid funds to some lonely abandoned place. It was Rash who needed the money—let *him* take the risk. At least she had drawn the draft on one of the jewelers who kept a table outside Market Gate, so he wouldn't have to pass any guards to get his payment.

RASA LOOKED AT her son and daughters, and Wetchik's two boys by other wives. Not the world's finest group of human beings, she thought. I'd be a bit more contemptuous of Volemak's failure with his two older boys, if I didn't have my two prize daughters to remind me of my own lack of brilliance as a parent. And, to be fair, all these young people have their gifts and talents. But only Nafai and Issib, the two children Volya and I had together, have shown themselves to have integrity, decency, and love of goodness.

"Why didn't you bring Issib?"

Elemak sighed. Poor boy, thought Rasa. Is the old lady making you explain again? "We didn't want to worry about his chair or his floats on this trip," he said.

"It's just as well we don't have him locked up in here with us," said Nafai.

"I don't think the general will keep us under arrest for long," said Rasa. "Once I'm thoroughly discredited, there'd be no reason to do something as clearly repressive as this. He's trying to create an image of himself as a liberator and protector, and having his soldiers in the streets here isn't helpful."

"And then we leave?" asked Nafai.

"No, we put down roots here," said Mebbekew. "Of course we leave."

"I want to go home," said Kokor. "Even if Obring is a wretched miserable excuse for a husband, I miss him."

Sevet said nothing.

Rasa looked at Elemak, who had a half-smile on his face. "And you, Elemak, are you also eager to leave my house?"

"I'm grateful for your hospitality," he said. "And we'll always remember your home as the last civilized house we lived in for many years."

"Speak for yourself, Elya," said Mebbekew.

"What is he talking about?" said Kokor. "I have a civilized house waiting for me right now."

Sevet gave a strangled laugh.

"I wouldn't boast about how civilized my house is, if I were you," said Rasa. "I see, too, that Elemak is the only one who understands your true situation here."

"I understand it," said Nafai.

Of course Elemak glared at Nafai under hooded eyes. Nafai, you foolish boy, thought Rasa. Must you always say the thing that will most provoke your brothers? Did you think I had forgotten that you have heard the voice of the Oversoul, that you understand far more than your brothers or sisters do? Couldn't you trust me to remember your worthiness, and so hold silence?

No, he couldn't. Nafai was young, too young to see the consequences of his actions, too young to contain his feelings.

"Nevertheless, it is Elemak who will explain it to us all."

"We can't stay in the city," said Elemak. "The moment the soldiers leave their watch, we have to escape, and quickly."

"Why?" asked Mebbekew. "It's Lady Rasa who's in trouble, not us."

"By the Oversoul, you're stupid," said Elemak.

What a refreshingly direct way of saying it, thought Rasa. No wonder your brothers worship you, Elya.

"As long as Lady Rasa is under arrest, Moozh has to see to it that no harm comes to anyone here. But he's set it up so that Rasa will have plenty of enemies in the city. As soon as his soldiers step out of the way, some very bad things will start to happen."

"All the more reason for us to get out of Mother's house," said Kokor. "Mother can flee if she wants, but they've got nothing against *me.*"

"They've got something against *all* of us," said Elemak. "Meb and Nafai and I are fugitives, and Nafai in particular has been accused of two murders, one of which he actually committed. Kokor can be charged with assault and attempted murder against her own sister. And Sevet is a flagrant adulterer, and since it was with her own sister's husband, the incest laws can be dredged up, too."

"They wouldn't dare," said Kokor. "Prosecute *me!*"

"And why wouldn't they dare?" asked Elemak. "Only the great respect and love people had for Lady Rasa protected you from arrest in the first place. Well, *that's* gone, or at least weakened."

"They'd never convict me," said Kokor.

"And the adultery laws haven't been enforced for centuries," said Meb. "And people are disgusted by incest between in-laws, but as long as they're at the age of consent . . ."

"Is *everyone* here criminally dumb?" asked Elemak. "No, I forget—*Nafai* understands *everything*"

"No," said Nafai. "I know we need to go out to the desert because the Oversoul commanded it, but I don't have any idea what *you're* talking about."

Rasa couldn't stop herself from smiling. Nafai could be foolish sometimes, but his very honesty and directness could also be disarming. Without meaning to, Nafai had pleased Elemak by humbling himself and acknowledging Elya's greater wisdom.

"Then I'll explain," said Elemak. "Lady Rasa is a powerful woman—even now, because the wisest people in Basilica don't believe the rumors about her, not for a moment. It won't be enough for Moozh just to discredit her. He needs her to be either completely under his control, or dead. To accomplish the former, all he needs to do is put one or all of Rasa's children on trial for murder—or Father's sons, too for that matter—and she'll be helpless. Lady Rasa is a brave woman, but I don't think she has the heart to let her children or Father's sons go to prison just so she can play politics. And if she *did* have that degree of ruthlessness, Moozh would simply up the stakes. Which of us would he kill first? Moozh is a deft man—he'd do only enough to communicate his message clearly. He'd kill *you*, I think, Meb, since you're the one who is most worthless and whom Father and Lady Rasa would miss the least."

Meb leaped to his feet. "I've had enough of you, fart-for-breath!"

"Sit down, Mebbekew," said Lady Rasa. "Can't you see he's goading you for sport?"

Elemak grinned at Mebbekew, who wasn't mollified. Mebbekew glowered as he sat back down.

"He'd kill *somebody*," said Elemak, "just as a warning. Of course, it wouldn't be *his* soldiers. But he'd know that Lady Rasa would see his hand in it. And if holding us as hostages for her good behavior didn't work, Moozh has already laid the groundwork for murdering Lady Rasa herself. It would be easy to find some outraged citizen eager to kill her for her supposed treachery; all Moozh would have to do is set up an opportunity for such an assassin to strike. It would be simple. It's when the soldiers *leave* the streets outside this house that our true danger begins. So we have to prepare to leave immediately, secretly, and permanently."

"Leave Basilica!" cried Kokor. Her genuine dismay meant that she had finally grasped the idea that their situation was serious.

Sevet understood, that was certain. Her face was tilted downward, but Rasa could still see the tears on her cheeks.

"I'm sorry that your close association with me is costing you so much," said Rasa. "But for all these years, my dear daughters, my dear son, my beloved students, you have all benefitted from the prestige of my house, as well as the great honor of the Wetchik. Now that events have turned against us in Basilica, you must share in paying the price, as well. It is inconvenient, but it is not unfair."

"Forever," murmured Kokor.

"Forever it is," said Elemak. "But I, for one, will not go out into the desert without my wife. I hope my brothers have made some provision for themselves. It *is* the reason we came here."

"Obring," said Kokor. "We must bring Obring!"

Sevet lifted her chin and looked into her mother's face. Sevet's eyes were swimming with tears, and there was a frightened question in her face.

"I think that Vas will come with you, if you ask him," said Rasa. "He's a wise and a forgiving man, and he loves you far more than you deserve." The words were cold, but Sevet still took them as comfort.

"But what about *Obring,*" insisted Kokor.

"He's such a weak man," said Rasa, "I'm sure you can persuade him to come along."

In the meantime, Mebbekew had turned to Elemak. "Your *wife?*" he asked.

"Lady Rasa is going to perform the ceremony for Eiadh and me tonight," said Elemak.

Mebbekew's face betrayed some powerful emotion—rage, jealousy? Had Mebbekew also wanted Eiadh, the way poor Nafai had?

"You're marrying her *tonight?*" demanded Mebbekew.

"We don't know when Moozh will lift our house arrest, and I want my marriage to be done properly. Once we're out in the desert, I don't want any question about who is married to whom."

"Not that we can't change around as soon as our terms are up," said Kokor.

Everyone looked at her.

"The desert isn't Basilica," said Rasa. "There'll only be a handful of us. Marriages will be permanent. Get used to that idea right now."

"That's absurd," said Kokor. "I'm not going, and you can't make me."

"No, I can't make you," said Rasa. "But if you stay, you'll soon discover how different life is when you're no longer the daughter of Lady Rasa, but merely a young singer who is notorious for having silenced her much more famous sister with a blow from her own hand."

"I can live with that!" said Kokor defiantly.

"Then I'm sure I don't want you with me," said Rasa angrily. "What good would a girl with no conscience be on the terrible journey that lies ahead of us?" Her words were harsh, but Rasa could taste her disappointment in Kokor like a foul poison on her tongue. "I've said all I have to say. You all have work to do and choices to make. Make them and have done."

It was a clear dismissal, and Kokor and Sevet got up and left at once, Kokor sweeping past, her nose in the air in a great show of hauteur.

Mebbekew sidled up to Rasa—couldn't the boy walk naturally, without looking like a sneak or a spy?—and asked his question. "Is Elya's wedding tonight an exclusive affair?"

"Everyone in the house is invited to attend," said Rasa.

"I meant—what if I were to marry someone, too. Would you do the ceremony tonight?"

"Marry *someone?* I assure you, Dolya may have been indiscreet, but I'll be surprised if she takes you on as a husband, Mebbekew."

Meb looked furious. "Luet told you."

"Of course she told me," said Rasa. "Half a dozen servants and Dolya herself would have told me before nightfall. Do you actually imagine anyone can keep a secret like *that* from me in my own house?"

"If I can persuade her to accept a piece of unworthy slime like myself," said Meb, his voice dripping with sarcasm, "will you condescend to include us in the ceremony?"

."It would be dangerous to bring you out into the desert without a wife," said Rasa. "Dolya would be more than enough woman for *you,* though she could hardly do worse for herself."

Mebbekew's face was red with fury. "I have done nothing to deserve such scorn from you."

"You have done nothing *but* to earn it," said Rasa. "You seduced my niece under my own roof, and now you contemplate marrying her—and don't think I'm fooled, either. You want to marry her, not to join your father in the desert, but to use her as your license to remain in Basilica. You'll be unfaithful to her the moment we're gone and you have your papers."

"And I swear to you in the eyes of the Oversoul that I will bring Dolya out into the desert, as surely as Elya is bringing Eiadh."

"Be careful when you make the Oversoul the witness of

your oath," said Rasa. "She has a way of making you hold to your word."

Mebbekew almost said something else, but then thought better of it and stalked out of Rasa's private receiving room. No doubt off to flatter Dolya into proposing marriage to *him*.

And it will work, thought Rasa bitterly. Because this boy, who has so little else going for him, *is* good with women. Haven't I heard of his exploits from the mothers of so many girls in Dolltown and Dauberville? Poor Dolya. Has life left you so hungry that you'll swallow even the poor imitation of love?

Only Elemak and Nafai remained.

"I don't want to share my ceremony with Mebbekew," said Elemak coldly.

"It's tragic, isn't it, that we don't always get what we want in this world," said Rasa. "Anyone who wants to be married tonight, will be. We don't have time to satisfy your vanity, and you know it. You'd tell me so yourself, if you were giving me impartial counsel."

Elemak studied her face for a few moments. "Yes," he said. "You're very wise." Then he, too, left.

But Rasa understood him, too, better than he imagined. She knew that he had sized her up and decided that, while she might be powerful in Basilica, she would be nothing in the desert. He would bow to her rule tonight, but once they got out into the desert he would delight in subjugating her. Well, I am not afraid to be humiliated, thought Rasa. I can bear much more than you imagine. What will your torments mean to me, when I will feel the agony of my beloved city, and know that in my exile I can do nothing to save it after all?

Only Nafai was with her now.

"Mother," he said, "what about Issib? And Gaballufix's

treasurer, Zdorab? They'll need wives. And Elemak saw wives for all of us, in his dream."

"Then the Oversoul must provide wives for them, don't you think?"

"Shedemei will come," he said. "She had a dream, too. The Oversoul is bringing her. And Hushidh. She's part of this, isn't she? The Oversoul will surely bring her. For Issib, or for Zdorab."

"Why don't you ask her?" said Rasa.

"Not *me*," said Nafai.

"You told me that the Oversoul said you would lead your brothers someday. How will that happen, if you haven't the strength inside yourself to face even a sweet and generous girl like Shuya?"

"To you she seems sweet," said Nafai. "But to *me*—and asking her such a thing—"

"She knows you boys came back here for wives, you foolish child. Do you think she hasn't counted heads? She's a raveler—do you think she doesn't already see the connections?"

He was abashed. "No, I didn't think of that. She probably knows more than I do about everything."

"Only about some things," said Rasa. "And you're still hiding from the most important question of all."

"No, I'm not," said Nafai. "I know that Luet is the woman I should marry, and I know that I will ask her. I didn't need your advice about that."

"Then I have nothing to fear for you, my son," said Rasa.

THE SOLDIERS BROUGHT Rashgallivak into his room and, as Moozh had instructed them beforehand, cast him down brutally onto the floor. When the soldiers had left, Rashgallivak touched his nose. It wasn't broken, but it was bleeding from its impact with the floor, and Moozh offered him nothing to wipe the blood. Since the soldiers had stripped Rashgallivak naked before bringing him here, there was nothing for Rashgallivak to do but let the blood flow into his mouth or down his chin.

"I knew I'd see you sooner or later," said Moozh. "I didn't have to search. I knew there'd come a time when you imagined that you had something I'd want from you, and then you'd come to me and try to bargain for your life. But I can assure you, I need nothing that you have."

"So kill me and have done," said Rashgallivak.

"Very dramatic," said Moozh. "I say I *need* nothing that you have, but I might *want* something, and I might even want it enough not to put your eyes out or castrate you or some other small favor before you are burned to death as a traitor to your city."

"Yes, so deeply you care for Basilica," said Rashgallivak.

"You gave me this city, you poor fool. Your stupidity and brutality gave it to me as a gift. Now it's the brightest jewel in my possession. Yes, I care deeply for Basilica."

"Only if you can keep it," said Rashgallivak.

"Oh, I assure you, I'll keep this jewel. Either by wearing it to adorn me, or by grinding it to powder and swallowing it down."

"So fearless you are, brave General. And yet you've got Lady Rasa under house arrest."

"I still have many paths that I can follow," said Moozh. "I can't think why any of them lead to anything but your immediate death. So you'll have to do better than tell me what I already know."

"Like it or not," said Rashgallivak, "I *am* the legal Wetchik and the head of the Palwashantu clan, and while no one has much love for me right now, if the disfranchised men outside the walls saw that I was in your favor and had some power to bestow, they would rally to me. I could be useful to you."

"I see that you harbor some pathetic dreams of being my rival for power here."

"No, General," said Rashgallivak. "I was a steward all my life, working to build and strengthen the house of Wetchik. Gaballufix talked me into acting on ambitions that I never had until he made me feel them. I've had plenty of time to regret believing him, to scorn myself for strutting around as if I were some great leader, when in fact what I am is a born steward. I was only happy when I served a stronger man than myself. I was proud that I always served the strongest man in Basilica. That happens to be yourself, and if you kept me alive and used me, you would find I am a man of many good gifts."

"Including unquestionable loyalty?"

"You will never trust me, I know that. I betrayed Wetchik, to my shame. But I only did it when Volemak was already exiled and powerless. You will *never* weaken or fail, and so you can trust me implicitly."

Moozh couldn't help laughing. "You're telling me that I can trust you to be loyal, because you're too much of a coward to betray a strong man?"

"I've had plenty of time to know myself, General Vozmuzhalnoy Vozmozhno. I have no desire to deceive either myself or you."

"I can put anyone in charge of the rabble of men who call themselves Palwashantu," said Moozh. "Or I can lead them myself. Why would I need you alive, when I can gain so much more from your public confession and execution?"

"You're a brilliant general and leader of men, but you still don't know Basilica."

"I know it well enough to rule here without losing the life of a single man of mine."

"Then if you're so all-knowing, General Vozmuzhalnoy Vozmozhno, perhaps you'll understand immediately why it is important that Shedemei bought a dozen drycases from me today."

"Don't play games with me, Rashgallivak. You know that I have no notion of who this Shedemei is, or what his buying drycases might mean."

"Shedemei is a woman, sir. A noted scientist. Very clever with genetics—she has developed some popular new plants, among other things."

"If you have a point . . ."

"Shedemei is also a teacher in Rasa's house, and one of her most beloved nieces."

Ah. So Rashgallivak *might* have something worth learning. Moozh waited to hear more.

"Drycases are used to transport seeds and embryos across great distances without refrigeration. She told me that she was moving her entire research laboratory to a faraway city, and that's why she needed drycases."

"And you don't believe her."

"It is unthinkable that Shedemei would move her laboratory *now*. The danger is clearly over, and ordinarily she would simply bury herself in her work. She is a very focused scientist. She barely notices the world around her."

"So her plan to leave comes from Rasa, you think."

"Rasa has been faithfully married to Wetch—to Volemak, the former Wetchik—for many years. He exiled himself from the city several weeks ago, ostensibly in obedience to some vision from the Oversoul. His sons came back to the city and tried to buy the Palwashantu Index from Gaballufix."

Rashgallivak paused, as if waiting for Moozh to make some connection; but of course Rashgallivak would know that Moozh lacked the information necessary to make this connection. It was Rashgallivak's way of trying to assert Moozh's need for him. But Moozh had no intention of playing this game. "Either tell me or don't," he said. "Then I'll decide whether I want you or not. If you continue to imagine you can manipulate my judgment, you only prove yourself to be worthless."

"It's clear that Volemak still dreams of ruling here in Basilica. Why else would he want the Index? Its only value is as a symbol of authority among the Palwashantu men; it reminds them of that ancient, ancient day when they were not ruled by women. Rasa is his wife and a powerful woman in her own right. Alone she is dangerous to you—in combination with her husband, they would be formidable indeed. Who else could unite the city against you? Shedemei would not be preparing for a journey like this unless Rasa asked her to. Therefore Rasa and Volemak must have some plan that requires drycases."

"And what kind of plan would that be?"

"Shedemei is a brilliant geneticist, as I said. What if she could develop some mold or fungus that would spread like a disease through Basilica? Only Rasa's and Volemak's supporters would have the fungicide to kill it."

"A fungus. And you think this would be a weapon against the soldiers of the Gorayni?"

"No one's ever used such a thing as a weapon, sir," said Rashgallivak. "I could hardly think of it myself. But imagine how well your soldiers would fight if their bodies were covered with an excruciating, unbearable itch."

"An *itch*," echoed Moozh. It sounded absurd, laughable. And yet it might work—soldiers distracted by an itching, ineradicable fungus would not fight well. Nor would the city be easily governed, if people were suffering from such a plague. Governments were never less imposing than when they showed themselves impotent against disease or famine. Moozh had used this fact against the enemies of the Imperator many times. Was it possible that Rasa and Volemak were so clever, so evil-hearted, that they could conceive of such an inconceivable weapon? To use a scientist as a weapon maker—how could God allow such a vile practice to come into the world?

Unless . . .

Unless Rasa and Volemak have, like me, learned to resist God. Why should I be the only one with the strength to ignore God's efforts to turn men stupid when they attempted to walk on the road leading to power?

But then, couldn't Rashgallivak also be a tool God was using to mislead him? It had been many days since God had attempted to block him from any action. Was it possible that God, having failed to dominate Moozh directly, might now be trying to control Moozh by leading him after foolish imagined conspiracies? Many generals had been destroyed by just such fancies as the one Rashgallivak had now brought to him.

"Couldn't the drycases be for something else?" asked Moozh, testing.

"Of course," said Rashgallivak. "I only pointed out the most extreme possibility. Drycases also work very well for transporting supplies through the desert. Volemak and his sons—his oldest boy, Elemak, in particular—are more familiar with the desert than most. It holds no fear for them. They could be planning to build an army. You *do* have only a thousand men here."

"The rest of the army of the Gorayni will be here soon."

"Then perhaps that's why Volemak needed only twelve drycases—he won't need to supply his little army for very long."

"Army," said Moozh scornfully. "Twelve drycases. You were found with a draft for jewels of very high value. How do I know you haven't been bribed to tell me foolish lies and waste my time?"

"I wasn't *found*, sir. I turned myself over to your soldiers deliberately. And I brought the draft instead of the jewels because I wanted you to see that it was Shedemei's own hand that wrote the note. This amount is far more than the drycases are worth. She is clearly trying to buy my silence."

"So. This is where you are now, Rashgallivak. A few days ago you thought you were master of the city. And now you betray your former master once again, in order to ingratiate yourself with a new one. Explain to me why I shouldn't retch at the sight of you."

"Because I can be useful to you."

"Yes, yes, I can imagine, like a vicious but hungry dog. So tell me, Rashgallivak, what bone do you want me to toss you?"

"My Life, sir."

"Your life will never be your own again, as long as you live. So again I ask you to tell me what bone you want to gnaw on."

Rashgallivak hesitated.

"If you pretend to have some altruistic desire to serve me or the Imperator or Basilica, I'll have you gutted and burned in the marketplace within the hour."

"We don't burn traitors here. It would make you look monstrous to the Basilicans."

"On the contrary," said Moozh. "It would make them very happy to see such treatment meted out to *you*. No one is so civilized as not to relish vengeance, even if later they're ashamed of how they loved to see their enemy suffer before he died."

"Stop threatening me, General," said Rashgallivak. "I've lived in terror and I've come out of it. Kill me or not, torture me or not, it doesn't matter to me. Just decide what to do."

"Tell me first what you want. Your secret desire. Your dream of the best thing that might come to you from all of this."

Again he hesitated. But this time he found the strength to name his desire. "Lady Rasa," he whispered.

Moozh nodded slightly. "So ambition isn't dead in you," he said. "You still have dreams of living infinitely above your station."

"I told you because you insisted, sir. I know it could never happen."

"Get out of here," said Moozh. "My men will take you to be bathed. And then dressed. You will live at least another night."

"Thank you, sir."

The soldiers came in and took Rashgallivak away— but this time without dragging him, without any brutality. Not that Moozh had decided to use Rashgallivak. His death was still an attractive possibility—it would be the most decisive way for Moozh to declare himself the master of Basilica, to mete out justice so publicly, so popularly, and so clearly in violation of all Basilican law and custom and decency. The citizens would love it, and in loving it they would cease to be the old Basilica. They would become something new. A new city.

My city.

Rashgallivak married to Rasa. That was a nasty thought, conceived in a nasty little mind. Yet it would certainly humiliate Rasa, and clinch the image of her in many people's minds as a traitor to Basilica. And yet she would still be a leading citizen of Basilica, with an aura of legitimacy. After all, she *was* on Bitanke's list. As was Rashgallivak.

It was a fine list, too. Well thought out, and quite daring. Bitanke was a bright man, very useful. For example, he was wise enough not to underestimate Moozh's powers of persuasion. He didn't leave people off his list just because he fancied that they'd never be willing to serve Moozh by ruling Basilica for him.

So the names that led the list were, unsurprisingly, the very names that Rashgallivak had mentioned as possible rivals: Volemak and Rasa. Rashgallivak's name, too, was there. And Volemak's son and heir, Elemak, because of both his ability and his legitimacy. Volemak's and Rasa's youngest, too—Nafai, because he linked those two great names and because he had killed Gaballufix with his own hands.

Was everyone who might serve Moozh's need linked to Rasa's house? That was no surprise to him—in most cities he'd conquered, there were at most two or three clans that had to be either eliminated or co-opted in order to control the populace. Almost everyone else on Bitanke's list was far too weak to rule well without constant help from Moozh, as Bitanke himself pointed out: They were too closely linked with certain factions, or too isolated from any support at all.

The only two who weren't tied by blood to Volemak or Rasa were nevertheless nieces in Rasa's house: The waterseer Luet and the raveler Hushidh. They were still only girls, of course, hardly ready to handle the difficult work of governance. But they had enormous prestige among the women of Basilica, especially the waterseer. They would be only figureheads, but with Rashgallivak to actually run things, and Bitanke to watch Rashgallivak and protect the figurehead from being manipulated against Moozh's best interest, the city could run very well while Moozh turned his attention to his real problems—the Cities of the Plain, and the Imperator.

Rashgallivak married to Rasa. It sounded so pleasantly dynastic. No doubt Rash's dreams included supplanting Moozh one day and ruling in his own right. Well, Moozh could hardly begrudge him those dreams. But there would soon be a dynasty that would surpass Rash's poor dreams. Rash might take the Lady Rasa, but how would that compare with the glorious marriage of the waterseer or the raveler with General Moozh himself? That would be a dynasty that could stand for a thousand years. That would be a dynasty that could topple the feeble house of that pathetic little man who dared to call himself the incarnation of God—the Imperator, whose power would be nothing when Moozh decided to move against him.

And, best of all, by marrying and using one of these chosen vessels of the Oversoul, Moozh would have the triumph that pleased him most: The triumph over God. You were never strong enough to control me, O Almighty One. And now I'll take your chosen daughter, filled with your visions, and make her the mother of a dynasty that will defy you and destroy all your plans and works.

Stop me if you can! I am far too strong for you.

NAFAI FOUND LUET and Hushidh together, waiting for him in the secret place on the roof. They looked very grave, which did nothing to calm the fear in Nafai's heart. Until now, Nafai had never felt himself to be young; he had always felt himself to be a person, equal to any other. But now his youth pressed in on him. He had not thought to marry now, or even really to *decide* whom to marry. Nor was it the easy, temporary union that he had expected his first marriage to be. His wife would probably be his only wife, and if he did badly in this marriage, he'd have no recourse. Seeing Luet and Hushidh, both looking at him solemnly as he made his way across the brightly sunlit roof, he wondered again if he could do this: If he could marry this girl Luet, who was so perfect and wise in the eyes of the Oversoul. She had come to the Oversoul with love, with devotion, with courage—he had come like a bratty child, taunting and testing his unknown parent. She had years of experience in speaking with the Oversoul; perhaps more important, she had had years in speaking *for* the Oversoul, to the women of Basilica. She knew how to dominate others—hadn't he seen it there on the shores of the lake of women, when she faced them down and saved his life?

Will I be coming to you as a husband or a child? A partner or a student?

"So the family council is over," said Hushidh, when at last he was near enough for easy speech.

He seated himself on the carpet under the awning. The shade gave him little enough respite from the heat. Sweat dripped under his clothing. It made him aware of his own naked body, hidden from view. If he married Luet, he would have to offer that body to her tonight. How often had he dreamed of such an offering? And yet never once had he thought of coming to a girl who filled him with awe and shyness, and yet who was herself utterly without experience; always in his dreams the woman was eager for him, and he was a bold and ready lover. There would be nothing like that tonight.

He had a wrenching thought. What if Luet wasn't ready yet? What if she wasn't even a *woman* yet? He quickly spoke a prayer in his heart to the Oversoul, but couldn't finish it, because he wasn't sure whether he hoped she *was* a woman, or hoped that she was *not*.

"How thickly woven are the bonds already," said Hushidh.

"What are you talking about?" asked Nafai.

"We're tied to the future by so many cords. The Oversoul has always told dear Luet, here, that she wants human beings to follow her freely. But I think she has caught us in a very tight-woven net, and we have about as much choice as a fish that's been dragged up from the sea."

"We have choices," said Nafai. "We always have choices."

"Do we?"

I don't want to talk to *you,* Hushidh. I came here now to talk to Luet.

"We have the choice to follow the Oversoul or not," said Luet, her voice coming soft and sweet, compared to

Hushidh's harsher tone. "And if we choose to follow, then we are not caught in her net, but rather carried in her basket into the future."

Hushidh smiled wanly. "Always so cheerful, aren't you, Lutya."

A lull in the conversation.

If I am to be a man and a husband, I must learn to act boldly, even when I'm afraid. "Luet," he began. Then: "Lutya."

"Yes?" she said.

But he could not ignore Hushidh's eyes boring into him, seeing in him things that he had no desire for her to see.

"Hushidh," he said, "could I speak to Luet alone?"

"I have no secrets from my sister," said Luet.

"And will that be true, even when you have a husband?" asked Nafai.

"I have no husband," said Luet.

"But if you did, I would hope that he would be the one you shared your inmost heart with, and not your sister."

"If I had a husband, I would hope that he would not be so cruel as to require me to abandon my sister, who is my only family in the world."

"If you had a husband," said Nafai, "he should love your sister as if she were his own sister. But still not as much as he loved *you,* and so you should not love your sister as much as you loved *him.*"

"Not all marriages are for love," said Luet. "Some are because one has no choice."

The words stung him to the heart. She knew, of course—if the Oversoul had told *him,* it would certainly have told *her,* as well. And she was telling him that she didn't love him, that she was marrying him only because the Oversoul commanded it.

"True," said Nafai. "But that doesn't mean that the husband and the wife can't treat each other with gentleness and kindness, until they learn trust for each other. It doesn't mean they can't resolve to love each other, even if they didn't choose the marriage freely, for themselves."

"I hope that what you've said is true."

"I promise to make it true, if you'll promise me the same."

Luet looked at him with a chagrined smile on her face. "Oh. Is this how I'm to hear my husband ask me to be his wife?"

So he had done it wrong. He had offended her, perhaps hurt her, certainly disappointed her. How she must loathe the idea of being married to him. Didn't she see that he would never have chosen to force such a thing on her? As the thought formed in his mind, he blurted it out. "The Oversoul chose us for each other, and so yes, I'm asking you to marry me, even though I'm afraid."

"Afraid of *me?*"

"Not that you mean me any harm—you've saved my life, and my father's life before that. I'm afraid—of your disdain for me. I'm afraid that I'll always be humiliated before you and your sister, the two of you, seeing everything weak about me, looking down on me. The way you see me now."

In all his life, Nafai had never spoken with such brutal frankness about his own fear; he had never felt so exposed and vulnerable in front of anyone. He dared not look up at her face—at their faces—for fear of seeing a look of wondrous contempt.

"Oh, Nafai, I'm sorry," whispered Luet.

Her words came as the blow that he had most dreaded. She pitied him. She saw how weak and frightened and uncertain he was, and she felt sorry for him. And yet even in the pain of that moment of disappointment, he felt a small bright fire of joy inside. I can do this, he thought. I have shown my weakness to these strong women, and still I am myself, and alive inside, and not defeated at all.

"Nafai, I only thought of how frightened I was," said Luet. "I never imagined that you might feel that way, too, or I would never have asked Shuya to stay here when you came to me."

"It's no great pleasure to *be* here, I assure you," added Hushidh.

"It was wrong of me to make you say these things in front of Shuya," said Luet. "And it was wrong of me to be afraid of you. I should have known that the Oversoul wouldn't have chosen you if you weren't a good-hearted man."

She was afraid of *him?*

"Won't you look at me, Nafai?" she asked. "I know you never looked at me before, not with hope or longing, anyway, but now that the Oversoul has given us to each other, can't you look at me with—with kindness, anyway?"

How could he lift his face to her now, with his eyes full of tears; and yet, since she asked him, since it would mean disappointment to her if he did not, how could he refuse? He looked at her, and even though his eyes swam with tears—of joy, of relief, of emotions even stronger that he didn't understand—he saw her as if for the first time, as if her soul had been made transparent to him. He saw the purity of her heart. He saw how fully she had given herself to the Oversoul, and to Basilica, and to her sister, and to him. He saw that in her heart she longed only to build something fine and beautiful, and how readily she was willing to try to do that with this boy who sat before her.

"What do you see, when you look at me like that?" asked Luet, her voice timid, yet daring to ask.

"I see what a great and glorious woman you are," he said, "and how little reason I have to fear you, because you'd never harm me or any other soul."

"Is that all you see?" she asked.

"I see that the Oversoul has found in you the most perfect example of what the human race must all become, if we are to be whole, and not destroy ourselves again."

"Nothing more?" she asked.

"What can be more wonderful than the things I've told you that I see?"

By now his eyes had cleared enough to see that *she* was now on the verge of crying—but not for joy.

"Nafai, you poor fool, you blind man," said Hushidh, "don't you know what she's hoping that you see?"

No, I don't know, thought Nafai. I don't know any of the right things to say. I'm not like Mebbekew, I'm not clever or tactful, I give offense to everybody when I speak, and somehow I've done it again, even though everything I said was what I honestly feel.

He looked at her, feeling helpless; what could he do? She looked at him so hungrily, aching for him to give her— what? He had praised her honestly, with the sort of praise that he could have spoken to no other woman in the world, and it was nothing to her, because she wanted something more from him, and he didn't know what it was. He was hurting her with his very silence, stabbing her to the heart, he could see that—and yet was powerless to stop doing it.

She was so frail, so young—even younger than he. He had never realized that before. She had always been so sure of herself, and, because she was the waterseer, he had always been in awe. He had never realized how . . . how *breakable* she was. How thinly her luminous skin covered her, how small her bones were. A tiny stone could bruise her, and now I find her battered with stones that I cast without knowing. Forgive me, Luet, tender child, gentle girl. I was so afraid for myself, but I turned out not to be breakable at all, even when I thought you and Hushidh had scorned me. While you, whom I had thought to be strong . . .

Impulsively he knelt up and gathered her into his arms

and held her close, the way he might hold a weeping child. "I'm sorry," he whispered.

"Don't be sorry, please," she said. But her voice was high, the voice of a child who is trying not to be caught crying, and he could feel her tears soaking into his shirt, and her body trembling with silent weeping.

"I'm sorry that it's only me you get as a husband," he said.

"And I'm sorry that it's only me you get as a wife," she said. "Not the waterseer, not the glorious being you imagined that you saw. Only me."

Finally he understood what she had been asking for all along, and couldn't help but laugh, because without knowing it he had just now given it to her. "Did you think that I said those things to the *waterseer?*" he asked. "No, you poor thing, I said those things to *you,* to Luet, to the girl I met in my mother's school, to the girl who sassed me and anybody else when she felt like it, to the girl I'm holding in my arms right now."

She laughed then—or sobbed harder, he wasn't sure. But he knew that whatever she was doing now, it was better. That was all she had needed—was for him to tell her that he didn't expect her to be the waterseer all the time, that he was marrying the fragile, imperfect human being, and not the overpowering image that she inadvertently wore.

He moved his hands across her back, to comfort her; but he also felt the curve of her body, the geometry of ribs and spine, the texture and softness of skin stretched taut over muscles. His hands explored, memorizing her, discovering for the first time how a woman's back felt to a man's hands. She was real and not a dream.

"The Oversoul didn't give you to me," he said softly. "You are giving yourself to me."

"Yes," she said. "That's right."

"And I give myself to you," he said. "Even though I, too, belong to the Oversoul."

He drew back a little, enough to cup the back of her head in his right hand as she looked up at him, enough to touch her cheek with the fingers of his left.

Then, suddenly, as if they both had the same thought at the same moment—which, quite certainly, they did— they looked away from each other, and toward the spot where Hushidh had been sitting through this whole conversation.

But Hushidh wasn't there. They turned back to each other then, and Luet, dismayed, said, "I shouldn't have made her come with me to—"

She never finished the sentence, because at that moment Nafai began to learn how to kiss a woman, and she, though she had never kissed a man before, became his tutor.

SIX

WEDDINGS

THE DREAM OF THE RAVELER

Hushidh saw nothing joyful about the wedding. Not that anything went wrong. Aunt Rasa had a way with rituals. Her ceremony was simple and sweet, without a hint of the false portentousness that so many other women resorted to in their desperate desire to seem holy or important. Aunt Rasa had never needed to pretend. And yet she still took great care that when the public passages of life—weddings, comings-of-age, graduations, embarkations, divinations, deathwatches, burials—were under her care, they took place with an easy grace, a gentleness that kept people's minds focused on the occasion, and not on the machinery of celebration. There was never a hint of anyone hurrying or bustling; never a hint that everything had to be *just so,* and therefore you'd better watch your step so you don't do anything wrong . . .

No, Rasa's wedding for her son Nafai and his two brothers—or, if you looked at it the other way, Rasa's wedding for her three nieces, Luet, Dol, and Eiadh—was a lovely affair on the portico of her house, bright and aromatic with flowers from her greenhouse and the blossoms that grew on the portico. Eiadh and Dol were astonishingly beautiful, their gowns clinging to them with the elegant illusion of simplicity, their facepaint so artfully applied that they seemed not to be painted at all. Or *would* have seemed so, had it not been for Luet.

Sweet Luet, who had refused to be painted at all, and whose dress really *was* simple. Where Eiadh and Dol had all the elegance of women trying—very successfully—to seem bright and young and gay, Luet really *was* young, her gown artlessly covering a body that was still more the promise than the reality of womanhood, her face bright with a grave and timid sort of joy that made Eiadh and Dol look older and far too experienced. In a way, it was almost cruel to make the older girls have their weddings in the presence of this girl who rebuked them by her very naivete. Eiadh had actually noticed, before the ceremony began— Hushidh overheard her urging Aunt Rasa to "send somebody up with Luet to help her choose a dress and to do something with her face and hair" but Aunt Rasa had only laughed and said, "No art will help that child." Eiadh took that, of course, to mean that Aunt Rasa thought Luet to be too plain to be helped by costume and makeup; but Hushidh caught Aunt Rasa's eye the moment afterward, and Aunt Rasa winked at her and rolled her eyes to let her know that *they* both understood that poor Eiadh hadn't a clue about what would happen at the wedding.

And it did happen, though fortunately Eiadh and Dol had no idea that when the watching servants and students and teachers whispered, "Ah, she is so lovely"; "Ah, so sweet"; "Look, who knew she was so beautiful," they were all speaking of Luet, only of Luet. When Nafai, as the youngest man, came forward to be claimed by his bride, the sighs were like a song from the congregation, an improvised hymn to the Oversoul, for having brought this boy of fourteen, who had the stature and strength of a man and the bright fire of the Oversoul in his eyes, to marry the

Oversoul's chosen daughter, the waterseer, whose pure beauty grew from the soul outward. He was the bright gold ring in which this jewel of a girl would glow with unreflected luster.

Hushidh saw better than anyone how the people belonged to Luet in their hearts. She saw the threads between them, sparkling like the dew-covered strands of a spider's web in the first sunlight of morning; how they love the waterseer! But most of all Hushidh saw the firming bonds between the husbands and wives as the ceremony progressed. Unconsciously she took note of each gesture, each glance, each facial expression, and in her mind she was able to understand the connection.

Between Elemak and Eiadh, it would be a strange sort of unequal partnership, in which the less Eiadh loved Elemak, the more he would desire her; and the more he treated her gently and lovingly, the more she would despise him. It would be a painful thing to watch, this marriage, in which the agony of coming apart was the very thing that would hold them together. But she could say nothing of this—neither one would understand this about themselves, and would only be furious if she tried to explain it.

As for poor Dolya and her precious new lover, Mebbekew, it was an ill-considered marriage indeed—and yet there was no reason to suppose it would be less viable than Elemak's and Eiadh's. At the moment, flushed with the glory of being, as they supposed, the center of attention, they were happy with the new bonds between them. But soon enough the reality would settle in. If they stayed in the city, they would hate each other within weeks—Dol because of Mebbekew's betrayals and unfaithfulness, Mebbekew because of Dol's clinging, possessive need for him. Hushidh imagined their domestic life. Dol would be forever throwing her arms around him in wonderfully enthusiastic hugs, thinking she was showing her love when really she was asserting her ownership; and Meb, shuddering under her profuse embraces, slipping away at every opportunity to find new bodies to possess, new hearts to ravish. But in the desert, it would be very different. Meb would find no woman who desired him except Dolya, and so his own lusts would throw him back into her arms again and again; and the very fact that he *could* not betray her would ease Dol's lonely fears, and she would not oppress him so much with her need for him. In the desert, they could make a marriage of it, though Mebbekew would never be happy with the boredom of making love with the same woman, night after night, week after week, year after year.

Hushidh imagined, with a pleasure she wasn't proud of, what Elemak would do the first time Meb made some flirting advance toward Eiadh. It would be discreet, so as to avoid weakening Elemak's public position by hinting that he feared being cuckolded. But Meb would never so much as look at Eiadh again afterward . . .

The bonds between Elemak and Eiadh, between Dol and Mebbekew, they were the sort of links that Hushidh saw every day in the city. These were Basilican marriages, made more poignant—and perhaps more viable—by the fact that soon the Oversoul would bring them out into the desert where they would need each other more and have fewer alternatives than in the city.

The marriage between Luet and Nafai, however, was not Basilican. For one thing, they were too young. Luet was only thirteen. It was almost barbaric, really—like the forest tribes of the Northern Shore, where a girl was bought as a bride before her first blood had stopped trickling. Only Hushidh's sure knowledge that the Oversoul had brought them together kept her from recoiling from the ceremony. Even at that, she felt a deep anger that she did not fully understand as she watched them join hands, make their vows, kiss so sweetly with Aunt Rasa's hands on their shoulders. Why do I hate this marriage so much, she wondered. For she could see that Luet was full of hope and joy, that Nafai was in awe of her and eager to please her—what more could Hushidh have hoped for, for her dear sister, her only kin in this world?

Yet when the wedding ended, when the newly married couples made their laughing, flower-strewn procession back into the house and up the stairways to their balcony rooms, Hushidh could not contain herself long enough even to watch her sister out of sight. She fled into a servants' corridor, and ran, not to her room, but to the rooftop where she and Luet had so often retreated together.

Even here, though, it was as if she could still see, in the gathering dark of evening, the shadow of Luet's and Nafai's first embrace, their first kiss. It filled her with rage, and she threw herself down onto the rug, beating on the thick fabric with her fists, weeping bitterly and sobbing, "No, no, no, no."

To what was she saying no? She didn't understand it herself. There she lay and there she wept until, weary with knowing too much and understanding not enough, she fell asleep in the cooling air of a Basilican night. Late in spring the breezes blew moist and cool from the sea, dry and warm from the desert, and met to do their turbulent dance in the streets and on the rooftops of the city. Hushidh's hair was caught in these breezes, and swirled and played as if it had a life of its own, and longed for freedom. But she did not wake.

Instead she dreamed, and in her dreams her unconscious mind brought forth the questions of fear and rage that she could not voice when she was awake. She dreamed of her own wedding. On a desert pinnacle, herself standing on the very tip of a high spire of rock, with no room for anyone else; yet there was her husband, floating in the air beside her: Issib, the cripple, blithely flying as she had seen him fly through the halls of Rasa's house during all his student years. In her dream she screamed the question that she had not dared to voice aloud: Why am I the one who must marry the cripple! How did you come up with my name for that life, Oversoul! How have I offended you, that I will never stand as Luet stood, sweet and young and blossoming with love, with a man beside me who is strong and holy, capable and good?

In her dream, she saw Issib float farther away from her, still smiling, but *she* knew that his smile was merely his own kind of courage, that her cries had broken his heart. As she watched, his smile faded; he crumpled, he fell like a bird taken out of the sky by a cruel miraculous arrow. Only then did she realize in the dream that he had been flying only by the power of his love for her, his need for her, and when she recoiled from him he had lost his power of flight. She tried to reach for him, tried to catch him, but all that happened then was that she herself lost her footing on the spire of rock and tumbled after him, downward to the ground.

She woke, panting, trembling in the cold. She gathered the free end of the carpet and pulled it over her and huddled under it, her cheeks cold from the tears drying there, her eyes puffy and sore from crying. Oversoul! she cried out silently with all her heart. O Mother of the Lake, tell me that you don't hate me so! Tell me that this is not your plan for me, that it was only accident that left me so bereft of hope on my sister's wedding night!

And then, with the perfect illogic of grief and self-pity, she prayed aloud, "Oversoul, tell me why you planned this life for me. I have to understand it if I'm going to live it. Tell me that it means something. Tell me why I am alive, tell me if some plan of yours brought me into this life as I am. Tell me why this power of understanding you gave me is a blessing, and not a curse. Tell me if I'll ever be as happy as Luet is tonight!" And then, ashamed of having put her jealousy and longing in such naked words, Hushidh wept again and drifted back into sleep.

Under the carpet she grew warm, for the night was not so cold yet, when she was covered. Her tears were replaced by sweat, drips of it tickling across her body like tiny hands. And again she dreamed.

She saw herself in the doorway of a desert tent. She had never seen a pitched tent before, except in holograms, yet this was not a tent she had seen in any picture. There she stood, holding a baby in her arms, as four other children, like stepstairs in height, rushed forth from the tent, and in the dream she thought it was as though the tent had just given birth to them, as though they were just now explod-ing into the world. If I had to, I would bear them all over again, and bring them here just to see them living so, brown and laughing in the desert sunlight. Around and around the children ran, chasing each other in some childish game while Hushidh watched. And then in her dream she heard the baby in her arms begin to fuss, and so she bared a breast and let the baby suckle; she could feel the milk flowing gratefully out of her nipple, could feel the sweet tingling of the baby's lips, kissing and sucking and smacking for life, warm life, wet life, a mingling of milk and saliva mak-ing a froth of tiny bubbles at the corners of the baby's mouth.

Then, through the door of the tent, there floated a chair, and in the chair a man. Issib, she knew at once. But there was no anger in her heart when she saw him, no sense that she had been cheated out of some good thing in life. In-stead she could see herself bound to him, heart to heart, by great ropes of glowing silk; she took the baby from her breast and laid it in Issib's lap, and he talked to the baby, and made her laugh as Hushidh lazily dried her breast and covered it again. All of them bound together, mother, father, children . . . she saw that this was what mattered, not some imagined ideal of what a husband ought to be. The children ran to their father and circled his chair, and he spoke to them, and they listened raptly, laughed when he laughed, sang with him when he sang. This Issib-of-dreams was not a burden for her to bear, he was as true a friend and husband as any she had ever seen.

Oversoul, she prayed in her dream, how did you bring me here? Why did you love me so much that you brought me to this time, to this place, to this man, to these children?

At once the answer came, with threads of gold and silver. The children connected to Hushidh and Issib, and then threads reaching out from them, backward, to other people. A rush, a haze of people, a billion, a trillion people, she saw them milling around, marching forward on some unknowable quest, or perhaps a migration. It was a fearful vision, so many people all at once, as though Hushidh were being shown every man and woman who had ever lived on Harmony. And among them, here and there, those same silver and golden threads.

All at once she understood: These are the ones in whom the connection with the Oversoul bred true. These are the ones who are best able to hear the voice of the Oversoul, in whom the genetic alteration of Harmony's founding has been doubled, redoubled, so that instead of receiving only vague feelings, a stupor of thought when they venture onto some forbidden avenue of invention or action, these special ones, these gold and silver ones can receive clear ideas, images, even words.

At first the gold and silver threads were short and thin, only glimpses here and there—mutations, chance connections, random variations in the genetic molecules. But here and there they found each other, these people, and married; and when they mated, gold to gold or silver to silver, some of their children were also linked to the Oversoul. Two

different strains, two different kinds of genetic link, Hushidh understood; when gold mated with silver, the children
were almost never gifted this way. Over the centuries, over
the uncountable multitudes, she could see that now the
Oversoul was nudging gifted people, trying to bring them
together, and after millions of years the gold and silver
were no longer threads, they were strong cords, passing
from generation to generation with much more regularity.

Until at last there came a time when one parent alone
could pass the gold thread on to all his children; and then,
many generations later, a time when the silver thread, too,
became a dominant trait, that one parent could pass on
regardless of whether the other parent was gifted or not.

Now the Oversoul grew more eager, and nudges became
intricate plots as people were drawn together over thousands of kilometers, improbable marriages and matings.
She saw a woman rise naked out of a stream to couple with
a man she had come a thousand kilometers to find, the
woman never knowing that this was the Oversoul's purpose. The man had in him both the gold and silver, strong
and true, and so did the woman, and their daughter was
born with cords of the brightest metal, shining as if with
its own light.

In her dream Hushidh saw the mother take her baby and
lay it in the arms of Rasa, who was herself linked to generations past with strands of gold and silver. And then the
same woman, the same mother, laying yet another daughter, brighter still, in Rasa's arms. Before her eyes the second baby grew and became Luet, and now Hushidh saw
what she had seen this very night, Luet and Nafai being
bound together, but now she could see that, more than the
cords of love and loyalty, of need and passion that Hushidh
always saw, there were also these gold and silver cords,
brighter in Luet and Nafai than in any others in the room.
No wonder their eyes shone with such grace and beauty,

thought Hushidh. They were created by the Oversoul, as surely as if she had come and smelted them out of perfect ore and touched them with the magic of life from her own hand.

Then Hushidh rose up as if she were flying over the portico, and she could see that all the couples being married there had these threads in them. Not as bright and strong as in Luet and Nafai, but they had them. Mebbekew and Elemak both had silver and gold in them; Dol had the silver only, and Eiadh the gold, with just a trace of silver.

Who else? How many others have you brought together, Oversoul?

Higher and higher she rose over the city, but because this was a dream she could still clearly see the people on the streets and in their houses. There were many bright traces of gold and silver here, far more than in any other place in all the world. Here in this city of women, many traders had come and brought, not just their goods, but their seed; many women had come on pilgrimage and stayed, at least long enough to bear a child; many families had sent their daughters and their sons to be educated; and now there was hardly a person in Basilica who was not touched with the gift to feel the influence of the Oversoul, to one degree or another. And those who were so touched could feel, not only the Oversoul, but also each other, though they never realized how much they understood. No wonder this is a holy city, thought Hushidh in her dream. No wonder it is known throughout the world for beauty and for truth.

Beauty and truth, but also darker things. The connection with the Oversoul did not mean that a person would be kinder or more generous. And unconscious knowledge of another person's heart could easily be turned to exploitation, manipulation, cruelty, or domination. Hushidh saw Gaballufix and realized that the threads in him were almost as bright as in Rasa or Wetchik. No wonder he knew so well how to lead the men of the Palwashantu, how to intimidate the women of Basilica, how to dominate those close to him.

Then Gaballufix as she saw in her dream stepped forth from his house, flailing about himself with his charged-wire blade as if a thousand invisible enemies attacked him. Hushidh understood that this was his own madness, and the Oversoul grieved at what he was doing. So she made Gaballufix stumble. He fell to the ground and lay there, still bright with gold and silver, but helpless and harmless for the moment.

As he lay there, another came: Nafai, she knew. She was being shown Luet's husband in his most terrible moment, for she could see how he stood over the body and pleaded with the Oversoul not to require him to do what he was being asked to do. Yet when he sliced off Gaballufix's head, he was not being controlled by the Oversoul. He had freely chosen to follow the Oversoul's path. Gaballufix was extinguished, and Nafai stood alone in the street, shining and ashamed.

Hushidh fairly flew over the city, catching glimpses of the brightest ones. Shedemei, alone in her laboratory, filling portable drycases with seeds and embryos. A man walking with Nafai toward the city gate, carrying a globe wrapped in a cloth—it had to be Zdorab, the one Nafai had told them about—and Zdorab was also bright with gold and silver. Sevet's husband, Vas. Kokor's husband, Obring. Both almost as bright as Rasa's and Gaballufix's daughters themselves. All these people brought together in this city, at this moment, and all the best of them were coming out into the desert to join Wetchik. The Oversoul had bred them for this, and now was calling them forth out of the world to take them to another place.

What will our children be? And our grandchildren?

Again she rose up over the city, rejoicing now to understand the Oversoul's plan, when she caught a glimpse of yet another gold and silver cord, as bright as any she had seen. She wanted to look, and because it was a dream she immediately swooped down and saw that the light came from Gaballufix's house, but the man was not Gaballufix. Instead he wore a strange uniform, and his hair was oiled and hung in wet-looking ringlets.

General Vozmuzhalnoy Vozmozhno, she realized. Moozh. He, too, has been brought here! He, too, is one that the Oversoul desires!

But as she watched, she saw Moozh stand up and draw his metal sword. Was he like Gaballufix, then? Would he flail about himself in a frenzy of killing?

No. He turned and saw the gold and silver cords that bound him to the Oversoul, and hacked at them with the blade. He cut them off, and then fled from them. Yet in a moment the cords grew back again, and once again he chopped them away and ran from where the cords had once led him. Again and again it happened, and Hushidh knew that he hated his connection with the Oversoul.

Yet he was here. However it had happened, the Oversoul had brought him here. And then she understood: The Oversoul, knowing how he hated her, how Moozh rebelled against her, had simply pushed him *not* to do whatever she actually wanted him to do. So easily he had been fooled! So easily he had been guided. And in her sleep she laughed.

Laughed and began to waken; she could feel the sleep falling away from her, could feel her body now, the real one, wrapped in a carpet, sweating even though the air was chill around her.

In that moment, as wakefulness drove away the dream, there came a sudden flash of vision that seemed different from all that had come before. She saw the image from her earlier dream, the one where she stood on the spire of rock and Issib floated in the air beside her, and he tumbled and fell and she also fell after him; it passed through her mind in a single flash, and then she saw something new: Winged creatures, hairy as animals and yet able to soar and fly; they swooped out of the sky and caught Issib and Hushidh by the arms and legs as they tumbled toward the ground, and with a great beating and pounding of their wings, they kept them from striking the rocks below, and instead carried them upward into the sky.

It terrified her, this sudden unexpected dream, for Hushidh knew that she was not really asleep, and no dream should have come at all, especially not one as clear and frightening as this. Hadn't the Oversoul already shown her everything she asked for? Why now did she bring her back to this old image?

And again, she flashed on a former moment in this night's dreams: She stood with Issib in the doorway of the tent, with the baby in Issib's lap and the children gathered around his floating chair. No sooner had she recognized the scene than it changed; they were no longer in the desert, but instead in lush forest, in the doorway of a wooden house in a clearing, and all at once giant rats rose up out of holes in the ground and dropped from the limbs of trees and rushed at them, and Hushidh knew they meant to steal their children, to carry them off and eat them, and she screamed in terror. Yet before the sound could even reach her lips, there came those flying creatures again, tumbling out of the sky to catch her children and lift them up out of the jaws and hands of the huge ravenous rats. Seeing what was happening, she snatched her own baby from Issib's lap and held it high above her head, and one of the flying creatures swooped down and snatched it from her hands and carried it away. And she stood there and wept, because she did not know if she had simply given her children from one predator to another . . . and yet she *did* know. She had made her choice, and when they came again she took Issib's arms and held them upward for the flying creatures to take him, to carry him away. Only before they could come, the rats were on them, tumbling them down, and a hundred tiny savage hands fumbled and seized at her, tugged at her—

She awoke with the sound of her own scream in her ears, and an unsoothable fear clawing at her heart. She was drenched in sweat, and the night was dark around her, the breeze chilling her, but her trembling was not from cold. She threw off the carpet that covered her and ran, stumbling, still half-blind from the sleep in her eyes and awkward from the stiffness of uncomfortable rest, to the gap in the gable that led her into an attic of the house.

By the time she got to her own room, she could see well enough, and walked smoothly and quietly, but she was still weak and terrified, and she could not bear the thought of being alone. For there was Luet's bed—Luet, who should be there to soothe her now—but it was empty, because Luet had gone to another bed, and held someone who needed her far less than Hushidh did tonight. Hushidh huddled on her own bed, alternating between silent trembling and great, gasping sobs, until she feared that someone in another room might hear her.

They'll think I'm jealous of Luet, if they hear me weeping. They'll think I hate her for marrying before me, and that isn't so . . . not now, anyway, not since the Oversoul showed me the meaning of it all. She tried to bring that dream back into her memory—of herself and her children and her husband at the door of the tent—but the moment she did, it transformed again and she was possessed by the terror of the rats coming out of their holes, out of the trees, and her only hope the desperate strangeness of the flying beasts—

And she found herself in the corridor outside her room, running away from a fear that she carried with her as she ran. Ran and ran until she hurled open the door to the room where she knew that Luet would be, for she couldn't bear this, she had to have help, and it could only be Luet, only Luet could help her . . .

"What is it?" The fear in Luet's voice was an echo of the terror in Hushidh's own. Hushidh saw her sister, sitting bolt upright on the bed, holding a sheet up to her throat as if it were a shield. And then Nafai, awakened more by her voice than by the door, sleepily rising from the bed, standing on the floor, coming toward Hushidh, not yet understanding who it was but knowing that if an intruder came it was his job to block the way . . .

"Shuya," said Luet.

"Oh, Luet, forgive me," Hushidh sobbed. "Help me. Hold me!"

Before Luet could reach her, Nafai was there, helping her, leading her into the room from the doorway. Then Luet was with her and brought her to sit on the rumpled bed, and now Hushidh could let out her sobs as her sister held her. She was vaguely aware of Nafai moving through the room; he closed the door, then found clothing enough for himself and Luet that they didn't need to be embarrassed when Hushidh stopped crying and came to herself.

"I'm sorry, I'm so sorry," Hushidh said again and again as she wept.

"No, please, it's all right," said Luet.

"Your wedding night, I never would have . . . but I dreamed, it was so terrible—"

"It's all right, Shuya," said Nafai. "Only I wish you could cry a little softer, because if anybody hears you they're going to think it's Luet sobbing her heart out on her wedding night and then who knows what they'll think of me." He paused. "Of course, come to think of it, maybe you should cry a little louder."

There was laughter and calm in Nafai's voice, and Luet also laughed a little at his jest. It was what Hushidh needed, to take away her terror: She could think of Luet and Nafai instead of her dream.

"No one has ever done anything as wretched as this," said Hushidh, miserable and ashamed and yet so deeply relieved. "Bursting in on my own sister's wedding night."

"It's not as if you interrupted anything," said Nafai, and then he and Luet both burst into laughter—no, *giggling* was what it was. Like little children with a ridiculous secret.

"I'm sorry to laugh when you're so unhappy," said Luet, "but you have to understand. We were both so bad at it." They both burst into giggles again.

"It's an acquired skill," said Nafai. "Which we haven't acquired."

Hushidh felt herself enfolded by their laughter, included in the calm that they created between them. It was unthinkable, that a young husband and his bride, interrupted in their first night together, should so willingly include and comfort an intruding sister; yet that was who they were, Lutya and her Nyef. She felt herself filled with love and gratitude for them, and it spilled out in tears, but glad ones, not the desperate tears born of loneliness and terror in the night.

"I wasn't weeping for myself," she said—for now she could speak. "I *was* jealous and lonely, I admit it, but the Oversoul sent me a kind dream, a good one, and it showed me and . . . my husband, and our children . . ." Then she had a thought that had not occurred to her before. "Nafai, I know that I am meant for Issib. But I have to ask—he *is* . . . capable, isn't he?"

"Shuya, he could hardly be *less* capable than I was tonight."

Luet playfully slapped at Nafai's hand. "She's asking a real question, Nafai."

"He's as much a virgin as I am," said Nafai, "and away from the city he has scant use of his hands. But he isn't paralyzed, and his . . . involuntary responses, well, *respond*"

"Then the dream *was* true," said Hushidh. "Or it can be, anyway. I dreamed of my children. With Issib. That could be true, couldn't it?"

"If you want it to be," said Nafai. "If you're willing to accept him. He's the best of us, Shuya, I promise you that. The smartest and the kindest and the wisest."

"You didn't tell me that," said Luet. "You told me *you* were the best."

Nafai only grinned at her with stupid joy.

Hushidh felt better now, and also knew that it wasn't right for her to remain between them like this; she had received all that she could hope for from her sister, and now she could return to her room and sleep alone. The shadow of the evil dream had passed from her. "Thank you both," she whispered. "I will never forget how kind you were to me tonight." And she arose from the edge of the bed and started for the door.

"Don't go," said Nafai.

"I must sleep now," said Hushidh.

"Not until you tell us your dream," he said. "We need to hear it. Not the sweet dream, but the one that made you so afraid."

"He's right," said Luet. "It may be our wedding night, but the whole world is dark around us and we must know everything the Oversoul says to any of us."

"In the morning," said Hushidh.

"Do you think that we can sleep, wondering what terrible dream could strike so hard at our sister?" said Nafai.

Even though Hushidh knew how carefully he had chosen his words, she was grateful for the good and loving impulse behind them. In his heart he might very well fear or resent her close connection with his new wife, but instead of trying to resist that closeness or drive them apart, Nafai was deliberately working to include himself in their sisterhood, and include Hushidh in the closeness of their marriage. It was a generous thing to do, on this night of all nights, when it must have seemed to him that his worst fears about Hushidh were true, what with her plunging into their bridal chamber sobbing her eyes out in the middle of the night! If he was willing to try so hard, could she do any less than accept the relationship he wanted to create? She was a raveler, after all. She knew about binding people together, and was glad to help him tie this knot.

So she came back and they sat together on the bed, making a triangle with their crossed legs, knee to knee, as she told her dreams, from beginning to end. She spared herself nothing, confessing her own resentments at the beginning so that they could understand how glad she was for the Oversoul's assurances.

Twice they interrupted her with their astonishment. The first time was when she told of seeing Moozh, and how the Oversoul was ruling him through his very rejection of her. Nafai laughed in wonderment. "Moozh himself—the bloody-handed general of the Gorayni, running away from the Oversoul into the very path the Oversoul laid out for him. Who could have guessed it!"

The second time was when Hushidh told of the winged beasts that caught her and Issib as they fell. "Angels!" cried Luet.

At once Hushidh remembered the dream that Luet had told her days before. "Of course," Hushidh said. "That's why they came into my dream—because I remembered your telling me about those angels and the giant rats."

"Don't reach conclusions now," said Luet. "Tell us the rest of the dream."

So she did, and when it was done, they sat in silence, thinking for a while.

"The first dream, of you and Issib, I think that was from yourself," said Luet at last.

"I think so, too," said Hushidh, "and now that I remember your telling me that dream of hairy angels . . ."

"Quiet," said Luet. "Don't get ahead of the dream. After that first vision that came from your fears about marrying Issib, you begged the Oversoul to tell you her purpose, and she showed you that wonderful dream of the gold and silver cords binding people together—"

"Breeding us like cattle," said Nafai.

"Don't be irreverent," said Luet.

"Don't be too reverent," said Nafai. "I sincerely doubt that the Oversoul's original programming told it to start a breeding program among the humans of Harmony."

"I know that you're right," said Luet, "that the Oversoul is a computer established at the dawn of our world to watch over human beings and keep us from destroying ourselves, but still in my heart I feel the Oversoul as a woman, as the Mother of the Lake."

"Woman or machine, it's developed purposes of its own, and I'm not comfortable with this one," said Nafai. "Bringing us together to make a journey to Earth, I accept that, I'm glad of it—it's a glorious undertaking. But this breeding thing. My mother and father, coupling like a ewe and a ram brought together to keep the bloodlines pure . . ."

"They still love each other," said Luet.

He reached out a hand to her and cupped her fingers gently in his. "Lutya, they *do*, as we will love each other. But what we've done, we've done willingly, knowing the Oversoul's purpose and consenting to it, or so we thought. What other plots and plans does the Oversoul have in mind for us, which we'll only discover later?"

"The Oversoul told me this because I asked," said Hushidh. "If she *is* a computer, as you say—and I believe you,

I really do—then perhaps she simply can't tell us what we haven't yet asked to know."

"Then we must ask. We must know *exactly* what she—what *he*—what *it* is planning," said Nafai.

Luet smiled at his confusion but did not laugh. Hushidh was not his loyal wife; she could not suppress a small hoot.

"However we think of the Oversoul," Nafai said patiently, "we have to ask. What it means for Moozh to be here, for instance. Are we supposed to try to bring him out into the desert, too? Is that why the Oversoul brought him here? And these strange creatures, these angels and rats—what do they mean? The Oversoul has to tell us."

"I still think the rats and angels came because Lutya dreamed them and told me about them and there they were, ready to give a face to my fears," said Hushidh.

"But why did they come into Lutya's dream?" asked Nafai. "*She* didn't fear them."

"And the rats weren't terrible or dangerous in my dream," said Luet. "They were just—themselves. Living their lives. They had nothing to do with human beings in my dream."

"Let's stop guessing," said Nafai, "and ask the Oversoul."

They had never done this before. Men and women did not pray together in the rituals of Basilica—the men prayed with blood and water in their temple, or in their private places, and the women prayed in water at the lake, or in *their* private places. So they were shy and uncertain. Nafai impulsively reached out his hands to Hushidh and Luet, and they took his hands and joined to each other as well.

"I speak to the Oversoul silently," said Nafai. "In my mind."

"I, too," said Luet, "but sometimes aloud, don't *you?*"

"The same with me," said Hushidh. "Luet, speak for us all."

Luet shook her head. "It was you who saw the dream tonight, Hushidh. It was you the Oversoul was speaking to."

Hushidh shuddered in spite of herself. "What if the bad dream comes back to me?"

"What does it matter which of us speaks?" said Nafai, "as long as we ask the same questions in our hearts? Father and Issib and I speak to the Oversoul easily, when we have the Index with us, asking questions and getting answers as if we spoke with the computer at school. We'll do the same here."

"We don't have the Index," Luet pointed out.

"No, but we are bound to the Oversoul with threads of gold and silver," said Nafai, glancing at Hushidh. "That should be enough, shouldn't it?"

"Speak for us then, Luet," said Hushidh.

So Luet spoke their questions, and then spoke aloud her own worries, and those Nafai had expressed, and the terror Hushidh had experienced. It was to that question that the first answer came.

I don't know, said the Oversoul.

Luet fell silent, startled.

"Did you hear what I heard?" asked Nafai.

Since no one knew what Nafai had heard, no one could answer. Until Hushidh dared to say the thing *she* had heard inside her mind. "She doesn't know," whispered Hushidh.

Nafai gripped their hands tighter, and spoke to the Oversoul, his voice now and not Luet's speaking for them all. "What don't you know?"

I sent the dream of the gold and silver threads, said the Oversoul. I sent the dream of Issib and the children at the door of the tent. But I never meant you to see the general. I never showed you the general.

"And the . . . the rats?" asked Hushidh.

"And the angels?" asked Luet.

I don't know where they came from or what they mean.

"So," said Hushidh. "It was just a strange chance dream in your mind, Luet. And then because you told your dream it became a memory in *my* mind, and that's it."

No!

It was as if the Oversoul had shouted into her mind, and Hushidh shuddered under the force of it.

"What, then!" cried Hushidh. "If you don't know where it came from, how do you know that it isn't just an ordinary frightening dream?"

Because the general had it too.

They looked at each other in amazement.

"General *Moozh?*"

To Hushidh's mind there came a fleeting image of a man with a flying creature on his shoulder, and a giant rat clinging to his leg, and many people—humans, rats, and angels—approaching, touching the three of them, worshipping. As quickly as it came, the image receded.

"The general saw this dream?" asked Hushidh.

He saw it. Weeks ago. Before any of you dreamed of these creatures.

"Three of us then," said Luet. "Three of us, and we have never met the general, and he has never met us, and yet we all dreamed of these creatures. He saw worship, and I saw art, and you saw war, Hushidh, war and salvation."

"If it didn't come from you, Oversoul," said Nafai, urgently pressing the question, holding tightly to their hands. "If it didn't come from you, then where could such a dream have come from?"

I don't know.

"Is there some other computer?" asked Hushidh.

Not here. Not in Harmony.

"Maybe you just didn't know about it," suggested Nafai.

I would have known.

"Then why are we having these dreams?" demanded Nafai.

They waited, and there was no answer. And then there *was* an answer, but one that they did not wish for.

I'm afraid, said the Oversoul.

Hushidh felt the fear return to her own heart, and she gripped her sister's hand more tightly, and Nafai's hand as well. "I hate this," said Hushidh. "I hate it. I didn't want to know it."

I'm afraid, said the Oversoul, as clear as speech in Hushidh's mind—and, she hoped, in the minds of the other two as well. I'm afraid, for fear is the name I have for uncertainty, for impossibility that is nevertheless real. Yet I also have a hope, for that is another name for the impossible that might be real. I have a hope that what you have been given is from the Keeper of Earth. That across these many light-years the Keeper of Earth is reaching out to us.

"Who is the Keeper of Earth?" asked Hushidh.

"The Oversoul has mentioned it before," said Nafai. "It's never been clear, but I think it's a computer that was set up as guardian of Earth when our ancestors left forty million years ago."

Not a computer, said the Oversoul.

"What is it then?" asked Nafai.

Not a machine.

"What, then?"

Alive.

"What could possibly be alive after all these years?"

The Keeper of Earth. Calling to us. Calling to you. Maybe my desire to bring you back to Earth is also a dream from the Keeper. I have also been confused, and did not know what I should do, and then ideas came into my mind. I thought they were the result of the randomizer routines. I thought they were from my programming. But if you and Moozh can dream strange dreams of creatures never known in this world, can't I also be given thoughts that were never programmed into me, that do not come from anything in this world?

They had no answer for the Oversoul's question.

"I don't know about you," said Hushidh, "but I was definitely counting on the Oversoul to be in charge of everything, and I really don't like the idea of her not knowing what's going on."

"Earth is calling to us," said Nafai. "Don't you see? Earth is calling to us. Calling the Oversoul, but not *just* the Oversoul. *Us.* Or you two, anyway, and Moozh. Calling you to come home to Earth."

Not Moozh, said the Oversoul.

"How do you know, not Moozh?" asked Hushidh. "If you don't know why or how or even *whether* the Keeper of Earth gave us these dreams, then how do you know that Moozh is not supposed to come out onto the desert with us?"

Not Moozh, said the Oversoul. Leave Moozh alone.

"If you didn't mean Moozh to join us, then why did you bring him here?" asked Nafai.

I brought him here, but not for you.

"He has the same gold and silver threads as we do," said Luet. "And the Keeper of Earth has spoken to him."

I brought him here to destroy Basilica.

"That tears it," said Nafai. "That really tears it. The Oversoul has one idea. The Keeper of Earth has another. And what are *we* supposed to do?"

Leave Moozh alone. Don't touch him. He's on his own path.

"Right," said Nafai. "A minute ago you tell us that you don't know what's going on, and now we're supposed to take your word for it that Moozh isn't part of what we're doing! We're not puppets, Oversoul! Do you understand me? If you don't know what's going on, then why should we follow your orders in this? How do you know you're right, and we're wrong?"

I *don't* know.

"Then how do you know I shouldn't go to him and ask him to come with us?"

Because he's dangerous and terrible and he might use you and destroy you and I can't stop him if he decides to do it.

"Don't go," said Luet.

"He's one of *us*," said Nafai. "If our purpose is a good one in the first place, then it's a good one *because* there's something right about *us*, the people that the Oversoul has bred, going back to Earth. If it's good it's good because the Keeper of Earth is calling us."

"Whatever sent me that terrible dream," said Hushidh, "I don't know if it's good or not."

"Maybe the dream was a warning," said Nafai. "Maybe there's some danger we'll face, and the dream was warning you."

"Or maybe the dream was a warning for you to stay away from Moozh," said Luet.

"How in the world could the dream possibly mean *that?*" he asked. He was shucking off the odd clothing he had thrown on in a hurry a short while before, and dressing seriously now, dressing to go out into the city.

"Because that's what I want it to mean," said Luet, and suddenly she was crying. "You've only been my husband for half a night, and suddenly you want to go to a man that the Oversoul says is dangerous and terrible, and for what? To invite him to come out into the desert? To invite him to give up his armies and his kingdoms and his blood and violence and travel with us in the desert on a journey that will somehow end with us on Earth? He'll kill you, Nafai! Or imprison you and keep you from coming with us. I'll *lose you*."

"You won't," said Nafai. "The Oversoul will protect me."

"The Oversoul warned you not to go. If you disobey . . ."

"The Oversoul won't punish me because the Oversoul doesn't even know that I'm not right. The Oversoul will bring me back to you because the Oversoul wants me with you almost as much as *I* want me with you."

I don't know if I can protect you.

"Yes, well, there's an awful lot that you don't know," said Nafai. "I think you've made that clear to us tonight. You're a very powerful computer and you have the best intentions in the world, but you don't know what's right any more than I do. You don't know whether all your plans for Moozh might have been influenced by the Keeper of Earth, do you—you don't know whether the *Keeper's* plan is for me to do exactly what I'm doing, and let your plot to destroy Basilica go hang. To *destroy Basilica,* of all things! It's your chosen city, isn't it? You've brought together all the people who are closest to you in this one place, and you want to destroy it?"

I brought them together to create *you,* foolish children. Now I'll destroy it to spread my people out again throughout the world. So that whatever influence I have left in this world will reach into every land and nation. What is the city of Basilica, compared to the world?

"The last time you talked that way, I killed a man," said Nafai.

"Please," said Luet. "Stay with me."

"Or let me come with you," said Hushidh.

"Not a chance," said Nafai. "And Lutya, I *will* come back to you. Because the Oversoul *will* protect me."

I don't know if I can.

"Then do your best," said Nafai. With that he was out the door and gone.

"They'll arrest him the minute he tries to go anywhere in the street," said Hushidh.

"I know," said Luet. "And I understand why he's doing it, and it's a brave thing to do, and I even think it's the right thing to do, and I *don't want him to do it!*"

Luet wept, and now it was Hushidh's turn to hold and comfort *her.* What a dance this has been tonight, she thought. What a wedding night for you, what a night of dreams for me. And now, what morning will it be? You could be left a widow without even his child inside you. Or—why not?—the great general Moozh might come with Nafai, renounce his army, and disappear with us into the desert. Anything could happen. Anything at all.

IN GABALLUFIX'S HOUSE, AND NOT IN A DREAM

Moozh spread out his map of the Western Shore on Gaballufix's table, and let his mind explore the shape of things. The Cities of the Plain and Seggidugu were spread out before him like a banquet. It was hard to guess which way to move. By now they all must have heard that a Gorayni army held the gates of Basilica. No doubt the hotheads in Seggidugu were urging a quick and brutal response, but they would not prevail—the northern border of Seggidugu was too close to the main Gorayni armies in Khlam and Ulye. It would take so many soldiers to take Basilica, even if they knew there were only a thousand Gorayni to defend it, that it would leave Seggidugu vulnerable to counterstrike.

Indeed, many faint hearts in Seggidugu would already be wondering if it might not be best to come before the Imperator now, as supplicants, begging him to take their nation under his beneficent protection. But Moozh was sure that these would have no more luck than the hotheads. Instead the coolest minds, the most careful men would prevail. They would wait and see. And that was what Moozh was counting on.

In the Cities of the Plain, there was no doubt already a movement afoot to revive the old Defense League, which had driven off the Seggidugu invaders nine times. But that was more than a thousand years ago, when the Seggidugu had first stormed over the mountains from the desert; it was unlikely that more than a few of the cities would unite, and even in supposed unity they would be quarreling and stealing from each other and weakening each other more than if each stood alone.

What was in Moozh's power to make happen? At this moment, if he sent a delegation with a sternly worded demand for the surrender of the nearest cities, they would no doubt receive quick compliance. But the refugees would gout out of those cities like blood from a heart-wound, and the other Cities of the Plain *would* unite then. They might even ask Seggidugu to lead them, and in that case Seggidugu might well act.

Instead he might demand Seggidugu's surrender. If they complied, then the Cities of the Plain would all roll over and play dead. But it was too big a gamble, if he could find a better way. He really *could* force the surrender of any one or even two of the Cities of the Plain, but he had far too few men—and far too tenuous a link with the main Gorayni armies—to make his ultimatum stick if Seggidugu decided to defy him. Great wars had been avoided, great empires had been created by just such dangerous bluffs, and Moozh was not afraid to take the chance if there was no better way.

And if there *was* a better way, he would have to find it soon. By now the Imperator himself would know that both Plod and the intercessor assigned to Moozh's army had been killed—by a Basilican assassin, of course, but no one had been able to question him because Moozh had killed the man with his own hands. Then Moozh took off with a thousand men and no one knew where he was. That bit of news would strike terror into the heart of the Imperator, for he knew quite well how fragile the power of a ruler is, when his best generals become too popular. The Imperator would be wondering how many of his own men would flock to Moozh if he raised a flag of rebellion in the mountains; and how many others, too loyal to defect, would nevertheless be terrified to fight against the greatest general of the Gorayni. All these fears would prompt the Imperator to put his armies in motion, and to have them moving south and west, knowing Khlam and Ulye.

All well and good . . . that would frighten the Seggidugu even more, and increase the chance that bluffing them into submission might work. And these army movements would *not* get far before the next news reached the Imperator— that Moozh's bold movement had succeeded brilliantly, that the fabled city of Basilica was now in Gorayni hands.

Moozh smiled in pleasure at the thought of how that news would strike terror in the hearts of all the courtiers who had been whispering to the Imperator that Moozh was a traitor. A traitor? A man who has the wit and courage to take a city with a thousand men? To march past two powerful enemy kingdoms and take a mountain fortress perched in their rear? What kind of traitor is this? the Imperator would ask.

But still, he would be afraid, for boldness in his generals always terrified him. Especially boldness in Vozmuzhalnoy Vozmozhno. So the Imperator would send him a legate or two—certainly an intercessor, probably a new friend, and also a couple of close and trusted family members. They would not have the authority to overrule Moozh—the Gorayni would never have conquered so many kingdoms if the imperators had allowed their underlings to countermand the orders of generals in the field. But they *would* have the ability to interfere, to question, to protest, to demand explanations, and to send word back to the Imperator of anything they didn't like.

When would these legates arrive? They would have to take the same desert route that Moozh had taken with his men. But now that road would be closely watched by Seggidugu and Izmennik, so there would have to be a ponderous bodyguard, and supply wagons, and many scouts and tents and all sorts of livestock. Thus the legates would have neither the desire nor the ability to move even half as quickly as Moozh's army had moved. So it would be at least a week before they arrived, probably longer. But when they came, they would have many soldiers—perhaps as many as Moozh had already brought—and these soldiers would almost certainly not be men who had fought under Moozh, men he had trained, men he could count on.

A week. Moozh had at least a week in which to set in motion the course he was going to follow. He could try his bluff against Seggidugu now, and risk deep humiliation if he was defied—the Cities of the Plain would certainly unite against him then, and he'd soon be defending Basilica from a siege. This would not lead to his ouster as general, but it would take the luster off his name, and it would put him back under the thumb of the Imperator. These last few days had been so delicious, not to have to play the games of deception and subterfuge that consumed half his life when he had to deal with a friend appointed by the Imperator, not to mention some career-advancing, meddlesome intercessor. Moozh had killed relatively few people with his own hands, but he certainly relished the memory of those deaths—the surprise on their faces, the exquisite relief that Moozh felt then. Even the necessity of killing that good soldier of Basilica, Smelost, even *that* did not take away the sheer joy of his new freedom.

Am I ready?

Am I ready to make the move of my life, to strike in vegeance against the Imperator in the name of Pravo Gollossa? To risk all on my ability to unite Basilica, Seggidugu, and the Cities of the Plain, along with every Gorayni soldier who will follow me and whatever support we can eke out from Potokgavan?

And if I am not ready for that, am I ready to set my neck back into the collar that the Imperator forces all his generals to wear? Am I ready to bow to the will of God's incarnation here on Harmony? Am I ready to wait years, decades for an opportunity that may never be closer than it is right now?

He knew the answer even as he asked the question. Somehow he must turn this week, this day, this hour into his opportunity, his chance to bring down the Gorayni and replace their cruel and brutal empire with a generous and democratic one, led by the Sotchitsiya, whose vengeance was long delayed but not one whit less sure for all that. Here Moozh stood with an army—a small one, but *his*—in the city that symbolized all that was weak and effete and cringing in the world. I longed to destroy you, Basilica, but what if instead I make you strong? What if I make you the center of the world—but a world ruled by men of power, not these weak and cringing women, these politicians and gossips and actors and singers. What if the greatest story told about Basilica was not that it was the city of women, but that it was the city of the Sotchitsiya ascendancy?

Basilica, you city of women, your husband is here for you, to master you and teach you the domestic arts that you have so long forgotten.

Moozh looked again at Bitanke's list of names. If he was looking for someone to rule Basilica in the name of the Imperator, then he would have to choose a man as consul: One of Wetchik's sons, if they could be found, or perhaps Rashgallivak himself, or some weaker man who might be propped up by Bitanke.

But if Moozh wanted to unite Basilica and the Cities of the Plain and Seggidugu as well against the Imperator, then what he needed was to become a citizen of Basilica by marriage, and to gain a place for himself at the head of the city; he needed, not a consul, but a bride.

So the names that intrigued him most were the two girls, the waterseer and the raveler. They were young— young enough that it would offend many if he married either of them, especially the waterseer—thirteen! And yet these two had the right kind of prestige, the kind that could include him in its aura if he married one or the other of them. Moozh, the great general of the Gorayni, marrying one of the most holy women of Basilica—humbling himself to enter the city as a mere husband instead of a conqueror. It would win their hearts, not just those who were already grateful to him for the peace he had imposed, but all of them, for they would see that he desired, not to conquer them, but to lead them to greatness.

With the raveler or the waterseer as his wife, Moozh would not longer merely *hold* Basilica. He would *be* Basilica, and instead of issuing ultimata to the southern kingdoms and cities of the Western Shore, he would issue a battlecry. He would arrest the spies of Potokgavan and send them home to their lazy waterlogged empire with presents and promises. And the word would sweep like wildfire through the north: Vozmuzhalnoy Vozmozhno has declared himself the new incarnation, the true Imperator. He calls upon all loyal soldiers of God to come south to him, or to rise up against the usurper where they are! In the meantime the word would be whispered in Pravo Gollossa: The Sotchitsiya will rule. Rise up and take what has belonged to you for all these years!

In the chaos that would result in the northlands, Moozh would march northward, gathering allies with him as he went. The Gorayni armies would retreat before him; the natives of the conquered nations would welcome him as their liberator. He would march until the Gorayni were thrown back into their own lands, and there he would stop—for one long winter in Pravo Gollossa, where he would train his motley army and weld it into a worthy fighting force. Then in the spring of next year he would move into the hill-fast land of the Gorayni and utterly destroy their capacity to rule. Every man of fighting age would have his thumbs cut off, so he could never wield either sword or bow, and with every thumb that was sheared off, the Gorayni would understand again the pain of the tongueless Sotchitsiya.

Let God try to stop him now!

But he knew that God would not. In these last few days, ever since he defied God and came south to seize Basilica, God had not tried to move against him, had not tried to block him in any way. He had half expected that God would make him forget these plans that he was laying out. But God must know now that it wouldn't matter if he did, for the plans were so true and obvious that Moozh would simply think of them again—and again and again, if it were necessary.

For me will be the overthrow of the Gorayni and the uniting of the Western Shore. For my son will be the conquest of Potokgavan, the civilizing of the northern forest tribes, the subduing of the northshore pirates. My son, and the son of my wife.

Which of you will it be? The waterseer was the more powerful of the two, the one with more prestige; but she was younger, too young, really. There would be a danger of people pitying her for such a marriage, unless Moozh could truly persuade her to come of her own free will.

The other one, though, the raveler, even though her prestige was less, would still do, and she was sixteen. Sixteen, a good age for a political marriage, for she had no former husbands and, if Bitanke was right, not even any lovers that anyone had heard about. And some of the prestige of the waterseer would still come to the marriage, because the raveler was her sister, and Moozh would see to it that the waterseer was well treated—and closely tied to the new dynastic house that Moozh would soon establish.

It was a very attractive plan. All that remained now was for Moozh to be sure—sure enough to act. Sure enough to go to Rasa's house and maneuver for the hand of one of these girls in marriage.

A single knock on the door. Moozh rapped once on the table. The door opened.

"Sir," said the soldier. "We have made an interesting arrest on the street in front of Lady Rasa's house."

Moozh looked up from the map on the table and waited for the rest of the message.

"Lady Rasa's youngest son. The one who killed Gaballufix."

"He escaped into the desert," said Moozh. "Are you sure it's not an imposter?"

"Quite possible," said the soldier. "But he did walk out of Rasa's house and straight up to the sergeant in charge and announce who he was and that he needed to speak to you at once about matters that would determine your future and the future of Basilica."

"Ah," said Moozh.

"So he's either the boy with balls of brass who cut off Gaballufix's head and wore his clothes out of the city, or he's a madman with a deathwish."

"Or both," said Moozh. "Bring him to me, and be prepared with an escort of four soldiers to take him directly back to Lady Rasa's house afterward. If I slap his face when you open the door to take him back, then you will kill him on Lady Rasa's front porch. If I smile at him, then you will treat him with courtesy and honor. Otherwise, he is under arrest and will not be permitted to leave the house again."

The soldier left the door open behind him. Moozh sat back in his chair and waited. Interesting, he thought, that I don't have to search for the key players in this city's bloody games. They all come to me, one by one. Nafai was supposed to be safely in the desert, beyond my reach—but he was in Lady Rasa's house all the time. What other surprises have we pent up in her house? The other sons? How had Bitanke summed them up . . . Elemak, the sharp and dangerous caravanner; Mebbekew, the walking penis; Issib, the brilliant cripple. Or why not Wetchik, the visionary plant-seller himself? They might all be waiting within Lady Rasa's walls for Moozh to decide how to use them.

Was it possible—barely possible—that God really *had* decided to favor Moozh's cause? That instead of opposing him, God might now be aiding Moozh, bringing into his hands every tool he needed to accomplish his purpose?

I am certainly not the incarnation of anything but myself, thought Moozh; I have no desire to play at holiness, the way the Imperator does. But if God is willing at long last to let me have some help in my cause, I will not refuse it. Perhaps in God's heart the hour of the Sotchitsiya has arrived.

NAFAI WAS AFRAID, but also he was not afraid. It was the strangest feeling. As if there was a terrified animal inside him, aghast that he was walking into a place where death was only a word away, and yet Nafai himself, that part of him that *was* himself and not the animal, was simply fascinated to find out what he might say, and whether he would meet Moozh, and what would happen next. It was not that he was unaware of the perpetual immanence of death among the Gorayni; rather he had simply decided, at some deep level of his mind, that personal survival was an irrelevant issue.

The soldiers had seemed, if anything, more perplexed

than alarmed at his accosting them on the street with the words, "Take me to the general. I'm Wetchik's son Nafai, and I killed Gaballufix." With those words he put his very life into this conversation, since Moozh now had witnesses of his confession of a crime that could lead to his execution; Moozh wouldn't even have to fabricate a pretext to have him killed if he wanted to.

Gaballufix's house had not changed, and yet it was entirely changed. None of the wall hangings, none of the furniture had been altered. All the lazy opulence was still intact, the plushness, the overdecoration in detail, the bold colors. And yet instead of being overpowering, the effect of all this ostentation was rather pathetic, for the simple discipline and brisk, unhesitating obedience of the Gorayni soldiers had the effect of diminishing everything around them. Gaballufix had chosen these furnishings to intimidate his visitors, to overawe them; now they looked weak, effete, as if the person who bought them had been frightened that people might see how weak his soul was, and so he had to hide it behind this barricade of bright colors and gold trim.

Real power, Nafai realized, does not demonstrate itself in anything that can be purchased for mere money. Money only buys the illusion of power. Real power is in the force of will—will strong enough that others bend to it for its own sake, and follow it willingly. Power that is won through deception will evaporate under the hot light of truth, as Rashgallivak had found; but real power grows stronger the more closely you look at it, even when it resides only in a single person, without armies, without servants, without friends, but with an indomitable will.

Such a man waited for him, sitting at a table behind an open door. Nafai knew this room. It was here that he and his brothers had faced Gaballufix, here that Nafai had blurted out some word or other that destroyed Elemak's delicate negotiations for the Index. Not that Gaballufix ever intended anything but to cheat them. The fact remained that Nafai had spoken carelessly, not realizing that Elemak, the sharp businessman, was holding back key information.

For a moment Nafai resolved inside himself to be more careful now, to hold back information as Elemak would have done, to be canny in this conversation.

Then General Moozh looked up and Nafai looked into his eyes and saw a deep well of rage and suffering and pride and, at the bottom of that well, a fierce intelligence that would see through all sham.

Is this what Moozh really is? Have I seen him true?

And in his heart, the Oversoul whispered, I have shown him to you as he truly is.

Then I can't lie to this man, thought Nafai. Which is just as well, because I'm not good at lying. I don't have the skill for it. I can't maintain the deep self-deception that successful lying requires. The truth keeps rising to the surface in my mind, and so I confess myself in every word and glance and gesture.

Besides, I didn't come here to play some game, to try my wits in some contest with General Vozmuzhalnoy Vozmozhno. I came here to give him the chance to join with us in our journey back to Earth. How could he do that if I tell him anything less than the truth?

"Nafai," said Moozh. "Please sit down."

Nafai sat down. He noticed that a map was spread out on the table before the general. The Western Shore. Somewhere on that map, deep in the southwest corner, was the stream where Father and Issib and Zdorab waited in their tents, listening to a troop of baboons hooting and barking at each other. Is the Oversoul showing Father what I'm doing now? Does Issib have the Index, and is he asking where I am?

"I assume that you didn't turn yourself in because your conscience overwhelmed you and you wanted to be put on trial for the murder of Gaballufix in order to expunge your guilt."

"No sir," said Nafai. "I was married last night. I have no desire to be imprisoned or tried or killed."

"Married last night? And out on the street confessing felonies before dawn? My boy, I fear you have not married well, if your wife can't hold you for even one night."

"I came because of a dream," said Nafai.

"Ah— *your* dream, or your bride's?"

"*Your* dream, sir."

Moozh waited, expressionless.

"I believe you dreamed once of a man with a hairy flying creature on his shoulder, and a giant rat clinging to his leg, and men and rats and angels came and worshipped them, all three of them, touching them with . . ."

But Nafai did not go on, for Moozh had risen to his feet and was boring into him with those dangerous, agonizing eyes. "I told this to Plod, and he reported it to the intercessor, and so it was known," said Moozh. "And the fact that you know it tells me that you have been in contact with someone from the Imperator's court. So stop this pretense and tell me the truth!"

"Sir, I don't know who Plod or the intercessor might be, and your dream wasn't told to me by anyone from the Imperator's court. I heard it from the Oversoul. Do you think the Oversoul doesn't know your dreams?"

Moozh sat back down, but his whole manner had changed. The certainty, the easy confidence was gone.

"Are you the form that God has taken now? Are you the incarnation?"

"Me?" asked Nafai. "You see what I am—I'm a fourteen-year-old boy. Maybe a little big for my age."

"A little young to be married."

"But not too young to have spoken to the Oversoul."

"Many in this city make a career of speaking to the Oversoul. You, however, God apparently answers."

"There's nothing mystical about it, sir. The Oversoul is a computer—a powerful one, a self-renewing one. Our ancestors set it in place forty million years ago, when they first reached the planet Harmony as refugees from the destruction of Earth. They genetically altered themselves and all their children—to us, all these generations later—to be responsive, at the deepest levels in the brain, to impulses from the Oversoul. Then they programmed the computer to block us from any train of thought, any plan of action that would lead to high technology or rapid communications or fast transportation, so that the world would remain a vast and unknowable place to us, and wars would remain a local affair."

"Until me," said Moozh.

"Your conquests have indeed ranged far beyond the area that the Oversoul would normally allow."

"Because I am not a slave to God," said Moozh. "Whatever power God—or, if you're right, this computer—whatever power it might have over other men is weaker in me, and I have withstood it and overwhelmed it. I am here today because I am too strong for God."

"Yes, he told us that you thought so," said Nafai. "But actually the influence of the Oversoul is even stronger in you than in most people. Probably about as strong as it is in me. If it was appropriate, if you opened yourself to its voice, the Oversoul could talk to you and you wouldn't need me to tell you what I'm here to tell you about."

"If the Oversoul told you that it is *stronger* in me than in most people, then your computer is a liar," said Moozh.

"You have to understand—the Oversoul isn't really concerned with individual people's lives, except insofar as it's been running some kind of breeding program to try to create people like me—and you, of course. I didn't like it when I learned about it, but it's the reason I'm alive, or at least the reason my parents were brought together. The Oversoul manipulates people. That's its job. It has manipulated you almost constantly."

"I'm aware that it has tried. I call it God, you call it the Oversoul, but it has not controlled me."

"As soon as it became aware that you intended to resist it, it simply turned things backward," said Nafai. "Whatever it wanted you to do, it forbade you to do. Then it made sure you remembered to do it and you obeyed almost perfectly."

"A lie," whispered Moozh.

It made Nafai afraid, to see how emotions were seizing this man. The general clearly was not accustomed to feelings he could not control; Nafai wondered if perhaps he ought to let him calm down before proceeding. "Are you all right?" Nafai asked.

"Go on," said Moozh acidly. "I can hear anything that dead men say."

That was such a weak thing to say that Nafai was disgusted. "Oh, am I supposed to change my story because you threaten me with death?" he asked. "If I was afraid to die, do you think I would have come here?"

Nafai could see a change come over Moozh. As if he visibly reined himself in. "I apologize," said Moozh. "For a moment I behaved like the kind of man I most despise. Blustering a threat in order to change the message of a messenger who believes, at least, that he is telling me the truth. But I can assure you, whatever I might feel, if you die today it will not be because of any words you might say. Please go on."

"You must understand," said Nafai, "if the Oversoul really wants you to forget something, you *will* forget it. My brother Issib and I thought we were very clever, forcing our way through its barriers. But we didn't really force it. We simply became more trouble than it was worth to resist us. The Oversoul would rather have us go along with its plans knowingly than to have to control us and manipulate us. That's why I'm here. Because my wife's sister saw in a dream how strong your link with the Oversoul is, and how you waste yourself in a vain effort to resist. I came to tell you that the only way to break free of its control is to embrace its plan."

"The way to win is to surrender?" Moozh asked wryly.

"The way to be *free* is to stop resisting and start talking," said Nafai. "The Oversoul is the servant of humanity, not its master. It can be persuaded. It will listen. Sometimes it needs our help. General, *we* need you, if you'll only come with us."

"Come with you?"

"My father was called out to the desert as the first step in a great journey."

"Your father was driven out onto the desert by the machinations of Gaballufix. I have spoken with Rashgallivak, and I can't be deceived."

"Do you honestly believe that speaking with Rashgallivak is a way to ensure that you *won't* be deceived?"

"I would know if he lied to me."

"But what if he believed what he told you, and yet it still wasn't true?"

Moozh waited, unspeaking.

"I tell you that, regardless of the immediate impetus that caused our departure at a certain hour of a certain day, it was the Oversoul's purpose to get Father and me and my brothers out into the desert, as the first step to a journey."

"And yet here you are in the city."

"I told you," said Nafai. "I was married last night. So were my brothers."

"Elemak and Mebbekew and Issib."

Nafai was surprised and a little frightened that Moozh knew so much about them. But he had set out to tell the truth, and tell it he would. "Issib is with Father. He wanted to come. I wanted him to come. But Elemak wouldn't have it, and Father went along. We came for wives. And for Father's wife. When we arrived, Mother laughed and said that she would never go out onto the desert, no matter what mad project Wetchik had in mind. But then you put her under arrest and spread those rumors about her. In effect, you cut her off from Basilica, and now she understands that there's nothing for her here and so she, too, will go with us into the desert."

"You're saying that what I did was all part of the Oversoul's plan to get your mother to join her husband in a tent?"

"I'm saying that your purposes were bent to serve the Oversoul's plans. They always will be, General. They always have been."

"But what if I refuse to allow your mother to leave her house? What if I keep you and your brothers and your wives under arrest here? What if I send soldiers to stop Shedemei from gathering up seeds and embryos for your journey?"

Nafai was stunned. He knew about Shedemei? Impossible—she would never have told anyone. What was this Moozh capable of, if he could come into a strange city and be so aware of things so quickly that he could realize that Shedemei's gathering of seeds had something to do with Wetchik's exile?

"You see," said Moozh. "The Oversoul does not have power where *I* rule."

"You can keep us under arrest," said Nafai. "But when the Oversoul determines that it's time for us to go, you will find that you have a compelling reason to let us go, and so you'll let us go."

"If the Oversoul wants you to go, my boy, you may be sure that you will *not* go."

"You don't understand. I haven't told you the most important part. Whatever this war is that you think you're having with whatever version of the Oversoul it is that you call God, what matters is that dream you had. Of the flying beasts, and the giant rats."

Moozh waited, but again Nafai could see that he was deeply disturbed.

"The Oversoul didn't send that dream. The Oversoul didn't understand it."

"So. Then it was a meaningless dream, a common sleeping dream."

"Not at all. Because my wife also dreamed of those same creatures, and so did her sister. All three of you, and these were not common dreams. They felt important to all of you. You knew that they had a meaning. Yet they didn't come from the Oversoul."

Again Moozh waited.

"It has been forty million years since human beings abandoned the Earth they had almost completely destroyed," said Nafai. "There has been time enough for Earth to heal itself. For there to be life there again. For there to be a place for humankind. Many species were lost—that's why Shedemei is gathering seeds and embryos for our journey. We are the ones that have the gift of speaking easily with the Oversoul. We are the ones who have been gathered together, here in Basilica, this day, this hour, so that we can go forth on a journey that will lead us back to Earth."

"Apart from the fact that Earth, if it exists, is a planet orbiting a faraway star, to which even birds can't fly," said Moozh, "you have still said nothing about what this journey might have to do with my dream."

"We don't *know* this," said Nafai. "We only guess it, but the Oversoul also thinks it might be true. Somehow the

Keeper of Earth is calling us. Across all the lightyears between us and Earth, it has reached out to us and it's calling us back. For all we know, it even altered the programming of the Oversoul itself, telling it to gather us together. The Oversoul thought it knew why it was doing this, but it only recently learned the real reason. Just as you are only now learning the real reason for everything you've done in your life."

"A message in a dream, and it comes from someone thousands of lightyears away from here? Then the dream must have been sent thirty generations before I was born. Don't make me laugh, Nafai. You're far too bright to believe this. Doesn't it occur to you that maybe the Oversoul is manipulating *you?*"

Nafai considered this. "The Oversoul doesn't lie to me," he said.

"Yet you say that it has lied to me all along. So we can't pretend that the Oversoul is rigidly committed to truthfulness, can we?"

"But it doesn't lie to *me.*"

"How do you know?" asked Moozh.

"Because what it tells me . . . *feels* right."

"If it can make *me* forget things—and it can, it's happened so many times that . . ." His voice petered out as Moozh apparently decided not to delve into those memories. "If it can do *that,* why can't it also make *you,* as you say, 'feel right'?"

Nafai had no ready answer. He had not questioned his own certainty, and so he didn't know why Moozh's reasoning was false. "It's not just me," said Nafai, struggling to find a reason. "My wife also trusts the Oversoul. And her sister, too. They've had dreams and visions all their lives, and the Oversoul has never lied to them."

"Dreams and visions all their lives?" Moozh leaned forward on the table. "Whom, exactly, did you marry?"

"I thought I told you," said Nafai. "Luet. She's one of my mother's nieces in her teaching house."

"The waterseer," said Moozh.

"I'm not surprised that you've heard of her."

"She's thirteen years old," said Moozh.

"Too young, I know. But she was willing to do what the Oversoul asked of her, as was I."

"You think you're going to be able to take the waterseer away from Basilica on some insane journey into the desert in order to find an ancient legendary planet?" asked Moozh. "Even if *I* did nothing to stop you, do you think the people of this city would stand for it?"

"They will if the Oversoul helps us, and the Oversoul *will* help us."

"And your wife's sister, which of your brothers did *she* marry? Elemak?"

"She's going to marry Issib. He's waiting for us at my father's tent."

Moozh leaned back in his chair and chuckled merrily. "It's hard to see who has been controlling whom," he said. "According to *you,* the Oversoul has a whole set of plans that I'm a small part of. But the way it looks to me, God is setting things up so that everything plays into my hands. I thought before you came in here that it looked as though God had finally stopped being my enemy."

"The Oversoul was never your enemy," said Nafai. "It was *your* decision to make a contest of it."

Moozh got up from the table, walked around it, sat down beside Nafai, and took him by the hand. "My boy, this has been the most remarkable conversation of my life."

Mine, too, thought Nafai, but he was too astonished to say anything.

"I'm sure you're very earnest about your desire to make this journey, but I can assure you that you've been seriously misled. You're not leaving this city, and neither is your wife or her sister, and neither are any of the other people you plan to take along. You'll realize that sooner or later. If you realize it sooner—if you realize it *now*—then I have another plan for you that I think you'll like a little better than puttering around among the rocks and scorpions and sleeping in a tent."

Again, Nafai wanted to be able to explain to him why he *wanted* to follow the Oversoul. Why he knew that he was freely following the Oversoul, and perhaps the Keeper of Earth as well. Why he knew that the Oversoul wasn't lying to him or manipulating him or controlling him. But because he couldn't find the words or even the reasons, he remained silent.

"Your wife and her sister are the keys to everything. I'm not here to conquer Basilica, I'm here to win Basilica's loyalty. I've watched you now for an hour, I've listened to your voice, and I'll tell you, lad, you're a remarkable boy. So earnest. So *honest*. And eager, and you mean well, it's plain to anyone with half an eye that you mean no harm to anyone. And yet you're the one who killed Gaballufix, and so freed the city from a man who *would* have been tyrant, if he had lived another day or two. And it happens that you've just married the most prestigious figure in Basilica, the girl who commands the most universal love and respect and loyalty and hope in this city."

"I married her to serve the Oversoul."

"Please, keep saying that, I want everyone to believe that, and when you say it it's amazingly truthful-sounding. It will be a simple matter for me to spread this story about how the Oversoul commanded you to kill Gaballufix in order to save the city. And you can even bruit it about that the Oversoul brought *me* here, too, to save the city from the chaos that came after your wife's sister, the raveler, destroyed Rashgallivak's power. It's all such a neat little package, don't you see? You and Luet and Hushidh and me, sent by the Oversoul to save the city, to lead Basilica to greatness. We all have a mission from the Oversoul . . . it's a story that will make the Imperator's nonsense about being God incarnate look pathetic."

"Why would you do this?" asked Nafai. It made no sense to him, for Moozh to propose making Nafai look like a hero instead of a killer, for Moozh to want to link himself with three people he was keeping prisoner in Rasa's house. Unless . . .

"What do you think?" asked Moozh.

"I think you imagine you can set *me* up as tyrant of Basilica instead of Gaballufix."

"Not tyrant," said Moozh. "Consul. The city council would still be there, quarreling and arguing and doing nothing important as usual. You'd just handle the city guard and the foreign relations; you'd just control the gates and make sure that Basilica remained loyal to me."

"Do you think they wouldn't see through this and realize I was a puppet?"

"They would if I didn't become a citizen of Basilica myself, and your good friend and close kin. But if I become one of them, a *part* of them, if I become the general of the Basilican army and do all that I do in your name, then they won't care who is puppet to whom."

"Rebellion," said Nafai. "Against the Gorayni."

"Against the most cruel and corrupt monsters who ever walked on Harmony's poor face," said Moozh. "Avenging their monstrous betrayal and enslavement of my people, the Sotchitsiya."

"So this is how Basilica will be destroyed," said Nafai. "Not *by* you, but because of your rebellion."

"I assure you, Nafai, I *know* the Gorayni. They're weak in the core, and their soldiers love me better than they love their pathetic Imperator."

"Oh, I have no doubt of it."

"If Basilica is my capital, the Gorayni won't destroy it. Nothing will destroy it, because I will be victorious."

"Basilica is nothing to you," said Nafai. "A tool of the moment. I can imagine you in the north, with a vast army, poised to destroy the army defending Gollod, the city of the Imperator, and at that moment you hear that Potokgavan has taken this opportunity to land an army on the Western Shore. Come back and defend Basilica, your people will beg. I will beg you. Luet will beg you. But you'll decide that there's plenty of time to deal with Potokgavan later, after you've defeated the Gorayni. And so you'll stay and finish your work, and the next year you'll sweep south and punish Potokgavan for their atrocities, and you'll stand in the ashes of Basilica and weep for the city of women. Your tears may even be sincere."

Moozh was trembling. Nafai could feel it in the hands that held his.

"Decide," said Moozh. "Whatever happens, either you will rule Basilica for me or you will die in Basilica— also for me. One thing is certain: You will never again *leave* Basilica."

"My life is in the hands of the Oversoul."

"Answer me," said Moozh. "Decide."

"If the Oversoul wanted me to help you subjugate this city, then I would be consul here," said Nafai. "But the Oversoul wants me to journey back to Earth, and so I will not be consul."

"Then the Oversoul has fooled you again, and this time you may well die for it," said Moozh.

"The Oversoul has never fooled me," said Nafai. "Those who follow the Oversoul willingly are never lied to."

"You never catch the Oversoul in his lies, is what you mean," said Moozh.

"No!" cried Nafai. "No. The Oversoul doesn't lie to me because . . . because everything that it has promised me has come true. All of it has been true."

"Or it has made you forget the ones that *didn't* come true."

"If I wanted to doubt, then I could doubt endlessly," said Nafai. "But at some point a person has to stop questioning and *act,* and at that point you have to trust something to be true. You have to act as if something is true, and so you choose the thing you have the most reason to believe in, you have to live in the world that you have the most hope in. I follow the Oversoul, I *believe* the Oversoul, because I want to live in the world that the Oversoul has shown me."

"Yes, Earth," said Moozh scornfully.

"I don't mean a planet, I mean—I want to live in the *reality* that the Oversoul has shown me. In which lives have meaning and purpose. In which there's a plan worth following. In which death and suffering are not in vain because some good will come from them."

"All you're saying is that you want to deceive yourself."

"I'm saying that the story the Oversoul tells me fits all the facts that I see. *Your* story, in which I'm endlessly deceived, can also explain all those facts. I have no way of knowing that your story is not true—but you have no way of knowing that *my* story isn't true. So I will choose the one that I love. I'll choose the one that, if it's true, makes this reality one worth living in. I'll act as if the life I hope for is real life, and the life that disgusts me— *your* life, your *view* of life—is the lie. And it *is* a lie. You don't even believe in it yourself."

"Don't you see, boy, that you've told me exactly the same story I told you? That the Oversoul has been fooling me all along? All I did was turn back on you the mad little tale you turned on me. The truth is that the Oversoul has played us both for fools, so all we can do is make the best life for ourselves that we can in this world. If you think that the best life for you and your new wife is to rule Basilica for me, to be part of the creation of the greatest empire that Harmony has ever known, then I'm offering it to you, and I will be as loyal to you as you are to me. Decide now."

"I've decided," said Nafai. "There will be no great empire. The Oversoul won't allow it. And even if there were such an empire, it would mean nothing to me. The Keeper of Earth is calling us. The Keeper of Earth is calling *you*. And I ask you again, General Vozmuzhalnoy Vozmozhno, forget all this meaningless pursuit of empire or vengeance or whatever it is that you've been chasing all these years. Come with us to the world where humanity was born. Turn your greatness into a cause that's worthy of you. Come with us."

"Come with you?" said Moozh. "You're going nowhere." Moozh arose and walked to the door and opened it. "Take this boy back to his mother."

Two soldiers appeared, as if they had been waiting by the door. Nafai got up from his chair and walked to where Moozh stood, half-blocking the door. They looked into each other's eyes. Nafai saw rage there still, unslaked by anything that had transpired here this morning. But also he saw fear, which had not been in his eyes before.

Moozh raised his hand as if to strike Nafai across the face; Nafai did not wince or shrink from the blow. Moozh hesitated, and the blow, when it came, was upon Nafai's shoulder, and then Moozh smiled at him. In his mind Nafai heard the voice that he knew as that of the Oversoul: A slap on the face was the soldiers' signal to murder you. I have this much power in the mind of this rebellious man: I have turned Moozh's slap into a smile. But in his heart, he wants you dead.

"We are not enemies, boy," said Moozh. "Tell no one what I've said to you today."

"Sir," said Nafai, "I will tell my wife and my sisters and my mother and my brothers anything that I know. There are no secrets there. And even if I didn't tell them, the

Oversoul would; my secrecy would accomplish nothing but my loss of their trust."

At the moment he refused to agree to secrecy, Nafai saw that the soldiers stiffened, ready to strike out at him. But whatever the signal was that they waited for, it didn't come.

Instead Moozh smiled again. "A weak man would have promised not to tell, and then told. A fearful man would have promised not to tell, and then would have not told. But you are neither weak nor fearful."

"The general praises me too highly," said Nafai.

"It will be such a shame if I have to kill you," said Moozh.

"It would be such a shame to die." Nafai could hardly believe it when he heard himself answer so flippantly.

"You truly believe that the Oversoul will protect you," said Moozh.

"The Oversoul has already saved my life today," said Nafai.

Then he turned and left, one soldier ahead of him, and one behind.

"Wait," said Moozh.

Nafai stopped, turned. Moozh strode down the hall. "I'll come with you," said Moozh.

Nafai could feel it in the way the soldiers nervously shifted their weight, though they didn't so much as glance at each other: This was not expected. This was not part of the plan.

So, thought Nafai. I may not have accomplished what I hoped for. I may not have convinced Moozh to come with us to Earth. But *something* has changed. Somehow things are different because I came.

I hope that means they're better.

The Oversoul answered in his mind: I hope so, too.

SEVEN

DAUGHTERS

THE DREAM OF THE LADY

Rasa slept badly after the weddings. She had, as a Basilican teacher should, kept her misgivings to herself, but it was emotionally grueling to give her dear weak Dolya to a young man that Rasa disliked as much as Wetchik's son Mebbekew. Oh, the boy was handsome and charming—Rasa wasn't blind, she knew exactly how attractive he could be—and she wouldn't have minded him as Dolya's first husband under ordinary circumstances, for Dolya was no fool and would certainly decide not to renew Meb after a single year. But there would be no question of renewals once they got into the desert. Wherever this journey would take them—Nafai's unlikely theory of Earth or some more possible place on Harmony—there would be no casual Basilican attitude toward marriage there, and even though she had warned them more than once, she knew that Meb and Dolya, at least, did not give her warnings even the slightest heed.

For, of course, Rasa was sure that Meb did not intend to leave Basilica. Married to Dol, he was now entitled to stay—he had his citizenship, and so he intended to laugh at any attempt by anyone to get him out of the city. If there weren't Gorayni soldiers outside the house, Meb would have taken Dolya and left tonight, never to show his face again until the rest of them had given up on him and left the city. So it was only the fact that Rasa was under house arrest that kept Meb in line. Well, so be it. The Oversoul would order things as she saw fit, and Mebbekew was hardly the one to thwart her.

Meb and Dolya, Elya and Edhya. . . . Well, she had seen nieces of hers marry miserably before. Hadn't she watched her own daughters marry badly? Well, actually, it was Kokor who married badly—Obring was a more moral man than Mebbekew only because he was too weak and timid and stupid to deceive and exploit women on Mebbekew's scale. Sevet, for her part, had actually married rather well, and Vas's behavior during the past few days had quite impressed Rasa. He was a good man, and maybe now that her voice had been taken from her Sevet would finally let pain turn her into a good woman. Stranger things had happened.

Yet when Rasa went to bed after the weddings, and could not sleep, it was the marriage between her son Nafai and her dearest niece, Luet, that troubled her and kept her awake. Luet was too young, and so was Nafai. How could they be thrust so early into manhood and womanhood, when their childhood was far from complete? Something precious had been stolen from both of them. And their very sweetness about the whole thing, the way they were trying so hard to fall in love with each other, only served to break Rasa's heart all the more.

Oversoul, you have so much to answer for. Is it worth all this sacrifice? My son Nafai is only fourteen, but for your sake he has a man's blood on his hands, and now both he and Luet share a marriage bed when at their age they should still be glancing at each other shyly, wondering if someday the other might fall in love with them.

She tossed and turned in her bed. The night was hot and

dark—the stars were out, but there was little moonlight, and the streetlights shone dimly in the curfewed city. She could see almost nothing in her room, and yet did not want to turn on a light; a servant would see it, and think she might need something, and discreetly enter and inquire. I must be alone, she thought, and so she lay in darkness.

What are you plotting, Oversoul? I'm under arrest, no one can come or go from my house. Moozh has cut me off so that I can't begin to guess whom I might or might not be able to trust in Basilica, and so I must wait here for his plots and yours to unfold. Which will triumph here, Moozh's malevolent scheming or your own, Oversoul?

What do you want from my family? What will you *do* to my family, to my dearest ones? Some of it I consent to, however reluctantly: I consent to the marriage of Nyef and Lutya. As for Issib and Hushidh, when that times comes, if Shuya is willing then I am content, for I always dreamed of Issib finding some sweet woman who would see past his frailty and discover the man he is, the husband he might be—and who better than my precious raveler, my quiet, wise Shuya?

But this journey in the wilderness—we aren't prepared for it, and can't very well *get* prepared here in this house. What are you doing about *that*, in all your scheming? Aren't you perhaps a little over your head in all that's going on? Have you really planned ahead? Expeditions like this take a little planning. Wetchik and his boys could go out into the desert on a moment's notice because they had all the equipment they needed and they had some experience with camels and tents. I hope you don't expect me or my girls to be able to do that!

Then, a little bit ashamed of herself for having told the Oversoul off so roundly, Rasa uttered a much more humble prayer. Let me sleep, she prayed, dipping her fingers into the prayer basin beside the bed. Let me have rest tonight, and if it wouldn't be too much bother, show me some vision of what it is you plan for us. Then she kissed the prayer water off her fingers.

As she did so, more words passed through her mind, like a flippant addendum to her prayer. While you're telling me your plans, dear Oversoul, don't be afraid to ask for some advice. I've had some experience in this city and I love and understand these people more than you do, and you haven't been doing all that well up to now, or so it seems to me.

Oh, forgive me! she cried silently, abashed.

And then: Oh, forget it. And she rolled over and went to sleep, letting her fingers dry in the faint drafts coming in at the windows of her chamber.

She slept at last; she dreamed.

In her dream she sat in a boat on the lake of women, and opposite her—at the helm—sat the Oversoul. Not that Rasa had ever seen the Oversoul before, but after all, this was a dream, and so she recognized her at once. The Oversoul looked rather like Wetchik's mother had looked—a stern woman, but not unkind.

"Keeping rowing," said the Oversoul.

Rasa looked down and saw that she was at the oars. "But I don't have the strength for this."

"You'd be surprised."

"I'd rather not be," said Rasa. "I'd rather be doing *your* job. You're the deity here, *you're* the one with infinite power. *You* row. *I'll* steer."

"I'm just a computer," said the Oversoul. "I don't have arms and legs. You have to do the rowing."

"I can see your arms and legs, and they're a great deal stronger than mine. Furthermore, I don't know where you're taking us. I can't see where we're going because I'm sitting here facing backward."

"I know," said the Oversoul. "That's how you've spent

your whole life, facing backward. Trying to reconstruct some glorious past."

"So, if you disapprove of that, have the cleverness if not the decency to trade places with me. Let me look into the future while you do the rowing for a change."

"You all push me around so," said the Oversoul. "I'm beginning to regret breeding you all. When you get too familiar with me, you lose your respect."

"That's hardly *our* fault," said Rasa. "Here, we can't pass side by side, the boat's too narrow and we'll tip over. You crawl between my legs, and that way the boat won't spill."

The Oversoul grumbled as she crawled. "See? No respect."

"I *do* respect you," said Rasa. "I just don't have any illusions that you're always right. Nafai and Issib say that you're a computer. A program, in fact, that lives in a computer. And so you're no wiser than those who programmed you."

"Maybe they programmed me to learn wisdom. After forty million years, I may even have picked up a few good ideas."

"Oh, I'm sure you have. Someday you must show me one of them—you certainly haven't done so well till now."

"Maybe you just don't *know* all that I've done."

Rasa settled herself in the stern of the boat, her hand on the prow, and she saw to her satisfaction that the Oversoul had a good grip on the oars and was able to give a good strong pull.

However, the boat merely lurched forward and then stopped dead. Rasa looked around to see why, and she realized that they weren't on water at all, they were in the middle of a waste of wind-rippled sand.

"Well, *this* is a miserable turn of events," said Rasa.

"I'm not terribly impressed with your helmsmanship,"

said the Oversoul. "I hope you don't expect me to do any serious rowing in *this*."

"My helmsmanship," said Rasa. "It's *you* that got us out into the desert."

"And you could have done better?"

"I should hope so. For instance, where are the camels? We need camels. And tents! Enough for—oh, how many of us are there? Elemak and Eiadh, Mebbekew and Dol, Nafai and Luet—and Hushidh, of course. That's seven. And me. And then we'd better take Sevet and Kokor, and their husbands if they'll come—that's twelve. Am I forgetting something? Oh, of course— Shedemei and all her seeds and embryos—how many drycases? I can't remember—at least six camels for her project alone. And our supplies? I'm not even sure how to estimate this. Thirteen of us, and that's a lot of us to feed and shelter along the way."

"Well, why are you telling *me?*" asked the Oversoul. "Do you think I keep some sort of binary camels and tents in my memory?"

"So, just as I thought. You haven't even prepared a thing for the journey. Don't you know that these things can't be done suddenly? If you can't help me, take me to somebody who can."

The Oversoul began to lead her toward a distant hill. "You're so bossy," said the Oversoul. *"I'm* the one who's supposed to be the guardian of humanity, if you'll be so good as to remember that."

"That's fine, you keep doing that job, while I look out for the people I love. Who's going to take care of my household after I'm gone? Did you ever think of that? So many children and teachers who depend on me."

"They'll go home. They'll find other teachers or other jobs. You're not indispensable."

They had reached the crest of the hill—as with all dreams, they were able to move very quickly sometimes, and sometimes very slowly. Now, at the top of the hill, Rasa saw that she was in the street in front of her own house. She had never known there was a way right down the hill to the desert from her own street. She looked around to see which way the Oversoul had brought her, only to find herself face-to-face with a soldier. Not a Gorayni, to her relief. Instead he was one of the officers of the Basilican guard.

"Lady Rasa," he said, in awe.

"I have work for you to do," she said. "The Oversoul would have told you all this already, only she's decided to leave this particular job up to me. I hope you don't mind helping."

"All I want to do is serve the Oversoul," he said.

"Well, then, I hope you'll be very resourceful and do all these jobs properly, because I'm not an expert and I'll have to leave a good many things to your judgment. To start with, there'll be thirteen of us."

"Thirteen of you to do *what?*"

"A journey in the desert."

"General Moozh has you under house arrest."

"Oh, the Oversoul will take care of that. I can't do *everything.*"

"All right, then," said the officer. "A journey into the desert. Thirteen of you."

"We'll need camels to ride on and tents to sleep in."

"Large tents or small ones?"

"How large is large, and how small is small?"

"Large can be up to a dozen men, but those are very hard to pitch. Small can be for two men."

"Small," said Rasa. "Everybody will sleep in couples, except one tent for three, for me and Hushidh and Shedemei."

"Hushidh the raveler? Leaving?"

"Never mind the roster, that's none of your business," said Rasa.

"I don't think Moozh will want Hushidh to leave."

"He doesn't want *me* to leave, either—*yet,*" said Rasa. "I hope you're taking notes."

"I'll remember."

"Fine. Camels for us to ride, and tents for us to sleep in, and then camels to carry the tents, and also camels to carry supplies enough for us to travel—oh, how far? I can't remember—ten days should be enough."

"That's a lot of camels."

"I can't help that. You're an officer, I'm sure you know where the camels are and how to get them."

"I do."

"And something else. An extra half-dozen camels to carry Shedemei's drycases. She might already have arranged for those herself—you'll have to check with her."

"When will you need all this?"

"Right away," said Rasa. "I have no idea when this journey will begin—and we're under house arrest right now, you might have heard—"

"I heard."

"But we must be ready to leave within an hour, whenever the time comes."

"Lady Rasa, I can't do these things without Moozh's authority. He rules the city now, and I'm not even the commander of the guard."

"All right," said Rasa. "I hereby give you Moozh's authority."

"You can't give that to me," said the officer.

"Oversoul?" said Rasa. "Isn't it about time you stepped in and did something?"

Immediately Moozh himself appeared beside the officer. "You've been talking to Lady Rasa," he said sternly.

"She's the one who came to *me*" said the officer.

"That's fine. I hope you paid attention to everything she said."

"So you authorize me to proceed?"

"I can't right at the moment," said Moozh. "Not officially, because at the moment I don't actually know that I'm going to want you to do this. So you have to do it very quietly, so that even I don't find out about it. Do you understand?"

"I hope I won't be in too much trouble if you find out."

"No, not at all. I *won't* find out, as long as you don't go out of your way to tell me."

"That's a relief."

"When the time comes for me to want this journey to begin, I'll order you to make preparations. All you have to say is, Yes sir, it can be done right away. Please *don't* embarrass me by pointing out that you've had it ready since noon, or anything like that to make it look as though my orders aren't spur-of-the-moment. Understand?"

"Very good, sir."

"I don't want to have to kill you, so please don't embarrass me, all right? I may need you later."

"As you wish, sir."

"You may leave," said Moozh.

Immediately the officer of the guard disappeared.

Moozh immediately turned into Rasa's dream image of the Oversoul. "I think that about takes care of it, Rasa," she said.

"Yes, I think so," said Rasa.

"Fine," said the Oversoul. "You can wake up now. The real Moozh will soon be at your door, and you want to be ready for him."

"Oh, thanks so very much," said Rasa, more than a little put out. "I've hardly had any sleep at all, and you're making me wake up already?"

"I wasn't responsible for the timing," said the Oversoul. "If Nafai hadn't run off half-cocked in the wee hours of the morning, demanding an interview with Moozh before the sun came up, you could have slept in to a reasonable hour."

"What time *is* it?"

"I told you, wake up and look at the clock."

With that the Oversoul disappeared and Rasa was awake, looking at the clock. The sky was barely greying with dawn outside, and she couldn't see what time it was without getting out of bed and looking closely. Wearily she groaned and turned on a light. Too, too early to get up. But the dream, strange as it was, had been this much true: Someone was ringing the bell.

At this hour, the servants knew they had no consent to open the door until Rasa herself had been alerted, but they were surprised to see her come into the foyer so quickly.

"Who?" she asked.

"Your son, Lady Rasa. And General Vozmoozh . . . the General."

"Open the door and you may retire," said Rasa.

The night bell was not so loud that the whole house heard it, so the foyer was nearly empty anyway. When the door opened, Nafai and Moozh entered together. No one else. No soldiers—though no doubt they waited on the street. Still, Rasa could not help remembering two earlier visits by men who thought to rule the city of Basilica. Gaballufix and Rashgallivak had both brought soldiers, holographically masked, in an attempt not so much to terrify *her* as to bolster their own confidence. It was significant that Moozh felt no need for accompaniment.

"I didn't know my son was out wandering the streets at this hour," said Rasa. "So I certainly appreciate your kindness in bringing him home to me."

"Surely now that he's married," said Moozh, "you won't be watching his comings and goings so carefully, will you?"

Rasa showed her impatience to Nafai. What was he doing, blurting out the fact that he had just married the waterseer last night? Had he no discretion at all? No, of course not, or he wouldn't even have been outside to be picked up by Moozh's soldiers. What, had he been trying to escape?

But no, hadn't there been something . . . in the dream, yes, the Oversoul had said something about Nafai going off half-cocked, demanding an interview with Moozh. "I hope he hasn't been any trouble to you," said Rasa.

"A little, I will confess," said Moozh. "I had hoped he might help me bring to Basilica the greatness that this city deserves, but he declined the honor."

"Forgive me for my ignorance, but I fail to see how anything my son could do might bring greatness to a city that is already a legend through all the world. Is there any city still standing that is older or holier than Basilica? Is there any other that has been a city of peace for so long?"

"A solitary city, madam," said Moozh. "A lonely city. A city for pilgrims. But soon, I hope, a city for ambassadors from all the great kingdoms of the world."

"Who will no doubt sail here on a sea of blood."

"Not if things work well. Not if I have significant cooperation."

"From whom?" asked Rasa. "From me? From my son?"

"I would like to meet, though I know the honor is inconvenient, with two nieces of yours. One of them happens to be Nafai's young bride. The other is her unmarried sister."

"I do not wish you to meet with them."

"But they will wish to meet with me. Don't you think? Since Hushidh is sixteen, and free to receive visitors under the law, and Luet is also married, and thus also free to receive visitors, then I hope you will respect both law and courtesy and inform them that I wish to meet with them."

Rasa could not help but admire him even as she feared him—for, at a moment when Gabya or Rash would have blustered or threatened, Moozh simply insisted on courtesy. He did not bother reminding her of his thousand soldiers, of his power in the world. He simply relied on her good manners, and she was helpless before him, for right was not yet clearly on her side.

"I dismissed the servants. I will wait with you here, while Nafai goes for them."

When Moozh nodded, Nafai left, walking briskly toward the wing of the house where the bridal couples had spent the night. Rasa vaguely wondered at what hour Elemak and Eiadh, Mebbekew and Dol would rise, and what they would think of the fact that Nafai had gone to General Moozh. They ought perhaps to admire the boy's courage, but Elemak would no doubt resent him for his very intrusiveness, meddling always in affairs that shouldn't concern him. Whereas Rasa didn't resent Nafai's failure to remember that he was only a boy. Rather she feared for him because of it.

"The foyer is not a comfortable place," said Moozh. "Perhaps there might be some private room, where early risers will not interrupt us."

"But why would we have need of a private room, when we don't yet know whether my nieces will receive you?"

"Your niece and your daughter-in-law," said Moozh.

"A new relationship; it could hardly bring us closer than we already were."

"You love the girls dearly," said Moozh.

"I would lay down my life for them."

"And yet cannot spare a private room for their meeting with a foreign visitor?"

Rasa glowered at him and led him out to her private portico—the screened-off area, where there was no view of the Rift Valley. But Moozh made no pretense of sitting in the place on the bench that she patted. Instead he made for the balustrade beyond the screens. It was forbidden for men to stand there, to see that view; and yet Rasa knew that it would weaken her to attempt to forbid him. It would be . . . pathetic.

So instead she arose and stood beside him, looking out over the valley.

"You see what few men have seen," said Rasa.

"But your son has seen it," said Moozh. "He has floated naked on the waters of the lake of women."

"It wasn't my idea," said Rasa.

"The Oversoul, I know," said Moozh. "He takes us down so many twisted paths. Mine perhaps the most twisted one of all."

"And which bend will you take now?"

"The bend towards greatness and glory. Justice and freedom."

"For whom?"

"For Basilica, if the city will accept it."

"We *have* greatness and glory. We *have* justice and freedom. How can you imagine that any exertion of yours will add one whit to what we have?"

"Perhaps you're right," said Moozh. "Perhaps I'm only using Basilica to add luster to my *own* name, at the beginning, when I need it. Is Basilican glory so rare and dear that we can't find a bit of it to share with me?"

"Moozh, I like you so much that I almost regret the terror that fills my heart whenever I think of you."

"Why? I mean no harm to you, or to anyone you love."

"The terror is not for that. It's for what you mean to my city. To the world at large. You are the thing that the Oversoul was set in place to prevent. You are the machineries of war, the love of power, the lust for enlargement."

"You could *not* have made me prouder than to praise me thus."

There were footsteps behind them. Rasa turned to find Luet and Hushidh approaching. Nafai hung back.

"Come with your wife and sister-in-law, Nafai," said Rasa. "General Moozh has decreed our ancient custom to be abrogated, at least for this morning, with the sun preparing to rise behind the mountains."

Nafai walked more briskly then, and they took their places. Moozh easily and artfully arranged them, simply by taking his place leaning against the balustrade, so that as they sat on the arc of benches, their focus, their center was Moozh.

"I have come here this morning to congratulate the waterseer directly on her wedding last night."

Luet nodded gravely, though Rasa was reasonably sure that Luet knew Moozh had no such purpose. In fact, Rasa rather hoped that Nafai had some idea of what he had in mind, and had briefed the girls before they got here.

"It was an astonishing thing, for one so young," said Moozh. "And yet, having met young Nafai here, I can see that you have married well. A fitting consort for the waterseer, for Nafai is a brave and noble young man. So noble, in fact, that I begged him to let me place his name in nomination for the consulship of Basilica."

"There is no such office," said Rasa.

"There will be," said Moozh, "as there was before. An office little called for in times of peace, but needful enough in times of war."

"Of which we would have done, if you would only go away."

"It hardly matters, for your son declined the honor. In a way, it's almost fortunate. Not that he wouldn't have made a splendid consul. The people would have accepted him, for not only is he the bridegroom of the waterseer, but also he hears the voice of the Oversoul himself. A prophet and a prophetess, together in the highest chamber of the city. And for those who feared he might be a weakling, a puppet of the Gorayni overmaster, we need only point out the fact that long before old General Moozh arrived, Nafai himself, under the orders of the Oversoul, boldly ended a great menace to the freedom of Basilica and carried out a just execution of the penalty of death already owed by one Gaballufix, for ordering, the murder of Roptat. Oh, the people would have accepted Nafai readily, and he would have been a wise and capable ruler. Especially with Lady Rasa to advise him."

"But he declined," said Rasa.

"He did."

"So what point is there in flattering us further?"

"Because there is more than one way for me to achieve the same end," said Moozh. "For instance, I could denounce Nafai for the cowardly murder of Gaballufix, and bring forth Rashgallivak as the man who heroically tried to hold the city through a time of turmoil. Had it not been for the vicious interference of a raveler named Hushidh, he might have succeeded—for everyone knew that Rashgallivak's hands were not stained with any man's blood. Instead he was the capable steward, struggling to hold together the households of both Wetchik and Gaballufix. While Nafai and Hushidh go on trial for their crimes, Rashgallivak is made consul of the city. And, of course, he quite properly takes Gaballufix's daughters under his protection, as he will also do with Nafai's widow after his execution, and the raveler after she is pardoned for her crime. The city council would not want these poor women under the influence of the dangerous, self-serving Lady Rasa for another day."

"So you *do* make threats, after all," said Rasa.

"Lady Rasa, I am describing serious possibilities— choices that I can make, which will lead me to the end that, one way or another, I *will* achieve. I will have Basilica freely allied with me. It will be *my* city before I go on to challenge the tyrannical rule of the Gorayni Imperator."

"There is another way?" asked Hushidh quietly.

"There is, and it is perhaps the best of all," said Moozh. "It is the reason why Nafai brought me home with him—so

I could stand before the raveler and ask for her to marry me."

Rasa was aghast. "Marry *you!*"

"Despite my nickname, I have no wife," said Moozh. "It isn't good for a man to be alone too long. I'm thirty years old—I hope not too old for you to accept me as your husband, Hushidh."

"She is intended for my son," said Rasa.

Moozh turned on her, and for the first time his sweet manners were replaced by a biting, dangerous anger. "A cripple who is hiding in the desert, a manlet whom this lovely girl has never desired as a husband and does not desire now!"

"You're mistaken," said Hushidh. "I *do* desire him."

"But you have not married him," said Moozh.

"I have not."

"There is no legal barrier to your marrying me," said Moozh.

"There is none."

"Enter this house and slay us all," said Rasa, "but I will not let you take this girl by force."

"Don't make a drama of this," said Moozh. "I have no intention of forcing anything. As I said, I have several paths open to me. At any point Nafai can say, 'I'll be the consul,' whereupon Hushidh will find the onerous burden of my marriage proposal less pressing—though not withdrawn, if she would like to share my future with me. For I assure you, Hushidh, that come what may, my life will be glorious, and the name of my wife will be sung with mine in all the tales of it forever."

"The answer is no," said Rasa.

"The question is not asked of you," said Moozh.

Hushidh looked from one to another of them, but not asking them anything. Indeed, Rasa was quite sure that

Hushidh was seeing, not their features, but rather the threads of love and loyalty that bound them together.

"Aunt Rasa," said Hushidh at last, "I hope you will forgive me for disappointing your son."

"Don't let him bully you," said Rasa fiercely. "The Oversoul would never let him have Nafai executed—it's all bluster."

"The Oversoul is a computer," said Hushidh. "She is not omnipotent."

"Hushidh, there are visions tying you to Issib. The Oversoul has chosen you for each other!"

"Aunt Rasa," said Hushidh, "I can only beg you to keep your silence and respect my decision. For I have seen threads that I never guessed were there, connecting me to this man. I did not think, when I heard his name was Moozh, that I would be the one woman with the *right* to use that name for him."

"Hushidh," said Moozh, "I decided to propose to you for political reasons, having never seen you. But I heard that you were wise, and I saw at once that you are lovely. Now I have seen the way you think and heard the way you speak, and I know that I can bring you, not just power and glory, but also the tender gifts of a true husband."

"And I will bring you the devotion of a true wife," said Hushidh, rising to her feet and walking to him. He reached for her, and she accepted his gentle embrace and his kiss upon her cheek.

Rasa, devastated, could say nothing.

"Can my Aunt Rasa perform the ceremony?" asked Hushidh. "I assume that for . . . political reasons . . . you'll want the wedding to be soon."

"Soon, but it can't be Lady Rasa," said Moozh. "Her reputation is none too good right now, though I'm sure that situation can be clarified soon after the wedding."

"Can I have a last day with my sister?"

"It's your wedding, not your funeral that you're going to," said Moozh. "You'll have many days with your sister. But the wedding will be today. At noon. In the Orchestra, with all the city as witnesses. And your sister Luet will perform the ceremony."

It was too terrible. Moozh understood too well how to turn this all to his advantage. If Luet performed the marriage, then her prestige would be on it. Moozh would be fully accepted as a noble citizen of Basilica, and he would have no need of any stand-in to be his puppet consul. Rather he would easily be named consul himself, and Hushidh would be his consort, the first lady of Basilica. She would be glorious in her role, worthy of it in every way—except that the role should not be played by anyone, and Moozh would destroy Basilica with his ambition.

Destroy Basilica . . .

"Oversoul!" cried Rasa from her heart. "Is that what you planned from the beginning?"

"Of course it is," said Moozh. "As Nafai himself told me, I was maneuvered here by God himself. For what other purpose, than to find a wife?" He turned again to Hushidh, who still looked up to him, still touched him, her hand on his arm. "My dear lady," said Moozh, "will you come with me now? While your sister prepares to perform the ceremony, we have many things to talk about, and you should be with me when we announce our wedding to the city council this morning."

Luet stood and strode forward. "I haven't agreed to play any part in this abominable farce!"

"Lutya," said Nafai.

"You can't force her!" cried Rasa triumphantly.

But it was Hushidh, not Moozh, who answered. "Sister, if you love me, if you have ever loved me, then I beg you, come to the Orchestra prepared to perform this wedding." Hushidh looked at them all. "Aunt Rasa, you must come. And bring your daughters and their husbands, and Nafai, bring your brothers and their wives. Bring all the teachers and the students of this house, even those who live away. Will you bring them to see me take a husband? Will you give me that one courtesy, in memory of all my happy years in this good house?"

The formality of her speech, the distance of her manner broke Rasa's heart, and she wept even as she agreed. Luet, too, promised to perform the ceremony.

"You will release them from this house for the wedding, won't you?" Hushidh asked Moozh.

He smiled tenderly at her. "They will be escorted to the Orchestra," he said, "and then escorted home."

"That's all I ask," said Hushidh. And then she left the portico on Moozh's arm.

When they were gone, Rasa sank to the bench and wept bitterly. "Why have we served her all these years?" Rasa demanded. "We are nothing to her. Nothing!"

"Hushidh loves us," said Luet.

"She's not talking about Hushidh," said Nafai.

"The Oversoul!" cried Rasa. Then she shouted the word, as if she were crowing it to the rising sun. "Oversoul!"

"If you've lost faith in the Oversoul," said Nafai, "at least have faith in Hushidh. She still has hope of turning this the way we want it to go, don't you realize? She took Moozh's offer because she saw some plan in it. Perhaps the Oversoul even *told* her to say yes, did you think of that?"

"I thought of it," said Luet, "but I can hardly believe it. The Oversoul has hinted nothing of this to us."

"Then instead of talking to each other," said Nafai, "and instead of getting resentful about it, perhaps we should listen. Perhaps the Oversoul is only waiting for us to spare it some scrap of our attention to tell us what's going on."

"I'll wait then," said Rasa. "But this better be a good plan."

They waited, all three with their own questions in their hearts.

From the look on Nafai's and Luet's faces, they received their answer first. And as Rasa waited, longer and longer, she realized that she would get no answer at all.

"Did you hear?" asked Nafai.

"Nothing," said Rasa. "Nothing at all."

"Perhaps you're too angry with the Oversoul to hear anything from her," said Luet.

"Or perhaps she's punishing me," said Rasa. "Spiteful machine! What did she have to say?"

Nafai and Luet glanced at each other. So the news wasn't good.

"The Oversoul isn't exactly in control of this," said Luet finally.

"It's my fault," said Nafai. "My going to the general put things at least a day ahead of schedule. He was already planning to marry one of them, but he would have studied it for another day at least."

"A day! Would that have made so much difference?"

"The Oversoul isn't sure that she can bring off her best plan, so quickly," said Luet. "But we can't blame Nafai for it, either. Moozh is impetuous and brilliant and he might have done it this quickly without Nafai's . . ."

"Stupidity," offered Nafai.

"Boldness," said Luet.

"So we're condemned to stay here as Moozh's tools?" asked Rasa. "Well, he could hardly misuse us more carelessly than the Oversoul has."

"Mother," said Nafai, and his tone was rather sharp. "The Oversoul has not misused us. Whether Hushidh marries Moozh or not, we will still take our journey. If she does end up as Moozh's wife, then she'll use her influence to set us free—he'll have no need for us once his position in the city is secured."

"Us?" asked Rasa. "Set *us* free?"

"All of us that we already planned for the journey, even Shedemei."

"And what about Hushidh?" asked Rasa.

"That's what the Oversoul can't do," said Luet. "If she can't prevent the wedding, then Hushidh will stay."

"I will hate the Oversoul forever," said Rasa. "If she does this to sweet Hushidh, then I'll never serve the Oversoul again. Do you hear me?"

"Calm yourself, Mother," said Nafai. "If Hushidh had refused him, then I would have agreed to be consul, and it would have been Luet and I who stayed behind. One way or another, it was going to happen."

"Is that supposed to comfort me?" Rasa asked bitterly.

"Comfort *you?*" asked Luet. "Comfort *you,* Lady Rasa? Hushidh is my sister, my only kin—you'll have all the children you ever bore with you, *and* your husband. What are you losing, compared with what I'm going to lose? Yet do you see me weeping?"

"You *should* be weeping," said Rasa.

"All the way through the desert I'll do my weeping," said Luet. "But for now we have very few hours to prepare."

"Oh, am I supposed to teach you the ceremony?"

"That will take five minutes," said Luet, "and the priestesses will help me anyway. The time we have must be spent in packing for the journey."

"The *journey,*" said Rasa bitterly.

"We must have everything ready so it can be loaded onto camels in five minutes," said Luet. "Isn't that so, Nafai?"

"There's still a chance that all will work well," said Nafai. "Mother, now is not the time for you to give up. All my life, you've held firm no matter what the provocation. Are you collapsing now, when we need you most to bring the others into line?"

"Do you expect *us* to get Sevet and Vas, Kokor and Obring to pack up for a desert journey?" asked Luet.

"Do you think Elemak and Mebbekew will take these instructions from *me?*" asked Nafai.

Rasa dried her eyes. "You ask too much of me," said Rasa. "I'm not as young as you. I'm not as resilient."

"You can bend as much as you need to," said Luet. "Now please, tell us what to do."

So Rasa swallowed, for now, her grief, and stepped back into her old familiar role. Within minutes the whole house was set in motion, the servants packing and preparing, the clerk drafting letters of recommendation for every teacher who would be left behind, and reports on the progress of every pupil, so that they could all find new schools easily after Rasa left and the school was closed.

Then Rasa walked the long corridor to Elemak's bridal chamber, to begin the grueling process of informing the reluctant travelers that they *would* attend the wedding, since soldiers would be marching them there, and they *would* prepare for a desert journey, since for some reason the Oversoul had decided that they would not have suffered enough until they were out among the scorpions.

AT THE ORCHESTRA, AND NOT IN A DREAM

This was hardly the way Elemak would have wanted to spend the morning after his wedding. It was supposed to be a leisurely time of dozing and lovemaking, talking and teasing. Instead it had been a flurry of preparations— hopelessly inadequate preparations, too, since they were supposedly preparing for a desert journey and yet had neither camels nor tents nor supplies. And it was disturbing how badly Eiadh had adjusted to the situation. Where Mebbekew's Dol was immediately cooperative—more so than Meb himself, the slug— Eiadh kept wasting Elemak's time with protests and arguments. Couldn't we stay behind and join them later? Why do *we* have to leave just because Aunt Rasa is under arrest?

Finally Elemak had sent Eiadh to Luet and Nafai to get her questions answered while he supervised the packing, to eliminate needless clothing—which meant bitter arguments with Rasa's daughter Kokor, who could not understand why her light and provocative little frocks were not going to be particularly useful out on the desert. Finally he had blown up, in front of her sister Sevet and both their husbands, and said, "Listen, Kokor, the only man you're going to be able to have out there is your husband, and when you want to seduce *him,* you can take your clothes *off."* With that he picked up her favorite dress and tore it down the middle. Of course she screamed and wept—but he saw her later, magnanimously giving away all her favorite gowns—or perhaps trading them for more practical clothing, since it was likely that Kokor had owned nothing serviceable at all.

If the ordeal of packing had not been enough, there was the mortifying passage through the city. True, the soldiers had done a fair job of being discreet—no solid phalanx of brutish men marching in step. But they were still Gorayni soldiers, and so passersby—most of them also heading for the Orchestra—cleared a space around them and then gawked at them as they passed. "They look at us like we're criminals," Eiadh said. But Elemak reassured her that most bystanders probably assumed they were guests of honor with a military escort, which made Eiadh preen. It bothered Elemak just a little, in the back of his mind, that Eidah was so childish. Hadn't Father warned him that young wives, while they had sleeker, lighter bodies, also had lighter minds? Eiadh was simply young; Elemak could hardly expect her to take serious matters seriously, or even to understand what was serious in the first place.

Now they sat in places of honor, not up among the benches on the upward slopes of the amphitheatre, but down on the Orchestra itself, to the righthand side of the low platform that had been erected in the center for the ceremony itself. They were the bride's party; on the other side, the groom's party consisted of many members of the city council, along with officers of the Basilican guard and a few—only a handful—of Gorayni officers. There was no sign of Gorayni domination here. Not that there needed to be. Elemak knew that there were plenty of Gorayni soldiers and Basilican guards discreetly out of sight, but close enough to intervene if something unexpected should happen. If, for instance, some assassin or other curiosity-seeker should attempt to cross the open space between the benches and the wedding parties around the platform, he would find himself sporting a new arrow somewhere in his body, from one of the archers in the prompters' and musicians' boxes.

How quickly things change, thought Elemak. Only a few weeks ago I came home from a successful caravan, imagining that I was ready to take my place as a man in the affairs of Basilica. Gaballufix seemed to be the most powerful man in the world to me then, and my future as the Wetchik's heir and Gabya's brother seemed bright indeed. Since then nothing had stayed the same for two days at a time. A week ago, dehydrating mind and body on the desert, would he have believed he might be married to Eiadh in Rasa's house not a week thence? And even last night, when he and Eiadh had been the central figures in the wedding ceremony, could he have imagined that at noon the next day, instead of Nafai and Luet being the childish, pathetic hangers-on at Elemak's wedding, they would now sit on the platform itself, where Luet would perform the ceremony and Nafai would stand as General Moozh's sponsor?

Nafai! A fourteen-year-old-boy! And General Moozh had asked *him* to stand as his sponsor for citizenship in Basilica, offering him to Hushidh as if Nafai were some important figure in the city. Well, he *was* an important figure—but only as the husband of the waterseer. Nobody could possibly think that he deserved any such honor in and of himself.

Waterseer, raveler . . . Elemak had never paid much heed to such things. It was all priestcraft, a profitable business but one he didn't have much patience with. Like the foolish dream that Elemak had had out on the desert—it was such an easy matter to turn a meaningless dream into a plan of action, because of the gullible fools who believed that the Oversoul was some noble being instead of a mere computer program responsible for pressing data and documents from city to city by satellite. Even Nafai himself was saying that the Oversoul was just a computer, and yet he and Luet and Hushidh and Rasa were all full of tales about how the Oversoul was trying to arrange things so the marriage wouldn't take place and they would all end up out on the desert, ready for the journey, before the day was over. What, could a computer program make camels appear out of nothing? Make tents rise up out of the dust? Turn rocks and sand into cheeses and grain?

"Doesn't he look brave and fine?" asked Eiadh.

Elemak turned to her. "Who? Is General Moozh here?"

"I mean your brother, silly. Look."

Elemak looked toward the platform and did not think Nafai looked particularly brave or fine. In fact, he looked silly, all dressed up like a boy pretending to be a man.

"I can hardly believe he would walk right up to one of the Gorayni soldiers," said Eiadh. "And go speak to General

Vozmuzhalnoy Vozmozhno himself—while everyone was still asleep!"

"What was brave about that? It was dangerous and foolish, and look what it led to—Hushidh having to marry the man."

Eiadh looked at him in bafflement, "Elya, she's marrying the most powerful man in the world! And Nafai will stand as his sponsor."

"Only because he's married to the waterseer."

Eiadh sighed. "She *is* such a plain little thing. But those dreams—I've tried to have dreams myself, but no one takes them seriously. I had the strangest dream last night, in fact. A hairy flying monkey with ugly teeth was throwing doo-doo at me, and a giant rat with a bow and arrow shot him out of the sky—can you believe anything so silly? Why can't *I* have dreams from the Oversoul, can you tell me that?"

Elemak was hardly listening. Instead he was thinking of how Eiadh had clearly been envious because Hushidh was marrying the most powerful man in the world. And how she had admired Nafai for his damnable cheek, in going out and accosting General Moozh in the middle of the night. What could he possibly have accomplished, except to infuriate the man? Pure stupid luck that it had ended up with Nafai on that platform. But it galled Elemak all the same, that it was Nafai who was sitting there, with all the eyes of Basilica upon him. Nafai who was being whispered about, Nafai who would be seen as the husband of the waterseer, the brother-in-law of the raveler. And as Moozh installed himself as king—oh, yes, the official word for it would be *consul,* but it would *mean* the same—Nafai would be the brother-in-law of majesty and the husband of greatness and Elemak would be a desert trader. Oh, of course they would restore Father to his place as Wetchik, once Father realized that the Oversoul wasn't going to be able to get anybody out of Basilica after all. And Elemak would again be his heir, but what would *that* title mean anymore? Worst of all would be the fact that he would receive his rank and his future back as a gift from *Nafai*. It made him seethe inside.

"Nafai is so *impetuous*," said Eiadh. "Aren't you proud of him?"

Couldn't she stop talking about him? Until this morning, Elemak had known that Eiadh was the finest marriage a man could make for himself in this city. But now he realized that in the back of his mind he had really been thinking that she was the finest *first* marriage a *young* man could make. Someday he would need a real wife, a consort, and there was no reason to think that Eiadh would grow up into such a one. She would probably always be shallow and frivolous, the very thing that he had found so endearing. Last night when she had sung to him, her throaty voice full of rehearsed passion, he had thought he could listen to her sing forever. Now he looked at the platform and realized that it was Nafai, after all, who had made a marriage that would be worth having thirty years from now.

Well, fine, thought Elemak. Since we *won't* get away from Basilica, I'll keep Eiadh for a couple of years and then gently ease her away. Who knows? Luet may not stay with Nafai. When she gets older she may begin to wish for a *strong* man beside her. We can look back on these first marriages as childish phases we went through in our youth. Then *I* will be the brother-in-law of the consul.

As for Eiadh, well, with luck she'll bear me a son before we're through. But would that truly be luck? Should my eldest son, my heir, be a boy with such a shallow woman for his mother? In all likelihood, it will be the sons of my later marriages, my mature marriages, who will be the worthiest to take my place.

Then, like a sudden attack of indigestion, there came the

realization that Father, too, might feel that way. After all, Lady Rasa was *his* marriage of maturity, and Issib and Nafai the sons of that marriage. Wasn't Mebbekew walking, talking proof of the unfortunate results of early marriages?

But not me, thought Elemak. I was not the son of some frivolous early marriage. I was a son he couldn't have dared to ask for—his Auntie's son, Hosni's son, born only because she so admired the boy Volemak as she introduced him to the pleasures of the bed. Hosni was a woman of substance, and Father trusts and admires me above his other children. Or *did,* anyway, until he started having visions from the Oversoul and Nafai was able to parlay that into an advantage by pretending to have visions, too.

Elemak was filled with rage—old, deep-burning rage and hot new jealousy because of Eiadh's admiration for Nafai. Yet what burned hottest and deepest was his fear that Nafai was not pretending, that for some unknowable reason the Oversoul had chosen Father's youngest instead of his eldest to be his true heir. When Issib's chair was taken over by the Oversoul and stopped Elemak from beating Nafai in that ravine outside the city, hadn't the Oversoul as much as said so? That Nafai would one day lead his brothers, or something to that effect?

Well, dear Oversoul, not if Nafai is dead. Ever think of that? If you can speak to *him* then you can speak to me, and it's about time you started.

I gave you the dream of wives.

The sentence came into Elemak's mind as clearly as speech. Elemak laughed.

"What are you laughing at, Elya, dear?" asked Eiadh.

"At how easily a person can deceive himself," said Elemak.

"People always talk about how a person can lie to himself, but I've never understood that," said Eiadh. "If you tell yourself a lie, then you know you're lying, don't you?"

"Yes," said Elemak. "You know you're lying, and you know what the truth is. But some people fall in love with the lie and let go of the truth completely."

As you're doing now, said the voice in his head. You prefer to believe the lie that I cannot speak to you or anyone else, and so you will deny me.

"Kiss me," said Elemak.

"We're in the middle of the Orchestra, Elya!" she said, but he knew she wanted to.

"All the better," he said. "We were married last night— people expect us to be oblivious to everything but each other."

So she kissed him, and he let himself fall into the kiss, blanking his mind to everything but desire. When at last the kiss ended, there was a smattering of applause—they had been noticed, and Eiadh was delighted.

Of course, Mebbekew immediately proposed an identical kiss to Dol, who had the good sense to decline. Still, Mebbekew persisted, until Elemak leaned across Eiadh and said, "Meb. Anticlimax is always bad theatre—didn't you tell me that yourself?"

Meb glowered and dropped the idea.

I am still in control of things, Elemak thought. And I am *not* about to start believing voices that pop into my mind just because I wish for them. I'm not like Father and Nafai and Issib, determined to believe in a fantasy because it feels so warm and cuddly to think that some superior being is in charge of things. I can deal with the cold hard truth. That's always enough for a *real* man.

The horns began. From all the minarets around the amphitheatre, the homers began their wailing cries. These were ancient instruments, not the finely-tuned horns of theatre or concert, and there was no attempt to create harmony between them. Each horn produced one note at a time, held long and loud, then fading as the horner lost breath. The notes overlaid each other, sometimes with winsome dissonance, sometimes with astonishing harmonies; always it was a haunting, beautiful sound.

It silenced the citizens gathered in the benches, and it filled Elemak with a trembling anticipation, as he knew it did with every other person in the Orchestra. The wedding was about to begin.

THIRSTY STOOD AT the gate of Basilica and wondered why the Oversoul had failed her now. Hadn't she been helped every step of the way from Potokgavan? She had come upon a canal boat and asked them to let her ride, and they had taken her aboard without question, though she could give them no fare. At the great port, she had boldly told the captain of the corsair that the Oversoul required her to have the fastest passage to Redcoast ever achieved, and he had laughed and boasted that as long as he took no cargo, he could make it in a day, with such a fair wind. In Redcoast a fine lady had dismounted from her horse and offered it to Thirsty on the street.

It was on that horse that Thirsty arrived at the Low Gate, expecting to be admitted easily, as all women always were, citizens or not. Instead she found the gate tended by Gorayni soldiers, and they were turning everyone away.

"There's a great wedding going on inside," a soldier explained to her. "General Moozh is marrying some Basilican lady."

Without knowing how, Thirsty knew at once that this wedding was the reason she had come.

"Then you must let me in," she said, "because I am an invited guest."

"Only the citizens of Basilica are invited to attend, and only those who were already inside the walls. Our orders allow no exceptions, not even for nursing mothers whose babes are inside the walls, not even for physicians whose dying patients are within."

"I am invited by the Oversoul," said Thirsty, "and by that authority I revoke any orders you were given by a mortal man."

The soldier laughed, but only a little, for her voice had carried, and the crowd at the gate was watching, listening. They had also been turned away, and were liable to turn surly at the slightest provocation.

"Let her in," said one of the soldiers, "if only to keep the crowd from turning."

"Don't be a fool," said another. "If we let her in we'll have to let them all in."

"They all want me to enter," said Thirsty.

The crowd murmured their assent. Thirsty wondered at this—that the crowd of Basilicans should heed the Oversoul so readily, while the Gorayni soldiers were deaf to her influence. Perhaps this was why the Gorayni were such an evil race, as she had heard in Potokgavan: because they could not hear the voice of the Oversoul.

"My husband is waiting for me inside," said Thirsty, though not until she heard herself say the words did she realize it was true.

"Your husband will have to wait," said a soldier.

"Or take a lover," said another, and they laughed.

"Or satisfy himself," said the first, and they hooted.

"We should let her in," said one of the soldiers. "What if God has chosen her?"

Immediately one of the other soldiers drew his lefthand knife and put it to the throat of the one who had spoken. "You know the warning we were given— that it's the very one that we *want* to allow inside who must be prevented!"

"But she needs to be there," said the soldier who was sensitive to the Oversoul.

"Say another word and I'll kill you."

"No!" cried Thirsty. "I'll go. This is not the gate for me."

Inside her she felt the urgency to enter the city increase; but she would not have this man be killed when it would not get her through the gate in any case. Instead she wheeled the horse and made her way back through the crowd, which parted for her. Quickly she made her way up the steep trail that led to the Caravan Road, but she did not bother trying the Market Gate; she made her way along the High Road, but she did not try to enter at High Gate or Funnel Gate, either. She hurried her mount along the Dark Path, which wound among deep ravines sloping upward into the forested hills north of the city until she reached the Forest Road—but she did not follow it down to Back Gate, either.

Instead she dismounted and plunged into the dense underbrush of Trackless Wood, heading for the private gate that only women knew of, that only women used. It had taken an hour for her to go around the city, and she had gone the long way, too—but there was no horsepath around the east wall, which dropped straight down to crags and precipices, and to clamber that route on foot would have taken far longer. Now the wood itself seemed to snag at her, to hold her back, though she knew that the Oversoul was guiding every step she took, to find the quickest path to the private gate. Even when she entered there, however, it would take time to make her way up into the city, and already she could hear the horns beginning their plaintive serenade. The ceremony would begin in moments, and Thirsty would not be there.

LUET MOVED AND spoke as slowly as she could, but as she stepped and spoke her way through the ceremony, she did not have the option of doing what she desired in her heart—to stop the wedding and denounce Moozh to the gathered citizens. At best she would merely be hustled from the platform before she could say a word, as a more responsible priestess took over; at worst, she might actually speak, might be stopped by an arrow, and then riot and bloodshed would ensue and Basilica could easily be destroyed before another morning came. What would that accomplish?

So she walked through the ceremony—with deliberation, with long pauses, but never stopping altogether, never ignoring the whispered promptings of the priestesses who were with her at every turning, at every speech.

For all the turmoil inside of Luet, though, she could not see that Hushidh felt anything but perfect calm. Was it possible that Hushidh actually welcomed this marriage, as a way of avoiding life as a cripple's wife? No—Shuya had been sincere when she said that the Oversoul had reconciled her to that future. Her calm must come from utter trust in the Oversoul.

"She is right to trust," said a voice—a whisper, really. For a moment she thought it was the Oversoul, but instead she realized that it was Nafai, who had spoken as she passed near him during the processional of flowers. How had he known what words he needed to say just then, to answer so perfectly her very thoughts? Was it the Oversoul, forging an ever-closer link between them? Or was it Nafai himself, seeing so deeply into her heart that he knew what she needed him to say?

Let it be true, that Shuya is right to trust the Oversoul. Let it be true that we will not have to leave her here when we make our journey to the desert, to another star. For I could not bear it to lose her, to leave her. Perhaps I would know joy again; perhaps my new husband could be a companion to me as Hushidh has been my dear companion. But there would always be an ache, an empty place, a grief that would never die, for my sister, my only kin in the world, my raveler who when I was an infant tied the knot that will bind us to each other forever.

And then, at last, the moment came, the taking of the oaths, Luet's hands on their shoulders—reaching up to Moozh's shoulder, so hard and large and strange, and to Hushidh's shoulder, so familiar, so frail by comparison to Moozh's. "The Oversoul makes one soul from the woman and the man," said Luet. A breath. An endless pause. And then the words she could not bear to say, yet had to say, and so said. "It is done."

The people of Basilica rose from their seats as if they were one, and cheered and clapped and called out their names: Hushidh! Raveler! Moozh! General! Vozmuzhalnoy! Vozmozhno!

Moozh kissed Hushidh as a husband kisses a wife— but gently, Luet saw, kindly. Then he turned and led Hushidh down to the front of the platform. A hundred, a thousand flowers filled the air, flying forward; those thrown from the back of the amphitheatre were picked up and tossed again, until the flowers filled the space between the platform and the first row of benches.

Amid the tumult, Luet became aware that Moozh himself was shouting. She could not hear the words he said, but only the fact that he was saying something, for his back was toward her. Gradually the people on the front row realized what he was saying, and took up his words as a chant. Only then did Luet understand how he was turning his own wedding now to clear political advantage. For what he said was a single word, repeated over and over again, spreading through the crowd until they all shouted with the same impossibly loud voice.

"Basilica! Basilica! Basilica!"

It went on forever, forever.

Luet wept, for she knew now that the Oversoul had

failed, that Hushidh was married to a man who would never love *her*, but only the city that he had taken as her dowry.

At last Moozh raised his hands—his left hand higher, palm out to silence them, his right still holding Hushidh's hand. He had no intention of breaking his link to *her*, for this was his link to the city. Slowly the chanting died down, and at last a curtain of silence fell on the Orchestra.

His speech was simple but eloquent. A protestation of his love for this city, his gratitude at having been privileged to restore it to peace and safety, and now his joy at being welcomed as a citizen, the husband of the sweet and simple beauty of a true daughter of the Oversoul. He mentioned Luet, too, and Nafai, how honored he felt to be kinsmen of the best and bravest of Basilica's children.

Luet knew what came next. Already the delegation of councilors had risen from their seats, ready to come forward and ask that the city accept Moozh as consul, to lead Basilica's military and foreign relations. It was a foregone conclusion that the vast majority of the people, overwhelmed with the ecstasy and majesty of the moment, would acclaim the choice. Only later would they realize what they had done, and even then most would think it was a wise and good change.

Moozh's speech was winding toward its end—and it would be a glorious end, well received by the people despite his northern accent, which in other times would have been ridiculed and despised.

He hesitated. In an unexpected place in his speech. An inappropriate place. The hesitation became a pause, and Luet could see that he was looking at something or someone that *she* could not see. So she stepped forward, and Nafai was instantly beside her; together they took the few steps necessary for both of them to be on Moozh's left, behind him still but able now to see whom he was looking at.

A woman. A woman dressed in the simple garb of a

farmer of Potokgavan—a strange costume indeed for this time and place. She was standing at the foot of the central flight of steps leading up into the amphitheatre; she made no move to come forward, so neither the Gorayni archers nor the two Basilican guards had made any move to stop her till now.

Because the general said nothing, the soldiers did not know what to do—should they seize the woman and hustle her away?

"You," said Moozh. So he knew her.

"What are you doing?" she asked. Her voice was not loud, and yet Luet heard it clearly. How could she hear so clearly?

Because I am speaking her words again in the mind of every person here, said the Oversoul.

"I am marrying," said Moozh.

"There has been no marriage," she said—again softly, again heard perfectly by all.

Moozh gestured at the assembled multitude. "All these have seen it."

"I don't know what they have seen," said the woman. "But what *I* see is a man holding his daughter by the hand."

A murmur arose in the congregation.

"God, what have you done," whispered Moozh. But now the Oversoul also carried *his* softest voice into their ears.

Now the woman stepped forward, and the soldiers made no effort to stop her, for they saw that what was happening was far larger than a mere assassination.

"The Oversoul brought me to you," she said. "Twice she brought me, and both times I conceived and bore daughters. But I was not your wife. Rather I was the body that the Oversoul chose to use, to bear *her* daughters. I took the daughters of the Oversoul to the Lady Rasa, whom the Oversoul had chosen to raise them and teach them, until the day when she chose to name them as her own."

The woman turned to Rasa, pointed at her. "Lady Rasa, do you know me? When I came to you I was naked and filthy. Do you know me now?"

Luet watched as Aunt Rasa shakily rose to her feet. "You are the one who brought them to me. Hushidh first, and then Luet. You told me to raise them as if they were my daughters, and I did."

"They were not your daughters. They were not my daughters. They are the daughters of the Oversoul, and this man—the one called Vozmuzhalnoy Vozmozhno by the Gorayni—he is the man that the Oversoul chose to be her Moozh."

Moozh. Moozh. The whisper ran through the crowd.

"The marriage you saw today was not between this man and this girl. She only stood as proxy for the Mother. He has become the husband of the Oversoul! And insofar as this is the city of the Mother, he has become the husband of Basilica. I say it because the Oversoul has put the words into my mouth! Now *you* must say it! All of Basilica must say it! Husband! Husband!"

They took up the chant. Husband! Husband! Husband! And then, gradually, it changed, to another word with the same meaning. Moozh! Moozh! Moozh!

As they chanted, the woman came forward to the front of the low platform. Hushidh let go of Moozh's hand and came forward, knelt before the woman; Luet followed her, too stunned to weep, too filled with joy at what the Oversoul had done to save Hushidh from this marriage, too filled with grief at having never known this woman who was her mother, too filled with wonder at discovering that her father had been this northern stranger, this terrifying general all along.

"Mother," Hushidh was saying—and *she* could weep, spilling her tears on the woman's hand.

"I bore you, yes," said the woman. "But I am not your

mother. The woman who raised you, *she* is your mother. And the Oversoul who caused you to be born, *she* is your mother. I'm just a farmer's wife in the wetlands of Potokgavan. That is where the children live who call *me* mother, and I must return to them."

"No," whispered Luet. "Can we only see you once?"

"I will remember you forever," said the woman. "And you will remember me. The Oversoul will keep these memories fresh in our hearts." She reached out one hand and touched Hushidh's cheek, and another to touch Luet, to stroke her hair. "So lovely. So worthy. How she loves you. How your mother loves you now."

Then she turned from them and left—walked from the platform, walked down into the ramp leading to the dressing rooms under the amphitheatre, and she was gone. No one saw her leave the city, though stories of strange miracles and odd visions quickly sprang up, of things she supposedly did but could not possibly have done on her way out of Basilica that day.

MOOZH WATCHED HER turn and leave, and with her she took all his hopes and plans and dreams; with her she took his life. He remembered so clearly the time he had spent with her—she was the reason he had never married, for what woman could make him feel what he had felt for her. At the time he had been sure that he loved her in defiance of God's will, for hadn't he felt that strong forbidding? When she was with him, hadn't he woken again and again with no memory of her, and yet he had overcome God's barriers in his mind, and kept her, and loved her? It was as Nafai said—even his rebellion was orchestrated by the Oversoul.

I am God's fool, God's tool, like everyone else, and when I thought to have my own dreams, to make my own destiny, God exposed my weakness and broke me to pieces before the people of the city. *This* city of all cities—Basilica. Basilica.

Hushidh and Luet arose from their knees at the front of the stage; Nafai joined them as they came to face Moozh. They had to come very close to him to be heard above the chanting of the crowd.

"Father," said Hushidh.

"Our father," echoed Luet.

"I never knew that I had children," said Moozh. "I should have known. I should have seen my own face when I looked at you." And it was true—now that the truth was known, the resemblance was obvious. Their faces had not followed the normal pattern of Basilican beauty because their Father was of the Sotchitsiya, and only God could guess where their mother might be from. Yet they *were* beautiful, in a strange exotic way. They were beautiful and wise, and strong women as well. He could be proud of them. In the ruins of his career, he could be proud of them. As he fled from the Imperator, who would certainly know what he had meant to attempt with this aborted marriage, he could be proud of them. For they were the only thing he had created that would last.

"We must go into the desert," said Nafai.

"I won't resist it now."

"We need your help," said Nafai. "We must go at once."

Moozh cast his eyes across the party he had assembled on his side of the platform. Bitanke. It was Bitanke who must help him now. He beckoned, and Bitanke arose and bounded onto the platform.

"Bitanke," said Moozh, "I need you to prepare for a desert journey." He turned to Nafai. "How many of you will there be?"

"Thirteen," said Nafai, "unless you decide to come with us."

"Come with us, Father," said Hushidh.

"He can't come with us," said Luet. "His place is here."

"She's right," said Moozh. "I could never go on a journey for God."

"Anyway," said Luet, "he'll be with us because his seed is part of us." She touched Nafai's arm. "He will be the grandfather of all our children, and of Hushidh's children, too."

Moozh turned back to Bitanke. "Thirteen of them. Camels and tents, for a desert journey."

"I will have it ready," said Bitanke. But Moozh understood, in the tone of his voice, in the confident way he held himself, and from the fact that he asked no questions, that Bitanke was not surprised or worried by this assignment.

"You already knew," said Moozh. He looked around at the others. "You all planned this from the start."

"No sir," said Nafai. "We knew only that the Oversoul was going to try to stop the marriage."

"Do you think that we would have been silent," asked Luet, "if we had known we were your daughters?"

"Sir," said Bitanke, "you must remember that you and Lady Rasa told me to prepare the camels and the tents and the supplies."

"When did I tell you such a thing?"

"In my dream last night," Bitanke said.

It was the crowning blow. God had destroyed him, and even went so far as to impersonate him in another man's prophetic dream. He felt his defeat like a heavy burden thrown over his shoulders; it bent him down.

"Sir," said Nafai, "why do you imagine that you've been destroyed? Don't you hear what they're chanting?"

Moozh listened.

Moozh, they said. Moozh. Moozh. Moozh.

"Don't you see that even as you let us go, you're stronger than you were before? The city is yours. The Oversoul has given it to you. Didn't you hear what their mother said? You are the husband of the Oversoul, and of Basilica."

Moozh had heard her, yes, but for the first time in his life—no, for the first time since he had loved her so many years before—he had not immediately thought of what advantage or disadvantage her words might bring to him. He had only thought: My one love was manipulated by God; my future has been destroyed by God; he has owned me and ruined me, past and future.

Now he realized that Nafai was right. Hadn't Moozh felt for the past few days that perhaps God had changed his mind and was now working *for* him? That feeling had been right. God meant to take his newfound daughters out into the desert on his impossible errand, but apart from that Moozh's plans were still intact. Basilica was his.

Moozh raised his hands, and the crowd—whose chanting had already been fading, from weariness if nothing else—fell silent.

"How great is the Oversoul!" Moozh shouted.

They cheered.

"My city!" he shouted. "Ah, my bride!"

They cheered again.

He turned to the girls and said, softly, "Any idea how I can get you out of the city without looking like I'm exiling my own daughters, or that you're running away from me?"

Hushidh looked at Luet. "The waterseer can do it."

"Oh, thanks," said Luet. "Suddenly it's up to me?"

"Pretty much, yes," said Nafai. "You can do it."

Luet set her shoulders, turned, and walked to the front of the platform. The crowd was silent again, waiting. She was still hooked up to the amplification system of the Orchestra, but it hardly mattered—the crowd was so united, so attuned to the Oversoul that whatever she wanted them to hear, they would hear.

"My sister and I are as astonished as any of you have been. We never guessed our parentage, for even as the Oversoul has spoken to us all our lives, she never told us we were hers, not in this way, not as you have seen today. Now we hear her voice, calling us into the wilderness. We must go to her, and serve her. In our place she leaves her husband, our father. Be a true bride to him, Basilica!"

There was no cheering, only a loud hum of murmuring. She looked back over her shoulder, clearly afraid that she was handling it badly. But that was only because she was unaccustomed to manipulating crowds—Moozh knew that she was doing well. So he nodded, indicated with a gesture that she must go on.

"The city council was prepared to ask our father to be consul of Basilica. If it was wise before, it is doubly wise now. For when the deeds of the Oversoul are known, all nations of the world will be jealous of Basilica, and it will be good to have such a man as this to be our voice before the world, and our protector from the wolves that will come against us!"

Now the cheering came, but it faded quickly.

"Basilica, in the name of the Oversoul, will you have Vozmuzhalnoy Vozmozhno to be your consul?"

That was it, Moozh knew. She had finally given them a clear moment to answer her, and the answer came as he knew it would, a loud shout of approbation from a hundred thousand throats. Far better than to have a councilor propose it, it was the waterseer who asked them to accept his rule, and in the name of God. Who could oppose him now?

"Father," she said, when the shouting died away. "Father, will you accept a blessing from your daughters' hands?"

What was this? What was she doing now? Moozh was confused for a moment. Until he realized that she wasn't doing this for a crowd now. She wasn't doing this to manipulate and control events. She was speaking from her heart; she had gained a father today, and would lose him today, and so she wanted to give him some parting gift. So he took Hushidh by the hand and they stepped forward; he knelt between them, and they laid their hands upon his head.

"Vozmuzhalnoy Vozmozhno," she began. And then: "Our father, our dear father, the Oversoul has brought you here to lead this city to its destiny. The women of Basilica have their husbands year to year, but the city of women has stayed unmarried all this time. Now the Oversoul has chosen, Basilica has found a worthy man at last, and you will be her only husband as long as these walls stand. But through all the great events that you will see, through all the people who will love and follow you through years to come, you will remember us. We bless you that you will remember us, and in the hour of your death you will see our faces in your memory, and you will feel your daughters' love for you within your heart. It is done."

THEY PASSED THROUGH Funnel Gate, and Moozh stood beside Bitanke and Rashgallivak to salute them as they left. Moozh had already decided to make Bitanke commander of the city guard, and Rash would be the city's governor when Moozh was away with his army. They passed in single file before him, before the waving, weeping, cheering crowd that gathered there—three dozen camels in their caravan, loaded with tents and supplies, passengers and drycases.

The cheering died away in the distance. The hot desert air stung them as they descended onto the rocky plain where the black chars of Moozh's deceiving fires were still visible like pockmarks of some dread disease. Still they all kept their silence, for Moozh's armed escort rode beside them, to protect them on their way— and to be certain that none of the reluctant travelers turned back.

So they rode until near nightfall, when Elemak determined where they would pitch the tents. The soldiers did the labor for them, though at Elemak's command they carefully showed those who had never pitched a tent how the job was done. Obring and Vas and the women looked terrified at the thought of having to do such a labor themselves, but Elemak encouraged them, and all went smoothly.

Yet when the soldiers left, it was not Elemak that they saluted, but rather Lady Rasa, and Luet the waterseer, and Hushidh the raveler—and, for reasons Elemak could not begin to understand, Nafai.

As soon as the soldiers had ridden off, the quarreling began.

"May beetles crawl into your nose and ears and eat your brain out!" Mebbekew screamed at Nafai, at Rasa, at everyone within earshot. "Why did you have to include *me* in this suicidal caravan?"

Shedemei was no less angry, merely quieter. "I never agreed to come along. I was only going to *teach* you how to revive the embryos. You had no *right* to force me to come."

Kokor and Sevet wept, and Obring added his grumbling to Mebbekew's screams of rage. Nothing that Rasa, Hushidh, or Luet could say would calm them, and as for Nafai, when he tried to open his mouth to speak, Mebbekew threw sand in his face and left him gasping and spitting—and silent.

Elemak watched it all and then, when he figured the rage had about spent itself, he stepped into the middle of the group and said, "No matter what else we do, my beloved company, the sun is down and the desert will soon be cold. Into the tents, and be silent, so you don't draw robbers to us in the night."

Of course there was no danger of robbers here, so close to Basilica and with so large a company. Besides, Elemak suspected that the Gorayni soldiers were camped only a little way off, ready to come at a moment's notice to protect them, if the need arose. And to prevent anyone from returning to Basilica, no doubt.

But they weren't desert men, as Elemak was. If I decide to return to Basilica, he said silently to the unseen Gorayni soldiers, then I will go to Basilica, and even *you,* the greatest soldiers in the world, won't stop me, won't even know that I have passed you by.

Then Elemak went to his tent, where Eiadh waited for him, weeping softly. Soon enough she forgot her tears. But Elemak did not forget his anger. He had not screamed like Mebbekew, had not howled or whined or grumbled or argued. But that did not mean he was any less angry than the others. Only that when he acted, it would be to some effect.

Moozh might not have been able to stand against the plots and plans of the Oversoul, but that doesn't mean that *I* can't, thought Elemak. And then he slept.

Overhead a satellite was slowly passing, reflecting a pinpoint of sunlight from over the horizon. One of the eyes of the Oversoul, seeing all that happened, receiving all the thoughts that passed through the minds of the people under its cone of influence. As one by one they fell asleep, the Oversoul began to watch their dreams, waiting, hoping, eager, for some arcane message from the Keeper of Earth. But there were no visions of hairy angels tonight, no giant rats, no dreams but the random firings of thirteen human brains asleep, made into meaningless stories that they would forget as soon as they awoke.

EPILOGUE

General Moozh succeeded as he had hoped. He united the Cities of the Plain and Seggidugu, and thousands of Gorayni soldiers deserted and joined with him. The Imperator's troops melted away, and before the summer was out, the Sotchitsiya lands were free. That winter the Imperator huddled in the snows of Gollod, while his spies and ambassadors worked to persuade Potokgavan to put an army like a dagger in Moozh's back.

But Moozh had foreseen this, and when the Potoku fleet arrived, it was met by General Bitanke and ten thousand soldiers, men and women of a militia he had trained himself. The Potoku soldiers died in the water, most of them, their ships burning, their blood leaving red foam with every wave that broke upon the beach. And in the spring, Gollod fell and the Imperator died by his own hand, before Moozh could reach him. Moozh stood in the Imperator's summer palace and declared that there *was* no incarnation of God on Harmony, and never had been—except for one unknown woman who came to him as the body of the Oversoul, and bore two daughters for the husband of the Oversoul.

Moozh died the next year, poisoned by a Potoku dart as he besieged the floodbound capital of Potokgavan.

Three Sotchitsiya kinsmen, a half-dozen Gorayni officers, and Rashgallivak of Basilica all claimed to be his successor. In the course of the civil wars that followed, three armies converged on Basilica and the inhabitants fled. Despite Bitanke's brave defense, the city fell. The walls and buildings all were broken down, and the teams of war captives cast the stones into the lake of women until all were gone, and the lake was wide and shallow.

The next summer there was nothing but old roads to show that once there had been a city in that place. And even though some few priestesses returned, and built a little temple beside the lake of women, the hot and cold waters now mixed far below the new surface of the lake, and so the thick fogs no longer rose and the place was not so holy anymore. Few pilgrims came.

The former citizens of Basilica spread far and wide throughout the world, but many of them remembered who they were, and passed the stories on, generation after generation. We were of Basilica, they told their children, and so the Oversoul is still alive within our hearts.